THE ROSE AND THE KEY

J. Sheridan Le Fanu

With a New Introduction by
Norman Donaldson
Author of *In Search of Dr. Thorndyke*

Dover Publications, Inc., New York

Copyright © 1982 by Dover Publications, Inc.

Published in Canada by General Publishing Company, Ltd., 30 Lesmill Road, Don Mills, Toronto, Ontario.
Published in the United Kingdom by Constable and Company, Ltd., 10 Orange Street, London WC2H 7EG.

This Dover edition, first published in 1982, is an unabridged republication of the edition published ca. 1895 by Downey & Co., London (first publication in book form: Chapman and Hall, London, 1871). A new introduction has been written specially for this Dover edition by Norman Donaldson.

Manufactured in the United States of America
Dover Publications, Inc., 180 Varick Street, New York, N.Y. 10014

Library of Congress Cataloging in Publication Data

Le Fanu, Joseph Sheridan, 1814-1873.
  The rose and the key.

  Reprint. Originally published: London : Downey, 1895.
  I. Title.
PR4879.L7R6   1982   823'.8   82-9569
ISBN 0-486-24377-X (pbk.)

INTRODUCTION TO THE DOVER EDITION

"They begin quietly enough, the tentacles of terror are applied so softly that the reader hardly notices them till they are sucking the courage from his blood." Thus E. F. Benson in a 1931 article, describing the masterly ghost stories of J. Sheridan Le Fanu, who, he wrote, "produces, page for page, a far higher percentage of terror than the more widely read Edgar Allan Poe."

The versatile Le Fanu also wrote the Gothic masterpiece *Uncle Silas*, which is redolent of what Benson called the "relentless drip, drip, drip of ominous and menacing incident." The question sometimes arises: What are this Irish writer's *other* novels like? Do any of them come close to matching the peculiar qualities of *Uncle Silas?* It is the chief purpose of this introduction to examine all fourteen of Le Fanu's novels, picking out for special remark those closest to the Gothic tradition, and to explain why the book you are fortunate enough to hold in your hand offers the best promise of sending up your spine the particular tingle that is Le Fanu's characteristic trademark.

Joseph Thomas Sheridan Le Fanu, born in Dominick Street, Dublin, on 28 August 1814, was descended from a Huguenot family that settled in the Irish capital around 1730 and intermarried with the Sheridan family, of which the playwright Richard Brinsley Sheridan, Joseph's great-uncle, was the most prominent member. The boy grew up at a military school in the city, where his father was resident chaplain, but in 1826 the family moved to Abington, a few miles east of Limerick in the southwest of the country. Here the quiet, studious youth led a peaceful existence, though as the son of a Protestant clergyman he was automatically regarded as an enemy by the oppressed Catholic peasantry and had some close calls during the violent skirmishes of the Tithe Wars.

Writing was his first and only love. His first story, "The Ghost and the Bone-Setter," was written in his early twenties while he was still a law student in Dublin, and though he was called to the Irish Bar in 1839 he never practiced. Instead, his urge to authorship turned him toward journalism and for some years he owned *The Warder*, an organ of Tory opinion, and held a part-ownership of several other Dublin newspapers. For ten years, beginning in 1842, his tenuous connection with the law brought him a small salary as tipstaff of the Court of Common Pleas, and this post in turn led to his wooing of Susanna Bennett, daughter of a prominent barrister, whom he married in 1844.

Not even the industrious W. J. McCormack, latest and most thorough of Le Fanu's biographers, can shed much light on Joseph's marriage, but in his *Sheridan Le Fanu and Victorian Ireland* (1980) Susanna emerges as a nervous woman prone to severe religious doubts and anxieties. Her husband noted in his diary: "If she took leave of anyone who was dear to her she was always overpowered with an agonizing frustration that she should never see them again. If anyone she loved was ill, though not dangerously, she despaired of their recovery."

She was taken ill of what McCormack calls a hysterical attack on 26 April 1858 and two days later she died, aged only thirty-four. Overcome by a grief that was not unmixed with feelings of guilt and insecurity, he was writing to his mother within the hour: "The greatest misfortune of my life has overtaken me. My darling wife is gone. The most affectionate the truest I think ... Oh, look through her letters to you & copy any words in which she said I loved her & was kind to her. I adored her."

The uneasy atmosphere of the marriage is echoed, McCormack believes, in the 1850 short tale "The Mysterious Lodger." A curiously ambivalent stance toward religion is evident in many of the later novels, not least in the present one.

In July 1861 Le Fanu made his most important investment: he purchased for £850 *The Dublin University Magazine*, a periodical that had been launched in January 1833 by Tory students at Trinity College while the young Le Fanu was a freshman there. It had been showing signs of decline since 1845, when Charles Lever quitted the editorial chair, but it did better under its new proprietor's guidance, and no fewer than eight of Le Fanu's novels were serialized in its pages between October 1861 and November 1869, including *Uncle Silas*, which was initially titled *Maud Ruthyn*. He also wrote numerous shorter pieces, not all of which have been identified as his. Between his editorial duties, his writing and the care of his four motherless children, he was left fully occupied, but he escaped to the seaside every summer, and in the middle 1860s spent some happy months at Beaumaris in Anglesey, from where he doubtless visited the mainland Welsh towns described in the early chapters of *The Rose and the Key*.

His home since 1851 had been his father-in-law's elegant Georgian house at 18 (now 70) Merrion Square, Dublin. He never possessed the funds to purchase the property, a fact that caused his children to be forced out after his death.

A quiet, unassuming man, Le Fanu is revealed by his portraits to have had a neatly trimmed beard, a hint of humor around his lips and a Gaelic twinkle in his eye. There is much we would like to know about the hidden depths below this outward appearance. E. F. Bleiler characterizes him as combining "the gentle weaknesses and terrible dreams of the visionary with the strengths of the very competent businessman." In the five years left to him after the sale of his magazine in 1869 he spent much time alone at home. His favorite hour for writing was after midnight; in the glimmering light shed by two tapers, his mind stimulated by strong tea, he would sit at the desk on which his great-uncle, nearly a century earlier, had written his original malapropisms.

Le Fanu was recovering from an attack of bronchitis when he died suddenly in his sleep, probably of a heart attack, before first light on 7 February 1873. The story is sometimes told of his oft-recurring nightmare in which a tottering old house was threatening to bury him. When the doctor was called to give a death-certificate he looked into the "terror-stricken eyes" and commented, "So the house has fallen at last." But the truth is that the writer's death was peaceful. "His face looks so happy with a beautiful smile on it," wrote his daughter Emmie in a letter. "It comforts me to think he is in Heaven, for no one could have been better than he was. He lived only for us, and his life was a most troubled one."

Le Fanu had planned another novel, *The House of Bondage*, for publication in 1873. McCormack believes that it would have been developed from "The Mysterious Lodger," and that the world was not denied another masterpiece by the author's death.

Sheridan Le Fanu's range was a wide one: ghost stories and patriotic ballads, historical romances and sentimental lyrics, innumerable articles and orthodox mystery novels. Among his ghost stories, "Green Tea"—the tale of a guilt-ridden clergyman haunted by a malevolent monkey—is perhaps the most famous. His sensuous vampire story "Carmilla" inspired Bram Stoker's *Dracula.* All the ghost stories—around thirty in all—have been issued by Dover in two volumes (*Best Ghost Stories of J. S. Le Fanu*, 1964, and *Ghost Stories and Mysteries*, 1975) with knowledgeable introductions by Bleiler, who perceptively observes that, among Victorian writers, "only Le Fanu seems to have recognized that there must be an aesthetic of supernatural terror . . . and was aware of the implications that supernaturalism would have for the other dynamics of the story."

Of Le Fanu's fifteen novels, *Morley Court* (1873) is a slightly revised reissue of his first book, *The Cock and Anchor*, and several others, including *Uncle Silas*, are developed versions of earlier short stories. Nevertheless, bearing in mind his abstention from novel-writing for sixteen years in mid-career and his death at fifty-eight, we have to conclude that his output was considerable.

The novels are widely varied in type and quality. Le Fanu set out as an author of Irish historical romances in the tradition of Lever, with no particular style of his own. But when he returned to the novel after his long absence, he found his stride immediately and with a vengeance as the proprietor and editor of *The Dublin University Magazine*. Four remarkable novels were serialized in its pages between October 1861 and July 1865: *The House by the Churchyard*, *Wylder's Hand*, *Uncle Silas* and *Guy Deverell*. The later books show a considerable falling off in quality, but the decline was not a steady one and there are fine titles to be found among mediocre ones. Le Fanu's career shows a remarkable similarity to Wilkie Collins's in this regard. The younger writer's decline is generally ascribed to the increasing doses of opium, in the form of laudanum, that he drank to ease a painful generalized gout, and David Brownell in a 1976 article has speculated that Le Fanu may also have had a secret drug habit. But the known facts point the other way: Le Fanu, a nonsmoker, seems to have partaken of nothing stronger than tea.

The Cock and Anchor, being A Chronicle of Old Dublin City (1845) and *The Fortunes of Colonel Torlogh O'Brien* (1847) are of little interest to the modern reader, lacking all the characteristics he hopes to find in a Le Fanu novel.

The House by the Churchyard (1863), of all Le Fanu's novels, is the subject of the widest differences of informed opinion. Nelson Browne, in his compact 1951 study of the author's works, places it with *Uncle Silas* in the first rank of the novels and quotes M. R. James, the ghost-story writer, as rating it even more highly. Elizabeth Bowen, in introducing a 1968 reprint, is enthusiastic but admits that admirers of *Uncle Silas* "may experience a setback when first they embark" on this earlier novel. She herself disliked it at first, and many, perhaps most, readers will find it a strange hodgepodge of incidents and characters from which only an occasional fragment can be detached and held up for admiration. Dorothy L. Sayers was impressed by the scene near the end in which a drunken young surgeon trepans the skull of a man lying unconscious after a murderous attack. (The hope is that the victim will recover sufficiently to name his attacker.) But the scene loses much of its effectiveness by taking place behind closed doors. A separate incident, not integral to the plot, concerns the haunting of the Tiled House, but this is available separately in Dover's *The Best Ghost Stories of J. S. Le Fanu* (1964).

With *Wylder's Hand* (1864), Le Fanu the novelist permanently abandoned the past as a subject and transported his scenes and characters from Ireland to Wales and northern England. From this time on, also, all his works were published in volume form in London rather than Dublin. *Wylder's Hand* is an excellent mystery dominated by the mysterious disappearance of a young naval lieutenant, Mark Wylder. Was he, we wonder, murdered by Captain Stanley Lake, his rival for the hand of a wealthy heiress? As these suspicions change to certainty, Wylder is reportedly seen in his old haunts, and all bets are off. S. M. Ellis in his pioneering work *Wilkie Collins, Le Fanu, and Others* (1951) declares it to be the best of the novels; so does Brownell. Fortunately it is now available as a 1978 Dover publication.

Though *Churchyard* and *Wylder* have their champions, there is no doubt that *Uncle Silas: A Tale of Bartram-Haugh* (1864) is the most celebrated of Le Fanu's novels. When M. R. James complained more than a half-century ago that the author was inaccessible in even the largest libraries, he was not including this novel in his lament, for it has never been out of print since its first publication. It is also the only one of Le Fanu's novels to be adapted as a movie (in 1947 with Jean Simmons; it was released in the United States four years later as *The Inheritance*).

The story of young Maud Ruthyn is developed slowly, but with enormous effect, until the chapter titled "The Hour of Death" is reached and the murderous plans of the heroine's evil uncle are put into effect. Among those deeply affected by the novel during its serialization was the novelist Anthony Trollope, who forthwith introduced into the novel he was writing, *The Claverings*, a character undoubtedly based on the hideous, gesticulating French housekeeper, Madame de la Rougierre. Dover's handsome 1966 reissue of the novel has an introduction by Frederick Shroyer.

Guy Deverell (1865) is a rather long-winded, but exceedingly well written, mystery novel set in a large country mansion. The owner, Sir Jekyl Marlowe, is a usurper who unfairly killed the original Guy Deverell in a duel twenty years before the story opens, and he is pitted against the sinister Monsieur Varbarriere, a disguised friend of the dead man. The affair between the rakish Sir Jekyl and Lady Jane Lennox is openly revealed and a droll irony new to Le Fanu runs through the book. The characterization is finely drawn and the inner thoughts and conversations are particularly brilliant. On many counts this can be viewed as the best of the novels, though when assessed more narrowly as a tale of mystery and terror in the style of *Uncle Silas*, it lacks the concentration and carefully crafted crescendo of the better-known work.

All in the Dark (1866) is unanimously regarded by every critic as a Victorian romance of little interest; Browne describes it as "very little more than the history of a village wooing," and the consensus declares it to be the poorest of Le Fanu's novels.

The Tenants of Malory (1867) must be regarded as another failure. Browne, in the main a generous critic, finds it "involved and tedious" and exhibiting "excessive sentimentality." Michael Begnal, in his slim 1971 study of Le Fanu, declares the plot "unfortunately stock." The novel is partly redeemed by a single character, Mr. Dingwell, whose true identity is the mainspring of the story and whom Begnal compares to "some of the best portraits of Dickens."

A Lost Name (1868) has its admirers; though Begnal labels it "little more than a murder mystery," that is hardly the kind of talk to repel admirers of *Uncle Silas*. But the beginning is tough going, and the beautiful, treacherous Agnes Marlyn is never fully explained to us. Moreover, the mystery is not solved during the progress of the novel, and the hasty explanation on the final page is neither surprising nor satisfactory. Serialization took place not in *The Dublin University Magazine* (as in the case of the preceding six novels and the two following) but in *Temple Bar*.

Haunted Lives (1868) has the advantage of a small cast, a London milieu (unusual for Le Fanu) and a simple plot. Browne was repelled by one of the chief characters: "He is oddly effeminate, and there is something neurotic and febrile in his wooing" of the heroine, Laura Challys Gray. Certainly these indoor scenes are somewhat repetitive but, as Bleiler remarks, the chief feature of the novel is "an incredibly sustained ambiguity: although the modern reader soon recognizes that one of the characters is in masquerade, and that there is no mystery in this aspect of the novel, he must admire the skill with which Le Fanu flaunts the ambiguity, instead of concealing it." Laura resists the appeals of the improvident, ruthless Guy de Beaumirail, who languishes in debtor's prison, for forgiveness of debts to her family. When she begins to receive threatening letters the handsome Alfred Dacre comes to her aid and soon falls in love with her. Laura's jealous cousin fights a duel with Dacre, with almost fatal consequences. Though Browne objects to the novel's sentimental ending, many will agree that Laura's acceptance of a second-best solution is fitting and satisfying.

The Wyvern Mystery (1869) marks the end of Le Fanu's eight-year association with his magazine. Despite its title it contains no real mystery but tells of the marriage — possibly bigamous — of Charles Fairfield. Modern critics have returned mixed verdicts on this novel. It does contain one scene of terror in which the first Mrs. Fairfield, now blind and hideously scarred, attacks the usurper, and there are several excellent character studies, including an ancient housekeeper and a cruel sergeant-major. The way the author achieves a happy ending when all seems lost is also impressive.

Checkmate (1871) was serialized in *Cassell's Magazine* between September 1870 and March 1871. Alma Murch in her *Development of the Detective Novel* (1958) picks it from among Le Fanu's works for special praise, but she is almost alone. Its one noteworthy feature is the disguising of the villain Longcluse by plastic surgery, but this is mentioned only incidentally. It is, as Bleiler says, a lengthy society novel, "overlong, rambling, and in places simply boring."

Willing to Die (1873), like *The Rose and the Key* (1871, to be discussed in detail below), first appeared in *All the Year Round.* Browne found it "a comparatively tame affair, and the reader waits in vain for any thrills of rapturous terror." Begnal sees the novel as the last stage in Le Fanu's progression from optimism to fatalistic nihilism, as his "final and most comprehensive statement of the meaninglessness of existence." The plot is unusually complicated, moving mindlessly from North Wales to London and from there to Golden Friars in the Lake District. Ethel Wade in middle age looks back on her life: on the shipwreck that casts up the mysterious Richard Marston, on his duel with another unaccountable young man, on her father's suicide, and on the Catholic priest who comes and goes without stated cause. For lack of a mystery a series of mystifications must serve, it seems. The result is a disappointing finale for an author who reached such heights only seven years earlier.

The Rose and the Key first appeared as a weekly serial between 21 January and 23 September 1871 in Charles Dickens's *All the Year Round*, which, following the death of its founder the previous year (like Le Fanu he died at the age of fifty-eight), was being edited by his son, Charles junior. The novel was published in three volumes by Chapman and Hall the same year.

With the notable exception of *The House by the Churchyard*, Le Fanu kept his ghost stories and mystery novels quite distinct. The latter are never dependent on apparitions or ghostly influences. His baleful forces are entirely human and often disguised as paragons: one thinks of Alfred Dacre, Longcluse and, of course, Uncle Silas. In *The Rose and the Key* the embodiment of malevolence is Barbara, Lady Vernon, mother of the heroine Maud and chatelaine of Roydon.

The novel begins quietly, and the only reason the reader does not imagine himself to be immersed in a low-keyed romance is the persistent shadowing of Maud and her elderly cousin Maximilla by the serpentine Elihu Lizard as they wend their way through northwest Wales, a favorite region of our author. (Incidentally, all the place names save one are authentic; Cardyllion with its castle seems modeled on Caernarvon.)

The ladies meet Charles Marston, a handsome young man of noble bearing, as they continue their sketching tour, and it should be mentioned that Le Fanu, who was fond of reusing names from story to story, had first used **Marston** in an early tale, "Some Account of the Latter Days of the Hon. Richard Marston of Dunoran," from which *A Lost Name* was developed twenty years later. But this Richard Marston is a villain, like his namesake in the final novel, *Willing to Die*, who survives a shipwreck and lures the heroine toward a bigamous marriage.

The Marston of the present story is a hero, though not a forceful one, and he therefore becomes enamored of Maud Vernon. She, being a more high-spirited — not to say capricious — young woman than Maud Ruthyn, spurns him and leaves for home without revealing her true identity. Of course, he duly traces her to Roydon, by which time the cast of characters has greatly expanded. Browne correctly describes the characterization in this novel as "always competent, sometimes masterly" and from among the minor personages selects "Mrs. Foljambe, the vicar's wife, ... whose one story is surely the most pointless ever related."

We can usually pick out Le Fanu's major villains by their telltale pallor, and, sure enough, Lady Vernon is so afflicted. Her alienation from, even distaste for, her daughter is soon made evident, but there are few readers who will not feel a pang of sympathy and awe as they discern her, in the twilit church, all but hidden in the dark archway above the congregation, looking down and "crying silently as if her heart would break."

At the same moment we perceive for the first time that this novel has deep mysteries yet to be revealed, though we can have no idea of how the story will proceed, or how terrible Maud's predicament will soon become at the hands of her mother, who is, Browne says, "a strange blend of fire and ice."

The dry, impressive figure of Lady Vernon's only confidant, Mr. Dawe, also engages our interest and respect, especially in the closing chapters, when it is to him we look, not to the nominal hero, to rescue the heroine.

We are now on the brink of revealing the mystery, but the aim of an introduction such as this must be to whet the reader's appetite, not to satiate it. Enough to say that the scene in which Maud thankfully leaves her home for a vacation at the home of Lady Mardykes is the last happy one in which she will appear or that we will experience. Because, in *Uncle Silas*, Maud Ruthyn is the narrator, we can assume she will survive to the last page of the book, but in *The Rose and the Key* nothing can be taken for granted.

Le Fanu, as Begnal remarks, had "an extraordinary sympathy for and understanding of the feminine mind. . . . In Rachel Lake [of *Wylder's Hand*], Maud Ruthyn, Laura Gray and Ethel Ware he offers living, breathing characters, and a reader's interest is held as much by their presentations as it is by the toils which involve them." Maud Vernon surely belongs in this gallery too. And the reader may well be tempted to place there her mother, the proud, obdurate Barbara Vernon, into whose heart we have been privileged to peer. Misguided, even wicked, she certainly is, but by no means irredeemably evil. It is a particular strength of this novel that Le Fanu is able to induce us to divide our sympathies between the oppressed and the oppressor — to experience fellow-feeling for the heroine while reserving for the villainess at least a crumb of compassion.

NORMAN DONALDSON

CONTENTS.

CONTENTS.

THE ROSE AND THE KEY.

CHAPTER I.

UNOCULUS.

THE level light of a summer sunset, over a broad heath, is brightening its brown undulations with a melancholy flush, and turning all the stalks of heather in the foreground into twisted sticks of gold. Insect wings sparkle dimly in the air; the lagging bee drones homeward, and a wide drift of rooks, cawing high and faint, show like shadows against the sea-green sky, flecked with faint crimson, as they sail away to the distant dormitories of Westwold Forest.

Toward the sunset end of this savage heath stand four gigantic fir-trees, casting long shadows. One, indeed, is little more than a rotten stump, some twelve feet high; all bend eastward, shorn of their boughs nearly to the top, and stretching the arms that remain, some yellow and stripped of their bark, in the same direction, as if signalling together to the same distant point. These slanting fir-trees look like the masts of a mighty wreck submerged; and antiquaries say that they are the monumental relics of a forest that lies buried under the peat.

A young lady, her dress of dark serge, with a small black straw hat, a little scarlet feather in it, and wearing a pair of boots such as a country artist might produce, made of good strong leather, with thick soles, but, in spite of coarse work and clumsy material, showing a wonderfully pretty little foot, is leaning lightly against one of these great firs. Her companion, an elderly lady, slight and merry, sits on a hillock of turf at her feet.

The dress of the elder lady corresponds with that of the younger. It is that of a person inured to the practice of a strict but not uncomfortable economy.

The young lady has dropped a japanned colour-box and a block-book at her feet. Is she an artist? Possibly a governess? At all events, she is one of the loveliest creatures eyes ever lighted on. Is there any light more becoming than that, low and richly tinted, that comes subdued through the mists of sunset?

With a pleased look—the listening look which such spiritual delight assumes—with parted lips, the light touching the edge of her little teeth, with eyes aglow with rapture, drinking in the splendour and beauty of the transitory hour and scene, as if she could look on in silence and beatitude for ever, the girl leans her little shoulder to the ancient tree.

With a long sigh, she says at last:

' I was going to ask your forgiveness, dear old cousin Max.'

'For what?' asked the old lady, turning up a face pleasantly illuminated with the golden light which catches the tip of her nose and chin, and the edge of her good-natured old cheek.

'For making you take so long a walk. I'm a little tired myself. But I don't beg your pardon, because I think this more than makes amends. Let us look for a minute more, before all fades.'

The old lady stood up, with a little shrug and screw of her shoulders.

' So I am—quite stiff—my old bones do complain; but oh, really, it is quite beautiful! I see it so much better standing here; that bank was in my way. How splendid—gorgeous!'

The scene was indeed worth a detour in their homeward route. Two grand and distant ranges of mountains, approaching from right and left, stop short in precipitous terminations that resemble the confronting castles of two gigantic lines of fortification, leaving an undulating plane between, with the sunset sky, and piles of flaming cloud, for a horizon; and, in the comparatively near foreground, rises between these points an abrupt knoll crowned by the ruined castle of Cardyllion, and, with the village studded with grand old trees, looking like a town on fire.

In nearer foreground, in the hollow, in solemn purple shadow, are masses of forest; and against the faint green and yellow sky are spread streaks of purple vapour, and the fading crimson and scarlet fires of sunset.

'This should reconcile us to very humble ways ; and more, I feel that through marble pillars, through great silk curtains, among mirrors, bronzes, china, and all the rest, looking out from a velvet sofa, I could not see, much less enjoy all this, as I do.'

Cousin Max laughed.

'Very wise ! very philosophical ! very romantic !' exclaimed she. 'But it is enough to be content with one's station in life, and not to grow too fond of any. To be content is, simply, not to wish for change. My poor father used to say that those who wished for change were like those who wished for death. They longed for a state of which they had no experience, and for which they might not be so fit as they fancied, for every situation has its liabilities as well as its privileges. That is what he used to say.'

'Dear Max, I withdraw it, if I said anything sensible, for whenever I do you grow so wise that you bore me to death.' She kissed her. 'Do let us be foolish, darling, while we are together, and we shall understand one another perfectly. See how quickly the scene changes. It is very beautiful, but not quite so glorious now.'

At this moment the sound of steps, close behind them upon the soft peat, made them both turn their heads.

A sleek, lean man, lantern-jawed, in a shabby, semi-clerical costume, passed them by in front, from right to left, in an oblique line. He was following a path, and was twirling a stick slowly in his hand by its crooked handle, and gazing up at the sky with one eye—the other was blind—with a smile that was meant to be saintly. In spite of his meek smile, and his seedy and mean exterior, the two ladies had come to connect ideas of the sinister and the dangerous with this man.

'Gracious me !' said the elder lady, after a pause, 'I do believe —I'm almost sure—that is the very man.'

'I am perfectly certain,' said the young lady, who had followed him with her eyes until he was hidden from view by a screen of furze and hawthorns, a little way to the left. 'I can't imagine what that odious, ill-looking man can possibly mean by following us about as he does.'

'Perhaps, after all, he is asking himself a question very like that about us ?' said the old lady, with a laugh.

'Not he. He *is* following us.'

'I saw him at Penmaen Mawr, but nowhere else,' said Miss Max.

'But I saw him at Chester, and there could be no mistake about his watching us there. I saw him look at our luggage, and look for our names there, and I saw him stand on the step of his carriage at Conway, until he saw us get out with the evident intention of staying there ; and then he got down with that little leather bag, that seems to be all that he possesses, and he came to our hotel, simply, I am certain, to watch us. You must recollect, when we returned from our walk, that I told you I saw him sitting in the room near the stairs, don't you recollect, writing—don't you remember ?'

'Yes, I remember your saying there was a man blind of an eye, the same we had observed at Penmaen Mawr, who had followed us, and was in the same place. But the people at the inn said he was a travelling secretary to some religious society, collecting money.'

'Did not you say,' persisted the young lady, ' when you first saw him, that he was a very ill-looking man ?'

'Yes ; so I did. So he is. He looks sanctimonious and roguish, and that white eye makes his face—I hope it is not very uncharitable to say so—almost villainous. I think him a very ill-looking man, and if I thought he was following us, I should speak to the police, and then set out for my humble home without losing an hour.'

'And you don't think he is following us ?' said the young lady.

'If he is travelling to collect subscriptions he may very well have come here about his business, and to Penmaen Mawr, and to Chester. I don't see why he must necessarily be following us. And Conway, too, he would have stopped at naturally. It does not follow at all that he is in pursuit of us because he happens to come to the same places.

> ' "The king himself has followed her
> When she has gone before."

We are not worth robbing, my dear, and we look it. You must not be so easily frightened.'

'Frightened ! I'm not the least frightened,' said the young lady spiritedly. 'I'm not what is termed a nervous young lady. You have no right to think that. But I don't believe he has any other business but tracking us from place to place.

What other business on earth could he have had—getting out at Aber, for instance? I forgot to mention Aber. It is very odd, you must allow. Let us walk on.' She had picked up her colour-box and her block. 'Very odd that he should get out of the train wherever we stop, always about business, we are to suppose, that has no connection with us; that he should follow us, by the same odd accident, where there is no rail, and where we can only get by a fly; that he should get always into the same quiet little inns, though, of course, he would like much better to be in noisier places, where he would meet people like himself; and that he should turn up this evening, so near our poor little lodgings, and go by that path which brings him there. What on earth can he want in that direction?'

'Yes, I do think it's odd, my dear; and, I say, I think he does look very villainous,' said the old lady.

'I don't pretend to account for it,' said the girl, as they trudged on side by side; 'but it is just possible that he may be a detective, who mistakes us for some people he is in pursuit of. I only know that he is spoiling my poor little holiday, and I do wish I were a man, that I might give him a good fright.'

The old lady laughed, for the girl spoke threateningly, with a flash from her splendid eyes, and for a moment clenched the tiniest little fist you can fancy.

'And you think he's gone before us to Pritchard's farm-house?' said the old lady, glancing over her shoulder in that direction, above which a mass of thunderous cloud was rising. 'Dear me! how like thunder that is.'

'Awfully!' said the young lady. 'Stop a moment—I thought I heard distant thunder. Listen!'

They both paused, looking toward those ominous piles of cloud, black against the now fast-fading sky.

CHAPTER II.

A GUIDE.

'Hush!' said the young lady, laying her fingers on her companion's arm.

They listened for a minute or more.

'There it is!' exclaimed the girl, as a faint rumble spread slowly along and among the mountains.

They remained silent for a minute after it had passed away.

'Yes, that certainly was thunder,' said the elder lady; 'and it is growing so dark; it would not do to be caught in the storm, and to meet our one-eyed persecutor, perhaps, and we have fully a mile to go still. Come, we must walk a little faster.'

'I hope it will be a good thunder-storm,' said the young lady, watching the sky, as they hurried on. 'It frightens me more than it does you, but I think I like it better.'

'You may easily do that, dear; and like our farm-house better than I do, also.'

'We are frightfully uncomfortable, I agree. Let us leave it to-morrow,' said the young lady.

'And where shall we go next?' inquired her companion.

'To Llanberris, if I'm to decide,' said the girl. 'But first we must look over the castle at Cardyllion, and there are one or two old houses I should like to sketch—only roughly.'

'You are making too great a labour of your holiday: you sketch too much.'

'Well, we leave to-morrow, and the day after is Sunday, and then—on Monday—my holiday ends, and my slavery begins,' said the young lady impetuously.

'You certainly do use strong language,' said the elder lady, a little testily. 'Why don't you try to be content? Dear me! How much nearer the thunder is!'

'It will soon be darker, and then we shall see the lightning splendidly,' said the young lady.

'Don't stop, darling, let us get on. I was going to say, you must study to be content—remember your Catechism. The Queen, I dare say, has things to complain of; and Farmer Pritchard's daughter, who has, as you fancy, a life of so much liberty, will tell you she is something of a slave, and can't do, by any means, quite as she likes. I only hope, dear Maud, we have money enough to take us home.'

'We can eke it out with my drawings. We shan't starve. We can have the ruins of Carnarvon Castle for breakfast, and eat Snowdon for dinner, and turn the Menai into tea. It is a comfort to know I can live by my handiwork. I don't think, cousin, I have a shilling I can call my own. If I could earn enough by my drawing to live on, I think I should prefer it to any other way of living I can imagine.'

'You used to think a farmer's life the happiest on earth,' said the old lady, trudging along. 'There's Richard Pritchard, why not marry him?'

'I might do worse; but there are half a dozen conclusive reasons against it. In the first place, I don't think Richard Pritchard would marry me; and, next, I know I wouldn't marry Richard Pritchard; and, thirdly, and seriously, I shall never marry at all, never, and for the reasons I have told you often; and those reasons can never change.'

'We shall see,' said her companion, with a laugh and a little shake of her head. 'Good Heavens!' exclaimed the old lady, as nearer thunder resounded over the landscape.

'Hush!' whispered the girl, as they both paused and listened, and when it had died away, 'What a noble peal that was!' she exclaimed. And as they resumed their march she continued, 'I shall never marry: and my resolution depends on my circumstances, and they, as you know, are never likely to alter—humanly speaking, they never can alter—and I have not courage enough to make myself happy; and coward as I am, I shall break my own heart rather than break my chains. Where are we now?'

As she said this she came to a sudden halt at the edge of a deep channelled stream, whose banks just there stand steep and rugged as those of a ravine, crowned with straggling masses of thorn and briars. She gazed across and up and down the stream, which was swollen just then by mountain rains of the night before.

'Can we have missed our way?' said the elder lady.

'What on earth has become of the wooden bridge?' exclaimed the younger one.

There was still quite light enough to discern objects, and Miss Max, catching her young companion by the hand, whispered:

'Good gracious, Maud, is that the man?'

'What man?' she asked, startled.

'The blind man—the person who has been following us.'

Miss Maud—for such was the young lady's name—said nothing in reply. The two ladies stood irresolute, side by side. Maud had seen the person who was approaching once only in her life. It was two days before, as she and her cousin were getting out of their fly at the Verney Arms, in the pretty little town of Cardyllion. She was a proud young lady; it would have taken a good deal to make her avow, even to herself, the slightest interest in any such person. Nevertheless, she recognised him a good many seconds before Miss Max had discovered her mistake.

She was standing beside that elderly lady.   They were both looking across the stream ; the young lady furthest from the stranger had turned a little away.

There is quite light enough to see faces still, but it will not last long.   The young man is very handsome, and also tall. He has been fishing, and has on a pair of those gigantic jack-boots in which fishermen delight to walk the rivers.   He wears a broad-leafed hat, round which are wound his flies.   A boy with his rod, net, and basket trudges behind.

The old lady speaks to him as he passes.   He stops, lowers his cigar, and inclines to listen.

' I beg pardon,' she says.   ' Can you tell me ?   There was—I am sure it was on this very spot—a bridge of plank across this stream, and I can't find it.'

' Oh ! They were taking that away to-day, as I passed by. It had grown unsafe, and the—the—— Oh, yes ; the new one is to be put up in the morning.'

The odd little hesitation I have recorded was caused by his seeing the young lady on a sudden in the midst of his sentence, and for the moment forgetting everything else.   And well he might, for he had been dreaming of her for the last two days.

He dropped his cigar, became all at once much more deferential, and with his hat in his hand said :

' Do you wish to cross the brook ?   Because, if you do, I can show you to some stepping-stones about a quarter of a mile higher up, where you can get across·very nicely.'

' Thanks ; I should be so very much obliged,' said the old lady.

The gentleman was only too happy, and having sent the boy on to the Verney Arms, talked very agreeably as he accompanied and directed their march.   He had come down there for a little fishing ; he knew the Verneys a little, and old Lord Verney was such a very odd man !   He told them stories of him, and very amusing some of them were, and his eye always glanced to see the effect of his anecdotes upon Miss Maud.   Two or three times he ventured to speak to her.   The young lady did not either encourage or discourage these little experiments, and answered very easily and carelessly, and, I am bound to say, very briefly too.

In the meantime the thunder grew nearer and more frequent, and the wild reflection of the lightning flickered on trees and fields about them,

And now they had reached the thick clump of osiers, beneath which the stepping-stones of which they were in search studded the stream. Only the summits of these stones were now above the water, and the light was nearly gone.

CHAPTER III.

PLAS YLWD.

'I HAVE not courage for this,' said the old lady, aghast, eyeing the swift current and the uncertain footing to which, in the most deceptive possible twilight, she was invited to commit herself.

'But you know, darling, we must get across somehow,' urged the girl cruelly. 'It is quite easy; don't fancy anything else.' And she stepped lightly over.

'It is all very fine, with your young feet and eyes,' she replied, 'but for an old woman like me it is little better than the tight rope; and it would be death to me to take a roll in that river. What on earth is to be done?'

'It *is* really a great deal easier than you suppose,' said the obliging young gentleman, not sorry to find an opportunity of agreeing with Miss Maud, 'and I think I can make it perfectly easy if you will just take my hand as you get across. I'll walk in the stream beside you. It is quite shallow here, and these things make me absolutely impervious to the water. Pray try. I undertake to get you across perfectly safely.'

So, supporting her across with his left hand, and walking beside her, with his right ready to assist her more effectually in case of a slip or stumble, he conducted her quite safely over.

When the lady had thanked him very earnestly, and he had laughingly disclaimed all right to her acknowledgments, another difficulty suddenly struck her.

'And now, how *are* we to find our farm-house? I know the way to it perfectly from the wooden bridge, but from this I really haven't an idea.'

'I'll make it out,' said the young lady, before their guide had time to speak. 'I like exploring, and it can't be far—a little in this direction. Thank you very much.'

The last words were to the young man, whose huge boots were pouring down rivulets on the dry dust of the little pathway on which they were standing.

'If I am not too disagreeable a guide in this fisherman's plight,' he said, glancing with a laugh at his boots, 'nothing would please me so much as being allowed to point out the way to you. I happen to know it perfectly, and it is by no means so easy as you may suppose, particularly by this light—one can hardly tell distances, ever so near.'

'Pray don't take all that trouble,' said the girl. 'I can make it out quite easily."

'Nonsense, my dear Maud. You could never make it out; and besides,' she added, in an undertone, 'how can you tell where that blind man may turn up that follows us, as you say? We are very much obliged to you,' she said, turning to him, 'and you are doing us really a great kindness. I only hope it won't be bringing you too far out of your way?'

Very pleasantly, therefore, they went on. It became darker rapidly, and though the thunder grew louder and more frequent, and the lightning gleamed more vividly across the landscape, the storm was still distant enough to enable Maud to enjoy its sights and sounds without a sense of danger.

The thunder-clouds are stealthily but swiftly ascending. These battlements of pandemonium, 'like an exhalation,' screen the sky and stars with black, and from their field of darkness leaps now and then the throbbing blue, that leaves the eye dazzled, and lights rock and forest, hill and ruin, for a moment in its pale glare. Then she listens for the rumble that swells into long and loud-echoing reverberations. He stays his narrative, and all stop and listen. He smiles, as from under his long lashes he covertly watches the ecstasy of the beautiful girl. And then they set out again, the old lady vowing that she can't think why she's such a fool as to stop at such an hour, and tired to death as she is, to listen to thunder.

Farmer Pritchard, happily for wandering Tintos in that part of the world, is not one of those scientific agriculturalists who cut down their hedgerows and square their fields. Our little party has now reached the stile which, under the shadow of some grand old elms, admits the rustics, who frequent Richard Pritchard, to his farmyard.

It is an old and a melancholy remark that the picturesque and the comfortable are hardly compatible. Here, however, these antagonistic principles are as nearly as possible reconciled. The farmyard is fenced round with hawthorns and lime-trees, and the farmhouse is a composite building, of which the quarter in which the ladies were lodged had formed a bit of the old Tudor manor-house of Plas Ylwd, which gave its name to the place.

A thatched porch, with worn stone pillars and steps, fronts the hatch, and from beside this, through a wide window of small panes, a cheerful light was scattered along the rough pavement, and more faintly on the hanging foliage of the tree opposite.

'What a pretty old house!' the young fisherman exclaimed, looking up at the gables, and the lattices, and the chimneys that rose from the deep thatch of the cobbled building.

'It may be prettier in this light, or rather darkness, than at noon,' said the old lady, with a shrug and a little laugh.

'But it really is, in any light, an extremely pretty old house.' said the girl, taking up the cudgels for their habitation, 'and everything is so beautifully neat. I think them such nice people.'

A few heavy rain-drops had fallen sullenly as they came, and now, with the suddenness of such visitations, the thunder shower all at once began to descend.

'Come in, come in,' said the old lady imperiously.

Very willingly the young gentleman stepped under the porch.

They all three stood there for a moment, looking out towards the point from which hitherto the lightning had been chiefly visible.

'Oh! but you must come in and take some tea,' said the old lady, suddenly recollecting. 'You *must* come in, really.'

Their walk and chat, and the climbing of stiles, and the rural simplicities that surrounded, had made her feel quite intimate. He glanced covertly at the young lady, but in her face he saw neither invitation nor prohibition; so he felt at liberty to choose, and he stepped very gladly into the house.

As you enter the old house you find yourself in a square vestibule, if I can call by so classic a name anything so rude. Straight before you yawns an arch that spans it from wall to wall, giving admission to the large kitchen of the farmhouse; at your right, under a corresponding moulded arch, opens the wide oak staircase of the manor-house, with a broad banister, on the first huge stem of which, as on a vestal altar, is placed a burnished candlestick of brass, in which burns a candle to welcome the return of old Miss Max and young Miss Maud Guendoline.

The young lady steps in with tho air, though she knows it not, of a princess into her palace.

As they enter, her ear is struck by an accent not Welsh, and a voice the tones of which have something of a cold, nasal, bleating falsetto, which is intensely disagreeable, and looking quickly through the arched entrance to the kitchen, she sees there, taking his ease in an arm-chair by the fireplace, the long-visaged man with the white eye.

He is holding forth agreeably, with a smile on his skinny lips. He gesticulates with a long hand, the nails of which are black as ebony. The steam of the saintly man's punch makes a halo round his head, and his hard cheeks are flushed with the pink that tells of inward comfort. His one effective eye addresses itself, although he is haranguing Richard Pritchard's wife, to Richard Pritchard's daughter, who is very pretty, and leans, listening to the ugly stranger, with her bare arms rolled in her apron, on the high back of one of the old-fashioned oak chairs.

CHAPTER IV.

HOW THEY ALL GOT ON.

Just for a moment, the appearance of this Cocles, domesticated under the same roof, spy, thief, whatever he might be, made the young lady wince. Her impulse was to walk straight into the kitchen, cross-examine the visitor, and call on Richard Pritchard to turn him out forthwith. But that was only for one moment; the next, she was chatting just as usual. Mrs. Pritchard, with her pretty Welsh accent, another candle, and her smile of welcome, had run out to accompany the ladies upstairs to know their wishes, and to make any little adjustments in the room they might require.

'I lighted a bit o' fire, please, 'm; the evenin' was gone rather cold, I thought.'

'You did quite right, Mrs. Pritchard; you take such good care of us; it looks so comfortable,' said the old lady.

'I'm very glad, 'm, thank you, ma'am; will you please to have tea, 'm?'

'Yes, as quickly as possible, thanks.'

And Mrs. Pritchard vanished noiselessly. The old lady's guest was delighted with everything he saw.

It is not a large room; square, with blackest oak panels, burnished so that they actually flash in the flicker of the fire that burns under the capacious arch of the fireplace. All the furniture, chairs, tables, and joint stools, are of the same black oak, waxed and polished, till it gleams and sparkles again. These clumsy pieces of ancient cabinet-making have probably descended, with this wing of the old house, to its present occupiers. The floor is also of polished oak, with a piece of thick old carpet laid down in the middle, and the window is covered with a rude curtain of baize. There are two sets of shelves against the wall, on which stand thick the brightly coloured delft figures, cups, and candlesticks, interspersed with mutilated specimens of old china—a kind of ornament in which the Welsh delight, and which makes their rooms very bright and cheerful. The room is a picture of neatness. For a king's ransom you could not find dust enough in it to cover a silver penny. The young guest looks round delighted. Margaret's homely room did not seem to Faust more interesting, or more instinct with the spirit of neatness.

'Well, now you are in our farmhouse, Mr. ——' The old lady had got thus far, when she found herself at fault, a little awkwardly.

'My name is Marston,' he said, smiling a little, but very pleasantly.

'And I think, for my part, I have seen much more uncomfortable drawing-rooms,' she resumed. 'I think it is a place one might grow fond of. Marston,' she murmured in a reverie, and then she said to him, 'I once met a Mr. Marston at ——'

But here a covert glance from Maud pulled her up again.

'I certainly did meet a Mr. Marston somewhere; but it is a long time ago,' she said.

'We are to be found in three different counties,' he said, laughing; 'it is hard to say where we are at home.'

'Aren't you afraid of those great wet boots?' the officious old lady began.

'Oh dear! not the least,' said he, 'if you don't object to them in your drawing-room.' He glanced at the young lady, so as to include her. 'But the little walk up here has shaken off all the wet, and as for myself, they are a sort of diving-bells in which one can go anywhere and be as dry as on *terra firma;* it is the only use of them.' He turned to the young lady. 'Very tempting scenery about here. I dare say you have taken

a long walk to-day.   Some lady friends of mine, last year, over-
did it very much, and were quite knocked up for some time after
they left this.'

'I'm a very good walker—better than my cousin,' said the
young lady; 'and a good long walk is one of the most delightful things on earth.   To see, as I have done, often, distant blue
hills grow near, and reveal all their picturesque details, and a
new landscape open before you, and finally to see the same hills
fall into the rear, and grow as dim and blue as they were before,
and to owe the transformation to your own feet, is there anything that gives one such a sense of independence?   Those fine
ladies who go everywhere in their carriages enjoy nothing of this,
and yet, I think, it is half the pleasure of beautiful scenery.
My cousin Max to-day was lecturing me on the duty of being
content—I don't think that is the speech of a discontented
person.'

'It is a very wise speech, and perfectly true; I have experienced the same thing a thousand times myself,' said Mr.
Marston.

Miss Max would have had a word to say, but she was busy
hammering upon the floor with a cudgel provided for the purpose of signalling thus for attendance from below.

Mrs. Pritchard enters with the tea.   Is there a cosier spectacle?   If people are disposed to be happy, is there not an
influence in the cups and saucers, and all the rest, that makes
them cheery, and garrulous, and prone to intimacy?

It is an odd little adventure.   Outside—

> 'The speedy gleams the darkness swallows,
> Loud, long, and deep, the thunder bellows.'

The pretty girl has drawn the curtain halfway back, and opened
a lattice in the stone-shafted window, the air being motionless,
to see the lightning better.   The rain is still rushing down perpendicularly, and whacking the pavement below all over.   Inside, the candles glimmer on oaken walls three hundred years
old, and a little party of three, so oddly made acquainted, are
sitting over their homely tea, and talking as if they had known
one another as long as they could remember.

Handsome Mr. Marston is chatting in the happiest excitement
he has ever known.   The girl can't deny, *in foro conscientiæ*, that
his brown features and large dark eyes, and thick soft hair, and

a certain delicacy of outline almost feminine, accompanied with his manly and athletic figure, present an *ensemble* singularly handsome.

'His face is intelligent, there is fire in his face, he looks like a hero,' she admitted to herself. 'But what do I know of him? He talks good-naturedly. His manners are gentle ; but mamma says that young faces are all deceptive, and that character does not write itself there, or tone the voice, or impress the manner, until beauty begins to wear itself out. I know nothing about him. He seems to know some great people, but he won't talk of them to *us*. That is good-breeding, but nothing more. He seems to enjoy himself here in this homely place, and drinks his tea very happily from these odd delft cups. He brings the kettle, or hammers on the floor with that cudgel, as my cousin orders him. But what is it all ? A masquerading adventure— the interest or fun of which consists in its incongruity with the spirit of his life, and its shock to his tastes. He may be cruel, selfish, disobliging, insolent, luxurious.'

In this alternative she wronged him. This Charles Marston, whose letters came to him addressed the 'Honourable Charles Marston,' was, despite his cleverness, something of a dreamer, very much of an enthusiast, and as capable of immensurable folly, in an affair of the grand passion, as any schoolboy, in the holidays, with his first novel under his pillow.

'He can't suppose, seeing us here,' thought the girl, 'that we are people such as he is accustomed to meet. Of course he despises us. Very good, sir. An eye for an eye,' and she turned her splendid dark eye for a moment covertly upon him, 'and a tooth for a tooth. If you despise us, I despise you. We shall see. I shall be very direct. I shall bring that to the test, just now. We shall see.'

Charles Marston stole beside her, and looked out, with her, at the lightning. This is an occupation that helps to make young people acquainted. A pity it does not oftener occur in our climate. The little interjections. The 'oh, oh, ohs !' and 'listens,' the 'hushes,' and 'wasn't that glorious !' 'you're not afraid ?' and fifty little useless but rather tender attentions, arise naturally from the situation. Thus an acquaintance, founded in thunder and lightning, may, like that of Macbeth and the witches, endure to the end of the gentleman's adventures.

Not much attended to, I admit, good Miss Max talked on, about fifty things, and, now and then, threw in an interjection, when an unusually loud peal shook the walls of the old farm-house, and was followed for a minute by a heavier cataract of rain.

But soon, to the secret grief of Mr. Marston, the thunder began perceptibly to grow more distant, and the lightning less vivid, and, still more terrible, the rain to abate.

The interest in the storm subsided, and Miss Maud Guendoline closed the lattice, and returned to the tea-table.

Had he ever seen in living face, in picture, in dream, anything so lovely? Such silken brown hair, such large eyes and long lashes, and beautifully red lips! Her dimples look so pretty in the oblique light and shadow, as her animated talk makes a pleasant music in his ears. He is growing more foolish than he supposes.

Miss Max, who knows nothing of him, who can't tell whether he is a nobleman or a strolling player, whether he is worth ten thousand a year, or only the clothes on his back and his enormous pair of boots, marks the symptoms of his weakness, and approves and assists with all the wise decision of a romantic old woman.

She makes an excuse of cold feet to turn about and place hers upon the fender. It is a lie, palpably, and Miss Maud is angry, and insists on talking to her, and keeping the retiring chaperon, much against her will, still in evidence.

The young man is not the least suspicious, has not an idea that good Miss Max is wittingly befriending him, but earnestly wishes that she may fall into a deep sleep in her chair.

The cruel girl, however, insists on her talking.

'I saw you talking to those American people who came into the carriage at Chester, didn't you?' said the girl.

'Yes, dear,' said Miss Max dryly; 'nothing could be more uninteresting.'

'I was in the waiting-room at Chester with that very party, I'm certain,' said Mr. Marston. 'There were two ladies, weren't there, and the man had a kind of varnished waterproof coat, and a white hat, and was very thin, and had a particularly long nose, a little crooked?'

'Yes, that is *my* friend,' answered Maud. 'That gentleman was good enough to take a great interest in me and my cousin. I had to inform him that my Christian name is Maud and my surname Guendoline; that a friend had made me a present of my first-class ticket; that my papa has been dead for many years ; and that mamma's business allows her hardly an hour to look after me ; that I have not a shilling I can call my own ; that I thought I could do something to earn a subsistence for myself ; that I can draw a little—I can teach——'

'Where have you ever taught, dear?' threw in Miss Max, apparently in great vexation at her companion's unseasonable frankness.

'I don't say I have yet taught for money, but I have learned something of it at the Sunday-school, and I don't see why I shouldn't do it as well as mamma.   Then there's my music—that ought to be worth something.'

'You must be tired, I think,' interrupted the old lady, a little sharply ; 'you have had a very long walk to-day.   I think you had better go to your room.'

'I have stayed, I'm afraid, a great deal too late,' said Mr. Marston, who could not mistake the purport of the old lady's speech.   'I'm afraid you are tired, Miss Guendoline.   I'm afraid you have both been doing too much, and you'll allow me, won't you, just to call in the morning to inquire how you are?'

'It is very inhospitable,' said Miss Max, relenting a little ; 'but we are very early people in this part of the world, and I shall be very happy to see you to-morrow, if we should happen to be at home.'

He had taken his leave ; he was gone.   A beautiful moonlight was silvering the quaint old building and the graceful trees that surround it.   The mists of night hung on the landscape, and the stars, the fabled arbiters of men's fortunes, burned brilliantly in the clear sky.

He crossed the stile, he walked along the white path, as if in a trance.   He paused under a great ash-tree, snake-bound in twisted ivy, and leaned against its trunk, looking towards the thatched gable of the old stone building.

'Was there ever so beautiful a creature?' he said.   'What dignity, what refinement, what prettiness, and what a sweet voice ; what animation !   Governess, farmer's daughter, artist, be she what she may, she is the loveliest being that ever trod this earth !'   In this rapture—in which mingled that pain of doubt and yearning of separation which constitutes the anguish of such violent 'fancies'—he walked slowly to the stepping-stones, and conning over every word she had spoken, and every look in her changing features, he arrived at last, rather late, at his inn, the Verney Arms, in Cardyllion.

CHAPTER V.

A SPECTRE.

THE two ladies sat silent for some time after their guest had departed.

Miss Max spoke first.

'I don't think it is quite honest—you make me ashamed of you.'

'I'm ashamed of myself. It's true; he'll think too well of me,' said the girl impetuously.

'He thinks very oddly of us both, I'm afraid,' said Miss Max.

'I'm not afraid—I don't care—I dare say he does. I think you hinted that he should carry you across the stream on his back. I got out of hearing before you had done. You all but asked him for his name, and finally turned him out in the thunder at a moment's notice.'

'It does not matter what an old woman says or does, but a girl is quite different,' replied Miss Max. 'You need not have said one word about our ways and means.'

'I shall say the same to every one that cares to hear, where I am not under constraint; and you shall keep your promise. Do let me enjoy my liberty while I may,' answered the girl.

'Are you a gipsy? You are such a mixture of audacity and imposture!' said Miss Max.

'Gipsy? Yes. We are something like gipsies, you and I— our long marches and wandering lives. Imposture and audacity? I should not mind pleading guilty to that, although, when I think it over, I don't remember that I said a word that was not literally true, except my surname. I was not bound to tell that, and he would have been, I dare say, no wiser if I had. I was not bound to tell him anything. I think I have been very good.'

'I dare say he is Lord Somebody,' said Miss Max.

'Do you like him better for that?' asked the girl.

'You are such a radical, Maud! Well, I don't say I do. But it just guarantees that if the man has any nice tastes, he has leisure and money to cultivate them; and if he has kind feelings he can indulge them, and is liberated from all those miserable limitations that accompany poverty.'

'I have made a very frank confession with one reserve. On that point I have a right to be secret, and you have promised secrecy. Am I under the miserable obligation to tell my real condition to everyone who pleases to be curious ?'

'You blush, Maud.'

'I dare say I do. It is because you look at me so steadily. I told him all I chose to tell. He shan't think me an adventuress; no one shall. I said enough to show I was, at least, willing to earn an honest livelihood. I said the same to that vulgar American, and you did not object. And why not to him? I don't care one farthing about him in particular. He will not pay us a visit to-morrow, you'll find. He has dropped us, being such as I suppose him, and we shall never see him more. I am glad of it. Let us cease to think of him. There's a more interesting man downstairs.'

In her slender hand she took the stick that she called the cudgel, and hammered on the floor.

Up came pretty Anne Pritchard, looking sleepy, her cheeks a little pale, her large eyes a little drowsy.

'Can I see your father, Mr. Pritchard ?' asked Maud.

'He's gone to his bed, please, ma'am, an hour ago.'

'Is he asleep, can you tell ?'

'He goes to sleep at once, if you please, miss.'

'How provoking ! What shall we do ?' She turned to Miss Max, and then to the girl. She said : 'I saw a man, a stranger —a man with a blind eye, here, when we came in. Is he here still ?'

'Yes, 'm, please.'

'He has a bed here, has he, and stays to-night ?' asked the old lady.

'Yes, 'm, please,' said the girl, with a courtesy.

'What do you think ? Shall we turn him out ?' said Maud, turning to Miss Max.

'Oh, no, dear ! don't trouble your head about him. He'll go in the morning. He's not in our way, at all,' answered Miss Max.

'Well, I suppose it is not worth making a fuss about. *There* is another advantage of the visit of our friend in the boots this evening. I could not find an opportunity to tell Mr. Pritchard to turn that person out of the house,' said Miss Maud, with vexation.

'Please, 'm, Mr. Lizard ?'

'Say it again, child, Mr. Who ?' asked Miss Max.

'Mr. Lizard, please, 'm. Elihu Lizard is wrote in his Bible, and he expounded this evening before he went to his bed. He's a very good man.'

'Was he ever here before?' asked Miss Maud.

'No, please, 'm.'

'And what is he?' demanded the young lady.

'I don't know, miss. Oh, yes, please, 'm, I forgot; he said he was gettin' money, please, 'm, for the good of the Gospel, and he had papers and cards, 'm.'

'The same story, you see,' she said, turning with a little nod and a faint smile to her companion.

'Do let the man rest in his bed, my dear, and let us go to ours; you forget how late it is growing,' said Miss Max, and yawned, and lighted her candle.

'That will do, thanks,' said Maud thoughtfully, 'and will you tell Mr. Pritchard, your father, in the morning, that we wish very much to see him before we go out?'

'And let us have breakfast a little before nine, please,' added Miss Max, looking at her watch, and then holding it to her ear. 'Come, darling,' she said, finding it was going, 'it really is very late, and you have a good deal, you know, to do to-morrow.'

'It is the most unpleasant thing in the world,' said the pretty young lady, looking thoughtfully at her companion. 'There can be no question he is following us, or one of us, you or me. Who on earth can have sent him? Who can it be? That odious creature! Did you ever see a more villainous face? He is watching us, picking up information about all our doings. What can he want? It is certainly for no good. Who can it be?'

'We can't find out to-night, and there is no good in losing your sleep. Perhaps we may make out something from old Pritchard in the morning,' said Miss Max.

'Yes, yes, perhaps so. All I know is, it is making me quite miserable,' said the girl, and she kissed the old lady, and went to her room. And Miss Max, having seen that the fire was nearly out, retired also to hers.

As neat and as quaint as their drawing-room was Miss Max's bedroom. But though everything invited to rest, and Miss Max was rather stiff from her long walk, and a little drowsy and yawning, she was one of those fidgety old ladies who take a prodigious time to get into bed.

Nearly an hour had passed, during which she had stuck armies of pins in her pincushion, and shut and opened every

drawer in her room, and walked from one table to another
oftener, and made more small dispositions about her room and
her bed, than I could possibly reckon, and, being now arrayed in
slippers and dressing-gown, she bethought of something to be
adjusted in the sitting-room, which might just as well have
waited till the morning, and so she took her candle and descended
the old oak stairs.

On the solid plank of that flooring, the slippered footfall of
the thin old lady made no sound. The moon was high, and
her cold blue light fell slanting through the window upon the
floor of the little lobby. Within and without reigned utter
silence; and if Miss Max had been a ghost-seeing old maid, no
scene could have been better suited for the visitation of a
phantom than this dissociated wing of a house more than three
hundred years old.

Miss Max was now at the drawing-room door, which she
opened softly and stepped in. It was neither without a tenant
nor a light.

At the far corner of the table, with a candle in his hand,
which he instantly blew out, she saw the slim figure and sly
lean face of Elihu Lizard, his white eyeball turned towards her,
and his other eye squinting, with the scowl of alarm, fiercely
across his nose at her.

Mr. Lizard was, with the exception of his shoes and his coat,
in full costume. His stockings and his shirt-sleeves gave him a
burglarious air, which rather heightened the shock of his ugly
leer, thus unexpectedly encountered.

He stepped back into a recess beside the chimney almost as
she entered.

For a moment she was not quite sure whether her frequent
discussions with Maud respecting this repulsive person had not
excited her fears and fancies, so as to call up an ugly vision. Mr.
Lizard, however, seeing that the extinction of his candle-light
was without effect, Miss Max's candle shining full upon him,
stepped forward softly, and executed his guileless smile and
lowly reverence.

Miss Max had recovered her intrepidity, and she said sharply:
'What do you mean, sir? What on earth brings you to our
private sitting-room?'

'I have taken the liberty,' he said, in his quavering tones,
inclining his long face aside with a plaintive simper, nearly
closing his eyelids, and lifting one skinny hand—it was the

tone and attitude in which the good Elihu Lizard was wont to expound, the same in which he might stand over a cradle, and pronounce a blessing on the little Christian in blankets, with whose purity the guileless heart of the good man sympathised— 'being a-thirst and panting, so to speak, as the hart for the water-brooks, as I lay in my bed, I arose, and finding none where I looked for it, I thought it would not be grudged me even in the chambers of them that go delicately, and therefore am I found here seeking if peradventure I might find any.'

Elihu Lizard, upon all occasions on which worldly men, of his rank in life, would affect the language of ceremony, glided from habit into that with which he had harangued from tables and other elevations at Greenwich Fair and similar assemblies, before he had engaged in his present peculiar occupation.

There was something celestial in the suavity of this person that positively exasperated Miss Max.

'That's all very fine. Water, indeed ! There you were, over Miss Maud's and my letters and papers, in our private sitting-room, and you show, sir, that you well knew you were about something nefarious, for I saw you put out your candle—there it is, sir, in your hand. How disgusting ! How dare you ! And I suspect you, sir, and your impious cant ; and I'll find out all about you, or I'll lose my life ! How can Mr. Pritchard allow such persons into his house ? I'll see him in the morning. I'll speak to the police in Cardyllion about you. I'll come to the bottom of all this. I'll consult a lawyer. I'll teach you, sir, be you who you may, you are not to follow people from place to place, and to haunt their drawing-rooms at dead of night. I'll turn the tables upon you ; I'll have you pursued.'

The good man turned up his effective eye till nothing but its white was seen, and it would have been as hard to say which of the two had a pupil to it, as under which of his thimbles, if thimble-rigger he be, the pea actually lies. He smiled patiently, and bowed lowly, and with his palm raised, uttered the words, 'Charity thinketh no evil.'

The measure of Miss Max's indignation was full. With her brown silk handkerchief swathed tightly about her head—for she had not yet got on her nightcap—and looking somewhat like a fez, in her red cloth slippers, and white cashmere dressing-gown, that, I must allow, was rather 'skimpy,' showing a little more of her ankle than was quite dignified, she was a rather striking effigy of indignation. She felt that she could have hurled her candlestick at the saintly man's head, an experiment which it is as well she did not hazard, seeing that she and her adversary would have been reduced to instantaneous darkness, and might have, without intending it, encountered in the dark, while endeavouring to make their retreat. Instead, therefore, of proceeding to this extreme measure, with kindling eyes, and a stamp on the floor, she said :

'Leave this room this moment, sir! How dare you? I shall call up Mr. Pritchard, if you presume to remain here another moment !'

I dare say that Mr. Lizard had completed whatever observations he intended to make, and his reconnaissance accomplished, he did not care to remain a moment longer than was necessary under fire. He withdrew, therefore, with the smiling meekness of a Christian enduring pagan vituperation and violence.

In the morning, when, at their early breakfast, the ladies made inquiry after him, they learned that he had taken his departure more than an hour before.

'More evidence, if it were needed, of a purpose, in tracking us as he does, which won't bear the light !' exclaimed Miss Max, who was now at least as strong upon the point as the handsome girl who accompanied her. 'I don't understand it. It is some object connected with *you,* most positively. Who on earth can be his employer ? I confess, Maud, I'm frightened at last.'

'Do you think it can be old Mr. Tintern ?' asked the girl, after a silence, looking curiously in the face of her companion. 'That old man may well wish me dead.'

'It may interest, possibly, a good many people to watch you very closely,' said the elder lady.

They both became thoughtful.

'You will now believe,' said the young lady, with a sigh, 'that the conditions of my life are not quite usual. I tell you, cousin, I have a presentiment that some misfortune impends. I suppose there is a crisis in every one's life; the astrologers used to say so. God send me safely through mine !'

'Amen, darling, if there be a crisis,' said Miss Max, more gravely than she usually spoke. 'But we must not croak any more. I have great confidence, under Heaven, in energy, my dear, and you were always a spirited girl. What, after all, can befal you ?'

'Many things. But let us think of to-day and Cardyllion and Llanberris, and let to-morrow take care of itself. What a beautiful day !'

CHAPTER VI.

THEY MEET A FRIEND.

' WON'T you wait and see Mr. Marston?' said Miss Max, a little later, when the young lady came down in her walking-dress.

' No ; I'm going to the castle. I have planned three drawings there, and two in the town, and then we set out on our drive to Llanberris, where I shall still have daylight, perhaps, to make one or two more.'

' Very industrious, upon my word ! But don't you think you might afford a little time to be civil?' said Miss Max.

' I don't know what you mean.'

' Mr. Marston said most pointedly, I mean particularly, that he would call this morning, and you allowed him to suppose we should be at home.'

' Did I? Well, that's past mending now,' said the girl.

' And he'll come and see *no* one,' said Miss Max, expanding her hands.

' He'll see the Pritchards,' said Miss Maud.

' I think it extremely rude, going out so much before our usual time, as if it was just to avoid him.'

' It *is* to avoid him. Put on your things and come,' said the girl.

' And what reason on earth can there be?' insisted Miss Max.

' I'm not in a Marston mood this morning, that's all. Do, like a darling, put on your things and come; everything is packed, and the people here know when the fly is coming to take our boxes, and I'll walk slowly on, and you will overtake me.'

So saying, she ran downstairs, and took a very friendly leave of the Pritchard family.

She was not afraid of meeting Mr. Marston, for Anne Pritchard had told her that he had inquired at what hour the ladies usually went out to walk, and that hour was considerably later than it now was.

Miss Max overtook her.

' It's plain we don't agree,' said that lady, as if their talk had not been suspended for a moment. ' I like that young man extremely, and I do think that it is rather marked, our leaving so unnecessarily early. I hate rudeness—*wanton* rudeness.'

The girl smiled pleasantly on her companion.

'Why do you like him?' she said.

'Because I think him so extremely nice. I thought him so polite, and there was so much deference and delicacy.'

'I'm afraid I've interrupted a very interesting acquaintance,' said Miss Maud, laughing.

'But tell me why you have changed your mind, for you did seem to like him,' said Miss Max.

'Well, don't you think he appeared a little more assured of his good reception than he would have been if he had thought us persons of his own rank—I mean, two great ladies such as he is in the habit of seeing; such as the people he knows? People like the Marstons—if he *is* one of them, as you suppose—make acquaintance with persons dressed in serge, like us, merely for amusement. Their affected deference seems to me insulting; it is an amusement I shan't afford him. From this point of view we can study human nature, because we can feel its meanness.'

'You are a morbid creature,' said Miss Max.

'I am trying to discover truth. I am trying to comprehend character,' said the girl.

'And making yourself a cynic as fast as you can,' said the old lady.

'It matters little what I am. We shan't see to-day a person so reckless of the future, a person with so little hope, a person who sees so little to live for, as I; or one who is so willing to die.'

'Look round, my dear, and open your eyes. You know nothing of life or of God's providence,' said Miss Max. 'I have no patience with you.'

'You were born free,' said the girl, more gently than before, 'I, a slave. Yes, don't smile; I call things by their names. You walk in the light, and I in darkness. The people who surround you, be they what they may, are at all events what they seem. When I look round, do I see images of candour? No; shadows dark and cold. I can trust no one—assassins in masquerade.'

'Everyone,' said Miss Max, 'has to encounter deceit and hypocrisy in this world.'

'It won't do; no, it won't do. You know very well that the cases are quite different,' said the girl. 'I have no one to care for me, and many that wish me dead; and, except you, I can trust no one.'

'Well, marry, and trust your husband.'

'I've too often told you I never shall, *never.* I need say so no more. How well the castle looks! I suppose it is from the rain last night; how beautifully the tints of the stone have come out!'

It was a brilliant, sunny morning. The grey walls, with patches of dull red and yellow stones, and cumbrous folds of ivy, looked their best, and tower, and arch, and battlement looked, in the soft summer air, all that the heart of an artist could desire.

Going to and fro from point to point, sometimes beyond the dry castle moat, sometimes within its grass-grown court, Miss Maud sketched industriously for some hours, and from her little tin colour-box threw in her tints with a bold and delicate brush, while Miss Max, seated beside her, read her book—for she loved a novel—and, through her spectacles, with glowing eyes, accompanied the heroine through her flirtations and agonies, to her final meeting with the man of her choice at the steps of the altar.

For a little time, now and then, pretty Miss Maud would lower her pencil, and rest her eye and hand, and think, looking vaguely on the ruins, in a sad reverie.

By this time Mr. Marston had, it was to be supposed, made his visit at the old farm-house, had sustained his disappointment and perhaps got over it, and was, possibly, consoling himself in his jack-boots, with his rod, in the channel of some distant trout-stream.

I can't say whether her thoughts ever wandered to this Mr. Marston, who was so agreeable and good-looking. But I fancy she did not think of him quite so hardly as she spoke. Whatever her thoughts were, her looks, at least, were sad.

'Whose epitaph are you writing, my dear?' inquired Miss Max, who had lowered her book, and, glancing over her spectacles, observed the absent and melancholy looks of the girl.

'My own,' said she, with a little laugh. 'But we have talked enough about that—I mean my life—and I suppose a good epitaph should sum that up. What do you think of these?' and she dropped her sketches on her cousin's lap. 'If I finish them as well as I have begun, they will be worth three shillings each, I dare say.'

'Yes; dear me! It is very good indeed. And this—how very pretty!' and so on, as she turned them over.

'But not one among them will ever be half so good as our

dear old farmhouse, that was so comfortable and so *uncomfortable*—so nearly intolerable, and yet so delightful; such a
pleasant adventure to remember. I am very glad to have it, for
we shall never see its face again.'

At these words, unexpectedly, Miss Max rose, and showed by
her countenance that she saw some one approaching whom she
was glad to greet. Her young companion turned also, and saw
Mr. Marston already very near.

He was so delighted to see them. He had been to the old
house, and was so disappointed; and the people there could not
tell where they had gone. He had hoped they had changed
their minds about leaving Cardyllion so soon. He had intended
going to Llanberris that day, but some of his people were coming
to Cardyllion. He had received orders from home to engage
rooms at the Verney Arms for them, and must stay that day.
It was too bad. Of course, he was very glad to see them; but
he might just as well have seen them in a week. Were they
(Miss Max and her companion) going to stay any time at Llanberris ?

'No. They would leave it in the morning.'

'And continue their tour? Where?'

'Nowhere,' said Miss Max. 'We go home then.'

He looked as if he would have given worlds to ask them
where that home was.

'My cousin returns to *her* home, and I to mine,' said the girl
gravely. 'We are very lucky in our last day; it would have
been so provoking to lose it.'

'She has made ever so many drawings to-day,' said Miss
Max; 'and they are really so very good, I must show them to
you.'

'There is not time,' said the girl to her cousin. 'It is a long
drive to Llanberris; it is time we were at the Verney Arms.
We must ask after our boxes, and order a carriage. It is later
than I fancied,' she said, turning to Mr. Marston; 'how time
runs away when one is really working.'

'Or really happy,' said the young man.

He walked with them down to Castle Street to the Verney
Arms, talking with them like an old friend all the way.

They all went together into the room to which the waiter
showed them. And Miss Max, who had the little portfolio in
her charge, said :

'Now, Maud, we must show Mr. Marston to-day's drawings.'

And very glad he was of that privilege.

Then she showed him the sketch of the old farmhouse.

'Oh! How pretty! What a sweet thing that is! What a beautiful drawing it makes!'

And so he descanted on it in a rapture.

'There is a place here where they do photographs; and I am going to have that old house taken,' he said to the young lady, as Miss Max was giving some orders at the door: 'I like it better than anything else about here. I feel so grateful to it.'

Miss Max was back again in a moment.

'Well, I do think they *are* very pretty indeed,' she said. 'We'll take the portfolio inside, dear. I'll take charge of it,' she said to Maud. 'And I hope none of our boxes were forgotten. I must count them. Five altogether.'

And she ran out again upon this errand; and Mr. Marston resumed:

'I shall never forget that thunder-storm, nor that pretty little room, nor my good fortune in being able to guide you home. I shall never forget yesterday evening, the most delightful evening I ever passed in my life.'

He was speaking in a very low tone.

Miss Maud looked embarrassed, almost vexed, and a beautiful colour flushed her cheeks, and gave a fire to her dark eyes.

Mr. Marston felt instinctively that he had been going a little too fast.

'Good Heavens!' he thought, 'what a fool I am! She looked almost angry. What business had I to talk so?'

There was a little silence.

'It is a misfortune, I believe, being too honest,' he said at length.

'A great one; but there are others greater,' said the girl, with eyes still vexed and fiery.

'What do you mean?'

'I mean being ever so little *dis*honest, and ever so little insolent. I hope I'm not that, at least to people I suppose to be my inferiors, though I may plead guilty to the lesser fault; perhaps I *am* too honest.'

Very proud, at least, she looked at that moment, and very completely 'floored' looked poor Mr. Marston.

I don't know what he might have said, or how much worse he might have made matters in the passionate effort to extricate himself, if Miss Max had not happened at that moment to return.

That he could be suspected of presuming upon her supposed position, to treat her with less deference than the greatest lady in the land, was a danger he had never dreamed of; he, who felt, as he spoke, as if he could have fallen on his knees before her. How monstrous! what degradation, what torture!

'Everything is ready, and the carriage at the door, my dear; and all our boxes quite right,' said Miss Max, in a fuss.

Mr. Marston came down to put the ladies into their carriage; and while Miss Max was saying a word from one carriage window, he leaned for a moment at the other, and said:

'I'm so shocked and pained to think I've been so mistaken. I implore of you to believe that I am incapable of a thought that could offend you, and that you leave me very miserable.'

The cheery voice of Miss Max, unconscious of her cruelty, interrupted him with a word or two of farewell, and the carriage drove off, leaving him not less melancholy than he had described himself.

CHAPTER VII.

FLIGHT.

THE old lady looked from the window as they drove on, watching the changes of the landscape. The girl, on the contrary, leaned back in her place, and seemed disturbed and thoughtful.

After a silence of nearly ten minutes, Miss Max, having had, I suppose, for the time, enough of the picturesque, remarked suddenly:

'Mr. Marston is, as I suspected, Lord Warhampton's son. His eldest, I believe his only living son. The people at the Verney Arms told me he had actually ordered horses for Llanberris, intending to go there to-day, when his plans were upset by his father's letter. Of course, we know perfectly why he wished to go there to-day. I mentioned last night that we intended visiting it this afternoon, and he really did look so miserable as we took our leave just now.'

'The fool! What right has he to follow us to Llanberris?' asked the girl.

'Why, of course, he has a right to go to Llanberris if he likes it, without asking either you or me,' said Miss Max.

'He has just the same right, I admit, that Mr. Elihu Lizard has.'

'Oh! come, you mustn't compare them,' said Miss Max. 'I should have been very glad to see Mr. Marston there, and so would you; he is very agreeable, and never could be the least in one's way; he's so good-natured and considerate, and would see in a moment if he was *de trop*. And it is all very fine, talking independence; but everyone knows there are fifty things we can't do so well for ourselves, and he might have been very useful in our walks.'

'Carrying us over rivers in his jack-boots.'

'He never did carry me over any river, if you mean that,' said Miss Max, a little testily, 'or anywhere else. But it is very well I had his arm to lean upon, over those stepping-stones, or I don't think we should have got home last night.'

'I dare say he thinks his title irresistible, and that the untitled and poor are made for his amusement. It is a selfish, cruel world. You ought to know it better than I; you have been longer in it; and yet, by a kind of sad inspiration, I know it, I'm sure, ever so much better than you do.'

'Wise-head!' said the old lady with a smile, and a little shake of her bonnet.

The young lady looked out, and in a little time took up a volume of Miss Max's nearly finished novel, and read listlessly. She was by no means in those high spirits that had hitherto accompanied every change of scene in their little excursion. Miss Max remarked this subsidence, thought even that she detected the evidence of positive fatigue and melancholy; but the wary lady made no remark. It was better to let this little cloud dissipate itself.

In a lonely part of the road a horse dropped a shoe, and brought them to a walk, till they had reached the next smithy. The delay made their arrival late. The sun was in the west when they gained their first view of that beautiful and melancholy lake lying in the lap of its lonely glen. They drew up near the ruined tower that caught the slanting light from the west, under the purple shadow of the hill.

As they stopped the carriage here and got out, they were just in time to see a man descend from the box beside the driver.

They were both so astounded that neither could find a word for some seconds. It was Mr. Elihu Lizard, who had enjoyed all the way a seat on their driver's box, and who now got down, put his bundle on the end of his stick, which he carried over his shoulder, and with a 'Heaven bless you, friend,' to the whip on the box, smiled defiantly over his shoulder at the ladies, and marched onward toward the little inn at the right of the glen.

'Well!' exclaimed Miss Max, when she had recovered breath. 'Certainly! Did you ever hear or see anything like that? Where did you take up that person, pray?'

Miss Max looked indignantly up at the fat, dull cheeks of the Welshman on the box, and pointed with her parasol at the retreating expounder. That gentleman, glancing back from time to time, was taken with a fit of coughing, or of laughter, it was difficult to say which at that distance, as he pursued his march, with the intention of refreshing himself with a mug of beer in the picturesque little inn.

'Call that man! You had no business taking any one upon the carriage we had hired, without our leave,' said Miss Max. 'Call him—make him come back, or you shall drive us after him. I will speak to him.'

The driver shouted. Mr. Lizard waved his hand.

'I'm certain he is laughing—insolent hypocrite!' exclaimed Miss Max, transported with indignation. 'I'll drive after him, I will overtake him.'

They got into the carriage, overtook Elihu Lizard, and stepped down about a dozen yards before him.

'So, sir, you persist in following us!' exclaimed the old lady.

'To me,' he replied, in a long-drawn, bleating falsetto, as he stood in his accustomed pose, with his hand a little raised, his eyes nearly closed, and a celestial simper playing upon his conceited and sinister features, 'to me it would appear, nevertheless, honourable lady, that it is you, asking your parding, that is a-following of me; I am following, not you, nor any other poor, weak, sinful, erring mortal, but my humble calling, which I hope it is not sich as will be disdained from the hand of a poor weak, miserable creature, nor yet that I shall be esteemed altogether an unprofitable servant.'

'I don't want to hear your cant, sir; if you had the least regard for truth, you would admit frankly that you have been following me and my friend the whole of the way from Chester, stopping wherever we stopped, and pursuing wherever we went. I have seen you everywhere, and if there was a policeman here, I should have you arrested: rely on it, I shall meet you somewhere, where I can have your conduct inquired into, and your cowardly persecution punished.'

'I have come to this land of Wales, honourable lady, and even to this place, which it is called Llanberris, holding myself subject and obedient unto the powers that be, and fearing no one, insomuch as I am upon my lawful business, with your parding for so saying, not with a concealed character, nor yet with a forged name, nor in anywise under false pretences ; but walking in my own humble way, and being that, and only that, which humbly and simply I pretend to be.'

The good man, with eyes nearly closed, between the lids of which a glitter was just perceptible, betraying his vigilance, delivered these words in his accustomed singsong, but with an impertinent significance that called a beautiful rush of crimson to the younger lady's cheeks.

' Your name is nothing to us, sir.   We are not likely to know it,' said the young lady, supporting Miss Max with a little effort. ' We shall find that out in good time, perhaps.   We shall make it out when we want it.'

'You shall have it when you please, honourable lady ; the humble and erring sinner who speaks to you is one who walks in the light, which he seeks not, as too many do, and have done, ay, and are doing at this present time, to walk as it were in a lie, and give themselves out for that which they are not. No, he is not one of those who loveth a lie, nor yet who is filled with guile, and he is not ashamed, neither afraid, to tell his name whithersoever he goeth, neither is he the heaviness of his mother ; no, nor yet forsaketh he the law of his mother.'

The same brilliant blush tinged the girl's cheeks ; she looked hard and angrily at the man, and his simper waxed more than ever provoking as he saw these signs of confusion.

' I believe I did wrong to speak to you here, where there are no police,' said Miss Max. ' I ought to have known that it could only supply new opportunity to your impertinence.   I shall find out, however, when I meet you next, as I have told you, whether we are longer to be exposed to this kind of cowardly annoyance.'

Miss Max and her young companion turned away.   The one-eyed Christian, apostle, detective, whatever he was, indulged silently in that meanest of all laughs, the laugh which, in cold blood, chuckles over insult, as with a little hitch of his shoulder, on which rested his stick and bundle, he got under way again toward the little inn, a couple of hundred yards on.

The driver took his horses up to the inn.

'Well,' said Miss Max, a little disconcerted, 'I could have told you that before. I thought him a very impertinent person, and just the kind of man who would be as insolent as he pleased to two ladies, alone as we are; but very civil if a gentleman were by with a stick in his hand.'

'I don't mean to make any drawings here. I've changed my mind,' said Maud. 'I'm longing to be at Wybourne again. Suppose, instead of staying here, we go to-night?'

'Very good, dear. To say truth, I'm not comfortable with the idea of that man's being here to watch us. Come, Maud, you must not look so sad. We have all to-morrow at Wybourne, before we part, and let us enjoy, as you say, our holiday.'

'Yes; on Monday we part. Don't mention it again. It is bad enough when it comes. Then the scene changes. I'll think of it no more to-day. I'll forget it. Let us walk a little further up the glen, and see all we can in an hour.'

So, with altered plans, the hour was passed; and at the approach of sunset they met the train at Bangor.

A fog was spreading up the Menai as the train started. To the girl it seemed prophetic of her own future of gloom and uncertainty.

Other people had changed their plans that evening. A letter had reached Mr. Marston, unluckiest of mortals, only two hours after the ladies had left Cardyllion for Llanberris, countermanding all his arrangements for his father, Lord Warhampton.

Instantly that impetuous young man had got horses, and pursued to Llanberris, but only to find that those whom he had followed had taken wing. As he looked from the uplands along the long level sweep that follows the base of the noble range of mountains, by which the line of rails stretches away until it rounds the foot of a mighty headland at the right, he saw, with distraction, the train gliding away along the level, submerging itself, at last, in the fog that flooded the valley like a golden lake.

His only clue was one of the papers, condemned as illegible, which Miss Max had hastily written for their boxes.

'Miss M. Guendoline,' was written on it, with the name of some place, it was to be supposed—but, oh, torture!—the clumsy hoof of the driver, thick with mud, had stamped this inestimable record into utter illegibility. *Viâ* Chester was still traceable, also England in the corner. The rest was undecipherable. The wretch seemed to have jumped upon it. The very paper was demolished. The gravel from the Vandal's heel was punched through it.

In the little inn where he had heard tidings of two ladies, with a carriage such as he described, he had picked up this precious but torturing bit of paper.

CHAPTER VIII.

WYBOURNE CHURCHYARD.

In a golden mist he lost her; but he does not despair. Mr. Marston pursues. Has he any very clear idea why?

If he had overtaken the ladies, as he expected, at Llanberris, would he have ventured, of his own mere motion, to accompany them on their after-journey? Certainly not. What, then, is the meaning of this pursuit? What does he mean to do or say?

He has no plan. He has no set speech or clear idea to deliver. He is in a state of utter confusion. He only knows that see her once more he must—that he can't endure the thought of letting her go, thus, for ever from his sight; she is never for a moment out of his head.

I don't know what his grave and experienced servant thought of their mysterious whirl to Chester by the night mail. He did not refer it, I dare say, to anything very wise or good. But the relation of man and master is, happily, military, and the servant's conscience is acquitted when he has obeyed his orders.

The fog has melted into clearest air, and the beautiful moon is shining.

What a world of romance, and love, and beauty he thinks it, as he looks out of the open window on the trees and mountains that sail by in that fairy light.

The distance is shortening. Everything near and far is good of its kind. Everything is interesting. It is like the ecstasy of the opium-eater. Never were such stars, and hedges, and ditches. What an exquisite little church, and tombstones! *Requiescat in pace!* What a beautiful ash-tree! Heaven bless it!

How picturesque that horse's head, poking out through the hole in the wall with the ivy over it ! And those pigs, lying flat on the manure-heap, jolly, odd creatures ! How delightfully funny they are ! And even when he draws his head in, and leans back for a moment in his place, he thinks there is something so kindly and jolly about that fat old fellow with the travelling-cap and the rugs, who snores with his chin on his chest—a stock-broker, perhaps. What heads and ledgers !—wonderful fellows ! The valves and channels through which flows into its myriad receptacles the incredible and restless wealth of Britain. Or, perhaps, a merchant, princely, benevolent. Well that we have such a body, the glory of England !

The fat gentleman utters a snort, wakes up, looks at his watch, and produces a tin sandwich-box.

That thin elderly lady in black, that sits at the left of the fat gentleman, who is champing his sandwiches, does not see things, with her sunken eyes, as Mr. Marston sees them. She is gliding on to her only darling at school, who lies in the sick-house in scarlatina.

They are now but half an hour from Chester. Mr. Marston is again looking out of the window as they draw near.

'Maud Guendoline,' he is repeating again. 'Guendoline—an odd surname, but so beautiful. Foreign, is it? I never heard it before. When we get into Chester I'll have the Army List, and the London Directory, and every list of names they can make me out. It may help me. Who knows?'

They are in Chester. Oh, that it were not so big a place ! His servant is looking after his luggage. He is in the ticket-office, making futile inquiries after 'an old lady, Miss Max, who left Bangor for Chester that very evening, and forgot something of importance, and I would gladly pay any one a reward who could give me a clue to find her by. I am sure only that she was to go *viâ* Chester.'

No ; they could tell him nothing. But if it was *viâ* Chester, she was going on by one of the branches. The clerk who might have written the new labels for her luggage was not on duty till to-morrow afternoon, having leave till two. 'He's very sharp ; if 'twas he did it—Max is a queer name—he'll be like to remember it ; that is, he may.'

Here was hope, but hope deferred. The people at Llanberris had told him that the label which he had picked up was the only one on which the name of the place was written, on which account it was removed, and all the rest were addressed simply 'Chester.' He has nothing for it but patience.

There is a pretty little town called Wybourne, not very far from a hundred miles away. Next evening, the church-bell, ringing the rustics to evening service, has sounded its sweet note over the chimneys of the town, through hedge-rows and bosky hollows, over slope and level sward, and Mr. Marston, with the gritty dust of the railway still on his hat, has tapped in the High Street at the post-office wooden window-pane, and converses with grave and plaintive Mrs. Fisher.

'Can you tell me if a lady named Miss Guendoline lives anywhere near this?' he inquires.

'Guendoline? No, sir. But there's Mr. and Mrs. Gwyn, please, that lives down the street near the Good Woman.'

'No, thanks! that's not it. Miss Maud Guendoline.'

Mrs. Fisher put an unheard question to an invisible interlocutor in the interior, and made answer: 'No, sir; please, there's no such person.'

'I beg pardon; but just one word more. Does a lady named Max—a Miss Max—live anywhere near this place?'

'Miss Max? I think not, sir.'

'You're not quite sure, I think?' says he, brightening, as he leans on the little shelf outside the window; and if his head would have fitted through the open pane, he would, I think, in his eagerness, have popped it into Mrs. Fisher's front parlour.

Again Mrs. Fisher consulted the inaudible oracle.

'No, sir; we don't receive no letters here for no person of that name,' she replied.

The disappointment in the young man's handsome face touched Mrs. Fisher's gentle heart.

'I'm very sorry, indeed, sir. I wish very much we could a' gave you any information,' she says, through the official aperture.

'Thank you very much,' he answers desolately. 'Is there any other post-office near? Do the people send a good way to you—about what distance round?'

'Well, the furthest, I think, will be Mr. Wyke's, of Wykhampton, about four miles.'

'Is there any name at all like Max, Miss Max, an old lady? I should be so extremely—I can't tell you—so very grateful.' He pleads, in his extremity, 'Do, do, pray ask.'

She turned and consulted the unknown once more.

'There is no one—that is, no surname—here, sir, at all like

Max. There's an old lady lives near here, but it can't be her. She's Miss Maximilla Medwyn.'

' Maximilla? Is she an old lady?'

' Yes, sir.'

' Thin?'

' She is, sir.' And Mrs. Fisher begins to wonder at the ardour of his inquiries, and to look at him very curiously.

' Has she been from home lately?'

' I think she was.' (Here she again consults her unseen adviser.) ' Yes, sir ; she returned only last night.'

' And where does she live, pray? In the town here—near this?' he pursues.

' In the Hermitage, please, sir ; any one you meet will show it you. It is just at the end of the town. But she'll be in church at present.'

' And how soon do you think it will be over—how soon will the people be coming out?'

' In about half an hour, sir.'

And so, with many acknowledgments on his part, and no little surprise and conjecture on that of sedate Mrs. Fisher, who wondered what could have fired this young gentleman so about old Miss Medwyn, the conference ends, and in ten minutes more, in a somewhat less dusty state, he presents himself at the open gate of the churchyard, and reconnoitres.

Over the graves in faint gusts peals the swell of the organ, and the sound of voices, sweetly and sadly, like psalmody from another world. He looks up to the gilded hand of the clock in the ivied tower, and conjectures that this must be the holy song that precedes the sermon. Devoutly he wishes the pulpit orator a quick deliverance.

He, on the whole, wisely resolves against going into the church, and, being provided with a seat, perhaps in some corner of difficult egress, whence, if he should see the objects of his pursuit, he might not be able to make his way out in time without a fuss.

At length, with a flutter at his heart, he sees the hats and bonnets begin to emerge from the porch. Taking his stand beside the gate, he watches. Not a single Christian in female garb escapes him. He sees the whole congregation pour itself out, and waits till the very dregs and sediment drop forth. Those who pray *in formâ pauperis*, and draw a weekly dividend out of the poors' box : old Mrs Milders, with the enormous

black straw bonnet, and the shaking head and hand; Bill
Hopkins, lame of a leg, who skips slowly down on a crutch; and
Tom Buzzard, blind of both eyes, a pock-marked object of
benevolence, with his chin high in the air, and a long cudgel in
his hand, with which he taps the curbstone, and now and then
the leg of a passenger who walks the street forgetful of the blind.

The clerk comes forth demurely with a black bag, such as
lawyers carry their briefs in. There is no good, Mr. Marston
thinks, in waiting for the sexton.

He joins the clerk, compliments him on his church and organ,
asks whether Miss Maximilla Medwyn was in church—(yes,
she was)—and where the house called the Hermitage is to be
found.

'You may go by the road, sir,' said the clerk, ' or by the path,
which you'll find it shorter. Take the first stile to your right,
when you turn the corner.'

Alas! what is the meaning of this walk to the Hermitage?
Miss Medwyn was in church; and could he not swear that, in
the review just ended, he had seen distinctly every female face
and figure in the congregation as it 'marched past?' His Miss
Max was assuredly not among them; and she and Miss Medwyn,
therefore, were utterly distinct old women—ah, well-a-day!

He crosses the stile. The path traverses a narrow strip of
meadow, the air is odorous with little dishevelled cocks of hay,
mown only the day before; the spot, cloistered in by very old
and high hawthorn hedges, is silent with a monastic melancholy.

He sighs more pleasantly as he enters this fragrant solitude;
beyond the stile at the other side is the gloom of tall old trees.
He is leaving the world behind him.

Butterflies are hovering up and down, along the hedge, at the
sunny side of the field. A bee booms by as he stands on the
second stile; it is the only sound he hears except the faint chirp
of the grasshopper. He descends upon that pleasant dark-green
grass that grows in shade.

Here is another field, long and narrow, silent and more gloomy
than the first. Up the steep, a giant double row of lime-trees
stretches, marking the line of the avenue, now carpeted over with
thick grass, of the old manor-house of Wybourne, some walls
and stone-shafted windows of which, laden with ivy, and canopied
by ancient trees, crown the summit. The western sun throws
long dim shadows down the slope. A thick underwood straggles
among the trunks of the lordly timber, and here and there a gap

leaves space, in which these patriarchal trees shake their branches free, and spread a wider shadow.

In this conventual obscurity, scarcely fifty steps up the gentle slope, he sees Miss Maud, Maud Guendoline, or whatever else her name may be, standing in her homely dress. She is looking toward him, no doubt recognises him, although she makes no sign. His heart thumps wildly once or twice. He is all right again in a moment. He quickens his pace. He is near enough to see her features distinctly. She looks a little grave, he thinks, as he raises his hat.

Here is a tall fellow, great in a town-and-gown row, full of pluck, cool as marble in danger, very much unnerved at this moment, and awfully afraid of this beautiful and slender girl.

CHAPTER IX.

THE YOUNG LADY SPEAKS.

'I'm so glad, I'm so charmed—how extremely lucky I am! I had not the least hope of this. And you have made your journey quite safely?'

As he makes this little confession and inquiry, his brown handsome face and large eyes are radiant with happiness.

'Safely! oh yes, my cousin and I are old travellers, and we never lose our way or our luggage. I am waiting here for her; she is paying a visit to—I really forget his name, farmer something or other, an old friend of hers, down there; you can see the smoke of his chimney over the hedge,' said the young lady, indicating the direction.

'And you're not fatigued?'

'Oh no! thanks.'

'And Miss Max quite well, I hope?' he adds, recollecting her right to an inquiry.

'Miss Max is very well, thanks,' said the young lady.

Had she blushed when she saw him? Was there not a gentle subsidence in the brilliant tint with which she met him? He thought her looking more beautiful than ever.

'I dare say you are glad to find yourself at home again?' says he, not knowing what exactly to say next.

She glanced at him as if she suspected a purpose in his question.

'Some people have no place they can call a home, and some who have are not glad to find themselves there. I'm not at home, and I'm not sorry,' she said, ever so little bitterly.

'There is a great deal of melancholy in that,' he said, in a lower tone, as if he would have been very glad to be permitted to sympathize. 'Away from home, and yet no wish to return. Isn't it a little cruel, too?'

'Melancholy or cruel, it happily concerns no one but myself,' she said, a little haughtily.

'Everything that can possibly concern your happiness concerns me,' said the young man audaciously.

She looked for a moment offended and even angry, but 'a change came o'er the spirit of her dream,' and she smiled as if a little amused.

'You seem, Mr. Marston, to give away your sympathy on very easy terms—you must have mistaken what I said. It was no confidence. It was spoken, as people in masks tell their secrets, and further because I don't care if all the world knew it. How can you tell that I either desire or deserve pity—yours, or any other person's? You know absolutely nothing of me.'

'I'm too impetuous; it is one of my many faults. Other fellows, wiser men, get on a thousand times better, and I have laid myself open to your reproof, and—and disdain, by my presumption, by my daring to speak exactly as I feel. It is partly this, that the last three days—they say that happy days seem very short—I don't know how it is, I suppose I'm different from everyone else; but that day, yesterday, and to-day, seem to me like three weeks; I feel as if I had known you ever so long——'

'And yet you know nothing about me, not even my name, said the young lady, smiling on the grass near her pretty foot, and poking at a daisy with the tip of her parasol, and making its little head nod this way and that.

'I do know your name—I beg pardon, but I do; I heard Miss Max call you Maud, and I learned quite accidentally your second name yesterday.'

Miss Maud looks at him from under her dark lashes suddenly. Her smile has vanished now; she looks down again; and now it returns darkly.

'I do upon my honour; I learned it at Llanberris yesterday,' he repeated.

'Oh! then you *did* go to Llanberris; and you did not disdain to cross-examine the people about us, and to try to make out that which you supposed we did not wish to disclose?'

'You are very severe,' he began, a good deal abashed.

'I'm very merciful, on the contrary,' she said bitterly; 'if I were not—but no matter. I think I can conjecture who was your informant. You made the acquaintance of a person blind of one eye, who is a detective, or a spy, or a villain of some sort, and you pumped him. Somehow, I did not think before that a gentleman was quite capable of that sort of thing.'

'But, I give you my honour, I did nothing of the kind,' ho pleads earnestly. 'I saw no such person, I do assure you.'

'You shall answer my questions, then,' she said, as imperiously as a spoiled child; 'and, first, will you speak candidly? Will you be upon honour, in no one particular, wilfully to deceive me?'

'You are the last person on earth I should deceive, upon any subject, Miss Guendoline—I hope you believe me.'

'Well, why did you go to Llanberris?'

'I had hopes,' he answered with a little embarrassment, 'of overtaking you and Miss Max—and I—I hoped, also, that perhaps you would permit me to join in your walk—that was my only reason.'

'Now, tell me my name?' said the young lady, suddenly changing her line of examination.

'Your name is, I believe—I think you are Miss Maud Guendoline,' he answered.

She smiled again darkly at the daisy she was busy tapping on the head.

'Miss Maud Guendoline,' she repeated, very low; and she laughed a little to herself. 'Maud and Guendoline are two Christian names,' she said. 'Do you really believe that I have no surname; or perhaps you believe that either of these is my surname? I need not have told you, but I do; that neither of these is the least like it. And now, why have you come here? Have you any real business here?'

'You are a very cruel inquisitor,' he says, with a very real wince. 'Is there any place where an idle man may *not* find himself, without well knowing why? Is your question quite fair?'

'Is your answer quite frank ?   Do you quite remember your promise ?   If we are not to part this moment, you must answer without evasion.'

This young lady in serge spoke as haughtily as if she were a princess in a fairy-tale.

'Well, as you command me, I will, I will, indeed.   I—I believe I came here, very much—entirely, indeed, from the same motive that led me to Llanberris.   I could not help it, I couldn't, upon my honour !   I hope you are not very angry.'

It is not usual to be constrained to speak, in matters of this kind, the literal truth ; and I question if the young man was ever so much embarrassed in all his days.

'Mr. Marston,' she said very quietly, he fancied a little sadly, ' you are, I happen to know, a person of some rank, and likely to succeed to estates, and a title—don't answer ; I *know* this to be so, and I mention it only by way of preface.   Now, suppose I pull off my glove, and show you a seamstress's finger, dotted all over with the needle's point ; suppose I fill in what I call my holiday by hard work with my pencil and colour-box ; suppose, beside all this, I have troubles enough to break the spirits of the three merriest people you know ; and suppose that I have reasons for preventing any one, but Miss Max, from knowing where I am, or suspecting who I am, don't you think there is enough in my case to make you a little ashamed of having pried and followed as you are doing ?'

'You wrong me—oh, *indeed* you wrong me !   You won't say that ; I did, perhaps, wrong—I may have been impertinent ; but the meanness of prying, you *won't* think it !   All I wanted was to learn where you had gone : my crime is in following you. I did not intend that you should think I had followed.   I hoped it might appear like accident.   If you knew how I dread your contempt, and how I respect you, and how your reproof pains me, I am sure you would think differently, and forgive me.'

I don't think there could have been more deference in his face and tones if he had been pleading before an empress.

The young lady's dark eyes for a moment looked full at him, and again down upon the little daisy at her foot ; and she drew some odd little circles round it as she looked, and I think there was ever so slight a brightening of her colour while the end of her parasol made these tiny diagrams.

If a girl be only beautiful enough, and her beauty of the refined type, it is totally impossible, be her position, her dress, her associates what they may, to connect the idea of vulgarity with her. There is nothing she does or means that is not elegant. Be she what she may, and you the most conceited dog on earth, there is a superiority in her of which your inward nature is conscious, and if you see her winnowing barley, as honest Don Quixote said of his mistress, the grains are undoubtedly pearls.

Mr. Marston, in the influence of this beauty, was growing more and more wild and maudlin every moment.

'The world's all wrong,' he said vehemently; 'it is always the best and the noblest that suffer most; and you say you have troubles, and you don't disdain to work, and are not ashamed of it; and I admired and respected you before, and I've learned to honour you to-day. You talk of rank: of course, there are things in its favour—some things; but there are ever so many more against it. I have little to boast of even in that, and I never was so happy as when I knew nothing about it. People are always happy, I am sure, in proportion as the idea of it fades from their minds. There is but one thing worth living for—and, oh, Heaven, how I wish I were worthy of you!'

'Now, Mr. Marston, you are talking like a madman. There must be no more of that,' she said in earnest.

'I spoke the truth, straight from my heart. I believe that is always madness.'

'I like truth pretty well. I speak it more boldly than most girls, I believe. But I quite agree with you, whenever one is noble one is inevitably foolish. I'm not very old, but I have heard a good deal of romantic talk in my time, as every girl does, and I despise it. It doesn't even embarrass me. If we are to talk till my cousin, Miss Max, comes back, do let it be reasonably; I shall tire of it instantly on any other terms.'

'When you told me to speak truth, just now, you did not think so,' says he, a little bitterly.

'Why can't you speak to me, for a few minutes, as you would to a friend? You talked just now about rank as if it should count for nothing. I don't agree with you. It is no illusion, but a cruelly hard fact. If I were the sort of girl who could like any one—I mean, make a fool of myself and fall in love—that person must be exactly of my own rank, neither above nor below it. The man who stoops is always sorry for it too late; and if he is like me, he would always think he was chosen not for himself, but for his wealth or his title. Now, if *I* suspected that, it would make my house a jail, every hour of my life ghastly, my very self odious to me. It would make me utterly wicked ; bad enough to be jealous of a human rival, though death may remove that. But to be jealous of your own circumstances, to know that you were nothing in the heart of your beloved, and they everything; that they had duped you ; that your wooing was an imposture, and your partner a phantom. That anything like that should be my lot, Heaven forbid ! It never shall. But were I a man, and found it so, I should load a pistol, and lie, soon enough, in my last strait bed.'

'Only think how cruel and impossible this is' he said gently, looking into her face. 'I ask you to be reasonable, and consider the consequences of your pitiless theory. As to wealth, isn't there always some inequality—and do you mean that an artificial social distinction should throw asunder for ever two people——'

'I mean to say this—I ought to beg your pardon for interrupting you, but I speak for myself—if I were a man, I could never trust the love of the woman who, being immensely poorer than I, and in an inferior place in life, consented to marry me. I never could ; and the more I loved her the worse it would be.'

'We are all lawgivers and law-breakers,' says he.

'I'm not, for one ; I observe, at least, my own precepts ; and so resolved, I shall never either love or marry.'

He looked at her sadly ; he looked down. Even this was more tolerable than if she had said she could neither love nor marry *him.*

'I wish, God knows, that *I* could rule my heart so,' he said sadly.

'Everyone who pleases can. There are good nuns and good monks. It is a matter of will and of situation. Man or girl, it is all the same ; if they know they can't marry, and have a particle of reason, they see that liking and loving, except in the way of common goodwill, is not for them. They resist that demon Asmodeus, or Cupid, or call him how you please, and he troubles them no more.'

'How can you talk so cruelly ?' he says.

There is pain in every line of his handsome face, in the vexed light of the eyes that gaze so piercingly on her, in the uneasy grasp of his hand, that leans upon the rough bark of the great tree which her shoulder touches lightly.

CHAPTER X.

FAREWELL.

As men who, in stories, have fallen in love with phantoms, Marston feels, alas! he is now in love with a beautiful image of apathy. Is the great gulf really between them, and he yearning for the impossible?

'If by any sacrifice I could ever make myself the least worthy of you; if you could ever like me ever so little——'

She laughed, but not unkindly.

'If I liked you, or were at all near liking you, you should know it by a certain sign,' she says, with a smile, though a sad one.

'How? Do tell me how—how I should know it!'

And he works off a great piece of the old bark with his sinewy hand as he talks.

'By my instantly leaving you,' she answered. 'And now we have talked sufficiently, haven't we, on this interesting theme? One day or other you'll say, if, by chance, you remember this talk under the walls of Wybourne, "That wise but threadbare young lady was right, and I was wrong, and it is very well there was some prudent person near to save me from an irreparable folly;" and having made this prediction, and said my say on what seems to me a very simple question, the subject is, for me, exhausted, and becomes a bore, and nothing shall tempt me to say or listen to another word upon it. What a sudden curious fog there was yesterday evening?'

Mr. Marston talked of the fog as well as he was able, and of the old city of Chester, and whatever else this young lady pleased; he was hardly half thinking of these themes. His mind was employed, in an undercurrent, upon far more interesting matter.

'Suffering,' he thinks, 'is the parent of all that is fine in character. This girl thinks, resolves, and acts for herself. How different she is from the youthful daughters of luxury! What originality—what energy—what self-reliance!'

Perhaps he is right. This young lady has a will of her own; she is a little eccentric; she thinks, without much knowledge of the world, very resolutely for herself. I don't know that she is more jealous than other women. But she is an imperious little princess.

While she is trifling in this cruel way, Miss Max comes through a little gate in the hedge at the foot of this sloping field. Urged apparently by the shortness of the time that remained, the young gentleman made one other venture.

'And do you mean to say, Miss Maud, that you, for instance, could never love a man whose rank you thought above your own?'

This was a rather abrupt transition from Carl Maria Von Weber, about whose music the young lady was talking.

'You don't keep treaties, it seems,' said the young lady; 'but as only two or three minutes remain, and we may never meet again, I'll answer you. Yes, perhaps I could. All the more readily for his superiority, all the more deeply for his sacrifices. But in some of my moods, vain or ambitious, I might marry him without caring a pin about him. There are the two cases, and I am never likely to be tempted by either, and—pray, let me say the rest—if I were, no one should ever suspect it, and I should assuredly accept neither.'

'You said we were never likely to meet again,' said the young man. 'Is that kind? What have I done to deserve so much severity?'

He glanced down the slope. Miss Max was toiling up. She was stumbling over the twisted roots that spread under the great trees, and seeing a man conversing with her young cousin, she had put up her parasol to keep the slanting sunlight from her eyes, and aid her curious scrutiny.

She could not reach them well in less than four minutes more.

Four minutes still. Precious interval.

'You go to the ball at Wymering?' she asked in a tone that had something odd in it; a strange little sigh, and yet how much apathy.

'Anywhere—yes, certainly,' he replies, in hot haste. 'Is there a chance—the least hope?' He remembered that she was not a very likely person to figure at a ball, and so he ended, 'I have often intended going there. Any hope of your being in the neighbourhood of Wymering about that time?'

'You see, I don't pretend to be a great person. No fairy has bedizened me for an occasion. I have no magnificence to dissolve at a fated hour,' she said, with a sad little laugh. 'Those balls are not such ill-natured things after all. They help poor girls who work at their needles. Yes, I always go to that, at least as far as the cloak-room.'

'Wherever you go, Miss Maud, there will be no one like you; no one like you anywhere in all the world ; and remember— though you can't like me now—how I adore you.'

'Stop—don't talk so to me,' she replied. 'You are rich. I am what I am, and language that might be only audacious if we were equals is insult now.'

'Good heavens ! won't you understand me ? I only meant, I can't help saying it, that I care to win no one else on earth, and never shall. If you but knew——'

'What need I know more than I do ? I believe, rather from your looks than from your words, that you talk your folly in good faith. But I have heard too much of that for one day. One thing more I have to say, you must leave this immediately ; and if from Miss Max, or any other person, you try to make out anything more, ever so little, about me, about my story, name, business, than I have told you, you never speak to me one word more. That's understood. Here, now, is my cousin.'

Miss Max, smiling pleasantly, said :

'Dear me, Mr. Marston, who could have fancied that you would have been here ! I could not think who it could be, as I came up the hill. Were you at Wybourne Church ?'

'Oh, no ! I wai——' He was going to say 'waited outside,' but he corrected himself. 'I arrived too late. A pretty little church it seems to be.'

'Oh ! quite a beautiful little church inside. Some one showed you the path here, I suppose ; those up there are the ruins of old Wybourne Hall : what an awful fog we had last night ! Do you know, it was really quite frightful, going through it at the fearful speed we did. You must come and drink tea with us, Mr. Marston.'

'No, dear, we must not have anyone to tea to-night; I have particular reasons, and besides, Mr. Marston has to leave this immediately,' said Miss Maud inhospitably.

He looked at her ruefully.

'You told me you were going immediately,' said the young lady gently, but with a slight emphasis.

'But I dare say you can manage to put it off for an hour or so, Mr. Marston—can't you ?' asked Miss Max.

He glanced at the inexorable Miss Maud, and he read his doom in that pretty face.

'I'm afraid—it is so very kind of you—but I'm really afraid it is quite impossible,' he answers.

'I don't like to bore you, Mr. Marston; but if you *can* stay to tea, just an hour or two—can't you manage that? I shall be *so* glad,' urged the old lady.

'Mr. Marston, I believe, made a promise to be at another place this evening,' said the girl; 'and Mr. Marston says he prides himself on keeping his word.'

Though she was looking down at the grass, and said this with something like a smile and in a careless way, Mr. Marston dares not disobey the reminder it conveys.

'That is perfectly true, what Miss Maud says. I made that promise to a person whom I dare not disappoint, whom I respect more than I can describe, and,' he added in a low tone to Maud, ' whom it is my pride to obey.'

'Good-bye, Mr. Marston,' she says with a smile, extending her pretty hand very frankly.

How he felt as he touched it!

'Good-bye, Miss Max,' he says, turning with a sigh and a smile to that lady.

'Good-bye, since so it must be, and I hope we may chance to meet again, Mr. Marston,' said the old lady, kindly giving him her thin old hand.

'So do I—so do I—thank you, very much,' says he, and he pauses, looking as if he was not sure that he had not something more to say. 'Good-bye, Miss Max,' he repeats, ' and good-bye,' he says again to the girl, extending his hand.

Once more, for a second or two, he holds her hand in his, and then he finds himself walking quickly under the straggling haw-thorns. The sprays are rattling on his hat as he crosses the stile. He is striding through the first narrow field over which his walk from the church had been. Lifeless and dimmed the hedges are, and the songs of the birds all round are but a noise which he scarcely hears. There is but one thought in his brain and heart, as he strides through this cloistered solitude as swiftly as if his rate of travel could shorten the time between this and the ball at Wymering.

This Mr. Marston was not so much a fool as not to know that, being a man of honour, he had taken a very serious step. The young lady—for be her troubles and distresses what they might, lady she surely was—whom he had pursued so far, and to whom he had spoken in language quite irrevocable, had now in her small hand his fate and fortunes.

There seemed to walk beside him along his grassy path an

angry father, and the sneers and gabble of kindred who had a right to talk were barking and laughing at his heels. He knew very well what he had to count upon, and had known it all along.

But it did not daunt him, either then or now.

Here was his first love, and an idol not created by his fancy, but undoubtedly the most beautiful girl he had ever seen. A first love devouring material so combustible; a generous fellow, impetuous, sanguine, dominated by imagination, and who had delivered eloquent lectures upon the folly of political economy, and the intrinsic tyranny of our social system.

These things troubled him, no doubt; but thus beset, he had no more notion of turning about than had honest Christian and Hopeful as they plodded through the Valley of the Shadow of Death. He felt, I dare say, pretty much as a knight when riding into the lists to mortal combat for the mistress of his heart.

He held himself now, so far as his own personal case went, irrevocably betrothed to his beautiful but cruel mistress; and so far from halting between two opinions, if what had passed this evening had been still unsaid, he would have gone round the world for a chance of speaking it.

Literally abiding by his promise, he left Wybourne as suddenly as he came.

Miss Max looked after him as the underwood hid him from view, with the somewhat blank and ruminating countenance which belongs to the lady about whose ears a favourite castle in the air has just tumbled.

'Well,' said she, turning to her young companion, nodding, and looking wise, 'that gentleman is gone on a fool's errand, I venture to say. Have you any idea where he's gone?'

'Not the least.'

'I liked him very much. I hope he's not going to make a fool of himself. I really thought he liked you. He is so full of romance. See how you blush!'

'I always do when I think I shall, and when I particularly wish not,' she said with a smile, but a little vexed.

'Well, I suspect, from what he said, that he is going to ask some young lady an interesting question; or perhaps he is actually engaged—goodness knows.'

Miss Max was walking under the lordly trees towards home and tea, with her young cousin beside her.

'That's a blackbird,' she says, listening for a moment. 'What a delicious evening !'

'Has your mother set out again upon her usual mysterious journey?' inquired Miss Max.

'I fancy not—not yet, at least,' answered the girl listlessly.

'Well, I may say to you, I can't understand your mother the least, my dear.'

The girl made no answer : she was looking up, with a list-less and sad face, towards the fleecy clouds that now glowed in the tint of sunset, and the rooks, that make no holiday of Sunday, winging homeward, high in air, with a softened cawing.

CHAPTER XI.

ROYDON.

NEXT day, about noon, the young lady, with an embrace and a little shower of kisses, took a loving farewell of her cousin, stepped into a fly, with her boxes on the roof, and with a sad heart began her journey homeward.

It was a good way, some thirty miles and upwards. She had borrowed Miss Max's novel, grew tired of it a dozen times, and resumed it as often ; and as she neared home, with the restless-ness that accompanies the conclusion of a journey, she threw her book on the opposite cushion, and looked out of the window, greeting, as it were, the familiar objects that in succession presented themselves to view.

Now they are passing the windmill on the little hillock over-looking the road. The day is sultry. There is not a breath to stir its sails, and the great arms stand bare and motionless. Mill and hillock glide backward, and are gone.

The road descends a little. They are between files of old elms. It grows broader ; there stands the old village tree, with a rude wooden bench encircling its trunk. The time-honoured tree sails back, and is lost, and quaint old diamond-latticed houses float into view, and pass. Here and there a familiar face is seen at door or window, or peeping from the shade over the hatch ; and the girl, from the fly-window, nods and smiles. They are now midway in the quiet little street, but they have not yet reached the home that she loves not.

At the other side are the stained walls of an antique church ;

the gilded vane, the grey tombstones, spread over the thick emerald grass, and the yew-tree, all go slanting off, hurry-scurry, as the fly-wheels whirl, by a wide circuit, through the piers of a great iron gate, which has just given egress to an old-fashioned family coach.

It is going the other way. It does not pass her. It and its liveried footmen are fast getting into perspective under the boughs of the trees that line the road. Through the window of the fly, as it turns, she has a momentary peep.

'Brown and gold,' she says, as listlessly she leans back again in her humble conveyance. 'The Tinterns. And so here I am, a black sheep, a scamp, and a reprobate, come home again, as curses do!'

There was not much remorse, but a good deal of bitterness in her tone, and the girl yawned, with her finger-tips to her lips, and looked for a moment a little peevish.

There is what is termed technically an 'approach' to the house up to which she is driving, a serpentine road, two miles long at least, through a wooded demesne. But, wisely, the old owner of Roydon, when consulting his new lights, and laying out, according to picturesque principles, the modern approach, would not allow them to obliterate or alter the old avenue of the mansion—broad and straight, something more than a quarter of a mile long, with a double line of trees at each side, wide enough apart to admit the entire front of the building.

It is up this broad, straight avenue she is driving now.

A lazy man, with a mind at ease, entering here for the first time, looking up the solemn lines of enormous boughs to the old-world glories that close the perspective, escaping from the vulgar world of dust and rattle into shorn grass, and clear, silent air, and the luxurious and melancholy grandeur of all that surrounds him, might fancy himself in the 'delicious land' once visited by the enchanted Sir Jeofry.

In the distance rises a grand Elizabethan structure—broad, florid, built of white stone, yellowed and many-tinted by time. A vague effect fills the eye of pinnacles and bell-mouthed chimneys, and curved and corniced gables, balustrades, a front variously indented and projecting; multitudes of stone-shafted windows, deep-curved scrolls, and heraldic shields and supporters; a broad flight of steps, and then another balustrade running at both sides the whole length of the base. All this rises before her, with its peculiar combination of richness, lightness, and solidity, basking drowsily in the summer sun.

As you approach, you discern a wide courtyard in front, with a second line of balustrade nearer to you.

On the summit of this, here and there, are peacocks sunning themselves, some white, others plumed in their proper gold and purple. They nod their crested heads as they prune their plumage, and hang their long tails to the grass, disturbing the slumbrous air, now and then, with a discordant scream.

As you draw nearer still, before you enter the court, two oblong ponds reveal their spacious waters, at the right and the left; you may hear the shower of the fountains playing in the middle; snowy coronals of water-lilies are floating near their banks, and swans are grandly gliding round and up and down.

Now the homely 'fly' is in the courtyard. A great Russian dog lies sunning himself on the dazzling gravel, near the steps, and whacks the ground twice or thrice with his tail, in lazy recognition, as he sees the young lady look from the window of her homely vehicle.

'I suppose that is the way of the world, Bevis,' she says; 'you know whom to get up for.'

Her attention is arrested by a carriage waiting a little way from the steps.

'That's the dean,' comments the young lady, as she sees that very neat equipage, at the window of which a tall footman, in light blue and gold livery, with powdered hair, is standing. He has just descended the broad flight of steps under the great shield which overhangs the door, and which displays in high relief all the heraldic insignia of that branch of the Vernons. He is delivering a message from Lady Vernon—Barbara Vernon—I give you the Christian name of this famous widow at once, as it is mentioned often in the sequel—to an old lady sitting in the carriage.

Old Miss Wyvel, the dean's sister, as usual, with her feet on a pan of hot water, sits in the carriage reading her novel and nursing her rheumatism, while her brother, the dean, makes his visit, with an apology from her for not coming in.

'We'll not mind Miss Wyvel this time. She'll be all the happier that I don't disturb her, and so shall I.'

Another tall footman, seeing who is in the fly, descends the broad steps quickly, and opens the door.

'The Dean of Chartry is here?' inquires the young lady.
'How long has he been here?'

'About ten minutes, please, miss.'

'Any other visitor?'

'No one, miss, at present, please.'

'Where is her ladyship?'

'In the library, please, miss.'

'Will you tell somebody, please, to tell my maid that I want
her in my room?' said the young lady.

And she ran up the steps lightly, and entered the great hall.
It runs backs into space, almost into darkness, with oak panelled
walls and tall pictures. She turned to the right, where the
broad oak staircase ascends.

Up she runs. There are more portraits in this house, one
must suppose, than the owners well know what to do with, for
you can hardly turn a corner without meeting a gentleman with
rosettes in his shoes, a ruff round his neck, and a rapier by his
side, or a lady in the toilet of Queen Elizabeth. All ages,
indeed, of English costume, from the court of Harry the Eighth
down to George the Second, are represented here; and, I suspect, there is now not a soul on earth who could tell you the
names of all these magnificos and high dames, who are fain to
lurk behind corners, or stand in their frames, with their backs
against the walls of galleries, passed, back and forward, by
gabbling moderns, who don't care twopence about them or their
finery.

Off one of these galleries the young lady enters her own room
—stately, comfortable, luxurious—looks around with a good-
natured recognition, and has hardly begun to take off her dusty
things, and prepare to make her toilet, when her maid passes in
through the dressing-room door, smiling.

CHAPTER XII.

BARBARA VERNON.

By no means old is this maid. Some six-and-thirty years, perhaps. She has carried Maud in her arms when she was a little
thing, and dressed her; sat by her bed and told her fairy-tales
in the nursery.

'Welcome home, Miss Maud,' smiles Jones.

'And how have you been ?' says the young lady, taking her by the hand, and kissing her affectionatcly on one cheek and the other. 'As for me, I've been flourishing. I almost think, old Jones, if I had only had you with me, I should never have come back again.'

'La, miss, how you talk !'

'I've been leading a wild, free life. Did you ever see so much dust, Jones, on any human being ?'

'Indeed, you are in a pickle, miss. Charles said you came in a fly with one horse. I wonder her ladyship did not send a carriage to Wybourne to meet you.'

'Mamma has other things and people to think about,' said the young lady, a little bitterly. 'But I dare say if I had asked I should have had it ; though, indeed, I shouldn't have liked it.'

'Your hand's all sunburnt, miss.'

'I've been sketching ; and I never could sketch with a glove on.'

'Well, dear me, it *was* a fancy going in these queer things ! Why, I would not be seen in such things myself, miss, much less you. You'd best bundle off that dress, miss, as quick as you can. La ! it is thick with dust. Phiew !'

'Help me, Jones, help me.' And as she continued her toilet she asked : 'Is mamma yet talking of making her usual journey ?'

'Not a word, miss, of any one stirring yet. Norris would know. She has not heard nothing.'

'The Tinterns' carriage was here to-day—I passed it at the gate. Do you know who called ?'

'Mr. Tintern and Mrs. They was here nigh half an hour. Leave them alone for 'aving their eyes about 'em, miss. There ain't a tack druv in the house, or a slate loose, but its known down at the Grange before it's noticed here.'

'I think, Jones, they reckon upon—don't pull my hair.' By this time she was sitting in her dressing-gown before the glass, with her dark, golden-brown hair hanging over her shoulders in such profusion, that it seemed incredible how such masses could find growing room in one little head. Jones was brushing out its folds.

'I'm not pulling it, indeed, miss,' she protested.

'Yes, you were, Jones. Don't ever contradict me. Has either of my special horrors—Mr. Smelt—he's the clergyman or Dissenter, something in black, the sleek fat man that comes so often —has he been here since ?'

'He may 'ave, miss ; but——'

'But you don't know. Well, the other—Doctor Malkin?'

'Oh, dear yes, miss. He was here, please, on Friday last.'

'You're sure?'

'Yes, miss, please. Her ladyship sent for me to the shield-room. She only asked whether I could remember for certain, miss, what day you were to return 'ome to Wybourne with Miss Medwyn.'

'Well?'

'Well, miss, she had it down in a book, and read it to me, and I said 'twas right. You said early—the seventeenth.'

'And did she say anything more?'

'No, please, miss, nothing more. Only she said, "That's all, you need not wait."'

'And what about Doctor Malkin?'

'He was showed in, miss, please, just as I was going out. And I heard her order Edward not to let any visitor in; and that was all, please.'

'Do you know the name of this place, parish, and county, Jones?' says the young lady carelessly.

'Well, I ought to by this time, miss,' laughs Jones.

'I don't think you do. The name of this place is Bœotia, and it is famous for its dulness, and Doctor Malkin is one of the six inhabitants who can think and talk a little. He is an agreeable man, and—put a pin there—an unpleasant-looking man. I like talking to him; but I think, on the whole, I should not be sorry if he were laid in the Red Sea, as poor nurse Creswell used to say. What do you think of him?'

'That is a gentleman, Heaven forgive me, I can't abide, miss,' answered Jones. 'I hate his face. I always feel in low spirits after I see it.'

'Well, anything more?' continues Miss Maud. 'When are the people coming to hear grandpapa's will read?'

'To-morrow, I believe, miss. But, as yet, Mr. Eccles has not got no orders about it. He said so after dinner in the 'ouse-keeper's-room yesterday.'

'And is there anything going to be—a tea and plum-cake for the school-children, or a meeting of missionaries, or anything of any kind?'

'Nothing, miss, please, as I 'ave heard of, but——'

'You'll knock down that china, Jones.'

'What, miss?'

'My ring-stand—my Dresden dancers.'

'Oh! The little man and woman with one arm akimbo and the other up. I saw them all the time.'

'Well, take great care. I'm sure I shall kill you if you break them. You were going to tell me there is nothing going to be, except something—what is it?'

'Oh! I know; yet, miss, the conseckeration of the monument in the church. That will be to-morrow evening, miss.'

'Oh! Really! Well, that *was* a whim! Give me those earrings. No, *not* those—the others; not those either. Don't you see the little ones. Thanks. Yes. I must run down and see mamma, I suppose, though I'm very sure she doesn't care if she did not see my face for a year, or—for ever.'

'La, miss! you must not talk like that. Your mamma's a very religious lady—the most so, as everyone knows, in the county—I might say in all England—and it's just her way; the same with everyone, a little bit high and distant like; but it ain't fit, miss, you should say that.'

'No, Jones, we can't agree, mamma and I. Give me that small enamel brooch—the little one with the lady's head set in gold. Thanks. She does not like me'—the young lady was standing before the glass, and I dare say was well pleased, for she looked splendidly handsome—'and the reason is just this, every one else flatters her—you and all the other sneaks. I never do, although I am sometimes a little afraid of her like the rest I'm nervous, I don't know why; but it's not cowardice—I never flatter her.'

'No, miss, it ain't that; it's only you don't try her. You won't go the right way about it.'

'There's no use, Jones—you only vex me. I've often felt that I would give the world to throw my arms about her neck and kiss her; but somehow I can't—she won't let me. Perhaps she tries; but she can't love me; and so it always was, as far back as I can remember, and so it will always be, and I've made up my mind to it; it can't be helped.'

So Miss Maud Vernon walked along the gallery, and went down the broad stairs, passing many ancestors who stood by, at the right and the left, against the wall, as she did so, and singing low to herself as she went, with a clear and rich voice, an Italian air quite new to the solemn people in the picture-frames at whom she looked listlessly, thinking neither of them nor of her song as she passed by.

Mr. Tarpey, the groom of the chambers, was fussing with the decorations of the hall as she passed.

'Can you tell me where her ladyship is ?' she inquired.

'Her ladyship, I think, is still in the library. Please, shall I see, miss ?'

'Don't mind. I'll try myself. Is her ladyship alone ?'

'I think so, miss.'

He crossed the hall, and opened the second door from the great entrance, which stood wide open, in this sultry weather, by Lady Vernon's command, the two tall footmen, in their blue and gold liveries, keeping guard there.

Maud glanced through the open hall-door as she crossed the hall; she would have been rather pleased to see a carriage approaching; she did not care for a very long interview with her mother; but there was no sign of a visitor in sight.

'Thanks, I'll go alone,' she said, dispensing with the escort of Mr. Tarpey; and passing through two spacious rooms, she reached the door of the library. Lady Vernon treated that apartment as her private cabinet, and from her childhood Maud had been accustomed to respect it.

Maud has no liking for the coming interview. She would, now, have liked to put it off, and as she crosses the Turkey carpet that muffles her tread, her step slackens. She stops at the door and raises her hand to knock, but she doesn't knock; she hesitates; she has a great mind to turn back, and wait till her mother sends for her. But perhaps that would not do. She has been at home nearly an hour, and it is time she should ask Lady Vernon how she does.

She knocks at the door, and hears a clear voice call 'Come in.'

She turns the handle accordingly, and steps into a spacious room, hung with gilded leather; the blinds are down, the sun by this time shining on this side of the house, and a mellow, cathedral-like dimness prevails. There are three or four antique book-cases, carved in ponderous relief, through the leaves and scrolls of which are grinning grotesque and ugly faces, rich with a cynical Gothic fancy, and overhung by fantastic cornices, crowned with the heraldic shield and supporters of the Vernons. They are stored with gilded volumes; portraits hang here, as in other parts of this rich old house, and cold marble busts gleam on pedestals from the corners.

Sitting at a table in the middle of this room is a very handsome woman of forty years or upwards, with skin smooth as ivory, and jet-black hair, divided in the middle, and brought down over her white temples and small pretty ears smoothly in the simple classic fashion, now out of date. Her finely pencilled black eyebrows, and her features with a classic elegance of outline, carry an expression of cold hauteur. Her slight embonpoint becomes her grave but rich dress, which is that of a woman of rank and wealth, by no means indifferent to the impression produced by externals.

This lady, with one handsome foot upon a stool, and a desk before her, is in a leisurely way writing a letter, over which she bends just the least thing in the world. Her pose is decidedly elegant.

The lady glances slightly toward the door. Her large grey eyes, under their long lashes, rest for a moment on her daughter. She does not smile; the pen is still in her fingers. She says, simply, in her clear and rather sweet tones, 'Oh, Maud! I will speak to you in a few minutes, when I have put this into its envelope. Won't you sit down?' And so she continues to write.

The young lady flashes back a rather fiery glance in return for this cool welcome, and does not sit down, but walks instead, with a quick step, to the window, pulls the blind aside, and looks out perseveringly.

CHAPTER XIII.

MOTHER AND DAUGHTER.

LADY VERNON having enclosed and addressed her letter, added it to the little pack of about six others at her left. Then, looking up, she said:

'So, you are quite well, Maud, and you arrived at a quarter past three?'

'Quite well, mamma, thanks. I suppose it was about that time; and I hope you are very well.'

'I am well, thanks; and I wished to mention that when you, as you told me, fixed the seventeenth for your return to the Hermitage with Maximilla Medwyn, I was under a mistake, and did not see, till too late, that the seventeenth would be Sunday; and I should not have given my sanction to your travelling for pleasure on Sunday. I wished to mention that particularly.

I told Maximilla I should be happy to receive her any day this week. Is she coming, do you know?'

'She would have come with me this morning, but she had so much to say to her servants, and so many things to arrange, that she could not leave home till after dinner at soonest, so she hopes to be here at ten to-night; and if anything should happen to prevent her, you are to have a note, by post, in the morning.'

'She will be in time, at all events, for the bishop's sermon to-morrow,' says Lady Vernon. 'The monument will be uncovered at five o'clock. The bishop arrives at six. He has to consecrate the new church at Eastover, before he comes here, and then he goes on, after his sermon, to Wardlake, for the evening meeting of the Church Missions.'

Miss Vernon is hardly so much interested in all this as her mother is, although even she recites the programme a little dryly. But dry as is her recital, it is not often that she volunteers so much information to her daughter.

'And what can the bishop have to say about the monument, to lead him so much out of his way, poor old man?'

'The bishop seems to think that his having been the dearest friend that Mr. Howard had on earth constitutes some little claim upon him,' says Lady Vernon haughtily, in a cold tone, and with her fine grey eyes fixed on her daughter.

'Oh! I did not know,' says Maud, a little apologetically.

'No, of course you did not; you seldom do know, or care to know, anything that interests me,' says the elder lady, with her fine brows a little higher.

Maud coloured suddenly, with an impatient movement of her head. She was not sitting down, only standing near the table, drumming on it with her finger-tips, and she felt for a moment as if she could have stamped.

She answered, however, without any show of excitement, except in her brilliant colour and eyes.

'I did not know, mamma, that this monument to Mr. Howard interested you particularly.'

'No, not particularly,' said handsome Lady Vernon sternly, for she was one of those persons who don't brook contradiction, and who interpret discussion as a contradiction. 'Mr. Howard was the best vicar we ever had here, or ever shall have; and, in his way, a benefactor to this parish. The bishop, who admired and loved him, as much as one man could another, suggested that for such a man, in the field of his labours, having lain in his grave more than a score of years unrecorded by a single line, it was time that a monument should be raised. He wished a beautiful one, and so I believe it is. His name is first in the list of subscribers, and it is his idea, and it is he who has taken a lead in it; and, therefore, though interested, I am not particularly interested in the personal degree which your emphasis would imply.'

' Well, all I can say is, I'm very unlucky, mamma.'

'I think you are unlucky,' replied her mother coldly, turning her head slowly away, and looking at the pendule over the chimney.

' Have you anything to ask me, Maud ?' inquired Lady Vernon, after a little interval.

'Nothing, thanks, mamma,' said Maud, with her head a little high. ' I'm afraid I have bored you, coming in when you were busy. But having been away ten days, I thought it would have been wrong, or at least odd, if I had not come to see you to ask you how you were.'

' So it would,' said Lady Vernon. ' Will you touch the bell ?' She did so.

' Well, mamma, I suppose there's nothing more ?'

' Nothing, Maud.'

Maud's heart swelled with bitterness as she left the room, and shut the door gently.

' No father, no mother, no near relation !' she thought impetuously. ' I love Cousin Max better than fifty such mammas. There are girls who would hate her. But I can't. Why am I cursed with this cruel yearning for her love? And she can't love me—she won't have my love. I think she wishes me to hate her.'

When Maud was a little thing, as far back as she could remember, her idea of a ' mamma' was an embodiment of power, and something to be afraid of. Seldom seen except when the spirited little girl became unmanageable ; then there would be a rustling of silk and a flutter of lace in the nursery, and the handsome figure, the proud still face and large grey eyes were before her. This phantom instantly awed her. It always looked severe, and never smiled, and its sweet cold tones were dreadful. The child's instinct could see dislike, hidden from maturer observers, in those fine eyes, and never heard a tender note in that harmonious voice.

Miss Maud passed out through the suite of rooms, and encountered Lady Vernon's footman going in to take her letters.

In the hall, serious Mr. Eccles, the gentlemanlike butler, was passing upon his business with the quiet importance and gravity of office.

The young lady had a word to say.

' Is any one expected to dinner to-day ?'

' Yes, miss—five ; the vicar and Mrs. Foljambe : his curate, the Reverend Mr. Doody ; and Mr. Puntles and Doctor Malkin. There was an invitation for Captain Bamme ; but he is absent on militia business, and it is thought not probable, miss, he will return in time.'

Anything was better than a *tête-à-tête* with Lady Vernon ; a situation which Lady Vernon herself seemed to deprecate as strongly as her daughter, for it did not occur usually six times in a year.

CHAPTER XIV.

GUESTS AND NEIGHBOURS.

WHEN, that evening, Miss Maud entered the vast drawing-room, it was some minutes past eight. The outer world was in twilight, but lamps glowed faintly here, upon the thick silken curtains, and lofty mirrors, and pictures, and treasures of china, and upon figures of people assembled for dinner. The little party was almost lost in the great void, as Miss Maud made her journey, over a comparatively gloomy desert of thick carpet, to the group illuminated by the soft light of the lamps.

Tall old Mr. Foljambe, the vicar, was entertaining Lady Vernon with his bland and dignified conversation. Doctor Malkin would have liked that post, but the vicar came first, and seized it.

The vicar is a well-connected old gentleman, related, in some remote cousinship, to the late Sir Amyrald Vernon, and knows very well what he is about. Has not Lady Vernon, the relict of that lamented kinsman, two extremely desirable livings in her gift, beside smaller things? And, old as the Reverend Mr. Foljambe is, are not the incumbents of these fat fields of usefulness older still ? Is not the Reverend Mr. Cripry seventy-nine ? And is not the venerable Doctor Shanks eighty-two, by the records of Trinity College, Cambridge? Compared with these mature ornaments of the Church, the vicar justly feels himself a stripling ; and being a young fellow, not yet in his seventy-first year, he may well complain of a selfish longevity which is sacrificing the interests of two important parishes which require a vigorous ministration.

The Vicar's shrewd old eye, from its wrinkled corners, observes Doctor Malkin's wistful look, and knows from experience that he likes to take possession of Lady Vernon's ear, and has suffered more than once from the tenacity with which he keeps it, when he can, to himself.

'Nothing of the kind shall happen to-night,' thinks the vicar, who, having a handsome bit of money in Consols, has sold out a hundred pounds to invest in a subscription to the monument of his predecessor, the Reverend Mr. Howard—a good work in which Lady Vernon takes a warm interest, as she always does in anything she takes up.

The vicar has her fast upon this, and the doctor thinks he can read sly triumph in his eye as once or twice it glides over to him, and their glances meet for a moment.

'Well, doctor, and how's all wid you ?' inquires the Reverend Michael Doody, with a grin that shows his fine white fangs, and a trifling clap of his enormous hand on the doctor's shoulder. 'Elegant, I suppose ?'

The doctor's slight frame quivers under the caress of the cleric, but he smiles politely, for who knows what influence this new importation may grow to in this part of the world ?

I'm very well, thanks—as well as a fellow so much knocked about as a doctor can be in this hot weather.'

The doctor is a little bald, with a high pale nose, a long upper lip, a receding chin, very blue, and a pair of fine dark eyes, set too close together, and with a slight obliquity which spoils them a great deal, and does not improve his countenance ; his shirt-front is beautified with needlework, and his rather tall choker, for his neck is long, is made up by his exemplary laundress with a snowy smoothness worthy of the neatness and decision with which the doctor ties it.

'My governor, the vicar, has Lady Vernon fast by the button,' continued Mr. Doody, with something like a wink. 'She must be a very conscientious woman, to listen so well to her clergy. He was talking about Vicar Howard's monument when I was near them just now.'

The doctor laughed and shrugged, and Mr. Doody thought for a moment he squinted a little more than usual.

'Our good vicar has but one subject at present,' says the

doctor,' who gives Mr. Doody, as a stranger, credit for a good
deal of waggish penetration. ' You have heard of the clarionet-
man who had but one tune, and played it always through the
key-hole till it answered its purpose, and extracted a gratuity;
and he made it pay very well, I believe.'

' And rayther hard, doctor, that you can't get your turn at the
key-hole, eh, my boy ?'

And the reverend gentleman utters a stentorian giggle, and
pokes his finger on the doctor's ribs.

' I don't quite see, Mr. Doody,' says Dr. Malkin, with a very
creditable smile, all things considered.

' Boo, docthor, my darlin' fellow, don't be comin' the simple-
ton over us. Don't we both know that every man in your profession likes to stand well with the women? And here you are,
and if it was to make a man of ye, not a word can ye edge in.
It's too hard, docthor, that the man of death should be blocked
out by a tombstone. Be the powers, it ain't fair ! He's takin'
her all over the monument; up on the pedestal, over the cornice,
down in the vault ! It's an unfair advantage. But never mind,
my boy, ye'll be even with him yet; ye'll attind him in his next
indisposition.'

This pleasant banter was accompanied by a running explosion
of giggles, and while the tall and rather handsome Irishman is
enjoying his little bit of farce with intense relish, the vicar and
Lady Vernon are discoursing thus :

' I thought, Lady Vernon, you would like, of course, in the
most private way in the world, to collect opinion upon the
monument; so, as he draws very nicely, my wife says, I allowed
my curate, Mr. Doody, just in the strictest privacy, quite to
ourselves, you understand, a peep at it for about five minutes
this morning. He thinks it very fine indeed—very fine—as,
indeed, every one who has seen it does. There is, I fancy, but
one opinion. I wish so much, Lady Vernon, I might venture to
invite you to pay my church—yours, indeed, I might more properly call it—a visit to-morrow, to look at what I may term your
beautiful gift to the sacred edifice.'

' No, thanks; I shall see it time enough.'

' But, as it owes its existence, Lady Vernon, to your extremely
munificent subscription——'

' I thought it was due, as the bishop said, to a very good
clergyman,' says Lady Vernon, quietly cutting it short; ' and I
gave what I thought right. That is all. And so your curate draws ?'

'I'm nothing of a draughtsman myself, but my wife under-stands it, and says he draws extremely nicely.'

'That tall young man, is he?'

'I ought to have presented him, Lady Vernon. It was an omission—an inexcusable omission—a very inexcusable omission.' He was trying to catch his curate's eye all this time. 'He has been with me only a week, and yesterday he did duty at Loxton. You remember, Lady Vernon, you thought an Irish-man would answer best.'

'The bishop says he has found them extremely energetic, and for very hard work unrivalled.'

'He's a very rough diamond, I must admit. But he's a con-vert from Romanism, and a very laborious young man, and a good scholar.'

He had beckoned Mr. Doody to approach, and accordingly that herculean labourer in the apostolic field drew near, a head and shoulders above all the other guests. The tall old vicar alone was sitting.

'Allow me, Lady Vernon, to present my curate, Mr. Doody,' says the vicar, rising to do the honours.

Mr. Doody is not the least overcome by the honour. His fine eyes have examined the lady, of whom he had heard so much, but of whom he has not had so near a view before, with the grave curiosity with which he would have scrutinised an interesting piece of waxwork.

The florid young man, with black whiskers and glossy black head, makes his best bow gravely, and inquires unexpectedly:

'How are ye, ma'am? A good evening, Lady Vernon.' A form of salutation with which it is his wont, as it were, to clench an introduction.

Lady Vernon does not mind answering or reciprocating these rather oddly placed greetings, but talks a few sentences with him, and then turns again to the vicar; and the curate, after a little wait, turns on his heel, and seeks employment for his active mind elsewhere.

Let me not be imagined to present an average Irish curate. Mr. Doody is almost as great a prodigy at home as anywhere else. His father, with his own hands, in his bare shins, with a dhuddeen stuck in his caubeen, cuts turf in the bog near the famous battlefield of Aghrim. He is not a bit ashamed of his father or his belongings. He holds him to be as good a gentleman as himself—being the lineal descendant of the

O'Doody of Tyr Doody—and himself as good as the primate. He sends his mother a present every now and then, but the farm is well stocked, and his parents are, according to primitive ideas, wealthy people in their homely way. His lapse into Protestantism was, of course, a sore blow. And when Dr. Pollard's wife mentioned to the priest, with perhaps a little excusable triumph, that Michael Doody had embraced the principles of the Reformation, his reverence scratched his tonsure, and said :

'I'm not a bit surprised, ma'am, for he was always an impudent chap ; but there was some good in the boy, also ; and go where he may at present, so sure as I'm a Catholic, he'll die one.'

CHAPTER XV.

DINNER.

OLD Mr. Foljambe takes precedence at dinner, in right of his cloth, connexions, and antiquity, and has taken Lady Vernon into the dining-room, and converses assiduously with that great lady.

Maud finds herself between the curate and Doctor Malkin. Middle-aged and agreeable Captain Bamme resents an arrangement which isolates him, and eyes the curate with disgust.

Captain Bamme does not count age by years. He knows better. As long as a fellow looks young, and feels young, he *is* young. The captain smiles more than any other two men in the parish. He is short and square, but he skips and swaggers like an officer and a gentleman. Who can talk to a girl like Charley Bamme ? Who understands that mixture of gaiety and gallantry—with now and then a dash of tenderness—like this officer ? To be sure, he's not a marrying man ; everyone knows that. It is out of the question. The captain laughs with a melancholy scorn over his scanty pittance. A fourth son, by Jove ! and put to a poor profession. But is he not the life and soul of a picnic, and the darling of the ladies ?

'I've been quartered in Ireland,' says little Captain Bamme, under cover of the surrounding buzz, to his more fortunate neighbour, Doctor Malkin ; 'I've been in every part of it ; I have talked to Irishmen of every rank and occupation, but such a brogue as that, I give you my honour, I never heard. Why, they wouldn't have him to preach to a congregation of carmen in Dublin. I never heard anything like it. How did old Fol-

jambe light on him? I really think, when people bring fellows
like that to a place like this, where people *must* know him, and,
for anything you or I can tell, that fellow may spend the rest of
his days down here—by Jove! it's pleasant—they ought to be
prepared to give an account of him. I suppose Foljambe can
say what he is? You never met such an insufferable creature.
I never spoke to the fellow before in my life; and he came up
to me in the hall here making some vulgar *personal* joke, I give
you my honour.'

'He seems to succeed very well,' says the doctor, 'notwithstanding. I suppose there's something interesting in it, though
you and I can't perceive it.'

'Upon my soul I can't!'

And with this declaration he turns to Mrs. Foljambe, who is
at his right, determined to make her account for her intolerable
curate.

Mrs. Foljambe is tall, deaf, and melancholy—a woman very
nearly useless, and quite harmless.

'I was saying just now to Doctor Malkin,' begins the captain,
'that I've been, at different times, quartered in Ireland——'

A footman here presents at the captain's right hand an *entrée*
which he loves, and on which he pounces.

'A daughter in Ireland?' repeats the drowsy voice of Mrs.
Foljambe, turning her dull and small grey eyes upon him, with
a heavy sigh.

'No; ha, ha! not yet; *quartered* in Ireland. No. Time
enough for that, I hope. I'm not married, Mrs. Foljambe—
thanks, that will do. I say, I have been a little puzzled by
your curate's accent.' He was speaking low, but with measured
articulation; for although the Reverend Michael Doody's voice
is loud and busy at the other side of the table, and the buzz of
conversation is general, that odious person's ears, for aught the
captain knew, might be preternaturally acute. 'And although
I know Ireland pretty well—Athlone, Limerick, Cork, Dublin,
and all that—yet I never heard his accent before in my life'.

Mrs. Foljambe bowed her patient grey head, and did not
seem aware that any answer was needed.

'Can you say what part of the country he comes from?'
persists Captain Bamme.

'I rather think Ireland,' replies Mrs. Foljambe, with an effort
and another sigh.

'I rather think so myself,' says the captain, in a disgusted aside, over his veal and truffles. 'The woman knows no more about him than my hat does of snipe-shooting,' he says, in the doctor's ear, and drowns his indignation in a glass of hock, which the butler at that moment charitably proffers.

The doctor has now got into talk with Miss Vernon. The captain has no wish to steal good Mrs. Foljambe's bothered ear from old Mr. Puntles, who is labouring to entertain her. So Captain Bamme attends to his dinner with great concentration and energy for some time. It was not until he came to the iced-pudding that he thought of the Reverend Michael Doody again, and his joke upon the captain's stature—'a fellow I had never exchanged six words with before !'—and raising his eyes, he saw, with a qualm, those of the florid divine fixed jocosely on him from the other side of the table.

'Upon my soul, it is very near intolerable !' the captain protests mentally, as he leans back with a flushed face. He resolves that this fellow must be snubbed, and laughed at, and sat upon, and taught to know his place, and held at arm's length.

As the captain has, however, nothing clever ready, he prefers not noticing the curate's expression ; and throwing into his countenance all the dignity which a not very tragic face can carry, he avails himself of Mr. Eccles's murmur at his right elbow, and take a glass of sherry.

'I'll drink a glass of wine widgye, captain,' insists the curate, recurring to a happily obsolete usage. 'Get me some white wine.'

The captain bows and stares, with a rather withering condescension and gravity, which, however, does not in the least tell upon the impervious curate, who, his glass replenished, observes with a hilarious smile, 'An agreeable way of makin' acquaintance with my flock ; better than a dhry domiciliary visit, captain, by a long chalk. I pledge you, my gallant parishioner —and here's to our better acquaintance.'

The captain nods curtly, and gulps down his wine, without half tasting it ; but even on these terms he thinks it is well to have escaped that brute.

Miss Vernon is again talking to the curate. How disgusting ! He turns, without thinking what he's doing, to his right, and his eyes meet the dull and innocent gaze of grey Mrs. Foljambe, who, recalled to the festive scene, makes an effort, and tells him her only story.

'We knew two very respectable poor women in this town. Anne Pluggs was one, and her sister, Julia Pluggs, was the other; there were two. They had both been servants, cooks, and they lived in the small house, last but one on your left, as you go towards the windmill.' A deep sigh here. 'You'll know it by wallflowers growing at the door; at least, there were, about a year or two ago; and they had saved a little money; and Mr. Foljambe had a very high opinion of them, and so had I.' The captain bows. 'And about sixteen years ago they gave up their house here, and went to Coventry; it is a good way off, you know."

The captain knits his brows and calculates rapidly.

'About forty-seven miles—by Jove, it *is* a good way.'

'And when they arrived there, they set up a confectioner's shop, in a small way, of course.'

'Oh?' says the captain, very much interested, 'that was very spirited of them.'

'It had a bow-window that was painted brown, it was at a corner of a street near one of the spires, and they did very well, and they are both alive still.'

Another deep sigh followed.

'What a pity !' says the polite captain, who is looking across the table, and thinking at the moment of quite another thing. The good lady does not hear his comment, and so its slight incongruity is harmless, and the captain, inviting the conclusion of the tale, says, 'And——?'

But the story is over. That is all. And good Mrs. Foljambe, contented with her contribution towards keeping the conversation alive, is looking, in a melancholy reverie, on the table-cloth.

As she has dropped off his hands in this gentle way the captain resigns her with a good grace, and listens undisturbed to other talk.

Lady Vernon has now taken the curate into council, and is leading the little cabinet. Mr. Michael Doody is attentive, and seems impressed by what Lady Vernon is saying. She has the reputation of being a clever woman, with a special talent for government.

Mr. Puntles is listening, and sipping his wine; and being a polite old man, now and then plagues Mrs. Foljambe with a question or a remark.

Doctor Malkin is in animated conversation with Miss Vernon.

He is perhaps, a little of an *esprit fort;* but in a rural region, always more pharisaical, as well as more pure than the city, he is very cautious, the more particularly as his great patroness, Lady Vernon, is a sharp and ready Christian, not High Church, not Low Church ; people at both sides of the controversy complain in whispers of ambiguities and inconsistencies; she is Broad Church. Yes, very Broad Church. She would throw the church-gates wide—as open as her heart—as open as her hand. She has built plain, sober churches—she has built meeting-houses—she has built florid chapels and churches, gleaming with purple and gold, and with saints and martyrs glowing in brilliant colours from stained windows, such as rejoice the heart of that learned and Gothic Christian, Archdeacon Complines. Her flatterers speak in this vein : and they are legion. The promoters of the projects which she vivifies by her magnificent bounty may hate their equally successful rivals, but they like her money ; and they are extremely careful not to offend her, for she has not the reputation of forgiving easily.

Doctor Malkin talks to Miss Vernon on her pet subjects, theories, and vagaries of all sorts, the abuses and corruptions begotten of an artificial system, bold social reforms, daring sentiments on all forms of civil government, treated romantically rather than very learnedly, or indeed, very wisely.

And now Lady Vernon, having established an understanding with old Mrs. Foljambe, rises, and with that dejected lady and Maud, takes her departure. Captain Bamme, gallantly standing as guard of honour, with the handle of the open door in his hand, smiles with supernatural sweetness, sees them off, and returns to complete the little party of five.

CHAPTER XVI.

A SKIRMISH.

PLUMP little Mr. Puntles is a cosy bachelor of two-and-sixty. Something of an antiquary, something of a herald, he is strong in county lore. He is the only man in Roydon who honestly likes books. He lives in the comfortable square brick house of Charles the First's date, at the northern end of the village. He usually takes a nap of five minutes after his dinner, and then is bright for all the evening after.

The Rev. Mr. Foljambe, who considers himself an aristocrat, talks with him upon genealogies, and such matters, with the condescending attention that befits his high descent and connections.

'No family has a right to powdered-blue in their liveries except this branch of the Vernons, one branch of the Lindseys, and two other families,' said Mr. Puntles, with his eyes closed, and his finger tracing diagrams slowly on the table-cloth. 'It is a very distinguished privilege, and I'll tell you how the Vernons came by it.'

Mr. Foljambe smiles blandly, and also nearly closing his eyes, inclines his ear; but a vociferation at another part of the table, where Captain Bamme and the curate were in hot debate, arrested the communication.

'Who consolidated your civil power in India?' urges the curate. 'I'll tell you, captain. It was Mr. Richard Colley Wellesley of Dangan, in the county of Meath. The Marquis Wellesley, as you are good enough to call him. And who commanded the Indian army, at the same critical period, when something more was wanted than blundering and plundering, a teaste of genius and a teaste for thundering?'

Before answering his own question the Reverend Mr. Doody applied his glass to his lips, his disengaged hand being extended all the time toward his gallant adversary, with a paddling of the fingers, intended to retain the ear of the company and the right of continuing his speech.

'So far as thundering is concerned, Mr. Doody,' said the vicar, with stately jocularity, 'it seems to me that your countrymen seldom want a Jupiter.'

The captain, with a rather inflamed visage, for more had passed between the curate and him, smirked angrily, and nodded at the vicar, and leaned back and tossed his head, and rolled a little in his chair, smiling scornfully along the cornice.

But the Reverend Mr. Doody could hear no one but himself, and think of no one but Captain Bamme and the Wellesley family at that moment, and he continued: 'Who, I repeat, saved India by his genius for arms, as the other consolidated the same empire by his genius for organization and rule? Who but that Irishman's Irish brother Arthur Wellesley, Jooke of Wellington? And I think I remember some trifling services that same county o' Meath man did you on other ground. But I'm speaking of India just now, and I ask again, who saved it, again, when its existence was imperilled by the natives? Who but my countryman, Irish Lord Gough, from Tipperary? It's easy for you, in quiet times, when you're enjoying the fruits of Irish gallantry and Irish genius, to make little of Ireland, but you know where to run for help when you're in danger.'

'Haven't you a rather uncomfortable way of putting it, Mr. Doody?' said the Reverend Mr. Foljambe, a little gravely.

'Why, I can prove to you,' began Mr. Doody, not hearing the vicar, 'if you take up the old chronicles, that the Irish were in the habit of continually invading England.'

'With what result?' inquired Mr. Foljambe, with a smile.

'Ship-loads of plundher and slaves,' answered Mr. Doody promptly.

'We had better look sharp,' said cosy Mr. Puntles, who rather enjoyed the debate.

'If they had but a regiment of tall Irish clergymen, no doubt they'd march through the country,' said the captain, laughing stingingly.

'If they had nothing but a regiment of small English captains before them,' said the curate, 'they'd do it easy enough. My dear friend,' continued the curate, 'I don't say, mind, that a mob can fight a trained army; but give us eighteen months to drill in, and see where you'll be; give us what ye must give us before long, Federalism, and before ten years we'll conquer England!'

Captain Bamme uttered a short laugh of scorn.

'I hope you'll spare my little collection of curiosities,' said Mr. Puntles merrily.

'If you're strong be merciful,' broke in Captain Bamme.

'Don't be frightened, captain; we'll spare them, and all other little curiosities too,' said Mr. Doody hilariously. 'But, seriously, as sure as you're sitting there, Ireland will conquer England, if she gets a fair chance.'

'That will be something new, won't it?' says the Reverend Mr. Foljambe. 'Shakespeare says something about a country

> '"That never yet did lie
> Under the proud foot of a conqueror." '

'Shakespeare said more than his prayers, sir; didn't he know as well as we do that there is no country in Christendom that has been so often and so completely conquered as England? "Did never lie?" ha, ha, ha! "The proud foot of a conqueror?"

Mighty fine! Did ye never lie undher the Romans? or the Saxons? or the Danes? or the Normans? and didn't they, one after the other, stay here and settle here, and take your houses, and live in them, and your fields, and make ye dig, and sow, and reap, and stack for them? and didn't they drive you hither and thither, and tax ye, and work ye, and put ye to bed at sunset, and make ye put out your candles and fires by sound of bell? And after all, England did never lie under the proud foot of a conqueror! Sure, my dear sir, ye oughtn't to be talking like a madman. It's enough to make a pig laugh. Can't ye buy books and read them?'

'But, sir, I'm very proud of those conquests,' interposed Mr. Puntles, smiling happily. 'All these invaders are blended down into one composite mass, and that fusion is the stuff that makes the modern Englishman.'

'It won't do, sir; a few thousands scattered among millions never changed the blood or nature of a nation yet—you're Britons still. You are Britons, the same as ever; by no means a warlike people, not gifted with any military aptitudes, pacific and thradesman-like, and the natural prey and possession of a nation with the spirit of conquest and a genius for arms. You're sinking into your natural hereditary state, that of Quakers and weavers, contented with your comforts and your opulence, knuckling down to the strong, and bullying the helpless, and leaving soldiering in earnest to nations that have the heart and the head for that sort of game, and just taking your chance, and hoarding your money.'

'Chance has answered pretty well up to this,' said Mr. Foljambe; 'we have escaped a military occupation tolerably well, I hope.

'So has Iceland, sir, so has Greenland; ye're out of the gangway, don't ye see, sir? I could show you in the Middle Ages——'

'Don't mind the Middle Ages,' said the captain, 'pray don't— we won't undertake to follow you there.'

'*You* won't follow me, captain, because ye're gone before me there, my dear fellow, ha, ha, ha!—ye're one of the middle ages of this place yourself, my dear captain; but never mind, age is honourable, and middle age is middling honourable, anyhow.'

The captain stared hard at the decanter from which he filled his glass. He so obviously meditated a retort that the neutral powers interposed.

'Now, now, now—pray Captain Bamme, take some wine, and send the decanters this way,' said the vicar, who was in charge of the party ; 'and Mr. Doody, I think we have stood the Irish invasion very well, and I vote we declare an armistice and a—eh—what do you think ?'

' We'll be better friends, captain, you and I,' said Mr. Doody generously, 'when we come to understand one another ; but don't ye be talking about things you don't understand. Stick to the cane and the pipeclay, my boy ; and my blessing attend ye ! and I pledge ye in a glass of clar't. Gentlemen, I give ye our gallant friend, Captain —— I give ye my word, I never heard your neeme. No matter ; our gallant friend the captain ; but I fill to ye all the same.'

'I think he's gone,' observed Doctor Malkin, rousing himself suddenly from a profound ' brown study.' So he was, although the Reverend Michael Doody, who, during his concluding remarks, had been staring at a claret jug, in the direction of which his powerful arm was extended, while he twiddled his fingers toward the handle, in general invitation to the company to push it within reach of his generous clutch, had not perceived his disdainful retreat.

'So he is ! There now ! Ye see what it is to be thin-skinned,' said the curate, filling his glass and drinking it off, without insisting on the presence of the object of the compliment, or the participation of the rest of the company. 'That's good clar't. I'll trouble, ye, sir, for the white wine—the madeira—thank ye, and I drink to our departed friend, the captain, and in solemn silence to the memory of his temper, the craiture !' Which ceremony, like the last, he had all to himself, and performed with a loud smack of his lips.

The Reverend Mr. Foljambe and Mr. Puntles had dropped into their quiet feudal talk again. Doctor Malkin would take no more wine, and the tall and courtly vicar, having collected the general suffrage in favour of joining the ladies, arose, and the little party retreated, talking listlessly, in the direction of the drawing-room.

CHAPTER XVII.

IN THE DRAWING-ROOM.

THE drawing-room is now in a blaze of wax-lights, and every object in it brilliantly defined. Miss Maximilla Medwyn has arrived, and stands near the fireplace, in a dark silk dress, with a good deal of handsome lace; otherwise the same erect figure and energetic and pleasant face that we have seen.

Two gentlemen have arrived to tea—a tall man, quiet and gentleman-like, of fifty years or upwards, who is talking to Lady Vernon, and a very short, vulgar man, fat and sleek-haired, with smooth chin and cheek, and ill-made, black, baggy clothes, and a general greasiness of hair, face, and habiliments. This is Mr. Zachary Smelt, a light in the firmament of Roydon dissent, who does not disdain to revolve, on occasions, round the munificent centre of so many religious charities, enterprises, and cliques.

Mr. Smelt has taught the muscles of his fat face to smile with a perseverance that must have been immensely fatiguing when he first tried it; but every fold and pucker in his cheeks was by this time as fixed as those of the great window-curtains opposite to him were by the tacks and hammer of the upholsterer. I am sure he sleeps in that smile, and that he will die with it on. When he is angry it still sits on his putty face, though his little black eyes look never so fell and wicked over it.

'I'm less in the world, Mr. Smelt, than you are,' Miss Maximilla is saying tartly enough to this good man, whom instinctively she loves not. 'What do you mean by telling me I live too much in and for the world? You don't say that to Lady Vernon, I venture to say. You like her money too well to risk it. I venture to say you have fifty times as many spites, and a hundred times as many schemes, in your head as I. I have just as good a commission to speak plainly as you have. There's your great gun, the Honourable Bagge Muggridge, as you take care to advertise him whenever he attends a meeting or makes a speech. He has gone out of the world, as you term it; that is, he shirks his duties as a public man and a country gentleman, surrounds himself with parasites and flatterers, and indulges his taste for notoriety by making dull speeches at canting meetings, and putting himself down for shabby contributions to all sorts of useless things. And this selfish creature, because he gratifies his indolence and his vanity, and rides his hobby, has, you tell us, retired from the world and become an apostle, and is perfectly certain of an eternal crown of glory. Those were your words, and I have seldom read anything more shocking.'

Perhaps Miss Medwyn had something more to say, and no doubt Mr. Z. Smelt had somewhat to rejoin, for he was smiling hard, and folding and rubbing his fat hands together ; but the Reverend Mr. Foljambe walked slowly up with a gracious smile, his head inclined and his hand extended, and said, with dignified affection :

' And how is my very dear friend, Miss Medwyn ?'

The vicar chose not to see Mr. Smelt, though the shoulder of his fashionably cut clerical coat almost touched the forehead of that fat thunderer against episcopacy, whose fixed smile acquired under this affront a character as nearly that of a sneer as anything so celestial could wear. So Zachary Smelt, folding his fat hands, turned on his heel with an expression of malignant compassion, and Mr. Foljambe inclined his long face and high nose over Maximilla Medwyn, smiling, in his way, as sweetly as his fellow-labourer; and as his ' very dear friend ' answered his affectionate inquiries, his shrewd eye was peering after Lady Vernon, and I am afraid he could not have given a very accurate account of what the good old spinster answered.

A cloud crossed the pure light of his brow as he saw the fat dissenter, who was always extracting money for the behoof of his sect from Lady Vernon, place himself before her exactly as the tall grave man with the iron-grey head was withdrawing.

Mr. Foljambe turned out of his way, and looked into a book of prints which Doctor Malkin was turning over.

' An unexpected pleasure that,' murmured the doctor, with smiling irony, as he glanced toward the short fat figure of Mr. Smelt.

' Oh ! That is—— ?' hesitated the vicar, compressing his eyelids a little as he glanced towards Mr. Smelt, whom he knew as well as the docter did. ' I stupidly forgot my glasses.'

' Mr. Zachary Smelt, the Independent preacher. I venture to say there is not a drawing-room in the country, except this, into which that fellow would be admitted,' said the doctor, who had no practice among that sect.

' Well, you know, Lady Vernon may do things that other people couldn't. Smelt ? Yes, he is a troublesome person, and certainly, I don't pretend to say—I don't stand, at all, I hope, on that sort of thing; but I should not suppose he can feel quite at home among gentlemen.'

Doctor Malkin smiled and shrugged his shoulders.

'This is, you know, a very distinguished house,' continues the vicar loftily, 'and not the place, as you say, where one would expect to meet people of a certain level in society; I don't object to it, though, of course, there are others who, I dare say, don't like it. But I do say it is a mistake, as respects the object of the distinction; it does not answer its purpose. I venture to say there is not a more uncomfortable man in this county to-night than this Mr.—Mr.—a—Smelt.'

'I'm not so sure; he is such an impudent fellow,' said the doctor.

'I shouldn't wonder if he had a good deal of that kind of thing, as you say. You possibly have more opportunities than I can boast. You see Doctor—a—Doctor—a—a—Malkin—' the Reverend Mr. Foljambe had a habit of hesitating rather over the names of small men with whom he was good enough to converse—'Lady Vernon, though she is a Church-woman, and a very staunch one, in a certain sense, has yet very vague views respecting the special sympathy due to those who, in a more intimate way, are of the household of faith; but she'll come all right, ultimately, with her powerful mind, and the supremacy she assigns to conscience in everything. I have had, from my position, opportunities, and I can safely say I have rarely encountered a mind so entirely under the guidance and control of conscience.'

The Reverend Richard Howard Foljambe looked with the affectionate interest of a good pastor and kinsman at that paragon of women.

'What a splendidly handsome woman she is!' observed the doctor. 'By Jove, for her time of life, she's perfectly wonderful.'

Everyone flatters Lady Vernon, and these gentlemen like to pay her compliments in each other's ears, though she does not hear them. This frank testimony behind backs prevents the least suspicion of adulation in what they may say in her hearing. But, in truth, Doctor Malkin's criticism is no flattery, though, perhaps, they hardly know that it is not, their critical faculties being a little confused, standing so much as they do in the relation of courtiers to her.

They are both covertly looking at her. They see a lady of some four or five and forty, still very handsome, according to the excellence of middle-aged beauty. How refined and elegant she looks, as she talks gravely with that little vulgar Dissenter. She is the representative of an ancient family. She is peculiar in appearance, in habits, in character. A fine figure, a little fuller than girlhood, but only a little. A Greek face, pale, proud, and very still.

' What a talent for command that woman has !' says the doctor.

' She's very clever—she's very able, I may say, is Lady Vernon,' says the clergyman, who, being a kinsman, does not quite like Doctor Malkin's calling her a woman.

' Did it ever strike you, sir, making allowance for the difference of sex, that her eye has a very powerful resemblance to that of a remarkable historic genius ?' asks Doctor Malkin.

' Ah—well, I can't quite say ; a—do you mean—I don't quite see,' says the vicar.

' A large wonderful grey eye that will be famous as long as history lasts—I mean Napoleon, the First Consul, Napoleon the Great. It is powerfully like some of the portraits.'

' Well, do you know, I should not wonder. I believe there is—very likely,' replies the vicar.

' Now, Miss Maud's, you see, although they are large and grey, they haven't got that peculiar character—a look of serene command, and what some people would call cold ; it is very fine.'

' Yes, and accompanied with that talent, she has so much administrative ability ! She is a Dorcas, but a Dorcas on a very princely scale indeed,' says Mr. Foljambe.

' More like my idea of Minerva Glaucopis, you know—just that marble brow and pencilled eyebrow, and cold, full, splendid grey eye. It is a study for Pallas ; it would be worth a fortune to some of our painters,' says the doctor.

The doctor's face looks a little sterner as he closes his little speech. It is not always easy to say what a man is looking at with an obliquity of vision like his ; but I think, of his two rather fine dark eyes, that one which he chiefly uses glanced at that moment on Miss Maud Vernon. Perhaps some association or train of thought, suddenly suggested, caused the change. The doctor's face is well enough when he is talking and animated. In repose it is not prepossessing; disturbed by any unpleasant emotion it is still less so.

CHAPTER XVIII.

DRESSING-GOWNS AND SLIPPERS.

CAPTAIN BAMME, who has been entertaining the young lady, is taking his leave. The doctor says good-night at the same time, and walks down the old avenue in the long streak of moonlight between the shadows of the trees in company with the captain, who is eloquent upon the treason against the peace and decency of the town perpetrated by old Foljambe in the importation of his Irish curate.

'I hope I have a proper respect for everything that's sacred; but, by Jove, if a fellow behaves like a rowdy, parson or no parson, sooner or later, he'll get what he wants—a devilish good licking; and I'd chuck him out of the window as soon as look at him :' a feat not only morally but physically worthy of admiration, considering their relative proportions.

The curate meanwhile has taken his departure, and very amicably, side by side with Mr. Smelt, is trudging after the captain and the doctor to the village. These apostolic men are manifestly deep in conversation, if we may so call a talk in which the loud and hilarious voice of the curate, interspersed with his peals of laughter echoing among the branches of the ancient trees, does duty for both. The captain quickens his pace on hearing these ominous sounds. He was going to light his cigar, but does not care to loiter, and with a sniff and a muttered word or two between his teeth, postpones that indulgence till he shall have reached the gate, where, as he knows, the curate turns to the right, and he to the left.

Mr. and Mrs. Foljambe, in their one-horse brougham, come rolling down the avenue, and oblige the fat Dissenter to skip out of the way as their wheel grazes his arm. He is, no doubt, grateful for his escape, but the fright does not abate his righteous abhorrence of prelatical pride ; and the boisterous and unfeeling banter of the Reverend Michael Doody fails to soothe him as he stands gazing, for some seconds, after the equipage, with his muddy elbow a little raised. The driver and the parson are of one mind, no doubt. If he had been a bishop, would they have made his 'lordship' cut that terrified caper? His blood boils as he looks after the carriage. The mud of the wheel, he could swear, is upon his shoulder. He half regrets, for the sake of the moral and the scandal, that he was not knocked down. Perhaps if he had possessed presence of mind he would have gone down at that touch, as adroit pugilists sometimes do in the ring.

Notwithstanding this little incident, however, Mr. Smelt and the curate proceed, side by side, in very friendly march toward the town.

The Churchman's jocularity has subsided, and he is now learning all he can about the religious state of the little town of Roydon, and the statistics of its poverty, from the preacher at his side, who is puzzled a little by the unaffectedly secular demeanour of the curate, by his utter repudiation of the doctrine of apostolic succession, and by his earnest and simple desire to go to the heart of his work, and do some good in his generation.

From the cold moonlight, and still shadows of the foliage on the broad avenue, we return to the great drawing-room of Roydon and the glow of other lights, where the clear voice of Lady Vernon is saying to the tall grey gentleman, with whom she has talked a good deal that evening, and who was on the point of going out to light his bedroom candle, and make his way to his room :

' I don't think I have introduced my daughter.'

The tall gentleman's eyes follow the direction of Lady Vernon's expectantly, and she says :

' Maud, I want to introduce you to Mr. Coke, who has been so good as to come with the papers for the trustees, who are coming to-morrow, and it may be right that you should be present.'

The elderly attorney looked at the young lady with interest as he made his bow, and he thought how high-spirited, how high-bred and beautiful she looked, and what a becoming representative of that great and ancient family she was.

' It is a good many years since I saw you, Miss Vernon, a long time in your life, that is—not in mine. You were only so high,' he says, with the familiarity of an old retainer, measuring a standard in the air with his hand.

Ten minutes later they have broken up and gone to their rooms, and Maud, in her dressing-gown, with her long hair loose over her shoulders, taps at her Cousin Max's door, which is near her own.

' Who's there ?'

' Maud. May I come in ?'

' Come in, my dear child, to be sure.'

Maximilla Medwyn is in her dressing-gown and slippers, and

smiles—rather an odd figure, her dressing-gown being 'skimpy,' as her maid tells her often, and her head being made up in an eccentric coiffure.

'What is the matter now ?'

'Nothing. Only I could not rest till I had seen you again. Mamma received me to-day just as usual.'

'She can't help it,' replies Miss Medwyn. 'My maid is gone to her bed; there's no one to hear us. She is the same to every one; it is her way; she was always cold. I tried to know her long ago—and I believe she liked me as well as she liked any one else—but I never could know her, young as she was. It is her nature, and she can't change it now.'

'I wish I could be cold and reasonable like other people. I wish I could care nothing about it, but—I'm such a fool.'

'You make too much of it.'

'I can't help it, and whenever I do speak out, we quarrel. It is so miserable.'

'You must treat different people differently, my dear, according to their natures. I make it a point to meet her just as coolly as she meets me, and I find we get on very well,' said Maximilla. 'She was always an oddity. Why, nothing odder was ever heard of than her marriage with your poor father. To me she always seemed unfathomable. All I know about her is, that she has the strongest will I ever heard of, and that she looks like a haughty lady superioress of a convent. Very handsome, of course, we all see that ; but with a countenance, it seems to me, incapable of sympathy, incapable of frankness, and dominated by pride, and dead to everything else.'

'You are frank enough, at all events,' says the young lady, a little dryly.

'Very frank always with you, Maud,' replies the old cousin, seating herself on the sofa at the foot of her bed.

'I see more good in her than that,' persists the girl.

'So do I ; but not in her face. She has a great deal of good. She is generous ; she is courageous ; she has many very fine points. But she seems to me to hold every one on earth at arm's length ; that's all I say. As for me, I gave up the idea of ever knowing her, twenty years ago. You must take her for what she is, and be content with so much love as she is capable of giving. She may give more than she shows, for anything we can tell, and I'm sure she'll do her duty. She has always been a pattern of all the virtues.'

'Yes, conscience, a strong sense of duty, everyone says that. I'm quite serious. But you said that she was odd. What was there about her marriage with papa?'

'Well, yes, that was extremely odd. I never was so surprised in my life. Your father had his baronetage, but that in your family was less than nothing; that title had been twice offered within the last hundred years to the Vernons of Roydon, and twice refused. He was a handsome man, and rather agreeable, and there ended his attractions. He had not a guinea. He was twenty years older than she. He liked nothing that she liked. He was a captain in the Guards, you know, and when he was ruined, had retired. He came down here, and tried to make love to her, without your grandfather's knowing anything about it; but she could not endure him, and treated him with utter contempt, and he grew to hate her. People thought, my dear, that he did not want anything but her money, and was furious at finding himself foiled. She certainly did hate him, then. He was of the same family—a Vernon—her third cousin.'

'Was not grandmamma alive then?'

'Yes, but in miserable health—slowly dying, in fact. They went away for a little tour, somewhere—a fancy of the doctor's, I believe; when she returned, which was in less than a year, your father came here, uninvited and unwished for. I was here at the time. Barbara seemed to hate him more intensely than ever. She would not even see him. She spoke of him to me, when I asked her to come down and take her place as usual, with a degree of detestation I could not understand.'

'Yet he was very gentle, I have always heard, and a great many people liked him,' said Maud.

'I dare say. I only tell you what I saw,' says Maximilla. 'I need not tell you I did not want her to like him. I thought his courtship, all things considered, a most audacious thing; and I could not believe, after all that had passed, that he had any serious idea of renewing it.'

'It was certainly very unequal in all things but birth,' said Maud.

'Yes, you know, she might have married any one, and he had no pretensions. Your grandfather plainly did not like his being here, though he did not choose to turn him out. I don't think, indeed, he saw what Amyrald Vernon was aiming at; but I could not help fancying that, for some reason, he was afraid of him. Your grandfather was a most upright, honourable man.

If he had ever been a reckless young man, or amongst objection-able companions, I could have understood the possibility of his dreading some awkward disclosure. But his whole life had been transparent, and, in all respects, honourable; and this puzzled me, for I could not account for his seeming embarrassed and timid in his own house, and so uneasy while Amyrald Vernon continued there. I had given up asking your mamma to appear as usual in her place while he was there. One morn-ing, however, she did come down, hating him just as much as ever, but thinking, I fancied, that it was making him too im-portant, keeping out of the way on his account. I remember so well her standing for a few minutes in the window, before breakfast, and his joining her there, and talking to her. They were both looking out, so I could not see their faces. But the next thing that happened was their taking a long walk, up and down the terrace, together, after luncheon; after that, her de-meanour changed entirely; he seemed to exercise an unaccount-able fascination over her; and one morning, in the drawing-room, she told me, as coldly as if it was a matter of going to take a drive, that she had made up her mind to marry Sir Amyrald Vernon. I don't think I was ever so astounded in all my life. I remonstrated and represented all I could, but it was in vain; whatever his fascination was, it had prevailed, and I might as well have tried to lift the house from its foundations by my eloquence. She must have fallen in love with him. Her father always made a pet of her; too much, indeed. She would, perhaps, under other management, have learned to be less wilful and less haughty. So, I suppose, he let her do as she pleased. But the end of it was that she did marry him; and, I think, her liking, if there was any, expired before two months were over, for when I saw them next, she seemed—begging your pardon, my dear—to hate him as much as ever. They did not quarrel; I don't mean that. She was too cold and dignified for any such exhibitions. But I could not mistake her. There was fixed dislike. And when, two years later, he lost his life by the fall of his horse, I don't think she cried a single tear, and I never heard her speak of him, except now and then, as coolly and curtly as you might mention a not very pleasant acquaintance who had gone to Van Diemen's Land.'

These recollections of Maximilla Medwyn's revived in Maud's mind a scene which often recurred of itself.

It was one of those short scenes, in the remembrance of which fear and disgust are mingled ; to disclosing which there grows up gradually an invincible repugnance, and on which the mind silently dwells with a sense of odious curiosity.

When she was a little thing, some five or six years of age, she was fond of old Margaret Creswell, who had been her mother's nurse. She used to run to her as a redresser of grievances, and to pour out her complaints and petitions at her knees. But a time came when her protectress was to take her last leave of her and of all things.

The old woman was dying, and found dying a hard and tedious piece of work. The child had not been in her room for four months, and one day, in a state of rebellion against some new rule of her mamma's, she broke from the nursery, and ran into old Margaret Creswell's room.

She was sitting up, in flannels, by the fire. The room was darkened. A little table, with her medicine bottles, her tablespoon and glasses, was beside her. With her one idea the child trotted into the room, prattled and sobbed through her story, and ended by saying, ' And that wouldn't be done to me if papa was alive.'

The figure in the flannels beckoned, and for the first time, a little awe stole over the child ; she drew near, trying to see her more distinctly in the obscurity. When she did, it was not the face she knew. There was no smile there. The face was hollow and yellow, a clammy blackness was about the lips, the eyes looked at her, large and earnest ; the child came beside her, returning her strange gaze in silence. She was frightened that such a thing should be Maggie Creswell.

The old woman placed her bony hand on the child's arm, and clasped it feebly. She spoke in a hard whisper, with a little quick panting at every word.

' That's Anne Holt has been saying that ; it's a shame to be putting things in your head against your good mamma. Well it is for you that you are under her, and not under him ; no blacker villain ever lived on earth than your papa. Keep that to yourself ; if you tell anyone in the nursery, I'll come to you after I'm dead, and frighten you.' She let go her arm, and said, ' Go now to your toys, and do as mamma bids you, and be thankful.'

Very much scared, and very quiet, the child stole back to the nursery, and kept the secret guarded by that menace.

That dark room ; the old woman, stern and changed ; the last words she was ever to hear from her ; and the dreadful terms of hatred applied to her father, which she tried to put away as a blasphemy, returned often, and drew her into conjecture.

'Was there any reason,' she asked her Cousin Max, after a little silence, 'for mamma's want of affection for poor papa?'

'No particular reason—no good reason. As a husband, I don't think there was anything against him. He devoted himself very much to his duties, and did his best to become a popular and useful country gentleman. I suppose she repented too late, and had acted on an impulse, and was disgusted to find, as many of us are, that the past is irrevocable.'

Old Miss Maximilla sighed. Perhaps she had a retrospect to regret, and Maud, with the world before her, looked for a moment on the carpet sadly.

'I don't know your mamma, my dear; she has been always a sealed book to me. I don't think she ever wanted either sympathy or advice. I don't think anyone ever knew her. *I* never could, and I have long given up the riddle. But, dear me, it is almost one o'clock. Run away, my dear, and let your poor old cousin get to her bed. I shan't go for a day or two, and we shall have time enough; I have fifty things to talk to you about. Good-night.'

And so they parted till next morning.

CHAPTER XIX.

BREAKFAST.

AT half-past nine in the morning, the roar of the gong spreads shivering and swelling through rooms and passages, up staircases, great and small, through lobbies and long galleries, calling all the inmates of Roydon Hall to prayers.

In a long room which projects, at the end, in a mass of stone-shafted window, they assemble. A hundred years ago and more, the then Vernon of Roydon gave to this great chamber, as nearly as he could, the character of a chapel. The light streams in through stained glass, brought from Antwerp, tradition says, flaming from the base up to the cornice with sacred story. The oak carving of this sombre room is admired by critics, who say that the spoils of some ancient church must have furnished it. Mr. Coke, the elderly attorney, with his head full of the strategy of the consulting-room and the rhetoric of the courts, is for a moment solemnized, as he enters and looks round him. He then falls to admiring, in detail, the stained glass. He and Miss Max

are the only guests at present in the house. It is a very small
party confronting so imposing an array of servants. There is
hardly another house in England where so prodigious a household assembles. Mr. Coke, whose business brings him, about
settlements and at other legal crises, to many noble houses, is
struck by the unusual superfluity of servant-kind here, and while
Mr. Penrhyn, Lady Vernon's secretary, who officiates when no
clergyman is present, is reading a chapter from the old Testament,
he tries to count them, but his polling always breaks down in
the middle, at the back rows; and then comes the thought,
'Here are just one lady and her daughter, a girl, to be attended
to, and this enormous piece of machinery is got up and main-
tained for that simple end;' and the words of 'the preacher'
stand good to this hour: 'When goods increase, they are increased that eat them: and what good is there to the owners
thereof, saving the beholding of them with their eyes?'

These morning prayers of Lady Vernon's are unusually long.
There are the psalms of the day, and the chapters, and, in fact,
a 'service,' which lasts about half an hour.

Mr. Penrhyn has had his breakfast an hour ago, in his own
little office, and having talked and smirked a little, remits himself,
in a fuss, to his work.

The breakfast-room still bears the ancient title of the 'parlour,'
and is a spacious and cheery apartment, hung with festive
tapestry, and opening into the dining-room. Here the little
party of four assembled.

'It is eleven years, Mr. Coke, I was counting up last night,
since I last saw you; and I believe you are one of the very
oldest friends I have,' said Miss Max. 'Why don't you pay
me a visit at Wybourne, when your excursions carry you to
points so near as Hammerton and Dake's Hall? I heard of you
there. I don't think it was kind.'

'It is all your fault,' said Lady Vernon. 'He went to Dake's
Hall to arrange settlements. Why don't you give him a reason
to visit you?'

'Thank you very much, Lady Vernon,' put in Mr. Coke
merrily.

'I think it is rather hard that an old woman should be put
into Coventry because she can't find anyone to marry her,'
replied Miss Max.

'A lady who might have married any one of a score of suitors,
every one eligible, has no case to make,' Mr. Coke said.

'I think Cousin Max is right. I think one's liberty is a great deal,' remarked Maud. 'Doctor Malkin said last night what I quite agree in,'that it is better to marry never, than once too often.'

'He says that a woman who marries once is a fool,' said Maximilla Medwyn ; 'but a woman who marries twice is a criminal.'

'Is not that rather violent doctrine ?' Mr. Coke inquired.

'I think he only said, who marries within a short time after the death of her husband,' said Maud ; 'and you recollect the curious stories he told us ? There was a woman who would not allow him to bleed her husband, whose life, he said, would certainly have been saved by it, pretending too great a tenderness for him to allow it, and, in a few weeks after his death, she married a person who lived in the house ; and there was another story of a woman who married immediately after her husband's death, without the slightest suspicion, who, ten years later, was convicted of having murdered him, by hammering a nail into his head while he was asleep.'

'But, seriously, I'm a mere slave, and can never command an hour, except when I get to the Continent, and letters can't find me any longer. Doctor Malkin was here last night ? I don't know the people—which was he ?' said the attorney.

'He is a pale man, with a high nose, and dishevelled black whiskers, and good eyes,' Miss Maud answered.

'My dear Maud, that doesn't describe him,' interposed Miss Max. 'In the first place, he squints ; next, he is bald, and he has a long upper-lip and a short chin, and an odious smile, that I think is both conceited and insincere, and you could fancy him just the doctor, if he did not like you, to bleed you to death, or poison you by mistake.'

'My dear Maximilla, how can you ?' said Lady Vernon gravely, with a glow in both cheeks that comes when she is either angry or otherwise agitated. 'My cousin, Mr. Coke, is not acquainted with Doctor Malkin. She does not know him, but I do, and I have the very highest opinion of him. I have great confidence in his skill, and still greater in his integrity. He is as conscientious a person as I ever met in my life. I know no one more entirely trustworthy than Doctor Malkin.'

Lady Vernon spoke coldly, after her wont, but she was evidently in earnest.

'Then his countenance does him great wrong,' answered Miss

Max cheerfully, 'that's all I say. It is quite true I don't know him, and I don't desire to know him.'

And she sipped her tea.

'I assure you, Mr. Coke, I speak from knowledge; there is no one of whose good sense and truth I have a higher opinion. I wished you to understand that,' said Lady Vernon. 'And I have an almost equally high opinion of his skill. For the last fifteen years he has been attending, in every illness, in this house; and he has been so attentive and so successful, it would be impossible not to have the highest opinion of him as a physician.'

Perhaps Mr. Coke thought it a little odd that Lady Vernon should make such a point of his believing this country doctor a paragon; and wondered why the peculiar flush by which she betrayed excitement should glow in her cheeks, and make her broad cold eyes fiery.

'Country doctors are often the ablest,' he remarked, letting the subject drop softly; 'they get to know the idiosyncrasies of their small circle of patients so thoroughly; and their dispensaries and the rustic population furnish an immense field of observation and experience. Does Lord Verney come to-day?'

'Yes; I'm sorry he does; he is such a bore, poor man! I should have preferred his staying away,' replied Lady Vernon, with plaintive disgust. 'Barroden comes, and so does Mr. Hildering.'

'And each, I think, brings his solicitor with him?' asked Mr. Coke.

'I wrote to them to do so, and I suppose they will,' answered Lady Vernon. 'Only Sir Harry Strafford doesn't come.'

'I don't think we are likely to hit upon anything very new. I have gone over it so often, and I don't think anything has escaped us,' ruminated Mr. Coke. 'Is there a solicitor to represent Miss Maud Vernon?'

'No; I did not think it necessary. Does it strike you that this room is lighter than it was when you were last here?' inquired Lady Vernon, a little irrelevantly. 'I'll show you how that happens.'

And breakfast being by this time over, she rose and walked to the great window that looks towards the east. Mr. Coke, a little thoughtful, followed her mechanically.

Two great lime-trees stood just there, where you see the grass a little yellow, and they were so shaken by the storm last year, that they were pronounced unsafe, and had to come down ; they were beautiful trees, but the room is a great deal lighter.'

' Yes,' said Mr. Coke. ' It is rather complicated, you see, and there might be a conflict of interests, and as the meeting is a little formal, it would have relieved me of a responsibility ; but I'll do my best.'

' I don't see that any conflict *can* arise, Mr. Coke,' said Lady Vernon coldly. ' At all events, if she wishes to ascertain her rights and opportunities, or whatever they are, separately, there is nothing to prevent her. What we do to-day can't fetter her in any way, and I thought you were quite competent to protect us both. It would be rather early to anticipate her litigating with her mother. I should hope there won't be an opportunity.'

' No,' acquiesced Mr. Coke ; ' I should have preferred that arrangement ; but I'll do my best. At what hour do you expect the trustees, Lady Vernon ?'

' They will all be here by three o'clock, if they keep their appointments. I think Mr. Hildering will come at one ; he said so.'

Mr. Coke was thoughtful ; and when Lady Vernon was gone, he looked over his note-book for a time, and raising his eyes a little after, he saw the slight figure of Miss Maximilla Medwyn walking up and down the long terrace before the house.

He went out and joined her.

CHAPTER XX.

LADY VERNON'S EXCURSIONS.

WHEN he overtook that cheerful sentry, he said : ' Can you tell me where I should be likely to find Miss Vernon ? I have a word to say to her.'

' Lady Vernon sent for her a few minutes ago, but she said she would not keep her long,' said Miss Max ; ' I told her I should walk up and down here till she came.'

Mr. Coke walked beside her without saying a word, till they had completed a walk to the end, and back again.

' Lady Vernon is as handsome as ever,' he remarked, on a sudden. ' Since I last saw her there is really no change that I can see.'

'But that is scarcely a year ago,' answered Miss Max.

'More than four,' replied Mr. Coke, smiling.

'You mean to say you have not seen Barbara for four years!' exclaimed Miss Max, stopping short and turning towards him.

'I come whenever I'm sent for,' said Mr. Coke, with a laugh. 'But though I don't see her very often, I very often hear from her, and very clear and clever letters she writes upon business, I can tell you.'

'But didn't you know she is in town for some time every year of her life?'

'I had not an idea. We hear from her generally about once a fortnight. But I should very often have liked a few minutes' talk with her. Those little points of *vivâ voce* explanation are very useful in a long correspondence. And so she is every year at Grosvenor Square?'

'I think you had better not say a word about it to Lady Vernon,' said Miss Max.

'Oh! of course not. I leave that to her. But I think it is a mistake, not giving us half an hour when she comes.' Thus said Mr. Coke, swinging his stick a little, and looking over the top of the terrace balustrades, across the court, and ponds, and peacocks, and swans, and the close-shorn sward stained with the solemn shadows of the trees, down the perspective of foliage, to the mighty piers and great carved urns of the iron gates, and the gables and twisted chimneys of the gate-house.

'Yes, that would be only natural, and her not doing so puzzles me more and more,' replied Maximilla Medwyn; 'you are such an old friend, and know everything about the affairs of this family so intimately, that I'll tell you ; but you are not to let it go further, for it is plain she does not want it talked about; and it is simply that which makes me very curious.'

'I've learned by this time to hold my tongue and to keep secrets, and I venture to say this is a very harmless one,' laughed Mr. Coke.

'Well, now, listen—what a time Maud is! Once a year—I think about July or August—my handsome cousin, Lady Vernon, is taken with what my maid terms a fit of the fidgets. She takes her maid, but never Maud with her, mind—never. Maud has never come out. I don't think she has been six times in London in her life. That is not right, you know ; but that is a different matter. Lady Vernon and her maid go up to Grosvenor Square, where the house is all locked up and uncarpeted, all except a room or two, and where there is no one to receive them but an old housekeeper and a housemaid. She tells old Mr. Foljambe, the vicar, that it is to consult a London physician. No great testimony, I think, to the surpassing skill of Doctor Malkin. But, I fancy, it is not about any such thing she goes to town, for her stay in Grosvenor Square never outlasts a day or two. Her fidgets continue. She leaves her maid there, and goes alone, I believe, from one watering-place to another.'

' Without her maid, you say ?'

' Yes, without her maid.'

' And how do they know she goes to watering-places ?'

' They never know where she is going. The only clue is, that now and then she sends a note of directions to her maid, in London, or to the house-steward, or the housekeeper, down here ; and these indicate her capricious and feverish changes of place, which you'll allow contrast oddly with the stillness and monotony of her life when she is at home. Then, after six weeks or so spent in this mysterous way, she appears again, suddenly, at her town-house, tells her maid that she is better, and so they return here. It is very whimsical, isn't it ? Can you understand it ?'

' Restlessness, and perhaps a longing for a little holiday,' he answered. ' She has, I may say, a very peculiar position in what they call the religious world; and the correspondence she directs, and even conducts with her own hand, is very large. Altogether, I think, she makes her life too laborious.'

' Well, as you and she, and you and I, are all old friends, I don't mind telling you that I don't think that's it. I don't believe a word of it. There is more in it than that; but *what* I can't divine ; and, indeed, it does not trouble me much ; if Barbara would only do what she ought about Maud, I should be very well satisfied. But she has never been presented, nor been to town for a single season, and Lady Vernon has never taken her out, and I don't think has any idea of doing so. Of course, you'll say that, with all her advantages, it can't matter much. But there can be no advantage in people's saying that she has lived all her life like a recluse; and I think there is always a disadvantage in despising what is usual. And really, Mr. Coke, as a confidential friend, I think you might very well say a word about it.'

He smiled and shook his head.

' All that sort of thing is quite out of my line. But I think, with you, it doesn't much matter; for she's the greatest heiress in England; and she is so beautiful, and—here's Miss Vernon at last.'

As Maud came down the steps she looked to the right and left, and seeing Miss Max, smiled and nodded, and quickened her approach.

Mr. Coke advanced a step or two to meet her, with his business looks on.

'I have been wishing to say a word, if you will allow me. I think it would be advisable that you should be represented at the conference we are to hold to-day, to prevent any course being determined on that might embarrass your interests under the will; and if you authorise me to do so, I will watch them for you this afternoon; and, in any case, I'll mention that a solicitor should be retained for you, as the instrument is unusually complicated, and you will be of age in a very little time.'

'I don't understand these things, Mr. Coke, but whatever mamma and you think right, I shall be very much obliged to you to do. What a charming day it is! I hope you are not to be shut up all day. When you were last here it was winter, and you will hardly know the place now; you ought to see Rymmel's Hoe to-day—it is looking quite beautiful,' said Miss Maud Vernon.

'I'm off, I'm afraid, to town this evening,' he answered; 'a thousand thanks. I must now go in and see Lady Vernon, if she's at leisure.'

So, with a smile that quickly disappeared, he turned and walked up the steps.

CHAPTER XXI.

THE CONFERENCE.

OF this muster of trustees, Miss Maud Vernon gave this account in one of her long letters to her friend, Miss Mary Mainard:

'On Tuesday we had a little parliament of trustees, opened with great solemnity by mamma. She was aided by an attorney, a Mr. Coke, who says that your humble servant ought also to have been furnished with an adviser of the same profession.

Old Lord Verney came similarly attended; and Lord Barroden also brought his attorney; Mr. Hildering, a great man in "the City," I am told, dispensed with that assistance, and, I suppose, relied on his native roguery.   Still, there was an imposing court of attorneys, sitting as assessors with the more dignified members of the assembly.   Sir Harry Strafford, who is also a trustee named in grandpapa's will, did not attend.   As all these were men of importance twenty years ago, when they were named in his will, you may suppose what a juvenile air the assembly presented.

'Mamma did not choose that I should attend, telling me that I should be sent for, if required; and I had begun to hope that my assistance had been unanimously dispensed with, when a servant came to tell me that mamma wished to see me in the library.   Thither I repaired, and found her presiding at her cabinet.

'Lord Verney and Mr. Hildering were a little red, and I fancy had been snubbing one another, for Mr. Coke mentioned, afterwards, that they are members of the same boards in London, and fight like "cat and dog" whenever they meet.   Mamma looked, as usual, serene, and old Lord Barroden was, I am sure, asleep, for he was the only gentleman of the company who did not rise to receive me.   There were printed copies of grand-papa's will, one of which was given to me; so I took a chair beside mamma, and listened while they talked in a language which I did not the least understand, about what they called real and personal reversions, contingent remainders, and vested remainders, and fees and tails, and more unintelligible names and things than I could remember or reckon up in an hour.

'They all seemed to treat mamma with great deference; not complimentary, but real; and I remarked that they said very little across the table to one another; but whenever they had anything to ask or to say, they looked to her, and she seemed to understand everything about it, better than anyone else in the room, and Mr. Coke told me afterwards, she is one of the best lawyers he ever met, and he explained a great deal that I did not then understand.

'The conference lasted nearly three hours!   You can't imagine anything so dull; I came away just as wise as I went there, except perhaps that I had learned a little patience.

'The Rose and the Key, which, as you know, figure on our shield, were talked of a good deal, and are mentioned very often

in the will, as indicating the families which are named particularly. Old Lord Barroden woke up at this part of the
conversation, and talked a great deal of heraldry, whether
good or bad I can't say; and then, as they were still very
garrulous upon crests, supporters, shields, chevrons, and all the
rest, mamma led the way to the state dining-room. I don't
know why, we never dine there now; I think it about the
prettiest room in the house—I don't think you saw it when you
were with us. It has great stone shields let into the wall all
round, and ours over the mantelpiece. They are all carved in
relief, and painted and gilded, according to heraldry; and you
can't think how stately and brilliant it looks. Old Mr. Puntles,
who is our antiquary in this part of the world, says that it was
an old English custom when a house was being built for the
owner to place the arms of the principal families in the county
thus round the state dining-room, by way of a compliment to
them; and now I saw what I never observed before, that in
every second one, or oftener, our device, the Rose and the Key,
is quartered in the corner. The rose red, and the key gold; *gules*
and *or* they call them, on a field azure: you see how learned I
have grown.'

Then the writer ran away to subjects more likely to amuse her
and her friend.

Mr. Coke did not stay to dinner. He took his leave nearly
three hours before that solemn meal. As he came downstairs
from his room he encountered Miss Vernon, who was going to
dress.

'You are going to hear the bishop's sermon, and see the statue
unveiled?' he inquired, stopping before her in the gallery.

'Yes, Miss Medwyn and I; mamma has a headache, and says
she can't come,' she replied.

'I'm afraid our long consultation tired her; I'm sure it tired
you, and I don't think you could have understood half we said.
If you have five minutes I'll describe to you now, just in outline, the leading provisions of your grandfather's will.'

'I have more than five minutes, I'm sure,' she answered;
but not so much interested as Mr. Coke thought she might have
been.

Young ladies are so much in the habit of being taken care of
by others, that they can without much magnanimity dispense
with the drudgery of taking care of themselves. They like
whole bones as well as we do, but the vicious habit of being

taken care of prevails, and what woman is quite capable of
taking care of herself over a crossing?

'You must have for life, if you outlive your mother, Lady
Vernon, at least ten thousand pounds a year, and you may have
ultimately one hundred and fifty thousand pounds a year in
land, and a great deal of money besides—I don't think there is
any lady of your age in England with such magnificent prospects. If Lady Vernon should marry, and have a son, the
estates will go to him, charged with ten thousand a year for you.
If she should not marry, then on her death they go to you. If
you marry, then your mother's power over the whole property
will be very limited indeed. If neither you nor she should
marry, then on your death the estates will go to some one to be
appointed among certain families who are connected with yours,
and who have a right to quarter the family device of the Rose
and the Key.'

'I've heard that before. Mr. Tintern of the Grange, near this,
represents one of those families, I've been told?'

'Yes, and in that event, you or Lady Vernon, whichever survives, would have the right to appoint.'

'I'm afraid, Mr. Coke, I have not mamma's talent for business.
I should very soon be lost in the labyrinth.'

'But so far, you do understand?'

'Yes, I think I do.'

'Well, there are also specific provisions in the event of your
marriage, Miss Vernon, and perhaps, until you are furnished
with a legal adviser, the best thing I can do for you will be
to send you as short and simple an abstract of the will and its
codicils as I can make out. The plan of the will is, to keep the
estates together, and to favour certain families, out of whom, in
the event of your both dying unmarried, an heir is to be appointed. If your mother marries, which I rather conjecture is
by no means unlikely——'

He looked very archly as he said this, and some complication of feeling made the young lady, though she smiled,
turn pale.

'Do you really mean—— ?' began Miss Maud.

'I only say conjecture, mind, but I am generally a tolerably
good conjuror, and we shall see. But, if Lady Vernon should
marry,' he continued, 'her power over the estates is increased
very considerably, but your reversion—I mean, your right of
succession—cannot be affected by any event but the birth of

a son. The provisions respecting the personal property—that is, money, jewels, pictures, everything but the estates—are very stringent also, and follow very nearly the dispositions respecting the real estate. There is an unusual provision, also, with respect to all savings and accumulations, which may be made either by your mother, Lady Vernon, or by you, and they are to be carried to the account of the personal estate under the trusts; and very searching powers for the discovery of any such are vested in the trustees, and they are obliged from time to time to exercise them : and any such sum or sums, no matter how invested, are to be carried to the credit of the trustees to the uses of the will. So you see, it is a very potent instrument.'

' I'm sure it is,' said the young lady, with a disappointing cheerfulness.

' Well, I'll do my best; I'll send you an abstract; and, is that the church-bell I hear ?' he asked, glancing through the open window.

' Yes, we hear it very distinctly,' said she.

' Oh, then you'll be going immediately.'

And again he took his leave.

CHAPTER XXII.

IN ROYDON CHURCH.

THE bell from the church tower sounds sweetly over town and field : and the sober-minded folk, who people the quaint streets of Roydon, answer that solemn invitation very kindly.

In this evening sun, as the parishioners troop slowly towards the church-gate, near the village tree, sad Mrs. Foljambe, hard of hearing, the gay Captain Bramme, and the new curate, the Reverend Michael Doody, accidentally encounter.

Mrs. Foljambe stops to receive their greetings. The level sunbeam shows all the tiny perplexity of wrinkles on her narrow forehead with a clear illumination.

' I'm going to the church to witness the ceremonial,' shouts the captain, with his best smile.

She turns with a little start.

'No wonder she's a bit hard of hearing, captain, if that's the way ye've been talking at her these ten years,' suggests Mr. Doody, in a tone to her inaudible.

'We have been sending up some china and cut-glass to the vestry-room, for the bishop's toilet-table,' says Mrs. Foljambe, and her head droops, and her sad eyes look dreamily on the road, as if she were thinking of passing the rest of the evening there.

'The bell has only ten minutes more to ring, ma'am,' says the curate, who is growing uneasy.

'It is a nice evening,' observes Mrs. Foljambe drearily.

'Quite so,' says the captain, waving his hand agreeably towards the firmament. 'Although we have sun, it's cool.'

'Your son's at school ?' repeats good Mrs. Foljambe, to let him know that she had heard him distinctly.

'Oh, oh, oh, that's rich !' ejaculates the curate, exploding.

The captain smiles, and darts a malignant glance at the Reverend Michael Doody, but does not choose to bawl a correction in the street.

So they resume their walk towards the church. The sun is drawing towards the horizon : it is six o'clock. The tombstones cast shadows eastward on the grass, and the people, as they troop upward toward the porch, throw their moving shadows likewise along the green mantle of the dead, and the grey churchyard wall catches them perpendicularly, by the heads and shoulders, and exhibits in that yellow light the silhouettes of worthy townsmen and their wives, and sharp outlines of hats and bonnets, gliding onward, to the music of the holy bell, to hear the good old bishop preach.

The bishop is robing in the vestry-room. The vicar does the honours with profound suavity, and the curate assists with a military sense of subordination and immense gravity.

A note awaits the bishop, in charge of the clerk, from Lady Vernon, pleading her headache, and begging the good prelate to come to Roydon Hall, and if his arrangements about the Church Missions meeting will not permit that, at least that on his way back to the palace he will give her a day or two, or as much longer a time as he can. One of her grenadiers in blue and gold and cockade waits at the vestry-door for an answer, looking superciliously over the headstones. But the bishop cannot accept these hospitable proffers.

In due time the statue is unveiled. In white marble, the image of a slender man, of some forty years or upward, with a noble pensive face, and broad fine forehead, his head a little inclined, stands forth, one hand laid lightly on an open book, the other raised, in pleading or in blessing. It is what we don't often see, a graceful, striking, and pathetic monumental image.

Dead two-and-twenty years, there were many present who remembered that energetic, charitable, and eloquent vicar well. And all who knew him adjusted themselves to listen, with earnest ears, to the words which were to fall from the lips of the good old prelate, who preached, after so long an interval, as it were, the funeral sermon of his gifted friend.

The Vernon family have a grand old-fashioned, square pew in the aisle; Maud Vernon and Miss Max Medwyn sit there now, and the bishop's chaplain has been, by special invitation, elevated to its carpeted floor, and sits on its crimson cushion, and performs his religious exercises on a level at least twelve inches higher than the rest of the congregation in the aisle.

Under the angle of the organ-loft, at each side, is a narrow entrance. And above that, at the right, is a straight stone arch, separating the loft from the side gallery, and looking diagonally across the aisle. Behind this, going back deep into the shade, is a narrow seat, with a door opened by a latch-key from the winding tower-stairs. Here you may sit between stone walls that are panelled with oak, hearing and seeing, and yourself unobserved. In old times, perhaps, it was the private observatory of some ecclesiastical dignitary or visitor, who looked in when he pleased, secretly, to see that mass was sung, and all things done decently and in order.

To those who look up, the arch seems empty, and nothing but darkness in the cavity behind it. But a human being in perturbation and bitterness of soul is there. It is hard for her to follow the benedictions of the psalm, to which the congregation read the responses that echo through the old church walls. In the corner of the deep and dark cell she occupies, there stands, as it were, an evil spirit, and there ripples in and fills her ears, with ebb and flow, the vengeful swell, but too familiar to her soul, of another psalm—a psalm of curses. Ever and anon, as if she would shake something from her ears, she shakes her head, saying :

'Is he not dead and gone? "Vengeance is mine, I will repay, saith the Lord." Let him alone. Don't think of him.'

But the gall returns to her heart, and fire and worm are working there, and the anathema goes on.

Why had she committed it, syllable by syllable, with a malignant meaning, to memory, and conned it over, with an evil delight?

Had she abused the Word of God; and was the spirit she had evoked her master now?

Though her lips were closed, she seemed to herself to be always repeating, fiercely :

'Set thou a wicked man over him, and let Satan stand at his right hand?'

'When he shall be judged, let him be condemned : and let his prayer become sin.'

'Let the iniquity of his fathers be remembered with the Lord; and let not the sin of his mother be blotted out.'

'Because he remembered not mercy, so let it be far from him.'

'As he loved cursing, so let it come unto him.'

She raises her head suddenly.

'I'm nervous,' she thinks, with her hands clasped over her dark eyes. 'God have mercy on me, and let me hear!'

The voice of the good bishop, clear and old, is heard uttering the brief prayer before his sermon.

She throws herself on her knees, listening with clasped hands, passionately. A dull life rolls away, and warm and vivid youth returns, and the fountain of her tears is opened, and the stream of remembrance, sweet and bitter, rushes in. The scene is unchanged : there is the same old church, there are the rude, familiar oak carvings, the self-same saints and martyrs in the vivid windows. The same sweet organ-pipes breathe through the arches from time to time the same tones to which, in summer evenings just like this, long ago, she had listened, when a loved hand pressed the notes, and. the melancholy sounds filled her ears as they do now. Oh ! the pain, how nearly insupportable, of scenes recalled too vividly, wanting the love that has made them dear to memory for ever.

Over the heads of the earnest and the inattentive, of dull and worthy townsfolk there assembled, the tremulous silvery tones of the white-haired bishop reach the solitary listener in this dark nook.

The old bishop tenderly enters on his labour of love. He eloquently celebrates his early friend. He tells them how gentle that friend was, how learned, how noble an enthusiast, modest and

simple as a child, yet a man of the finest genius. Many of those
who heard him now remembered Mr. Howard in the prime of
manhood. Two-and-twenty years were numbered since his
beloved friend died. They two were once young students
together—it seemed but yesterday ; and he, the survivor, was
now an old man ; and if the companion whom he had deplored,
with foolish sorrow, were now living, he would be but the
shadow of the man they remembered, with hair bleached, and
furrowed brows, and strength changing fast to weakness. But
time could not have changed the fine affections and noble
nature that God had given him, and would have only improved
the graces that grow with the life of the Spirit. Then follow
traits of the character he described, and some passages, perhaps
unconsciously pathetic, on the vanity of human sorrows, and
the transitoriness of all that is splendid and beautiful in mortal
man.

The feeble voice of the bishop is heard no more.

The organ peals, and voices skilled in the mystery of that
sublime music rise in a funeral anthem : voices called together
from distant places chant the magnificent and melancholy
passages in Holy Writ that speak on the awful and plaintive
theme of death.

Then in one long chord the voices faint and die, like a choir
of angels receding from the earth. A silence follows, the organ
peals once more, and the people begin slowly to disperse.

Old Mrs. Clink, who opens and locks the pews, is waiting at
the foot of the tower-stairs to receive Lady Vernon, whose
brougham is to come to the church-doors, when the people are
gone, and there will be few to canvass the great lady's secret
visit to the church.

The funereal swell of the organ still rolls and trembles along
the roof, and fills the building, now nearly empty. The sun has
just gone down ; the fading mists of rose are still on the western
sky. She ventures now to the front of the arch, in the shadow
of which she has hitherto been hidden. The early twilight,
dimmed by the stained windows, fills the church with a misleading and melancholy light ; white shafts of marble rise faintly
through the obscurity, and she, from her lonely place, unseen,
looks down, crying silently as if her heart would break.

CHAPTER XXIII.

THE PARTY AT ROYDON HALL.

COLDLY handsome, an hour later, looked Lady Vernon, at the head of her table, with old Lord Verney beside her. Lord Barroden and her other guests, who had assisted at the legal consultation, were also of the party. The Dean of East Copely was there, very natty in his silk stockings, and apron, and buckles, and Sir Thomas Grummelston, Lady Grummelston, and Miss Grummelston, with several others who had attended the unveiling of the statue and the bishop's sermon.

Lady Vernon was never very gay; but she was this evening more than usually conversable and animated.

'What an admirable sermon the bishop gave us to-day,' remarked the Dean of East Copely. 'He always preaches well, I need not say; but to-day there was so much feeling; it really was, even for him, an unusually fine sermon. Didn't it so strike you, Lord Verney?'

'I have had,' said Lord Verney, looking across the table with his dull grey eyes solemnly upon the dean, 'the advantage, Mr. Dean, of listening to the bishop of your diocese, in, as we say, another place. But I had been applying my mind to-day, I may say, to business a good deal, and although I have, people say, rather a facility of getting through business and things——'

Lord Verney's dull eyes at this moment had wandered to the bald head, flushed pink with champagne, of his attorney, Mr. Larkin, who instantaneously closed his eyes and shook his tall head with a mysterious smile, and murmured to the dean at his side:

'I wish I had his lordship's faculty; it would be an easy thousand a year in my pocket!' Which graceful little aside Lord Verney heard, and dropped his eyelids, raising his eyebrows with a slight clearing of his voice, and turning his face more directly towards the dean, suppressed in his own countenance, with an unusual pomp, a tendency to smile at the testimony of the man of business.

'People will form opinions and things, you know; and I was a little tired about it, and so I didn't mind, and I took a walk, and other people, no doubt, heard the bishop preach, and he seems to have gone somewhere.'

'I wanted him to take his dinner here,' said Lady Vernon, interpreting Lord Verney's rather vague but probable conjecture, ' but he could not manage it.'

'You were a little tired, also, I fear, Lady Vernon,' said Mr. Foljambe. 'A great many people, as well as I, were disappointed on missing Lady Vernon from her place.'

'I had intended going, but I did feel a little tired; but I made an effort afterwards, though very late, and I glided into our nook in the gallery without disturbing any one, and I heard the sermon, which I thought very good, and the anthem, which was better than I expected. I like our bishop so much; he's not the least a prig, he's not worldly, he is thoroughly simple—simple as a child; his simplicity is king-like; it is better, it is angelic. He is unconsciously the most dignified man one could imagine; and so kind. I have the greatest respect and affection for him.'

'He was a good deal moved to-day,' said Mr. Foljambe, leaning back a little grandly. 'It is charming, so much sensibility; I saw him shed tears to-day while he spoke of the early years of Mr. Howard, my predecessor.'

Mr. Foljambe blinked a little, as he said this, being always moved by the tears of people of any considerable rank, hereditary or otherwise.

Lord Verney being thus addressed by the stately vicar, whom he assumed to be a man of some mark, made answer a little elaborately.

'Sensibility and all that, I think, very well in its place; but in public speaking—and I hope I have had some little experience, I ought—sensibility, and that kind of very creditable feeling, ought to be managed; there's a way of putting up the pocket-handkerchief about it—all our best speakers do it—to the face, because then, if there *are* tears, and things, the faces they make are so distressing, and you see, by means of that, it is always managed; I can do it, you can do it, any one may do it, and that is the way it is prevented.'

'Very true,' said Mr. Foljambe, thoughtfully nodding, as he helped himself to a new *entrée*, a something *aux truffes*, which piqued his curiosity; 'one learns something every day one lives.'

'You don't, of course, recollect Mr. Howard very distinctly, Lady Vernon?' inquired the Dean of East Copely.

'Perfectly—I was past twenty when he died.'

'A plain man, I should say, judging from that statute?' inferred the dean.

'He was not that—no—he had a very agreeable countenance, and his features were well-formed—his forehead particularly fine,' she replied.

'His opinions were, I've been told, very unsettled indeed,' said the dean.

'It did not appear from his preaching, then. It was admired and approved, and the then bishop was not a man to permit any trifling with doctrine, any more than the present,' answered Lady Vernon. 'Mr. Howard was very much beloved, and a most able teacher—his influence was extraordinary in this parish—I am speaking, of course, upon hearsay a good deal, for at that time I did not attend as much as I ought to such things, and my father was still living.'

'Mr. Howard was, I believe, very highly connected?' said the dean.

'Quite so,' answered Mr. Foljambe. 'In fact, as far back as we can go, there was Chevenix, and then Craven, and Vernon, one of this house; and then Percy, one of the old Percys and Dormer, and Stanley, and Bulkeley, and Howard; and, in fact, it is really quite curious!—the people here do seem always to have liked to be taken care of by gentlemen,' said Mr. Foljambe grandly.

'I can't see that there is anything very curious in that,' said Lord Verney. 'I can't concede that. One naturally asks one's self the question, why should not a gentleman be preferred? And one answers, he should be preferred, because he is naturally superior to persons who are inferior to him; and we know he has certain principles and things that all gentlemen have, about it, and that, I conjecture, will always account for gentlemen and things being considered in that sort of light.'

'I entirely concur,' said Mr. Foljambe, who always concurred with peers. 'I only meant that it is a little curious that the vicarage of Roydon should have been always filled by a person of that stamp.'

'That is what I have been, I hope, endeavouring to say, or, rather, what I have not said, because I have endeavoured to say something different; in fact, that it is *not* curious. I'll take some sherry about it.' The concluding remark was addressed to the butler.

And so the conversation proceeded very agreeably.

But—

'Pleasures are like poppies spread,
You pluck the flower, its bloom is shed.'

The most agreeable dinner-party, its cutlets and conversation, its wit and its wines, are transitory, and the hour inevitably arrives when people prefer their night-caps and the extinguisher.

Lord Verney has uttered his last wise and lucid exposition for the evening, and the stately vicar, who would not object to a visit to Lord Verney's hospitable house at Ware, has imbibed his latest draughts from that fountain of illumination. Lord Barroden has said his say to Lady Vernon, and enlivened by a nap, has made some agreeable sallies in conversation with Lady Grummelston; and to that happy lady, in the drawing-room, Mrs. Foljambe has told her story about the two young women in whom she took an interest, who left Roydon and set up a confectioner's shop in Coventry, and prospered.

The pleasures of that festive evening are over; and Miss Max and Miss Vernon are having their chat together in their dressing-gowns.

Miss Max has a little bit of fire in her grate, for this is, thanks to our variable climate, by no means like last night; not at·all sultry, rather chilly, on the contrary.

'Well, we shall soon hear something, I fancy, about mamma's annual trip to town,' says Maud, speaking from a very low-cushioned chair in a corner of which she is nestled, with her feet on the fender.

The young lady's dressing-gown is of rose-coloured cashmere, some of the quilted silk lining of which, in her careless pose, appears. She is extremely pretty, looking up from her cushioned nook at the old lady, who sits, in her odd garb, before the fire in a more formal arm-chair.

'And why do you think so? Have you heard anything?' asks the old lady.

'Only that Jones says that Latimer is making the usual preparations,' answers Miss Maud.

'Latimer's her maid, I suppose?'

'Yes.'

'And why doesn't she ask Latimer directly?' demanded Miss Max.

'Because Latimer would be afraid to tell, and *she* would be afraid to ask. Mamma finds out everything she chooses to find out. You don't know mamma as well as I do in this house. Whatever she chooses to be secret is secret, and whatever she chooses to know she does know ; and the servants are awfully afraid of her. You might as well ask that picture as Latimer ; and Jones would not be such a fool as to ask her, for she does not know the moment mamma might say, "Latimer, has any one been asking you anything about my going to London ?" and so sure as she did, Latimer would tell her the truth, for there is no fault she is so summary upon as a falsehood : and the servants think that she somehow knows everything.'

'Well, at all events, Jones thinks she is going in a week ?' says Miss Max.

'Yes. Do you know what Mr. Coke said to me to-day ?'

'No. What ?' says Miss Max, looking drowsily into the fire.

'He said he thought, or had reason to think, or something of that kind, that mamma is going to marry.'

Miss Max turned, with a start, and looked for a few silent moments at Maud.

'Are you sure ?'

'Perfectly sure.'

'Well, that is very odd. Do you know, I've been thinking that, this long time. Did he say why he thought so ?'

'No.'

'Nor who the person is ?'

'No; nothing. He only said that, and he looked very sly and mysterious.'

'Mr. Coke is a very shrewd man. I don't think he had heard before of your mamma's excursions, and when I told him to-day I saw that his mind was working on what I said, and I suspect he has connected something he may have learned from a different source with what I told him, and has put the whole case together, and formed his conclusions. I wonder you did not make him tell you all he knew. I wish he had said so much to me. I should have made him say a great deal more, I promise you.'

'He talks to me as if I were a child, and it came so much by surprise, and really I don't think I could have asked him one word about it ; I felt so insulted somehow, and disgusted.'

'Suppose she has fallen in love with some one of whom, for some reason or other, she is a little ashamed, and suppose there is an engagement ? I don't understand it. I have been suspecting something for some time, and I did not like to say so, but you see it has struck Mr. Coke the same way. If it is that, there is a disparity of some kind, you may be sure.'

'I dare say. I don't care,' says the young lady, who looks, nevertheless, as if she did care very much. 'I shall have as much money as I want. Mr. Coke said I should have ten thousand a year, and I should go and live with you. You would take me in. Here nothing on earth should induce me to remain. She merely took a fancy to papa, soon grew tired of him, and ended by disliking him. But I shan't stay here to see his place filled and his memory insulted, and to be hectored and ordered about by some low man.'

'I shall be only too glad to have you at any time, as long as you will stay with me. But don't be in too great a hurry. You are assuming a great deal; and even if she does marry, it may turn out very differently; and you know, my dear, widows will marry, without intending any particular affront to the memory of their first husbands.'

'It is not a pleasant home to me as it is,' says the young lady, glancing fiercely along the hearth; 'but if this takes place I shan't stay here to see it; that I am resolved on.'

'In about a week she'll go, Jones thinks?' asks Miss Max. 'I have grown very curious. I should like to see what sort of swain she has chosen. You never know what fancy a woman may take. He may be a very third-rate man. I was thinking he may possibly be in the army. Mrs. Stonix swears she saw her alone in Chatham last year. But it is growing awfully late. Good-night. We'll get to our beds and dream it over.'

CHAPTER XXIV.

A GENTLEMAN IN BLACK.

THEY had both risen preparatory to Miss Maud's flitting and a parting kiss and good-night, when Miss Max said, suddenly : -

'And what about Mr. Marston?'

'Well, what about him?' answered Miss Vernon, a little crossly, for she had not recovered the conversation that had just occurred.

'Nothing very particular—nothing at all, in fact—only I had intended talking about him fifty times to-day, and something always prevented. He's coming to the ball at Wymering, isn't he?'

'I don't know ; he said so. I don't care,' said the handsome girl drowsily. And she advanced her hand and her lips a little, as if for her final salutation.

But Miss Max had not quite done.

'I like him so much. I think him so clever, and so good-natured, and so nice. I wish so much, Maud, that you and he were married,' said Miss Max, with audacious directness.

'And I wish so much that you and he were married,' retorted Maud, looking lazily at the flame of her bedroom candle, which she held in her hand. 'That would be a more natural conse-quence, I think, of your liking and admiring.'

'You can't deny that he is wildly in love with you,' said Miss Max.

'I can't deny that he was perhaps wildly in love with a poor seamstress in a dark serge dress a few days ago, and may possibly be in love with another to-day. That is wildly in love, as you say. I don't think there is anything very flattering in being the object of that kind of folly.'

'Well, he will be a good deal surprised, I venture to say, when he comes in quest of his seamstress to the Wymering cloak-room,' remarked Miss Max, with a pleasant anticipation of the éclaircissement.

'That depends on two things : first, how his seamstress meets him ; and secondly, whether she meets him there at all. Good-night. It is very late.' And with these words she kissed her genial old friend, and was gone.

Miss Max looked after her, and shook her head with a smile.

'There goes impracticability itself !' she says, and throws up her hands and eyes with a shrug. 'I pity that poor young man; Heaven only knows what's in store for him. I shall engage in no more vagaries, at all events. What an old fool I was to join in that madcap project of rambling over the country and conceal-ing our names ! What will Mr. Marston think of us ?'

When she laid her busy, rheumatic little head, bound up in its queer night-cap, on her pillow, it began at once to construct all manner of situations and pictures.

Here was a romance in a delightful state of confusion ! On this case her head may work all night long, for a year, without a chance of exhausting its fertile problems ; for it presents what the doctors call a complication. Barbara Vernon, with her whole heart, hates the Warhamptoms ; and the Warhamptons, with all theirs, detest Barbara Vernon. It is too long a story to tell all the aggressions and reprisals which have carried the feud to the internecine point.

'I must certainly tell Maud. I'll tell her in the morning,' thought Miss Max.   'It's only fair.'

Perhaps this incorrigible old matchmaker fancied that it might not prejudice Mr. Marston if Maud knew that her mother had placed him under anathema.

By noon next day Lord Verney and Lord Barroden, and their attorneys, had taken flight, and Miss Maximilla Medwyn had gone on to see friends at Naunton, with an uncertain promise of returning in a day or two to Roydon Hall.

There is no life in that grand house but the phantom life on its pictured walls, and the gliding life of its silent servants. The hour is dull for Maud, who sits listlessly looking from one of the great drawing-room windows. Lady Vernon, who has seen, in succession, two deputations in the library, returns, and in stately silence sits down and resumes her examination of a series of letters from the late Bishop of Rotherham, and notes them for transmission to Mr. Coke.

Maud changes her posture, and glances at her mother. Why is there never any love in the cold elegance of that face ? Why can't she make up her mind and be patient ? The throb of life will as soon visit that marble statue of Joan of Arc, by the door ; Psyche at the other side, in her chill beauty, will as easily glow and soften into flesh.

Miss Vernon leans on her hand, listless, gloomy—in a degree indignant.

The room is darkening.   The darker the better, she thinks. It is no metaphoric, but a real darkness ; for clouds portending thunder or heavy rain or hail have on a sudden overcast the sky, and are growing thicker.

The light is dying out, the shadow blackens on Lady Vernon's letters ; she raises her eyes.   One can hardly see to read.

Lady Vernon lays her letter on the table.   She can no longer see the features of the Titian over the door, and the marble statues on either side have faded into white drifts. Some heavy, perpendicular drops fall, plashing on the smooth flags outside the window, and the melancholy rumble of distant thunder-booms, followed by a momentarily aggravated downpour and a sudden thickening of the darkness.

This was a rather sublime prelude to the footman's voice, announcing:

'Mr. Dawe.'

Maud glanced toward the door, which was in obscurity, and then at Lady Vernon, who, sitting full in the light of the window, had turned with a stare and a frown, as if she had heard something incredible and unwelcome, towards the person who was entering.

By no means an heroic figure, nor worthy of being heralded by thunder, has stepped in somewhat slowly and stiffly, and halts in the dim sidelight of the window, relieved by the dark background. It is a small man, dark visaged, with a black wig, a grave, dull, mahogany face, furrowed with lines of reserve. Maud is certain that she never saw that small, insignificant-looking man before, who is staring with a very grave but not unfriendly countenance at her mother.

He is buttoned up in a black outside coat, with a cape to it; he holds a rather low-crowned hat in his hand, and wears those shining leather coverings for the legs which are buckled up to the knees. Getting in and getting out of his posting carriage he has scrupulously avoided dust or mud. His boots are without a speck. His queer hat is nattily brushed, and, in stable phraseology, has not a hair turned. His black coat is the finest possible, but it has great pockets at either side, each of which seems laden with papers, mufflers, and other things, so that his hips seem to descend gradually and culminate near his knees.

This man's brown face, smoothly shaved, is furrowed and solemn enough for five-and-sixty. In his dress and air there is nothing of the careless queerness of a country gentleman. His singularities suggest rather the eccentricity of a precise and rich old City humourist.

There is something characteristic and queer enough in the buttoned-up and black-wigged little man to interest Maud's curiosity.

He has not been ten seconds in the room, and stands poised on his leather-cased legs, looking gravely and quietly at Lady Vernon, and, like a ghost, says nothing till he is spoken to. One can reckon the tick, tick, tick of the Louis Quatorze clock on the bracket by the chimney-piece.

Lady Vernon stood up with an effort, still looking hard at him, and advancing a step she said :

'Mr. Dawe? I'm so surprised. I could scarcely believe my ears. It is such an age since I have seen you here.'

And she put out her hand hospitably, and he took it in his brown old fingers with the stiffness of a mummy, and as he shook it slightly, he said in his wooden tones quietly :

'Yes, it is. I was looking into my notes yesterday—it *is* a good while. You look well, Barbara. Your looks are not much altered ; no—considering.'

'It is very good of you to come to see me ; you mustn't stay away so long again,' she replied in her silvery tones.

'This is your daughter?' he interrupted, with a little wave of his dark, thin hand towards the young lady.

'Yes, that is she. Maud, shake hands with Mr. Dawe.'

'Maud Guendoline she was baptized,' he said, as he advanced two stiff steps toward her, with his prominent brown eyes fixed upon her.

She rose and placed her pretty fingers on that hand of boxwood, which closed on them.

CHAPTER XXV.

THE COUNTY PAPER.

WHEN he had inspected her features for a time, he turned to her mother and spoke.

'Not like her father,' he said, still holding her hand.

'Don't you think so?' answered Lady Vernon coldly. 'I can see a look—very decidedly.'

Maud was wondering all this time who this Mr. Dawe could be, who seemed to assert a sort of dry intimacy with Lady Vernon and her family very unusual in the girl's experience.

'I think it is more than a look. I think her extremely like him,' insisted Lady Vernon, resuming in the same cold tone, and without looking at Maud, as if she had that resemblance by heart, and did not like it.

'She has some of the family beauty, wherever she got it,' said Mr. Dawe deliberately in his hard quiet tones, and he let go her hand and turned away his inflexible face and brown eyes, a good deal to the young lady's relief.

Lady Vernon was still standing. She did not usually receive

such guests standing. There was a hectic red in each cheek, also unusual, except when she was angry, and she had not been angry.

'Her eyes resemble yours,' said Mr. Dawe.

'Oh no. Perhaps, indeed, the colour; but mere colour is not a resemblance,' answered Lady Vernon, with a cold little laugh, that, in Maud's ear, rang with cruelty and disdain. 'No, Maud's good looks are all her own. She doesn't, I think, resemble me in any one particular—not the least.'

Maude was wounded. She felt that tears were rising to her eyes. But her pride suppressed them.

'H'm!' Mr. Dawe hummed with closed lips.

'Of course, Mr. Dawe, you are come to stay a little? It is so long since you have been here.'

'I'm not so sure about staying. It is a long time—sixteen years and upwards. You have been well; you have been spared, and your daughter, and I. We have all reason to be grateful to the Almighty. Time is so important, and eternity so long!'

'Very true,' she said, with a deep sigh, 'and death so irremediable.'

Mr. Dawe took his big silver snuff-box from his coat-pocket, and tapped it. He nodded in acquiescence in the sentiment, leaned a little forward, and took a large pinch, twiddling his fingers afterwards, to get rid of any snuff that might remain on their tips. Perhaps the little superfluous shower that fell to the carpet suggested unconsciously his funeral commentary.

'Ay, dust to dust.'

Whereupon he applied his Indian silk handkerchief, not to his eyes, but lightly to his nose.

'By-and-by I shall have a word to say to you,' he said, with a solemn roll of his brown eyes.

She looked hard at him, though with a half-flinching gaze, as if to read the character of his news. But the solemn reserve of his wooden face never changed.

'We shall be quite to ourselves in the library,' she said.

'Then suppose we go there now.'

'Very well; let us go,' she said, and led the way.

At the door he made, with his stiff backbone, a little inclination to Miss Maud.

The door closes, and the young lady is left to herself, with matter for speculation to amuse her.

Quite alone in that vast and magnificent room, she looks wearily round.   The care of Mr. Tarpey, on whom devolves the arrangement of flowers and of newspapers, has spread a table in a corner near the window with these latter luxuries.

Maud looks out ; the rain is still tumbling continuously and plashing heavily, though the sky looks lighter.   She turns her eyes on the newspapers, and goes over to the table, and looks down upon them with listless eyes.

She carelessly plucks the county paper from among its companions, and in that garrulous and homely broad-sheet a paragraph catches her suddenly earnest eye.   She reads it twice. The annual Wymering ball is to come off three weeks earlier than usual.   She takes the paper to the window and reads it again.   There is no mistake about it.   ' Three weeks earlier than the accustomed day !'   There is an unusual colour in her cheeks, and a lustre in her eyes.   She fancies, as she muses, that she hears a step in the passage, and she drops the 'paper. She is afraid of Lady Vernon's all-seeing gaze, and the dreadful question, ' Have you seen anything unusual in the paper ? Allow me to look at it.'   And she feels that her face would proclaim, to all who cared to look, that the Wymering ball was to take place three weeks earlier than usual.

No one is coming, however.   She hastens to replace the paper on the table, and she sits down with a pretty flush, determined to think.

She does not think very logically, or very much in train, and the effort subsides in a reverie.

Well, what is to be done now ?   The crisis has taken her by surprise ; then fancy leads her into the assembly-room at Wymering.   There are lights, and fiddles, and—oh, such a strange meeting !

Cousin Max must be with her.   With that spirited veteran by her side she would fear nothing.

Very glad she was when one of Lady Vernon's broughams drove up to the door a few minutes later.

In that great house you cannot get as quickly to the hall as, on occasions like this, you may wish.   But Maud overtakes her at the foot of the stairs, as in her cloak and bonnet Maximilla Medwyn is about to ascend to her own room.

' Mamma is in the library ; and there are three men, with ill-made clothes and lank hair, a deputation, as usual, waiting in the shield-room to talk to her about a meeting-house at Heppsborough ; and two clergymen are waiting in the blue drawing-room, to see her afterwards about plate for the church of Saint Hilary. So you and I shall be very much to ourselves for a time ; and do you know we have had a new arrival—a guest. I dare say you know him. Such an odd little figure, as solemn as a conjurer. His name is Dawe.'

'Dawe ? Why, for goodness sake, has Richard Dawe appeared again ?' exclaims Miss Max, stopping on the stair, and leaning with her back against the massive banister in great surprise.

'His name is certainly Dawe, and I'll tell you what he's like.'

And forthwith Maud describes him.

'Oh ! there's no mistaking the picture,' cries Miss Max ; and then she is taken with a fit of laughing, very mysterious to Miss Maud.

Recovering a little, she continues :

'Mr. Dawe ? We are very good friends. I like him—at least, all I could ever know of him in twenty years. He keeps his thoughts to himself a good deal. I don't think anyone else in the world had half his influence with your poor grandpapa ; but certainly I never expected to see him here during Barbara's reign. My dear ! I thought she hated him. He was the only person who used to tell her, and in the simplest language, what he thought of her. Have they been fighting yet ?'

'No, I think not—that is, they had not time. I don't know, I'm sure, what may be going on now.'

'Where are they ?'

'In the library,' says Maud.

'I think he is the only person on earth she ever was the least afraid of. I wonder what he can have to say or do here. He has never been inside this door since—yes, he did come once, for a day or two, a few years after your poor papa's death, and that, I think, was simply because he had some direction of your grandfather's about the Roydon vault, which he had promised to see carried out ; but, except then, he has never once been here, till now, since your poor grandpapa's death.'

'How did he come to have such an influence here ?' asked Maud.

They had resumed their ascent, and were walking up the stairs side by side.

'I believe he understands business very well, and he is, I

fancy, the best keeper of a secret on earth. His influence with your grandpapa increased immensely toward the close of his life; and he knew he could talk to him safely about that wonderful will of his.'

'I wonder he allowed him to make that troublesome will,' said Maud.

Miss Max laughed.

'I said the very same thing to him once, and he answered that he could not dissuade him, but that he had prevented a great deal. So, here we are.'

The latter exclamation accompanied her entrance into her room.

Maud was more curious than ever.

'He's not the kind of person, then, who would have come here, under all the circumstances, without good reason,' she said.

'Not he. He has a reason—a strong one, you may be very sure of that. It is very odd. I can't imagine what it can possibly be about. Well, leave him to me. I think he's franker with me than with anyone else; and I'll get it from him, one way or other, before he goes. You'll see.'

In this sanguine mood Miss Maximilla Medwyn put off her things, and prepared very happily for luncheon.

Mr. Dawe and Lady Vernon are, in the meantime, holding a rather singular conference.

CHAPTER XXVI.

COLLOQUY.

On reaching the library, Lady Vernon touched the bell.

'You know this room very well, Mr. Dawe? You see no change here?'

'This house has seen many generations,' said he, looking up to the cornice and round, 'and will see out a good many generations more.'

He steps backward two or three steps, looks up at the Vandyck over the mantelpiece, nods to that very old acquaintance, and says 'Yes.'

Then he rolls his prominent eyes again about the room, un·
usually shadowy on this dark day, and spying a marble bust between two windows, the little man walks solemnly towards it.

'That is Mr. Howard, who was our vicar, long ago,' says Lady
Vernon.

The blue livery is standing, by this time, at the opened door.

'Poor papa placed that bust there,' she continues, 'and it has
remained ever since.'

'Indeed !' says Mr. Dawe, and peers at it, nose to nose, for
some seconds.

'They took casts from it,' she continues, 'for the statue that
the bishop wished to place to his memory in the church.'

'*Here ?*' says Mr. Dawe, turning his profile, and rolling his
brown eyes suddenly on her.

'Yes, in the church of Roydon, of course, where, as vicar, he
preached for so long.'

'I see,' says Mr. Dawe.

'I shall be engaged for some time, particularly, on business,'
says Lady Vernon to her footman, 'and you are to admit no
one.'

'Yes, my lady.'

And the apparition of gold, azure, and powder (for they still
wore powder then) steps backward, the door closes, and they are
alone.

Lady Vernon is smiling, with bright hectic patches in her
cheeks.   There is something a little piteous and deprecatory in
her smile.

'We are quite alone now.   Tell me what it is,' she says, in a
voice that could have been scarcely heard at the door.

Mr. Dawe turns on his heel, walks briskly up, and seats himself near her.   He takes out his old silver box, with groups of
Dutch figures embossed on it, and takes a pinch of snuff preparatory, with his solemn eyes fixed on her.

'Is it anything—alarming—what is it?' she almost gasps.

'There has been illness,' he says, with his unsearchable brown
eyes still fixed on her.

'Oh, my God ! Is he gone?' she says, turning as white as
the marble Mr. Dawe has just been looking at.

'Captain Vivian has been very ill, yes, Elwyn has been very
dangerously ill,' says the imperturbable little man in the black
wig ; 'but he's out of danger now, quite—that's all over.'

There was a silence, and Lady Vernon was trembling very

much. She placed her finger-tips hard against her forehead, and
did not speak for a few minutes.

Mr. Dawe looked at her with stoical gravity, and taking his
spectacles from a very shabby case, put them on, and occupied
himself with a pocketbook, and seemed to be totting up some
figures.

'You guessed, of course, that I must have something to say
on that subject?' he said, raising his eyes from the page.

'I thought it possible,' she answered, with an effort.

'I could not in the drawing-room, you know——'

'No, of course,' she said hastily, and the colour returned with
two hot flushes to her cheeks.

There was in her bearing to this elderly gentleman an odd
embarrassment, something of pain and shame ; a wounded pride
struggling through it.

She rose, and they walked together to the window.

'He has got his leave. His troop is still at Chatham. The
doctor says he must go to some quiet country nook. He has
been thinking of Beaumaris,' said the old gentleman.

'Is he as beautiful as ever?' she asked. 'Oh, why should I
ask? What does it matter? Is there any gift that God gives
his creatures that is not more or less a curse?'

'You should not talk in that wild way, Barbara. If people
can't control their feelings, they can, at least, control their words.
It is only an effort at first. It easily becomes a matter of habit.
You shan't talk so to me.'

She looked at him angrily for a moment of silence.

'You treat me with a contempt, sir, that you never could have
felt if I had not trusted you so madly,' she cried passionately.

The tone, fierce and plaintive, was lost on the phlegmatic old
man in the black wig.

He delivered a little lecture, with his thin brown finger raised,
and his exhortation was dry, but stern.

'You have been rash and self-willed; you have been to blame.
Your unjust imputation shan't prevent my saying that, and
whatever else truth requires. Your difficulty is the creation of
your own passions. I don't say look your difficulty in the face,
for it will look you in the face ; but take the lesson it teaches,
and learn self-control.'

'Don't blame me for this. I met him first in a railway
carriage, nearly two years ago. Who can prevent such accidental
acquaintances? He was so attentive, and so agreeable, and so

gentleman-like. I had chosen to travel alone, without even a
maid. You'll say I had no business doing so. I say, at my
years, there was nothing against it; it was more than four
hours; there were other people in the carriage. I never meant
to seek him out afterwards; it was the merest accident my
learning even his name. When I met him next, it was in town,
at Lady Stukely's. I recognised him instantly, but he did not
know me, for my veil had been down all the time.' This narrative Lady Vernon was pouring out with the rapid volubility of
excitement. 'I was introduced to him there. Perhaps I have
been a fool; but there is no good, now, in telling me so. I have
seen him since, more than once, and gone where I thought I was
likely to see him, and I succeeded. If I have been a fool, God
knows I suffer. My difficulty, you call it! My difficulty! My
agony is the right word. To love as I love, without being loved,
without being loved ever so little!'

' So much the better,' said Mr. Dawe phlegmatically. ' What
are you driving at? You ought to consider consequences. Don't
you know the annoyance, and possibly insane litigation, to
which your folly would lead? In a woman of your years,
Barbara, this sort of thing is inexcusable.'

'Why did you come at all? Why did you come in so
suddenly, and—before people? Would not a letter have answered? Hast thou found me, oh! mine enemy?' she suddenly
almost cried, and clasped her fingers for a moment wildly upon
his arm.

'A letter?' he repeated.

'Yes, a letter. You should think. It would have been more
merciful,' she answered vehemently.

' Not when I had so many things to talk to you about,' he
retorted quietly.

'I would have met you anywhere. You ought not to have
come into the room so suddenly,' she persisted. 'You alone
know my sad secret. You might have remembered that people
are sometimes startled. You say I have no self-command. I
think I have immense self-command. I think I am a stoic.
I know how you tasked it, too. I knew you had something
important to tell me, and that *he* was probably involved.'

'H'm! Yes; I'm an old friend of yours, and I wish you
well. And I'm Captain Vivian's friend, and was once his
guardian, and I wish him well. And this kind of thing I
don't approve of. And you'll get yourself spoken about; you

are talked of. People saw you alone at Chatham last year; and if they come to connect your movements with his, think what it will be.'

' He's the only person on earth I love, or ever shall love.'

'Barbara, you forget your child, Maud Vernon,' said the old man, with hard emphasis.

' I don't forget her,' she answered fiercely.

The old man turned away his head. There was no change of countenance ; that, I believe, never changed ; but the movement indicated disgust.

' I say I love him, with all my love, with *all*,' she repeated.

' Be it so. Still, common prudence will suggest your keeping that love locked up in your own heart, a dead secret.'

' I am determined, somehow or other, to meet him, and talk to him, and know him well,' she persisted; ' and you shall assist me.'

' I'm wholly opposed to it.'

' You'd not have me see him again ?

' No.'

' Why ? What are you ? Who are you ? Have you human sympathy ? Good Heavens ! Am I a free woman ?' she broke out again wildly.

' Certainly, quite free,' said Mr. Dawe, cutting her short with a little tap on his snuff-box. ' You can do it, Barbara, when you please ; however, whenever, wherever you like best; only you have a right to my judgment, and I'm quite against it.'

' I know, Mr. Dawe, you are my friend,' she said, after a brief pause. ' I know how I can trust you. I am impetuous, perhaps. I dare say you are right. You certainly would speak wisely if your counsels were addressed to some colder and happier woman. Why is it that to be cold, and selfish, and timid, is the only way to be happy on earth ? If I am sanguine, audacious, what you will, I can't help it. You cannot under-stand me—God knows all ; for me to live any longer as I am is worse than death. I'll endure it no longer. Oh ! if I could open my lips and tell him all !'

' There, that's it, you see ! You are ready to die now to be on more intimate terms with him ; and if you were you would be ready to die again, as you say, to open your heart to him. Don't you see ? Don't you perceive what it is tending to ? Are you prepared for all that ? If not, why approach it ? You

would be in perpetual danger of saying more than you think
you should.'

Mr. Dawe had probably not spoken quite so long a sentence
for more than a month.

'I may be a better listener, Mr. Dawe, in a little time.   Let
us sit down.   I want to ask you about it.   Tell me everything.
What was his illness ?'

' Fever.'

'Fever ! and he was in great danger.   Oh ! my darling, my
darling, for how long ?'

'For two days in great danger.'

Her hands were clasped as she looked in his face, and she
went on.

'And there is no danger now ?   It is quite over ?'

'Quite,' he repeated.

She looked up, her fingers raised a little, and a long shud-
dering sigh, like a sob, relieved her.

'I had the best advice—the two best men I could get from
London.   He's all right now ; he's fairly under way, and nothing
can go wrong; with common prudence, of course.   I have the
account here.'   He held his pocket-book by the corner, and
shook it a little.

'He was near dying,' she repeated.   'Why didn't you tell
me ?   I knew nothing of his danger.'

'The doctors did not tell me the extent of it till it was over,'
he replied.

'Think what it would have been if he had died !   I should
have been in a madhouse.   I should have killed myself.'

'Don't, don't, don't.   Nonsense.   Come, you must not talk
so.   I admit it is a painful situation ; but who has made it ?
You.   Remember that, and control your—your vehemence.'

'Has he been out ?   Is he recovering strength ?'

'Yes.   He has been out, and he has made way ; but he is
still an invalid.'

'I want to know; I must know.   Is there any danger
still apprehended ?'

'None; I give you my word,' said Mr. Dawe dryly.

'He is still very weak ?' she urged.

'Still weak, but gaining strength daily.'

'How soon do the doctors think he will be quite himself ?'

'In five or six weeks.'

'And his leave of absence, for how long is that ?

'It has been extended; about four weeks still to run.'

'I think I know everything now,' she said slowly.

Mr. Dawe nodded acquiescence.

'He's not rich, Mr. Dawe; and all this must cost a good deal of money. It is only through you I can be of any use.'

'Yes; I was his guardian, and am his trustee. I had a regard for his father, and his grandfather was essentially kind to me. But I have learned to regret that I ever undertook to interest myself specially in his affairs; and you, Barbara, are the cause of that regret.'

'You mustn't reproach me; you know what I am,' she pleaded.

Mr. Dawe responded with his usual inarticulate 'H'm!' and an oracular nod.

'I can't help it; I can't. Why are you so cruelly unreasonable? Do you think I can learn a new character, and unlearn the nature that God gave me, in a moment?'

'I say this. If you cultivate Captain Vivian's acquaintance further, it is against my opinion and protest. I don't expect either to have much weight. I think you incorrigible.'

Lady Vernon coloured, and her eyes flashed. But she would not, and could not, quarrel with Mr. Dawe.

'Surely you can't pretend there is anything wrong in it?' she said fiercely.

'I did not say there was. Extreme imprudence; reckless imprudence.'

'You always said everything I did was reckless and imprudent.'

'Not everything. Some things extremely. And what you propose, considering that you are no longer young, and know what the world is, appears to me a positively inexcusable folly.'

'It is possible to prescribe limits and impose conditions upon one's self,' she said, with an effort; 'and if so, there need be no rashness in the matter, not the slightest.'

'Possible? We know it's *not* possible with some people.'

'You always hated me, sir.'

'Tut, tut!'

'You never liked me.'

'Pooh, pooh!'

'You have always thought ill of me.'

'I have always wished you well, Barbara, and accident, I

think, enabled me to understand you better than others. You have great faults, immense faults.'

'All faults and no virtues, of course,' she said, with a bitter little laugh.

'You are capable of strong and enduring attachments.'

'Even that is something,' she said, with an agitated smile, and burst into tears.

'This is very painful, Barbara,' said the little man in the black wig, while a shadow of positive displeasure darkened his furrowed face. 'I believe my first impression was right, and yours too. I begin to think I had no business coming to Roydon.'

Lady Vernon got up, and walked toward the window, and then turned, and walked to the further end of the room, standing before a picture.

He could see that her handkerchief was busy drying her eyes.

With a womanly weakness she walked to the mirror close by, and looked into it, and perhaps was satisfied that the traces of this agitation were not very striking.

She returned to her place.

'I have been a fool. My saying so will perhaps save you trouble. I want to put you in funds again.'

'When you please,' said the old man. 'Any time will answer. I have the figures here.' His pocket-book was still in his hand. 'But he has money enough of his own. He must think me a fool, paying all these expenses for him. And I think, Barbara, your doing so is a mischievous infatuation.'

'And you would deny me this one pleasure !' she said.

'Enough, enough,' he answers. 'It was not about that I came here ; that we could have settled by a letter. But I knew you would have fifty questions to ask. He has made up his mind to try change of air. I'm ignorant in such matters, and he has not made up his mind where to go.'

'I have quite made up my mind upon that point,' she answered.

'Well; and where ?'

'Here,' said Lady Vernon, once more, in her cold quiet way. 'I'll ask him here.'

'H'm !' said Mr. Dawe.

'Here,' she repeated, with her old calm peremptoriness. 'Here, at Roydon Hall. I'll receive him here, and he can't be quieter or better anywhere else, and you shall come with him.'

It was now Mr. Dawe's turn to get up, which he did with a kind of jerk, and, checking some impulse, walked slowly round his chair, looking down on the carpet, and with a pretty wide circuit he came behind it, and resting his hands on its high back, and leaning over, he said, with a little pause, and a wag of his head to each word :

' Is there the least use in my arguing the point ?'

' None.'

' H'm !'

Mr. Dawe looked to the far corner of the room, with eyes askance, ruminating, and took a pinch of snuff, some of which shed a brown snow upon the cut pattern of the Utrecht velvet on the back of the chair.

' I can't say it is anything to me ; nothing. I should be officious were I to say more to dissuade you from it. Only remember, I have no share in the responsibility of this, excuse me, most strange step. As I suppose he will be brought here, one way or other, in any case, I think I had better come with him, and stay a day or two. It will excite less observation, so——'

' Thank you so very much, Mr. Dawe,' said Lady Vernon, extending her hand, with an odd, eager gratitude in tone and countenance. ' That is like yourself.'

Mr. Dawe's usual ' H'm !' responded to this little effusion, and with an ominous countenance he took her profferred hand in his dry grasp, and let it go almost in a moment.

Looking down on the carpet, he walked to the window, with his hands behind his back, and as, with furrowed jaws and pursed mouth, and a roll of his prominent eyes, he stood close to the pane of glass, down which the rain was no longer streaming, Lady Vernon opened her desk, and wrote a cheque for two hundred pounds, and coming to his side, she said :

' He does not suspect that he has a friend concealed ?'

' Certainly not—certainly not,' said Mr. Dawe sharply.

' Will you apply this for me, and we can account another time ? And you think me very ungrateful, Mr. Dawe, but indeed I am not. I only wish an opportunity may occur, if you could only point out some way. But you are so rich, and so happy. Well, some day, notwithstanding, I may be able to show you how I thank you. Let us return to the drawing-room.'

As she passed the mirror, the lady glanced at her face again, and was satisfied.

'Yes,' said Mr. Dawe, recurring to the matter of business, 'I'll do that, and with respect to coming here, I say no more. Under protest, mind, I do it. Only let me have a line to say when you can receive us.'

CHAPTER XXVII.

THE NUN'S WELL.

MAUD was found by her elders, on their return, nestled in a low chair, in one of those lazy moods in which one not only does nothing, but thinks nothing.

They were talking as they entered, and Maud turned her eyes merely in their direction, being far enough away to feel herself very little observed.

'You will surely stay to-night, Mr. Dawe?' said Lady Vernon.

'No, certainly; thank you very much. I have made up my mind,' replied Mr. Dawe dryly.

Miss Maud was observing this little man in the wig with increased interest. There was in his manner, looks, and voice something of the familiarity of an old friend, she thought, without much of the liking.

Whatever the business which they discussed in the library, her mamma, she thought, was perfectly unruffled; but there were traces of displeasure in the old gentleman's demeanour.

'I ought to have told you that my cousin, Maximilla Medwyn, is staying here.'

'She has returned, mamma; she will be down in a few minutes,' said Maud.

'Oh! and we shall certainly have her here for some days. Will that tempt you to stay?'

'I like her well—very well, but I shall be off, notwithstanding,' said the old gentleman, with a rigid countenance.

The sound of the gong announced luncheon.

'We are a very small party,' she said, smiling. 'I'm glad you're here to luncheon, at all events.'

'I've had a biscuit and a glass of sherry.'

'But that is not luncheon, you know,' said Lady Vernon.

Maud wondered more and more why her mamma should take such unusual pains to conciliate this odd, grim old man. For her part, she did not know what to make of him. Ungainly, preposterous, obsolete as he was, she yet could not assign him a place outside the line that encircles gentlemen. There was not a trace of vulgarity in the reserved and saturnine inflexibility of his face. There was something that commanded her respect, in the obvious contrast it presented to the vulgar simper and sycophancy of the people who generally sought 'audiences' of her mother.

And Maud fancied, when he looked at her, that there was something of kindly interest dimly visible through his dark and solemn lineaments.

'Luncheon and dinner,' he said, 'are with me incompatible; and I prefer my dinner. My train, I think, is due at six-twenty P.M. I suppose your servant can find a Bradshaw, and I'll consult it while you are at luncheon. Go, Barbara. Go, pray; you make me uncomfortable.'

The little man sat himself down in an arm-chair, took out his pocket-book, and seemed to forget everything but the figures over which he began to pore.

Miss Max joined the ladies at luncheon.

'Well, we shall find him in the drawing-room,' she said, reconciling herself to her disappointment. 'It is a long time since I saw him. But I dare say he's not much changed. Wigs wear wonderfully.'

'So do ugly men,' added Lady Vernon carelessly.

So luncheon proceeded. And when it was over, the three ladies came to the drawing-room, and, looking round, discovered that Mr. Dawe was gone.

A minute after, Maud saw him walking under the trees of the avenue, with his broad-leafed, low-crowned hat on, and a slow, stiff tread, and his silk umbrella in his hand doing the office of a walking-stick. It was pleasant sunshine now.

The blue sky was clear and brilliant, and only a few white clouds near the horizon accounted for the rain-drops that still glittered on the blades of grass. Stepping carefully in the centre of the path, little Mr. Dawe, now and then shouldering his umbrella, and turning and looking about him, like a man reviving old recollections and scanning alterations, disappeared slowly from view, over the stile, leaving Miss Maud very curious.

'I'll put on my things and try to find him,' said Miss Max, in a fuss, and was speedily seen emerging from the hall-door in pursuit.

His walk being slow and meditative, his active pursuer did succeed in overtaking him. She knew very well that he was glad to see her, though his rigid features gave no sign, and he shook hands very kindly.

When these greetings were over, he answered her question by saying briefly :

'No, I shan't dine. I'm off.'

'Without bidding Barbara good-bye! exclaimed Miss Medwyn, drawing herself up in amazement.

'I've left my farewell in the hall. The footman will find it.'

'A note, I suppose ?

'H'm,' acquiesced the little gentleman. 'My carriage will take me up in the village ;' and he nodded gravely to the distant tower of Roydon Church, which happily did not return that salutation, though he continued to stare solemnly at it for some seconds, and ended by a second slighter nod.

'That is not a pretty compliment to me,' she said. 'I think you might have stayed till to-morrow.'

He nodded only, and silence followed.

'Well, I see you won't.'

Another pause, and a more impatient 'H'm,' and a quick shake of the head.

'So as that can't be,' she resumed, 'and as all things are so uncertain in this life, that we may possibly never meet again, I'll walk a little way with you towards the village.'

Mr. Dawe nodded his usual sign of acquiescence.

'And now you must tell me,' she said, as they walked at a leisurely pace along the path which winds gently among the old timber, 'what on earth brought you here? Has anything wonderful happened ; is anything wonderful going to happen?'

'A word or two with Barbara,' he said.

'You don't mean to tell me it is a secret?' said she.

'If it be, it is none of mine,' he replied.

'Well, but you can tell me generally what it is about,' she insisted.

'H'm! Ask Barbara,' she answered.

'You mean, it is a secret, and you won't tell it?' she said.

Mr. Dawe left this inference unanswered.

'You found Barbara very little altered?' said Miss Max.

'As self-willed and unwise as ever,' he replied.

'Ho! Then she wants to do something foolish?'

'She can do that when she pleases,' he remarked. 'Do you know the Tinterns, who live near?'

'Yes, pretty well,' she answered, rather curious to know why he should ask.

'What do you think of them?'

'I rather dislike Mr. Tintern, I neither like nor dislike his wife, and I like his daughter very much indeed. His son I don't know; he is with his regiment in India,' she answered. 'Why do you ask?'

'You are as inquisitive as ever, Maximilla,' he said.

'I've just satisfied your curiosity about the Tinterns, and you can't complain fairly of my question. I think your business with Barbara had something to do with them.'

'You are sagacious,' he observed; but whether he spoke in good faith or in irony his countenance helped her nothing to discover.

'Come, you must tell me. Are the Tinterns involved in the foolish thing she is going to do?' the lady insisted.

'She is going to do a foolish thing, and you, probably, will never know what makes it so particularly foolish; that is, unless she carries out her folly to its climax.'

'I may possibly guess more than you suppose,' Miss Medwyn said.

But this remark led to nothing.

'You don't know young Tintern, you say, but you like his sister. Why?' asked Mr. Dawe.

'I like her because she is really nice—one of the very nicest girls I ever knew.'

'Ha! Then, I hope she doesn't depend altogether on her father, for they say he has lost money, said Mr. Dawe.

'She is not well provided for, although her mother was an

heiress, you know; but there is something trifling settled on
her.'

'Well for her she doesn't depend altogether on Tintern.
I'm told he is a distressed man, or likely soon to be so,'
he said.

'But, to come back to Barbara,' resumed Maximilla: 'I
think you ought to exercise your influence to prevent her
from taking any foolish step, particularly one which may affect
others.'

'I have none.'

'If you haven't, who has?'

'No one ever had, for her good.'

'For my part, I never knew what to think of her,' said Miss
Medwyn.

'I did,' said Mr. Dawe.

He stopped short, and looked straight at her, being about
her own height, which, even for a woman, was nothing very
remarkable. His dark face looked darker, and his prominent
brown eyes were inflexibly fixed on her, as he spoke a rather
longer harangue than usual.

'She is a great dissembler,' said Mr. Dawe. 'She is proud.
She has the appearance of coldness, and she is secretly passionate and violent. She is vindictive. All that is concealed.
She has a strong will. People know that; but it is not inflexibility founded on fixed data. It is simply irresistible impulse. There is nothing fixed in her but a few likings and
hatreds. Principles in the high sense, that is, involving the
submission of a life to maxims of duty, she has none; and she
thinks herself a paragon.'

Maximilla laughed, and they resumed their walk, when Mr.
Dawe had ended his speech.

'That seems rather a severe delineation, Mr. Dawe,' said
Maximilla Medwyn, with another little laugh and a shrug.

'It is true. I would repeat it to herself, if it could do her
any good.'

They followed the path, Miss Medwyn chatting after her
manner, gaily, until they had nearly reached the stile at the
village road.

'So here we part, Mr. Dawe.'

Mr. Dawe gave her one of his oracular looks, and took her
hand in his hard fingers.

' And it is very ill-natured of you not telling me what I asked you,' she called after him.

Bestriding the stile, he looked back with the same solemnity raised his broad-leafed hat, and disappeared on the other side, and Maximilla could not help laughing a little at the awful gravity and silence of the apparition which went down behind the wall.

The day was now brilliant, and Miss Medwyn was tempted to walk home by a path still prettier, though a little circuitous.

It was a favourite walk of hers long ago. Perhaps it was the visit of Mr. Dawe, with whom in old times she had often walked these out-of-the-way paths, that suggested this little ramble.

The lofty trees close about the path that she had now chosen, and gradually beset and overhang it in the densest shadow. Walking in the open air, on a sunny day, you could not fancy so deep a darkness anywhere. This is, of course, in the leafy days, when the tall elms, whose boughs cross and mix above, are laden with their thick dark foliage.

The darkness and silence of this narrow path are here so curiously deep, that it is worth going a mile or two out of one's way to visit it ; and fancy will play a nervous wayfarer as many tricks in this strange solitude as in a lonely night walk.

At the side of this path, nearly in its darkest part, is a well, under an arch. It is more properly a spring, rising at this point, and overflowing its stone basin, and escapes, in a gush, through a groove cut in the flag that encloses it in front. Two iron cups, hanging by chains, invite the passengers to drink of the icy water that with ceaseless plash and gurgle descends from the opening.

With a slow step on the light mossy turf she draws near this remembered point of interest. Her eyes have grown accustomed to the clear shadow. Two steps lead down to the level at which one can take the iron cup and drink from this cold well.

If outside all is shadowy, you may suppose how obscure it is within this low arch.

As she looks, she sees something rise within it. It is the figure of a man, who has just been stooping for a draught from the spring. His back is turned toward her.

We do not know how habitually we rely upon the protection of the upright among our fellowmen, until accident isolates us, and we confront a possible villain in a lonely place. There was no reason to suspect this man above other strangers. But a sense of her helplessness frightened her.

She stepped back, as most old ladies, with presence of mind, would have done under the circumstances. And very still, from her place of comparative concealment, she sees this faint shadow emerge in shade less deep, and she discerns the long neck, lank jaws, and white eyeball of Elihu Lizard.

The lady pursed her mouth and frowned, as she might at a paragraph in the newspaper describing a horror; and she drew a little further back, and as much behind the huge trunk of the tree at the edge of the path as she could with the power of still peeping at Mr. Lizard.

That lank wayfarer, in such a place, having, we must suppose, a quieter conscience than Miss Max, did not trouble himself to grope and peep about for spies, or other waylayers, among the trees, and having wiped his mouth on his sleeve, he sopped his lank face·all over with his coloured handkerchief, which he rolled into a ball, and pitched into his hat. Next he replaced his hat on his head, and gave it a little adjusting jerk.

Then Mr. Lizard threw his head back, so as to look up to the groining of branches above him. She could not tell exactly, so dark it was, what expression his odious countenance wore. Her active fancy saw a frown one moment, a smile the next, and then a grimace. Though these uncertain distortions seemed to flicker over it, I dare say his lean face was quiet enough then, and having popped something, which I conjecture to have been a plug of tobacco, into his mouth, he shouldered his stick with a little preliminary flourish, and set out again upon his march in the direction from whence she had just come.

This apparition gave a new direction to her thoughts. She waited quietly till she could hear his steps no more. She wondered whether he had been up to the Hall; but she recollected that this particular path crossed the park; there was a right of way by it, and therefore he need not have diverged to the house, nor have asked any one's leave to cross the grounds by it.

There remained the question, why was he here? Were she and Maud never to get rid of that odious attendant? She quickened her step homeward, and was glad when she emerged into the open light.

CHAPTER XXVIII.

INQUIRY.

TURNING into another walk, at her left, she approached the house, and saw Maud looking about her, as she stood in the midst of the scarlet and blue verbenas in the Dutch garden at the side of the Hall.

She signed to the old lady, smiling as she emerged.

' I have been looking all round for you, and almost repenting I had not gone with you. I really began to think he had run away with you.'

' Walked away, you mean; he does everything deliberately. He never ran in his life,' replies the old lady.

' Well—well—and——' The young lady stole a quick glance over her shoulder to be sure they were not observed, and lowering her voice very much as they got nearer, she continued eagerly, ' and tell me what he said. Did he tell you anything?'

' Well, he thinks he told me nothing, and intended to tell me nothing, but he did tell me a great deal,' answered Miss Max, smiling shrewdly ; ' and I don't know whether you will be glad or sorry, but the upshot is, putting everything together, I am nearly certain that your mamma intends marrying, and that he is strongly against it.'

' Really !' exclaimed Maud, stopping short, for they were walking very slowly, side by side.

' He did not say so in so many words, mind, but I can't account for what he said on any other supposition,' said Miss Max. ' Has not she been very diplomatic? I don't know that any living creature but I suspected what those mysterious excursions could be about. You see Mr. Coke jumped to the same conclusion when I told him the facts. I can't understand that kind of thing. What can be the pleasure of going through life, without a human being to whom you ever tell anything you either feel or intend? But she was always the same. She never trusted anyone, as long as I remember her.'

Maud listened to all this very thoughtfully.

' Tell me, like a darling, what you collect it from ; tell me everything he said,' after a considerable silence, Maude asked.

So Maximilla Medwyn repeated her conversation with Mr. Dawe with praiseworthy minuteness.

'What do you think of it ?' she asked in conclusion.

'I think it looks extremely like what you say,' Maud replied, looking down thoughtfully.

'And do you like it?'

'I can't say I do. It is not a thing I have much thought about—mamma's marrying ; but if she wishes——'

She stopped suddenly, and Maximilla saw, to her surprise, that she was crying.

'Pooh, pooh ! my dear child, take care,' said Miss Max. 'Goodness knows who may see you. I had not an idea you cared so much. When I talked to you before about it you didn't seem to mind.'

'I don't know ; it didn't seem so likely or so near,' she said, making an effort, and drying her eyes hastily. 'And really, I don't know, as you say, whether I ought to be glad or sorry.'

'Well, for the present, we'll put that particular inquiry aside, for I want to tell you that horrid one-eyed man has pursued us, and I saw him at the old well, in the dark walk, just now. We must make out whether he was at the house. I dare say Jones can find out all about him.'

Full of this idea, they returned together to the house ; but no such person, so far as they could make out, had been there.

Jones, again charged to inquire, failed to discover anything.

'You see, he has no business, or even pretence of business, at the house,' said Miss Max. 'I think he's watching you. It can be for no good purpose ; and if I were you, I should tell your mamma.'

'Why mamma?   I mean, why should I tell anyone ?' She looked uncomfortably at Miss Medwyn.

'I think your mamma ought to know it, and I think it is better that people should know that you observe it.'

Their eyes met for a moment, and were again averted.

'Yes, I think I will go to mamma, and tell her,' said the young lady.   'Shall I find you here when I come back ?'

They were in the hall at the time.

'Yes, I'll wait here,' she answered.

Lady Vernon was alone in the library. Maud knocked at the door, and her mother's voice told her to come in.

She did so, and found Lady Vernon writing. She raised her eyes only for a moment, and said, with a cold glance at her daughter :

'Have you anything to say, Maud ?'

'Only this. I wish to tell you, mamma, that a very ill-looking, elderly man, who has been following my Cousin Max and me from place to place, during the whole of our little excursion, evidently tracking and watching us, for what purpose we can't guess, has turned up, to-day, in the grounds. Maximilla saw him at the Nun's Well, in the dark walk, to-day. He is blind of one eye, and pretends to be travelling for a religious society, and his name is Elihu Lizard.'

She paused.

Lady Vernon had resumed her writing, and said, with her eyes on the line her pen was tracing:

'Well?'

'I only wanted to ask, mamma, whether you knew anything of any such person?' said Maud.

'A man blind of one eye?—what was he doing?' said Lady Vernon, dropping each word slowly, as she continued her writing.

'Following us from place to place, everywhere we went, and we really grew at last quite frightened and miserable,' said the young lady.

'I think, Maud, you should endeavour to be less governed by your imagination. There is no one admitted to Roydon who is not a proper person, and in all respects unexceptionable. You must know that,' said Lady Vernon, looking in her face with a cold stare; 'and I don't think, within the precincts of Roydon, that you or Max have anything to fear from the machinations of blind elderly men, and I really have no time to discuss such things just now.' And Lady Vernon, with imperious displeasure, turned and wrote her letter diligently.

So Maud turned and left the stately seclusion of that apartment, and returned through the other rooms to the hall, where she found Miss Max.

'I don't think she knows anything about him,' said Maud.

'If she does not, that only makes it more unpleasant,' answered the old lady.

And they went out again together for a walk.

The interrogation of Lady Vernon had not resulted, I think, in anything very satisfactory. Maud, however, did not venture to renew it; and in their after rambles in the grounds or the village of Roydon, neither she nor Miss Max encountered any more the ill-favoured apparition of Elihu Lizard.

The monotonous life of Roydon went drowsily on.

At the entreaty of Maud, Miss Medwyn prolonged her stay, which she interrupted only by a visit of a day or half a day, now and then, to a neighbouring house; and so a week or more had flown, when an incident occurred which, in the end, altered very seriously the relations of many people in and about Roydon Hall.

CHAPTER XXIX.

CAPTAIN VIVIAN.

ONE evening, Maximilla Medwyn and Maud returned from a drive just in time to dress for dinner. The sun was setting as they descended from the open carriage and mounted the steps.

Compared with the flaming sky and ruddy sunlight outside, deep was the shadow of the hall as they entered. But Miss Max discerned in that shade the figure of a little man standing in the background.

She stopped for a moment, exclaiming :

'Good gracious ! Is this you, Mr. Dawe ?'

'How do you do, Miss Medwyn ?' replied the small figure, advancing into the reflected glow that entered through the hall-door, and revealing the veritable black wig and mahogany face of that saturnine humorist.

'I hope you are not going already ?' said she. 'We have not been out two hours, have we, Maud ?'

Thus brought into prominence, Maud greeted the old gentleman, who then made answer to Miss Medwyn.

'I stay till to-morrow or next day.'

'Well, that's an improvement on your last visit, short as it is,' she replied. 'Do you know, I had quite made up my mind that we were never to meet in this world again.'

'So much for prescience. We are not witches, Maximilla,' observed the little gentleman dryly.

'Though we should not look the part badly, you and I,' she rejoined, with a laugh ; 'one thing I do predict : you'll meet Mr. Tintern at dinner to-day ; you were asking about him, you remember.'

'H'm !' he responded, with a roll of his eyes.

And with this brief greeting the ladies went up to their rooms, and Mr. Dawe, more slowly, followed to his.

When Miss Maud returned to the drawing-room, Mr. Tintern, having been at the Wymering Sessions to meet his brother magistrates, had not yet arrived. Lady Vernon had not returned, but a stranger was there.

There was no one in the room, except a young man, rather tall and slight. He had brown hair and light moustache, and was, if not actually handsome, certainly good-looking, and nothing could be more quiet and gentleman-like than his air and dress.

He had the pallor and general languor of an invalid. He appeared about thirty ; but he had been ill, and was possibly younger. He was leaning on the chimney-piece, and, I think, was actually looking at himself in the great mirror over it, as Maud came into the room.

It was a little awkward, perhaps, there being no one to introduce him ; but, notwithstanding, in a little while they were very cheerfully engaged in conversation, though not exactly of importance or novelty enough to very deeply interest my readers.

They had not been so employed very long, when Lady Vernon appeared.

'Captain Vivian, I must introduce you to my daughter.'

Captain Vivian bowed.

'You have never been in this part of the world before ?' said Lady Vernon. 'I think you said so ?'

'No. Coventry, I think, is about the nearest point of any interest I'm acquainted with.'

'Oh ! That is quite a journey ; but there is a good deal worth seeing near us ; we can plan all that to-morrow. I only hope our fine weather may continue,' said Lady Vernon. 'Oh, Mr. Dawe ! you came in so quietly, I did not see you. I dare say you knew your old room again. You used to like it long ago, so I thought I'd put you into it.'

'Thanks. Yes—h'm !' said Mr. Dawe solemnly, with a mysterious ogle, as if it was a good room to conjure in. 'I remember it.'

Captain Vivian was talking to Miss Vernon.

'How pale he looks !' Lady Vernon almost whispered to Mr. Dawe, her eyes covertly following the young man's movements. 'He is fatigued—he is doing too much. Make him sit down,'

Mr. Dawe nodded. He approached the young man and said a few words to him.

'Thank you very much, Mr. Dawe; but I really am not the least fatigued. I have not felt so strong I don't know when.'

'Yes; but you *are* fatigued, and you must sit down,' said Mr. Dawe, raising his brown hand and laying it on the young man's shoulder with an imperious pressure.

But before he had accomplished his purpose, Mr. Tintern, who had arrived, claimed his attention by playfully taking his disengaged hand, and saying:

'You won't look at me, Mr. Dawe. You are not going to cut your old friend, I hope?'

Mr. Dawe looked round. Tall Mr. Tintern stood before him, with a sort of wintry sunshine in his smile, which was not warm; his false teeth and light eyes were shining coldly on him.

Since they last met, Mr. Tintern's hair has grown almost white, but, as it was always light, this does not alter the character of his countenance, which, however, has grown puffy and wrinkled, with an infinity of fine lines, that indicate nothing bolder or higher, perhaps, than cunning.

Mr. Tintern is one of those pleasant fellows who is always glad to see everybody, and whose hand is always open to shake that of his neighbour; who can smile on people he does not like, as easily as he laughs at jokes he does not understand. For the rest, he parts with his condolences more easily than with his shillings, and taking on himself the entire burden of sympathy, he leaves to others the coarser enjoyment of relieving suffering by sacrifices of money or trouble.

'I never cut my friends,' says Mr. Dawe. 'I don't think I have five in the world. That is a luxury for people who have money.'

'You have some very good ones, out of the five, in this part of the world, at all events, and I only hope you remember them as well as they remember you,' replies Mr. Tintern, with a playful effervescence.

Mr. Dawe makes one of his stiff bows; but they shake hands, and Mr. Tintern holds the hard brown fingers of his 'friend' longer in his puffy white hand than Mr. Dawe seems to care for.

'Time flies, Mr. Dawe,' says Mr. Tintern, with a little plaintive smile and a shake of the head,

' Yes, sir; and we alter very much,' answers Mr. Dawe.

' Not all—not all,' says Mr. Tintern, who does not acquiesce in the approaches of senility ; ' at least I can vouch for you.'

And he lays his soft hand caressingly on Mr. Dawe's arm.

' H'm !' says Mr. Dawe.

And the interval that follows hears from him no return of the little flattery.

' We have been considering a good many things to-day after our session ; putting our heads together. It will interest Lady Vernon,' says Mr. Tintern cheerfully. ' By-the-bye, Lady Vernon, a question is to be submitted to you for your decision, and we so hope you will say "Yes." We are thinking, if you approve, of moving for a presentment next assizes, for a short road, only three and a half miles, connecting the two roads from the northern end of Wymering across by Linton Grange, to meet the Trafford road, about a quarter of a mile at this side of Stanbridge. But it is nearly all Roydon property, I need not tell you, and of course all depends upon you, and we were consulting as to how best to submit it, so as to obtain your sanction and assistance.'

' I think something ought to be done,' says Lady Vernon. ' I said so before, and I shall be very happy to talk with my steward about it, and the surveyor can call here ; but I'm not so sure that those are the best points. I shall look at the map to-morrow. I traced the line; I'm nearly certain I did what I thought best. You shall hear from me in time for the assizes.'

Miss Max had entered, and Mr. Dawe, in his grim, ungainly way, presented Captain Vivian. You might see that the old lady looked a little inquisitively at him, of course very cautiously, and that something was passing in her mind.

There was not much time, indeed, for speculation, and hardly any for a little talk with this young gentleman, for the whole party in a few minutes went away to the dining-room, where they were all presently much more agreeably employed.

Nothing very worthy of record occurred during dinner, nor after that meal, until the gentlemen had followed the ladies to the drawing-room, and then a little psychological discussion arose over the tea-table.

' I have been reading a novel, Barbara,' said Miss Max, ' and the heroine is made to fall in love with the hero before he has made a sign, and, for anything she knows, he is quite indifferent. Now, it strikes me that I don't remember a case of that kind, and I am collecting opinions. Maud says it is impossible. Mr. Dawe, on the contrary, thinks it quite on the cards. Captain Vivian agrees with Maud that the thing could not be, and now I want to know what you and Mr. Tintern can add for the enlightenment of an old maid in her perplexity ?'

Now this question interrupted a dialogue very earnest, and spoken very low, between Lady Vernon and Mr. Tintern, who were sitting quite far enough apart from the others to make their conversation inaudible to the rest of the party. That dialogue had been carried on thus :

'You may suppose what it has been to me,' Lady Vernon said, 'the suspense and torture of mind, although, possibly, of course, it may never be.'

'You have my warmest and deepest sympathy, Lady Vernon ; I need not tell you,' answered Mr. Tintern, closing his eyes, with a look of proper concern, and a plaintive shake of his head, ' and I feel very much honoured, I assure you, by your selecting me for this, I may say, very deplorable confidence ; and I shall, I need hardly add, consider it a very sacred trust. But you have, of course, mentioned it to other friends ?'

'Only to one, of whose good sense I have a very high opinion indeed,' said she.

'Mr. Dawe ?' suggested Mr. Tintern.

'Certainly not,' said Lady Vernon, with a quick glance towards that solemn little figure. 'He is about the last person I should speak to on the subject.'

'Oh, I see,' murmured Mr. Tintern deferentially, throwing at the same moment a vast deal of caution into his countenance ; 'it is a kind of thing, of course, that requires immense circumspection.'

'Yes,' replied the lady, 'and I intended——' It was at this word that Miss Max's inopportune inquiry broke in.

'I did not hear your question,' says Lady Vernon, a little bored by the interruption.

Miss Max repeated it.

'Well, Mr. Tintern, what do you say ?' she asked.

'Why, really,' said Mr. Tintern, working hard to get up a neat reply, and smiling diligently, 'where there is so much fascination of mind or of beauty, or of both, as we often see, in this part of the world, I can hardly fancy, eh ?—the lady's being allowed time to be the first to fall in love—ha, ha, ha !—really —upon my honour—and that's my answer.'

And he looked as if he thought it was not a bad answer.

'And now, Barbara, what do you say?' persisted Miss Max.

'I? I've no opinion upon it,' said Lady Vernon, with a little laugh; but a close observer could have discovered anger in her eye. 'I will think it over, and, in a day or two, I shall be able to aid you with my valuable opinion.'

And she turned again to Mr. Tintern, who asked, glancing at Captain Vivian:

'Mr. Dawe, does he make any stay in the country?'

'I don't know. I shall be very happy to make him stay here as long as I can. Captain Vivian, that young man, is his friend, and, it seems, was his ward, and as he could not leave him—he has been ill, and requires looking after—Mr. Dawe asked me if he might bring him here, and so I make him welcome also.'

'A very gentleman-like, nice young fellow he is,' said Mr. Tintern.

And so that little talk ended.

Mr. Tintern went his way, and the little party broke up, and the bedroom candles glided along the galleries, and the guests had soon distributed themselves in their quarters.

But that night an odd little incident did occur.

Miss Max had, after her usual little talk with Maud, bid her good-night, and her busy head was now laid on her pillow. The glimmer of a nightlight cheered her solitude, and she had just addressed herself seriously to sleep, when an unexpected knock at her door announced a visitor.

She thought it was her maid, and said:

'Do come in, and take whatever you want, and let me be quiet.'

But it was not her maid, but Lady Vernon, who came in, with her candle in her hand, and closed the door.

'Ho! Barbara? Well, what is it?' she said, wondering what she could want.

'Are you quite awake?' asked Lady Vernon.

'Perfectly; that is, I was going to settle; but it doesn't matter.'

'Well, I shan't detain you long,' said Lady Vernon, placing the candle on the table. 'I could not sleep without asking you what you meant, for I'm sure you had a meaning, by asking me the question you did to-night.'

She spoke a little hurriedly, and her eyes looked extremely angry, but her tones were cold.

'The only question I asked was about first love,' began Miss Max.

'Yes; and I ask you what did you mean, for you did mean something, by putting so very odd a question to me?' she replied.

'Mean? What did I mean?' said Miss Max, sitting up straight in a moment, so that her face was at least as well lighted as her visitor's. 'I assure you I meant nothing on earth, and I don't know what you mean by putting such a question to me.'

The handsome eyes of Lady Vernon were fixed on her doubtfully.

'You used to be frank, Maximilla. Why do you hesitate to speak what is in your mind?' said Lady Vernon sharply.

'Used to be—I'm always frank. As I told you before, there was nothing in my mind; but I think there's something in yours.'

'I only wanted to know if you intended any insinuation, however ridiculous. I fancied there was a significance in your manner, and as I could not comprehend it, I asked you to define, as one doesn't care to have surmises affecting one's self afloat in the mind of a friend, without at least learning what they are.'

'I had no surmises of the kind; but you have certainly gone the very way to fill my heart with them. What could you have fancied I meant?'

'Suppose I thought that you meant that I had made overtures of marriage to my husband before he had declared himself. That would have been untrue and offensive.'

'Such an idea never entered my mind—never could have— because I knew all about it as well as you did. That's mere nonsense, my child.'

'Well, then, there's nothing else you could mean, and so I'm glad I came. I believe it is always best to be a little outspoken, at the risk of a few hot words, than to keep anything in reserve among friends, and you and I are very old friends, Max. Good-night. I have not disturbed you much?'

And she kissed her.

'Not a bit, dear. Good-night, Barbara.'

And Lady Vernon disappeared as quickly as she came, leaving a new problem for Maximilla's active mind to work on.

CHAPTER XXX.

A VISIT.

In the morning Lady Vernon was more than usually affectionate when she greeted Miss Max.

When the little party met in the small room that opens into the chapel, where, as we know, Mr. Penrhyn, the secretary, officiated at morning prayers, Lady Vernon actually drew her cousin Maximilla to her and kissed her.

'Making reparation, I suppose,' thought Maximilla. 'But there was no occasion ; I was not hurt.'

And by the suggestion involved in this unusual demonstration, good Miss Max's fancy was started on a wild tour of entertaining conjecture respecting her reserved cousin Barbara, and the possible bearing of that curious question upon the sensibilities of the handsome woman of three-and-forty, who had not yet contracted a single wrinkle or grey hair ; and I am sorry to say that the measured intonation of Mr. Penrhyn, the secretary, as he duly read his chapter from the First Book of Chronicles, sounded in her ears faint and far away as the distant cawing of the rooks.

This morning service was now over, and the little party gathered round the breakfast-table.

Seen in daylight, Captain Vivian looked ill and weak enough. He was not up to the walking, riding, and rough out-door amusements of a country house. That was plain. He must lounge in easy-chairs or lie his length on a sofa, and be content, for the present, to traverse the country with his handsome but haggard eyes only.

Those eyes are blue, his hair light brown and silken, his moustache soft and golden. It is a Saxon face, and good-looking.

There is no dragoonery or swagger about this guest ; he is simply a well-bred gentleman, and, in plain clothes, as completely divested of the conventional soldierly manner as if he had never stood before a drill-sergeant.

Whether it is a consequence of his illness I can't say, but he looks a little sad.

In a house now and then so deserted and always so quiet as Roydon, the sojourn of a guest so unexceptionable, and also so agreeable, would have been at any time very welcome.

A little time ago, indeed, Maud might have thought this interruption of their humdrum life pleasanter. She had a good deal now to think of.

'What an inheritance of pictures you have,' said Captain Vivian. There is a seat outside the window, and on this the invalid was taking his ease, while Miss Max and Maud Vernon, seated listlessly within, talked with him through the open window. 'I think portraits are the most glorious and interesting of all possessions ; I mean, of course, family portraits.'

'If one could only tell whose portraits they are,' said Maud, with a little laugh. 'I know about twenty, I think, and, Max, you know nearly forty, don't you ? And I don't know who knows the rest. There is a list somewhere ; grandpapa made it out, I believe. But they are not all even in that.'

'I look round on them with a vague awe,' he said ; 'artists and sitters, so long dead and gone ; I wonder whether their ghosts come back to look at their work again, or to see what they once were like. I envy you all those portraits. Aren't you proud of them, Miss Vernon ?'

'I suppose I ought to be,' replied Maud. 'I dare say I should be if they were treated with a little more respect. But when one meets one's ancestors peeping from behind doors, shouldering one another for want of room in galleries and in lobbies, hid away in corners or with their backs to the wall half-way up the staircase, they lose something of their dignity, and it becomes a little hard to be proud of them.'

'Such long lines of ancestors, running so far back into perspective !' said the invalid languidly. 'Think of those who look back without a single lamp to light the past ! I knew a man who was well born, his parents both unquestionably of good family ; first his mother, then his father died, when he was but two years old,' Captain Vivian continued, looking down, as he talked, on the veining of the oak seat, along which he was idly running his pencil. 'His fate was very odd. He found himself with money bequeathed to him by his father, and with a guardian who had hardly known that father, but who, I dare say half from charity, the father being on his death-bed, undertook the office. Of course, if my friend's father had lived a little longer, the guardian would have learnt from his own lips all particulars respecting his charge. But his death came too swiftly. There was no mystery intended, of course ; the money was in foreign stocks, and was collected and brought to England as the will directed, and neither he nor his guardian know as much as they would wish of the family of either parent. So there he is, quite isolated ; a good-natured fellow, I believe. It gives him something to think about ; and I assure you it is perfectly true. I was thinking what that poor fellow would give for such a flood of light upon his ancestry as your portraits throw upon yours.'

'Perhaps he has made it all out by this time,' suggested Miss Max.

'I don't think he has,' said Captain Vivian.

'And what is his name?' inquired the old lady.

'Well, I'm afraid I ought not to mention his name,' he said, looking up. 'It does not trouble him much now, I think, and I dare say it has caused him more pain than it is worth. Here comes a carriage,' he said, raising his head. 'Your avenue is longer than it appears, it is so wide. What magnificent trees !'

'Who are they, I wonder; the bishop or the dean?' said curious Miss Max.

'It may be the Manwarings. We called there a few days ago,' said Maud.

'The liveries look like brown and gold, as well as I can see,' said Captain Vivian, who had stood up and was looking down the avenue.

'Oh, it is the Tinterns, then,' said Maud.

'Chocolate and gold, yes,' assented Miss Max. 'I hope so much that charming creature, Miss Tintern, is in the carriage. You'd be charmed with her, Captain Vivian.'

'I dare say I should. But I am an awfully dull person at present, and I rather shrink from being presented. Mr. Tintern, from what I saw of him last night, appears to be a good-natured, agreeable man?'

This was thrown out rather in the tone of an inquiry, but Captain Vivian did not wait for an answer, and, instead, moved slowly towards the hall-door, and before the Tinterns' carriage had reached the low balustrade of those ponds on which the swans and water-lilies float, he was in the drawing-room.

'I'm ashamed to say I'm a little bit tired,' said he to Miss Max, and pale and languid he did, indeed, look. 'And I think till this little visit is over I'll get into the next room, and look over some of those books of prints. You must not think me very lazy; but if you knew what I was a week ago, you'd think me a Hercules now.'

So, slowly Captain Vivian withdrew to the quieter drawing-room beyond this room, and sat him down before a book in the window, and turned over the pages alone.

In the meantime, agreeable Mr. Tintern has arrived, and his extremely pretty daughter has come with him.

She and Maud kiss, as young lady friends will, with more or less sincerity, after a long absence.

They make a very pretty contrast, the blonde and the dark beauty, Miss Tintern having golden hair and blue eyes, and Maud Vernon large dark grey eyes and brown hair.

So these young persons begin to talk together, while Lady Vernon and Mr. Tintern converse more gravely, a little way off, on themes that interest them more than flower-shows, fashions, and the coming ball at Wymering. Good Miss Max, who, in spite of her grave years, likes a little bit of frivolity, joins the young people, and has her laugh and gossip with them very cosily.

Having disposed of the Wymering ball, and talked over the statue of Mr. Howard in the church a little, and passed on to some county marriages likely to be, and said a word or two on guipure work, and the fashions, Miss Max said :

'I did not see your flowers at the Grange; I'm told they are perfectly lovely. The shower came on, you know; I was to have seen them.'

'Oh, yes, it was so unlucky,' says Miss Tintern. Yes, I think they are very good. Don't you, Maud?'

'Yes, wonderful,' answers Maud; 'they throw us, I know, quite into shade.'

'I think you are great florists in this part of the world,' says Miss Max. 'I thought I was very well myself; but I find I'm a mere nobody among you. You have got, of course, that new Dutch hyacinth. It is so beautiful, and so immense—white, and so waxen. What is its name, Maud?'

Maud gave the name of this beautiful monster.

'No; I'm sure we haven't got it,' answers Ethel Tintern. 'I should have liked so to see it.'

'We have one,' says Maud, 'the last, I think, still in its best looks; they are very late. I saw it in the next room. Come and see.'

In the histories of a thousand men, I suppose it has not

happened six times, possibly in that of ten thousand not half so often, that a young man should be surprised, in a deep sleep, over a book, by two young ladies so beautiful, and in whose eyes he wished, perhaps, to appear agreeable.

When the young ladies had pushed open the door, they stood for a moment beside it talking, and then, coming in, Maud Vernon pointed out the flower they had come to examine.

And, as they looked, admired, and talked, accidentally her eye lighted on the invalid, as he sat in the window, one hand on his book, his book slanting from his knee, and he with closed eyes and head sunk on his other hand, in a deep sleep. She exchanged a glance with her companion, and a faint smile and a nod.

The young ladies returned to the drawing-room; and when they had left the room a very few seconds, the slumbering invalid, without disturbing his attitude, looked after them curiously from the corner of his now half-opened eye, and listened. Then he turned his chair, so as better to avert his face, and, without stirring, continued to listen.

But they did not return. And as Mr. Tintern proposed lunching at Hartstonge Hall, he and his pretty daughter very soon took their leave, and Captain Vivian watched them quietly from the window, as they got into the open carriage and drove away.

'What a nice girl Ethel Tintern is. I like her so very much,' said Miss Max.

'Yes,' said Lady Vernon, 'but I did not think her looking well, did you?'

'Very pretty, but perhaps a little pale,' acquiesced Miss Max.

'Very pale, indeed,' says Lady Vernon; 'when she was going I was quite struck with it. Did you ever see her before, Mr. Dawe?'

'No,' answered that gentleman promptly from the recess of the window, where he was reading a note.

'I saw you look at her a good deal, Mr. Dawe,' said Maximilla, 'and I know you thought her very pretty.'

'H'm!' said Mr. Dawe oracularly.

'And I think she observed your admiration, also, for I saw her eyes follow you about the room whenever she fancied no one was looking, and I think there is more in it than you intend us to understand, and that you are a very profound person.'

'It's time I should be,' said Mr. Dawe, and the gong began to sound for luncheon as he spoke.

<hr/>

CHAPTER XXXI.

A LETTER.

THE invalid came slowly in now, and the little party, roared for by the gong, as I said, went away together to luncheon very merrily.

When this social meal was ended, Maximilla said to Maud, as they were going through the door, side by side :

'Some letters have come here from the Hermitage, and one among them that concerns you. Come up to my room with me, and we can read it.'

'Who is it from?' asks Maud, with excusable impatience.

'You shall see when we get upstairs—come.'

'But what is it about?'

'You.'

And the agile old lady ran up the stairs before her, laughing.

'Come in and shut the door,' says Miss Max, as Maud reached the threshold ; 'bolt the door ; it is no harm. Come here, to this window, and nobody can hear.'

She recollected the dressing-room door, and turning the key in it, rejoined Maud, whose curiosity was a good deal piqued by these precautions.

'Well, who is it from?' said Miss Max, with a provoking smile, as she raised it by the corner.

'If you don't tell me this moment, I'll push you into your chair, and take it by force.'

'Well, what do you say to Mr. Marston? I don't know a more exemplary lover ; the letter is from him. You shall hear,' answered Miss Max, as she opened it, and adjusted her glasses, smiling all the time a little mysteriously.

Maud looked grave, and a brilliant colour dyed her cheeks.

'Listen,' said Maximilla, very unnecessarily, and began :—

'DEAR MISS MEDWYN,—You have been so extremely kind to me that I venture to write a very short note, which I can no longer forbear, although I scarcely know myself what it is going to be. Miss Maud Guendoline, as I still call her, although she told me that I still have to learn her surname, imposed a command upon me, when taking my leave on that happy and melancholy Sunday evening, which I can never forget, a command which I need hardly assure you I have implicitly obeyed. I am, therefore, as entirely in the dark as ever respecting all I most ardently long to hear. Every day that passes makes me long more intensely for the hour when I may again see that one human face which alone of all others has ever interested me——'

'Mine, of course,' suggested Miss Max, raising her eyes for a moment. 'Well:'

'—Has ever interested me. Are you aware that the ball at Wymering is to come off nearly a fortnight earlier this year than usual? I have been so miserable lest the change of time should in any way endanger the certainty of Miss Maud Guendoline's attendance at it. Your nature is so entirely kind, that I know you will pardon my entreating you to write two or three words, only to reassure me, and tell me my misgivings are groundless. Till I shall have heard from you that your beautiful friend is to be at Wymering on the evening of the ball, I cannot know an hour's quiet.'

'Poor thing! I can't bear to keep him in suspense another hour,' said Miss Max.

Maud said nothing—neither 'Yes' nor 'No,' not even 'Read on.' Miss Max, however, went on diligently, thus:

'I am going, if you allow me, to make a confidence, and implore a great kindness. If you think you can do what I ask, and will kindly undertake it, I cannot describe to you how grateful I shall be. I am tortured with the idea that your young friend has undertaken too much. From some things she said, I fear that her life is but a dull and troubled one, beset with anxieties and embittered by conditions, for which she is utterly unfitted. You are our friend—hers and mine—and do, I implore, permit me to place at your disposal what will suffice to prevent this. You must not think me very coarse. I am only very miserable as often as I think of her troubles and vexations, and entreat you to intervene to prevent them, acting as if entirely from yourself, and on no account for another. If I were only assured that you would undertake this, I could wait with a lighter heart for the moment when I hope to meet her again. You can understand what I suffer, and how entirely I rely upon your kind secrecy, in the little commission I so earnestly implore of you to undertake.'

'And see how religiously I keep his secret!' said Miss Max. 'But, poor fellow! doesn't it do him honour? He thinks, at this moment, that you are living by the work of your fingers, and he not only lays his title and his title-deeds, with himself, at your feet, but he is miserable till he rescues you from the vexations of your supposed lot in life. I know very well that you think him an arrant fool. But I think him a hero—I know he's a hero.'

'Did I say I thought him a fool?' said Maud. 'I don't know who is a fool and who is a sage in this world; and if he is a fool, I dare say I'm a greater one. I believe, Max, we are wise and foolish where we least suspect it. I think we are most foolish when we act entirely from our heads, and wisest when we act entirely upon our feelings, provided they are good. I said so to Dr. Malkin, and he agreed; but, indeed, it is a dreadful life. I don't know where there is happiness. I was thinking if I were really the poor girl he believes me, how wild with happiness all this would probably have made me.'

'It ought, as you are, to make you just as happy,' said Maximilla.

'It ought, perhaps, but it doesn't. If I were that poor girl, gratitude and his rank would make me like him.'

'And you don't like him?'

'No, I don't like him.'

'Well. How inexpressibly pig-headed! How ungrateful!' exclaimed Miss Max, almost with a gasp. 'There is everything! Such kindness, and devotion, and self-sacrifice. I never heard of such a lover—and no possible objection!'

'I don't like him. I mean I don't love him.'

'And I suppose you won't go to the ball?' said Miss Max, aghast.

'I will go to the ball.'

'Do you know, Maud, I'm almost sorry I ever saw that poor young man. I'm sorry I ever beheld his face. One thing I am certain of, we must not go on mystifying him. I'll write to him instantly, and tell him everything. I'll not let him suppose I take a pleasure in fooling him ; I like him too well for that. I don't think, in this selfish world, I ever met any one like him. I shall wash my hands of the whole business ; and I'm very sorry I ever took any part in practising this unlucky trick upon him. I must seem so heartless !'

'If you write any such letter I'll not go.'

'Not go to the ball !' cried Maximilla. 'Well, certainly, that will seem good-natured—that is the climax !'

'I say to the ball I'll not go if you write him any such letter,' said Maud.

'And you will go if I don't ?' persisted good-natured Miss Max.

'Certainly,' said Maud decisively.

'I don't see why he should be mystified,' said Maximilla, after a considerable pause.

'He shall be mystified as long as I like. It is the only way by which we can ever know anything of him. What could you have known of him now, if it had not been that he was all in the dark about us ? No ; you shall write to him to-day, if to-day it must me, and tell him, in whatever way you like to put it, that you can't think of accepting his offer of money, as I and my mother have, one way or other, quite enough.'

And at this point these two wise ladies, looking in one another's eyes, laughed a little, and then very heartily, and Miss Max said :

'It is a great shame. I don't know how we can ever look him in the face again when he discovers how we have been deceiving him !'

'You have much too mean an opinion of your impudence, Max. At all events, if we can't we can't, and so the acquaintance ends.'

'Well ? What more ? What about your going to the ball ?' says Maximilla.

'Say that we shall certainly be there—you and I. You know you must stay for it.'

'I suppose I must.'

'And, let me see, it will be on Friday week ?'

'Yes; I'll tell him all that.'

'But wait a moment. I haven't done yet. The ball begins at ten exactly. Yes, ten, and you and I shall be in the gallery at nine precisely.'

'In the gallery !'

'Yes, in the gallery,' repeated Miss Maud.

'Why, my dear Maud, no one sits in the gallery but towns-people, and musicians' wives, and dressmakers. I don't know, I'm sure, what on earth you can mean.'

'You shall know, of course, everything I mean.'

'And, you know, I object to our having any more of that masquerading—remember that.'

'Perfectly; I'll do nothing but exactly what you like. I promise to do nothing unless you agree to it. You shall know all my plans—isn't that fair ?'

'Yes; but what are they ?'

'I have only a vague idea now ; but we can talk them over when you have written your letter ; recollect, in little more than half an hour the servant takes the letters to the post. But write on your own paper with the Hermitage at the top of the sheet, and—yes—if you can be very quick, I'll send the letter to the post-office at Dalworth ; it will be better than the Roydon post-mark.'

'Yes, Roydon might set him thinking, if you don't want to tell him now.'

'No, nothing, except what I have said. I'll never see him more if you do—you promise me that ?'

'Certainly, you shall read the letter when it is written.'

'There now, you are a good girl, Max ; I'll stay here for it ; and I'll get Lexton to send a man riding to Dalworth.'

'Now you mustn't talk, or make the least noise,' said Miss Max, as she opened her desk. 'I must not make a mistake.'

And soon the scraping of her industrious pen was the only sound audible in the room.

In the meantime, Maud took Mr. Marston's letter to the window, and leaning lightly with her shoulder to the angle of the wall, she looked it over, and thought what a gentle-man-like hand it was, and then she read and re-read it, and with a pretty glow in her cheeks, and her large eyes fired and sad-dened, she laid it on the table beside Maximilla, just as that romantic accomplice, having written the address on the en-velope, turned round to place it in her hand.

'No, there isn't time to read it. Shut it up now, and let me have it. Lexton will put a stamp on it.'

And with these words Maud kissed her with a fond little caress, and ran away with the note in her hand.

CHAPTER XXXII.

DRIFTING.

AND now people begin to observe and whisper something strange. Now, in fact, begins an amazing infatuation. It shows itself in the cold, proud matron, Lady Vernon, at first covertly, afterwards with less disguise.

The young officer, Captain Vivian, is to make a stay of some weeks.

For a day or two Lady Vernon appears to take no particular interest in him. But gradually, by the third day of his sojourn, her manner, either disclosing a foregone liking, or indicating the growth of a new passion, changes.

It changes at first covertly ; afterwards the signs that excite general comment show themselves with less disguise.

As Miss Max remarks to Maud, with a little pardonable exaggeration, 'She can't take her eyes off him, she can hear no one else speak, while he is talking in the same room to any one. She is quite rapt up in him.' As Miss Jones, Maud's maid, phrases it in her confidential talk, she is 'light on him,' meaning thereby, under the influence of a craze.

People who come in upon her solitude in her room, suddenly, say they find her agitated, and often in floods of tears. All agree that she has grown silent and absent, and seems never happy now but when she is near him.

It was one of those mysterious cases which honest Jack Falstaff would have accounted for by the hypothesis, 'I'm be-witched with the rogue's company. If the rascal have not given me medicines to make me love him, I'll be hanged ; it could not be else ; I have drunk medicines.'

I suppose she guarded her language very carefully, and even her looks, in actual conversation with Captain Vivian, for that which appeared plain enough to other people seemed hidden from him. It was discussed in the servants' hall and in the housekeeper's room.

The unanimous opinion was that Captain Vivian had only to speak and that the new year would see him the chosen of the handsome widow and lord of Roydon Hall. People wondered, indeed, how he could be so stupid as not to see what was so plain to everyone else. But they could not know how cautious Lady Vernon was in her actual conversation with him, not, by sign or word, to commit herself in the least degree.

It was clear enough, however, to the household of Roydon in what direction all this was tending, and a general agitation and uneasiness trembled through every region and articulation of that huge and hitherto comfortable body.

Such was the attitude of affairs when Maud Vernon, with her cousin Maximilla, drove over to the Grange to pay the Tinterns a visit.

Mr. Dawe had taken his departure after a day or two with a promise, made upon consideration, as one might conjecture, for undivulged reasons of his own, to return in less than a week.

The prominent brown eyes and furrowed, inflexible face removed, a sense of liberty seemed to visit Captain Vivian suddenly. His spirits improved, and he evidently began to enjoy Maud Vernon's society more happily. They took walks together; they talked over books; they compared notes about places they had visited, and she began to think that the intellectual resources of Roydon were improved, since the time when she used to insist that Dr. Malkin alone redeemed that region of the earth from darkness.

'Take care, my dear, that our plaintive invalid doesn't turn out instead a very robust lover,' said Miss Max, in one of her nocturnal conferences with Maud. ' *There* will be a pretty comedy !'

'How can you like to make me uncomfortable ?' said Maud.

'Upon my word, if I don't, I think Barbara will,' replied Maximilla. 'Don't you see how she is devoted to him ?'

'I can't understand her. Sometimes I think she is, and sometimes I doubt it,' said Miss Vernon.

'Well—yes. She is, perhaps, in a state of vacillation—a state of struggle ; but she thinks of nothing else, and, it seems to me, can scarcely hear, or even see, any other human being.'

'You may be very sure I shan't allow him to make love to me,' said Maud, with proper dignity.

'Unless you wish to come to pulling of caps with your mamma, for the amusement of the rest of the world, you had better not, I think,' answered Miss Max, with a laugh.

'But, I tell you, I should not permit it, and he never has made the slightest attempt to make love to me,' repeated Maud, blushing.

'Well, it is rather a good imitation. But Barbara does not seem to see it—I don't think, indeed, she has had an opportunity—and if she's happy, why should I interfere?' said Miss Max.

And so that little talk ended.

Coming out of church on Sunday, the three ladies from Roydon and Captain Vivian, who felt strong enough for one of Mr. Foljambe's sermons, and sat in the corner of the great Vernon pew, stood for a moment on the step of the side porch, while the carriage drove up to receive them. The grenadier footmen in blue and gold opened the door and let down the steps, and Lady Vernon, following Miss Max, stepped lightly as a girl into her carriage. The Tinterns, Mr., Mrs., and Miss, at the same moment emerged from the holy shadow under the stained and grooved Gothic arch with a similar intent. Lady Vernon from the carriage bowed to them with her cold, haughty smile, which Mr. Tintern answered with his hat in his hand, high above his head, in the ceremonious old fashion, and with a countenance beaming all over with manly servility.

The chocolate and gold liveries, standing at the flank, awaited the departure of the blue and gold to do their devoir by the more ponderous carriage of the humbler Grange family.

While Mr. and Mrs. Tintern made their smiling salutations, and answered the remark which Maximilla Medwyn called out to the effect that it was a charming day, Maud thought she remarked from pretty Ethel Tintern a quick and odd glance at Captain Vivian, who, not having been presented to the Tintern ladies, was industriously poking a tiny stalk of groundsel from a chink in the old worn step, at the flank of which he stood.

It was very natural that the young lady should steal that quick glance at the unobservant stranger. It was the undefinable character of it that struck Maud.

There seemed neither curiosity nor recognition. It was momentary—a dark look, pained and shrunken. It was gone, quite, in a moment, and Ethel, as Maud with a hurried pressure

of her hand was about to take her place in the carriage, said
softly :

'You must come to see me to-morrow or next day.   You owe
us a visit, you know.   *Do.*'

'I will, certainly,' promised Maud, smiling.   And in a
moment more she was in her place, and, followed by Captain
Vivian, the door closed upon her ; and the smiling faces and
stately liveries whirled away over the gritty gravel of the churchyard road.

'This has been your first Sunday at church since your illness.
It was rather longer than usual.   Mr. Foljambe's sermons don't
often exceed twenty minutes.   I hope you are not doing too
much ?'

This question of Lady Vernon's, and Captain Vivian's polite
disclaimer, were the only essays toward conversation which
enlivened the little party as they drove home.

'Mr. Mapleson told me that mamma said she would have the
main street of the village watered every Sunday, and she hasn't
given any order, I suppose, about it.   See what a state we are
in !   Covered with dust.   I must ask Mr. Mapleson why,' said
Maud to Miss Max in the hall.

'Well, it is a bore,' she answered ; 'we can't sit down in
these things.   Come up.   I want to tell you I've just found a
note on the table.   No, it's not from the person you think.   I
see you're blushing.'

'Now, don't be a goose,' said Maud.

'Although it's not so bad a guess, as you shall hear when you
come to my room.   I told you, you remember, that my gossiping maid said that Captain Vivian sent two letters to the
Grange ; Captain Vivian's man told her, but she could make
out nothing more.   She has not an idea to whom they were
written.   He does not know Miss Tintern nor Mrs. Tintern,
and I don't see what he could write to old Tintern about ; but
the note I have got is from such a charming creature, younger
than Barbara, and a widow—Lady Mardykes.   She is a sister
of Mr. Marston's, and she has, besides her place at Golden Friars,
such a pretty place about five-and-thirty or forty miles from
this, and she is one of my very dearest friends.   She asks me
to go and see her immediately, and I must introduce you.
You will be charmed with her, and she, I know, with you.'

'Is there any chance of Mr. Marston's being there ? If there
is, I certainly shan't go,' said Maud.

'None in the world. He is to be with his father till Thursday, don't you recollect, he tells us all about it in his letter, and on Friday he will be at the ball at Wymering. Suppose we go and see her to-morrow. Do you know, I have been suspecting a little that Captain Vivian's letter was to her. But she could not be such a fool as to throw herself away upon him.'

'Very well, then, let us take the carriage and go to the Grange to-morrow. So that's agreed.'

In pursuance of this plan they did actually drive over to the Grange next day.

Artful Miss Max was rather anxious to induce Captain Vivian to accompany them. It would have amused her active mind to observe that gallant gentleman's proceedings. But, as if he suspected her design, he very adroitly, but politely, evaded the suggestion. So she and Maud went alone.

The Grange was a pretty house, a little later than the Tudor style. Driving up through the rather handsome grounds, they had hardly got a peep at the comfortable steep-gabled house, when Maud exclaims:

'There is Ethel—who is that with her?'

'Dear me! That is Lady Mardykes, I'm sure. I'm so glad to see her! They are looking at the flowers; suppose we get out.'

So down they got, and the ladies before the hall-door, among the flowers, looked up, and came toward them with smiles.

CHAPTER XXXIII.

A WARNING.

A GREAT kissing ensued upon the grass, and a shaking of hands, and Maud was introduced to Lady Mardykes, whom she liked instantaneously.

A face that must have been very pretty, and was still interesting—gentle, gay, and frank—was before her. But she was much older than her brother: a daughter by an earlier marriage.

This lady evidently took a fancy to Maud, and when they had talked a little, and began to grow to know one another better, after a short conversation aside with Maximilla, during which Maud saw that good-natured old maid look once or twice at her, Lady Mardykes, coming over to her, began to talk to her again.

' I should have gone to Roydon to see Lady Vernon,' she said ' only that I had doubts as to her liking it ; and perhaps it is better to put it off to another time. There have been so many unlucky vexations, and I know she and papa don't visit, so you will understand why I don't go to see you at Roydon. But you must promise to come to me for a few weeks to Carsbrook. I shan't be going to Mardykes till next year, perhaps ; I should rather have had you there. All about Golden Friars is so very beautiful. But I think you will say that Carsbrook is a pretty place, and if I can persuade Maximilla Medwyn to come to meet you, I'm sure you will find it pleasant. I'll consult with her as to how best to arrange it all.'

Maud was very well pleased with this little plan ; and now old Mr. Tintern came forth upon the grass, with his agreeable greetings and chilly smiles, and Maximilla and he began to talk, and their talk grew gradually, it seemed, a little earnest. And when the gong summoned them to luncheon, he seemed still thoughtful now and then during that repast.

They walked out again through the glass-door after luncheon, and Mr. Tintern, in the same mood, accompanied them, and once more fell into talk with Miss Max.

Ethel Tintern was now beside Maud, and the two young ladies sat down upon a rustic seat among the flowers.

' We are forlorn damsels here ; our gentlemen have all gone off to fish at Dalworth. Papa wanted Lady Mardykes and me to go in the carriage, and I am so glad now we did not. We should have missed you. Do you know, I think we girls have much more resource than men. They won't entertain themselves as we do, and it is so very hard to amuse them. You have a guest at present at Roydon ?'

' Yes, Captain Vivian.'

' Yes ; and Miss Medwyn thinks he is a little taken with you ?'

' She divides him between me and Lady Mardykes at present, and when you are acquainted, I dare say she'll give you a share.'

Ethel laughed, and said suddenly :

' By-the-bye, I was so near forgetting the pyracanth ! It is beginning to look rather *passé ;* it is the very last, but you can judge pretty well what it must be when it is in its best looks.'

So she got Miss Max to look at the flower, which she held up for inspection in its glass, and there ensued an animated bit of floral gossip, in which Mr. Tintern, who was skilled in flowers, and had won a few years since two or three prizes, one especially, which made a great noise, for his ranunculuses, took a leading part.

Then Mr. Tintern withdrew, and Miss Max, Lady Mardykes, and Mrs. Tintern talked together, and Ethel, alone once more with Maud Vernon, said, as if the long parenthesis counted for nothing :

'About that Captain Vivian—take my advice, and don't allow him to pay you the slightest attention.'

'Really ——'

'Yes,' says Miss Tintern, who is cruelly plucking a white rose, petal by petal, asunder, and watching the process intently.

'Yes, but I assure you he hasn't,' said Maud.

'Miss Medwyn thinks differently,' said Miss Tintern, with gentle diligence continuing the process of discerption.

'I don't perceive it, if he does,' answered Maud. 'But why do you warn me ?' and she smiled a little curiously as she put her question.

'Because I know certain things about him, and he is aware that I do, that ought to prevent him. You mustn't repeat a word I say, mind. Does he seem to wish to avoid me ?'

'Quite the contrary. He talks as if he should like so much to make your acquaintance.'

'That I don't understand,' said Ethel, plucking three or four leaves together from her dishevelled rose.

'I understood him to wish that I should take the first opportunity of introducing him.'

'I should not like that at all,' said Ethel, with a tone and look of marked annoyance, her eyes still watching the flower she was stripping.

'Is it anything discreditable ?' asked Maud.

'No, not that, certainly not, but it might easily become so. You see, I'm talking riddles, but indeed, I can't help it. I can't say anything more at present than I have told you, and so much I had a right to say, and am very glad I have had an opportunity, and for the present, as I said, I can give you nothing but that, my earnest piece of advice. And take care of yourself, I counsel you, in this false, shabby, wicked world.'

With these words, Ethel Tintern got up, and broke what remained of the rose between her fingers, and crumpled it up and threw it away. She saw Miss Max walking quickly toward them, with the air of a chaperon in search of her charge, and she guessed that the hour had come for saying good-bye.

'My dear Maud, I had no idea how late it was,' said Maximilla, before she reached them. 'I'm so afraid we shall be late for our appointment with your mamma, It is twenty minutes past three now. Had not we better go ?'

Maud was a little alarmed, for with her to be late for an appointment with her mother was a very serious matter indeed, so she consulted her watch, which, for a lady's timepiece, was a very fair one, being seldom more than twenty minutes wrong, either way, and finding there signs corroborative of Miss Max's calculations, 'there were sudden partings,' and time for little more than a hurried inquiry whether Ethel was going to the Wymering ball.

'Yes, she thought so ; that is, if her papa went ; her mamma was not well enough.'

And so, kissing and good-byes, and a very friendly reminder from Lady Mardykes, who said she expected to be at home at Carsbrook in ten days, and that Maud would be sure to hear from her about that time.

And now they are whirling homeward, at the brilliant pace of the high-bred horses of Roydon, and Maud says to her companion :

'Ethel has just been warning me, for reasons she won't tell, against permitting Captain Vivian to pay me attentions. Not a very likely thing, but I'm sure she means it kindly, and she was really quite earnest, but she charged me not to tell it to mortal, so you must promise not to mention it.'

So you see how well the secret was guarded.

'Upon my life, this Captain Vivian, invalid though he be, is beginning to grow into a very formidable sort of hero. Mr. Tintern was talking about him, and I said, just to try what he would say, that I thought Barbara had taken rather a fancy to him, and he took it up not at all jestingly, but very seriously indeed, and he told me, confidentially, that he had heard the same thing from another quarter, and that he believed it. So, my dear Maud, I rather think,' continued Miss Max, who saw

as far into millstones as must old ladies, 'that we may connect
Miss Ethel's warning with her father's curious information.
Don't you see?'

'Upon my word, the situation grows tragical!' said Maud,
with a laugh.

'It would be an unlucky business for Mr. Tintern, of course,
if Barbara took it into her head to marry, because it might
extinguish any chance, and you may be sure he thinks it a
better one than it is, of his succeeding to a share of the Vernon
property. Dear me, who are those?'

The exclamation and question were suggested by the emer-
gence of Lady Vernon and Captain Vivian from the church-
door of Roydon, which the carriage was now almost passing.

'Rehearsing the ceremony, I suppose,' laughed Miss Max.

A footman was waiting outside, and the sexton followed the
lady and gentleman out, and locked the old church-door.

Lady Vernon had been showing Captain Vivian the monument, which he had seen but imperfectly the day before. Lady
Vernon saw them, and nodded and smiled to Miss Max as they
passed.

'I sometimes think Barbara is not looking very well—pale
and tired. I don't know why she fags herself so miserably, I'm
sure. But if I told her so, I should only have my head in my
hand. There are some people, my dear, who hate advice, and,
on the whole, do you know, I rather think they are right.'

They were driving up the avenue by this time, and were soon
in the court-yard.

CHAPTER XXXIV.

MR. TINTERN HAS SOMETHING TO SAY.

MR. TINTERN arrived next day, and was fortunate enough to
find Lady Vernon alone in the drawing-room.

He had some county business to tell her of, and some gossip
to report; but there was still something palpably on his mind
which he did not very well know how to express.

He stood up, and she thought he was going to take his leave;
it was time he should; but he went to the window instead, and
talked of the two gigantic chestnut trees that overshadow the

balustrade of the court, in a sentimental and affectionate vein, as remembering them from the earliest time he could remember anything; and he spoke of her father with great regard, affection, and veneration. And then he spoke of the friendship that had always existed between the Grange and Roydon Hall, and then he mentioned that most interesting family memorial, the 'shield-room,' with the quarterings of the Rose and the Key; of his right to quarter which, proving the early connection of his family with the Vernons, he was prouder than of any other incident in their history. And having ended all this, he seemed to have still something more to say.

The lady's large grey eyes lighted on him with a cold inquiry. She was growing impatient. If he had anything to say, why did he not say it? Her look disconcerted him, and his light eyes went down before her dark gaze, as with an effort he said:

'I'm going to take my leave, Lady Vernon, and I don't know whether you will, by-and-bye, be vexed with me for having gone without mentioning a circumstance, which, however, I believe to be of absolutely no importance. But, you see, you have so often told me that you like, on all occasions, to be put in possession of facts, and that you insist so much on candour and frankness as the primary conditions of all friendship, and you have honoured me, more than once, with so large a measure of confidence, which has extremely flattered me, that even at a risk of appearing very impertinent, I had almost made up my mind to tell you what I have ascertained to be a general—a very general—topic of—of interest among neighbours and people down here; but, on the whole, I should rather not, unless, indeed, you would command me, which I rather hope you will not.'

'I shan't command you, certainly. I have no right even to press you; but if it concerns me, I should be very much obliged if you would let me know what it is.'

'I'm sure you will forgive me, but feeling how much, in a matter of so much more delicacy, you have already honoured me with your confidence, I felt myself, you will understand, in a little difficulty.'

'You need have none, Mr. Tintern, in speaking perfectly frankly to me. Pray say what it is.'

'As you say so, I shall, of course.'

And then, with all the tact and delicacy, and polite and

oblique refinement, on which he piqued himself, Mr. Tintern
did at length distinctly inform Lady Vernon that it was said
that she meant to honour Captain Vivian with her hand.

'If people had some useful occupation of their own they
would have less time to spare in settling other people's affairs.
I shan't take the slightest notice of any such rumours. They
don't amount even to that. They are not rumours, but the
mere speculations of two or three idle people. I am forty-two'
—she was really forty-three, but even for the force of her argument she would not forego that little inaccuracy—'and I have
not married since my husband's death, twenty years ago nearly.
It is a little odd, that one can't have a guest in one's house,
without being made a topic for the coarse gossip of low people.
I only wish I knew to whom I am obliged for taking this very
gross liberty with my name. They should never enter the
doors of Roydon again.'

Mr. Tintern was a little frightened at the effect of his own
temerity, for he had never seen Lady Vernon so angry before,
and a quarrel with her was the last thing he would have provoked.

'I shall certainly contradict it,' he hastened to say. 'I shall
take every occasion to do so.'

'You may, or you may not. I shan't prevent you, and I
shan't authorize you. I don't want it circulated or contradicted.
I am totally indifferent about it.'

'Of course—entirely; you must be—entirely indifferent.
But you understand, although I didn't believe it, yet as I was
supposed to be a not unlikely person to hear anything so
interesting, I thought you might not choose, as my sitting by
and not being in a position to contradict it appeared to some
people very like countenancing the—the gossip——'

'Pray understand me, Mr. Tintern. I don't the least care
whether it is countenanced or contradicted. It does not interest
me. I shan't either directly or indirectly take the smallest
notice of it. I look on it simply as an impertinence.'

'I hope, Lady Vernon, you don't suppose for a moment
that I viewed it otherwise than as an impertinence. That
was my real difficulty, and I felt it so much that I really
doubted whether I should mention it. But, on the other hand,
I think you will say that I should have been wanting in loyalty
to the house of Vernon, if I had not given you the option of
hearing, or of not hearing, as you might determine.'

'I think, Mr. Tintern, you did no more than was friendly in the matter,' said Lady Vernon, extending her hand, 'and I am extremely obliged to you. As to the thing itself, we shan't talk of it any more.'

Lady Vernon took an unusually cordial leave of that near neighbour and distant kinsman, who departed in good spirits, and well pleased with himself.

As he rode homeward, however, and conned over the conversation, he began to perceive with more distinctness that upon the main question Lady Vernon had left him quite as much in the dark as ever.

'But she could not express all that contempt and indignation if there was anything in the report, and she certainly would not have been so much obliged to me for repeating it to her.'

But this reasoning did not so entirely reassure him as he fancied it ought.

Six words would have denied it, and set the matter at rest, and that short sentence had not been spoken.

He began to grow very uncomfortable. If he had known what was occurring at that moment in the library at Roydon Hall, it would not have allayed his uneasiness.

In that room there is a very pretty buhl cabinet, with ormolu Cupids gambolling and flitting over its rich cornice. You would not suppose that this elegant shell contained within it a grimy iron safe. But on unlocking and throwing open the florid and many-coloured doors, the homely front of the black safe appears, proof against fire and burglars.

Lady Vernon unlocks a small bronze casket over the chimney-piece, and from it takes the big many-warded key of the safe. She applies it, and the doors swing open.

A treasury of parchment deeds discloses itself. She knows exactly where to place her hand on the one she wants. The organ of neatness and order is strong in her. She selects it from a sheaf of exactly similar ones. No ancient deeds, yellow and rusty with years. This is a milk-white parchment. Its blue stamp and silver foil look quite pretty in the corner. A short square deed, with scrivenry that looks black and fresh as if the ink were hardly dry upon it, and there are blanks left for names and dates. It is a deed as yet unexecuted. She takes it out, and lays it with its face downward on her desk, locks the safe and the cabinet, and restores the key to its casket over the mantelpiece.

The angry colour is still in Lady Vernon's cheeks as she slowly reads this deed, filling in, with careful penmanship, all the dates, and writing, in no less than four blank places at full length, the words ' Alexander Wyke Tintern, of the Grange, in the county of ——, Esquire.'

Was Lady Vernon rewarding friendly Mr. Tintern, then and there, by a deed of appointment—for these have been prepared, at her desire, by Mr. Coke—securing his succession, in certain contingencies, to a share in a princely reversion?

No. Alas for the aspirations of the Grange! these little deeds, quite sufficient and irrevocable, are for the eternal cutting-off of the condemned.

All being ready now, Lady Vernon touches the bell, sends for her secretary, and having doubled back the deed so that the signing place only is disclosed, seals, signs, and delivers it in his presence, who little dreams that these few magical symbols are taking off the head of a neighbour, and laying his airy castle in the dust.

And now he has duly ' witnessed' it, and Lady Vernon despatches it that evening, registered, with a letter enjoining the strictest secrecy, to Mr. Coke in London.

So good Mr. Tintern, if he knew but all, need trouble himself no further whether Lady Vernon or Maud marry, or pine and die singly; for go where it may, not one shilling of the great reversion can, by any chance or change, ever become his.

CHAPTER XXXV.

CINDERELLA.

CAPTAIN VIVIAN is now very much better; he has lost the languor of an invalid, and is rapidly recovering the strength and tints of health, and with them the air and looks of youth return.

The uneasiness of Mr. Tintern grew apace, for he heard authentic reports of the long walks which the handsome young captain used daily to take about the romantic grounds of Roydon with the beautiful lady of that ancient manor.

' The idea,' he said to Mrs. Tintern, ' of that old woman—

she's forty-six, if she's an hour—marrying that military adventurer, not five-and-twenty, by Jove ! Such infatuation !'

As respected the young man, there was, indeed, no exaggeration in this. He might have been taken for even a younger
man, now.

Old Tintern saw the captain one day fishing his trout-stream
diligently, and pretending not to know him at that distance, he
shouted, in arrogant tones, to the keeper :

'Holloa ! I say, Drattles, go down there, will you, quick,
and see who the devil that is fishing my brook !'

The gamekeeper touched his hat, and ran down, and Mr.
Tintern, from his point of observation, strode at a more leisurely
pace, in a converging line, towards the offender.

He found Captain Vivian in parley with the keeper.

'Oh, Captain Vivian !' he exclaimed very naturally, 'I had
not an idea. I'm so glad to see you able to take a rod in your
hand.'

'Lady Vernon told me you were so good——'

'My dear sir, don't say a word. I begged of Lady Vernon
to send you here, if you cared for trout-fishing, and indeed all
Roydon guests are welcome. I hope you have had some sport.
You must come up and take luncheon with us. I ought not,
indeed, to say I'm glad to see you so well, for I am afraid it is
a sign we are to lose you very soon. You'll be joining your
regiment, I suppose. Those big-wigs are so churlish about
holidays. They forget they ever were young fellows themselves.
Do come and have some luncheon.'

This invitation, however, Captain Vivian very politely declined.

'You are going to the ball to-night—Wymering—eh ?' inquired Mr. Tintern.

'Yes, I intend going ; and your party are going, I suppose ?'
said the young man.

'Oh yes, we always show there; and Lady Vernon, is she
going ?' pursued Mr. Tintern.

'No, Lady Vernon don't feel quite up to it.'

'Sending him,' thought Mr. Tintern, 'to put people off their
guard. Perhaps she doesn't wish them to criticize her looks
and demeanour in presence of the aspiring captain.'

'Dear me, I'm so sorry ; she complains sometimes of headache,' said Mr. Tintern affectionately. 'By-the-bye, there's
about a mile of very good pike-fishing at the other side. The

men are busy cleaning the ponds just now ; but if you are here in three weeks' time——'

'No, I'm afraid I shan't, thank you very much.'

'Well, we must make an effort, and say a fortnight; will that do ?'

'A thousand thanks, but I'm afraid I have little more than a week.'

'Oh ! nonsense. I won't believe it,' exclaimed Mr. Tintern very cheerfully.

'I'm awfully sorry,' said Captain Vivian ; 'it is such a beautiful country, and so charming in every way. I could live here all my life with pleasure.'

'I'm so glad to hear it has made so agreeable an impression. We may look to see you here again, I dare say, before long.'

'You are very kind. I don't know anything yet with certainty about my movements ; they depend upon so many things. I've a note, by-the-bye, which I promised to leave at the Grange.'

'As you won't come to the house, I'll take charge of it,' said Mr. Tintern. 'I see it is for my wife. I dare say about the ball. She's out ; she'll not be home for some hours. I think I may venture to open it.' He did, and glanced through it.

'Oh yes, pray tell Miss Vernon, my wife will be only too delighted to meet her and Miss Medwyn in the cloak-room. We shall be there at exactly half-past ten. I hope that will answer Miss Vernon. My wife would write, but she has gone to Dallerton ; but you will be so kind as to say Miss Vernon may look on it as quite settled.'

So they parted very pleasantly ; for Mr. Tintern, who was a shrewd man, had heard two or three things that cheered his heart in this little talk with Captain Vivian. He felt, indeed, in better spirits about Roydon and the probable continuance of Lady Vernon's widowhood than he had enjoyed for nearly a fortnight.

He had had losses lately. It would be too bad if everything were to go wrong.

If we could sum up the amount of the sins and sorrows of the human race, purely mental and unexpressed, for the most part, that result from contingent remainders, destructible reversions, and possible godsends and windfalls, the total would be possibly rather shocking.

The little old-fashioned town of Wymering is in a wonderful

fuss this night. It is its great anniversary—its night of dis-sipation and glory. It is not only for the town a crisis and an event, but the country all round, with Wymering for a centre, feels the radiation and pulse of the excitement. For ten miles round almost every good county house sends in its carriage and horses and liveries, and for fifteen—ay, even twenty miles round—roll in occasional carriages with post-horses; and traps besides, of all sorts, come rattling into the High Street with young fellows in hilarious spirits, thinking of nothing but dances and flirtation; and sometimes of some one pretty face, without which the ball and the world would be dark.

The clock of the town-hall has struck nine, and the Roydon carriages and liveries stop at the door of the Old Hall Hotel. Miss Max and Miss Vernon get down, and their two maids also.

Captain Vivian, with Captain Bamme, who has begged a seat to Wymering, are coming on later.

The ladies have run upstairs to their rooms; the maids and boxes follow.

Miss Max cowers over the little bit of fire that smoulders in the grate of the large room. Miss Vernon is looking from the window to the lights of the Town Hall over the way, and up and down the High Street, in a glow of excitement, which, to a town young lady, after a season or two, would have been incom-prehensible and amusing.

Maud touched the bell, saying:

'We must see Mr. Lomax.'

The host of the Old Hall appears forthwith, in answer to the summons of his Roydon guests.

'Mr. Lomax,' says Maud, as soon as he appears at the stair-head, 'you must give me an order for Miss Medwyn and her maid to go to the gallery of the Town Hall. She wishes to see how the room looks.'

Mr. Lomax makes his bow, and in the lobby writes the order, and gives it to Miss Vernon's maid.

A few minutes later Jones was spreading, with light and care-ful fingers, upon the wide coverlet of the bed, the dress which had arrived only that morning from London.

In very marked contrast with this and the splendours which Jones was preparing, including the diamond stars which were to flash from her dark brown hair, and were now strewn on the dressing-table, was the present costume of pretty Miss Vernon.

Before the glass she stood in the identical dark serge dress and little black hat, and the very boots and gloves which she wore at Cardyllion. The beautiful face that looks out of the glass smiles darkly in hers.

'Come, dear Max, here is the order. It is only a step across the street.'

Jones and Maximilla's maid were fussing over gloves and satin boots, and fifty things in the dressing-room.

'Didn't you say a quarter-past nine in the gallery of the Town Hall?' said Maud, looking still at her own pretty face in the glass.

'Yes, dear; and mind, Maud, this is the very last piece of masquerading I'll ever be led into; I don't care how you coax and flatter me. What an old fool I have been!'

With this protest, Miss Max shook her head with a smile, and lifting her hands she said:

'With this act I take leave of my follies for ever, remember. I really don't know how it is you make such a fool of me, whenever you please; I don't understand how you have got such an unaccountable influence; I only know that there doesn't exist a person on earth for whom I would have perpetrated so many absurdities, and told so many fibs, and I say, once for all, that this is the very last time I'll ever be a Jack-pudding for anyone, while I live.'

Miss Maud was before the cheval-glass, so Maximilla had to betake herself to a mirror of more moderate dimensions, before which she made a few slight adjustments of her staid brown silk, and her bonnet, and her velvet cloak, and then turning to Maud, she exclaimed:

'Oh, my dear, are you really coming in that serge? You are such a figure.'

'Now come, you say this is to be the last appearance of Cinderella in her work-a-day costume, and you must not interfere. You shall change all with a touch of your wand when the hour comes. But, in the meantime, I'm to be as shabby and threadbare as I please. Come, it's ten minutes past nine; I should like to be in the gallery before he comes. You told him not to be there a moment before the hour?'

'To be sure I did, poor fellow; and I don't know which, he or I, is the greater fool.'

With these words Maximilla Medwyn led the way down the broad staircase, and the two ladies, side by side, tripped swiftly

across the village street.   Miss Max handed her order from Mr.
Lomax to the woman who already kept guard at the door,
through which they reached the flight of narrow stairs.

They mounted quickly, and entered the gallery.   At the
opposite end of this really handsome room is a corresponding
gallery allotted to the musicians, half a dozen of whom were
already on the benches, in high chat, pulling about their music,
and uncasing their instruments.   A quart pot, from the Old
Hall, and a frothy tumbler stood in the ledge, showing that they
were already disposed to make merry.   The gas candelabra were
but imperfectly lighted ; workmen were walking up and down
the long room, with light tread, in tenderness to the waxed
floor, completing arrangements, while their employers bawled
their orders from one end of the room to the other ; one steward
was already present, garrulous and fussy, whom Maud, with
some alarm, recognised as young Mr. Hexton, of Hexton Hall.
Devoutly she hoped he might not take it into his head to visit
the galleries.

They were quite to themselves, she and Maximilla, except for
a little knot of Wymering womankind, who were leaning over
at the other end of the gallery, far too much engrossed by their
own conversation to take any notice of them.

As the moment approached, the question, ' Will he come ?
will he come ?' was repeating itself strangely at Maud's heart.
The noise in the lower part of the building had subsided, having
moved away to the refreshment and cloak-rooms, from which its
hum was but faintly heard ; and the confidential murmur of
the party at the other end of the gallery, who were discussing
dresses, which they have, no doubt, been making for this great
occasion, was rather reassuring.

' I think I'm fast,' said Miss Max, holding her watch to her
ear.   ' I wish we had not told him not to come before the time ,
we should have found him waiting.'

At that moment the bells from the old church steeple,
scarcely a hundred yards away, chimed the quarter, and, like a
spirit evoked by the summons, Mr. Marston opened the door of
the gallery and came in.

Smiling, to cover his real agitation, he came quickly to Miss
Max, who rose with a very kind alacrity to greet him.

' Was ever mortal more punctual ?   It is quite a virtue nowadays, being in time to meet a friend,' she said approvingly, as she
gave him her hand.

'It is only too easy not to be late,' he said, with glowing eyes and a smile, extending his hand in turn to the young lady in the dark serge ; 'the difficulty is not to be too soon.'

He came next Miss Maud, and seating himself beside her, took her hand again very gently, and said, very low, looking in her eyes, 'It is so like a dream.'

CHAPTER XXXVI.

A LEGEND.

'WHAT a beautiful clear evening it is,' says Miss Max, doing her best to find a topic. 'The stars look as brilliant almost as they do in a winter's frost. You have come a long way, Mr. Marston, I dare say.'

'Coming here, it seemed nothing,' he says, with a look at the young lady.

'It was a very fine night also when we took leave after our little tea-party at Cardyllion, do you remember ?'

'I do remember,' he said very gently.

'You'll turn up at the ball, of course ?' says Miss Max.

'That depends on who are going,' he answers. 'Is there the least chance of your being there ?'

'Who ? *I* ?' with a little laugh, says Miss Maud, to whom, nearly in a whisper, the question had been addressed.

To his ear there was something sad in that laugh ; he was sorry he had asked, for he might easily have known what the answer would be.

'I think that was a cruel question,' she continued, 'that is, if you remembered what I said when we last spoke about this ball.'

'I remember every syllable you spoke, not only about this ball,' he answers, 'but about everything else we talked of. I ought not to have asked, perhaps, but changes, you know, are perpetually occurring, and you, I think, forget how very long it is since I last saw you.'

'The interval has brought no change for me—no good change, I mean,' she answered. 'I shall be rather busy to-night and tired enough in the morning, I dare say. My gay Cousin Maximilla is going—or coming, shall I say, as we are here, to the ball with a young lady whose dress I have seen.' And here Miss Maud laughed very merrily. 'And I shall have, I think, to help her maid to put it on her.'

'Maud, will you be quiet,' said the old lady, very much vexed. 'I—I—well, it is very disagreeable—and see! you have made me drop my locket. Would you mind, Mr. Marston, trying if you can see it?'

He was already in search of it.

'It vexes her by telling it; but it is quite true,' whispered Maud. 'I must see that young lady's maid in ten minutes.'

'You don't mean to say you are going so soon?' exclaims Mr. Marston.

'I must—you know.'

'Know what?' said Miss Max, thus appealed to.

'I must leave this in about ten minutes,' said Maud.

'Well, I believe you must; and so must I, for that matter. And, Mr. Marston, your sister is to be at the ball, she is coming with the Tinterns; of course you will look in? And I really want to introduce you to a very particular friend, and you must look in; if you don't, I give you my word, I'll never answer a note of yours again as long as I live.'

'Under that threat, I shall certainly turn up. What a very pretty locket!' said he, presenting it to its owner. 'And that little bit of work, the rose in rubies, and the key in yellow topaz, the Rose and the Key, that is the device of the Vernons.'

'Yes,' said Miss Max, 'a very dear friend gave it to me.'

'I was in hopes you wore it as your own,' he said; 'it would have given me a right to claim a cousinship.'

'Well, I am a cousin,' she said, and added, with a smile, 'but not near enough to adopt their quarrels.'

'I should be very ungrateful if I did not acknowledge that.'

'But tell me—I have a very particular reason for asking—have you really a right to bear the Rose and the Key?' urged Maximilla.

'It is quite true,' he answered, smiling. 'One of our family, a lady named Rhoda Marston, married a Vernon five hundred years ago, at least, the College of Heralds, while there was such a thing, used to tell the story; and we intermarried after, and that gave us a right to quarter the Rose and the Key. In our old shield it is often quartered. I think it such a pretty device. I wonder why our people gave it up.'

' I'm a very bad herald ; I did not know there had ever been such a cousinship,' said Miss Max.

' Oh yes, I recollect hearing the paper read when I was a boy. It is more than a hundred years old, and it is said that our name was originally Vernon, but that we took the name of Marston from the place granted to our ancestor by the Conqueror. And that a Marston, Sir Guy Marston, it said, I think, was in love with a lady called the Lady Rhoda Vernon.'

' A Marston in love with a Vernon!' exclaimed Miss Max. ' That's not very likely to be repeated in modern history. The two houses don't hit it off nowadays quite so well.'

' A long time ago, of course. The lady, from her name, was called the Rose, the Rose of Wyke it is in the legend. In one of their raids the lady was carried off by the lances of the Earl of Northumberland, and imprisoned, and held to ransom, in one of his many castles; but in which Sir Guy could not learn. But the lady, I'll not undertake to say whether she could write or not, contrived from her place of captivity to send him a rose, which he took as the emblem of *his* rose ; and learning from what castle it was sent, he raised his hand to the wall, and taking down his battle-axe, he said, " Behold the key of Percy's Keep," and so, the story says, he undertook the adventure, and won and wed the lady, and hence came the device of the Rose and the Key.'

' Then there were Vernons on both sides, and you are a Vernon,' said the young lady, looking over the rail of the gallery into the great room.

' My ancestors have borne the name of Marston for five hundred years, but our real name is Vernon.'

' The moral of that legend is,' she continued, ' that every one is ready to help a great lady.'

' That every one is ready to serve a beautiful and brilliant lady, rather ; the ideal of the knight-errant is simply that of the gentleman a little in extravagance.'

' So I think. I fancy it has been always the same. The great have the lion's share of charity, as well as every other good thing,' said Maud carelessly.

' Where will you be when the ball commences ?' he inquired, with a hope that he might have divined the cause of those looks. ' Here?'

' Certainly not. Oh no !'

'And, surely—I have so much to say. It is two months since I saw you, and you can't think how I have longed for this little meeting; and lived, ever since, upon the hope of it. You can't think of reducing it, after all, to a few minutes?'

Miss Max understood, though she did not hear the terms of it, this ardent murmur close to Maud's pretty ear, and she said, good-naturedly:

'I have not had time yet to read old Heyrick's letter, and I really must finish it, Mr. Marston. I know you'll not mind me for a moment.'

And this spacious document, which she luckily had about her, Miss Medwyn unfolded, and proceeded to peruse, with her glasses to her eyes, greatly to the relief of Mr. Marston.

'I have ever so much to say, and I've been looking forward to this chance of telling you a great deal—everything; and—may I say it? yes, I do say it—I thought you did not seem so friendly as our old acquaintance might have warranted. You were cold and indifferent—I am sure it is all right; but, oh! if you knew how it pained me—as if you did not care ever so little to see your old Cardyllion friend again. And I, who have never thought of any one but you, all that time. Not one moment of solitude ever since in which you've not been before me. And—oh, Heaven!—if you knew how it tortures me, thinking of the cruel injustice of fortune that condemns you to a life of so much trouble and anxiety, and how I have longed to tell you how I honour you, how, if I dare speak it, I adore you, and tell you all; how every day I long to lay myself and all my hopes at your feet. But you will never like me; you will never care for me. It never yet was the way to be loved, to love too madly.'

'What am I to say to all this? Who am I? You may know something of Miss Medwyn, my cousin Maximilla, but of me you can know nothing. There are inequalities everywhere,' she said with agitation; 'I have often wished that fortune had placed me exactly where she is. But good people tell us that whatever is is best, and now you must promise me this—you must, if our acquaintance is to go on—that you will not talk to me so wildly any more. Why can't we be very good friends, and grow better acquainted, and come, at last, to know one another? Why should you try to force me to say good-bye, and to lose an acquaintance—I, who have so few? I think that is utterly selfish.'

Her cheeks were flushed with a beautiful colour, and there was an angry fire in her vexed eyes as she said this.

'I must go away in a few minutes, but I shall be back again somewhere about this room to-night, and you will have little difficulty in finding me again to say good-bye. Miss Max, Maximilla Medwyn, my cousin here, is bent on introducing you to her kinswoman, Miss Vernon. She is to be at the ball to-night.'

'What Miss Vernon is that?'

'She is the daughter of Lady Vernon, of Roydon Hall.'

'I know,' he said, 'and I don't think Miss Vernon is very likely to encourage that. Lady Vernon and my father have not been on particularly friendly terms, and if she has used the very decided language I have been told, I don't think any one of that family would care to know a person bearing my name, and certainly the honour of being presented, under all circumstances, I should rather shrink from, if Miss Max will kindly let me off.'

Mr. Marston said this, not that he cared very much whether the introduction were essayed or not, but that he was, in a sort, pained to think that Maud was humiliated by the contrast of Miss Vernon's brilliant fortunes, and from this obscure point of observation, should look down on the scene with wounded pride and a sad heart.

'When Cousin Max takes a fancy to do a thing, like me, she is not easily put off. As for me, I feel sad to-night; I feel as if I were parting with an old friend and a quiet life. I am half sorry I came here. I shall go now.'

She pressed Miss Max's arm lightly as she spoke, and that lady, lowering her letter, looked rather sharply round on her, a little vexed.

If she had spoken exactly what was in her mind she would have said: 'I wish you would try to know your own mind. I've been at the trouble, pretending to read this old letter that I know by heart, to contrive a *tête-à-tête* for you, and simply for the whimsical pleasure of teasing Mr. Marston, you spoil it.'

What she did say was:

'What is it, dear? I wish you would allow me to read my letter.'

'It is time to go. *I* must, at least,' says Maud.

'Well, go you shall,' says the old lady, crumpling up her letter, and standing erect, with her head a little high. 'There's nothing to delay me a moment.'

And relenting a little, she added :

'Mr. Marston, would you mind seeing me across the street? We are going to the Old Hall Inn, exactly opposite.'

You may suppose that Mr. Marston was very much at her service.

'Shall I be sure to find you?' he murmurs, very earnestly, to Maud, as they turn to go.

'I think so,' she says. 'Now, you must take care of my cousin.'

The young lady goes down, and crosses the street at the other side of Miss Max, and seeing her maid about to mount the staircase of the inn, she joins her, passes her by with a word, and runs up the stairs without once turning her pretty head to look back on her friends in the hall.

Maximilla was vexed for her friend, Mr. Marston.

'I did not say, in my answer, because it embarrasses me, sometimes, trying to write what I feel, how very nice I thought your letter—how particularly nice !'

'Oh, Miss Medwyn, do you think she will ever like me ?'

'I only know she ought, Mr. Marston ; but, as you see, she is an odd girl. One thing I assure you, you have a very fast friend in me, and so you ought, and mind you don't fail me. You must come to the ball, for I want to introduce you to the only person living who, I think, has an influence with her. I shall expect you at about a quarter to eleven. I shall be sure to be there about then, and so shall my friend. Good-bye for a very short time.'

And without giving him time to answer, and with a very kind smile, she nodded, and ran up the broad stairs, and disappeared.

CHAPTER XXXVII.

THE BALL.

A BALL, a meeting, a review, a crowd, said in one word, presented to the mind as a unity, regarded truly, is, of course, nothing of the sort.

Consider a ball. Each man and woman there is, as before, a separate microcosm, with distinct aims, thoughts, history, and secrets. The very dishes in the supper-room are individuals,

and every separate morsel they contain. Every plate and wine-
glass there has had its separate hour of birth, its distinct adventures, and will have its particular hour of dissolution, and
consignment to the dust-pit. This ball at Wymering we cannot
treat like a plum-pudding, 'in globo.' I must take its bits apart,
and tell you what two or three people were doing in it.

Mr. Marston loitered a little in the cloak-room, he rambled
through the building into the refreshment and waiting rooms,
wherever he thought it possible the beautiful girl who alone
gave this trumpery scene its magical interest, might be waiting
to see Miss Max again.

He was a little late, and a little dispirited. He began to fear
horribly that she might not appear again that night.

What a bore it was, his having in such a mood to look out
Miss Max among the chaperons, and to be introduced to some
insupportable person, girl or matron, he forgot which.

Here and there, as he makes his way up the room, a friendly
voice among the men recognised Marston, and cries :
'I say ! Is that you, Marston ?' or ' What brings you here,
Marston, old fellow ?'

At length he catches a glimpse of Miss Medwyn, in high chat
with his sister ; and she is hidden again, as he slowly gets up
through the people ; the band is braying and thundering now
obstreperously over their heads from the gallery, and the
stewards clearing a space for the dancers.

And now, again, he sees Miss Medwyn, much nearer, and she
advances a step or two with her cheery smile to greet him. She
says something pleasant to him, smiling and nodding toward his
sister, Lady Mardykes, who is busy at that moment talking to
old Lord Fondlebury ; Mr. Marston does not hear it, for his attention has been fixed by a figure standing near Miss Medwyn,
the outline of which bears a marked resemblance to the lady he
is thinking of ; her face is turned away ; she is speaking to a
tall, rather handsome young man, with good blue eyes, and light
golden moustache.

Miss Medwyn taps her glove gently, and the lady turns.

She is dressed, I am enabled to tell you, in 'a pale blue tulle,
with a very graceful panier, the whole dress looped and studded
with pale maize roses.' It is the work of the great Madame
Meyer. All these particulars I learn from the county paper.

She has diamond stars in her rich brown hair, diamond earrings, and, being a very great lady, and choosing to wear her

brilliants, a diamond necklace.   These are remarkably large diamonds, and the effect of the whole get up is dazzling, rich, and elegant.

Old Mr. Tintern is a little pleasurably flushed and excited in the consciousness of having, in that room, such unparalleled brilliants under his wing.

She has turned about, at the touch of Miss Max's hand, with a regal flash, and as the old lady introduces Mr. Marston to Miss Vernon, he grows pale, and hesitates :

'I am introducing only a name, you see.   You have known the lady some time,' says Miss Max, smiling very cheerfully.

Maud is looking beautiful as a princess in a fairy-tale ; but in all her splendour more good-natured and somehow more simple than ever.

She was smiling gently, and put out her hand a little, as it seemed, almost timidly.

He took it, and said something suitable, I suppose.   Perhaps it seemed a little cold and constrained, contrasted, at least, with his talk at other times—happier times (were they ?)—when he suspected nothing of her great name and fortunes.

Has he been trifled with ?   Has he been fooled ?   How do these ladies regard him ?

These questions were quieted.   Neither was capable of enjoying his strange mortification.   Whatever had passed was in good faith.   But however good-natured the masquerading, still the truth, now revealed, broke up and dissipated, with an indescribable shock, his more Quixotic, but in many respects happier, estimate of their relations.

What had become of his unavowed confidence in his rank and reversions ?   Here was no longer the poor and beautiful idol of a half-compassionating love.   The Gretchen of his romance, who made the homely old house of Plas Ylwd and all its surroundings so tenderly beautiful for ever, is dead and gone ; and in her stead—

> 'In Belmont is a lady richly left,
>   And she is fair ;
> Nor is the wide world ignorant of her worth ;
> For the four winds blow in from every coast,
> Renowned suitors, and her sunny locks
> Hang on her temples like a golden fleece,
> Which makes her seat of Belmont Colcho's strand,
> And many Jasons come in quest of her.'

Here was, in fortune absolutely, and in pure patrician blood nearly, the highest lady in England. Despair was stealing over his once sunny prospects. He began, in an expressive phrase, to feel very small. Being proud and sensitive, he was not only a little stunned, but wounded.

Something, however, must be said and proposed. It would not do to stand there absolutely dumb.

Mr. Marston asks Miss Vernon to dance. She has number one. Has she kept it for him? There is not a moment to lose. It is a quadrille, as is the inflexible practice at public balls.

They take their places in a set just forming, with Lady Helen de Flambeaux and Captain Vivian *vis-à-vis*. Mr. Marston recognises the tall young man with azure eyes and yellow moustache, to whom Miss Vernon has been talking.

The music is roaring over their heads, so that people cannot in the least overhear their neighbours' talk.

'You did not half like, to-night, when my cousin Maximilla proposed it, the idea of being introduced to Miss Vernon,' says that young lady. 'Perhaps the feud of Marston and Vernon is more a matter of conscience than I supposed, and that I have not been as loyal as I ought to the vendetta.'

'I don't know what to answer to that cruel conjecture,' he replies, smiling. 'I am very bad at finding an answer where I am in earnest;' but before he can get further their *vis-à-vis* are in motion, and away they sail, and cross over and return, and set, and not until that figure is over, and the side couples in action, can they begin to talk again.

'I have been very much surprised this evening,' he says.

'And shocked,' she adds.

'No, Miss Vernon; amazed a little—dazzled.'

'It is so odd a sensation, being ceremoniously introduced to an old friend,' she says.

'It is, somehow, so like losing an old friend and finding only an acquaintance in exchange,' he answers; 'when first impressions, very much cherished, are proved to be illusions, and circumstances change so entirely, everything becomes uncertain, and one grows melancholy—it is enough to make one suspicious.'

'That is very tragical,' laughs the young lady.

'Happy are those, say I, for whom life is a holiday, and the world a toy—I mean the people who have a good deal of

satire and very little compassion, who are not unkind, but very cold, who enjoy the comedy of life, and can even smile at its tragedy; they can afford to laugh when others suffer,' says Mr. Marston. 'It can be of no consequence to you, Miss Vernon, how the strange delusion I have—I don't deny it—in a measure practised on myself affects me.'

'Well, I hope it won't embitter you for ever, Mr. Marston; it is a comfort, at all events, it has not made you give up dancing.'

At this interesting moment Mr. Marston was obliged to advance and retreat, *chassé* to the right and to the left, cross over, and all the rest; and when he had set to his partner, and turned that splendid lady about, it devolved on her to execute the same manœuvres with handsome Captain Vivian for *vis-à-vis*.

The next subject was not so interesting.

'I don't think our Wymering friends have done all they might for the floor,' she remarks.

To which he makes suitable answer, and artfully endeavours to lead back the conversation into more interesting channels.

But Miss Vernon holds him fast during the remainder of the quadrille to the decorations, the music, the room, and the other details, and he begins to think it is all over with him, and with his hopes, and that he has had his last serious talk with Miss Vernon.

'When this is over,' he thinks, 'she will ask me to take her back to the Tinterns, and leave her again with Miss Max, and so she will take a friendly leave, and I shall have a theme to think of for the rest of my life.'

But he was mistaken. Miss Vernon, when the dance was over, said:

'Would you mind, Mr. Marston, taking me to the tea-room? I have not had any yet.'

Very happy this little reprieve made him.

How the light touch of her hand upon his arm thrilled him as he led her in.

'What dances can you give me? Surely you can give me one?' he asks imploringly, as they get along.

'I can give you a great many,' says the young lady gently; 'but I don't mean to give you one more.'

Mr. Marston stared.

'You must not think me very unkind. I might have said I

have not one to give—not one—earlier than number twelve, and long before that we shall be on our way home to Roydon. But I mean to be very honest to-night; and if we can find a quiet place at the table in the tea-room, we can talk a little there.'

'I half dread that little talk, Miss Vernon. Some people have more power of inflicting pain than they perhaps suspect. I scarcely think that can be your case; but—don't—I think I may ask that; don't, I entreat, say anything that may give me very great pain to-night. Give me an opportunity of speaking first. I hope that is not a very unreasonable petition.'

He spoke very low and gently, but very earnestly.

'What a crowd!' says Miss Vernon, as if she had not heard a word.

As they slowly make their way many an admiring and many an envious eye is directed on that princess, and many a curious one upon the handsome young gentleman on whose arm her hand is lightly placed. She continues: 'This is the best ball we have had at Wymering for two years. It is my third. I begin to feel very old.'

'Eh! Hallo! Hi! How d'ye do, Miss Vernon?' bawls old Sir John Martingale, of Whistlewhips, short and square, pulling up and blocking half the passage, with his wife on one arm and his elderly daughter, Arabella, on the other, with both of whom Miss Vernon has to exchange greetings. 'You're not turning your back on the dancers so soon, hey?'

His shrewd little grey eyes that lighted up his mulberry-coloured features were scrutinizing Mr. Marston with very little disguise.

'Oh, tea is it? And right good tea it is, I can tell you. Old Mother Vaneil in the High Street here, the confectioner, is doing the refreshments this time. And, by the law! I have just been telling my old woman, Lady Martingale, I han't got so good a cup o' tea this twel'month.'

'Don't mind him, Miss Vernon. We treat him a great deal too well, and he's always grumbling,' interposes Lady Martingale, 'half joke, and whole earnest,' as the good old phrase is.

Here, Miss Martingale, who had been secretly squeezing and plucking at his arm, having secured half an hour before an eligible old bachelor, Mr. Plimby, of Cowslip Meads, for 'number two,' prevails, and Sir John, with a jocular 'I won't stand no more of your rot-gut for breakfast, mind ye, my lady, and a wink at Miss Vernon, in which Mr. Marston, though a stranger, is included, pulls his women through, as he phrases it, with a boisterous chuckle, interrupted, alas! soon by as boisterous a fit of coughing.

By this time Mr. Marston has led Miss Vernon to the long tea-table, that, like a counter, traverses one end of the tea-room, and at an unfrequented part of this they take their stand, and he calls for a cup of tea for the young lady.

CHAPTER XXXVIII.

A MAN WITH A SQUARE BLACK BEARD.

THERE are few loiterers left in the room; the distant roar of the band accounts for this desertion. The damsel who administers tea is stricken in years, thin, and anxious with the cares of boiling kettles behind the scenes, and many teapots, and plum and sponge cakes, and soup and ices in immediate perspective. I shouldn't wonder if she was the identical 'Mary Vaneil, confectioner,' who, as we have heard, has contracted with the committee for 'the supply of tea, ices, soup, and supper,' for this momentous ball. At all events, just now she has not a thought for other people's business, and is the most convenient possible attendant upon two people who have anything of the slightest interest to say to one another.

'Yes, it is a very nice tea,' says the young lady; 'and, I forgot, I promised this dance to Mr. Dacre. I suppose I'm in disgrace, but I can't help it.' She glances up at the cornice, and thinks for a moment. 'I want you, Mr. Marston,' she says, more gravely—and her diamonds make a great flash as she lowers her head, 'to remember this: that if we are to continue to be good friends, you must never be offended at anything I do, or ever ask the meaning of it.'

Marston laughed. It was a pained laugh, she thought.

'You can't suppose me so unreasonable,' he says. 'I know, perfectly, I have not the least right to ask a question, far less to be offended. In fact, you can hardly feel, more than I do, how very little claim an acquaintance founded in so much ignorance and misapprehension can give me to more than, perhaps, a very slight recognition.'

'Well, I don't quite agree with you, Mr. Marston; I think on the contrary, that I know you a great deal better than I possibly could under other circumstances, in so short a time; and I think we ought to be better friends—I think we are better friends—for that very reason.'

That was the sweetest music he ever heard in his life, and he could not answer immediately. It seemed to him, as she spoke, that her colour was a little heightened, and, for a moment, a strange soft fire in her eyes. But was this real, or only one of those illusions which, before the gaze of devout enthusiasts, have, in a moment of ecstasy, lighted up sad portraits with smiles, or crossed their beauty with a shade of sorrow?

The next moment she looked just as usual.

'I saw my sister for a few minutes in the cloak-room,' he says suddenly, 'and she told me that she had asked Miss Vernon to her house in Warwickshire. It did not interest me, for I little knew, then, who Miss Vernon really was. Do you think you will go to her?'

'I hope I shall—that is, if I can, I certainly will. Miss Medwyn is going, I believe, and I could go with her; but I don't know yet what mamma will say to it; and mamma is the only person living who can prevent my doing exactly what I please.'

'But Lady Vernon, I hope, won't dream of preventing it?' he says, very anxiously.

'Mamma decides for herself in all things, and acts very strictly according to her ideas of duty, and sometimes thinks things, that appear to me of no importance whatever, very important indeed; and you know that there has been some—something very like a quarrel—and Lord Warhampton doesn't like her, and I'm afraid mamma doesn't like him—and I really don't know whether that might not make a difficulty in her allowing me to go to Lady Mardykes'; but a few days will decide.'

'God grant it may be favourably!' murmurs the young man vehemently.

'And you have asked me to say nothing to-night that could give you pain,' says the young lady, referring to a speech that she had not before noticed, 'and I, in return, exact the same promise from you. You must say nothing that may make us part worse friends than we met.'

'And I have so much to tell you, that is, ever so much to say; and, oh! how I hope you will not refuse my sister's invitation.'

'I like her so very much,' says the young lady. 'And this dance will soon be over. You must take me now to Miss Medwyn—she is with the Tinterns—and remember I have a reason for everything I do, although you may not understand it. You are not to speak to me again to-night when you have taken me back to the Tinterns.'

'Then,' says Mr. Marston, with a look of sadness, almost reproach, 'am I to take my leave in something worse than uncertainty?'

'Uncertainty?' with a half-angry, half startled glance, the girl repeats, but in the moment that follows she places her fingers lightly on his arm, and says: 'Shall we come? I'm afraid the passage will soon be crowded. Let us come before the dance is over.'

As they passed together toward the great room where the dancers, gentle and simple, townsfolk and rural, skilled and clumsy, were all whisking and whirling their best to the inspiring thunder of the band, she repeats:

'You understand? You are not to speak to me, or look at me, or come near where I am again to-night—not in the cloak-room, not anywhere—and you must leave me the moment you place me beside my cousin Maximilla. I should not like you to think me capricious or silly,' she added, he fancied a little sadly. 'So, as a proof of your friendship, I ask you to believe that I have good reasons for what I ask. No, not this door; let us come in by the other. Good-night,' she said, as they reached Miss Medwyn's side.

That lady stood a little behind Mr. and Mrs. Tintern and Lady Mardykes, and the door by which they entered brought Miss Vernon beside her cousin without passing before the other figures in this group.

'Good-night,' she repeated, a little hurriedly.

'God bless you,' he said, very low, holding in his the hand she had given him, longer than he ever had before, 'and come what may, I will see you very soon again.'

'Well, dear, you have been to the tea-room?' says Miss Max, greeting her young cousin with a smile, 'and where is Mr.— wasn't it Mr. Marston who took you?'

' Yes, I think he's gone,' says the young lady.

Miss Max was looking round to find him, but he had left by the door through which they had just entered.

' He has vanished,' she continued, ' but of course he'll turn up.'

' How extremely pretty Lady Mardykes is looking to-night,' says Maud to Maximilla, who was standing beside her.

' I was just going to say so when you anticipated me,' replies Miss Max.

' How very young she looks. What a pity she won't dance,' Maud suggests.

' I think so, and I don't—no, no—it is a good many years since her husband died. Let me see ; how many ? Yes, she was thirty-two then. Yes, my dear, she's forty at least, and I shan't press her to dance after that. But to look at her now you would not suppose her more than three-and-thirty.'

She seems so happy as she talks to the people who recognise her ; she looks so gracious. There is such a light of gaiety, good-nature, and candour in her face that it is quite a pleasure to look at her.

' Who is that man with the black beard, and strange eyes, and solemn, pale face, who is looking towards Lady Mardykes?' asks Maud, after a silence of a minute or two.

' I don't know ; I may have seen him ; rather a remarkable face ; clever, I think,' answers Miss Max ; ' she knows every one that is worth knowing. Her house is quite delightful. Warhampton having held office so often, and only awaiting the next division, they say, to be Minister again, she knows all the clever people of her party, in both Houses, and the foreign Ministers, and all the people distinguished for talent. I do so hope Barbara will let you go to her.'

But we have not yet done with that remarkable-looking man, pale, with a statuesque regularity of feature, with long, smooth, coal-black hair, and a black, square-cut beard, all the life of whose face seems concentrated in his extraordinary eyes. He is slowly and methodically, through the crowd, approaching Lady Mardykes. Those eyes of his are oddly set, intensely cold and hard, and their colour a sort of grey-green, with very con-tracted pupils.

At length this man, all in black, with a black waistcoat, cut very low, so as to show a great deal of the snowy shirt that covers his deep broad chest, stands, no one any longer interposing, in front a little to her right, and smiles movelessly, with his eyes fixed on her.

She was looking the other way when he came, but when her eyes lighted on that remarkable face she almost started.

She smiled uncomfortably, and flushed a little, and extended her hand, approaching a step, you would have said, with a little tremor.

The pallid smile continued, and he took her hand.

'You did not expect to see me here?' he said softly, in his resonant bass tones, with a slight foreign accent.

'No, indeed,' she replied, very low.　'It is a long time since we last met.'

'Eight years, Lady Mardykes,' he makes answer.　'Do you find the room too hot?　Perhaps you will permit me to get you an ice?'

Lady Mardykes seems a little embarrassed, as if she would have wished this acquaintance, friend, whatever he is, a hundred miles away at that moment.

'I think I should prefer, if you don't mind, going to the room where the ices are, and taking it there.'

In a moment more her fingers were laid lightly on the arm which he proffered, and they disappeared in the crowd.

A few minutes later she had returned, and was sitting on one of the sofas which were placed along the walls of the dancing-room, with this marble-featured, black-haired man beside her, now very grave, conversing, as it seemed, earnestly.

The grave man with the black beard now made his bow and smile, and turned away and disappeared in the crowd, and before Maud had time to ask Lady Mardykes who he was, Captain Vivian appeared to claim number three, promised to him.

Marston did not dance this, nor the next, and he saw Miss Vernon give both dances to the handsome young man with blue eyes and golden moustache, whom he had seen in conversation with her at the beginning of the evening.

'Fine girl, Miss Vernon, Miss Vernon of Roydon, you know; that's she with the diamonds, and devilish good diamonds they are,' said Marston's schoolfellow, Tom Tewkesbury, who, after an absence of five years, was just what he always was, only a little fonder of his bottle, 'by Jove she is; positively lovely, by Jove!　Don't you think so?　I do.　I wonder who that fellow is she's dancing with—not a bad-looking fellow. I say, Marston,

I wonder whether a fellow would have a chance of getting a
dance from her? By Jove! They are going it. Do you think
it's a case? I've a great mind to go and try. She's with the
Tinterns. Shall I? What do you say?'

'You had better be quick. She's not likely to remain long
standing,' said Marston, who was not sorry, in his present mood,
to lose his agreeable conversation.

Marston shifted his point of observation to see more distinctly
how his friend Tewkesbury fared.

That gentleman had made his way by this time to Mr.
Tintern.

'Here I am—come to ask a favour,' said Tewkesbury, fiddling
with a button of Mr. Tintern's coat, and looking persuasively in
his face. 'I want Miss Vernon to give me a dance, and you
must introduce me. Do.'

Tewkesbury has more than twelve thousand a year, represents
an old county family, is a popular man, and not the kind of
fellow to excite a romance. Miss Vernon being, as he thinks,
a fastidious young lady, rather, he is just the person whom Mr.
Tintern would have chosen to dance with the heiress of Roydon.
But he says, with a very amused chuckle:

'I'll introduce you with pleasure. Certainly, if you wish
it; but I've just done the same thing for Lord Hawkshawe,
and she had not a dance. However, I'll introduce you with
pleasure.'

Perhaps Tom Tewkesbury thought that he could afford in
this game to give Lord Hawkshawe, who was fifty, and had a
couple of thousand a year less than he, some points, and was not
very much daunted by his failure.

Did he succeed? Alas! no. She was again carried off by
the victorious Captain Vivian; and she and he beheld Mr. Marston, who had seen this early enough to secure Miss Chevron,
figuring in the next set to theirs. There he was chasséeing, for
it was a quadrille, and setting to that young lady, and turning
her about, looking the while black as thunder.

His eyes stole, in spite of his resolution, now and then, in the
direction of Miss Vernon. Once he thought their eyes met; but
he could not be certain, for hers betrayed not the slightest sign
of consciousness, and no more shrank or turned aside than the
gleam of her diamonds.

And now, the dance ended, Miss Vernon returned to the
Tinterns, and said a word to Miss Max, and Captain Vivian led

her away to the refreshment-room, where people were sipping soup or eating ices.

There they loiter. The next dance has begun. She does not intend to dance it. She has refused it to half a dozen distinguished competitors. Every one is inquiring who that fellow with the yellow moustache is, and no one seems to know exactly. He is by no means popular among the aspiring youth of Wymering.

The dance is nearly over by the time they return to Miss Medwyn, and the shadow of Mrs. Tintern's protection.

The youth of the county, with here and there a sprinkling of middle age, are dancing number seven, and are pretty well on in it, when Miss Vernon resolves to take wing, and drive home to Roydon under the care of Maximilla Medwyn.

She has taken leave of the Tinterns and Lady Mardykes. The devoted Captain Vivian attends to put on her cloak and sees her into her carriage, with a last word, and a smile, and a goodnight to Miss Max.

Miss Max yawns, and leans back. Miss Vernon does not yawn, but she looks tired, and leans back also, no longer smiling, listlessly in her corner.

'Home,' says the young lady to the footman at the window.

With the high-blooded trotters of Roydon, the carriage rolls swiftly through the High Street, and in a few minutes more is gliding through old hedge-rows in the soft moonlight, among misty meadows and silent farm-steads.

CHAPTER XXXIX.

THOUGH SOME PEOPLE GO HOME, THE BALL GOES ON.

FOR a time neither lady seemed disposed to talk.

Maud's ruminations were exciting and unsatisfactory. She had acted a good deal from impulse, and, as she now, perhaps, secretly thought, neither very wisely nor very kindly. She expected a lecture from Maximilla. She would have preferred combat to her own solitary self-upbraidings. At all events, she quickly grew weary of her reflections, and, turning her eyes to her silent companion in the shadow of her own corner, she said;

'I quite forgot to ask Lady Mardykes who her solemn friend, with the black square beard, is. Did you?'

'Yes—if you mean did I forget; at least, I don't think I had an opportunity. But, to tell you the truth,' here Miss Max yawned, 'I don't much care. He looks like a foreigner.'

'He has good eyes. There is something quiet and masterly in his air. I saw him afterwards talking to Doctor Malkin.'

'Yes, so did I. I can't endure that man,' exclaimed Miss Max. 'What on earth brings him to a ball, of all places? It might have been wiser if he had stayed at home. I dare say Barbara would have had him to tea if he had looked in, and he would have had the advantage of a *tête-à-tête*,' said Maximilla.

'The advantage—what do you mean?' asked Maud.

'Why, Mr. Foljambe told us yesterday—you must have been thinking of something else—that your mamma will have in the course of the year, I think it was four medical appointments virtually in her gift, including the supply of medicines to the county jail, which will be given to whatever candidate she supports. And they are altogether worth between eleven and twelve hundred a year, I think he said, and that's the reason why Doctor Malkin is so frequent a visitor just now.'

'I should be very glad,' said Maud.

'I don't care twopence who gets them,' said Maximilla resignedly.

'Did Ethel Tintern dance much to-night?' asked the young lady.

'Not a great deal. I don't think she seemed to care for the ball.'

Here came a silence. And after two or three minutes Miss Max said suddenly:

'It strikes me you have been sowing the wind to-night, my dear.'

'Sowing the wind! How? What have I done?'

'Come, Maud, you know as well as I what you have been doing. You have treated Mr. Marston very ill; and you have prepared, you may be sure, an animated scene at home. I can tell you, Barbara will be extremely angry; and not without very good reason.'

'You mean about Captain Vivian?' said Maud, a little sulkily.

'Of course I mean about Captain Vivian,' replied Miss Max.

'Well, there's no good in talking about it now. It's done, and

I can't help it, and, indeed, I could not have prevented it; and I don't want to talk about it,' said Maud pettishly.

'And what is Mr. Marston to think?'

'What he pleases,' Maud answered. 'You know what mamma thinks of the Marstons. I think my chance of going to Lady Mardykes' would have been pretty well ended if she heard that I gave Mr. Marston a great many dances, and she will know everything about this ball. It was not my fault, Captain Vivian asking for all those dances. I'm very glad he did. I hope people remarked it. I hope mamma will hear of it. If she does she will think of nothing else, I dare say.'

The young lady laughed, and then she sighed.

'Upon my word you are complicating the situation very prettily,' said Miss Max.

'I suppose I am doing everything that is wrong and foolish; yet I believe it is best as it is,' said the young lady. 'I did not want to vex Mr. Marston; and if he has any sense he'll understand perfectly that I did not; and what need I care whether old Lord Hawkshawe, or Mr. Tewkesbury, or Mr. Wylder, or any of the people who intended I should stay all night, dancing with them in that hot room, are pleased or not?'

'Captain Vivian was determined certainly to make the most of his opportunity,' observed Miss Max.

And again the conversation flagged, and Miss Medwyn's active mind was employed upon the problem, and busy in conjecturing Captain Vivian's motive.

'Either he wishes to pique Barbara,' she thought, 'or he means to try his chances of success, in good faith, with Maud. I can quite understand that. But he is not the kind of person Maud would ever like, and I do think she likes Mr. Marston.'

Then again she recalled Captain Vivian's sayings and doings that night at Wymering, to try to discover new lights and hidden meanings, to guide her to a right reading of that little episode.

While these two ladies are driving along the moon-lit road towards Roydon Hall, the festivities of Wymering have lost nothing of their energy.

I shall ask you, therefore, to peep into the ball-room for a few minutes more, where you will find that Captain Vivian has just begged of old Mr. Tintern to introduce him to Miss Tintern. That young lady says to Mr. Tintern hastily:

'Oh, don't please!'

But her papa, not hearing, or, at least, not heeding, does present Captain Vivian, who carries off the young lady on his arm.

'If you don't mind, I should prefer not dancing this time. It is so crowded,' says Miss Tintern.

'I'm so glad,' says he. 'There is a quadrille after this. You must come where we shall be quiet for two or three minutes.'

In the recess outside the ball-room, on the lobby at the head of the great staircase, an old-fashioned sofa is placed.

Skirting the dancers, to this he led her. When she had sat down,

'Ethel,' he said, 'you are very angry—that is to say, very unjust. What have I done ?'

'What have you done ?' she repeats. 'You have placed me in the most miserable situation. How am I to look Maud Vernon in the face again ? What will papa think of me ? Is not concealment enough ? Why should you practise positive deception ? I don't like it. I'm entirely against it. You make me utterly miserable.'

'Now, Ethel, don't be unreasonable. You must not blame me for that which neither you nor I can prevent. When the time comes I'll speak out frankly enough. I could not help coming to Roydon. I could not refuse, without a risk of vexing Mr. Dawe very much, and that, for fifty reasons, would never do. I can't tell you all I've suffered, being so near, and unable to contrive a meeting, with scarcely an opportunity even of writing. Don't suppose that the vexation has been all yours ; I have been positively miserable, and I knew very well all the ridiculous things that were said, and how they must have pained you. A little patience, a little time.'

'I know all that very well, and I have suffered from those strange rumours, and I have suffered to-night. I feel so treacherous and deceitful. I won't be made an accomplice in such things. I hate myself for hesitating to tell Maud how it really is.'

'My dear Ethel, you must not be foolish. Living down here so much in the country, you make too much of trifles. What can it signify, my dancing a few dances, more or less, with Miss Vernon ? Do you fancy she cares about me, or that any one seriously thinks there can be anything more than that she likes my dancing, and that I admire her diamonds ? Why, dancing two or three dances at a ball means absolutely nothing. Everyone knows that. There is nothing in it but this—that people won't guess anything of the real state of things. They won't see anything, for instance, in our quiet little talk here.'

Miss Buffins here passing by, with her hand on Captain Bamme's arm, stops, her cheeks flushed and radiant with her triumphs, and remarks what a jolly ball it is, and how hot the room is, and how every one seems to be enjoying it so much, and so she gabbles on. Captain Bamme, smiling, with his mouth open, and his face hot and shining, is not able to get in a word, facetious or complimentary, and Miss Buffins, as she entertains Miss Tintern, is scanning her dress, and estimating its value in detail, while, more slyly still, she inspects Captain Vivian.

At length, the crowd setting in towards the supper-room in a stronger current, Captain Bamme and his fair charge are hurried away, smiling, towards chickens, tongue, lobster-salad, and those other comforts which the gallant captain loves with a secret, middle-aged affection that quite supersedes the sentimental vanities of earlier years. I think, with all his ostentatious gallantry, just then, the gay deceiver, who is jostling among elbows and shoulders, and bawling to waiters for cold salmon or lobster for this lady with a chivalric self-sacrifice, wishes her all the time, if the truth were known, at the bottom of the Red Sea. But he will return, after he has restored her to her mother, in quiet moments, when people, who know less of life, are busy dancing, and, with a shrewd *gourmandise,* will task the energies of the waiters, and strip chickens of their liver-wings, crunch lobster-salad, plunge into Strasbourg *patés,* drink champagne, and, with shining forehead and reckless enthusiasm, leave to-morrow's headache to take care of itself.

CHAPTER XL.

LADY VERNON GROWS ANXIOUS.

THE morning after the ball Mr. Tintern was prodigiously uncomfortable. He was now, indeed, pretty easy about Lady Vernon's fancied matrimonial designs; but relief at one point is too often accompanied by an acute pressure at another.

Captain Vivian had been audacious, nay, ostentatious, in his devotion to Miss Vernon at the Wymering ball. Whatever his reason, he seemed to wish that people should remark his attentions, and the young lady had certainly shown no unwillingness to permit them.

Next morning, before twelve o'clock, Mr. Tintern was at Roydon Hall, full of the occurrences of the night before.

Mr. Tintern has observed, with satisfaction, that for more than a year his relations with Lady Vernon have been growing in confidence, and even intimacy. Call when he may, Lady Vernon is never denied to him now.

'Her ladyship is in the library, sir!'

'Oh!'

And Mr. Tintern follows the tall footman through the silent, stately rooms, to the door he knows so well.

He is announced, and very graciously received.

'You have come to consult about your projected road, I suppose? And, oddly enough, I had just been looking over the map with Mr. Penrhyn.'

'Well, thanks. Yes, any time, you know, that suits you, Lady Vernon, would do for that; but I happened to be passing this way, and I thought I might as well look in and tell you one or two things that struck me last night at the ball. You'll not be surprised, perhaps, but I was, a good deal: it is so unaccountable, except, indeed, on one supposition. I know how you feel about it, but, certainly, it does confirm my very high ideas, Lady Vernon, of your penetration. Only think, I'm going to tell you what I heard from the man himself! Miss Vernon obtained from old Lomax, the keeper of the Old Hall Inn, you know, an order of admission to the gallery of the Town Hall for Miss Medwyn and her maid. And with this order Miss Medwyn went; and who do you think with her? Not her maid; by no means; no. It was Miss Vernon, and dressed in some old stuff—such a dress, I'm told, I suppose a lady's-maid would not be seen in it; and Miss Medwyn, I'm assured, tried to dissuade her, and they had a little dispute about it. But it would not do, and so Miss Vernon of Roydon carried her point, and presented herself as Miss Medwyn's servant!'

'It is a continuation of the same vein—nothing new. It only shows how persistent it is,' says Lady Vernon, closing her fine eyes with a little frown, and running one finger-tip meditatively to and fro over her finely pencilled black eyebrow.

'Only think,' repeats Mr. Tintern, with a little shrug, lowering his voice eagerly, and expanding his hands like a man making a painful exposition, ' without the slightest temptation, nothing on earth to make it intelligible.'

'I am afraid, Mr. Tintern, it is not very easy to account for all this ; upon any pleasant theory, I mean.'

'I thought it my duty, Lady Vernon, considering the terms of, I may say, confidence to which you have been so good as to admit me, to mention this ; and, also, perhaps another circumstance which excited, I may say, very general observation last night at the ball, and I fancy you would prefer my being quite straight and above-board in giving you my opinion and the result of my observation.'

' Certainly, I shall thank you very much,' said the lady, raising her eyes suddenly, and fixing them upon him with a rather stern expectation.

' Well, I believe it is but right to tell you that your guest, Captain Vernon, devoted himself in, I may say, an extraordinary way to Miss Vernon, your daughter.   Now, I don't know what that young man's position or expectations may be ; but it is of course quite possible he may be in many respects an eligible *parti* for Miss Vernon.   But if he be, perhaps, considering all you have been so good as to tell me, don't you think, a—eh? he ought to be a—a—warned, don't you think ?'

' Captain Vivian,' she answered, with the fire that comes with excitement in each cheek, ' Mr. Dawe tells me, has scarcely four hundred a year, and has no chance of succeeding to anything, unless, indeed, Mr. Dawe should leave him something, which, of course, may never happen.   I need not tell you that nothing could be more amazing than any such pretensions.   Pray let me know why you suppose them possible.'

' The evidence,' replied Mr. Tintern, ' was patent to everyone at Wymering last night.   Nothing could be more marked, and I am bound to say, speaking to you, Lady Vernon, what I should hesitate to say to anyone else, I say he was received as favourably as he could have hoped.   In fact, if he were the greatest muff in England, and he is far from being anything of the kind, he could not have failed to see it, and see it he did.'

Lady Vernon was looking down upon the table, following with her pencil's point the lines of her monogram upon the side of her blotting-book, and continuing to do so with a very black countenance, smiling sourly on the interlacing initials, she said :

'There has been a great deal of duplicity then ; I fancied one evening I did see something, but it seemed quite to have died out by next day, and never was renewed—great duplicity ; it is morbid, it is not an amiable trait, not attractive, but, of course, we must view it with charity.'

'I hope I have done right in telling you, Lady Vernon?' said Mr. Tintern, who was in no haste to see Miss Vernon married, no more, indeed, than Lady Vernon was. ' Of course, you know, we should all be glad, the whole county, I mean, to see her suitably married,' he continued, 'and suitably in her case would, of course, mean splendidly ; and less than that would not, I think, satisfy expectation. But a creature—a—a whipper-snapper like that,' he said, with his head on one side, and his hands expanded, with a mixture of disgust and compassion, 'an adventurer, and I—really for the life of me, I can't see anything to make up for it.'

' People see with different eyes, Mr. Tintern,' she said, looking on the rings that covered the fingers of her finely formed hand ; ' and you saw this yourself ?'

' I saw it, and you may trust my report. I say there is—I don't say a romance—but, possibly, a great deal more than a romance, established in that quarter—and—you know, it would amount to this, that the young lady would be simply sacrificed !'

And Mr. Tintern threw back his arms with his hands open, and a look of wild stupefaction, which plainly conveyed the despair in which such a catastrophe would plunge this loyal county.

' But a ball is a kind of thing,' said Lady Vernon meditatively, 'at which unreal flirtation is always carried on. You may be looking at this in much too serious a light, Mr. Tintern.'

' Oh, pardon me, Lady Vernon. I make every allowance, but this was nothing of the kind. It would be misleading you most unjustifiably if I were to acquiesce in any such supposition.'

' Well, you know, it would be, as you say, utterly untenable and monstrous,' began Lady Vernon. ' And, of course——'

' One moment,' he interrupted, lifting his finger suddenly, as something caught his eye outside the window. ' I beg pardon a thousand times, but—but—yes—there they are !' exclaimed Mr. Tintern.

He had approached the window, and was pointing with his extended hand toward the terrace-walk before the house.

'There, there, there, you see ; it is, upon my life ! Only look. You see, eh ?'

He stepped backward a pace or two a little into the shade.

Lady Vernon watched them darkly as they passed, and what Lady Vernon saw did not please her.

The young lady yielded a flower she had in her fingers to the young gentleman, who placed it in his button-hole over his heart, to which he pressed its stem with an expressive glance at her.

Lady Vernon changed colour a little, and looked down again on the table.

Quite unconscious of being observed at that moment, the young people passed on.

'She has always been perverse and ungovernable, always,' said Lady Vernon, with cold bitterness ; 'and a want of self-restraint induces the violent and hysterical state in which she often is. I leave to other persons the task of explaining her whims and extravagances, her excursion to Cardyllion, and such eccentricities as that of her visit to the gallery last night, dressed as a lady's-maid.'

'And a very humble sort of maid too,' said Mr. Tintern. 'And —what is one to think ? *I* entirely agree with you. What can one say ?'

Lady Vernon's large dark eyes, hollow and strangely tired now, were lowered to the little cluster of seals upon the table, with which the tip of her taper finger played softly. There was the same brilliant flush in each cheek, and an odd slight drawing of her handsome lips—a look like that of a person who witnesses a cruel, but inevitable operation.

Lady Vernon is too proud to betray to Mr. Tintern the least particle of what she really suffers by the smallest voluntary sign.

It is not the belief that forms the desire, but the desire that shapes the belief. Little originates in the head. Nearly all has its inception in the heart. The brain is its slave, and does task-work. That which it is your interest or your wish to believe, you do believe. The thing you desire is the thing you will think. Men not only speak, but actually think well of those with whom they have a community of interest and profit, and evil of those who stand in their way. Government, by party, proceeds upon this ascertained law of humanity. As a rule, the brain does not lead. It is the instrument and the slave of the desire.

There is another occult force, a mechanical power, as it were, always formidably at the service of the devil and the soul. The inclined plane by which the mind glides imperceptibly from perversion into perjury.

I once heard an attorney of great ability and experience remark : ' You may take it as a rule that in every case, if your client says an untruth in support of his own case, when the time comes for filing his affidavit he will also swear it.'

It is the desire that governs the will, and the will the intellect. Let every man keep his heart, then, as he would his house, and beware how he admits a villain to live in it.

Mr. Tintern is a gentleman of sensitive honour and unexceptionable morality. Forty years ago, when duels were still fought, he perforated the Honourable Whiffle Newgate's hat with a pistol-bullet, for daring to call his veracity in question. And did he not proceed criminally against the Radical county paper, simply to gain the opportunity of filing his affidavit, and afterwards of undergoing examination and cross-examination in the witness-box, in vindication of his probity ?

And does not Lady Vernon walk this world a pattern and a reproach to sinners, and a paragon among the godly ? And, alas is not the heart of man deceitful above all things, and desperately wicked ?

Something we can do for ourselves. Not a great deal, but still indispensable. As much as his friend could do for Lazarus. ' Take ye away the stone,' and when that is done, into the sepulchre enters the miraculous influence—actual life and the voice of power, where before was the silence of darkness.

' It is all very painful, Mr. Tintern, miserably painful,' she says faintly, still looking down. And then, with a sigh, she picks up the pretty little cluster of seals, and drops them into their place in the desk, and shuts it down and locks it.

CHAPTER XLI.

LADY VERNON TAKES EVIDENCE.

WHEN Mr. Tintern had taken his departure, with the comfortable feeling that he had done what was right, Lady Vernon sighed deeply.

'Mr. Tintern,' she thought, 'lives in castles of his own building. He is always thinking of poor papa's will, and the reversion of Roydon, and the money in the funds. If he knew all he would be easy enough respecting them. All the better he doesn't. I can't spare him yet. He is very sensitive about Maud's marrying. He exaggerates, I dare say. I'll see Maximilla; she tells truth. Poor Mr. Tintern can think of nothing but himself. How nervous he has made me. What business has Maud walking out alone with *him ?* I think Maximilla might have prevented that. A selfish world. No, no, no ! My God ! it can't be. That would make me mad—quite mad. Oh, if I could go back to childhood and die !'

She went to the window, but she did not any longer see Maud and Captain Vivian.

Her clouded dark eyes swept so much of the landscape as was visible from the window in which the stood, in vain.

In answer to her bell, a footman appeared.

'Have you seen Miss Medwyn ?'

'Miss Medwyn is in the first drawing-room, my lady.'

'Tell Miss Medwyn, please, that I'm coming to her in a moment,' said Lady Vernon.

She got up and sighed heavily, with her hand pressed to her heart.

'Barbara, Barbara, you must command yourself. Say what they will, you can do that.'

She frowned and shook her head a little, and so seemed to shake off the bewildered look that had settled on her features ; and she resumed her usual air and countenance, except that she was very pale ; and she walked serenely into the great drawing-room.

'I have just got rid of my tiresome neighbour, Mr. Tintern, who has been boring me about fifty things, and I want you to tell me all about the ball last night, and I was so afraid you might run away before I had locked up my letters.'

Miss Max lowered her little gold glasses and the newspaper she had been reading, and looked up from her chair near the window into Lady Vernon's face.

'Well, my dear, it was, I should say—you know it is four years, or five, since I was last at one of your Wymering balls; but I think it was a very good ball, and seemed to go off very spiritedly. There were the Wycombes, and the Heydukes, and the Forresters, and the Gystans; and Hawkshawe was there.'

And so she went on with an enumeration interesting to country people, but scarcely so much so to others; and then she went into the events, and the soup, and the ices, and the flirtations, and the gossip of the chaperons, Lady Vernon now and then reviving a recollection, or opening a subject by a question.

'And how did Maud look ?' she asked at last, carelessly.

'Perfectly lovely,' answered Miss Max, with decision.

'Did she dance ?'

'Not a great deal.'

'About how many dances do you suppose ?'

'I think she said, coming home, two quadrilles and three round dances.'

'That was very little.'

'Oh, I need not tell you she could have danced everything if she had liked,' said Miss Max complacently.

'To whom did she give the fast dances ?' asks Lady Vernon.

'To Captain Vivian.'

'Well, but there were three.'

'All to Captain Vivian.'

'Really ? She must have been very rude, then, to other people,' said Lady Vernon.

'It can't have pleased them, I fancy. Lord Heyduke, a very good-looking young man, and clever they say, looked so angry. I really thought he and old Lord Hawkshawe would have been rude afterwards to Captain Vivian.

'That is so foolish of Maud,' said Lady Vernon. 'She knows nothing, absolutely, about Captain Vivian, except that he is gentleman-like and good-looking. But I happen to know that, over and above his commission, he has not three hundred a-year in the world.'

'But you know Maud as well as I do ; *that* consideration is not likely to weigh with her for a moment,' said Maximilla.

'She is so perverse,' said Lady Vernon, darkening with great severity.

'Well, Barbara, it isn't all perversity. That kind of impetuosity runs very much in families, and you certainly did not marry for money.'

'That is a kind reminder,' said Lady Vernon, with a fierce smile. 'I beg pardon for interrupting you, but some of my friends (you among them) know pretty well that I have never ceased to repent that one hasty step; and if I was a fool, as you remind me a little cruelly, I'd rather she regarded me in that great mistake of my life, not as an example, but as a warning; and certainly neither you nor I, at our years, should encourage her.'

'She is the last person on earth to be either encouraged or discouraged by our opinions—mine, perhaps, I should say,' answered Miss Max. 'But don't let us quarrel about it, Barbara, for I rather think that upon this point we are both very nearly agreed.'

Hereupon she very honestly related her reasons for thinking Captain Vivian very much in love with Maud, and added her opinion that, 'unless she likes him, which I don't believe, and has made up her mind not to trifle with him, she ought not to encourage him.'

Lady Vernon looked out of the window, and, still looking out, said carelessly:

'And you don't think there is anything in it?'

'I did not say that. I don't think it possible that a young man could be for so long in the same house without being impressed by her; she is so very beautiful. I should not be at all surprised if he were very much in love with her; and you know, my dear Barbara, if he has any ambition, and thinks himself an Adonis, what is likely to follow? As to Maud, my belief is she is not in love with him. I don't think she cares about him; but young ladies are so mysterious, I can only speak on conjecture, and she may—it is quite possible—she may like him. I should be sorry to take it on me to say positively she does not.'

'It has set people talking, at all events,' said Lady Vernon carelessly, 'and nothing could be more absurd. But, as you say, there may be nothing in it.'

'I think, perhaps, it might not be amiss to let her go about a little to friends' houses, and make some visits, and she will soon forget him, if she ever cared about him. I should be delighted to have her, but I have promised so soon to go to Lady Mardykes', and I know she wishes ever so much to have Maud. She saw her at the Tinterns, and liked her so much, and I said I would ask you, and I think she could not visit a better house. I'm to be with her in a fortnight or less, and we should meet there. What do you say ? Will you let her go ?'

'I don't see anything very particular against it at present,' said Lady Vernon, thinking. 'But you know I have not seen her since her marriage, and all that fraud, I may call it, and violence, on Warhampton's part, has occurred since. I certainly should not have her here, nor any member of that family. But Maud may choose her friends for herself. I need not know them. I have reasons for not caring to send or take her to the Wycombes, or old Lady Heyduke's or the Frogworths, or the Gystans, and a great many more I could name. I should prefer Lady Mardykes', and your being there at the same time would make me feel quite comfortable about her. We can talk it over, you and I, Max, by-and-bye.'

And with a more cheerful countenance she left the room.

Miss Max had a little good-natured mischief in her, and was, if the truth were spoken, a little disappointed at the equanimity with which haughty, jealous Barbara took the news, the irritating nature of which she had been at no special pains to mitigate.

'She may smile as she pleases,' she thought, looking after her as the door closed, 'but I am certain she is nettled. I think she likes him, and I'm a little curious to see what she will do.'

CHAPTER XLII.

THE SKY CLEARING.

LADY VERNON passed from the great drawing-room, smiling ; but as she traversed the two rooms that lie between it and the hall, the light rapidly faded from her features, and her face grew dark. Across the hall she went, and entered first one lonely room, then another, until she found herself, at last, in the shield-room,

In deep abstraction, she walked slowly round it, gazing, one after the other, at the armorial bearings, with their quarterings, 'gules' and 'or,' of the Rose and the Key. Looking on her face, you would have thought that she was reading malignant oracles on the wall. She did not see these things. The eyes of her spirit were opened, and she saw, in the abstraction of horror, far beyond them, the pictures of a tragedy.

Then she stood still at the window, looking out upon a cloistered square, hedged round with yew. Dark yew-trees, trimmed into old shapes, stand in files along the sward, and many arches are cut in the quadrangle of yew hedge that forms the inner and narrower square, and white statues gleam faintly in the shadow.

Neither did she see this funereal cloister, rising as it recedes, and backed by the solemn foliage of masses of Roydon timber.

She sighed heavily again and again at long intervals. She was restless, and looked round the room, and then left it, going through a corridor, and passing up a narrower staircase, to her own room.

It was her custom to read in the morning-room every day, for only five minutes, or fifteen, or sometimes for nearly an hour, between one and two.

Latimer, her dark, silent, active maid, by no means young, was in attendance, as was her wont, in the dressing-room, from which opens Lady Vernon's smaller morning-room.

Into this the lady passed; Latimer, stiff and angular, following her to the door, with soft tread, and there awaiting orders.

'Are you quite well, please, my lady?' she asked, with the privilege of an old servant, looking a little hard at her mistress.

'Quite, thanks—that is, very well—yes, I'm very well. I think, Latimer, I shan't want you,' she said, seating herself at the table, and placing her hands on the large, noted Bible that lies there, and sighing again heavily.

She opened it, she turned over the leaves slowly; they lay open at the Gospel of St. John.

Latimer, with a tread soft as a cat's, withdrew.

'Have I lost the power to collect my ideas?' said Lady Vernon. 'I'm excited. If my heart did not beat quite so fast! Ah, yes, I know how that must end.'

She got up and walked restlessly to the rows of prettily bound books, and stood as if reading their backs for a time, and passed on in abstraction. The first thing that recalled her was the sight of her features in the porcelain-framed mirror.

'Yes, I do look a little ill,' she said, as she saw her altered face. 'My God! that such a thing should have befallen!' she almost cried suddenly, lifting her hand to her temple. 'I have lost him—I have lost him—I have lost him! What has gone right with me? Oh, God! why am I pursued and tortured?'

She trembled like a person pierced with cold, and this trembling became more violent. It was a continued shudder. After a long time it subsided. She felt faint and ill.

She knelt, but she could not 'lift up her heart,' or fix her mind.

She sat down again, and looked on the open Bible. Her eye rested on the text:

'Ye shall seek Me, and shall not find Me : and where I am, thither ye cannot come.'

It glared on her from the page, like the sudden reality of her smouldering despair.

'Yes, the Redeemer has hidden His face for ever from me. I seek Him, and cannot find Him, and where He is, thither I cannot come,' she repeated again and again.

An idea had taken possession of her. It did not make her love Maud better. It was that she had heard, or guessed at, the suspicions which were conveyed in the rumour that officious Mr. Tintern had mentioned—the rumour that she, Lady Vernon, liked Captain Vivian—and this demonstration of Maud's, she thought, whether she cared or not about him, was meant to take him away from her. She would not yet be quite sure that Maud liked him. She had watched that closely. What insane malice that girl must have!

But a woman of her strong will, pride, and ability, could not be very long incapacitated, and in a little time she resolved upon several things.

She shut the big Bible, that still lay open, with an angry clap.

'I have asked for help, and it is denied me,' she said fiercely to herself, with an odd mixture of faith and profanation. 'I shall see what I can do without it.'

The first thing she resolved was to send instantly for Mr.

Dawe. Once she decided upon a measure, she did not waste time over its execution.

She glanced at her image in the glass. She was looking a little more like herself. She felt better. Her confidence was returning.

Not a human being should trace in her features, manner, conversation, the least evidence of her sufferings and her resolution. She would meet them more easily and cheerfully than ever.

She paused at the door, till she had decided what would be the most rapid and potent mode of invoking Mr. Dawe. She stood in deep thought for a minute, with stern lips and brows knit, and her dark eyes wandering—the image of a beautiful Thessalian witch.

This point at last determined, she opened the door quickly, and Mr. Dawe himself stood before her in the lobby. Mr. Dawe, in his black-caped coat, shiny leather leggings, and black wig, his low-crowned hat in his left hand. His right arm was extended, for he was on the point of knocking, if he had not been arrested by the unexpected opening of the door.

The figure stood with arm extended and knuckle bent, and dark features lighted by the fixed eye-balls that were staring at her.

Very unusually for him, he was first to speak.

'Latimer said you were here. I was going to knock. You are pretty well ?'

'Very well, thanks ; I'm so glad to see you. You remember this room ?'

He followed her in, and shut the door.

'Perfectly,' he answered, rolling his eyes round the room.

'Sit down. The gong will soon sound for luncheon. Let us talk a little first, and tell me—it seems an inhospitable way of putting it, but it is so difficult to move you in the direction of Roydon—what has brought you here ? Nothing that is not pleasant, I hope ?'

She looked in his face.

'Something—I am not at liberty to tell what—that may affect Captain Vivian very seriously.'

'Nothing in his profession ?' said the lady, in alarm.

'Nothing,' says Mr. Dawe.

'Surely you can tell me what it is ?' she urged.

'Certainly I cannot,' he answered.

'Is it money?'

'I shall answer nothing at present. You ask in vain.'

'Surely you will say yes or no to that?'

'To nothing. No. If that guess were not right you would go on to another, and so my refusing at last to answer would imply that you were right.'

'Well, I shall learn by-and-bye whether you won't yield a little.'

'You shall,' he answered.

'You mean you won't. Tell me, then, generally, what you are going to do,' said the lady.

'To remain here two or three days with Captain Vivian,' he answered.

'No,' she said. 'You have come to take him away.'

'H'm!' replied Mr. Dawe; and his prominent eyes stared in her dark ones. 'How soon?'

'This afternoon,' she answered decisively.

'That's untoward,' he said, lowering his hand, and looking down.

'Why untoward?' she persisted.

'I can't tell you yet.'

'It may be; if it be I'm sorry; but it is inevitable. He must go this afternoon.'

As she thus spoke, the old gentleman's eyes fixed on her with a look of inquiry, and were then lowered again; and he nodded once or twice slightly, as if affirmatively to some thought of his own.

'He can return—he shall return,' she said softly, laying her pretty hand on the old man's arm.

'In the meantime, you begin to feel that you were precipitate?' he said dryly.

'No,' she answered passionately. 'He shall return in a few days. I will lose my life rather than lose him. I will write, and he shall come again.'

'How soon?'

'Ten days—a fortnight perhaps; perhaps in a week. But at present he must go.'

'So be it,' he said. 'I wanted to tell you that they have extended his leave four weeks.'

'I thank Heaven,' she said gently and fervently. 'I thought they would.'

'I came to your door here to tell you. It is near your

luncheon hour.   Yes ; eight minutes to two.   Vivian will be at luncheon.   I don't lunch, but I don't mind going in.   I must not let him slip through my fingers.'

'You're not offended with me ?' she pleaded.

'Who?   I?   I never was offended in my life,' said the dark little gentleman, in perfect good faith.

'It seems so unaccountable and unkind,' she continued ; 'but I can't help it, and I can't explain yet, any more than you can ; at least, you won't ask me.'

'No, certainly,' he interposed.

'And you have been very kind in this matter,' she added.

'Respecting Captain Vivian ?'

'Yes, very kind,' she repeated.

'No, not kind—savage.   But I have done what, all things well considered, I thought wisest.   That is all,' he said, and took the pinch of snuff he held in his fingers.

'Well, I am grateful.   I thank you from my heart, and I am going to beg another favour,' she went on.   'You will not tell him that it is I who wish him to leave Roydon at present, but give him some other reason.

'I'll give him no reason,' said Mr. Dawe.

'Will you take it on yourself ?'

'Certainly.'

'You have not seen him since you came ?' she asked.

'No.'

'So much the better ; and you must come as well as he : you promise ?'

'Yes, I must come, and the sooner the better, for him at least.'

'You will find them now at luncheon.   I'll follow you when I have put up my books.'

She did not care to enter the room at the same moment with Mr. Dawe, or that people should suppose that they had been conferring.

CHAPTER XLIII.

ANTOMARCHI.

DOCTOR MALKIN was the only guest present, except Mr. Dawe, for by this time we have come to regard Captain Vivian almost as one of the family.

Maud, looking quite lovely, but professing to be very much fatigued by her exertions at the Wymering ball, was chatting gaily with Miss Max and Captain Vivian as Lady Vernon came in.

That handsome lady was the only one of the party whom fatigue, to judge by her looks, had touched. Quite at her ease she seemed, and joined very gaily in the general talk.

Doctor Malkin at first was too busy to contribute much to the conversation, but he soon became less absorbed.

'I saw you, Doctor Malkin, at the ball last night,' said Maud, 'but I don't think you danced?'

'No, certainly,' said Doctor Malkin.

'Well, I think you were right,' put in Miss Max, who did not like him. 'Would not a dance of doctors be rather like a dance of death?'

'Awfully grisly,' acquiesced the doctor, with a laugh. 'No, I don't go to frighten the people; I attend merely as a spectator, to evidence my loyalty. You know, it is a very loyal celebration; and, besides, one meets one's friends; and then there is supper; and, after all, a nobody who doesn't dance may slip away whenever he pleases, and no one miss him.'

'Except his friends,' said Miss Vernon; 'and I'm so glad you mentioned them, because I wanted so much to ask you about one in particular, whose appearance I thought very striking. You told me you remarked him also, Captain Vivian?'

'I know, yes; the man with the dark face, and very odd eyes, and black beard, cut as square as a book,' said the fair-haired captain. 'If he had not been so very odd-looking, I should have thought him almost handsome.'

'I thought him quite handsome,' said Maud; 'he had such a strange, energetic, commanding countenance. I felt that I could not quite decide whether he looked like a great man, or only a great charlatan, but still there was something so striking about him, and so interesting, that it was hard to take one's eyes off him while he was in sight.'

'I was trying to remember last night, after we came home,' said Maximilla Medwyn, 'where I had met him before, for I know I did meet him somewhere, and now I recollect perfectly, it was at Lady Mardykes', whose house is, I think, one of the most charming and wonderful places in the world. She has every one that is worth seeing or knowing, I do believe, in the habitable world, and she is such good company herself, and so clever, and I have been trying to remember his name.'

'Would you remember it if you heard it?' asked the doctor, who had once or twice essayed to put in a word, with a smile.

'I'm certain I should—I think I should,' answered Miss Max.

'Was it Antomarchi?'

'The very thing,' said Miss Max, much relieved. 'The same name, I think, as the physician's at St. Helena—Napoleon's, I mean?'

He nodded.

'Then he is the very person I remember meeting at Lady Mardykes'. What is he?'

'A physician; a very accomplished one,' said Doctor Malkin. 'He has written some of the ablest papers extant in our medical journals.'

'Is he any relation of Napoleon's physician?' asked Miss Vernon.

'Very distant, if any,' answered the doctor.

'Have not we talked enough about doctors?' said Lady Vernon, a little impatiently.

'Only one word more,' pleaded Miss Max. 'I do assure you, Barbara, if you had seen him you would have been just as curious as I.'

'I don't know a great deal about him,' said Doctor Malkin, suddenly cooling upon the subject, in which, up to then, he had appeared very well up.

'Where does he practise?' asked Miss Max.

'He tried London, where his writings had made him a reputation, but it did not do,' Doctor Malkin answered, smiling a little uncomfortably, as if some awkward recollections were disturbing him, and the obliquity of his dark, close-set eyes looked, as whenever he was put out, a little more marked and sinister. 'I can't say he practises anywhere as a physician. He is consulted, and he writes. The profession have a very high opinion of him. I don't know him, that is, I can't say I am more than a—a—hardly an acquaintance, and an admirer.'

' Where does he live ?' asked Miss Max.

' Oh—a—it is very stupid, but I really totally forget the name of the place,' said Doctor Malkin.

' How far away?' persisted Miss Medwyn.

' How far away ? I am the worst guesser of a distance in the world,' says the doctor, looking up to the cornice, as if in search of an inspiration.

' You must let me ask a question, Max, if you think for the present we have talked enough about this Mr.—whatever his name is. I want to trouble Doctor Malkin with an inquiry,' said Lady Vernon, who seemed to grow more and more irritable under Mr. Dawe's inscrutable stare from the other side of the table. He seemed suddenly to become conscious that he had been treating the handsome face of that great lady a little too like a picture, and he rolled his eyeballs in another direction. Lady Vernon continued, ' And how did you find poor old Grimston to-day?'

' She's a shade better, but you know she is a very old woman. I suppose she was here sixty years ago ?'

' I dare say ; more, perhaps,' said Lady Vernon. ' You know poor Rebecca Grimstone?' she asked Maximilla, who acknowledged the acquaintance. ' Well, poor thing, she had a fainting fit, about ten o'clock to-day. She had one about three months ago, and recovered so slowly that this alarmed me a good deal.'

' Dear me ! I had not an idea. I must have seemed so unfeeling, delaying you so long about Doctor Antomarchi. But I am so glad to hear she is better.'

Lady Vernon had ever so many questions still to put to Doctor Malkin, and the doctor seemed to take a very special interest in old Mrs. Grimston's case, and grew more and more animated and confidential.

Miss Max was now talking to Mr. Dawe, and now and then a little to Maud, and to Captain Vivian.

' I saw an old flame of yours at the ball last night,' said Miss Max. ' I'm sure you know who I mean.'

' I don't,' said Mr. Dawe conclusively.

' You have had so many, I dare say. But this one you will remember when I tell you. It was Diana Rowley.'

' Diana Rowley !' repeated Mr. Dawe. ' Is Miss Rowley still living ?'

'What a gallant question ! Do you know she made precisely the same inquiry, in the same tone of wonder, when I mentioned you. Lovers dissemble their feelings so.'

'She must have been eight or nine-and-twenty then.'

'When ?' interposed Miss Max.

'In the year 'thirty-one ; June. Let me see, she must be sixty-three or sixty-four now ; this is the twenty-eighth of August.'

'She was slight, very good figure, and fine eyes,' said Miss Max.

'Yes, she was comely,' assented Mr. Dawe reflectively.

'You used to say she was a little too thin,' said Miss Max, ' but she has improved. She is the fattest woman in the county now.'

'Really !' exclaimed Mr. Dawe.

'Yes, and she has given up the only folly you used to complain of—she has given up riding to the hounds.'

'H'm !' said Mr. Dawe.

'Well ; then she is still approachable,' continued Miss Max cheerily. 'She might have been married, I'm told, often ; but —I don't know who she has been waiting for.'

'She must have known very well that Richard Dawe was not a marrying man. Tut, tut, Maximilla ; you always liked quizzing people,' said the old bachelor.

' 'You'd have done very well to marry her, though,' said Maximilla.

'I don't see any good it would have done me.'

'An infinity. She'd have given you a good shaking,' said Maximilla, as they got up.

Miss Medwyn and Maud went together into the drawing-room, and then out among the flowers. Mr. Dawe signed to Captain Vivian, as he was leaving the luncheon-room, and he turned. Mr. Dawe led him to a window, where they had a quiet and earnest talk.

As Maud and Maximilla stood among the flowers, doubtful whether they would take a walk into the woods, or visit the conservatory first, Miss Max, who was looking in that direction, said suddenly :

'Oh, look there ! Who can that be ?'

Maud looked round, and saw a hired carriage, with luggage on the top, driving down the avenue.

'It can't be Mr. Dawe, for he told me, when he arrived, that he intended staying two or three days, and that Captain's Vivian's leave was extended.'

The ladies stood side by side looking after the carriage, until it was lost to sight.

'I should not be a bit surprised,' said Miss Max, "if Barbara has ordered Captain Vivian to make a march to head-quarters. Come in, and let us find out what it is.'

There was no one in the hall as they passed. But in the drawing-room they found Lady Vernon.

'Who has gone away, Barbara?' inquired Miss Max.

Lady Vernon looked up, so as to see Maud's face as well as Maximilla's.

'One of Mr. Dawe's imperious whims. He has gone, and taken away Captain Vivian with him.'

Maud felt that Lady Vernon's all-seeing eyes rested upon her for a moment as she said this, and her colour changed.

Lady Vernon did not seem to observe her embarrassment.

'Very sudden,' said Max.

'And mysterious,' added Lady Vernon. 'He came with the intention of remaining a few days, but he had a long talk with Captain Vivian, and the end of it was a total change of plans, and they came in here and took leave. It was all so sudden. I dare say Mr. Dawe will write to say something more. In the meantime we must only command our curiosity.'

She laughed carelessly.

'But aren't they coming back?' asked Miss Max.

'They have not obliged me with any information. I don't know, either, that I could have them very soon, because I shall be going for some weeks to town, and Maud, I suppose, will be going to Lady Mardykes'. I don't think, Maximilla, you care about drawings like these' (there was an open portfolio before her), 'ecclesiastical architecture and decoration?'

'No, not the least,' she answered; 'but I suppose you are busy just now.'

'I'm obliged to look at these, to say what I think of them. I should rather have left it to the committee, but as I have subscribed a good deal, they choose that I should tell them what I think.'

'Then we may as well take our little walk to the woods, Maud.'

And away they went.

But Miss Max, instead of going out, stopped in the hall, and said, all radiant with satisfaction, to Maud:

'Well, that is settled very quietly, and I am glad of it. You *are* to go to Lady Mardykes'. I was afraid to say a word, Barbara is so odd and suspicious, sometimes, and if she saw how pleased I was, it might have put it into her head to recall her leave. I'll write to Lady Mardykes this moment to tell her she may ask you, with every confidence that your mamma will make no difficulties.'

So, instead of going to the woods, Miss Max ran up to her dressing-room, and wrote a note to that effect.

CHAPTER XLIV.

FACES SEEN BEFORE.

LADY MARDYKES had left the Grange the morning after the Wymering ball, but Miss Medwyn's note followed her; and a few days more brought to Roydon three envelopes, addressed, in her pretty hand, one to each of the three ladies at present at Roydon.

That to Lady Vernon was very polite, though a little formal, and not very long, asking leave for Maud. But that to Maud herself was playful and animated, and extremely good-natured. She named an early day for her visit, and she insisted it should not be a flying one, as there were a great number of people coming to Carsbrook, who would interest and amuse her.

To Maximilla, she mentioned some of these foreign ministers, authors, artists, parliamentary celebrities. 'I know she would think it amusing, and you must not let her disappoint me. You have never failed me, so I put you down as certain. Don't allow her to leave Carsbrook before she is really tired of it. You know that there are more bedrooms there than I can ever find guests to occupy. Don't, therefore, let her fancy that I shall want her room; and you and she will be glad, I think, to meet where you can do exactly as you please, which, I conjecture, is scarcely the case at Roydon.'

'I think I shall be pretty sure to meet a very particular friend of mine at Carsbrook,' said Miss Max, after a little silence.

'Who is it?' inquired Maud, misled by her grave simplicity.

'Charles Marston, my dear,' she said, lighting up with a smile. Of course you don't care, but I do.'

'I don't think that very likely. I should not wonder if I were never to see him again,' said the young lady.

'I should very much,' laughed Miss Max.

'I mean he was so vexed at that odious Wymering ball.'

'No wonder. But he has had time to cool since then, in one sense only. He will be there, as sure as I am here. You'll see. Put on your things, and come out, and we'll have a comfortable talk, quite to ourselves.'

So these two cronies went out together, busy with the future, and already in imagination at Carsbrook.

'It is a huge house,' said Miss Max. 'One of those great black and white houses, with really an infinitude of bedrooms. When I was there last, we mustered sixty people every day to dinner—a noisier place, you see, than Roydon, and yet, I assure you, there were whole galleries perfectly deserted. She told me it would be much more crowded this year. I think, between ourselves, she takes a pride in collecting celebrities. It is her vanity, and certainly it is one of the very most amusing houses I ever was in. Of course, one would grow tired of it after a time; at least, an old girl like me would. But for a little time it is quite delightful. She is very rich, you know.'

'Indeed!'

'I don't say rich compared with you Roydon people, but she is what seems very rich to me; that is, her jointure is five thousand a year, and she has more than fifteen thousand a year that belonged to her mother, the first Lady Warhampton; so she has more than twenty thousand a year.'

'Well, tell me more about Carsbrook,' said Maud.

'We used to pass our time so agreeably, when we were not going out driving, or picnicking, or sight-seeing. There is a great square flower-garden, with old-fashioned, trim hedges all round, and such quantities of pretty flowers, in the old Dutch style. As you look down on them from the terrace, they seem like the pattern of a thick-piled carpet. This is like a border all round, for the centre is kept in grass as smooth as velvet. And there is a very old mulberry-tree, with so many curious stories about it, in the centre. And ever so many parties used to play croquet or lawn billiards. It was such fun. And there were so many amusing affairs of the heart to interest old people like me.

Such a comedy perpetually going on. You can't think what a charming house it is to stay at.'

'I'm very glad we are going,' said Maud.

'But you don't look very glad, my dear.'

'Well, I suppose I am discontented a little. I was just thinking what a pity it is mamma keeps such a dull house here.'

'So it is. I have often told her so,' said Miss Max. 'She could do, you know, whatever she liked. I don't think, indeed, she could get together so many remarkable people, but that kind of thing may be a little overdone, and, certainly, once or twice when I was there, there were some very absurd people at Carsbrook; but, taken for all in all, it is one of the most delightful houses in the world.'

Full of these pleasant anticipations, which, to a girl who had never seen a London season, had something even exciting in them, and in the certainty of a very early meeting with Maximilla Medwyn, Maud bore the hour of separation much more cheerfully than she otherwise would.

That hour had now arrived, and Miss Max, having bid Lady Vernon good-bye, and taken many leaves of Maud, drove away at last, with maid and boxes, down the old avenue of Roydon.

It was three o'clock when she set out, having a ten miles' drive before reaching the train she was to catch.

It was about six o'clock, when the train in which she was now gliding toward her destination stopped at the Drongwell station.

Here some of her fellow-passengers got out, and a gentleman with a small leather bag, a slender silk umbrella, and a rug, stepped nearly in, but arrested his foot at the door, and would probably have receded had it not been that he was followed a little too closely by another person, who, with a despatch-box in his hand, had scaled the steps.

Miss Max saw his momentary hesitation, and a little maliciously said:

'How d'ye do?' with a nod and smile of recognition.

Dr. Malkin, for he it was, smiling his best, and squinting viciously, with a surprised and glad recognition, returned her salutation, and took his place beside her. His companion took his seat at the opposite side, in the corner next the window, placed his despatch-box on the seat beside him, and unlocked it.

There was no mistaking the marble features, strange eyes, and coal-black square beard. The gentleman with the despatch-box, who now leaned across and murmured low a word or two in Dr. Malkin's ear, was that Antomarchi, whose appearance had so strongly excited Miss Maximilla Medwyn's curiosity at the Wymering ball.

The clapping of the doors was over now, the whistle skirled its horrid blast, the engine communicated its first jerk through all the articulations of the snake-like train, and the carriages were again gliding forward.

Doctor Malkin for a few minutes was busy stowing away his bag and umbrella, and having rid his mind of these cares, he smiled again, turning to Miss Max, and observed on the beauty of the weather and scenery.

'How soon we glide from summer into autumn,' he observed. 'The change of the leaf does not remind us so powerfully of our approach to winter, as the perceptible shortening of the days.'

'It is so long since I glided into autumn myself, that these changes in nature don't trouble me much,' answered Miss Max gaily. 'Certainly, the days are shortening, and so are mine, but that does not vex me either. There are younger people—for instance, Lady Vernon, I think her looking by no means well. I can't define what it is; she looks hectic, and odd, as if there were something decidedly wrong. She told me one day, when I remarked that she was not looking well, that she had a little palpitation, and she seemed almost vexed that she had mentioned it.'

'Yes, there is a little; the action of the heart is a little eccentric,' said Doctor Malkin. 'Of course, we must not mention it; people are so stupid, it would be sure to come back to her, and the fact of its being talked of would only make her worse.'

'You know I'm a homœopathist, but that's of no importance. What I want to know is, does she suffer under any actual disease of the heart ?'

'Why, as to the heart, it is very hard to say,' observed the doctor a little evasively; 'because a man might pass the severest examination of the ablest physicians in England, and having been pronounced perfectly sound, might drop down dead as he quitted the room where the consultation was held. But there is no evidence of organic complaint in Lady Vernon's case, and I'll tell you frankly, if there were, I should not admit it; I am a great stickler for keeping faith with a patient. No one likes their ailments or infirmities to be disclosed; but, of course,' he added, thinking he had been a little brusque, 'to so very near a friend and relation as you, Miss Medwyn, it would be different. The truth is, however, just as I have told you.'

Miss Max sat quite far enough away to mention Doctor Antomarchi, the noise of the train allowed for, without danger of his overhearing what she said.

'I was going to say I think Doctor Antomarchi a rather interesting man, and I should, I think, like to make his acquaintance.'

'Well, I don't know that you would like him. He thinks of nothing but his science, his art; and to a listener not *éclairée*, I fear it can scarcely be entertaining.'

'He seemed to have a great deal to say for himself at Wymering, to Lady Mardykes, the other evening,' said Miss Max.

'I did not remark. But the truth is, I have scarcely made his acquaintance myself,' observed Doctor Malkin, smiling. 'I found him on the platform, and he followed me in here.'

'How far does he go?'

'I don't know. I've to get out at Wakesworth.'

'Wakesworth? That is not a great many miles away from Lady Mardykes'. You know Carsbrook, of course?' says Miss Max. 'It is such a broken, roundabout journey by rail, however. From Roydon it is more comfortably reached by the high road. What a huge old house it is,' she continued, breaking again into the description of it she had given to Maud a few days before; 'black and white, you know, and the great, old, square flower-garden, with the clipped hedges round it, and the croquet-ground in the centre, and the old mulberry-tree.'

As Miss Max concluded the description, she thought she saw a listening smile of secret intelligence on the still face of Antomarchi, who was busy noting the papers he took from his box, and did not raise his eyes.

Her curiosity was piqued.

Did Doctor Malkin know more about this Antomarchi than he pretended? Were their routes really as disconnected as the Roydon doctor would have her believe? Had their journey anything to do with Lady Mardykes and Carsbrook?

These inquiries must rest unspoken for the present. She leaned back, and was silent for a time, with her eyes all but closed.

'I'm sure it is a fine place,' resumed Doctor Malkin ; 'but I've never seen it, and I don't know Lady Mardykes. I hear she is perfectly charming.'

'So she is, and extremely clever. Her poor mother was ; and her father is. You know Warhampton ?'

'Yes, by fame, of course. Very able man. I've had to come here all the way about a patient,' he added, as if to quiet further conjectures.

The sun was at the edge of the horizon. It would, after two or three golden glorious minutes, be grey twilight.

Miss Max raised her eyes, and those of Antomarchi met, or rather seemed to hold, hers with a sensation the most unpleasant and overpowering she had ever experienced.

His eyes almost immediately looked another way, and were bent again upon his papers.

Twilight came. He then locked up his despatch-box, and looked out of the window.

'Is not your friend, Mr. Antomarchi, something of a mesmerist ?' inquired Miss Max.

'He is ; a very potent one ; at least, he is so reputed. I have never seen him exercise his faculty,' answered Doctor Malkin.

A few minutes more passed, and the train, with a long whistle, came to a standstill at the platform of Wakesworth station.

Doctor Antomarchi stood up, with his despatch-box in his hand, and signed to the porter to open the door.

Miss Max was glad, somehow, that he was gone, and took leave of Doctor Malkin, who was also going, without much reluctance.

She watched their movements slyly from the window, close to which she had moved. But there was to-ing and fro-ing on the platform, and the steam from the engine had eddied in, and was confusing objects, and it was already nearly dark. She thought, however, that the two gentlemen went up the steep road from the station side by side.

In another minute the train was moving away, and she had left Wakesworth and the two doctors far behind.

Those two doctors did walk up, side by side, into the little town, and entered the White Lion, and, while they were eating a hasty cold dinner, horses were put to a carriage, which stood ready at the door so soon as the gentlemen emerged.

Some of the people who were at the door looked darkly at Doctor Malkin, and whispered to one another, as, aided by the

lamp over the inn-door, and by the faint silvery beams of the
moon, which by this time was showing her light, they saw him
get in and take his seat.

The doctors smiled amusedly on each other as the carriage
rolled away through the quiet street of Wakesworth, and lighting their cigars, they smoked as they drove up the narrow road,
over the hedges of which hung the dewy boughs and fruit of
orchards in the moonlight.

CHAPTER XLV.

THE JOURNEY'S END.

FOR nearly three miles they drove in silence, each too comfortable to disturb the serenity of his ruminations.

There is a soothing influence in the subsidence of colour and
the indistinctness of outline that surround one in a drive through
a wooded country, when the thin mists arise by moonlight; and
this seemed to prevail with the spirit of each gentleman, as he
looked listlessly from his window.

Doctor Malkin broke the silence first.

'What asses young fellows are !' he declaimed. 'I had an
uncle the head of a great legal firm, and two first cousins
solicitors, and they, one and all, wished me to go to the bar. I
might have been making four thousand a year easily by this
time. I might have been on the high road to the bench. Everyone said I had a turn for it. But, like a fool, I took a fancy to
be a doctor—and even so, I might have stayed in London. If I
had—it was on the cards—I might have done some good. I
know something about my business, I believe. And much good
has it done me ! What's the good of a fellow's making a slave
of himself, if he doesn't put by something worth while ? Better
to enjoy what he has.'

'Regretting is the greatest waste of time except wishing,' said
Antomarchi, in his cold, resonant bass tones.

'I have not much, very little : but liberty is something,' said
Doctor Malkin.

'Life without progress is death,' insisted the same marble
oracle, with something of scorn ringing in his deep voice.

'Think what Paris is, or Vienna, and think, then, of being in such a cursed little hole as Roydon,' said Doctor Malkin, with disgust.

'Your liberty and your vices are not resources enough for a life. A man of any mind must have a game of some sort to play at,' observed Antomarchi.

'You may laugh. I don't say you are not a man of merit; I think you about the ablest man I ever met,' said the Roydon doctor; 'but you have found a short cut to fortune.'

'You must count on a good deal of mud before you turn up a nugget,' said the man with the square beard, and yawned. 'I was on my way to London this morning,' Doctor Antomarchi suddenly resumed; 'I am not the first man who has so changed his purpose. A lady's billet has brought me back. Try one of these.'

And so saying, he tendered his cigars.

'Thanks. I tell you, at a single jump you have reached a fortune,' said Doctor Malkin. 'I wish I could woo the goddess as successfully.'

'Have you never tried the language of the eyes?' said Antomarchi.

'In ten years' time you'll be a baronet—you know how .to rule men—and before fifteen more are passed you will have got a peerage. Of course, I assume that your energies will be directed to get it.'

'And I will take for my crest, what device?' said Antomarchi. 'Let me see. Just that,' he said, nodding his head toward the resplendent moon. 'A full moon argent, on a field azure, and three razors proper, and by way of motto, *tondit oves*.'

They were now approaching a village, with the tower of a country church shining silver white among dark trees and glimmering roofs.

Antomarchi's resonant voice brought the driver to a halt.

'We get out here,' he cried sternly. 'Drive on to the gatehouse, and give the man these things, and he will pay you.'

'All right, sir,' replied the driver, and the carriage rolled away toward the village.

They were now standing on the white road, dappled by the intense shadow of a motionless tree, under the brilliant moon. Skirting the road at the left hand ran a high park wall, here and there clustered with ivy, and overtopped with high old trees.

A narrow, arched door in this opened to Antomarchi's latch-key, and he and his companion entered, to find themselves in a fine old park.

The grounds were studded with clumps of lofty timber. The two doctors walked up a gentle, undulating slope, and when this was surmounted, close before them, on the low ground, stood a huge black and white house, its white showing, in the moonbeams, in dazzling contrast with the oak-bars that crossed it perpendicularly, horizontally, diagonally. They stood just overlooking a great, square, Dutch flower-garden, which interposed between them and the house, surrounded by tall, trim hedges, in the bygone Dutch taste. The flowers made a wide border in fantastic patterns all round, the centre was laid out in grass, and in the middle of this wide, green carpet stood a lonely old mulberry-tree.

In a long line of windows on the second story a ruddy light glowed out hospitably, as well as here and there from other windows above, and in the lower story.

They stopped for a minute without premeditation. The scene was too pretty, the contrast between the lights in the house and the cold, silver brightness of the landscape so striking, and the character of the whole so festive and hospitable, that each silently enjoyed the picture.

'There is a ball to-night,' said Antomarchi, 'but it is too late for you and me to dress and appear at it. Come.'

And he led the way towards the house. They soon reached a path, and under the wide shadow of tall trees, arrived at a door, like that which they had already passed in the wall that begirt the garden.

The latch-key again opened this, and they entered the silent alleys of lofty clipped hedges, tall and straight as prison walls, making a profound shadow. They passed under the first arch of the many that pierced these thick curtains of foliage, and so found themselves, after passing the broad border of flower-beds, upon the shorn grass, in the light of the moon, among the croquet hoops, that in this cloudless weather make their bivouac all night on the ground they have taken up by day.

It was, as I have said, a great black and white house, and, as they approached, its walls and windows seemed to expand, and the whole building to grow almost gigantic.

The latch-key of the privileged Doctor Antomarchi did here for Doctor Malkin the office which the feather from the cock's tail did for Micyllus, and all doors opened before it.

Ascending two steps he opened a door in the wall, and led the way into the house.

They were in a long, dimly lighted passage, that seemed to go right through it, with doors on each side opening from it. Up this Antomarchi walked quietly, his hat still on, as confidently as if he were master of all around him.

Another passage, longer still, crossed this at right angles, dimly lighted like the first. A footman in livery was walking along it quickly. Antomarchi signed to him, and he approached.

'Mr. Drummond in his room?' he asked.

'Yes, sir.'

'You won't mind coming a few steps this way?' he said, taking Doctor Malkin's acquiescence for granted.

He walked down the transverse passage to the left, where, more than half-way on, a folding screen blocked nearly half the width of the corridor, protecting a door at the left from the draughts that sometimes eddied up the passage. At this door Antomarchi knocked.

'Mr. Drummond?'

Mr. Drummond, a serious, quiet man, with rosy cheeks, a little stout, and dressed in black, who had just been reading his paper and drinking his tea, appeared, swallowing down a bit of bread-and-butter which he was munching at the moment.

'Lady Mardykes came this morning?' inquired Antomarchi.

'Yes, sir,' said Drummond, waiting just a second, to be certain that he had quite swallowed his bit of bread-and-butter.

'She was satisfied with the preparations in the rooms?'

'Quite, sir; and she placed some papers in my hands, by-the-bye, sir, which she said were deeds affecting Mardykes Hall.'

'Very good; place them under lock and key in the long press, under the proper letter. They belong to Mr. Mardykes. How soon does her ladyship return?'

'She said in two or three days, sir.'

Antomarchi nodded, and, turning on his heel, led the way at a swift pace. They passed a staircase, and then reached another, the grand staircase, and a great hall, in which were many footmen in livery, and some female servants peeping in at an open door, from which issued the sounds of music and dancing, and laughter and talking.

'Peep in if you like. They won't mind you.'

He did, and—

'Wow! Tam saw an unco sight.'

The Wymering ball was dulness itself compared with this. There was such a variety of character in the guests, and in their dancing. Some so stately, grave, and ceremonious; others so hilarious; some working with hearty, but rather grave goodwill; others wild with glee—all so animated and amusing, that Doctor Malkin could have kept his post at the door I know not for how long.

'There is a tall, dark man, with long hair, rather handsome; he looks about forty. He smiles haughtily round, and stands with his arms folded—a remarkable-looking fellow!'

'Does he wear steel buckles in his shoes?' asked Antomarchi.

'Yes, by Jove! and point-lace to his white neck-tie.'

'That is his excellency the Spanish minister,' continued Antomarchi.

'Oh?' said Doctor Malkin. 'And there's a fellow, almost a dwarf, with straw-coloured hair, and a long, solemn face, with a sharp chin. He is close to the door here, and he has a set of ivory tablets in one hand and a pencil in the other. He must be a queer fellow.'

'Queer fellow! You may well say so. He is the greatest mathematician, astronomer, and mechanic on earth. He has lately discovered, among other things, an instrument by which you may see the reverse side of the moon, and, oh, look there; do you see that lady, in purple satin, sitting on the sofa near the window?' said Antomarchi, peeping cautiously over Doctor Malkin's shoulder. 'I don't think you'll recognise her, do you?'

'No, I don't think I do. Ought I to know who she is?'

'I think so. That's the Duchess of Falconbury. But come, or they'll see me. I will conduct you to your room. Come,' said Antomarchi.

They crossed the great hall, ascended a broad oak staircase, and then marched half the length of a long gallery. Their progress was arrested by a ponderous door, which appeared to be sheathed with iron. This opened, they passed in. It closed with a spring lock.

'Here we are private. This is your room; only two doors from mine.'

Antomarchi pointed with his open hand towards his own. He opened the door, and led the way into a large and very comfortable room.

Doctor Malkin looked round on the curtained bed and windows, and the handsome furniture, with a feeling of rather angry envy.

'You are lucky,' he said. 'How well housed you are.'

'Patience, and shuffle the cards,' the other answered. 'Lady Vernon, I'm told, has some pretty things in her gift. You will be rich yet, if you are not in too great haste to marry.'

'Would you mind talking the matter over, where we are, we are so quiet here?' said Doctor Malkin, again looking round.

'Here, there, where you please; all one to me, provided we are not interrupted,' replied Antomarchi. 'Will you have your supper before or after?'

'When we have done, please,' he replied. 'I should like it here, if it doesn't upset arrangements. A broiled bone and a glass of sherry.'

They entered on their business, and talked for some time, Antomarchi being chiefly a listener, but now and then putting a short, sharp question, and keeping the more discursive man very rigidly to the point.

Under the control of such a conductor, the discussion did not last very long.

And now it was over, and the point settled, and both gentlemen stood up, and Doctor Malkin, while his broiled bones were coming, looked round the room again.

Over the chimney hung a rather remarkable portrait; it was that of a handsome, but forbidding woman, in a nun's dress. The face expressed resolution, contempt, and cruelty, with a strange power; but it was death-like.

Under this picture hung a crooked Malayan dagger.

'That kreese was my father's,' said Antomarchi. 'He killed a renegade priest with it in a row in Egypt. So it has made its mark.'

'Ha!' exclaimed Doctor Malkin softly, as, smiling with increased interest, he handled its heft, and tried its point with his finger-tip. 'Very sharp, too.'

'It has some magical characters engraved there,' observed Antomarchi. 'It is in keeping with the portrait; it looks as if it had slipped out of that sinister virago's fingers.'

Doctor Malkin looked round, but there was nothing else by way of decoration in the room that interested him.

And now he had his supper, and Antomarchi, who wished

to look in at the ball, took his leave, and went to make a rapid toilet.

His tray and sherry gone, Doctor Malkin prepared for bed.

The moon was high, but as yet her beams only entered the window obliquely. He drew the curtains, freely to admit the air. Partly in consequence of being in a strange house, and partly from other causes, he felt, perhaps, just a little nervous. He looked in the two presses, and other possible hiding-places in the room, to satisfy himself that there was no lurking intruder there. Then he secured his door, and, lastly, he made his prayerless preparations for bed, extinguished his candle, and was soon comfortably extended with his head on the pillow. He thought of the ball he had stolen a glimpse at to-night, and then of the Wymering ball, and the image of Lady Mardykes talking with so much earnestness to Antomarchi, came before him. Lucky rascal, Antomarchi! And finally, he was overcome by drowsiness, and slept soundly.

There are abnormal states in which the partners, the spirit and the animal, that jointly constitute man, are oddly divorced. The body will lie with eyes closed in deep slumber. The spirit will sit up with its interior vision and hearing opened, and see and hear things of which, in other states, it is not permitted a perception.

Here was Dr. Malkin, with his watch under his pillow and his head upon it, snoring, as was his wont, moderately but regularly.

But the doctor had eaten supper, which was not a habit of his, and seldom agreed with him; and the spirit, finding its tenement hot and uncomfortable, I suppose, slipped out of it, and sat up in the bed and looked about.

It saw the 'still life' of the room accurately. The bed-curtains drawn back to the posts, the window-curtains to the frame at either side. The moon by this time was full in front of the broad window, and shone with an intense lustre into the old-fashioned room, right before the foot of the bed.

Doctor Malkin supposed nothing but that he was wide awake. He was looking about him, as I said, and, turning his eyes toward the fireplace at his left, he wondered what had become of the long Malayan knife with its wavy blade, that had hung under the portrait over the chimney-piece. He raised his eyes to the repulsive monastic portrait; but he could not see it! Had it melted into shadow?

The canvas seemed to present one surface of black. Perhaps the moonlight had dazzled his newly awakened eyes a little. He shaded them with his hand, but still the frame presented nothing but a black canvas. All the odder his dulness of vision seemed, that the dress of this mother abbess was in great measure white. While he was looking, a voice at his right whispered: 'Ha! Tempter, my child!'

Looking round instantly, he saw standing close to the bedside the figure of the portrait, but not the features. The face was that of Lady Vernon, white, gleaming, and quivering with fury, and the knife was in her hand. He sprang on the floor at the other side, and the phantom was gone. Over the chimney-piece the kreese was glimmering undisturbed, and the lady-abbess was scowling down from her frame with a grim smile.

Doctor Malkin went to the window and looked out. The flower-garden lay beneath.

He could see the arabesque pattern of the beds, in which the flowers were now closed and drooping. He could see in the broad grass-plat in the midst, which looked bright silver-grey all over, the faint lines of the croquet hoops, and at the other side the sharp black shadows of the tall, trim hedge, and the bush-like mulberry-tree in the centre, with its blotch of shadow on the grass.

He had never had a fright of this kind since his nursery years, and he was very nervous.

The unaccustomed view failed to reassure him. He lighted his candles again, and then one of his cigars, and smoked diligently from the open window, thinking of Lady Vernon, and assuring himself that never was vision more preposterous. He smoked on, looking out of the window, doing his best to obliterate the uncomfortable impression of his visitation or his nightmare. But he could not.

It answered uncomfortably to a latent horror of his conscience, which yet he boldly seized, examined, and pronounced upon most satisfactorily whenever it tormented him sufficiently. He did nothing he was afraid of, he shrank from no scrutiny; not he.

At last he lay down again, with candles burning still on his table, and, after a long and uncomfortable waking interval, he fell asleep, and the moment he awoke again in the morning, his thoughts were once more five-and-forty miles away at Roydon Hall.

He felt nervous and ill, and despise it as he might, his vision worried him.

CHAPTER XLVI.

GRIEF.

AT Roydon Hall, whither Doctor Malkin's thoughts had led him this morning, dulness reigned.

Maud was relieved of the embarrassment of a *tête-à-tête* with her mother at breakfast, by Lady Vernon's remaining in her room, in consequence of a cold.

She missed her cheery and energetic cousin. How on earth could she dispose of the day? She could have a carriage, of course, if she pleased, and drive where she liked. Whom should she visit?

About one o'clock her doubts on this point were ended by the arrival of Miss Tintern, who came to see her, having a great deal to say, and looking unhappy. She had come alone. Her father had ridden over to the Wymering Sessions.

'·Is Lady Vernon coming down?' she asked, immediately after their salutation.

'I can't say. But do you wish that we should be to ourselves?'

'Immensely. I have ever so much to tell you.' The young lady was in great distress. 'I don't know, Maud, whether I ought to tell you. It would, I fear, only embarrass you; but I have no one to speak to.'

'What would embarrass me?'

'Your having my secret to keep, dear Maud.'

'Never mind—not a bit. I'm not the least afraid,' said Miss Maud eagerly; for what young lady objects to hearing a secret?

'It is a secret that you must not tell to any living creature for the world.'

'Of course; I quite understand that. Rut I have no one to tell anything to, if I wished it. Mamma——'

' Oh, not *that*, for the world !'

' Not to mamma ? No, of course. But why particularly must it be concealed from her ?'

' Well, I'll explain by-and-bye. Do you think she will come here ? I should not like to be surprised. Would you mind walking out among the flowers ? We could not be taken unawares there.'

' I was thinking of that myself,' said Maud, and the two young ladies walked into the garden.

As soon as they got to a quiet spot, under the three acacia trees, with the scarlet and blue verbena in front, Miss Tintern looked round softly, and being assured that they were not observed, she began to pour forth her sorrows.

She began by narrating how Mr. Plimby, of Cowslip Meads, that detestable old bachelor, had wanted to dance very often with her at the Wymering ball, and how, after her papa had at last made her give him a quadrille, he had hardly left her for ten minutes all the rest of the evening.

' Oh, my dear Ethel, is he in love with you ? Is he in love ? I know he is. Oh, how delightful !' cried Maud, in an ecstasy of laughter.

' There's nothing to laugh at,' said Ethel Tintern, a good deal hurt. ' Don't you see how vexed I am, Maud ?'

' He is such a figure ! He is such a wonderful creature !' and again she broke into peals of laughter.

' Well, Maud, perhaps I had better come another day.'

' Oh, oh, oh !' almost sobbed Maud, recovering a little, with tears in her eyes. ' I'm so sorry I've interrupted you so shamefully. But he always struck me as so delightfully ridiculous ; do tell me the rest.'

' I suppose it is ridiculous, at least to everyone who does not suffer from it ; but for me it is the greatest vexation. I wish it was no worse, but it is a great deal worse—vexation is no name for it.'

' You must tell me all about it,' said Maud. ' You look so tragical, Ethel. Why, after all, it can't be so very awful. I don't think Mr. Plimby will run away with you against your will.'

' Listen now, and judge ; but, oh, Maud, remember what a confidence it is ! I am going to tell you things, that but one other person in the world knows anything of.'

' I'll not tell, I assure you ; mamma never gives me an

opportunity; and, besides, she is the last person on earth I
should volunteer to tell anything to.'

'No; I was thinking more of Miss Medwyn.'

'Max shan't hear one word about it; no, upon my honour,
not a living being shall ever hear a word about it. till you give
me leave.'

And the young lady drew Miss Tintern towards her and
kissed her.

'I know you won't tell. Where did I leave off? Oh yes,
he has been, at one time or another, every day since the ball,
calling at the Grange.'

'And do you mean to tell me that all this mischief has been
done by one quadrille at the Wymering ball ?'

'No; it seems he has been paying me pretty little attentions,
though I never perceived it, for more than a year, and I suppose
he thinks he has made an impression, and that the time has
come for being more explicit. And he has actually spoken to
papa, who sent him to me.'

'Well ?'

'I refused him, of course. You could not suppose anything
else ?'

'Well, then, if you did, where's the distress ? I can't see
what there is to trouble you.'

'Well, listen. After I had refused him, papa, who was
waiting to see him before he went, persuaded him that it was
all a mistake, and that I did not know my own mind. This
occurred yesterday, and he fixed to-morrow for his return to the
Grange, where he is to have another interview with me. Only
think !'

'Well, there's no great danger from that, is there ?' said
Maud.

'Wait till I've told you all. Papa returned, having spoken
to him, and sent for me. He seemed very ill and pale, and I
soon perceived he was very much agitated. I can never forget
his face. And then he told me, oh, Maud, Maud ! what I had
not a suspicion of. He has been making immense speculations
in mines, and they have turned out badly, and he says he is
ruined, and Mr. Plimby is his principal creditor, and that his
being able still to live at the Grange depends altogether on my
saying "yes," and marrying him.'

'Oh, darling ! I'm so awfully sorry,' said Maud, in consternation. 'But it can't possibly be. Oh no ! I believe everyone

exaggerates when they lose. You'll find it's nothing so bad as he thinks.'

But Maud's consolation failed to comfort Miss Tintern— failed even to reassure herself.

'Well, Ethel, if things do go wrong, remember I shall be my own mistress very soon. I intend to go to my Cousin Maximilla, and live with her, and you shall come—I'm quite serious —and live with us. We shall be the three happiest old maids in England. But, after all, Mr. Plimby, they say, is very rich, and no one, that I know of, ever said anything against him. I don't recommend him particularly, but he might be a better husband than a great many men who are thought very eligible indeed.'

'No, no, *no*, Maud, dear. I know it is kindly said, but all that tortures me—it is totally impossible—and oh, Maud, darling, I am in such misery! Oh, Maud, you will think me so odious, and yet I could not help it. It was not my secret, but I have been concealing something ever so long, and I know you'll hate me.'

'Hate you! Nonsense; what is it?'

And upon this invitation, with an effort, Miss Tintern told the story of her engagement to Captain Vivian.

'It was when I was at the Easterbrokes', last summer; and it has been ever since; and he has insisted on its being a secret; and I'm ashamed to look you in the face, Maud. And oh, what am I to do?'

And she threw her arms round Maud's neck and cried.

Maud, if the truth must be told, was a little affronted. The idea of having been duped and made use of by Captain Vivian to conceal his real attachment to another young lady, stung her pride.

'What am I to do, what am I to do?' sobbed poor Ethel's voice.

'What are you to do? By all means marry him, if you like him well enough. But I don't think he is the least worthy of you. I don't know a great deal of him. Very little, considering that he was so long here. He dances very nicely, that I do know, for I danced two or three dances with him at the ball. It may be that I don't know him as well as other people, but he seems nothing like good enough for you.'

Miss Tintern met this with a protest, and a torrent of the

sort of eulogy with which the enamoured astonish those who still enjoy their senses, and then she continued :

'Oh, Maud, it is such a lesson to me. I ought never to have consented to this miserable concealment, and the idea of giving up Elwyn is simply despair—I should die.'

'Well, don't give him up.'

'I could not if I wished.'

'Some way or other it will all come right, you'll find. How is Mr. Tintern? not ill, I hope?'

'He seems absent and anxious, but he bears up wonderfully; and he goes to sessions, and everything else, just as usual. I never was so astonished as when I learned the awful news from him.'

'I don't think it is quite so bad as he would have you believe; that is, I am sure he is making the worst of it.'

'Well, darling Maud, I feel better since I told you. I think I should have gone mad if I had not some one like you just now to talk to ; and remember, Maud, not a word to Miss Medwyn.'

'Not one word, I promise, to a living creature.'

'I'll not ask to see Lady Vernon. You can tell her I came in, but she was not down. I'll get into the carriage now. Good-bye.'

And so she departed, and Maud returned to the house wondering.

CHAPTER XLVII.

ROYDON PARK.

In the evening of that very lonely day Maud took a ramble in the park of Roydon.

There is nothing very bold or striking in the park, but it is prettily varied, with many rising undulations and rocky, fernclad knolls, and many winding hollows. Here the yellow gorse perfumes the air, and brambles straggle over the rocks ; the hawthorn and birch trees stretch from their clefts, and pretty wild flowers show their many hues in sheltered nooks, while all around, in groups or singly, stand the nobler forest trees, casting their mighty shadows along the uneven sward.

Maud was passing through a gentle hollow, almost a little glen, when she heard the tramp of running feet near her. A little boy was scampering along the summit of the narrow hollow at the other side.

She called to him, and he halted. She observed that the boy had a note in his hand, and beckoned him to approach. After a moment's hesitation, he descended the bank at his leisure, and stood before her.

'What are you doing here, my little man ?' she asked. 'Aren't you afraid that the keepers will find you ?'

'I was taking a message up to the Hall yonder, but the lady's not there. Happen you'll be her ?'

'What is her name ?'

'Miss Mack—Mack-something—Medwyn !'

'Oh ! Miss Maximilla Medwyn ?'

'Ay, that will be it,' replied the boy.

'No, she's not there now. Miss Medwyn left the Hall yesterday,' said the young lady, looking with an unconscious scrutiny at the note he held clutched in his dirty little fist.

'Ay,' said the boy.

'And you can tell whoever wishes to send the letter, that anyone by asking at the house can learn where Miss Medwyn is at present.'

'Ay, sure,' said the boy again, and started once more to find his employer.

Very curious was Maud ; but she did not continue her walk in its former direction. She turned about, and at the same quiet pace began to saunter towards home.

She had not reached the end of this shallow glen when she was again overtaken, and this time it was Charles Marston who was beside her.

'I hope you are not vexed. I am sure you won't be when you hear.'

Maud was more startled than she would have cared to betray, and there followed a very short silence. She had set down Captain Vivian as Maximilla's correspondent, and had never suspected such a move on Mr. Marston's part. It was unlike him. It was hardly consistent with his promise to her. Yet she was glad.

'I'm not vexed, I assure you,' she said, smiling a little, and blushing very much, as she gave him her hand. 'A little boy overtook me just now, when I was going in the opposite direction, and told me he had been looking for Miss Medwyn at the house, to give her a note. I dare say he was your messenger?'

'He was. I sent to find her, that I might ask her fifty things, and, above all, whether she thought she could persuade you to see me for a very few minutes.'

'Well, it has come about, you see, by accident.'

'And that is better, and—don't, I entreat, walk so fast—you won't refuse me a few minutes?'

She did walk slower.

'Our walk must not be very far,' she said. 'Why have you come here? You ought to consider me. It was hardly kind of you to come here, knowing all that Miss Medwyn told you.'

'I am not to blame for this chance meeting; but a letter would not have done, indeed it would not; no, nothing but a few—ever so few—spoken words. And if I had failed to see you, I think I should have despaired.'

'I hate the word despair; you must not talk tragedy.'

With a saddened change of voice and look, he said :

'I can't understand you, Maud; I think you might be more frank with me. I think, knowing the torture of my suspense, you might tell me how you wished me to understand all that passed at the Wymering ball. Tell me frankly, and I shall trouble you no more ; do you wish all over between us, or will you give me a chance?'

'What do you speak of as having occurred at the Wymering ball?' asked the young lady evasively.

'Oh, you must know,' replied Charles Marston, his jealousy overcoming all other considerations. 'I mean your having given so many dances to Captain Vivian, when you refused me more than one ; and you had thrown over other men for him.'

'Suppose I tell you that I have a right to do as I please, and that I will neither be questioned nor lectured by anyone, there would be an end of all this.'

'Certainly, Miss Vernon ; and you make me feel that I have, for a moment, forgotten myself.'

'But I won't say that. I tell you, frankly, that I don't care if I never see Captain Vivian again. I had reasons of my own for all I did ; I told you so beforehand ; and it seems a little strange that you should assume that there can be none but unkind ones.'

The reply, that had opened with so much fire and spirit, grew gentle, reproachful almost, as it ended.

They had come now, from walking very slowly, quite to a standstill under a hawthorn-tree, that stretched a friendly shelter from the steep bank.

'Heaven bless you for that reproof, because there is hope in it. Oh! how I wish, Miss Vernon, you were what you seemed to me at first, poor and almost friendless. I think my devotion might have moved you, and the proudest hope I cherished was that some day you would permit me to lift you from your troubles. But now I feel it is all changed. When I saw who you were, my heart sank. I saw my presumption, and that I ought to renounce my folly, but I could not; and now what dare I ask ?—only, perhaps, that you will allow me still to be your friend.' He took her hand. 'No, Maud, I don't think that could be. I could not live and be no more to you than a friend.' He spoke in great agitation, and kissed the hand he had taken. 'Oh, don't withdraw it. Listen for one moment, in mercy. I am going to say what is quite desperate. You will tell me now, Maud, can you ever like me ?'

'We have been on strange terms for a long time—I hardly understand them myself. We may meet again, and we may never see one another more in this uncertain world. If I were to answer you now, as you ask me, I should speak as recklessly as you say you have spoken. But I won't answer. I don't know you well enough to give you a promise, and I like you too well to take leave of you for ever. I like no one else. Perhaps I never shall; perhaps I shall never like anyone. Let all remain as it has been a little longer. And now I have said everything, and I am very glad I met you. Will you agree to what I have said ? Are you content?'

'I do agree; I am content,' he answered.

A mountain of doubt and fear was lifted from his heart in the assurance, 'I like no one else.' And the words, 'I like you too well to take leave of you for ever,' had made him tumultuously proud and happy.

'And now we must say good-bye. If you want to hear of me, write to Miss Medwyn, but not to me, and you are not to come here again. I don't act from caprice. I have good reasons for all I ask. Now I must go home, and you must not follow me one step more. Good-bye.'

He held her hand for a moment, and said :

'Good-bye, darling, but only for a little. Good-bye.'
And he kissed it passionately.

She turned and left him hurriedly, and with hasty steps walked homeward.

CHAPTER XLVIII.

A SURPRISE.

So Maud had all but confessed her love. Filled with a strange and delightful agitation, she followed the path towards the Hall.

Crossing the stile, she stopped for a minute and looked back. How infinitely fonder that vague love had grown! In that one hour her character was saddened and softened for ever. For the first time, on leaving him, she felt a great loneliness. She almost repented that she had not ended all doubt and hesitation in the matter. But there was an alarm when she thought of Lady Vernon. She did not know what powers she might have under that terrible will, in the shadow of which she had for the last few weeks begun to feel herself dismayed.

In the sweet reverie in which already the melancholy of a care quite new to her was mingling, how incredibly short the walk home proved !

She lifted up her eyes before the door, and saw the flight of white steps, and the noble doorway with its massive florid carving, friendly too, as all things seen unchanged since childhood are. Sad a little now, for the first time, it looks to her, with an altered face, in the evening glow, and a smile of reproach seems to light it mournfully. She will take her flight, as others have done, from the old home, generation after generation, for two hundred and fifty years. It does not look like home, quite, any longer.

Great heiress as she was, if all went right, she knew generally that her position might be immensely modified by certain possible events. She knew that under certain circumstances her mother had what amounted very nearly to a veto on her marriage, and that she hated the Marstons. Was she likely to sacrifice her feud to please a daughter, of whom she scarcely concealed her disdain ?

Who quite understood that complicated and teazing will of her grandfather's? He had spent half his life pulling it to pieces and putting it together again. It was his hobby. Wherever he went, or whatever he seemed to be doing, his mind was always working upon it. He left it, he confided, a few days before his death, to his attorney, in a very unfinished state. He left behind him, nevertheless, such a tesselation of puzzles, so many provisoes, exceptions, conditions, as no layman could disentangle; and his chief earthly regret on his death-bed was, that he had not been spared some six years longer, to elaborate this masterpiece.

There was uncertainty enough in her actual position to make the future anxious.

On the shield over the hall-door stands forth the sculptured Rose and Key, sharply defined in the oblique sunlight. The interest of those symbols of heraldry, after a moment's contemplation, made her think of the 'shield-room,' as the peculiar chamber I have already described was called, and to it she turned her steps.

She passed through the smooth-floored, silent hall, and along a corridor, and opened the door of the shield-room. It is so spacious a room that she did not hear a sharp voice speaking at the further end, with great animation, until she had entered it.

Her eyes, on entering the room, were dazzled by the dim western sky glaring through the three great windows, and for a moment or two all the rest looked but shadow. But she soon saw better, and the picture, touched with light, came out of the darkness.

It was Mr. Tintern's voice that was exerting itself with so much spirit. He was leaning back, in an easy posture, with his legs crossed, his arm resting on the table, and his hat and walking-cane in his other hand, reposing on his knee.

Round the corner of the table, which was not a very large one, and fronting the door, sat Lady Vernon, with a pretty little pocket-book in her hand, in which she seemed to have been making notes with a pencil; near her sat Doctor Malkin. The angle of the room, which formed a background for him, was a good deal in shadow, but a sunbeam glanced on his bald head, which shone in that light as red as blood.

There was one figure standing, and that completed a rather odd party of four. It was the slim figure of a long-necked, lantern-jawed man, with long hands, folded one over the other, a saintly smile, a head a little plaintively inclined to one side, and something indefinably villainous in his one eye. He seemed to be undergoing an examination, and Mr. Tintern rose suddenly, gazing upon Maud, and suspended his question as she advanced.

The same light that flamed on Doctor Malkin's burnished head, also showed this lank, roguish face very distinctly, and Miss Maud instantaneously recognised Elihu Lizard.

Nearly all the party seemed put out by the interruption. Mr. Lizard made a soft step or two backwards, receding into shadow. Doctor Malkin stood up, staring at her, as if not quite sure whether he saw Miss Maud or a spectral illusion. Mr. Tintern, who, as I said, had started up, advanced, after a moment's hesitation, jauntily, with his hand extended gallantly.

But the young lady had stopped short, looking very much confounded.

Lady Vernon was the only one of the party who did not appear disconcerted.

'Come in, dear, come in,' she said, employing the very unusual term 'dear.' 'There is nothing to prevent you, that is, if you have anything to say.'

'Nothing, thanks; no, mamma. I had not an idea you were busy—how do you do, Mr. Tintern and Doctor Malkin?' she said, but without delaying her retreat beyond the brief space it took to utter these hasty salutations, and gave them each a little bow.

What could they be about? This vague wonder and misgiving filled her as she ran upstairs.

Mr. Tintern she knew to be a magistrate. That odious Elihu Lizard, the sight of whom chilled her, was plainly under the ordeal of examination, when she had surprised them all together.

Why had Doctor Malkin looked at her, with an expression she had never seen before, as if she were something horrible?

What was the meaning of Mr. Tintern's cringing smile, and deprecatory, almost agitated air?

Maximilla Medwyn had always told her that Mr. Tintern had an interest under that will which was adverse to hers. She would spend that night over the printed copy of the will, which Mr. Coke had given her, and would try to understand it.

Her mother! Yes, she appeared just as usual, and not at all disconcerted. But she never was the least put out by anything. Never. Her mother! What was she thinking of? No, if there was anything under discussion which could injure her, her mother was surely unconscious of it.

She was in her own room alone, standing at the window with her hands folded together, thinking, or rather, thunderstruck.

Except her mother's, which was always negative, and therefore inflexible and inscrutable, every countenance she had seen, even the features of Elihu Lizard, wore a new and ominous expression which dismayed her.

'I wish I had my cousin Max to talk to,' she thought, ' or any living creature to consult. How lonely I have always been ! Is there any creature in the house who, under a risk of mamma's displeasure, would tell me the plain truth ?'

So, wishing in vain, she at last rang for her maid. It was time to dress for dinner.

'Jones, do you know why mamma saw Doctor Malkin and Mr. Tintern in the shield-room to-day? She does not usually sit there ?'

No, Jones did not know.

'Did you see that ill-looking man, blind of one eye, who was also in the room ?'

' No, miss, not I.'

'Well, Jones, I'm very curious, and you must try to make out all about it, mind, and tell me to-night when I come up to-bed. Don't forget.'

So Jones promised, and did her best; but nothing was to be learned, except that the blind man in question had refreshments in the housekeeper's room, and that the housekeeper was of opinion that he was one of those missionary folk, whom Lady Vernon was pleased to encourage.

There are some pictures which, we scarcely know why, seize the imagination, and retain their hold on the retina; and ever and anon, during a troubled night, the obscure background of that spacious room, and the figures touched by the horizontal glare of sunset, were before Maud.

Miss Vernon was one of those people who rely very much upon instincts and intuitions : she felt uneasily that the spectacle of that strange quartette conveyed to her a warning ; and that all that was needed was the faculty of reading it aright.

CHAPTER XLIX.

MOTHER AND DAUGHTER.

MAUD and her mother were *tête-à-tête* at dinner that day.   Lady Vernon scarcely spoke ; she seemed fatigued.

Such meetings seldom happened.   They embarrassed both mother and daughter, between whom there was an undefined but incurable estrangement.

Under such circumstances a ladies' dinner does not last very long ; and they were soon, each provided with a book, taking a very unsociable tea in the drawing-room.

A wood fire smouldered in the grate.   The evening was a little chilly, and made it pleasant.

Maud sat by it in a low chair with her feet on a stool.   She leaned back with her book before her.   The silence was only broken by the rustle of the pages as she turned them over.

At length Maud lowered the book to her lap, and raised her eyes.

They met the large grey eyes of Lady Vernon fixed on her, and the flush that indicated some secret agitation was in her cheeks.   The mutual gaze continued for some two or three seconds, and then Lady Vernon turned her eyes away, as it seemed to Maud, haughtily.

It had not lasted long ; but it made Maud uncomfortable. She knew her mother's face so well, that she read danger in that glance.

She waited some time, expecting something to come.   But as Lady Vernon remained silent, Maud took up her book again, and read a page or two ; but her mind did not follow the lines with her eyes.

In a little time she put down her book again, and looked up.

Her mother was again looking at her, and this time she spoke.

' Did you hear,' she asked, in her coldest tones, ' that Captain Vivian drove through the town of Roydon to-day ?'

' Did he, really ?'

' I should not have thought it necessary to ask you a second time,' she said, with a sneer.   ' Don't you know he did ?'

' No, I did not hear that he was in the town since he left this,' Maud replied.

' It is so nice of you, answering me so honestly,' said Lady Vernon.

Maud looked at her, not quite certain whether the irony she suspected in her tone was real or fancied.

'Did you see anyone to-day?' Lady Vernon reopened her conversation, after an interval, more dangerously.

'Miss Tintern was here to-day. She came in hoping to see you, and then I took her a little walk.'

'Oh! Then this has been a day of walking,' said Lady Vernon, with something derisive in her tone, that terrified Maud for her secret, and Maud blushed.

Lady Vernon, deadly pale, held her with her steady grey eyes, and an insulting smile, for some seconds.

Then the elder lady turned slowly away, still smiling, and Maud felt that she could breathe.

How much hatred there seemed to Maud in that pale, cruel smile; how much hatred in those cold, strange tones, low and sweet as the faintest notes of a flute!

Maud was in momentary fear of a renewal of the torture. But a minute passed, five minutes, and there was no renewal of the attack. Her mother seemed to have forgotten her, and to have returned to her book, with no further intention of disturbing her studies.

Ten minutes passed. The room was still as death. Suddenly that soft, cold, sweet voice was again in her ear. If it had been a clap of thunder it could not have startled her more.

'Pray, Maud, did you meet anyone to-day in your walk?'

There was in Lady Vernon's tone, air, and look that which fired the girl's indignation.

She returned her mother's look, undecided whether she would answer her at all.

Suddenly losing command of her temper, Lady Vernon exclaimed sternly:

'How dare you look at me, your mother, so? Answer my question, and speak truth. Whom did you meet to-day?'

'I shan't answer,' said Maud, flushing crimson. 'What have I done that you should attack me with so much bitterness?'

'Come, Maud, recollect yourself,' said Lady Vernon, recovering her colder manner. 'You seem to forget that, as your mother, I have a right to know, from your own lips, whom you met to-day. Who was it?'

'I question your right to catechize me,' returned Maud, now thoroughly roused. 'If I am to remember your rights, you must remember mine. I shall be of age in a few weeks, and my own mistress. You are not to treat me any longer like a child.'

'While you remain in my house you shall be amenable to me. I can't command affection, but I can command respect. You shall obey me. I'll make you obey me.'

The flush had quite left her cheeks, her face was unnaturally white, and her lip, as white as her face, was trembling. Maud had never before seen her so terribly angry. But she was now past being daunted. She was herself very nearly as angry, and so the spark had started into flame, and the flame had gathered to a conflagration.

'That is not the way to make me obey you. That is not what you want. You wish to wound me, and to trample on me. You never loved me ; you hate me ; yes, you hate me—your own child, your only child. And what have I done ? All my life trying to bring you to love me. That's over. I'll try no more—never. You'll teach me at last to hate you, as you hate me. I wish it were God's will to take me. Oh ! this dreadful world !'

'Wicked people make it dreadful to themselves and to others, said Lady Vernon.

But Maud went on with her wild tirade.

'That poor girl who drowned herself in the mere at Golden Friars—they said she was wicked—she looked like an angel. Oh ! for courage like hers to take the leap out of this frightful world !'

'That's a threat of suicide, as I understand it, unless I forego, not my rights, but my duty. You shan't deter me from doing it,' said Lady Vernon. 'You shall confess.'

'I will not answer you. I will not confess. I have nothing to confess. Why do you use that insulting word ? There has been nothing in my life I need ever have been ashamed or afraid to disclose.'

Lady Vernon looked at her intently for a moment, and then laughed a cold little laugh of disdain.

But that counterfeit merriment did not last long. The false smile faded, and left a deeper shadow of menace on her face.

'Another person would answer a daughter who presumed to talk to them so, very differently. But I know only too well your lamentable weakness and violence ; and I'll tell you, as you have not the grace or candour to admit it, that you cannot conceal the fact from me. You saw Captain Vivian to-day.

You talked and walked with him, and returned to the house only a few minutes before you came into the shield-room this evening. You might as well have spoken frankly.'

If it had not been for the anger provoked by Lady Vernon's language and manner, Maud would, I dare say, have undeceived her, now. But the devil of perverse pride had been evoked, and Maud answered :

'If you knew all this, why need you have asked me to tell you ? I said I should answer nothing ; and I shall not.'

'You shall do more than answer,' said Lady Vernon, rising to her feet, with a new access of passion, and confronting her daughter. 'You shall now and here write me a letter renouncing Captain Vivian. Sit down at this desk and write it.'

'No,' answered Maud, also rising, 'I'll do nothing of the kind. I'll place myself in no such ridiculous position.'

Lady Vernon was astounded. Maud had never disputed a distinct command of hers before.

'Think again, Maud, you had better. I fear you are losing your head a little,' she said coldly.

'I need not think again ; I won't write anything. I've said so, and I won't,' answered Maud, with all the fiery blood of the Vernons careering in her veins.

'Then take the consequences of your insanity,' said Lady Vernon, almost in a whisper, but with an audible stamp on the floor.

These two pair of large eyes were encountering, all this time, in defiance.

So the unnatural alienation that had for so many years existed between mother and child had now at last spoken out, and the angry passions of both were declared and active.

'I think I had better go to my own room,' said Maud, in tones which trembled a little.

'Do so,' said Lady Vernon.

Maud walked straight to the door. She had opened it, and paused with the handle in her hand. It was only to say, hastily :

'Good-night, mamma.'

'Good-night,' returned Lady Vernon, in a tone that sounded like 'begone.'

And so Maud stepped out, with heightened colour, blazing eyes, and a countenance wild and heart-broken.

She walked upstairs with a humming in her ears, as if she

had received a blow. Her dry, hot lips were whispering :

' No, never again : we never can be again even what we were
before. It is all over ; there is nothing ever to reconcile us.
No, never; it can never be again.'

When she got to her room, her maid Jones, advancing with
her accustomed smile, exclaimed, with a sudden halt and a change
of countenance :

' La ! Miss Maud, dear, what's the matter? you do look pale
and queer !'

' Do I ?' said Maud vaguely. ' No, not much. I'm sorry,
Jones.' And she burst into a wild flood of tears.

' What is it, Miss Maud, my dear child ; what's the matter ?'

' Oh, Jones ! if all the world were like you !'

And she placed her arms round her trusty maid's neck and
kissed her.

' What is it, my dear ? There, there, don't ! Tell me, like a
good child, what's the matter ?'

' I'll tell you all, Jones, by-and-bye. It has come at last; it's
as well it should   Mamma has been so unkind, and cruel, and
insulting, and I was angry, and we've quarrelled—desperately.
It can never be made up again, Jones ; never, never.'

' Nonsense, Miss Maud, what a fuss you make ; it will all be
nothing at all.'

' I was violent—I was wrong—I spoke as I ought not—I
blame myself. But, no, Jones, it can never be made up—it is
folly to think it. I know mamma too well. It is past that ;
she never forgives ; and she never loved me ; there is no use in
trying to think it. She hates me now, and always will, and I'm
sorry, but it can't be helped.'

So she sobbed on, sitting in the great chair, with her face to
the wall beside it, and honest Jones, who was disturbed and
even shocked, said, with her hands on the big arm of the chair,
leaning over her, and employing a powerful superlative of her
own invention :

' Her ladyship's the very most religiousest lady in England,
and the most charitablest, and you mustn't say or think *so*.
She's strict, and will have her will obeyed, and you mustn't
gainsay her when she thinks she's right. But she's a just
woman, and good. Now don't be crying so, darling, for you
have only to say what you should say to her, and everything

will be as it used, and you'll say so yourself in the morning.
There now, don't take on so.'

Thus honest Jones poured consolation into an inattentive and
incredulous ear, and the young lady, answering never a word,
wept on for a long time. It was her leave-taking of a dream
that could never come again, the hope that her mother might, at
last, come to love her.

CHAPTER L.

LADY VERNON.

WHEN Maud had closed the door, the bitter smile that had
gleamed on her mother's face with a wintry light departed, and
left the bleakest darkness instead.

She remained sitting as in a dream where Maud had left her,
with her hands clasped hard together in her lap ; she looked
down on the carpet a yard or so before her feet darkly, and drew
her shoulders together, as if a chill air were about her, and
shuddered.

How sudden had been the alarm ! and now that the danger
was upon her, how fast events were driving on !

The tiny ring of the clock over the mantelpiece recalled her.
It was twelve o'clock. More than an hour had passed since
Maud had left her. It had not appeared five minutes.

She lit her candle, and ascended the great stairs, still in her
dream. Without effort, almost without consciousness of motion,
she moved like a ghost along the galleries. The homely figure of
lean Mrs. Latimer, in her plain black silk dress, startled her like
the sight of a stranger.

Lady Vernon did not talk to Latimer that night ; she had no
questions to ask her. Her veteran maid had never known her so
darkly absent before. She told her to leave the two candles on
the dressing-table burning, and the maid departed, wondering
what had gone wrong, or who had vexed ' my lady.'

Left to herself, Lady Vernon lay still, in that grisly vigilance
that in outward seeming simulates the quietude of slumber.
Sometimes, for five minutes, her eyes were closed ; sometimes
wide open for as long. She heard the pulse of the artery in her
temple drum on her pillow ; and her heart beat harder than a
heart at ease is wont to throb.

Lady Vernon had now lain awake in her bed for an hour. She grew hopeless of the rest she felt she wanted. At last she got up, unlocked her dressing-case, and took out one of its pretty cut-glass bottles, with a golden cap over it stopper. It contained the infusion of opium in water, which De Quincy mentions as the fluid approved by those who use that drug on a large scale.

Lady Vernon had recourse to its potent magic only when sleep forsook her, as at present. This of late had happened often enough to cause her to apply to it with increasing doses.

It failed on this occasion, and produced, instead of quiet, exaggerated excitement.

At length the lady rose, and in her dressing-gown and slippers sat down at her table, and wrote a passionate letter to Captain Vivian, summoning him to Roydon, and promising to open her heart to him if he would come.

This letter written, she again had recourse to the little cut-glass bottle, and this time with success. In a few minutes she lay in a deep, motionless sleep.

In the morning when she awoke the vengeful drug exacted its compensation. She felt stunned by the potent medicine.

She had locked the letter in her dressing-box. The first thing in the morning she took it out and read it.

No; it would not do. The glamour of the opium was over it. She burnt it at the candle that was still flaring at her bedside, pale and smoky, in the early light of morning which she had admitted at the open shutter.

That letter must be very carefully written, she thought; and other measures must be taken first. It seemed doubtful, alto-gether, whether it might not be as effectual and wiser to write only to old Mr. Dawe.

She did not come down to breakfast that morning. Maud was infinitely relieved; she dreaded the idea of meeting Lady Vernon; and to her great delight, there came a letter from Lady Mardykes, naming the day for receiving her at Carsbrook. It said :

'Your mamma has been so good as to tell Maximilla Medwyn that she will allow you to come to Carsbrook any day you please. If you can, do come on Monday next; Maximilla has promised to be here early, so if you arrive any time in the afternoon, you will be sure to find her here. I tried to get Ethel Tintern to come; but she can't, she says, for some time. You will find my house very full, and there are some odd, and, I think, very amusing people here.   Maximilla tells me that you and she were interested by the rather striking appearance of Doctor Anto-marchi.   I wrote to ask him for a day or two; so you shall meet him at Carsbrook.   He is a wonderful mesmerist.   Two young ladies are talking in my room as I write.   I hope I am not quite unintelligible in consequence.   I hope you like dancing. We dance a great deal ; but you will learn all our ways in a little time.'

There was a note from Maximilla Medwyn also, seconding Lady Mardykes' invitation, and promising to be punctually at Carsbrook on the morning of Monday.   She mentioned also that she had written to Lady Vernon, and was certain, from what had passed, that she would place no difficulty in the way of Maud's visit to Carsbrook.   Of this, however, Maud was by no means so sure.

Lady Vernon did not meet her at luncheon.   Maud had gone to the room in secret trepidation.   The respite was very wel-come ; if she could only make her escape to Carsbrook, what a happy change !

She was glad to learn from Jones that Sir Paul and Lady Blunkett were to dine at Roydon, and stay till next day, and that Mr. and Mrs. Foljambe and Captain Bamme were to meet the worthy baronet and his wife.

She was in hopes of getting away to Carsbrook—if she were indeed to be allowed to visit Lady Mardykes, of which she had very uncomfortable doubts since the scene of the night before —without the agitation of another *tête-à-tête* with her mother.

She sent for Jones, and ran up to her own room, trembling lest she should meet Lady Vernon on the stairs.

I don't know whether Lady Vernon had any secret shrink-ings of a similar kind.   If she had, she would have disdained them, and played out her game, whatever it was, disdainfully.

Jones found her young mistress standing at her own window, looking out in an anxious reverie.

'Jones, do you know where mamma is ?' Maud asked.

'Her ladyship went down more than an hour ago to the library, and I think she is there still, for it is only about ten minutes since she sent for Mr. Penrhyn to go to her there.'

'I'm so afraid of meeting her.   I should rather put off seeing her as long as I can. Did Latimer say anything of her having been vexed with me last night ?'

'Not a word, miss; I dare say you are making too much of it.'

Maud shook her head.

'We'll not talk about that. I wish I were sure that she would allow me to go to Lady Mardykes'. You would have great fun there, Jones.'

'Well, indeed, miss, a bit o' fun would not hurt neither of us. Her ladyship does keep things awful dull here.'

At this moment came a knock at the door.

Miss Vernon looked at Jones, and Jones at Miss Vernon, and there was rather alarmed silence, during which the knock was repeated.

'Who is there ?' asked Maud, after another pause.

It was Latimer.

'Come in, Latimer. Are you looking for me ?' said the young lady.

'Please, miss, her ladyship wishes to see you in the library,' said Latimer, in her dry way.

'Immediately ?' asked Maud, changing colour.

'So she desired me to say, miss.'

'Oh, very well, Latimer. Tell mamma, please, that I'll follow you in a moment.

Latimer was gone, and the door shut.

'I wish it was over,' said the young lady, very pale. 'Stay here, Jones, till I come back.

'I will, miss,' said Jones, whose heart misgave her now, respecting the visit to Carsbrook. 'And you won't mind me saying, miss, 'twill be best you should not contradict her ladyship in nothing.'

'I don't think she'll keep me very long. When I come back I'll tell you whether we are going or not.'

And with these words Miss Vernon left the room, and proceeded along the gallery, and down the stairs, at a much more sedate pace than usual.

It was a very unpleasant excitement, and she felt for a moment almost a little faint as she approached the well-known door.

She hesitated before it. She wondered whether any one was with her mother, and with something nearly amounting to the sinking of panic, anticipated the coming scene.

With an effort of resolution she knocked.

'Come in,' said the sweet, cold commanding voice she knew so well.

Maud entered the room, and drew near with the embarrassment of one who knows not what reception may be awaiting her.

Her eyes, fixed on Lady Vernon, saw nothing unusual in the serene and cold expression of her handsome face. She heard nothing unusual in her clear, harmonious tones. Her manner was perfectly unembarrassed. Judging by external signs, Maud might have concluded that no recollection of their fiery encounter of the night before remained in her mother's mind.

'There has come a note from Maximilla Medwyn, to-day, telling me that Lady Mardykes wishes you to go to Carsbrook on Monday next. There is nothing to prevent your telling her that you will go.

Maud was afraid to say how delighted and relieved she was. She could not say what untoward caprice too strong an expression of her feeling might excite; but a flush of pleasure glowed brilliantly in her cheeks.

'It is too late to-day for the Roydon post; you can write to-morrow. I have written to Maximilla to say what your answer will be,' said Lady Vernon. 'Some people are coming to dine here to-day, and I don't think we are likely to be alone while you remain at home. I only wished to mention that; and you had better tell Jones, as she is to go with you; there's nothing more.'

'I hope you are pretty well now, mamma?'

'Quite well, thanks,' said Lady Vernon, cutting short any possible prolongation of these civilities. 'You remember the story of—Talleyrand, was it. I forget—a Frenchman of the world, who, being bored at every posting-house, through half the journey to Paris, with messages from a gentleman who was travelling the same road, to inquire particularly how he was, requested the messenger at last to say to the gentleman who was so good as to make so many inquiries, that he was very well all the way to Paris. So we'll take that hint, I think, and save one another some trouble, and I'll say I'm very well all the way to Monday afternoon. And now, dear Maud, I'm busy, and I think I'll say good-bye.'

And with this gracious speech, accompanied by a cold little laugh that was indescribably insulting, she turned to her papers once more, leaving Maud to make her exit with a very full and angry heart.

'I'm always sorry when I try to show her the least sign of affection. Well, while I remain here, I'll not be such a fool again.'

So, with flashing eyes, Maud resolved, as she passed from the library through the suite of rooms beyond it.

CHAPTER LI.

DOCTOR MALKIN CONFERS.

ABOUT two hours later, Maud was walking beyond the avenue, in that part of the grounds in which, some weeks before, Miss Max and old Mr. Dawe had taken a little ramble together.

Suddenly she lighted on Doctor Malkin, who was walking up the wooded path from the village. Maud saw that the quick eye of the doctor had seen her at the same moment that she saw him. He happened to be in a part of the path which makes its way through a very shadowy bit of wood, and possibly the doctor thought that he might have been unobserved, for he hesitated for a second, and she fancied was about to evade the meeting by stepping quickly among the trees. But it was only a momentary thought, for he would not of course allow the young lady to suppose that he shrank from a recognition. So, pretending to look up among the boughs of the tree under which he stood, in search of a bird or a squirrel, or some other animated illustration of that natural history which was one of his studies, he resumed his walk toward her, affecting not to see her until he had approached more nearly; then raising his hat, with a surprised smile and a deferential inclination, he quickened his pace, and, as he reached her, observed on the weather and the beauty of the tints beginning to discolour the summer foliage, and then mentioned that he fancied he saw a kite, whose scientific name he also mentioned, among the boughs of a very dark tree, a little way off, but he was not quite sure. She was taking a rather solitary walk, he observed; how very much she must miss her companion in so many pleasant rambles—Miss Medwyn. What a charming old lady she is, so agreeable, and such exhilarating spirits !

There was a sort of effort and embarrassment in all this that was indefinable and unpleasant. If he had been half detected in a poaching expedition to snare the rabbits, or on any other lawless design, he could scarcely have looked more really disconcerted, and more anxious to appear at his ease.

The doctor appeared to be made up for a journey ; he had a rug and a muffler for the night air, still five or six hours away, across his arm, and carried his thin umbrella, in its black shining case, in his hand, as well as a small black leather bag. A fly was to meet him at the back gate of Roydon, and wherever he was going he wished to have a word with Lady Vernon before setting out on his travels.

'Lady Vernon was a little uneasy,' he said, 'lest that attack of the young woman at the gate-house should turn out to be diphtheria, and I promised to see her and report, and I'm glad to say it is nothing of the kind. So, as I shan't be home till to-morrow, I thought it best to look in to-day to set Lady Vernon's mind at ease. Good-bye, Miss Vernon.'

The doctor took his leave, as I have said ; and Maud saw the shower of dotted sunlight, as he strode on the path toward the Hall, flying through the interstices of the leaves across the glazed black bag he carried, or, more softly, mottling his rug and his hat. She could not account for the slight awkwardness that seemed to affect everything he said or did during those two or three minutes, and she observed that the pale gentleman with the long upper lip and short chin, smooth and blue, smiled more than was necessary, and that the obliquity that spoiled his really fine eyes was a good deal more marked than usual.

The doctor was soon quite beyond her ken, and pursued his way at a brisk place to the house, where he was instantly admitted to the library.

He had thrown down his rugs and other property in the hall, and had merely his hat in his hand as he entered.

Lady Vernon got up and took his hand, and smiled faintly and wearily, and, with a little sigh, said :

'I did not think the time had arrived. I have had, as usual, some business to get through ; but you are punctual.'

She glanced at the French clock over the chimney-piece.

'Sit down, Doctor Malkin ; I have been thinking over

what I said, and I don't recollect that I have anything very
particular to add.   There are only two things that occur to me
to say : the first is, that I have quite made up my mind upon
the main point ; and the second is, that it must take place immediately.'

The doctor bowed, and his eyes remained fixed on the table
for a minute.   The lady did not speak.   She was also looking
down, but with a little frown, and affected to be diligently arranging her letters one over the other.

Doctor Malkin felt himself called upon to say something.

'It is as well often—generally—*I* don't see any difficulty ; in
fact, I know there can't be, unless it should exist *here*,' he said
in a low tone, speaking by fits and starts.

'There is none,' said Lady Vernon, with a little irritation in
her look and tone.   Perhaps she did not understand Doctor
Malkin's affectation of embarrassment.   ' I have made a note of
the day I now wish to appoint, and of my reason for greater
promptitude ; I thought it would be more satisfactory to you to
have it in that form.'

'Thanks ; it is so considerate,' said Doctor Malkin, taking the
note she dropped before him.   ' I'll just, if you allow me, run
my eye over it.'

He opened it.   It was not a very long memorandum.

'Perfectly clear,' he said, when he had read it through ;
'and I must say, your reason appears to me a very powerful one
—very.'

'Mr. Pembroke Damian is a very admirable man,' said the
lady, after an interval of silence.   'He was one of the most
eloquent preachers I ever heard, and a man whose life was
more eloquent still than his preaching, and he is so able, so wise.
I look upon him, taken for all in all, as one of the worthies
of England.'

Lady Vernon had raised her dark, cold eyes, and was looking,
not indeed at the doctor, but straight before her, to the wall, as
she spoke this high moral testimony.

'He certainly is a most remarkable man,' said Doctor
Malkin.

'He is a benefactor to the human race,' said the lady.   'When
I think of all the suffering he has alleviated, and the despair
to which he has been the instrument of admitting comfort and
peace, I am justified in regarding him, as I do, as the minister

and angel of Heaven. I have boundless confidence in that good and able man.'

Doctor Malkin acquiesced.

'And I thank Heaven there is such a person living, and in his peculiar position,' continued Lady Vernon. 'Will you be so good as to give him this note ?'

Doctor Malkin deferentially took the letter she handed him.

'It is a very happy reflection that my confidence, inevitable as it is, should be placed in so sagacious and pious a man,' she added.

'He has certainly been a useful man,' said the doctor, still looking down on the envelope, with the address, the 'Rev. Pembroke Damian, M.A.' etc., in the clear and graceful hand of Lady Vernon, 'and a most conscientious person—a truly religious man. You, Lady Vernon, can speak with much more authority than I upon that point ; and certainly, I will say, his ideas have been in advance of his time ; his has been a most influential mind, and in some points has led the opinion of his age.'

'I would trust my life, as I am ready to trust that which, you will say, ought to be dearer still to me, in his hands,' said Lady Vernon.

'He does not quite take the leading part he did, you know,' said Doctor Malkin. 'For the last two or three years he has not done a very great deal.'

'That is a rather unpleasant piece of information, you must suppose, for me,' Lady Vernon said, with an angry flush 'If I did not suppose it a little exaggerated, I think I should almost hesitate.'

Doctor Malkin knew that the lady wished him to understand that he had made a stupid speech. He had put his foot in it. He said hastily :

'Of course, I don't mean that Mr. Damian has abdicated, or anything of the kind. Of course, he takes a very essential part, and is, in so far as your interests and feelings are personally concerned, everything he ever was.'

'I have always assumed that to be so,' said Lady Vernon severely, 'and I should be obliged to you, Doctor Malkin, if you would report to me any dereliction of duty on the part of Mr. Damian, which, I must tell you frankly, I can't suppose. I know so, much of him ; he is in all respects so consistent a Christian. I relied upon this, and upon his principal and actual responsibility.'

The lady's eyes still flashed, and she spoke sharply. Doctor Malkin saw, too late, that she possibly construed his words as casting an undesirable responsibility upon her. He hastened, therefore, to reply.

'My meaning was, I assure you, very far from that. On the contrary, I believe Mr. Damian was never more vigorous in mind. He deputes nothing involving a responsibility. I'm afraid I must have expressed myself very clumsily indeed.'

Lady Vernon did not care to discuss the point further.

'I need not tell you how much I have suffered,' she said. 'It may come, very soon, all right again. Let us hope the best. I hope, at least, it may not be very protracted. I shall see you to-morrow?'

'Yes, certainly, Lady Vernon, at any hour that suits you best. And I don't anticipate the slightest trouble.'

'There will be some trifling arrangements still to complete, which we can then talk over. You set out, I suppose, immediately on leaving this?'

'Immediately,' said he. 'I think I have very full instructions now. You don't recollect anything more?'

'No. The rest had better wait till to-morrow. So I will say good-bye.'

Lady Vernon gave her hand to Doctor Malkin without a smile, and he was more than usually deferential and solemn as he took it.

At the room door, Doctor Malkin recollected his accidental meeting with Miss Vernon, and returned for a moment to mention the circumstance to Lady Vernon, as it had obliged him to allege a pretext for his visit to Roydon Hall.

'Well,' said the lady, growing a little red, 'I should have preferred saying nothing. But it can't be helped now. Where did you meet her?'

He told her.

She looked down in momentary misgiving—thoughtful. But she had learned that Captain Vivian, who had undoubtedly driven through the town of Roydon the evening before, had left again for the station, and had gone away by train, and she was sure to hear more particularly in the morning about his movements from Mr. Dawe, to whom she had written a very agitated letter of inquiry and alarm.

She would take her, if possible, to the Tinterns next day, and somewhere else the day following, and keep her, should any uncertainty arise, out of the way of any further meeting with that perverse gentleman.

So Lady Vernon, recollecting that the silence had been rather long, said suddenly :

'I was thinking, I may tell you, as I have taken you so unreservedly into council, whether, under all circumstances, the grounds here are quite a suitable place for Maud to take these solitary walks in?'

'Well, as you say Lady Mardykes' invitation was for Monday, she will be leaving this so soon, it is scarcely——'

'Well, *yes;* we can talk of that to-morrow,' interrupted Lady Vernon.

So again giving him her hand, she and the doctor, who was not himself looking very well or very merry, made a second leave-taking, and he took his departure.

His allusion to Maud's departure on the Monday following was in the tone of her own very decided feeling.

Lady Vernon had particular reasons for being glad that Lady Mardykes had fixed so early a day for her daughter's visit to Carsbrook.

CHAPTER LII.

MERCY CRESWELL.

NEXT day an humble but unlooked-for visitor appeared at Roydon Hall.

Miss Vernon, on returning in the afternoon from her short walk to inquire at the gate-house for the sick girl, encountered the slim, dark figure of Latimer, her mother's maid, in the hall.

Latimer had evidently been looking for her, for the demure angular figure, which had been crossing the hall toward the drawing-room as she entered, turned sharp to the left, and approached her with a quick step, and making a little inclination before Maud, Lady Vernon's maid said, in her low, dry tones :

'Please, miss, my lady desires me to say that Mercy Creswell, which you recollect her, perhaps, in the nursery long ago, being niece of old Mrs. Creswell, that died here when you was but a child, miss, has come here to see her ladyship and you, also, if you please.'

'I do remember her very well. I must have been a very little thing, Latimer, when she went away.'

'About six years old you was, miss, when she left. Where will you please to see her ?' replied Latimer.

'Where is she now ?'

'In my lady's morning-room, please, miss. But you can see her, my lady says, anywhere you please,' answered Latimer.

'Then I should like to see her quietly, if you would tell her to come to my dressing-room, and tell some one to send Jones there, please, and I will go myself in two or three minutes to see her.'

Latimer disappeared; and Maud in a minute more was running up the stairs to her room.

We all lean a little fondly to the recollections of childhood, especially those images of very early memory, from which chance has long widely separated us.

But Maud could not get up any great interest in this particular woman, Mercy Creswell. She was, as Maud remembered her, a red-haired, stunted, freckled girl of perhaps some sixteen years ; plump, and broad, and strong, with a cunning and false gaiety in her fat face, and who laughed a great deal, not pleasantly, but rather maliciously, and at untoward times.

Maud had a remembrance of an occasional slap or pinch, now and then, slyly bestowed by this short, freckled, laughing young lady, who rather liked getting her into a scrape at times, and who used in playful moods, when they were running about the rooms together, and no one by, to run her into a corner, hold her to the wall, and make ugly faces, with her nose almost touching Maud's, till the child would scream with fright and anger; and then she would fall into shrieks of laughter, and hug and kiss her a little more roughly than was necessary, and after this somewhat sore and uncomfortable reconciliation, she would charge her —for the love she bore her own, own poor little Mercy Creswell, who would be sent away if she did, never more to dress her doll, or trundle her cart, or roll her ball for her—not to tell nurse, or nursery-maid, or Miss Latimer, that they had had 'a falling out.'

Her recollections of this early attendant and, under the rose, playmate, therefore, were not quite as sunny as they might be. Still, they were connected with happier days, or what now seemed happier, than those which had come later; and perhaps if Mercy Creswell was sometimes a disagreeable companion, it was to be attributed, in great measure, to the boisterous, and occasionally mischievous, spirits of very early girlhood.

When she reached her dressing-room, Maud Vernon beheld, for the first time for fourteen years, this same Mercy Creswell.

The interval had not improved her personal appearance. Short and square, with a very fat, and rather flat face, mottled with very large freckles, and her red hair showing under her bonnet, she might have passed for a woman of the age, at least, of Don Quixote's housekeeper. No one could have supposed that her age did not exceed thirty years. She smiled so ecstatically that she nearly shut up her cunning little eyes in rolls of fat wrinkles, while she blinked them very fast, as if tears were forcing their way from them; of which, I don't think, there was any other sign. She was not prepossessing; but Maud could not find it in her heart to repulse her when, whisking aside her green veil, she rose on tip-toe, put her short arms round Maud's neck, and kissing her energetically, said:

'Ye'll excuse the liberty, Miss Maud, dear, but it is such a time since your own poor little Mercy has saw'd you. La! what a beautiful young lady you have growed up since then; well, to be sure, and me as small as ever. Well, la! it is a queer world, miss. I 'a bin in many a place since Roydon nursery. La, miss! do you mind the big ball o' red leather, and the black man with the cymbals, and all the toys and trumpets, dollies, and donkeys? Well, dearie me! so there was, wasn't there? La! and we was great friends, you and me, ye'll excuse me saying so; and many a day's play together we two has had; and I thought I'd 'a heard o' you married long ago, miss, but there's time enough yet. 'Twill be a lord, nothing less, whenever he comes; bless him.'

'And you, Mercy, you have not married yet?' said Maud.

'Me? La bless ye! not I, by no means, miss. Oh, la! what would I be doin' with a husband? Oh, la! no.'

'Well, as you say, there is time enough, Mercy; and what have you been doing ever since?'

'La, miss! I could not answer that in a week. I was at service after leaving here, first with Lady Mardykes.'

'At Lady Mardykes'? I know her. I'm sure you had a pleasant time in her house?' said Maud eagerly.

'That it was; no pleasanter, miss; no end of great folks there, and music, and fine clothes, and all sorts, and play-acting, and dancing by night; and croquet and lawn billiards, and the like o' that all day; or driving off, with cold luncheons, to this place or that, nothing but grand people, and all sorts of fun; high jinks the gentlemen used to call it.'

'I'm going there, to Carsbrook, on Monday next,' said Maud, who was full of this visit.

'Well to be you, miss,' said Mercy Creswell, looking down and coughing a little; 'and I would not wonder, miss, if I was to be there myself,' she added, looking up again, and screwing her mouth together, and drawing in her breath through the circular orifice, while she raised her eyebrows with a lackadaisical ogle at the window.

'Oh? Really! Well, mind you must make me out if you should,' said Maud gaily.

'I'll be sure to,' she answered, with one of her sly giggles.

'It is a great black-and-white house, very large, ain't it?' said Maud, smiling.

'La! how did ye find that out?' Mercy Creswell continued, with the same irrepressible giggle.

'You see, I know more about it than you fancied,' continued Maud. 'It is three stories high, and close under the windows there is an old-fashioned flower-garden, with the croquet-ground in the middle, and the lawn billiards and all that, and an old mulberry-tree growing in the middle of it; and it is surrounded on three sides by a tall hedge clipped like a wall, with here and there an arch cut through it, something like the yew cloisters behind the shield-room here, only very much larger.'

'Why, you must 'a bin there, miss,' her visitor cried, half stifled with laughter.

'No, never; and there are ever so many bedrooms, and more guests generally than you could number—all kinds of great, and wise, and clever, and famous people.'

As Maud proceeded, her short, fat visitor, in her shawl and big bonnet, was actually obliged to get up and stump about the room, so extravagant her laughter by degrees became.

'You see, I know something about it,' continued Maud, laughing also. 'As you used to say to me long ago, a little bird told me. But I shall soon be there, I hope, to see for myself; and I believe everyone is made to feel quite at home there, immediately; and it is such a hospitable house everyone says. Your only difficulty is, how to get away; and oh! tell me, do you know Doctor Antomarchi?'

' I 'a heard of him once or twice,' screamed Mercy Creswell, almost suffocated with laughter.

' Now listen to me. We have laughed enough,' said Maud. ' You mustn't laugh. I can't get you to tell me anything ; you do nothing but laugh ; and I really wished so much to hear about him. I and Miss Medwyn saw him at the Wymering ball, and we were both so curious. Can you tell me anything about him ?'

' Not I, miss.'

' Well, if you like, Jones shall make you a wager that he will be there at the same time,' continued the young lady, a little puzzled by her fat friend's irrepressible and continued screams of laughter, and beginning to feel the infection a little more herself ; ' and the Spanish ambassador ; *he* will be there also.'

' Oh ! Oh, la ! Oh, miss, stop ! Oh, oh, oh, you're a killing of me. I'm—I'm—I'm not able to—to—oh, la ! ha, ha, ha ! catch my breath.' And fat Mercy Creswell, clinging to the corner of a wardrobe, actually shook with laughter till tears rolled plentifully down her big cheeks ; and Maud, and her maid Jones, who was nevertheless disgusted by the vulgar familiarity and noise of the clumsy Miss Creswell, were drawn in in spite of themselves, and joined at last vehemently and hilariously in the chorus.

' Well, don't mind me,' at last sobbed Miss Creswell, recovering slowly, ' I always was one, oh, ho, ho ! that laughs at nothing. I do ; I'm as tired now, my dear—oh, ho, ho !—as if I ran up to the top o' the fells of Golden Friars, and la ! but that's high enough ; but how did you hear all about it, so exact, Miss Maud, dear ? where in the world——'

' I may as well tell you then,' she answered, also recovering. ' I heard everything about it from Miss Medwyn ; you must remember her very well. She has been there very often, and she, I know, will be staying there at the same time that I am.'

But at this moment Miss Mercy experienced another relapse, nearly as long and violent, every now and then, half articulately, blurting out, in sobs and gasps amidst the screaming roulades of her laughter : ' Oh la ! ha, ha ! Miss Med—Med—oh, ho ! ho ! —Medwyn—la ! ha, ha, ha ! She's so staid, she is—she's so nice. La ! ha, ha, ha !' and so on.

When at length a lull came, Miss Vernon, who was protected by its impertinence from any tendency to join in this last explosion of her old under-nursery-maid's merriment, said gravely :

'Mamma has not been very well : she has been complaining of headache ; and I think we are making a good deal of noise. I don't know how far off it may be heard.'

'Well, dear Miss Maud, I hope you ain't offended, miss ; but, dearie me, I could not but laugh a bit, thinking of old Miss Medwyn among all them queer dancers, and fiddlers, and princes, and play-actors, and flute-players ; I hope you'll hexcuse the noise I 'a made, seein' I really could not help it, miss, by no chance. I know Lady Mardykes well ; why shouldn't I, having lived in her service for a many years ? And a very great lady she is, and well liked, as I well know ; and her papa, Lord Warhampton, a'most the greatest man in England ; no wonder she should have all the highest in the land in her house, when- ever she so pleases. But, la ! ha, ha, ha ! It's a queer world. Who'd a thought? There is such queer things happens.'

This time her laughter was but an amused giggle, and she did not lose her command over it.

'Have you had luncheon ?' inquired Maud.

'I thank you, miss, hearty, in the 'ouse-keeper's room, before I came up to see her ladyship,' answered short Miss Mercy, with a comfortable sigh, blowing her nose a little, and adjusting her big bonnet and old green veil, and smoothing her red tresses, while, still out of breath, she tried to recover the fatigues of her long fit of laughter. 'Well, Miss Maud, dear, and how are ye ?' inquired Mercy, suddenly returning from gay to grave.

'Oh, very well, thanks, and so are you ; and you haven't married, you tell me, so you have nothing on earth to trouble you. I wish we were all like the trees, Mercy ; they live very long and very happily, I dare say—longer, certainly, and more quietly than we do a great deal, and I don't hear of any marry- ing or giving in marriage among them.'

'Not they, not a bit ; they're never married, and why should we, miss? That's a very wise saying,' acquiesced Mercy Cres- well, very gravely looking at her.

'If you really think so,' said Maud, 'you are a wise woman ; I have been trying to convince my maid Jones, but I'm afraid she is still rather in favour of the vulgar way of thinking.'

'Well, miss, you'll not find me so. I make my own clothes,

miss, and I think my own thoughts,' said Mercy, with a wise nod.

'You are a woman after my own heart then,' said Maud gaily.

'And how are you, miss?' repeats Mercy Cresswell.

'I told you I am very well, thanks,' said Maud.

'None o' them headaches you used to have when you was a little thing?'

'Oh, no! I sometimes have a little nervous pain from cold over my eyebrow, neuralgia they call it; but that is nothing, it never continues very long.'

'It never gets *into* your eye?' asked Mercy, staring steadily and gravely at the suspected organ, and screwing her lips together uneasily all the time. 'Them pains—they—say, sometimes begins—in the eyes, miss.'

Maud laughed.

'But Heaven only knows, as you say, miss. I dare say you are right, whatever you think; for every one knows best about their own pains. Sich is the will of Heaven—so we leave them things to wiser heads, miss, and I'm sure where you're going you'll be comfortable and amused.'

'If I'm not, Mercy, I shall be the first visitor at that pleasant house who ever had such a complaint to make.'

Mercy was suddenly very near exploding in a new fit of laughing, but she mastered it.

'Well, miss, I'll be there, I think—not unlikely,' said Mercy.

'As a servant?' asked Miss Maud.

'Well, as an attendant, I would say,' answered she.

'Oh!'

'And if I am, I'll be sure, I hope, to see you, miss, if you gives permission; and I'm sure I desires nothing but your 'ealth and 'appiness, miss. Why should I? And I must be going now, Miss Maud. Good-bye to you, miss.'

And again, but most solemnly, the short woman extended her thick arms, and rising to her toes, kissed Miss Vernon, and with a more ceremonious politeness took her leave of 'Miss Jones,' the lady's-maid, who regarded her with polite disgust.

So the squat figure of Miss Mercy Creswell disappeared, and Maud, for a time, lost sight of that uncouth reminder of old times and the Roydon nursery.

CHAPTER LIII.

THE DOCTOR RETURNS.

THE laughter of this uncomfortable Mercy Creswell remained in Maud Vernon's ears. She would have fancied that there was something odd about Lady Mardyke's house, if she had not known, by inference, from her mother, and directly from Maximilla Medwyn, that it was in every way unexceptionable. The woman could hardly have been tipsy. So Maud referred her unexplained merriment to something ridiculous which might have befallen in her own social level, the recollection of which irresistibly tickled her.

Lady Vernon was happier that day. A letter had reached her from her true but scarcely loving friend, old Richard Dawe. It told her that Captain Vivian had made an excursion, *he* knew not whither, on the day on which he had passed through the town of Roydon ; but that he had returned the same evening, and that the doctor having pronounced that he had been doing too much, he, Mr. Dawe, had exacted a promise from him not again to attempt a journey for ten days. He had named that time particularly, in consequence of Lady Vernon's letter.

' I am not qualified,' he said, ' to speak about such feelings ; but I will say, cure yourself of your excessive fondness for that young man. You have placed yourself in an agonizing position. Make the effort ; see him no more. I spare you. Commiserate yourself.'

Notwithstanding its severe tone and unpalatable advice, this letter had cheered her. Maud would have left Roydon before his possible return. Her soul may have acquiesced, in secret, in the wisdom of old Dawe's advice. But it was the recognition of one beholding himself in a glass, and straightway oblivion followed.

Lady Vernon had some charitable visits to pay, on two days in the week, in Roydon. Some fifty pensioners, more or less decayed, endured her occasional calls and lectures in consideration of the substantial comforts that attended a place on her list. On some days she would visit two, on others nearly a score.

Lady Vernon filled the *rôle* of the Christian matron with punctilious completeness. She had her great charities and her small. The will placed at her disposal, and entirely at her discretion, a great fund for such public and charitable uses. She had her tens of thousands to bestow, and her sixpences ; her influential committees and powerful societies, and her grumbling and querulous old women in their garrets.   She would make a flannel petticoat or build a church.

Lady Vernon bore herself to all her friends and acquaintances as an unexceptionable type of Christian life.   She would tell herself, as she meditated in her solitude, that she could not remember having ever acted in a single instance contrary to her conscience.

Lady Vernon had violated authority a little once or twice. She and authority had differed, and she had taken her own course.   But who was right, she or authority ?   Need I say ?

Of course she had things to vex her.   She had more ; secret afflictions and dreadful recollections, of which but one person now living, except herself, knew anything.

For years she had been silently, though unconsciously, battling with remorse.   She was battling with the same fiend now.   But was not Satan writhing under her heel ?   Did she not stand, resting on her spear, unscathed in her panoply, like the angel of wisdom, purity, and courage ?   What were these internal questionings, doubtings, and upbraidings, but the malignant sophistries of the Evil One accusing the just ?

Lady Vernon had made two or three of her domiciliary visits, and was emerging from between the poplars that stood one at each side of old Mr. Martin's door, when her eye lighted upon the figure of Dr. Malkin, in his black frock-coat, newly arrived from his journey, looking a little fagged, but smiling politely, and raising his hat.

The doctor had just made his toilet, and was on his way to Roydon Hall to pay his respects to his patroness.

Lady Vernon smiled, but looked suddenly a little paler, as she saw her family physician thus unexpectedly near her.

'How d'ye do, Doctor Malkin ?   I did not think you could have been home so early,' said Lady Vernon.   'You intend calling at Roydon Hall to-day ?'

'I was actually on my way,' said Doctor Malkin, smiling engagingly, with his hat still in his hand, and the sun glancing dazzlingly on his bald head.   'At any hour that will best suit you, Lady Vernon, I shall be most happy to wait upon you.'

'I shall be going home now ; I have made my little round of visits.'

' And left a great many afflicted hearts comforted,' interpolated the appreciative doctor.

' And I mean to return by the path,' she continued, not choosing to hear the doctor's little compliment. ' Open that door, please,' she said to the footman, who contrived with a struggle, without dropping the volumes he was charged with, to disengage a key from his pocket, and open a wicket in the park wall, which at this point runs only a few yards in the rear of the houses. ' And as you say you were on your way to Roydon Hall, you may as well, if you don't mind, come by the path with me.'

The doctor was only too happy.

The footman stood by the open door, which was only about a dozen steps away ; and Lady Vernon stopped for a moment, and said to him :

' You must see old Grimwick, and tell him to send up to Mrs. Mordaunt at six o'clock this evening for the blankets that I said he should have.'

' Yes, my lady.'

So now she and Doctor Malkin were walking in the perfect quietude of a secluded path among the trees, and he began by saying :

' You will be glad to hear, Lady Vernon, that I saw Mr. Damian. He read the copies of the papers, and pronounced them more than sufficient.'

A silence followed. Lady Vernon was looking straight before her with an inflexible countenance. They walked on about twenty steps before either spoke.

' We had a visit from Mercy Creswell to-day,' said Lady Vernon.

' Oh ! Had you ? But I don't think I quite recollect who Mercy Creswell is.'

' She was once a servant here, and now she is in the employment of Mr. Damian.'

' Oh ! I understand ; actually in his service at present ?'

' Yes.'

The doctor looked intelligently at Lady Vernon.

' I wished to see her. I knew she would have a good deal to tell me ; and I had some ideas of making her particularly useful, which on seeing her, and ascertaining that she is clever, I have made up my mind to carry into effect.'

' I have no doubt that anything resolved on by Lady Vernon will be most judicious and successful.'

'It is five years since I saw Mr. Damian; how is he looking ?'
asked Lady Vernon.

'Very well. His hair has been white a long time. I think
he stoops a little now; but in all other respects he is unchanged.
His sight, his hearing, his mind, are quite unimpaired. He is
very active, too; everything, in short, you could wish. He is
going for a few days, at the end of the week, to his place near
Brighton. But it is a mere flying visit.'

'I suppose you have had a conversation with Mr. Damian ?'

'A very detailed and full one; a very satisfactory conversation, indeed. I explained every point of difficulty on which he
required light, and he is quite clear as to his duty.'

'And I as to mine,' she said abstractedly, looking with
gloomy eyes on the grass; 'I as to mine.' She was walking,
unconsciously, more slowly.

'You have had a great deal of anxiety and trouble, Doctor
Malkin,' she said, suddenly raising her eyes. 'I think you
have acted with kindness, and tact, and energy, and *secrecy.*'

'Certainly,' he interposed; '*religious* secrecy. I should
consider myself dishonoured, had I not.'

'I'm sure of that; I'm quite sure of that, Doctor Malkin;
and I am very much obliged to you. You have done me a
great kindness, and I hope yet to make you understand how
very much I feel it. I have still, I am afraid, a great deal of
trouble to give you.'

'I should be a very ungrateful man, Lady Vernon, if, in a
case of this painful kind, I were to grudge any trouble that
could contribute to make your mind more happy. I should
perhaps say less anxious.'

'I know very well how I can rely upon you, Doctor Malkin,'
said Lady Vernon abstractedly. 'It will be quite necessary
that you should go on Sunday. We can't avoid it. I don't
like travelling on Sundays, when it can be helped. But in this
particular case it is unavoidable.'

'Quite; of course you can command me. I am entirely at
your disposal.'

'And no one knows where you go ?'

'That of course. I—I manage that very easily. I do all I
can by rail, and take the train at an unlikely station.'

'You know best,' she said, with a heavy sigh. 'I wish it
were all over. Doctor Malkin, it comforts me that I am so well

supported by advice. I know I am right; yet I do not think I could endure the responsibility alone.'

A little pink flush showed itself suddenly in Doctor Malkin's pale cheeks; he looked down.

'I have relied a good deal on Mr. Tintern,' he said. 'He has had a great deal of experience, and you know he is perfectly conversant with the mode of proceeding, and all responsibility rests ultimately, neither upon you nor upon any of those whom you have honoured with your more immediate confidence, but entirely with other people,' said Doctor Malkin.

'If you don't mind, I should thank you to call on Sunday afternoon. I don't care to part with the papers until then. Will six o'clock suit you?'

'Perfectly.'

'Well, I'm sure I ought to thank you very much, you have relieved my anxiety. Perhaps it is as well that we should part here. Good-bye, Doctor Malkin.'

'Entirely,' acquiesced Doctor Malkin. 'I will call on Sunday, at the hour you name. Charming weather we have got, and what a delightful serenity pervades this place always,' he added, raising one hand gently, with a faint smile round, as if to imply that he need have no scruple in withdrawing his escort under conditions so assuring and delightful. 'One thing only, I hope, perhaps, without being very impertinent, I may suggest.'

Doctor Malkin hesitated here, and Lady Vernon answered easily:

'I should be happy to hear anything you may think it well to say.'

'I was thinking, perhaps, that it might be desirable, Lady Vernon, not indeed to quiet any doubts, for I don't see that any can anywhere exist, but merely by way of technical authority—I was going to say, that some communication, either with Mr. Coke, or some other London lawyer of eminence, would be perhaps desirable.'

'I don't mind telling you, Doctor Malkin, that I have already taken that step,' said the lady. 'You shall have the papers on Sunday, when you call, and for the present, I think I will say good-bye.'

And so they parted.

CHAPTER LIV.

MR. HOWARD'S GRAVESTONE.

LADY VERNON's correspondence with Mr. Dawe was at this time carried on daily.

One of the old gentleman's letters intensified her alarms. It said :—

'I thought for a time I had discovered a different object of the young gentleman's devotions—Miss Tintern, of the Grange. I did not open my conjectures to him, nor did he speak on the subject to me. I think I was mistaken, and I can't now tell how it is. There is some powerful attraction, unquestionably, in the neighbourhood of Roydon.'

Lady Vernon's panic continued, therefore, unabated.

On Saturday by the late post a letter reached Roydon, addressed to Miss Vernon, which took Maud a good deal by surprise. It was from Lady Mardykes, and was to this effect.

'The Forest, Warhampton, Friday.
'MY DEAR MISS VERNON,
'You will be surprised when you see that I write from the Forest. I was suddenly called here yesterday by a message from dear papa. I found him so much better, and so entirely out of danger, that I sent by telegraph to my aunt, at Carsbrook, to prevent my friends going away ; and to beg of her to stay till Tuesday, where I am quite sure you will find her very happy to take charge of you when you arrive, as you promised, on Monday. I hope to be at home early on Tuesday. Pray do not postpone your coming, or make any change in our plans, unless Lady Vernon should think differently. Your cousin, Maximilla Medwyn, will arrive early on Monday, and you will find her quite an old inhabitant by the time you reach Carsbrook in the evening. I will write to Maximilla to-day, and tell her not to put off coming, and that I have written to you to rely upon her being at Carsbrook early on Monday. Pray write to me here by return, when you have ascertained what Lady Vernon decides.'

So the note ended.

Maud was dismayed. Was this one of those slips between the cup and the lip, by which the nectar of life is spilled and

lost ? With an augury of ill, she repaired with the note to her
mother.

'What is this, Maud ?' inquired Lady Vernon, as Maud held
Lady Mardykes' letter towards her.

Maud told her, and asked her to read it, and waited in trepidation till she had done so.

'I see no reason why you should not go on Monday, just as
if nothing had happened. That will do.'

She nodded, and Maud, immensely relieved, went to her
room, and wrote her note to Lady Mardykes accordingly.

'So now,' thought she, 'we have reached Saturday evening ;
and if nothing happens between this and Monday, I shall be at
Carsbrook on Monday night.'

So that day passed in hope, Sunday dawned, and the sweet
bell in Roydon tower sent its tremulous notes in spreading
ripples far over fields, and chimneys, and lordly trees.

In church, Maud observed that Ethel Tintern was looking far
from well. She reproached herself for not having driven over
to the Grange to see her.

This Sunday the Sacrament of the Lord's Supper was administered in Roydon Church, and among those who knelt
round the cushioned steps of the communion-table was Lady
Vernon. Miss Tintern and Mrs. Tintern also were there, and
Maud Vernon, who, once a month, from the time of her confir-
mation, had, according to the rule of Roydon Hall, been a
regular attendant.

Lady Vernon has risen, pale and stately, and is again in the
spacious Vernon pew, kneeling in solitary supplication, while
the murmured words of the great commemoration are heard
faintly along the aisle, and reverent footfalls pass slowly up and
down.

And now it is ended ; the church seems darkened as she rises.
It is overcast by a wide, black thunder-cloud. By the side-door
they step out. Lady Vernon's handsome face does not look as
if the light of peace was upon it. In the livid shadow of the
sky, the grass upon the graves is changed to the deep tint of the
yew. The grey church-tower and hoary tombstones are darkened
to the hue of lead.

Mr. Foljambe joins them ; Mrs. and Miss Tintern are standing by Lady Vernon and Maud. Mrs. Tintern is talking rather
eagerly to Lady Vernon, who seems just then to have troubled
thoughts of her own to employ her. She is talking about a

particular tombstone; Lady Vernon does not want to look at it, but does not care to decline, as Mrs. Tintern is bent on it; and Mr. Foljambe is only too anxious to act as guide.

They walk round the buttress at the corner of the old church, and they find themselves before the tombstone of the late vicar, Mr. Howard. It stands perpendicularly; the inscription is cut deep in the stone; and there is no decoration about it but the clustering roses, which straggle wide and high, and are now shedding their honours on the green mound.

As they walked toward this point, very slowly, over the churchyard grass, Ethel Tintern seized the opportunity to say a word or two to Maud.

'You go to Carsbrook to-morrow, don't you?'

'Yes,' said Maud, 'and I have been blaming myself for not having been to the Grange to see you; but I really could not help it—twice the carriage was at the door, and twice mamma put it off.'

'A great many things have happened since I saw you—I dare not try to tell you now,' she said, scarcely above a whisper. 'It would not do; if we were alone, of course——'

'Can you tell me, Ethel, whether the carriage is here?' said Mrs. Tintern, looking over her shoulder at her daughter.

'Oh, yes—I saw it—it is waiting at the church porch.'

And she continued to Maud, when her mother had resumed her talk with Lady Vernon and Mr. Foljambe:

'I have made up my mind, nearly, to take a decisive step. I daren't tell you; I daren't now, you understand why,' she glanced at the group close before them; 'but I think I will write to you at Carsbrook, if I do what I am thinking of, that is, what I am urged to, under a pressure that is almost cruel; a terrible pressure. Hush!'

The last word and a look were evoked by her observing, for her eye was upon them, although she spoke to Maud, that the three elder people of the party had suddenly slackened their pace, and come to standstill by the vicar's grave.

They had gone to the other side. Mr. Foljambe was leading the discussion; he was advising, I believe, some change in the arrangements of the vicar's grave, which he had persuaded Mrs. Tintern to admire; and which I'm afraid he would not have troubled his head about, had he not fancied they would have been received with special favour by Lady Vernon.

Maud and Miss Tintern were standing at this side of the

gentle mound that covered the good man's bones, and neither thinking of the conversation that was proceeding at the other side.

On a sudden, with a malignant look, Lady Vernon's cold, sweet voice recalled Maud with the words :

'Don't tread upon that grave, dear.'

Maud withdrew her foot quickly.

'No foot looks pretty on a grave,' she continued with the same look, and a momentary shudder.

'I don't think my foot was actually upon the grave, though it looked so to you,' Maud pleaded, a little disconcerted.

'Many people have a feeling about treading on a grave. I think it so horrible an indignity to mortality. I was going to say, I hope, Mr. Foljambe, that you, who are obliged, pretty often, to walk among them, feel that peculiar recoil; but I need hardly ask—you are so humane.'

Uttered in cold, gentle tones, this was irritating to spirited Maud Vernon.

'But I do assure you, mamma,' she said, with a heightened colour, 'my foot was *not* upon it. I am quite certain.'

'There, there, there, there, dear,' said Lady Vernon, 'I shan't mention it any more. Pray don't allow yourself to be excited, Maud; that kind of thing can't be good for any one.'

Maud's fine eyes and beautiful colour were brighter. But Lady Vernon went on talking fluently, in very low tones, to old Mr. Foljambe, and she turned as they walked away, and said to Mrs. Tintern gently :

'I scarcely like to ask poor dear Maud to do or to omit anything. She becomes so miserably excited.'

Maud, I dare say, had a word of complaint to utter in Miss Tintern's ear as they returned to take leave, and get into their carriages at the church-door.

In a dark and sour mood Lady Vernon bid old Mr. Foljambe good-bye.

'What bores people are! To think of those two stupid persons taking me there to hear all that odious nonsense.'

Lady Vernon did not come to luncheon, and hardly eat anything at dinner. She was by no means well that Sunday evening. Doctor Malkin came and departed, the sun set, and Maud was glad, as her maid dropped the extinguisher on her candle, that the day was over, and that she would sleep next night at Carsbrook.

CHAPTER LV.

THE JOURNEY BEGINS.

MONDAY came; and it was now evening, and about the hour at which Lady Vernon had ordained that Maud was to set out upon her long drive to Carsbrook.

The carriage was at the door. The boxes were on top, and Jones, ready dressed for the journey, was in the hall.

Maud was also in travelling costume, the pleasant excitement of her excursion for a moment quelled by the pending interview with her mother.

Oh, that she could have gone without seeing her!

In the hall she told Jones to get into the carriage. The sight of her maid in her place, smirking through the carriage window on the familiar front of the old house, at which she peeped at intervals when she was not busy with the internal arrangements of the carriage, was satisfactory; it reassured her that her journey to Carsbrook was a reality. The feeling of uncertainty, until she should be well out of reach of Roydon and the practicable range of a capricious recall, made her a little feverish.

Jones's fussy frown had left her quite. As she simpered through the open window at her young mistress, Maud smiled in return, in spite of her little alarm. Then she receded into the shadow of the hall, and peeped at the door opening into the suite of drawing-rooms, trying to gather courage for the dreaded leave-taking.

She entered the first drawing-room, and passed from one to another in succession, with the nervous feeling of one who is taking possession of a hostile magazine, and does not know the moment when an unseen train may explode it and blow all into air.

She had now passed through all the drawing-rooms, but her mother was not in any one of them. She must seek her in that room which was not cheered by a single pleasant association, a room of which Maud had the secret dread with which a suspected person eyes the council chamber.

She knocked at the door, but Lady Vernon was not there.

Maud was relieved by her failure; she returned to the drawing-room, and touched the bell. A footman entered.

The footman did not know whether her ladyship had gone

out, or whether she might be upstairs; but she was not in the shield-room, or in any of the rooms at that side. The butler, having something particular to tell her, had looked there only a few minutes before.

'Could some one send mamma's maid to me?'

In due time Latimer appeared in the drawing-room, and Maud said:

'Mamma told me, Latimer, that I was to go at four o'clock, and the horses are waiting, and I don't know where to find her, to bid her good-bye. Can you tell me?'

'I think she is in her morning-room upstairs, miss. Do you wish me to see?'

'Yes, Latimer, please. Will you tell her what I have said, and find out what she wishes?' answered Maud.

Latimer returned in a few minutes, and said:

'Her ladyship says, miss, if you'll please to wait a short time, she'll send for you so soon as she is at leisure.'

'Very well; thanks, Latimer,' said Maud, and she went to the window and looked out upon the court-yard, very ill-pleased at the delay.

In a little time she saw the coachman drive the horses, at a walk, a short way up and down the avenue, and round the court-yard; she thought the delay would never end; wondered what her mother could intend by it, and went from window to window, and sat down, and stood up again.

More than half an hour passed, before a footman arrived to inform Maud that Lady Vernon awaited her in the shield-room.

Thither she took her way, and found Lady Vernon alone in that stately and spacious room. She was standing at the further end, looking from one of the windows, when Maud entered.

Hearing the door close, she turned.

'I am not sorry, Maud, that you don't leave this quite so early as I at first intended. No, I am rather pleased.'

'I think,' said Maud, who was vexed profoundly at the delay, 'that it is almost a pity. But of course, whatever you think best. They tell me it will take a little more than five hours to reach Lady Mardykes' house; and it would be uncomfortable, I'm afraid, getting there very late.'

'Your arriving half an hour late, or an hour late, or two hours late, will cause Lady Mardykes no uneasiness,' said her mother; 'nor any other person. Pray allow me to direct the manner in which my own servants, carriages, and horses shall be employed, and you will find that I am quite competent to carry out any arrangements which, while you remain in my charge, may seem desirable.'

Though Lady Vernon spoke, as usual, with a calm manner and in cold tones, her faint smile expressed something of positive antipathy, and there were, in her measured emphasis, evidences of strangely intense and bitter temper, to which Maud was not accustomed.

These signs irritated, but also awed, Miss Vernon. There was something of the malignity of suffering in the gloom of her address, and Maud instinctively shrank from any betrayal of feeling which, in Lady Vernon's mood, might possibly lead to a sudden countermand of the entire expedition.

'From me you don't deserve confidence,' she said suddenly. 'You have given me none. I should not accept it now. But I know all I need know; from whom you receive letters among the rest. Don't speak; don't answer. I will have no altercation. What I allude to, I know. You have been no child to me. I have been, you'll say, no mother to you. It is false. I look into my heart and life, of which you know nothing, and I see that I have done, am doing, and, with Heaven's help, will do, my duty. I am sacrificing myself, my feelings, for you and for others. Yes, for *you*—for you, at this moment. I don't care, with that comfort, what may be said or fancied. What can it be to me what the wicked and frivolous may say or think? I do my duty by you always, steadily, and I defy them. I and you, we are what we are. There; go. No good-byes. Only remember, wherever you are, duty rules my life; my care shall follow you.'

With these odd words she turned away, and left the room by the side-door, and Maud was alone. Glad she was that the interview was over, and she at liberty.

The shadow of this cloud did not rest long upon her, black as its transit had been.

She and her maid were presently driving at a swift trot away from Roydon. She had not driven a mile away, when that unnatural parting began to recede in her mind, before the free and sunny prospect opening before her at Carsbrook.

'You never were at Carsbrook, Jones?' said Miss Vernon to her maid, for the tenth time during the last week. 'No. I forgot I asked you that before. I should not wonder, Jones, if

I were to leave you there. Miss Medwyn is a great matchmaker, and three of her own maids have been married from her
house.'

'Marriages is made in heaven, miss, they say : but I don't
see many wives that would not be maids again if they could.
I might 'a been married a many a time if I would. And if I
would change my mind there's many a one would take me, if
they thought I'd have them, without going all the way to Carsbrook.'

'Oh, yes ; but I mean a very eligible match. No matter ;
my cousin Max will look about, and we'll be satisfied with
nothing less.'

'La, miss ! do give over your nonsense !'

'We change horses five or six times on the way to Carsbrook.
What o'clock is it now ?' She looked at her watch. 'About
half-past four. What a good pace he is driving at. We shall
be there before ten, I think.'

The evening tints were over the landscape by the time they
reached the Green Dragon—a lonely posting-house near Dorminbury Common.

'We'll tell them to make us some tea here, Jones, what do
you think ? Should not you like it ?'

'Thanks, miss, very much ; I should like it very well, miss,
please.'

By this time the horses came to a standstill before the pretty
little inn ; the ostlers shuffled out to take the horses off ; and
Maud ran into the house under a fragrant bower of jessamine
and honeysuckle.

They look out upon the quiet slopes and rather hungry sheep-
walks that surround the Green Dragon, and make it solitary,
through a little window that makes a frame of dark leaves and
roses round.

Here they take their tea in high spirits. And this little
repast over, they walk out upon the platform before the
porch.

The horses are, by this time, put to ; and from this elevated
point of view Maud looks towards Roydon Hall, now seventeen
miles away, exactly in the direction where the sun is now sinking from view.

It is a strange, wild, ominous sunset. Long floods of clear
saffron flush into faint flame, and deep purple masses, like piles
of battle-smoke, load the pale sea of green above. The sun

dives into its abyss of fire. Black clouds, like girding rocks, with jagged edges dazzling as flame, encircle its descent with the yawn of a crater ; and, high in air, scattered flecks of cloud, like the fragments of an explosion, hang splendouring the fading sky with tongues of fire. The sun is now quite down ; all is gradually darkening. The smoke is slowly rolling and subsiding, and the crater stretches up its enormous mouth, and breathes out a blood-red vapour that overspreads the amber sky, and meets the sinking masses ; and so the vaporous scenery fades and blackens, leaving on Maud's mind a vague sense of the melancholy and portentous.

When she takes her place in the carriage she is silent ; she is thinking of her mother's oracular and incoherent leave-taking, and she sees her pale, handsome face, and flitting smile, and does not know whether they indicate more suffering or dislike.

But is she not leaving Roydon and its troubles fast and far behind her, and is she not driving now with four good trotters, at an exhilarating pace, towards her dear old cousin Max, towards Carsbrook, and its pleasant excitements, towards her new and hospitable friend, its charming hostess, and towards a possible meeting still more interesting ?

CHAPTER LVI.

THE PIG AND TINDER-BOX.

Soon the pleasant moon was shining, and silvered all the landscape.

In one of Swift's picturesque illustrations he describes the hilarity with which a party of friends ride out on a journey ; in the morning how spruce they look, how they talk and laugh, and admire all they see, and enjoy everything ; and how bespattered, silent, and spiritless, after some hours in the saddle, the same party arrive at their journey's end.

Something of this, in a modified way, our travellers experienced, as they approached the Pig and Tinder Box, the fourth posting-house, where they were to change horses.

It is a larger building than the Green Dragon, and older a great deal, with a porch of Charles the First's time, and a portion of the building as old as Queen Elizabeth's.

This inn, like the others along the posting line, depends in no sort upon its neighbourhood for support. A well-kept road across a melancholy moor, called Haxteth Heath, passes its front. The Pig and Tinder-box is nine-and-twenty miles away from the chimneys of Roydon Hall, and about sixteen from Carsbrook.

Maud has ceased to enjoy the mere sense of locomotion, and has got into the state in which the end of the journey is looked forward to with satisfaction. She looks out of the carriage window, and sees the road stretching over the black moor, in the moonlight, like a strip of white tape.

Beside it show, at first dimly, the gables and chimneys of the Pig and Tinder-box, with the outlines of its stables and offices, and the poplars and chestnuts that grow near it.

Listlessly she looks on, and thinks she sees a carriage before its door.

'Look out, Jones, and tell me, is that a carriage before the door of the inn ?'

Jones stretches her neck from the window twice as far as is necessary.

'A waggon, miss, I think,' said she, without interrupting her scrutiny to pull her head in. 'No—is it ? Well, I do believe —it does look like a carriage, rayther.'

'Let *me* look, Jones,' said Miss Maud, with her fingers on her shoulder. 'I hope they are not taking our horses.'

Miss Vernon looked out, and now plainly saw a carriage standing upon the road, with the horses' heads turned towards them. A post-boy in top-boots was in front, at the horses' bridles. The moonlight showed all this distinctly, and his comrade, partly hid in the black shadow of the old building, and partly revealed by the lamp-light that shone from the porch, was talking to some one inside.

It was plain that these people now heard the clink and rumble of the approaching coach-wheels, for the man at the porch, pointing along the road in their direction, turned towards his companion, who forthwith led his horses toward them a little, drawing up at the side of the road.

The Roydon carriage passed this swiftly by, and drew up before the porch of the Pig and Tinder-box.

The landlady waddled out swiftly in front of the threshold, to receive her distinguished guests.

'You had a letter from Lady Vernon, hadn't you?' inquired the young lady eagerly, thinking what a mortification it would be to find no horses, and be obliged to put up till morning at this melancholy old roadside inn.

'Yes, miss, sure, everything is ready, as her ladyship ordered; and will your ladyship, miss, please to take a cup of tea? I made it when we saw your ladyship's carriage a-coming, jest two minutes ago.'

Tea is always tempting on a journey, and although they had taken some scarcely two hours before, Maud agreed, and their hostess showed them into a comfortable panelled room, where tea-things were on the table.

The fat landlady of the Pig and Tinder-box stood with her apron against the table, on which her knuckles leaned, and said:

'I hope, miss, you may find the carriage comfortable.'

'Thanks, we are travelling in mamma's.'

'But Lady Vernon said in her note, please, miss, that her own was not to go further than this, and I was to furnish a carriage, on——'

'Oh, I did not know; I'm sure it is very nice; I have no doubt we shall find it very comfortable. Jones, you had better go and see that they make no mistake about our boxes and the things in the carriage that are coming on with us.'

Jones 'went off in a fuss. The room in which she left her young mistress is at the end of a passage, which runs to the left from the hall, with some doors opening from it toward the front of the building.

When Jones, in obedience to her young mistress's orders, had got to the foot of the stairs in front of the open hall-door, she saw standing in the entrance of the corresponding passage, at the other side of the hall, a man, with a dark, determined face and good forehead, about the sternest and gravest-looking man she had ever seen. Judging by his dress, you would have supposed him a person in the rank of an upper servant, and he wore a black outside coat buttoned up to his throat. His hat was in his hand. But judging by his air and countenance you would have taken him for a Jesuit, on a secret service of danger. There was in his face the severity of habitual responsibility, and in the brown eye, that glanced from corner to corner, the penetration and cold courage of a man of action.

He stepped forward as gravely as an undertaker, and speaking low but rapidly, said :

'Are you Miss Jones, please ?'

'Yes, my name is Jones,' said that young lady, with ears erect.

'Miss Vernon's maid ?' continued the inquirer.

'Yes, sir,' she replied, with dignity and some disdain, for she was not accustomed to be questioned by strangers.

'You have just come, Miss Jones, with the young lady from Roydon ?' he added politely.

'Yes, sir,' she again answered dryly.

'Then, Miss Jones, if you'll be good enough to come this way for a moment, I'll give you a message and a note from Lady Vernon,' he continued.

'Certainly, sir,' answered Miss Jones, with her eyes very wide open. A slight sinking at her heart acknowledged the ominous character of the occurrence.

The dark stranger had a candle in his hand, and led Miss Jones down the passage, at the opposite side of the hall from which he had just emerged.

As she followed him into the room, the door of which stood open, she thought she saw a fat, unpleasant face, which she little expected to see there, smiling from the further end at her.

She stepped back from the door, and looked steadily down the passage ; but if it had really been there, it was gone.

There was a pair of candles in the small room to which he had conducted her, one upon the chimney-piece, the other he had himself placed on the table ; and he now snuffed it.

'Lady Vernon desired me, Miss Jones, by letter received this morning, to look after Miss Vernon's luggage here, and to see it transferred all right to the carriage she is going on in. That is done, except your two boxes, which are not to go on.'

'But I can't get on at Carsbrook without my two boxes, sir,' exclaimed Miss Jones, alarmed for her get-up and decorations. 'I shall want every single individual thing I took with me from Roydon !'

'Perhaps, Miss Jones, you would prefer sitting,' said the imperturbable stranger, placing a chair, and sliding the candle along the table towards her. 'This is the letter which Lady Vernon desires me to give you with my own hand.'

At the same time he placed a note in the alarmed young lady's fingers.

She opened it, and read these words :

'Roydon Hall, Monday.

'REBECCA JONES,—

'I require your presence here. Therefore, immediately on receiving this note, you will return to Roydon Hall in the carriage in which you left it. Miss Vernon will continue her journey with, for the present, another maid.

'BARBARA VERNON.'

Miss Jones sniffed once or twice, and felt an odd chill, as she laid this note on the table ; and looking with flushed cheeks and undisguised scorn at the courier, she asked, with a little toss of her head :

'And who are you, sir, if I may make bold to inquire ?'

'As regards you, Miss Jones, in this present matter, I am Lady Vernon's messenger, and nothing more,' he answered phlegmatically, and smiled, after a pause, showing a row of even white teeth.

'I think it's a very odd way I'm treated,' said Miss Jones, whisking the note, with a little jerk, by the corner. 'I don't know no reason why I should be sent to and fro, between Roydon and this, and this and Roydon, back and forward, as if I was good for nothing but to be tossed here and there like a shuttlecock !'

'Very likely, miss,' acquiesced the serene messenger.

'And I'll acquaint my young lady, and see what she will say to it,' continued Jones, in her indignation preparing to go direct to her young mistress.

'But we are forbidden to do that, Miss Jones,' said this grave person calmly. 'You know Lady Vernon's handwriting ?'

'I rayther suppose I ought to,' answered Miss Jones scornfully, with her head very high, and dismay at her heart.

'My directions are strictly to prevent any such thing. Will you be good enough to read this.'

He doubled back a piece of the letter, and permitted her to read the following lines :

'I have ordered Rebecca Jones to return immediately to

Roydon. She will, therefore, *without speaking to Miss Vernon*, take her place again in my carriage, into which you will be so good as to put her, and my servant will immediately drive the carriage back to Roydon, as you advise.'

'I have given them their directions,' said the man, putting up his letter, 'and the carriage, with your two boxes, Miss Jones, waits at the door, to which I will, if you permit me, conduct you now.'

'Well, as for me, I'm but a lady's-maid, and I ought to be thankful to stand anything. Having been Miss Maud's own maid, which no one can deny what I have been to her through many a troubled day and night, ever since she was old enough to have a maid, anything is good enough, and too good for me.'

'I think, Miss Jones, Lady Vernon won't like it if you delay here any longer,' remarked the quiet man, approaching the door.

'And who's to go with Miss Maud? I'd like to know that, if it's no treason; 'tain't every one that can dress a young lady like she is, and I don't suppose her ladyship could 'a meant I was to leave my young lady without knowing who was to take care of her, and be in charge of her things; and so I should like to know better, before I leave here, who's to go on with her to Carsbrook?'

'Lady Vernon is a very particular lady, I'm told, and she has arranged all that herself, and I have no directions to give you, Miss Jones, except what I have said.'

'Well, it is a queer way, I am sure! I suppose I must do as her ladyship desires. I hope Miss Maud mayn't be the sufferer; and it does seem a bit queer I mayn't so much as say good-bye to her.'

There was here a little interrogative pause, as she looked in his face in the hope that he might relent.

'Lady Vernon's directions are plain upon that point,' observed the dark-featured man; 'and we have delayed too long, I'm afraid, Miss Jones.'

'It ain't me, then,' said Miss Jones quickly. 'I'm making no delays; I'm ready to go. I said so when I saw her ladyship's note, that instant minute.'

'Be so good as to follow me, miss,' said the stranger.

And he led the way down the passage, through the kitchen, into the stable-yard, and through the gate forth upon the road, where the Roydon carriage, with the tired horses, which had just brought them there, were waiting to take crestfallen Miss Jones back to the Green Dragon.

That young lady was quickly shut up, left to her angry reflections, and the prompt man in black said a word to the coachman, who was again on the box, and another to the footman, who handed his pewter pot, just drained, with some flakes of foam still on its side, to the ostler.

The footman took his seat, and Lady Vernon's carriage and servants, including Jones, much disgusted at her unexpected reverse, began to roll away toward Dorminbury Common and distant Roydon.

CHAPTER LVII.

A DESPATCH.

Miss Vernon rang her bell, and the landlady looked in.

' Where is my maid ? Can you tell me ?' she inquired.

' In the hall, please, miss, at present, talking with Mr. Darkdale about the luggage, please, my lady,' she answered in good faith, not knowing which maid she inquired for.

' Well, as soon as she has seen after those things, I should like her to come here,' continued Miss Vernon.

' Do you wish to see Mr. Darkdale, miss ?'

' No.   Who is Mr. Darkdale ?'

' We all thinks a deal of Mr. Darkdale down here,' said the woman reservedly.

' And why do you think so much of him ?' inquired the young lady.

' Well, he brings a deal of business one way or other, going and coming, and he's a very responsible man, he is.   And Mr. Darkdale, please, miss, has a note from Lady Vernon for you.'

' A note from mamma ? Why, I have come straight from Roydon.'

' He says, please, miss, that a letter came by the late post about an hour after you left, and your mamma sent him partly by rail, and partly on horseback, to overtake you here. If you please, miss, I'll fetch the letter.'

'Thank you very much,' said Maud, suddenly alarmed.

She stood up, and awaited the return of the landlady of the Pig and Tinder-box almost without breathing.

In a minute she reappeared with a large envelope, which she placed in the young lady's fingers. It contained a note from Maximilla Medwyn to Maud, which consisted of a few lines only, rather hastily written, and said :

'You have heard of Warhampton's illness. He is better ; but I have not had a line from Lady Mardykes, and don't know whether she would yet like to have us at Carsbrook. I think we had better wait for a day or two. I will write to you the moment I hear from her. I am sure you agree with me.'

At the corner of this letter Lady Vernon had written a few words in two oblique lines, thus :

' "Go on, notwithstanding. Don't think of turning back. I write to Maximilla by this evening's post.

' "B. E. V.' "

So she was to go on, and find neither Lady Mardykes nor her cousin at Carsbrook.

Well, Max would get Lady Vernon's letter at nine o'clock the next morning, and, we may be sure, would lose no time in join-ing Maud at Carsbrook, and before the day was over very likely Lady Mardykes herself would arrive. Max would make a point of coming forthwith to relieve Maud from the oddity of her solitary state. She need not come down to breakfast, she deter-mined ; and on arriving she would go straight to her room. At all events, it was a mercy that her mamma, in the existing state of things, had not ordered her back to Roydon.

'Would you mind telling my maid to come here and take some tea ?' said the young lady.

In a few minutes the shoes of the hostess were heard patter-ing along the tiles of the passage, and coming in with a curtsey, she said :

'She's very thankful, miss, but if you'll allow, she'd rayther sit in the carriage till your ladyship comes out.'

'Very well. So she may,' said the young lady. 'How far is Carsbrook—Lady Mardykes' house—from this, do you happen to know ?'

'We count it just twenty-two miles, miss. It might be half a mile less if the new bridge was open, but it ain't.'

'Two-and-twenty. I thought it was only sixteen. Well, I'm not sorry, after all. The night is so very fine, and the moonlight so charming, it is quite a pleasure travelling to-night.'

The young lady was really thinking that it would be better not to arrive until the guests had gone to their rooms. She did not hurry herself, therefore, over her cup of tea, which she drank from the state china of the Pig and Tinder-box.

She looked from the narrow window, and saw the carriage with four horses and two postilions at the door, and saw, also, the energetic figure of the grave man in the black greatcoat, pacing slowly, this way and that, in the neighbourhood of the carriage-door, and now and then turning towards the hall of the inn, and looking at his watch in the light that shone through the door.

It was plain that the people outside were growing impatient, and Miss Vernon made up her mind to delay them no longer.

She took leave of her new acquaintance, the hostess, in the hall. The man in the black coat opened the carriage-door, and Miss Vernon, handing in first a roll of music she was taking with her to Carsbrook, said: 'Take this for a moment, and don't let it be crushed,' was received by a dumpy gloved hand from the dark interior, and took her place beside her attendant, to whom, assuming her to be her old maid, Rebecca Jones, she did not immediately speak, but looked out of the window listlessly on the landscape, as the carriage rolled away toward its destination from the inn-door.

'I wonder, Jones, you preferred sitting alone to coming in and drinking tea. It was better than they gave us at the what's-its-name?—the Green Dragon.'

The person accosted cleared her voice with a little hesitation.

Trifling as was the sound, Miss Vernon detected a difference, and looked round with an odd sensation.

The figure in the corner was broader and shorter than Jones's, and wore a big obsolete bonnet, such as that refined lady's-maid would not be seen in.

'You are not Jones?' said the young lady, after a pause.

A deprecatory giggle was the only answer.

'Who *are* you?' demanded the young lady, very uncomfortably.

'La! Miss Maud, don't you know me, miss?'

'I—I'm not sure. Will you say, please, who you are?'

'Dear me, miss, you know me as well as I know you.'

She sat forward as she spoke, giggling.

'Yes, I see who you are. But where is Jones, my maid? She is not sitting outside?'

'Not she, miss; she's gone home to Roydon, please.'

'Who sent her away?—I want her. It is quite impossible she can have gone home!'

'Please, miss,' said the woman, in a tone of much greater deference, for there was something dangerous in Maud's look and manner, 'I got a written order from Lady Vernon yesterday, Miss Maud, directing me to be in attendance here to go on with you as your maid in place of Miss Jones.'

The carriage in which they now were was something like the old-fashioned post-chaise. Miss Vernon, without another word, let down the front window, and called to the post-boys to stop.

They did accordingly pull up, and instantly the stern man in the black greatcoat was at the side of the window.

'Anything wrong?' he said in an undertone to Mercy Creswell.

'No,' she whispered, with a nod, 'nothing.'

'Now, if you please, Creswell, you'll show me that note of mamma's. I must see it, or I shan't go on.'

The man stood back a little, so that Maud could not see him at the open window; but with this precaution, he kept his ear as close to it as he could, and was plainly listening with the closest attention.

'Certainly, miss, you shall read it,' said Mercy, fumbling in haste in her pocket. Indeed, she seemed, as she would have said, in a bit of a fluster.

She did produce it, and Maud had no difficulty in reading the bold writing in the moonlight.

It was a short, very clear, very peremptory note, to the effect she had stated.

'How did my maid go without my being so much as told of it?' demanded Miss Vernon fiercely.

Half a step sideways brought the man in the black coat to the window.

'Please, Miss Vernon,' said he, very quietly, but firmly, 'I received instructions from Lady Vernon to send Miss Jones

home to Roydon, precisely as she has gone, by the return
horses, in her ladyship's carriage, as far as the Green Dragon
on Dorminbury Common, and so on, in charge of her ladyship's
servants, and without any interview beforehand with you, all
which I have accordingly done. If her ladyship did not acquaint you beforehand, or if any disappointment results to you
in any way, I regret having had to disoblige you.'

For some seconds Maud made no answer. Those who
knew her would have seen in her fine eyes the evidence of
her anger. I dare say she was on the point of ordering
the drivers to turn the horses about, and of going back to
Roydon.

But that impulse of her indignation did not last long.
She looked at the man, whose intelligent, commanding, and
somewhat stern face was new to her, and asked, with some
hesitation :

'Are you a servant of Lady Vernon's ?'

'Only for this journey, miss.'

'But—but what are your duties ?'

'I look after your luggage, miss, and pay the turnpikes, and
settle for the horses, and take your orders, please, miss.'

Although this man was perfectly civil, there was something
in his manner by no means so deferential and ceremonious as
she was accustomed to. He looked in her face with no awe
whatever, and at her dress, and leaned his hand on the carriage window. And when she leaned back a little, to recollect
what next she should ask him, he touched Mercy Creswell's arm
with his finger, and whispered some words in the ear which she
placed near the window.

'I've made up my mind. I shall go on. Tell them to go
on,' said the young lady, indignant at these free-and-easy
ways.

Mercy Creswell gave the man a clandestine look from the
window, which he returned with a stern smile, and instantly
calling to the post-boys 'All right,' he mounted the seat behind,
and the journey proceeded.

CHAPTER LVIII.

LAMPS IN THE DARK.

THE carriage drove on. Lady Vernon had certainly, Maud thought, treated her very oddly. It was not the first time, however, that she had snubbed or puzzled her daughter; and when Maud had a little got over her resentment, she resolved that she could not think of visiting her vexation upon the innocent Mercy Creswell.

She was leaving constraint and gloom behind her at Roydon. Nearer and nearer were the friendly voices, the music and laughter of Carsbrook, and she could fancy the lights of that festive place already visible on the horizon.

'I dare say something has suddenly happened to make it unavoidable that mamma should have Jones back again with her at Roydon,' said the young lady. 'I wonder what it can be. I hope it is nothing that could vex poor Jones; have you any idea, Mercy?'

'Me! La! no, miss!' said Mercy. 'I do suppose Miss Jones will come after you hot-foot. Like enough your mamma has heard of some grand doings she didn't know of before, and means to send some more jewels, or fans, or finery, or dresses, after you, and that is what I thinks.'

'Well, that is possible; it can't be, after all, anything very wonderful, whatever it is. What is the name of that man who is acting as a sort of courier for this journey?'

'I don't know, miss,' said Mercy Creswell instantly.

'If he is a servant he certainly knows very little about his business,' said the young lady. 'However, that need not trouble us much, as we are to part with him at the end of our journey. You know the country, I suppose, between this and Carsbrook?'

'Oh?' she said with a prolonged and dubious interrogation in the tone. 'Do I know the country betwixt this and there? Well, yes, I do. Oh, to be sure I do—hevery inch! We'll change next at Torvey's Cross, unless Mr. Darkdale have made other arrangements.'

'Oh! Darkdale? Is that the name of the man?' asked Maud.

'Well, I won't be too sure, but I think I heard some one call

him Darkdale—Daniel Darkdale. It may 'a bin down there
at the Pig and Tinder-box; but I don't suppose his name is of no
great consequence,' answered Miss Mercy Creswell, endeavouring
to brazen out a good deal of confusion.

'And what is Mr. Darkdale? Is he a servant; or what
is he? He looks more like a poor schoolmaster,' said Miss
Vernon.

'La, miss! What could I know about him!' exclaimed
Mercy Creswell oracularly. 'Next to nothing, sure. Did they
say I knewed anything about him? La! Nonsense!'

'I want to know what he is, or what he was,' said Miss
Vernon, unable to account for her fat companion's fencing with
her questions.

Miss Creswell plainly did not know the extent of Maud's
information, and hesitated to say anything definite.

'The old woman down there at the Pig and Tinder-box—she
doesn't know next to nothing about him, or me. I don't know
what she was saying, I'm sure; not a pin's-worth.'

There was a slight interrogative tone in this discrediting of
the hostess, who, for aught she knew, had been talking in her
gossiping fashion with Maud.

But Maud did not help her by saying anything.

'He was a postmaster, I'm told, somewhere in Cheshire, and
kept a stationer's shop. I'm sure I don't know.'

'But what is he now?' asked Maud, whose suspicions began
to be roused by Mercy Creswell's unaccountable reluctance.

'What is he now? Well, I believe he is a sort of under-
steward to a clergyman. That's what I think.'

'You seem not to wish to tell me what you know about this
man; and I can't conceive why you should make a mystery of
it. But if there is any difficulty I am sure I don't care, provided he is a person of good character, which I suppose mamma
took care to ascertain.'

'That I do know, miss. He is a most respectable man is
Daniel Darkdale; he is a man that has been trusted by many,
miss, and never found wanting. La! He has had untold
wealth in his keeping, has Mr. Darkdale, many times, and there
is them as would trust him with all they has, and knows him
well too.'

'And you say our next change of horses will be at a place
called Torvey's Cross?' said Miss Vernon, interrupting, for her
interest in Mr. Darkdale had worn itself out. 'This is a very

wide moor. Have we a long way still to go before we reach Torvey's Cross?'

Mercy put her head out of the window, and the moonlight fell upon her fat, flabby face.

'Ay, there'll be near four miles still to go. When we come to the Seven Sallies—I can see them now—there will be still three miles betwixt us and it.'

'How do you come to know this road so very well?' inquired Maud.

'Well, I do; and why shouldn't I, miss, as you say, seeing I was so long a time in Lady Mardykes' service, and many a time I drove the road to Carsbrook before now. Will you 'ave a sangwige, miss?'

She had disentangled by this time, from a little basket in her lap, a roll of rather greasy newspaper, in which the proffered delicacies were wrapped up.

Maud declined politely, and Miss Mercy, with a word of apology for the liberty, stuffed them, one after another, into her own mouth.

Maud was a good deal disgusted at the vulgarity and greediness of her new waiting-maid, as well as upset, like every other lady in similar circumstances, by the loss of her old one. She was sustained, however, in this serious bereavement by agreeable and exciting anticipations of all that awaited her at Carsbrook.

'When were you last at Carsbrook?' asked the young lady, so soon as Miss Creswell had finished her sandwiches, and popped the paper out of the window, brushed away the crumbs from her lap, and wiped her mouth with her handkerchief, briskly.

'This morning, miss,' she answered with that odd preliminary hesitation that made Miss Vernon uncomfortable.

'Are you there as a servant, or how is it? I should like to know exactly whether you are my servant, or whose servant.'

'Lady Vernon's at present, miss, to attend upon you, please,' said Mercy Creswell, clearing her voice.

'Were you ever a lady's-maid?'

'Oh, la! yes, miss; I was, I may say, Lady Mardykes' maid all the time she was down, three years ago, at Mardykes Hall, near Golden Friars; you have heard of it, miss; it is such a beautiful place.'

Maud could hardly believe that Lady Mardykes could have had such a person for her maid, as she looked at her square

body and clumsy hands, in the dim light, and bethought her
that she had never heard that Mercy Creswell had shown the
smallest aptitude for such a post. Certainly, if she was a
tolerable lady's-maid she looked the part very badly. It was
unspeakably provoking.

By this time they had passed the Seven Sallies and changed
horses again at Torvey's Cross; and now, a mile or two on, the
road, which had hitherto traversed a particularly open and
rather bare country, plunged suddenly into a close wood of lofty
fir-trees.

The post-boys very soon slackened the pace at which they
had been driving. It became, indeed, so dark that they could
hardly proceed at all without danger.

It is a region of wood which might rival the pine forests of
Norway. No ray of moonlight streaked the road. It is just
wide enough for two carriages to pass, and the trunks of the
great trees rear themselves at each side in a perspective, dim
enough in daylight, and showing like a long and irregular
colonnade, but now so little discernible, that the man in the
back seat called to the drivers to pull up.

His voice was easily heard, for this road is carpeted with the
perpetually falling showers of withered vegetation that serves
for leaves upon the sprays and branches that overhang it, and
hoofs and wheels pass on with dull and muffled sounds.

Now that they had come to a standstill, Maud lowered the
window, and asked a question of Mr. Darkdale—a name not in-
appropriate to such a scene—who had got down, and stood,
hardly discernible, outside, opening something he had just taken
from his breast-pocket.

'Can we get on?' inquired she, a good deal alarmed.

'Yes, miss,' he answered.

'But we can't see.'

'We'll see well enough, miss, when I light the lamps.'

'I say, Daniel, there's lamps a-following of us,' exclaimed
Miss Creswell, who, hearing some odd sounds, had thrust her
head and shoulders out of the window at her own side.

'There are lamps here,' he answered.

'No, but listen, and look behind you,' said Mercy Creswell,
with suppressed impatience.

The man turned and listened; Maud, whose curiosity and
some slight sense of alarm were excited, partly by the profound
darkness, and partly by the silence, looked from the window at

her side, and saw two carriage-lamps gliding toward them, and faintly lighting the backs of four horses jogging on, with postilions duly mounted, just visible, and still pretty distant.

Mr. Darkdale bestirred himself, for these postilions were palpably quickening their pace, a rather reckless proceeding in a pass so profoundly dark. He took down one of the carriage-lamps, and lighting it with a match, shouted :

'Hallo ! Look ahead !'

The warning light that sprang thus suddenly out of darkness, and the voice, seemed hardly to act as a damper on the ardour of the postilions ; and Maud heard distinctly those sounds to which, probably, quick-eared Mercy Creswell had referred.

She mistook them first for the laughter and vociferation of a rollicking party on their way home from supper. But she soon perceived, with alarm, that they indicated something very different.

They were sounds of fury and terror. She heard a voice exerting itself in short gasps and shrieks, and declaiming with frightful volubility :

'I say Vivian's my name ! Murder, murder—my God !—two to one—they're murdering me !' yelled this voice, which, disguised as it was with rage and terror, she nevertheless fancied she knew, and exactly as the chaise drove by, at a suddenly stimulated pace, the window was broken, and the jingling glass showered on the road close beside the wheels ; and, in the flash of the lamp, Miss Vernon had a momentary glimpse of the cantering horses and the postilions lashing them, and of the hands and faces of men struggling within, and, as the strange phantasmagoria flew by—

'Hallo ! I'm here—Daniel Darkdale. Pull up ; stop ! Hallo !' yelled Mr. Darkdale grimly.

And he ran on in the direction in which the carriage had passed, shouting, as he followed, 'I'm Daniel Darkdale. Hallo !'

There was a magic in this name which brought the chaise, a very little way further on, to a sudden stop.

CHAPTER LIX.

MR. DARKDALE'S GUEST.

'This will never do,' said Mr. Darkdale sharply, striding up to the carriage window, from which cries of 'murder' were still proceeding. 'What's going on here?'

'Two assassins trying to murder me, here in this carriage, sir. For God's sake, sir, see me safe out of this. They have pinioned me.'

Mr. Darkdale put his hand through the broken window and let it down a little, and then withdrawing it, let the window down altogether, and popped his head in, holding the lamp, which he still carried, close to the window, so as to light up the interior with a rather fierce and sudden glare.

Who are you, sir?' he asked of the young man, who, with a torn shirt-front, disordered hair and necktie, and a very pale face, across which a smear of blood showed rather ghastlily, was staring with wild eyes.

There were two powerful-looking men, sitting one at each side, hot and blown after the struggle. With these Mr. Darkdale exchanged a significant glance, and said :

'You'll give me your names, you two. You know Mr. Darkdale, you know me—Daniel Darkdale?'

The two men exchanged a sheepish look, as if they would have winked at one another, and gave their names.

'I'm the constable of this county, sir,' said Mr. Darkdale, in a loud voice. 'I'm pretty well known. I'll set all this right. If they have injured you they shall be made examples of. They have secured your hands somehow?'

'Yes. I'm a cavalry officer. My name is Vivian—that is, it will do as well as another. My enemies want to call me Vivian Mardykes, but I won't have it,' cried the gentleman, in high excitement, gabbling at that gallop which recognises no stop longer than a comma, and hardly that. 'I had been down in that part of the country behind us a good way, you know, and I wanted to get back to my quarters, and this man had a carriage, and I could not get another'—the injured man was talking at such a pace that the foam appeared at the corners of his lips—'and he undertook to give me a lift to Chatham ; and this other fellow—d—— them, they are both murderers, I say, get my arms out.' And he began to tug again.

'Wait a moment. I have a reason. You'll say I'm right in a moment,' Mr. Darkdale, leaning in, sternly whispered in his ear.

He opened the door.

'I say, you come out, till I hear this gentleman's complaint,' he said to the man next the door.

He obeyed, and walked a little to the rear of the chaise, and the officer sat close to the window next Mr. Darkdale.

'Don't you be listening,' said Darkdale to the other. 'Now, sir, we shan't be overheard; tell me the rest, pray.'

'He asked for leave to take in that fellow, who said he wanted to go on to Chatham, and they wished to play "blind-hooky" with me, and I like the game, and said yes, and they had cards, and I told them how I was used, very badly, I'll tell you by-and-bye, and they seemed very agreeable, and I had been kept awake all night, last night, by half a dozen scoundrels drilling in the room next mine, with a couple of sergeants and a drum, you can't conceive such an infernal noise, like so many ghosts out of hell, I knew very well why it was done; there's a fellow, Major Spooner, he has been doing everything imagination can devise, by Heaven, to make the army too hot for me, but I think I have a way of hitting him rather hard, ha! ha! and when I was asleep, as sound as if I had made three forced marches without a halt, those two robbers, agents they are of the same villain, gambling, rascally murderers, tied my arms behind my back, and only for you, sir, I should have been robbed and murdered by this time.'

'I should not wonder, sir,' said Darkdale. 'I should not wonder. But I have them pretty fast, now. I have their names, and I know their faces; I have seen them long ago; and I'll have them up for it. Don't you be listening; allow me, sir, to whisper a word in your ear. You'll be at the next posting-house very soon, an hour or less. Those fellows are frightened now, and they will try to make it up with you. Don't you be such a muff. They would be very glad, now, to loose your hands; don't you allow it. I'll get up behind as soon as they are in, without their knowing it, and I'll have them arrested the moment we arrive, and I'll have witnesses to see how they have tied your hands, and I'll compel them to disclose their connection with that blackguard Major Spooner, and I'll lay you twenty pounds they'll split. Do you like my plan?'

'Uncommonly,' whispered the young man close to his ear.

'Well, when he gets in, do you pretend to be asleep, and if they try to undo the pinion, don't you let them—hush! Mind what I say. We'll pay the whole lot off.'

'Will you?' gasped the pinioned traveller. 'By Heavens, then, I'll do it, I'll bear it, I say I will; anything to bring it home to Spooner, he's so cunning; the villain, he's as hard to catch as a ghost, never mind, I'll have him yet, the scoundrel, I wish this thing wasn't quite so tight, though, by Jove, it does hurt me, never mind, it is worth some trouble; we'll catch them, it's a serious thing, this outrage, and if you can show they aimed at my life, it will be a bad business for Spooner, ha! ha! and if I can't hang him, whenever I get a fair chance I'll shoot him, by Heaven! I'll shoot him—I'll shoot him—I'll shoot him dead, if it was in church!'

'Hush—don't mind. Here comes the fellow. We understand one another—you and I—eh?'

'All right.' And the voluble gentleman, with his arms tied behind him, and extremely uncomfortable, would have run on again with a similar declaration, if Mr. Darkdale had not said, with a peremptory gesture of caution:

'They'll hear us; not another word.'

He drew back, and walked toward the man whom he had just ejected from the carriage, and he said very low, and without turning his head, a few words to his ear, ending with:

''Twill be all right now; get on at the best lick you can. You must be there in forty-five minutes sharp.'

The man gave his orders to the postilions, and got into the carriage, and away they whirled at a great pace, flashing a fiery streak from their lamps along each brown trunk as they flew by on the close forest road.

Mr. Darkdale stood, lamp in hand, for a minute, watching the retreating equipage; and then turned and approached his own carriage, which he had left standing about a hundred paces in the rear.

CHAPTER LX.

ARRIVED.

'WELL, what is it, Mr. Darkdale?' inquired Maud, eagerly, as soon as he had reached the side of the carriage.

'Two bailiffs, miss, in charge of an officer, arrested for debt, and something worse; they have had a bit of a row in the coach; he's a troublesome fellow. I knew something about him; he has been up before, and I think there's a criminal warrant this time.'

'Was he hurt?'

'A scratch, I fancy. It isn't easy, always, keeping those dangerous cases from hurting themselves: he's very strong, and always slipping away if he can. But they have him fast enough this time; and the road's clear of them now; so I suppose I had best tell our post-boys, miss, to get on?'

'Please do; it is growing late. How long will it take to reach Carsbrook?'

'About an hour, miss.'

Maud leaned back in the carriage, the unpleasant excitement of their recent adventure still tingling in her nerves.

Could it be that Captain Vivian had got into a scrape, and was really in the hands of bailiffs? A sad hearing for poor Ethel Tintern; rather a shock even to other people.

'Do you know anything of that officer those people were taking away in the carriage?' inquired the young lady, suddenly, of her attendant, so soon as they were again in motion.

'I may, miss, or I mayn't. I could not say for certain, unless I was to see him,' answered the servant.

'Have you ever seen an officer named Vivian, who is tall, and has light hair; a young man rather good-looking?' persisted Maud.

'Well, I—I think I did,' she replied, watching Maud's face. 'I *have* seen some one like that. Veevian? Yes. He used to call hisself Veevian.'

'The person who passed us by, who said they were murdering him—how horrible his voice was!—said his name was Vivian. You heard him, of course?'

'Well, I made shift to hear; but there was a noise, you know,' answered Mercy Creswell evasively.

'Oh, you must have heard him call out that his name was Vivian; you are not at all deaf,' said the young lady, irritated.

'I did hear something like it, for certain,' she replied.

Miss Mercy would have been very glad to know, while under these examinations, what the extent of Miss Vernon's information actually was, for however willing she might be to tell stories, she was especially adverse to being found out at this particular juncture. The sense of this inconvenience a good deal embarrassed her accustomed liberty of speech.

All this time Maud was possessed by the suspicion that, for some reason or other, Mercy Creswell was deliberately deceiving her, and that she knew just as much as Darkdale did about this Mr. Vivian. More than ever she disliked being assigned this particular attendant, and more and more puzzled she became in her search for her mother's motive.

For a while she looked from the window. The wood had gradually thinned, and now but a few scattered and decayed firs stretched their bleached boughs under the moonbeams, and stooped over the peat.

'Why should you try to deceive me?' said Miss Vernon, suddenly turning to Mercy Creswell, who, with her mouth screwed together, and her cunning eyes looking from her window upon the moonlit prospect, was busy with her own thoughts.

'Me deceive you? La, Miss Maud! Why should I deceive you, above all? I would not, for no consideration, miss. I hope I have a conscience, miss. I'd be sorry, I assure you, Miss Maud.'

'Why, then, did you not tell me, at once, that you knew something about that gentleman, Mr. Vivian? You know as much about him as Mr. Darkdale does.'

'Well, now, indeed, I do not, miss, no sich thing. I may 'a seen him, and I think I did at Lady Mardykes'; he's a cousin, or something, to her.'

'Oh, really? A relation of Lady Mardykes?'

'Yes, miss. If it be the same I mean.'

Maud mused for a minute or two.

'How far are we now from Carsbrook?' she asked.

'Well, miss, I'd say little more than three mile. Here's the finger-post, and down there, among the trees, is the Red Lion, and there we'll get into the right road, without another turn, right on to the house.'

' I'm not sorry,' said Maud, looking from the windows with more interest than before. ' It has been a long journey. You were at Carsbrook this morning ?'

' Yes, miss,' said the maid, who had gradually grown to look careworn and pallid, as they neared their destination.

' Was Lady Mardykes there ?'

' No, miss,' answered Mercy.

' She was expected there, wasn't she ?'

' Expected there ?' repeated Miss Creswell. ' Let me think. Oh, la ! yes, to be sure, she was expected.'

' How soon ?'

' How soon ? 'Twill be to-morrow morning. Oh, yes, to-morrow morning. To-morrow's Tuesday ? Yes, to-morrow morning, for certain.'

They were now driving through a pretty wooded country. On the· left was a great park wall, grey and moss-streaked, mantled here and there with ivy, and overlapped by grand old trees. On the right were hedge-rows, and many a sloping field ; and, a little in advance, the chimneys and gables of a village, and the slender spire of a rural church, white in the moonlight.

' We're near home now, miss,' said Mercy.

' Oh,' said Maud, looking out more curiously. ' What wall is that ?'

' The park wall, miss.'

' It would not be easy to climb that; higher, I think, than Roydon wall.'

' It is very high, miss.'

' And how soon is Miss Max expected to arrive ?'

' Miss Medwyn ?' exclaimed the maid, laughing, all at once, in spite of herself.

' Why do you laugh ? Miss Medwyn is coming here, and I thought she would have been here to-day,' said Maud, a little haughtily.

' Like enough, miss,' said Mercy, drying her eyes, ' La, ha, ha, ha ! it is funny—I beg your pardon, miss. I suppose she will—time enough. But she was not here when I left this morning.'

' We'll hear all about it when we reach the house. I suppose there is nothing like a dance, or anything of that kind, while Lady Mardykes is away ?'

'Oh, la! yes, miss. No end of dancing and music and everything that way,' answered Mercy, with a great sigh, and a haggard look, after her brief merriment. 'There's a—what do you call it ?—of singing and music to-night.'

'A concert ?'

'Yes, that's it, miss, a concert. A concert of music. La! they does it so beautiful, you wouldn't believe. I wish Miss Medwyn was here to try her pipe at it. Hoo, hoo, hoo—la! I beg your pardon—she's so staid and wise, miss !'

Mercy was stuffing her handkerchief into her mouth to stifle her laughter. But this time it was over quickly.

At this moment the postilions wheeled their horses to the left, and pulled them up, calling lustily, 'Gate, gate !'

'So we have arrived,' said Maud, letting down the window, and looking out with the curiosity of long-deferred expectation.

The leaders' heads seemed almost touching the bars of a great iron gate, over which burned a solitary lamp, acting lighthouse fashion, rather as a warning than as an effectual light.

They were under the shadow of gigantic elms, that threw their branches from side to side; the carriage-lamps dimly lighted a few clusters of their dark foliage, and the light over the gate showed, for a few feet round and above it, the same moveless leafage.

'We shan't be long reaching the house ?' she inquired of Mr. Darkdale, who was walking by the window toward the gate, for she remembered 'approaches' three miles long after you enter the gate, deceiving you with a second journey before you reach the hall-door.

'Not five minutes, miss,' said the man, hardly turning his head as he passed.

Was he growing a little gruffer, she thought, as they approached their destination ?

Darkdale was talking earnestly in a low tone with the man who had come to the gate at their summons; and then he called :

'Be alive, now—open the gate.'

In a minute more they were driving up the approach at a rapid pace under rows of trees. Suddenly the shadowy road they followed turned to the right, and took a direction parallel to the high road; about a hundred yards on they drove up to the front of the house, along which this road, expanding before it into a court-yard, passes. And now they pull up before the steps of the hall-door. And the horses stand drooping their heads, and snorting, and sending up each a thin white vapour, through which the metal buckles of their harness glimmer faintly in the moonlight.

Mr. Darkdale was already on the steps ringing the bell.

CHAPTER LXI.

IN THE HOUSE.

MAUD was looking at the house—a huge structure of the cage-work sort, which stood out in the light broad and high, its black V's and X's and I's traced in black old beams, contrasting like gigantic symbols with the smooth while plaster they spanned and intersected, and which showed dazzlingly in the moon's intense splendour, under which also many broad windows were sparkling.

A footman in livery stood before the open door, in the shadow of a deep porch, and Maud observed that Mr. Darkdale seemed to speak to him as one in authority, and by no means as one servant to another.

Maud was looking from the carriage window; and the hall was full of light, which came out with a pleasant glow, showing the gilt buttons and gold lace on the servant's livery, flushing the white powder on his head, and making Mr. Darkdale, who stood at the threshold, look blacker against its warm light. Some figures, gentlemen in evening dress, and ladies in brilliant costume, passed and repassed a little in perspective.

There came from the interior, as the hall-door stood partly open, the sounds of violins and other instruments, and the more powerful swell of human voices.

Mr. Darkdale turned and ran down the steps, and at the carriage window said :

'There's a concert going on, and a great many of the people moving about in the hall. Perhaps you had better come in by a different way ?'

'That is just what I wished,' said Miss Vernon.

But Darkdale did not seem to care very much for her sanction, and in fact had not waited for it. He was now talking to
the drivers, and the hall-door had been shut. He returned, and
said, at the window :

'Your boxes shall be taken up to your room, Miss Vernon,
and as the night is so fine, you will have no objection, I dare
say, to walk round to the entrance to which I will conduct you
and Mercy Creswell.'

He opened the carriage-door, and the young lady got out
and found herself in the court-yard. Looking along the face
of the great house to the right, a mass of stables and other
offices closed the view, behind a broken screen of fine old elms ;
and to the left it was blocked by dark and thicker masses of
towering trees.

In this latter direction, along the front of the house, Mr.
Darkdale led the way. In the still air his swift steps sounded
sharp on the hard ground. He did not seem to care whether she
liked his pace or not.

As she hurried after him, from the open windows, whose
blinds, transparent with the lights within, were down, she
heard, it seemed to her, very fine voices singing, as she thought,
that brilliant staccata air, 'Quest un' Nodo,' etc., from 'Ceneren-
tola,' and so unusually well that she was almost tempted to pause
and listen.

Mr. Darkdale did not consult her, however, but glided on
to the extremity of the house, where a high wall confronted
them, and with a latch-key opened a door, beside which he
stood, holding it wide, for Miss Vernon and her attendant, and
shutting it immediately on their passing in.

They were now in the great quadrangle which lies against
the side of the house, with the quaint Dutch flower-beds, like
fanciful carpet pattern, surrounding it, and the tall yew hedges
giving it a cloister-like seclusion. Miss Vernon easily recognised this by the description ; the trim yew hedges were visible,
overtopped by a dense screen of trees at the other side, every
distance marked by the thin mist of night; and in the centre
stretched the smooth carpet of grass, in the midst of which
stood the old mulberry-tree.

'Oh ! This is the croquet-ground ?' said Miss Vernon to her
attendant, as they passed on.

'Ay, that will be the croquet-ground,' answered her maid, a

little absently, as if a gloom and suspicion had come over her. Her fat face had grown more than usually putty-coloured, and she was screwing her lips together and frowning hard.

Mr. Darkdale spoke never a word until he had reached the door through which Antomarchi, some nights before, had admitted himself and Doctor Malkin to the self-same house.

A servant, not in livery, stood by this door, which was ajar, and opened it wide at their approach.

Darkdale whispered a few words to him, the purport of which Maud did not catch, and was not meant to hear, and in this same tone the man replied a word or two.

It was rather a chill reception. But then her hostess was absent, and certainly was not accountable for the uncomfortable ways of the odd attendants whom it had pleased her mother to assign her.

The servant hied away through the door; it seemed, to execute some behest of Darkdale's in haste; and Darkdale himself stood at the entrance instead, to receive them.

'So, in Carsbrook at last,' said Maud, with a smile, as she placed her foot on the oak flooring of the very long passage with which we are already acquainted.

Mercy Creswell screwed her lips harder, and raised her eyebrows, 'pulling,' as they say, in her abstraction, an old and dismal grimace.

'Now, miss? Oh, ay, to be sure,' said Mercy Creswell, as it were, half awaking, and looking vaguely about her.

Mr. Darkdale shut the heavy door, which closed by a spring bolt, with a clang that boomed through the long passage, and then, with an odd familiarity with internal arrangements, he drew the bolts with noisy rapidity, and turned the key which was in the lock, and drew it out.

'Now, miss, you'll not be long getting to your room,' said Mercy Creswell, her eyes wandering along the wall, and something sunken and weary in her unwholesome face.

'Well, I should hope not,' thought Maud, a little surprised.

Darkdale was walking along the passage with rapid strides, having merely beckoned to them to follow.

Miss Maud was a good deal disgusted at this procedure. She was obliged, in order to keep this man in view, to follow at a rapid pace, and as he turned a corner, which she had not yet reached, Maud saw a person emerge from a side-door in

the perspective of the passage, the sight of whom very much
surprised her.

It was Doctor Malkin who stepped out under the lamp which
overhung that door, his bald head flushed, and his disagreeable
countenance smiling grimly.

With the smile still on his thin lips, he turned his head and
saw Miss Vernon.

He thought, I dare say, that she had not seen him, for he
instantly drew back into the recess of the doorway.

Perhaps he had not recognised her, perhaps he did not
choose to be recognised in this part of the house. But a few
days ago he certainly was not even acquainted with Lady Mardykes. But he had a good many friends, and she an infinitude,
and an introduction might, of course, have been very easily
managed.

This all passed in her mind nearly momentarily, as she
walked quickly into the side passage after Darkdale, Mercy
Creswell keeping hardly a foot behind, and a little to the other
side.

The impression this odd little incident left upon her mind
was, notwithstanding, unpleasant.

Having turned to the left, she saw the large screen I mentioned on a former occasion, that protected the door at which
Darkdale was now tapping. It was hardly opened when Maud
reached it.

' Can my room be on this floor?' she wondered.

No; it was no such thing. Mr. Drummond, short, serious,
and benevolent, with rosy cheeks and brown eyes, and bald
head, and a pen behind his ear, was standing in a short office-
coat at the threshold.

' This is Miss Maud Vernon, daughter of Lady Vernon, of
Roydon Hall,' said Darkdale, performing this odd office of introduction in a dry, rapid way.

' Half an hour later than we expected,' said Mr. Drummond,
pulling out a large old-fashioned silver watch by the chain, from
which dangled a bunch of seals and keys on his comfortable
paunch ; and then, glancing back, it was to be presumed at a
clock, in the interior, ' no, twenty-five, precisely five-and-twenty
minutes late,' and he turned from the corners of his eyes upon
Miss Vernon a shrewd glance, and quickly made her a respect-
ful bow.

' I'll tell you about that by-and-by,' said Darkdale.

'I hope the young lady will find everything to her liking,
I'm sure.'

'Miss Vernon's come for a short visit to *Lady Mardykes* here, a
few weeks or so,' interrupted Darkdale. 'And there are two boxes,
largest size, and two middle size, and a dressing-case, and a
bonnet-box, and here's Lady Vernon's list of the jewels she's
brought; and—come here, Creswell—she's to wait on Miss
Vernon. Which is Miss Vernon's room?'

Mr. Drummond dived into his room, and returned in a
moment with a big book like a ledger.

'Miss Vernon? Yes. Here it is. This will be it—A A,
Fourteen.'

'A A, Fourteen,' repeated Darkdale, musing. 'That is at
the west side of the cross-door, eh?'

'Yes, so it is.'

'I—I didn't think that,' said Darkdale, drawing nearer
to him, with an inquiring glance and a dubious frown of
thought.

'Yes, it's all right; and here's the voucher and "question"
wrote with his own hand across it.'

Darkdale read the paper, and returned it to the plump fingers
of the secretary.

'It is—that's it,' he said.

'I'm a little tired. I should like to get to my room, please.
I suppose my maid knows where it is?' said Miss Vernon, who
was beginning to lose patience.

'In one moment, presently, please, Miss Vernon.' Darkdale
whispered a word in the ear of Mercy Creswell. 'Now, Miss
Vernon, please, we have only a moment to delay on the way,
and then your maid shall show you to your room.'

At the same quick pace he led her through a passage or two,
and opened a door, which she entered after him.

'You shan't be detained a moment here, Miss Vernon,' he
repeated.

It is a spacious and oval room, panelled massively up to the
ceiling, and surrounded, as it seems, with doors all alike in very
heavy casings. It is rather bare of furniture. A thick Turkey
carpet covers the floor. There are four enormous armchairs on
castors, and a square table, covered with stamped leather, and
with legs as thick as cannons on castors, stands in the centre of
the room. A ponderous oak desk lies upon the table, and is, in
fact, attached to it, the whole heavy structure forming one

massive piece. Except these articles of furniture, there is not a movable thing in the room.

The chamber is lighted from the ceiling, over the table, by a small oval line of gas-jets, which looks like a continuous ribbon of flame.

There is something queer, and almost dismaying, in the effect of this bare and massive room, with its four huge, modern, purple-leather chairs.

The immense solidity of the mouldings and panelling that surround it, as well as its peculiar shape, would reflect back and muffle any sound uttered within it. And, somehow, it suggests vaguely the idea of surgery, the strap, the knife, and all that therapeutic torture.

The effect of the mild equable light is odd, and the monotony with which the doors, or the sham doors, match one another all round, has something bewildering and portentous in it.

While she looks round at all this, Mr. Darkdale has left the room; and turning about, she finds that Mercy Creswell, perhaps, never entered it. At all events, she certainly is not there now, and Maud is quite alone.

One thing is obvious. It certainly is pretty evident that Mercy Creswell spoke truth, and that Lady Mardykes is not at home.

'There must, however, be some servant, I think, who can show me my room. I'll try,' Miss Vernon resolves.

Maud accordingly tries the handle of the particular door through which she thinks she had entered, but it will not turn; then another, with the same result. It is rather a disconcerting situation, for by this time she cannot tell by what door she had come in, or by which of all these Mr. Darkdale had gone out, each door is so like its neighbour.

She looked about for a bell, but she could discover nothing of the kind.

Before another minute had passed, however, one of the doors at the other side of the room opened noiselessly, and a marble-featured man, with strange eyes, and black, square beard, stood before the panel, like a picture. It was Automarchi.

'Oh, I'm afraid the servant has made a mistake,' said Miss Vernon, who was vexed at her absurd situation. 'He showed me in here, to wait till my maid returned to show me the way to my room.'

'She will be here in a moment, Miss Vernon ; there has been no mistake. I hope your head is better ?'

'Thanks, a great deal better.'

She was surprised at his knowing that she had complained of a slight headache on her journey.

'I'm glad of that. My friend, Lady Mardykes,' he said, with a fixed smile, 'will be here in the morning. I am a doctor, and she makes me accountable for the health and spirits of all the guests in this big house.'

The pallor and stillness of his face, and the strange metallic vibration of his bass tones, produced in Maud a sensation akin to fear, and made even his pleasantries formidable.

'Your maid must, by this time, be at the door.'

He opened a door, beckoned, and Mercy Creswell came into the room.

'If you permit me, Miss Vernon, I'll try your pulse.' And he took the young lady's wrist before she could decline. 'You don't often drive so far. You'll be quite well in the morning ; but you must not think of coming down to breakfast.'

'Is Miss Medwyn here ?' inquired Maud, before committing herself to stay in her room all the morning.

'No, Miss Medwyn is not here.'

'I wonder what can have happened. Lady Mardykes wrote to me to say she would certainly be here, to stay some time, this morning.'

'An uncertain world !' he observed, with the same smile. 'But Lady Mardykes is seldom mistaken. Whatever she *said* one may be sure she *believed ;* and what she thinks is generally very near the truth. You had an alarm on the way ? But you did not mind it much ?'

'It did startle me a good deal for the moment ; but it was soon over. I think the whole party were startled.'

'I dare say ; but you don't feel it now ? It won't interfere with your sleep, eh ?'

'Oh no,' laughed the young lady ; 'I assure you I'm quite well—I'm not the least likely to be on your list of invalids, and so I think I'll say good-night.'

'Good-night,' said he, with his peculiar smile, and a very ceremonious bow, and he opened the door and stood beside it, with the handle in his fingers.

Mercy Creswell took the bedroom candle that stood, lighted, on a table outside the door. The young lady walked on.

Antomarchi's smile was instantly gone, and the stern, waxen face was grave as before.

Antomarchi's eyes rested for a moment on Mercy Creswell as she passed. He nodded, and made her a slight sign.

You would have judged by her face that she stood in great awe of this man. She positively winced; and with a frightened ogle, and very round eyes, and mouth down at the corners, made him a little courtesy.

He shut the door without waiting for that parting reverence, and Maud saw no more of him or the oval room for that night.

CHAPTER LXII.

MAUD'S BEDROOM.

MERCY CRESWELL led the young lady by a back stair. She was interested; everything was so unlike Roydon. As they traversed the passage leading to the hall, the sounds of music again swelled faintly on her ear; and she saw servants going to and fro, in the corridor, in the fuss and jostle of trays, ices, and claret-cup, glasses, soup and tea-cups.

Up the stair went Maud and her *femme de chambre*, and the sounds died out. The stairs and passages were lighted, rather dingily, by small muffed lamps, which seemed to be fixed in the ceilings. Only at two points, on the level which they had now reached, a yard or two apart, did they encounter any living persons. They were a pair of strong middle-aged housemaids, who, each in turn, stopped and looked at Maud with a transitory and grave curiosity as she passed.

'Isn't she pretty, poor little thing?' said the fatter of these two to her companion.

'Pretty and proud, I dare say; 'tis a good house she's come to; it won't do her no harm, I warrant you,' answered the darker-visaged and leaner woman, following the young lady with a half-cynical smile.

They were now in the long passage through which, a few nights before, Dr. Malkin had approached his room. A man in a waistcoat with black calico sleeves to it seemed to be awaiting them at the other end, leaning against the great door that closed the perspective, with his arms folded, and one leg crossed over the other, an attitude in which we have seen ostlers smoking in inn-yards at stable-doors.

Seeing them, the man stood erect, with the key in his fingers.

'This way, please, Miss Maud,' said Mercy, pushing forward, as she observed the young lady hesitate, as if doubtful whether she was to pass that barrier.

'Miss Vernon, A A, Fourteen,' said Mercy briskly, to this janitor, who forthwith opened the heavy door.

They saw now before them the continuation of the long gallery which is interrupted by this massive door.

The man held out his hand as she gave him a little printed check; he looked at it, and said:

'Yes, all right, A A, Fourteen.' And he opened the first door to the left.

On a little disk of ivory sunk in the door-post, were the number and letters, but so small that you might not have observed them.

At home at last! There was Miss Vernon's luggage on the carpet. A muffed glass lamp, the same as those she had observed in the lobbies, only much more powerful, shed a clear light over every object in the room, from the ceiling.

It was the same room which had been assigned to Doctor Malkin a short time before; but some alterations tending to improve the style and convenience of its arrangements had been made; and now it looked not only a spacious and comfortable, but even a handsome bedroom.

'Heaven defend us! What an awful picture that is!' exclaimed Maud, as she stood before the picture of the abbess, that was placed over the chimney-piece. 'What a deathlike, dreadful countenance! Who is it? No relation of Lady Mardykes, I hope?'

'I don't know, indeed, miss,' answered Mercy, thus appealed to. 'I was never in this room before.'

The kreese, no suitable decoration for a lady's apartment, had been removed.

Maud turned away.

'I wonder why Lady Mardykes lights her rooms and galleries so oddly,' she pursues, talking half to herself, as she looked up at the lamp in the centre of the ceiling; 'I fancy myself in an immense railway carriage.'

A dressing-room opened from this apartment to the right,

and beyond that lay Mercy Creswell's room, accessible in turn
by a door from the dressing-room. Each of these rooms was
lighted in the same way.

'Are all the bedrooms in this house marked with numbers
and letters like this?'

'Every one, miss.'

'I can't say I admire that arrangement, nor the lighting.
One thinks of an hotel. If Miss Medwyn were here,' she
added, more merrily, 'I should certainly, late as it is, dress and
go down to the concert. I should like to see the dresses and
the people. I fancy the house is very full.'

'It is always that, miss; I never knew it hotherwise.'

'And a very gay house?'

'Too gay for me, miss. Always something going on. A too
much of a racket. I don't think it's good for no one,' said
Mercy, half stifling a dreary little yawn. She had not been
laughing since their approach to the house, even at mention of
Miss Medwyn's name; but on the contrary, as she would have
said herself, was 'rayther in the dismals.'

'Lady Mardykes' aunt is here; Mrs. Pendel, of Pendel
Woods? You have seen her often, of course?'

'The Honourable Mrs. Pendel? Oh dear yes, miss, hoften-
times.'

'She was here a day or two ago, certainly. Can you tell me
whether she is here now?'

'No; she's not here now, miss.'

'That's very odd, for Lady Mardykes wrote to beg of her
not to go away. You had better go down and ask.'

'No use in life, miss; I know she's not here—she's gone.
We was talking about her this morning, before I left here.'

'Well, it doesn't so much matter. Lady Mardykes will be
here in the morning. Don't mind those dresses to-night; you
can do all that in the morning; just lay my dressing-case there,
and give me my dressing-gown. Thanks; and I think I'll go
to my bed.'

'Would you please like a bit of supper or something first,
miss?'

'Nothing, thanks; but perhaps you would, Mercy?'

'I had my supper, miss, thanks, at the Pig and Tinder-box.
Servants never sups so late here, miss; it is against the rule of
the house.'

The young lady, in her dressing-gown and slippers, sat before the glass, with her long, thick hair about her shoulders; and Mercy Creswell stood by, brush in hand, arranging it.

When all this was over the young lady, beginning to feel a little sleepy, was glad to get to her bed.

A double cord, with a ring like an old-fashioned handle of a bell-rope, hung by her bed, and the use of this Mercy Creswell explained. Drawing the cord in one direction had the effect of moving a shade under the lamp in the ceiling, and of thus reducing the room to darkness, and in the opposite direction of removing this shade again, and readmitting the light. Having tried this two or three times, and found that she could manage it perfectly, she dismissed her maid, lay down and drew the shade; and the room being in total darkness, she addressed herself to sleep.

But there is a tide in the affairs of men other than that which Shakespeare wrote of at least, and which, taken at the flood, leads on to slumber, but which once passed may never come again for half a night; and Maud soon began to fear she had suffered it to escape her; for after lying for some time still, with eyes closed, she felt more wide awake than when she had first tried to sleep.

She turned on her other side, and lay still; but in vain she tried and exhausted all the common expedients for inducing sleep; they all failed.

An hour had passed, and sleep seemed further than ever.

Perhaps a question which mingled unbidden in all her speculations had something to do with the postponement of her sleep. Was she likely to see Mr. Marston next morning among the guests?

She was listening now with excited attention for far-off sounds of music; but the house was too vast, and if the concert was still going on, which was not indeed very probable, its harmonies were lost in distance long before they could reach her ear. The silence was intense, and more unfriendly to sleep than some little hum of distant life might have been.

Now and then came one of those odd creeks or cracks in the woodwork of the room, which spiritualists assign to mysterious causes, and more sceptical philosophers simply to a change of temperature; and ever and anon a moth would bob against the window-pane with a little tap. But these sounds were far enough between to be a little startling when they did come; and the silence of the long intervals was intense.

She listened; but not a footstep could she hear—not a distant barking of a dog, not a sound of life anywhere.

It was an oppressive and melancholy silence. At length she thought she heard a distant clock strike two, and the sound died away, leaving the silence deeper.

It continued. Some time passed. She lay in the dark with her eyes open, her head on the pillow, without a stir, but awake and excited.

But on a sudden her ears were startled by a loud and horrible sound.

Close to her door, in the gallery, there arose a howling and weeping, and a clang at the bolts of the massive cross door. This was followed by loud ironical laughter. Then came a silence, and then more of the same slow, jeering laughter, and then another silence.

Maud had started up in her bed, and sat with her heart throbbing violently, almost breathless, listening with the chill of terror.

To her relief this horrid sound next time was heard at a comparative distance. She heard other men's voices, now in low and vehement dialogue, and sounds of shuffling feet, of gasping, tugging, and panting, as if a determined struggle were going on; once or twice a low laugh was heard; and then came a yell loud and long, which seemed passing further and further away, and was soon lost quite in the distance; a door clapped, and the place was silent.

For some minutes Maud was afraid to stir. But summoning courage she sprang from her bed, intending to lock the door. But she could discover neither lock nor bolt; but, to her comfort, found that it was nevertheless secured. She made her way to the window, drew the curtain, opened the shutter a little, and looked out.

CHAPTER LXIII.

MORE SIGHTS AND SOUNDS.

THE moon was low now; all was motionless and silent. Long shadows were thrown from the tall hedges and trees upon the misty grass; and the croquet-ground and flower-garden, with all the pleasant anticipations associated with them, lay full in view beneath.

Encouraging the cheerful train of thought to which this prospect gave rise, she sat in her dressing-gown and slippers for some time at the window, and then, intending to question Mercy Creswell on the subject of the uproar that had so scared her, and no doubt her maid also, she tried the dressing-room door; but the handle at this side was gone, and the door fast shut.

So she must be content to wait till morning, for an explanation of the noises that had startled the unusual quiet of the night.

I dare say she would soon have grown drowsy, for she really needed sleep, and the healthier associations that were by this time again uppermost in her mind would have prepared the way for its approach, had she not again been disturbed, just as she was about to return to her bed, by noises which she could not account for.

This time they proceeded from the quadrangle under her window; men's voices were talking low, and steps were audible on the gravel-walk that runs along that side of the house.

She placed herself close to the glass and looked down.

The terrace that passes under the windows, the same along which she had that night approached the house, is very broad, affording a wide belt of grass between the gravel-walk and the wall of the house. This distance enabled her without difficulty to observe the people who were now on the path.

The elevation of this terrace raised it above the level of the shadows, and clear in the moonlight she saw the figures that appeared distinctly. The window from which she was looking was as nearly as possible over the door through which she had entered the house.

Some half-dozen men, with their hats on, were waiting on the broad walk before it. Two or three more in a short time

came out from the house and joined them. The three gentlemen dressed in those black cloaks, with which undertakers
drape chief-mourners, entered the terrace walk, from the point
at her left, at which the door from the courtyard communicates
with it. They were walking very slowly side by side, and he
who was in the middle had a handkerchief in his hand, and
appeared to be weeping.

They passed the window, and the group of men on the walk
drew back toward the house as they did so ; and the three
gentlemen in black continued to walk slowly up and down that
portion of the promenade that lay to her left.

The group of men who are standing before the door breaks
up: some half-dozen go into the house, and only three remain
where they were.

Maud is becoming more and more curious.

A man whose square build looks squarer, as she looks down
upon him, steps out. He looks along the terrace after the three
men who are walking down it. He looks up towards the moon.
There in no mistaking that pale still face, with the jet-black
beard. He is Antomarchi.

The three gentlemen turn about, and are now approaching
him. He advances two or three steps toward them, and
takes off his hat, and makes a particularly low and ceremonious bow. One of these gentlemen advances at a quick
pace, makes him a bow in return, and they talk together. The
other two continue to pace, as before, slowly up and down
the walk.

Antomarchi approaches the door, and the gentleman who
joined him a few minutes before is at his side. They stop.
The three men who were lounging near the door are suddenly, as it were, called to attention. Antomarchi waves his
hand slightly towards the door, and says something to his
companion, who turns about, and at his quickest walk rejoins his
two friends.

These gentlemen, hearing what he says, stop and turn about,
and slowly walk towards the door. There is some little fuss
there ; first one and then another man emerges from it and
returns, and now, with white scarfs and hat-bands, bearing a
long coffin on a bier, come forth the men who had gone in first.
A man steps out last, and shuts the door softly. Is it Darkdale ?
She can't be quite sure.

It is not easy to distinguish colours, at any distance, by

moonlight; but Maud thinks that this coffin is covered with red velvet, and that the large plate and big nails upon it are gilded.

Immediately behind this coffin the three gentlemen walk, and Antomarchi after them, till it disappears round the corner of the house, away to her left, at which the door she had passed that night gives access to the court-yard.

A strange feeling of disgust and fear now, for the first time, steals over her. What is she to think of a house in which, while an inmate lies dead and coffined, all the fiddling and singing, and vanities and feasting of a banquet proceed unchecked? What is she to think of the right feeling and refinement of a hostess who can permit so extraordinary a profanation?

The sombre images summoned to her fancy by the scene she had just witnessed, gave for the time a sickly character to the moonlit prospect, and the now solitary walk so lately traversed by the scanty and mysterious funeral procession.

Maud left the window, and drew the shade from the lamp, and in a moment the warm light filled the room cheerily.

Closing the shutters, and drawing the curtains, she now bethought her seriously of the necessity of getting a little sleep, if she was not to look like a ghost next morning, which certainly was very far from her wish.

So into her bed she got again, and drawing the cord once more, the light vanished, and she lay down determined at last to go to sleep.

All was profoundly silent again, and Maud was now, after the lapse of some eight or ten minutes, beginning at last to feel the approaches of sleep, when she fancied she heard something brushing very softly by the great arm-chair near the side of her bed.

Was she ever to get to sleep in this unlucky bed? Even the idea that a cat had got into her room was not pleasant; for nursery tales of the assassin-like propensities of the tribe (especially of black cats, and why should not this be black?) when their tendency to throttle and murder sleepers in the dark was favoured by opportunity, crowded upon her recollection.

She listened intently. She heard in a little time a slight click, as if a trinket or coin was stirred on the table near. There was no other noise, and nothing very formidable in that. But still she could bear the uncertainty no longer. The darkness and silence were oppressive; she put her hand out and drew the cord, and in an instant the soft light from the lamp in the ceiling filled the room, and disclosed every object.

She was not alone. A figure, perfectly still, was standing about a yard from the side of the bed, toward the foot. She stared at it for some time, hardly believing that what she saw was real, before she recognised in the short squat person in a woollen night-gown Mercy Creswell, her ugly *femme de chambre.*

'How on earth did you come in?' at length Maud exclaimed.

'La! miss, how?' repeated Mercy, who gained a little time for reflections by such repetitions. 'How did I come in? I came as quiet as I could, through the dressing-room door, please, miss.'

'What do you want here?' demanded Miss Maud, a little peremptorily, for she was losing patience. 'I did not call for you, and I think I should have been asleep by this time, if you had remained quietly where you were. What *do* you want?'

'I? I came, miss—what I wanted was—I came to see was you sleeping comfortable, having been, as you was, complaining of your head.'

'Well, don't mind trying to see in the dark any more, please. I wonder you did not tumble over the furniture. You'd have frightened me out of my wits if you had; I have been made so awfully nervous. There were such horrible noises in the gallery, just outside my door; and I hardly got over that, when, of all things in the world, a funeral passed out of this house.'

'La! though, *really*, miss?'

'Yes, *really*, such a grisly idea! Didn't you hear the people under the windows? What are you made of? But you *must* have heard the person who made a hideous uproar in the gallery.'

Maud paused with her eyes upon her.

'Well, I wouldn't wonder if it was, miss, that might easy be,' said Mercy.

'But didn't you *hear* it; what can you mean by affecting to doubt it? You won't allow that you know, or see, or hear anything. You *must* have heard it.'

'Yes, I did hear it,' said Mercy, who resolved, at length, to be candid; 'a man hollooing and crying and laughing, and I think I should know pretty well what it was, miss.'

'That's just what I want you to tell me.'

'Well, I heard this morning there's a servant of one of the great people here that's got fits and raving, saving your presence, miss, from drink.'

'My gracious! that horrible complaint that Doctor Malkin told me about! And why don't they send him to an hospital?'

'So they will, miss, I am told, in the morning.'

'But what about the funeral? You were here this morning, and know the servants. It was evidently some person of rank, and you must have heard of it. A person of that sort could not have been lying dead in the house, without your knowing something of it.'

'Well, no—really, miss, I knew there was some one, I forget his name, a lord, I do believe, lying very bad, some days ago, and gave over—and most like it is the same—but Lady Mardykes, she'll be here in the morning; she can tell you all about it.'

'But do you mean to say that such things happen, in the midst of balls and concerts, in Lady Mardykes' house? Do you mean to say that if I had a fever and died here, Lady Mardykes would not suspend her gaieties till I was buried?'

'Oh! miss, la! you know, miss, Lady Mardykes does things her own way. She's not that sort, neither; but there's a part of the house down at that end farthest from the hall-door, there is sometimes people in she does not know from Adam, saving your presence, miss.'

'I don't in the least comprehend you,' said the young lady, in unaffected amazement.

'I mean this, when people is ordered the waters here for a week, miss, there being no hotel, miss, nor inn, nor nothing of no sort, near Lady Mardykes', if it should 'appen to be a lady or gentleman of consequence, a lord or a countess, or sich like, she would give them the use of a room or two in the house, you see, and so, now and then, of course, it can't be helped. There will be a lady or gentleman die, seeing all as comes to drink the waters is more or less sick and ailing always; and I have known a many a one die here.'

'And without any interruption of the amusements—the music and dancing?' persisted Miss Vernon.

'La! none in life, miss, why should there? Let them go out as they come in, private. When you have seen as many corpses as I have, here, laid out in their caps and sheets, you'll think no more of them than you would of so many yellow wax statues—what's a coffin but a box of cloth? If there's no one I don't care for in it, why should I fret my eyes out? Not I. I wouldn't look over my shoulder to see corpse or coffin; I wouldn't think twice about it; 'tis all fancy, miss.'

'Well, as you say, I shall probably know all about it from Lady Mardykes to-morrow, and now really you must go; and pray don't return till it is time to call me in the morning. Good-night.'

'Good-night, miss.'

And the maid withdrew.

'Well,' thought Maud, as she lay down, 'I have heard that Lady Mardykes keeps an odd house; but anything like this could anyone have conjectured?'

And very soon after this reflection Maud Vernon did, at length, fall fast asleep.

CHAPTER LXIV.

AT THE TERRACE DOOR.

NEXT morning, when Maud awoke, she saw Mercy Creswell sitting near the window, playing a 'devil's tattoo' on the window-stool, and staring out with all her eyes, and a strained neck, on the scene below.

'Oh! Mercy, you are there?' said the young lady drowsily, with her head still upon her pillow.

'Yes, miss, please,' said Mercy, standing up promptly, with a grave countenance.

'What o'clock is it, do you know?' inquired Miss Vernon.

Miss Mercy consulted the big silver watch which she wore at her belt, and which, if not quite so pretty as some little gold ones we may have seen, had the advantage of keeping time a good deal better.

'Half-past ten, miss.'

'Half-past ten!' repeated the young lady, sitting up. 'And

why did not you call me before? Breakfast over, I suppose, and—and Lady Mardykes, has she come?' she added, recollecting that if her hostess were still absent, she would not after all have cared to go down to the breakfast-room.

'Yes, ma'am—yes, miss, half an hour ago Lady Mardykes harrived.'

'Oh? I'm so glad, that is quite charming; now, if Miss Medwyn were here, I think I should have nothing left to wish for.'

And in high spirits, notwithstanding the alarms of the night before, Miss Vernon addressed herself to her toilet, while her breakfast came up on a pretty china tray to the adjoining dressing-room, which was a large and comfortable apartment, commanding precisely the same view of the croquet-ground as she saw from her bedroom window.

As Miss Vernon entered the dressing-room, a dark-featured, low-browed housemaid, standing by the gallery-door, with a pale frown, and in low tones was saying to Mercy Creswell, who was listening with a dark gaze and compressed lips, with the corners of her mouth drawn grimly down.

'An oak stool, all in *that*,' and she clapped her hands. 'You never seed sich another smash in the dead-house. Tom Rose was nothing to it. Lauk! it was a turn! I couldn't eat not that big o' breakfast!'

Mercy saw the young lady coming in, and shifting her place, she said in a quick aside:

'Here's Miss Vernon.'

And with a glance at her, the broad-shouldered lass in housemaid's uniform withdrew and closed the door.

'What was she talking of?' asked the young lady, when she had gone.

'An old story, miss; a man that was killed here years ago; poachers, I dessay, or the like.'

'Oh, a keeper?'

'Well, yes; something that way, miss. Shall I pour you out tea or coffee, please, miss?'

Her breakfast equipage Maud thought a great deal handsomer than was required for the careless service of a bedroom. The china was old and quite exquisite; and the silver, an antique Dutch miniature service, was covered with grotesque figures, trees, windmills, cocks and hens. Every detail in the little breakfast service was pretty and even elegant, a great deal prettier certainly than her mamma would have allowed her at Roydon.

Looking down, she saw from the window a very animated scene ; people in gay dresses were walking on the terrace, and upon the gravel walks that surround the croquet-ground, on which were already assembled some lounging groups, who were knocking the balls about in a desultory way. The cheerful sounds of talking and laughing filled the air. Some of these people, foreigners she supposed, were very demonstrative in their talk and gestures. And a dozen or so of the heterogeneous company who were making the large squares, with the background of old Dutch hedges, and lofty timber, as amusing for her to look at as a fair-green, or a race-course, were dressed extremely oddly, not to say grotesquely. There were at least ninety or a hundred people in that pretty enclosure. Some might possibly be merely visitors for the hour, but still the number assembled testified to a very splendid hospitality.

As Maud was looking out, she saw Lady Mardykes enter the terrace from the door in the side of the house, almost directly under her window.

This, as you may suppose, was a very welcome sight to her.

Antomarchi was walking at her side, and they seemed to be talking incessantly, as they walked slowly round the croquet-ground, and sometimes with very earnest gravity.

Did it strike her that Lady Mardykes was distinguishing this stern and striking man in a very marked way ? He seemed to engross her. She stopped and spoke to but one other person as she walked round and round the quadrangle. She had seen her guests, no doubt, since her arrival before now ; but she seemed at present to have neither eye nor ear for anyone but Antomarchi.

He seemed very devoted, she thought. Might he not possibly entertain hopes which she had not suspected before respecting this rich and brilliant widow ? What was the meaning of her delegating to him, as he had said she did, even playfully, a commission to see after the health and spirits of her guests during her absence ?

And now Maud remembered a laughing warning given to her by this same Lady Mardykes, in answer to some speculations of hers about mesmerism. She said, ' Don't allow anyone to mesmerise you, unless you want to fall in love with him.' Then came her special mention of Doctor Antomarchi, in the letter in which she promised to have him at her house, to meet Maud, as a potent mesmeriser.

Was this clever foreigner really on the high road to fortune and social position ?　Things as strange had happened.

Some illustrated papers had been sent to her at the same time with her breakfast, and Maud, taking one of them up, looked into her room, intending to take her paper-cutter from the table beside her bed, but it was not there.

She had left it on the table herself, beside her book, and she had seen it there afterwards ; and by one of those accidents that sometimes fix trifles in the memory, she had remarked it as it lay in the same place, on her return, after her long look out from the window the night before, to her bed.

'Mercy, did you take my paper-knife from the table beside my bed ?　*I* did not remove it ; look for it, please, and fetch it to me.'

'Me move it !　Certainly not me, miss.　La ! miss, I would 'av' knewed you put it there, but I wasn't a step nearer than the window till you woke up and called me.'

She was fidgeting about the table by this time.

'No, miss, I don't see no sign of no knife, paper or hotherwise.　No, miss, nothing.'

'But I would not lose that pretty little paper-knife on any account, and it *must* be there ; no one has been in the room to take it, and you really *must* find it.'

But nowhere could the paper-knife be found.　It was hardly the sort of thing which a thief would have selected for a prize, seeing on the table close by all the rings and trinkets that might have been as easily picked up.

'It was given me by a person I was very fond of, who is dead, and I won't lose it,' said Miss Vernon, joining in the search, after an interval ; but it did not turn up.

'La ! miss, it must be a mistake.　Where could it go to ?　If it was there, miss, last night, 'twould be there still ; there's no signs on it ; 'tis only worriting yourself, miss, to suppose it was ever there at all.'

'I happened to know it was,' said the young lady, nettled at this irritating line of reply, 'and you must find it.　I shan't go downstairs till I am satisfied about it.'

'What was it like, please, miss ?'

'It is a small mother-of-pearl paper-cutter, that answers as a marker beside, and it has my initials, M. G. V., on the side.'

Maud was really vexed, and was resolved not to lose it; her attention was, however, called to another quarter by a gentle but distinct knock at the dressing-room door. A visit from Lady Mardykes, she thought, with a smile, as she stepped into the dressing-room, and called to her visitor to come in.

It was Doctor Antomarchi who opened the door, and made her a grave and very ceremonious bow. Maud was a little surprised.

'I fancied it was Lady Mardykes who knocked at my door,' she said; 'I was thinking of going out; I saw her from the window.'

'Oh? I'm commissioned to make this little visit, to inquire how you have passed the night. Your nerves were more disturbed than you would allow by the shock of that unlucky rencontre on the road. I'll try your pulse, if you don't mind. Yes—yes—still nervous. You can have your walk quite safely in the croquet-ground, but don't think of taking a drive to-day, and you had better lunch and dine quietly upstairs; to-morrow you will be, I hope, all right, and then, of course, you can do as you please.'

Antomarchi remained for a few minutes, and chatted on agreeably upon other things. He is apparently anxious to please; nothing could be more polite; but his smile is not winning. There is something in it she can't describe, death-like and cruel. In his manner, soften it all he can, there is a latent sternness that might be prompt and terrible.

His large, strange eyes, as if conscious of their power, he has not turned upon hers. In this slightly but studiously averted gaze, there is a hinting of treason.

When he is gone, Maud says to herself:

'Well! is it possible that nice creature can have taken a fancy to that horrible man? She certainly can't see him as I do. However, I suppose there is a charm, if one could only see it, in the sinister as there is in the beautiful.'

'I have looked everywhere, miss, high and low, and I can't find no sich a thing; you couldn't have forgot it at Roydon, unbeknown to you?' said Mercy, returning from her search for the paper-knife.

Maud extinguished this theory peremptorily, and asked:

'Are you quite sure that no one was in that room except you and me?'

'Not a living soul, miss. Who could?'

Maud was now putting her things on for a little walk, and she called for her scissors from the dressing-case.

'You can have mine, miss, please.'

But the young lady preferred her own.

'I don't see no scissors there, miss——'

'Well, my penknife must do.'

'Nor no knife, miss; only a few things.'

Now came another alarm, another search, and a new disappointment.

'I can't understand it!' exclaimed Maud. 'It *is* just possible, to be sure, as you say, that Jones may have left them out, and forgotten them. I'll write to her. But it is so unlikely, that I can't believe it. I really don't understand all this. I can't account for these things.'

Maud's fiery eyes were upon Mercy Creswell as she thus spoke.

The fat, freckled maid, with her chin rather high, tossed her head, with an air of offended dignity. But her eyes could not bear the frank gaze of her young mistress, and were unsteady and confused. She looked, in fact, extremely put out.

'I hope, miss, you don't suppose there's no one about you miss, as would do any sich a thing as to make free with a lady's dressing-case. There never was none in this house but honest servants, nor none, I expects, as would so much as think of any sich things, no, not for the minds of Peru! And as for myself, I hope, miss, you don't think or imagine you're not as safe as the queen's jewels with Mercy Creswell, which I can get a character, as many as I likes, from Lady Mardykes, or from your own mamma, miss, Lady Vernon of Roydon, not to mention a many a lady besides, as would travel a many a mile to say the same for me, if so it was I stood in need of any sich a thing.'

But Maud, not a bit daunted, had nothing more satisfactory to add.

'Charming!' thought Maud, 'if in addition to her other accomplishments she should turn out a thief! I wonder when mamma will allow me to have poor Jones back again.'

The young lady, with her hat and jacket on, was now ready to go down.

'I'm not sure, Mercy, that I should know the way; you must come with me to the top of the stairs. I shall find out the rest of the way myself.'

So they set out together, and Maud looked about her with some curiosity.

It was a vast house, and the gallery, the flooring of which was warped and ridged with age, was dark and dismal enough almost for an ogre's dwelling. On the way to the head of the stairs other passages crossed, in gloomy perspective, and in them they passed, here and there, two or three of the same sort of housemaids whom she had remarked before, with something, she could not exactly say what, a little unusual about them. They were in a sort of uniform, all wearing exactly the same strong, plain, dark-blue dress, white aprons, and neat caps. 'Lady Mardykes,' she thought, 'enlists her servants and rules her house with a military eye.' Those servants all looked, she fancied, a little reserved and thoughtful, but, for the most part, good-natured; they were all above thirty, and some past forty, and all looked remarkably firmly knit and strong; an extremely serviceable corps.

Finally, Maud and her guide had to make several zigzags.

In one respect, among others, before reaching the great stair-case, these lofty and sombre galleries differed very pointedly from those of Roydon; from end to end, not a single picture hung upon their dark panelling, and Maud felt relieved when she had escaped from this monotonous gloom, and stood at last at the broad stair-head.

She heard voices in the hall, and when more than half-way down the stairs, she saw a footman near the foot, and asked him:

'Can you tell me whether Lady Mardykes is in the drawing-room?'

'No, please, my lady. She's not there. I think her ladyship's in the croquet-garden.'

'Will you please show me the way?'

So the servant preceded her deferentially, and led her at last to the door in the side of this great house, and opened it.

Maud paused for a moment. The spectacle before her was very different indeed from that which she had seen issuing from the same door, by moonlight, on the night before.

As a mere picture nothing could be gayer or more amusing. Such brilliant costume, so much animation, such curious contrasts! Such very odd people!

CHAPTER LXV.

MAUD WALKS IN THE CROQUET-GROUND.

MAUD descended the steps, and took the direction of the door opening into the court-yard. She looked at the people as they approached, lest by accident Lady Mardykes should pass her by on the broad gravel-walk. People who had made their mark in the world, no doubt, many of them. She longed to meet her hostess, and learn who was who, in this curious assembly.

In this distinguished and multitudinous company she was glad to perceive that she seemed to excite little or no attention. She was now near enough to the corner to be certain that Lady Mardykes was not upon this walk ; at the end of it she turned to the right, down a new side of the square. Many groups, and many people walking singly, passed her. But neither did she see Lady Mardykes upon this walk.

She paused for a minute at its further angle, and looked across the croquet-ground, where two or three games were by this time in full activity, and the hollow knock of the roquet, and the bounding balls, and all the animated sights and sounds that attend the game, for a moment drew her thoughts from Lady Mardykes, and her eyes from the search.

Among the players or spectators about the hoops, Lady Mardykes was not visible. Maud was beginning to feel a little uncomfortable. If Ethel Tintern had been there, or even Doctor Malkin, whom she had seen the night before, not to mention Maximilla Medwyn, she would have felt comparatively at her ease. But it was very awkward finding herself among such a crowd, without seeing a single face she knew.

She turned about. A very tall yew hedge, clipped in the old Dutch taste, rises there like a dark wall (those at the sides are comparatively low), and traverses the whole length of the quadrangle, opposite to the sides of the house, high as the arcades of a cathedral aisle, with lofty and narrow doorways here and there, cut in this dark and thick partition. Possibly there is a walk within its shadow, and there she may at length discover her hostess.

As a little anxiously she is beginning to explore, intending to resume her search, she is accosted by a person whom she has observed before, as about the most singular if not the most grotesque of the figures she has passed.

He has been making a short promenade in the sun, backward and forward upon the walk close by, like a sentinel. He is one of the few persons there who seem to have observed her. He has bowed slightly, but very ceremoniously, as he passed, but without raising his hat.

He is a tall man and well formed, with a short black cloak thrown Spanish fashion, in spite of the heat of the weather, across his breast and over his shoulder. He has a broad-leafed black felt hat looped at the front with something that looks like a little buckle of brilliants. His face is dark and handsome, with an expression of the most ineffable pride and self-complacency. His chin is high in the air, his movements are slow and graceful, he wears white kid gloves, and carries in his hand an ebony walking-cane, with a gold head, formed something like a crown, in which glimmers a brilliant. He is evidently dressed in 'shorts,' for the more advantageous exhibition of his handsome legs; he wears black silk stockings, and he turns out his toes as he walks like Sir Christopher Hatton.

In Spanish first, which Maud understood not at all, and then, with better fortune, in French, in which she had no difficulty in conversing, he, with a lofty but smiling courtesy, asked the young lady whether he could direct her, or give her any information.

Maud thanked him, and asked if he had seen Lady Mardykes, or could say where she was.

He had seen her a little time ago, but he deeply regretted he could not say whether she was now in the garden or not.

'May I now,' he said, drawing himself up to his full height with a smile of haughty urbanity, 'venture a question in return?'

'Certainly,' said the young lady. They were conversing still in French.

'It is this. Have you observed, I entreat, any peculiarity in me? I anticipate your reply. You have. You remarked that in accosting you I merely touched, without removing, my hat. The reason of that is not dishonourable. I have the very great honour to represent her Majesty the Queen of Spain' (there was such a personage then) 'at the Court of St. James's. I cannot therefore uncover to a subject. You understand. It is alike my painful prerogative and my loyal duty. I must in all but a royal presence retain my hat. I need not say more. I see, with infinite satisfaction, how fully you assent. My servants, if indeed they were in attendance, as they ought to be, I should send with pleasure in quest of Lady Mardykes; but, alas! here, in the country, they always claim a privilege of irregularity, and are never to be found.'

He made another stately bow, drew back a step or two to indicate that the audience was over, folded his arms, threw back his head, and smiled, with half-closed eyes, haughtily.

Miss Vernon passed under the tall arch in the dark green wall of yew, and found herself in a long and sombre walk, fenced in by two solemn hedges of shorn foliage, between which but a few groups were now to be seen in the perspective. Some were walking before her in the same direction, diminished in the distance; others slowly approaching. The people who made their promenade in this walk were, possibly, of a graver turn of mind than those who kept the sunnier haunts. Nevertheless, now and then they would pause in their sauntering walk to stand before one of the open archways, and look out upon the croquet-ground and its amusing vicissitudes and garrulous players.

A gentleman walking with two ladies, and conversing gravely, seemed to observe her solitary state and evident search for some missing friend, and politely inquired, taking off his hat, whether he could be of any use. In reply to her question, he told her that it was more than half an hour since he had seen Lady Mardykes, and rather thought she had left the croquet-ground, but could not be quite certain. If she would permit him, he added, perhaps prompted to this heroism by her striking beauty, he would have pleasure in assisting her in her search—an exertion which Maud, with many thanks, declined.

Mr. Darkdale, in a long, ungainly black coat, such as she thought she had seen Jesuits wear, and with a book under his arm, passed her by, a few moments later, at a brisk pace. His stern mouth and dark face were thoughtful, and his broad forehead lowered, and as he passed her, from their corners, his penetrating brown eyes for a moment fixed on her face; he made no sign of recognition, however, but glided with a light tread, in a straight line, upon his way.

'That man never was a servant,' thought Maud, as she passed him with a chill feeling of suspicion. 'I thought he said, or mamma, or Mercy Creswell said, *some* one did, I'm sure, that he was simply to take care of me here, and then to go—I forget where—to some other place, and yet here I still find him domesticated! And I am nearly certain I saw him directing the men

who were conducting that funeral last night. He is not what he
pretends. A Jesuit, I dare say, he is. He is one of the first
persons I shall ask Lady Mardykes to explain.'

As she reached the further end of this cool and shadowy walk,
she saw, at her left, the walls of what had been an old-fashioned
square tea-house, two stories high, such as used to fill an angle
in the wall of a Dutch garden. Roof and floorings were now
gone, and the brick was covered with ivy, and looked very dark
under the spreading branches of the tall trees that overhung the
outer wall.

She turned aside to peep into this ruin. She had expected
to find it empty; but it was no such thing. Inside was a thin
old gentleman, with stooped and narrow shoulders, and a very
long and melancholy face: he had a conical fur cap on, and
large tortoise-shell spectacles, and a long white-peaked beard,
and was seated at a table, with an enormous ink-bottle beside
him, totting up figures in a mighty book like a ledger. He
might have done very well in a pantomime for either a miser
or a magician. There were innumerable sheaves of papers,
neatly folded and docketed, placed in order, upon the table at
each side; and under it, and beside him, on the ground, was a
huge litter, consisting chiefly of files stuck up to the very hooks
with papers, and several leather bags stuffed, no doubt, with
old balance-sheets and account-books. On a row of nails along
the wall were hanging a series of 'stock-lists,' with the sparrows
twittering above, and bees and flies buzzing about them in
the ivy.

With a grimace as if he had suddenly crunched a sour
gooseberry, this sage rose, with a stamp on the ground, and,
jerking his pen behind his ear, gazed angrily at Maud, and
muttered:

'Is not the garden wide enough for you and for me, madam?
Saints and angels! How is it possible for an overworked old
man to get through his business, interrupted as I am? Pray
don't go for a moment; on the contrary, wait; the mischief is
done. I claim this, because I want to prevent the occurrence
of another such intrusion. It is something to keep the complicated and never-ending accounts of this enormous house. It is
something to make and direct all the prodigious investments
that are going on, and to be able at an instant's notice to tell to
a fractional part of a farthing what the entire figure is, and
each item stands at, every day of the week. It requires an

arithmetical secretary such as England does not see every day,
to get all that within the circle of his head, madam.　But when
you are ordered to make up a tot of forty years' figures on pain
of losing your splendid rights, at a single voyage, between
morning light and setting sun, it screws, you see, on an old
fellow's temples too tight.'　He pressed three fingers of each
hand on his temples, and turned up his eyes.　'It is enough
to make them burst in or out, by Heaven, like a ship.　I
remember the time I could have done it like *that*' (he snapped
his fingers), 'but we grow old, ma'am, and always interrupted,
never quiet.　Some one looks in; just as I have it, some one
laughs, or a cock crows, or the light goes out; and I, simple as
you see me, entitled to all that stock, unclaimed dividends, if I
could only finish it, and bring my tots into court.　It is a hard,
hard thing all that, and so exquisitely near it, to be still
doomed at my years to a life of slavery !　Always so near it,
always so near; always interrupted.　Here I came out to-day
to take the fresh air in this place a little ; shut up perpetually
in my office ; and just as I had got midway in the tot *you* look
in, and—immortal gods ! blessed patience ! hell and Satan !—
all is lost in one frightful moment of forgetfulness !　Always so
near.　It makes one's thumbs tremble !　Always blasted.　It
makes one squint.　It is enough to make a man stark, staring
mad !　Pray make no excuses, madam ; they waste time.　You
looked in ; do so no more, and I'll forgive you.'

He made her a short bow, placed his finger on his lip,
turned up his eyes, and shook his head, with a profound groan,
and addressed himself forthwith to his work again.

With a mixture of compassion and amusement, she left the
den of this old humourist, into which she had unwittingly
intruded, and continued her search.

A prepossessing young lady, dressed in very exquisite taste,
walking slowly, and looking about her with an air and smile of
quiet enjoyment and hauteur, hesitated as Maud approached,
stood still, looking on her with a gracious and kind expression,
and a countenance so *riant* that Miss Vernon hesitated also in
the almost irresistible attraction.

CHAPTER LXVI.

HER GRACE THE DUCHESS OF FALCONBURY.

IN this pleasant green shade they had come to a standstill.

'Pretty creature,' said this lady, in very sweet tones, 'you are looking for somebody, I think. You have not been long here; I have not seen your face before. First tell me who it is you want; I may be able to help you.'

'Thank you very much; I have been looking everywhere for Lady Mardykes, and no one seems to know where she is.'

'Oh! Lady Mardykes? You'll find her time enough. You are very young, dear; Lady Mardykes is a charming companion. But if you knew as much as I do of this curious world, you would hardly be in such a hurry to find her; you would wait with a great deal of patience until she found you.'

The young lady looked in the face of her new acquaintance, who spoke so oddly of her hostess. That unknown friend laughed musically and softly, and looked very archly from the corners of her eyes, and nodded a little more gravely, as if to say, 'Although I laugh I mean it seriously.'

What she did say in continuation, was this:

'Come through this arch; there is a seat here that commands a very good view of the croquet-ground and the open walks. And what is your name, child?' she continued, as they walked side by side; 'you are sweetly pretty; but by no means so pretty as I.'

This little qualification Maud, of course, accepted as a pleasantry, which yet might be quite true, for this lady, although by no means so young as she, was extremely pretty.

'You, now, begin by telling me who you are,' said this lady, taking her place on the rustic seat, to which she had led the way, and, pointing with her parasol, invited her to sit down also, 'and then you shall hear everything about me.'

'My name,' said Maud, 'is Vernon, my mamma is Lady Vernon; we live at Roydon, a little more than forty miles from this.'

'Indeed! Lady Vernon, of Roydon? We ought to know one another then. I knew your mamma at one time, when I was a very young girl; it is twelve years ago. You have heard her speak of me, the Duchess of Falconbury. My greatest misfortune overtook me very early.'

She turned away, and sighed deeply.

Maud had heard of that lady's bereavement. It had been a marriage of love. The young duke died in the second year of what promised to be a perfectly happy union, and the beautiful dowager had refused to listen to any solicitations to change her widowed state ever since.

'I like your face, I love your voice, which, for me, has a greater charm than even the features,' said the Duchess. And she placed her hand on Maud's as it lay upon the seat, and looked for a moment earnestly in her face. 'Yes, we shall be very good friends; I can trust you; I ought to trust you, for, otherwise, I cannot warn you.'

'Warn me?' repeated Maud.

'Yes, *warn* you. I see you looking round again for Lady Mardykes.'

'I don't see her anywhere,' said Maud.

'So much the better,' said the Duchess, this time with a little shudder.

Maud looked at her. But her dark look was but the shadow of a passing cloud. The sunshine of her smile immediately succeeded, but was soon darkened again.

'For five years a miserable secret has lain heavy at my heart; I breathed it but once, and then to a person who visited me under circumstances so strange, that I scarcely know whether he is of this world or of the next. Can you keep a secret? Will you, while you live?' she whispered, drawing near to Maud.

I wonder whether priests and physicians, who have so many secrets thrust upon them, in the way of their trade, have any curiosity left for those which fortune may throw in their way? But people who enjoy no such professional obligations and opportunities, have for the most part a large and accommodating appetite for all such mental aliment.

Maud looked for a moment in the pretty face which had so suddenly grown pale and thoughtful, and with hardly a hesitation she accepted the proffered trust.

'You like Lady Mardykes?' asks the Duchess.

'Extremely—all I know of her.'

'Well said. Well guarded—"all you know of her." You shall know more of her before you leave me. She is a pretty woman still, but, of course, *passée.* When I knew her first she was beautiful ; how beautiful you could not now believe. But always something, to my sense, *funeste ;* a beautiful flower dedicated to death. Yet she seemed the analogy of some exquisite and wonderful flower that grows somewhere in dreamland, in enchanted gardens, where you will, but always in the shade, never in light. Her face was beautiful, gentle, melancholy, but, to my eye, baleful. I should have liked to have held my parasol between it and me. Do you understand that feeling? Those flowers are associated in my mind with a poison that infects the air.'

'An odd guest,' thought Maud, 'to speak so of her entertainer.'

'You think it strange,' said the Duchess, oddly echoing Maud's thoughts, 'that I should speak so of Lady Mardykes. You shall hear and judge.'

This lady spoke, I may parenthetically mention, in a particularly low, sweet voice, and with a curious fluency, which, if one had only heard without seeing her, would have led one to suppose that she was reading a written composition rather than talking in colloquial English. She continued thus :

'You know her. She is very winning and gentle ; she is, or was, one of the most fascinating persons I ever met. She is radiant with the beauty of candour. Her expression is soft and quite angelic; and she, of all living women, possesses the blackest heart and is capable of the most enormous crimes.'

As she murmured these words, the lady, with a dismal gaze in her face, pressed her hand on Maud's wrist.

'You can't believe that I am serious,' said the Duchess. 'I'll convince you. You think it odd I should know her and meet her. I'll convince you in a way you little expect. The days of detection are marked in this little red book. No one reads it but myself, and that only for a date.' She showed a little book about two inches square, bound in scarlet leather. 'I'm talking to you in an unknown tongue; you will understand me perfectly another time,' she continued, a little embarrassed. 'I'll tell you at present enough to justify what I have said of her. I am fettered and she is fettered. You cannot yet understand that ; and, as sometimes happens, from the first moment we met there was a mutual embarrassment, that is, mutual fear and dislike ; even more, mutual horror and antipathy, the reasons of which depend on——. Well, by-and-by I may speak of it again ;

but for the present we let that pass. There is the cause of my permitting her to live, and of her permitting me to live. Those are strong terms, but true. Listen. I make no half-confidences. She liked my dear husband before his marriage. Gentle and soft as she looks, she is an ambitious and daring woman. He suspected nothing of it. She loved him passionately, and in proportion as jealousy began to infuse itself into it, that passion became atrocious. Here is the secret. Sit closer to me. My husband died by the hand of a poisoner; and that hand was afterwards directed against my life.'

'Gracious Heaven!' exclaimed Maud, feeling as if she were still in a horrible dream.

'Hush! Dear child, it is of the last importance that no human being should suspect that I have imparted a secret to you. Your life would be practised upon immediately, and the ultimate vindication of justice be defeated. You shall know, by-and-by, the curious circumstances which, for a time, prevent the sword from descending upon Lady Mardykes, and which, although she knows that a movement of my finger may bring it down, yet compel her to tolerate my existence, and constrain both to live on mutual terms of exterior friendliness. Do you see that man coming towards us?'

'Doctor Antomarchi?' said Maud.

CHAPTER LXVII.

MAUD CHANGES HER ROOMS.

DOCTOR ANTOMARCHI was walking slowly in that direction, with his eye upon them.

'I see you know him. He is a very particular friend, and has been for many years, of Lady Mardykes. I never smell any perfume, no, not even a flower, that he presents. You will do wisely to follow my example. Lady Mardykes chooses her instruments astutely. See how he watches us. Let us get up; he will think, if we seem so absorbed, that we are talking of that which—might not please him.'

The Duchess rose as she spoke, and Maud with her.

Could Maud Vernon credit one particle of the shocking

melodrama she had just been listening to ? One thing was certain : her new friend had not been mystifying her. Her colour came and went as she told her story, and the expression was too genuinely that of a person pursued by an agitating and horrible recollection to be counterfeited.

'You can't believe all this ?' resumed the Duchess. 'I shall be here for a walk at eleven in the morning ; meet me, and we shall have another talk. Till then, upon this subject we are mute.'

Antomarchi was now near. To the Duchess he made a very ceremonious bow, and one not quite so profound to Miss Vernon.

'Oh, Doctor Antomarchi,' said the Duchess loftily, drawing up, 'can you tell us where Lady Mardykes is ? Miss Vernon has been looking for her.'

'I believe, your grace, she is not likely to see her to-day ; Lady Mardykes has been called away. But she will certainly be here again in the morning.'

Doctor Antomarchi had to address the conclusion of this speech to Maud only, for the Duchess of Falconbury turned her head away with an air of scarcely concealed disdain, which implied very pointedly how exclusively in the interest of her companion her inquiry respecting Lady Mardykes had been made.

'And can you tell me,' said Maud, 'whether Miss Medwyn has arrived, or how soon she is expected ?'

'I know that Miss Medwyn has not come; I do not know when she may come, but certainly she is not expected to-day,' he answered. 'I think, Miss Vernon, I need scarcely ask you whether you feel a good deal knocked up to-day ?'

'I am a little tired.'

'And a little nervous.'

'I slept so little last night, and went to bed rather tired, and I really do think there is nothing else.'

'Well, you must consent to remain perfectly quiet for the remainder of the afternoon, and get to bed before ten to-night, and to-morrow you will be quite yourself. You are more tired, and your nerves more shaken, than you suppose. You may bring on an attack of illness else.'

'But if Lady Mardykes should come to-night I should like so much to be ready to go down.'

'She will not be here to-night, assure yourself of that. Or

I'll put it, if you please, in a way you may like better.   If she does come to-night, I undertake that she shall certainly pay you a visit in your room the very first thing she does.'

'That is very good of Doctor Antomarchi,' said the Duchess, with a satirical smile on her lips and irony in her tone. 'I shall be going out for a drive after luncheon, so I suppose, dear, I shan't see you, unless Doctor Antomarchi should give leave, again to-day, but to-morrow we shall meet, and I think till then I shall say good-bye.'

She nodded prettily to Maud, and smiled lingeringly over her shoulder as she turned away and re-entered the shady walk from which they had lately emerged together.

Doctor Antomarchi, although not included in the lady's leave-taking, took off his hat with another ceremonious bow, and at the same moment a servant stationed on the terrace began to ring a bell.

'That is the luncheon-bell,' said the doctor.

The polite company assembled on the croquet-ground threw down their mallets at the sound of it, and they and all the loiterers on the walks, and among the flowers, began to troop toward the door through which she had entered, and in a very short time this pretty quadrangle was nearly emptied, while, more slowly, Doctor Antomarchi walking by her side, the two moved in the same direction.

Maud did feel a little, indeed, a good deal, tired, and this, together with the dispiriting absence of her hostess, and the agitating stories, false she was certain, communicated by her fanciful new friend, the Duchess, predisposed her to adopt Antomarchi's advice.

Maud found Mercy Creswell awaiting her in the passage. She ducked a little courtesy, with a face of awe, to Doctor Antomarchi as he passed her, and then told her young mistress that 'she had been moved to much more beautifuller rooms.'

On reaching them, under Mercy Creswell's guidance, she found that they were next the suite which she had occupied on the night before, but at the near side of that strong door which seemed to form a very marked boundary in the house.

They consisted of four rooms, a bedroom, a dressing-room adjoining it, and a sitting-room beyond that ; there was also a narrow room for her maid, with a door of communication with the young lady's room, and another opening on the passage.

Nothing could have been devised more charming than the taste in which the rooms intended for Miss Vernon's use were furnished and got up. If they had been prepared by some wealthy vassal for the reception of a royal visitor, they could not have been more elegant, and even magnificent. Who could have fancied that these bare, gloomy corridors led to anything so gorgeous and refined? Maud looked round, smiling with surprise and pleasure.

'They were only finished this morning, miss,' said Mercy, also turning round slowly, with a fat smile of complacency, for she participated in the distinction.

'Was all this done for me?' Maud inquired at last.

'Every bit, miss,' rejoined her maid.

'How extremely kind! What taste! What beautiful combinations of colour!'

Maud ran on in inexhaustible admiration for some time, examining now, bit by bit, the details of her sitting-room.

'Lady Mardykes will be here to-morrow morning,' said Maud at last; 'it really will be a relief to me to thank her. I hardly know what to say.'

Her eloquence was interrupted by the arrival of luncheon.

When she had had her luncheon, she began to question Mercy about the people whom she had seen in the croquet-ground under the windows.

'Do you know the appearance of the Spanish Minister?' she asked.

'Spanish Hambassador? Oh! La, yes, miss. Don Ferdnando Tights they calls him in the servants' hall.'

'What kind of a person is he?'

'Well, he's a quiet creature; there's no harm in him, only, they say, he is woundy proud.'

'That is pretty plain. And the Duchess of Falconbury? She was talking to me a good deal of Lady Mardykes. Are they good friends?'

'Oh! bless you, that's a troublesome one. Never a good word for no one has she. I would not advise no one that's here to make a companion of that lass; she has got many a light head into trouble, not that there's nothing dangerous about her, only this, that she is always a-trying to make mischief.'

'That is a good deal, however. Do you mean that she tells untruths?'

'Well, no; I do believe she really half thinks what she says, but her head is always running on mischief, and that's the sort she is.'

'How do you mean that she has got people into trouble?'

'Well, I mean by putting mischievous thoughts in their heads, you see, and breeding doubt and ill-will.'

'Do you recollect any particular thing she said of that kind?' asked Maud curiously.

'Not I, miss. Ho! bless you, miss, she'd talk faster than the river runs, or the mill turns. That's the sort she is with her airs and her grandeur, fit to burst with pride.'

Miss Vernon was pleased at this testimony to the dubious nature of this great lady's scandal. A mist, however, not quite comfortable, still remained. She wished very much that she had never heard her stories.

Maud had still a slight flicker of her nervous headache, and was really tired besides, and not sorry of an excuse to spend the rest of the day quietly with her pleasant books and music, for a piano had been placed in her sitting-room, now and then relieved by so much of Mercy Creswell's gossip as she cared to call for, and, in this way, before she was well aware, the curtain of night descended upon her first day.

CHAPTER LXVIII.

THE THIEF.

It was past nine o'clock next morning, notwithstanding her resolution to be up and stirring early, when Maud got up.

Lady Mardykes was expected, as we know, to arrive that morning; and Maud peeped often from the window, as she sat at her dressing-table near it.

In her dressing-gown and slippers, she went into the sitting-room on hearing the maid arrive with her breakfast things.

'Can you tell me,' asked Maud, 'whether Lady Mardykes has arrived?'

'Please 'm, is that the lady that is coming from——'

'No matter where's she coming from,' interrupted Mercy Creswell sharply; 'it is Lady Mardykes, the lady that came yesterday, and is expected again this morning. She's a new

servant, not a week in the house,' says the *femme de chambre*
to Maud, in a hasty aside. ' I think you might know whether
her ladyship's harrived or no,' and she darted at the maid a look
black as thunder.

' Yes 'm, I'm quite new here, please. I don't half know the
ways of the 'ouse yet. I was 'ired by——'

' Don't you mind who you was 'ired by. I'll make out all
about it, miss, myself, if you please, just now,' again interposed
Mercy.

And before she had time to reflect upon this odd dialogue
between the maids, Miss Vernon's attention was pleasantly engaged by satisfactory evidence on the subject of her inquiry, for
she saw Lady Mardykes enter the now quiet croquet-ground
from the further side in company with Antomarchi. Except for
these two figures the large quadrangle was deserted.

Antomarchi was speaking earnestly to her ; she was looking
down about the walk. The distance was too great to read faces
at ; but Maud saw Lady Mardykes apply her handkerchief once
or twice to her eyes. She was evidently weeping.

Her father had not died. Her dress was as brilliant as good
taste would allow, and the morning paper said that there were
no longer any grounds for uneasiness about him. Had Maud's
eye accidentally lighted on a scene ? Was this strange, and as
she thought, repulsive man, urging his suit upon this lady over
whom he had succeeded, possibly, in establishing a mysterious
influence ?

Lady Mardykes glances up toward this long line of windows,
as if suddenly recollecting that she may be observed.

Then she walked with more of her accustomed air ; and she
and Antomarchi, crossing the grass-plot, ascended the broad flight
of steps that scale the terrace, at its middle point, exactly opposite to the door in the side of the house, nearly under Maud's
window. Through this door they entered the house, and Miss
Vernon, for the present, lost sight of them.

On the breakfast table lay the *Morning Post*, where, among
other interesting pieces of news, she read : ' Lady Mardykes
is at present entertaining a distinguished circle of friends at
Carsbrook ;' and then followed a selection from the names.
Among which figured his Excellency the Spanish Minister,
and her Grace the Dowager Duchess of Falconbury. Her interest more than revived as she read this long list of names,
containing so much that was distinguished. There was one

omission.   The Honourable Charles Marston did not figure
with other honourables in the list.   But that list was but a
selection, and Charles Marston had not yet made his mark in
the world, and might easily be omitted, and be at Carsbrook,
notwithstanding.

She would not ask Mercy Creswell; for she did not choose
Lady Vernon to hear anything that might awake her suspicions.
And that reserved and prevaricating *femme de chambre* had
written, she knew, the day before, to Lady Vernon, and considered herself as in *her* employment, and not in Maud's.   It
behoved her, therefore, to be very much on her guard in talking
to that person.

Maud never found Mercy Creswell so slow and clumsy in
assisting at her toilet as this morning.   There was very little to
be done to equip her for her ramble in the croquet-ground ; but
that little was retarded by so many blunders, that Maud first
laughed, and then stared and wondered.

She saw Mercy Creswell frequently look at her big watch,
and not until after she had successfully repeated it pretty
often, did she perceive that this sly young woman was pointing out to her in the quadrangle below, which was now beginning to fill, persons, and little incidents in succession, which
tempted her again and again to look from the window, and
delayed her.   All this time the *femme de chambre*, affecting
to laugh with her young mistress, and to be highly interested
in the doings of the croquet-ground, was plainly thinking with
some anxiety of something totally different, and watching the
lapse of the minutes whenever she thought she could, unobserved, consult her watch.

Maud looking in the glass, saw her do this, with an anxious
face, and then hold it to her ear, doubtful if it were going, time
seemed, I suppose, to creep so slowly.

Why was it that this maid, this agent of her mother's,
seemed always occupied about something different from what
she pretended to be about, and to have always something to
conceal ?

Another delay arose about the young lady's boots.   Her maid
had put them out of her hand, she could not for the life of her
remember where.

'Surely Jones put up more than one pair.   Will you
try ?'

'They're not come up yet, please, miss.'

'It seems to me, Mercy, you have made up your mind not to let me out until your watch says I may go ; so unless you find them in a minute more, I shall walk out in my slippers.'

As the young lady half in jest said this, the great clock of the old house, which is fixed in that side of it that overlooks the croquet-ground, struck eleven. And the clang of its bell seemed to act like magic upon Mercy Creswell, for she instantly found the boots, and in a minute or two more had done all that was required of her, and her young mistress went out, full of excited expectation, and not a little curious to observe more closely the odd relations of confidence and sympathy which seemed to have established themselves between the wealthy lady of Carsbrook and the clever foreign adventurer who had, she fancied, marked her for his own.

The gallery that passes her door is a very long one, and exactly as she entered it from her dressing-room, there emerged from a side-door near the further extremity, to her great surprise, two persons, whom she saw to be Lady Mardykes and Doctor Antomarchi. The lady stepped out quickly ; their way lay towards the head of the stairs. They were in low and earnest conversation, and plainly had not seen her.

Lady Mardykes walked with a quick and agitated step, intending, it seemed, to avoid observation. Had it been otherwise, Maud would have run to overtake her. What was she to think ?

She would try to keep Lady Mardykes in sight, and when she got down-stairs there would be no awkwardness in speaking to her.

Lady Mardykes and Antomarchi had but just appeared, and Maud had hardly made two steps towards them from the door, when Mercy Creswell peeped out.

'Lord ! There's her ladyship !' gasped the maid, in unaccountable consternation, and with a stamp on the floor she called to her young mistress, still in a suppressed voice, as she tried to catch her dress in her hand. 'Come back, miss, you must not follow her ladyship. It's as much as my place is worth if you do.'

'What on earth do you mean ? What *can* you mean ?' said Maud, turning toward her for a moment in astonishment. 'I'm going downstairs, I'm going to the croquet-ground. Go back to my room, please, and wait for me there.'

The *femme de chambre* glared on her irresolutely, with her

finger-tips to her under-lip, and the other hand extended in the attitude in which she had grasped with it at the lady's dress. Suddenly she drew back a step, with a look a little demure and frightened, and dropping a short courtesy, she dived back into the room again.

This woman, to whose care Lady Vernon had consigned her toilet, was becoming more and more unaccountable and unpleasant every day. But there were subjects of curiosity that piqued her too nearly to allow the image of Mercy Creswell a place in her thoughts just now.

As she moved along the gallery, she saw the door, through which Lady Mardykes and Antomarchi had just passed, open, and a man's head and a part of his figure protruded; it was only for a moment while he dropped a black leather bag at the side of the door next the stairs, and then withdrew, closing but not quite shutting the door; but she had no difficulty in recognising the peculiar countenance of Mr. Darkdale.

As she passed she heard a voice she recognised. It was the same she had heard from the carriage that passed them in the pine-wood on the night of her journey, and which, allowing for the hoarseness produced by shouting, had, she fancied, so nearly resembled that of Captain Vivian.

'Imprisoned by Lady Mardykes, you know as well as I, I can't get away, no one ever can from this d—d house: I shall never leave this room alive——'

These odd words reached her, and the door was shut, as they were rapidly spoken. It was not the voice of an angry man. It was spoken in a tone of utter despondency. Some people, however, have an exaggerated way of talking; and this was not worth a great deal.

Maud knew her way to the great staircase perfectly now. As she went down she met the Duchess of Falconbury coming up. This great lady was dressed, as usual, in a very elegant taste, and looked quite charming. She stopped at the landing where she met Maud.

'So I have found my friend at last. Come to my arms, my long lost swain!' she exclaimed, and smiling, placed her arms about her neck and kissed her, before Maud had well time to be even astonished. The Duchess laughed a little silvery laugh. 'I really began to fear I was never to see you again, and I have so much to tell you. So much *more*,' she whispered, 'and you don't know what it is to have a confidence to make, and no one with either honour or sympathy to hear it ; and that was my sad case, until I met you. I forgot my watch in its case on my dressing-table. I don't mind sending ; I go myself. I lock up everything,' she said in a still lower whisper, and held up a little ormolu key, and she added significantly, ' you had better do so, while you remain here. I used to lose something or other every day till I took that precaution ; they steal all my penknives and scissors. Where are you going now ?'

' I'm trying to find a friend.' (She did not care to mention Lady Mardykes particularly, as her name might easily set the Duchess off upon one of her ' hominies,' as they call such stories in the north country.) ' I think I shall have no difficulty, now, in finding her.'

' And *then ?* Where shall I look for you ?'

' I suppose I shall go where every one seems to go, here, to the croquet-ground.'

' Yes—the croquet-ground, that will do very nicely, and I will meet you there.'

She nodded, and smiled over her shoulder as she ran up the stairs, and Maud ran down, in hopes of recovering Lady Mardykes' track, but, for the time, she had effectually lost sight of her.

There was no footman at this moment in the hall near the stairs. The servant who was at the hall-door had not seen her. She had probably taken the way to the croquet-ground, the general muster before luncheon.

She made a wrong turn in threading the long passages, and found herself at the door of the odd oval room in which her interview with Doctor Antomarchi, on the night of her arrival, had taken place.

The door was a little open. It occurred to her that possibly Lady Mardykes might be there. She tapped at the door. There was no answer ; she pushed it more, opened it, and stepped in.

This room had a peculiar character, as I have said. Something sternly official and mysterious. It might be the first audience-chamber, in a series, in the Inquisition. Maud looked about her. She was alone.

On the massive table I have mentioned, near the large desk which stood at one end of it, was spread a square piece of letter-paper, on which were laid, side by side, three trifling toys, of very little collective value, but which at once riveted the attention of Miss Vernon.

She stooped over them; there could be no doubt as to their identity. There was the tiny paper-cutter she had missed, with its one little steel blade in the handle. There were the scissors with the gold mounting of her dressing-case, from which they had been stolen, and there, finally, a little penknife, also stolen from her dressing-case, but which she had not missed. The pretty little pen-knife had her monogram, M. G. V., upon it. The paper-knife had this, and the device of the Rose and the Key besides; and about the scissors there could be no doubt whatever. If there had been any, it would have been removed by a memorandum written in a clear, masculine hand upon the sheet of paper on which they lay.

It was simply these words :

'Septm. —th, 1864.
'Miss Vernon. Roydon Hall.
'See K. L. L., vol. iii., folio 378.
'Three articles ; viz. scissors, paper-cutter, pen-knife.
'Questionable.'

'Questionable ! What can he mean ? Is this a piece of insolence of that foreigner, about whom Lady Mardykes appears infatuated ? Questionable ? What on earth can he mean or suspect ?'

Her first impulse was to seize her own property, and the paper, and bring the whole thing before Lady Mardykes. But her more dignified instinct told her differently. She would leave these stolen trifles where they were, and mention the discovery, perhaps, after consultation with her Cousin Maximilla, whom she was sure to see in a day or two.

Maud turned about now, and walked out of the door, almost hoping to meet Doctor Antomarchi. She did not; for he returned through another door, and too late discovered his oversight. But he little suspected that Miss Vernon had herself visited the room, and by a perverse accident had seen and recognised her missing property. He glanced jealously round the room, with eyes that, whenever he was roused, became wild and burning.

'Strange forgetfulness ! But nothing has been stirred. That dear Lady Mardykes, she is so excitable ! One can't avoid being disturbed.'

He shut the door sharply, opened a large cabinet, and popped these trophies of larceny into one of a multitude of pigeon-holes.

'What will Damian say? What will Damian think? He's past the age of thinking against a hard head like this,' and he tapped his square forehead with his pencil-case, smiling and musing.

CHAPTER LXIX.

ODD PEOPLE.

IN the meantime, Maud had reached the steps of the door which opens on the terrace-walk of the quadrangle; and from that elevation she made a survey of the ground.

This fruitless pursuit of her hostess was beginning to grow ridiculous; she would have laughed, I dare say, if she had not been, also, very near crying. For her comprehensive survey was unrewarded by a sight of Lady Mardykes; and here was she already in the third day of her visit, without having yet exchanged a word with her hostess, or having been introduced to a single person; and were it not for the absurdly magnificent proofs of Lady Mardykes' very marked attention to her comforts and luxuries, displayed in the number of rooms assigned to her use, and the exquisite taste in which they were furnished, she would have begun to suspect that Lady Mardykes had quite forgotten that she had ever invited her to Carsbrook.

If she was in the croquet-ground she was not in prominence; she could not see her.

She might possibly be concealed by the thick yew hedge at the opposite side of this pretty square, and if she were walking in that shadowy alley she could easily find her. So Maud this time turned to her right, intending to walk round to the further side.

She was met on the terrace-walk by a lady, very little, with a grey silk shawl on that swept the gravel-walk behind her; she had an open book half as big as herself in both hands before her eyes, and was reading to herself, her lips forming the words silently with great rapidity and emphasis. She stopped suddenly

before Maud, and eyed her grimly over the top of her open
book, without moving her long and grotesque face, and then in
a stern voice she asked :

'Hast thou thy catechism at thy fingers' ends?   Hast thou by
rote the morning and evening services, the Litany, and the Com-
munion Service, and, above all, the Burial of the Dead?   I will
examine thee in all, by-and-by, and receive thee as heavenly
or else brand thee, of the earth earthy, as being the soul of a
pagan in the body of a milliner.   There is one here as ignorant, mayhap, as thou; as ignorant as *dirt*, whose god is his
belly.   Take care thou art not weighed in the balance also,
and found wanting; for it seems to me *thy* god is thy back!
Why not dress as *I* do?   Get thee behind me.   Go and
ponder.'

And with a severe frown she passed on.

A very gentleman-like elderly man came running up at this
moment, and raised his hat from his grey head.

'Will you excuse my saying a word?   I made all the haste I
could, fearing you might be frightened by that very singular old
lady.'   He smiled and shrugged.   'I assure you, when first I
came here she frightened me into working up my catechism.
But, I wanted to tell you, you need not stand the least in awe
of her; when she sees you don't mind her, she'll not speak to
you.   She's a very clever woman, you know; and was quite a
wonderful preacher, I'm told, when she was young; that is all
over, of course; but, absurd as she is, she was a kind of intellectual celebrity.   I only wished to prevent your being made
uncomfortable by her, and to assure you that no one here minds
her, ever so little.'

He bowed again with his hat in the air, after the old fashion,
and once again to acknowledge her thanks with a kindly smile,
and so passed on.

The side-walk, to the right, into which she had now turned,
seemed to be less frequented than the corresponding one opposite ;
a young lady, with pretty evidently a lover standing at her side,
was making a sketch in water-colours of a fine old beech, that
spreads its foliage near that spot; the young man was talking
in low tones, and she, with a gentle blush, was smiling down
upon her work.   The young lady passed quickly by, with sym-
pathetic care not to interrupt the tender little scene or seem to
observe it.   There was a tall yew hedge at this side, as at the
others of the square, but beyond it no walk, only an ivy-covered

wall, as might be seen through an opening now and then, over-lapped here and there by clumps of fine old trees.

A noble sycamore, such as she had never seen approached in size, at one of these openings in the hedge, stood close to the other side of the wall, which being a particularly high one, she mounted a little grass hillock at the side of the walk, to command a better view of the tree.

As she looked, she heard a sound a little like the cooing of a wild pigeon, from the midst of its dark foliage. This sound grew louder soon, and the leaves began to rustle furiously, and the boughs which formed the leafy flooring and ceiling of one of those black chasms which separate the masses of foliage in great trees, were agitated and shook fiercely. At the same time she saw emerging from this recess a lean figure, clinging with long arms to the branch above, and with feet on that beneath, advancing with a sort of dance towards the front, and uttering a shriller hooting as it did so. It looked like a monstrous ape; unable as she was to measure the distance with her eye, the figure seemed to her at least seven feet from head to heel. She could see its white eye-balls and teeth in the shadow, and faintly the outline of a head. As the figure half danced and half climbed forward, shifting its hands along the boughs to which it clung with curious rapidity, all doubt as to its human type was put an end to by its crying in a hoarse and piercing voice, which soon rose to a yell of menace, ' Bella, bella ! carissima mia ! catch him : vivo-vivissimo-tu-tu-tuto. Receive my love, or I'll wring your long neck, Moloch !'

And at the same time springing from the branches, and aided by their swing, he leaped from his overhanging elevation, very nearly across the wall. He failed, however, and, instead, struck its summit, dislodging a stone or two, and himself falling backward, on the other side.

Maud was frightened, as well she might be, although the wall was still between them. It must have been a dangerous fall, for the height was no trifle. Instantaneously she heard shouting within the boundary, and footsteps running in the direction of the fallen acrobat.

She had been riveted to the spot as people are by a suspense, and now a good deal alarmed, for she had almost expected to see the odious grotesque alight on the grass, at her side.

That human ape who attempted such a feat, and looked as that being did, *must* be out of his mind. Her thoughts were, however, suddenly and forcibly diverted from this spectacle by the appearance of Lady Mardykes.

There could be no doubt it was she.

She was walking with inseparable Antomarchi by her side, along the terrace toward the further side of the grounds. Perhaps she had been looking for her, in the princely suite of rooms which she had assigned her, and had now come out in search of her long unseen guest.

Miss Vernon determined to cross the grass, keeping a little below the croquet-hoops, so as to arrive at a point of the walk on the opposite side, which Lady Mardykes should not yet have reached.

This manœuvre, in high spirits, notwithstanding her strange adventure, and all the odd stories and suggestions which had lately reached her about her hostess, Maud instantly began to execute.

She kept her eye steadily upon Lady Mardykes. She was resolved not to lose her this time. By crossing the grass at the pace she had started at she would reach the walk at the other side, much lower down, of course, at about the same moment at which Lady Mardykes would enter it from the terrace-walk, and then they would meet face to face, and the long-deferred greeting at last take place.

Lady Mardykes was talking earnestly, and looking down on the gravel as she did so. Antomarchi's eyes, on the contrary, were everywhere, and Maud felt instinctively that his piercing eyes had lighted upon her. That did not matter, however; she was certain now to meet her.

But there was, after all, another 'slip between the cup and the lip,' for, instead of turning down the side-walk, as Maud expected, Antomarchi and the lady passed out of the quadrangle by the latch-key door at the far corner of the terrace, through which, on the night of her arrival, Miss Vernon had been admitted by Darkdale.

This was really too bad. Maud hurried forward, and reached the door in hopes of finding it still unlocked. But it was immovably shut. She hastened to the house-door opening upon the terrace, and made her way to the hall. The footman informed her that he had just seen Lady Mardykes get into her carriage and drive away.

How soon would she return?

He could not say

So Maud, disappointed and a little offended, returned with a slower step to the place from whence she came, wondering whether she was ever to meet Lady Mardykes again.

Her guests certainly did not seem to trouble her a great deal, and, so far as Maud could see, she was pleased to leave them very much to amuse and take care of themselves.

Well, it was disappointing; but, after all, Lady Mardykes was sure to be home for luncheon, possibly an hour before it. In the meantime other people might introduce themselves, as had happened yesterday, and so her acquaintance might grow.

Her anticipations were quickly justified, for as she was walking down, by this time pretty well resigned to her disappointment, toward the yew-hedge walk, a singular-looking person accosted her.

He was almost a pigmy in stature, and his air ineffably pompous; his face was long and pallid, with a turn-up nose and an expression of conceit and scorn as he eyed passers-by, such as Miss Vernon could not have believed in except perhaps in the caricature of a pantomime. He walked slowly, rising on his toes as he did so, and carried a big portfolio and a small shagreen case under his arm, and a quadrant strapped across his back. To Miss Vernon he made a slight bow and a smile, so transitory that it amounted to little more than a momentary grimace, the effect of which was rather odd than alluring.

His long chin terminated in a lank white beard, unaccompanied by either whisker or moustache. A solemn gloom overspread his countenance, and an habitual look of surprise made his small eyes round, except when a smirk of contempt or of self-esteem lighted his face.

It seemed to be the rule in this house not to wait for introduction. The appearance of this dwarfish sage aroused Miss Vernon's curiosity, and she was rather glad that she had so quickly found some one willing to entertain her.

How he did so is related in the next chapter.

CHAPTER LXX.

A RIOT.

'You have heard, madam,' said he, walking at her side, 'of Laplace, of Newton, you have heard of Watt, you have heard of Davy. I see by your head and eye, that you have an intellect and an interest for the physical sciences, and I need scarcely add, you have heard of Sidebotham, and the perpetuum mobile. He is at present a guest at this place, and, of course, he comes and goes as he pleases.'

'Oh? Indeed!' said Miss Vernon, affecting a greater interest in the worthies of science than perhaps she felt, and ashamed to admit that she had never before heard of Sidebotham in that brilliant muster-roll. 'Lady Mardykes has so many distinguished guests that one is scarcely surprised to meet any great name among them.'

He simpered with gratified self-complacency and made his bow, and in an instant was more solemn than ever.

'I am pretty well known in Germany, I rather think. The King of Prussia has my portrait, full length.' (And he rose on his toes.) 'It is hung in his library. You have seen engravings? You recognised me? Eh? Ha? Most people do.'

Maud explained that she lived so much in the country, and in so quiet a place, that she was not in the way of hearing all she ought of English and European celebrities.

He rose on tip-toe again and touched her arm, saying merely, with a look that anticipated wonder:

'The individual who has the honour of addressing you is Sidebotham, the machinist, the mechanical genius of this, and *all* ages, as I have had the honour of being termed.'

At this moment a sweet voice inquired:

'Well, Mr. Sidebotham, how goes on the perpetual motion?'

And raising her eyes, Maud saw the Duchess of Falconbury before her, smiling.

'That is a question that answers itself,' sneered the professor, slowly averting his face with upturned nose. 'How goes on the perpetuum mobile? Why it goes on *for ever!* Ha, ha, ha!'

And he laughed as demons do in melodramas, in three distinct 'Ha's.'

Her grace was not in the least ruffled, for her attention was engaged by a melancholy but gentleman-like looking man who was approaching.

'You see that man,' whispered the Duchess in Maud's ear; her eyes looking down the shady walk which they had now entered.

'The Spanish ambassador?' inquired Maud, who saw that Minister in the antique costume which he affected, approaching with toes turned out, at a slow and grand pace, in the rear of the melancholy man.

'Ambassador. He's *no* ambassador, my dear; he has lost his head a little; he's a Mr. Ap-Jenkins, who has a slate quarry in Carnarvonshire, but it is not about him. You see this man in black who walks towards us, looking down on the gravel over his shoulder. Did you ever see such a comically miserable face? When he comes up we'll talk to him; he'll amuse you.'

Maud thought that such pining misery and malignity as were expressed in that lean, dark face, could not have been conveyed in the human countenance.

The Duchess said, as he was passing by, unheeding:

'I hope, Mr. Poinders, you will find that boiling sensation a little better to-day?'

'*Sensation?*' he repeated, stopping suddenly, and raising his dreadful face. 'Heat and motion tell pretty plainly, when water, much less *blood*, is bubbling at a boil. No, not better, *worse*. My blood boils; *as* yesterday, so to-day, and so, for ever *and* ever, amen!'

'I'm so sorry,' said the Duchess, pressing her hand ever so little on Maud's arm, by way of showing her enjoyment of what was passing. 'And those wheels?' she inquired, with a look of concern.

'Yes, those wheels, in my inside—whir-r-r, whir-r-r, whir-r-r-r. Where are your ears? Listen, ha, ha! don't you hear them? They never stop. That is the way perpetually!'

'Perpetually! Perpetual motion! A rival discoverer, I'm afraid, Mr. Sidebotham,' said her grace wickedly; 'but you are a mechanist, don't you think you might do something to stop, or at least retard, those wheels?'

'Pish!' said the philosopher, in high disdain.

The sufferer, about to resume his walk, added:

'And I am subject, to-day, to violent shocks of electricity.'

He ground his teeth, and muttered to himself, and so passed on. The Duchess was laughing quietly, as she turned again to Maud, who was anything but amused; she was very much shocked, on the contrary.

'The poor man is perfectly mad,' whispered the Duchess.

Miss Vernon felt a hand laid softly on her shoulder, before she could speak; and looking round, saw that frightful face.

He said rapidly, with his eyes close to hers:

'I am beyond the hope of salvation !'

And he turned and pursued his slow, solitary walk. What on earth could induce Lady Mardykes to permit a madman to walk about these grounds ? A filmy suspicion was stealing over Maud, too terrific for utterance.

The Spanish ambassador in full fig arrived. There was an opening just here in the yew-hedge, and a low hedge of sweet-briar, running for some yards, at the edge of the walk, made the air at this spot fragrant.

His excellency the Spanish Minister, having arrived, the little party came to a halt, here commanding a view of the house and the croquet-ground, as well as one of the long and sequestered alleys in both directions.

The Minister made his king-like greeting. They were standing on the grass that with a broad belt skirts the walk. The croquet-ground before them, the little sweet-briar hedge in the rear.

His excellency, notwithstanding the sultry weather, wears, as before, the skirt of his black mantle flung across his breast, over his shoulder. He is now in high chat. He is speaking loud, throwing his chest well out; his head is thrown back, his dark eyes half-closed. His clear brown complexion and black moustache, white, even teeth, and handsome features, lend a cavalier-like grace to the contemptuous smile with which he surveys the pigmy of perpetual motion, and flouts him with a lofty irony.

The dialogue grows a little more spirited, as the ambassador with folded arms persists in his intangible banter. The homunculus becomes more fiercely voluble on his perpetual motion, and treats his excellency with a good deal less ceremony than he likes. Both parties are waxing fiery.

'Mechanic ! perpetuum mobile ! Professor ! Philosopher !' said his excellency, smiling on, and quite closing his eyes for a short time. 'A great European name. Sidebotham and Co., grocers, Cheapside. Why, no one who lives near you can fail to discover the perpetual motion. It exists in your tongue, ha, ha! your tongue—it is nowhere else about you—and *it* never ceases.'

The sage gasped ; sprang back two or three steps ; and rose, as usual, to his toes, with his fists clenched, trembling all over, and his eyes starting from their sockets.

'You have no business talking so,' said the Duchess haughtily ; 'if we spare you all inquiry into the authenticity of your diploma, or whatever you please to call it, I think you might, at least, remember what is due to rank ; you can hardly suppose that it can be an agreeable pastime to the Duchess of Falconbury to witness a low quarrel between two such persons as Mr. Sidebotham and Mr. Ap-Jenkins.'

But the Minister, nothing moved from his faith in his own representative dignity, smiled superbly, with folded arms, his black cane, tipped with its golden crown, held gracefully in his French-gloved hand, and with his chin high in air, he observed, in a tone of cold ridicule :

'Duchess of Falconbury ! Ha! ha! ha! How charmingly that comes from the lips of Mrs. Fish, of New York !'

And he made the lady a satirically ceremonious bow.

The eyes of the Duchess gleamed actual fire ; her face, her very lips grew white. She stood open-lipped and breathless. It was hard to say whether the great lady or the pigmy was most furiously agitated.

To the latter his excellency turned again, with a haughty wave of his white-gloved hand, and observed :

'As for you, you illiterate dwarf and grocer, I shall order my secretary to take you by your cocked nose, and jerk you over that wall, like one of your own bad red-herrings.'

The lady uttered a sudden scream of fury, and the philosopher jumped in the air, and slapped his forehead, with a roulade of blasphemies, yelling still more shrilly, 'Let *me*—let *me*—I'll annihilate him ! I'll *annihilate* him !' and they rushed nearly together upon his excellency the Spanish Minister, who smiled in haughty scorn, as well he might, of such an attack.

The homunculus, strung to double his natural strength by fury, was first to reach the object of assault, and grasping the Goliath in his arms below the knees, and nothing daunted by the untoward interference of his own quadrant, which, in the feat, swung over his head, and hit him a smart blow upon the nose, lifted the Minister fairly off his feet ; and this superb personage, in spite of a frantic effort to recover his equilibrium, fell backward, with an undignified souse, and a grunt, through the tangled hedge of sweet-briar, so that half his person lay on the grass, at the other side, and his shapely legs were struggling wildly for escape at this.

With the acumen and promptitude of her sex, the enraged Duchess caught up the jet-black cane with its head of gold, that had flown from his hand, and with immense rapidity discharged a shower of whistling cuts, right and left, on the silken calves of the ambassador, who kicked high and right and left with grotesque activity, shrieking horrible threats and wild appeals to his sovereign, to heaven, to the law of nations, to his servants, in the vain endeavour to struggle through the thick fence, while the professor of mechanics, who had transferred himself to the other side, seized his hair and moustache in both hands, and with his heels against his shoulders, tugged till the ambassador's roars were heard above the shrieks and gabble of his executioners.

The sudden uproar, wilder and fiercer, alarmed the loungers and the croquet-players. Mallets were dropped and balls abandoned. Some whooped, and threw up their hats in saturnine ferocity. Others broke into screeching laughter. A dumpy woman, with a yellow face, dropped on her knees, turned up her eyes, and began to tell a rosary of enormous beads, signing herself all over with the cross. The little preaching woman cast her book before her on the grass, lifted up her right hand, and standing stiff as a post, commenced a homily on the Day of Judgment, in a stentorian sing-song. An elderly gentleman, with a military air, bawled to anyone who chose to execute his behests, to send up a troop of his light dragoons. And a gentleman dressed in deep mourning danced a hornpipe, sailor-fashion, snapping his fingers with austere gravity.

At the same time several strong, grave-looking men, who acted unobserved as a patrol in those pleasure-grounds, came running up at the top of their speed to quell the outbreak.

Professor Sidebotham let go the moustache and dropped the ambassador's head on the ground, as an Irishman would say, like a hot potato, re-arranged his quadrant and recovered his hat, concealed his bleeding nose with one hand, and affected to be a sedate professor and an ornament to society.

Not so the Duchess. She had become 'blooded,' and plied the supple cane with shrieks and Billingsgate, resolutely and even ferociously resisting all interference. She turned now upon the men who had caught her wrists and disarmed her; she scratched, she stamped, she kicked, she even bit.

Darkdale emerged in the midst of this struggle. He had a strange short garment in his hand with enormously long sleeves. The duchess seemed to recognise this, for at sight of it she shrieked; she redoubled her struggles, she became quite furious.

By a kind of magic, in spite of all, without violence, by a sinister dexterity, Darkdale, with the aid of the other men, got it on her. The arms were drawn across her breast, and the long sleeves crossed and tied behind, so that no force or skill which she could exert could in the least avail to extricate her.

Now her struggles, being hopeless, became frightful; she yelled, she foamed, the veins of her forehead started and darkened, and her eyes rolled. Her handsome figure writhed and quivered in the contortions of the pythoness. But all could effect nothing. She was quietly and completely overpowered, and hurried, now uttering long despairing screams, but no longer offering active resistance, swiftly across the grass to the terrace, and so disappeared into the door through which she had lately emerged in so different a mood.

'What is that you have just put upon that lady?' Maud, who was horribly agitated, inquired of a broad-shouldered, dark-faced man in a dark fustian coat.

He looked on her silently for a minute, and smiled cynically.

'It is a thing we calls a strait-waistcoat,' he answered.

'But that is for people who are quite *mad*,' said Maud.

'Well, I take it,' he replied, 'you don't want to see no one madder than that.'

CHAPTER LXXI.

UPBRAIDINGS.

THERE were two other sturdy fellows in jackets in the same group with the man who had just spoken to Maud.

These two were bleeding from their faces, scratched or switched in the struggle just ended ; and the three were laughing over a quiet bit of chaff together, as they wiped off the blood with their knuckles.

Maud heard one of them say :

'Well for you, Tom, her leddyship had not her scissors handy, like Mrs. Spiffles, that time ; wouldn't she 'a gev you a punch.'

'She han't a scissors or penknife this six months. Old Martha telt me she's bin wrote down questionable.'

This last observation told a startling story in Maud's ears.

The Ambassador had got up and made some hasty readjustment, forgetting only one of his well-waxed moustaches, which stands up nearly perpendicularly to the corner of his eye, just as the last tug of the mechanical genius had left it. He advanced with stately pace, with folded arms, and a scornful smile, unconscious of a dab of ink across his face, from Sidebotham's shagreen writing-case, and says aside to Maud, with a wave of his hand to the three men in jackets :

'These are gentlemen in my service. Fear nothing. The conspirators will suffer as they deserve. I abandon them to justice.'

And with a ceremonious bow, carefully observing his rule, however, not to remove his hat, he turned, and in rather disordered plight, and no doubt smarting severely, marched, with out-turned toes, slowly and grandly away, among the titters, and jabberings, and scowls of some of the company who bore him no goodwill.

Not one word he had said did Miss Vernon hear. She felt stunned.

It seemed to her that she did not breathe once from the time she left the scene of the too significant buffoonery she had just witnessed until she found herself in her own dressing-room.

She awoke there,

She saw Mercy Creswell standing with her back against the wall, pale as a ghost, with a dark stare, and the corners of her mouth screwed down hard as she gazed at her. She looked guilty, and as if she expected mischief; her hands she held folded together as tightly as the joints could clasp; she was motionless as the wooden door-case behind her, and never took her frightened eyes off her young mistress.

There was something in the look and mien of the young lady, you may be sure, to account for the panic of the maid.

Miss Vernon sat down trembling, and then got up, pressing her hands to her temples, with a terrible look of helplessness. She walked round and round the room, with long stifled moans.

After a time she stopped, and looked slowly about her.

'My God!' she gasped, 'I'm terrified! *Did* it happen?'

She glided over to the window, and looked out on the gaily dressed and busy crowd, and with a sudden cry of despairing terror, she covered her eyes with her hands.

Now she is passing swiftly from one room to another, back and forward; she runs towards Mercy Creswell, and stands fixed, like an apparition, before her.

'I see it all; I understand it now! Help me to think. Do you know what has happened? My God! they have inveigled me into a madhouse! What is it? Oh, you wretch—*you* have got me into a madhouse!'

The sentence broke into a shriek at the close.

'Now don't, Miss Maud, don't now, there's a darling!' cried Mercy Creswell, as quick and shrill as the words could fly from her lips, and with her hands extended towards her. 'Ye'll take a parrokism, ye will, indeed; indeed ye will; ye'll take a parrokism, if ye don't be quiet; ye will, ye'll have it.'

'*You* have done it; and mamma; and Lady Mardykes; and Cousin Max! Merciful God! *All* the people—all my friends! And Cousin Maximilla! There's no one left—I have none to help me! Where shall I hide? Help me to think of something, Mercy Creswell, my old friend; you could not forsake me—you would not. Poor Miss Maud! Oh, think of long ago, at Roydon; if ever you hope for God's mercy, get me out of this horrible place.'

'It wasn't me, miss, so it wasn't; so 'elp me, miss; 'twas your mamma. I've no more to do with it, as God's my 'ope, than the hinfant babe unborn,' gabbled Mercy Creswell, in a shrilly whine.

' I'll not stay in this dreadful place. I'll lose my life, or I'll get out of it. Oh! mamma—mamma—how could you—could you—could you? I shall go mad. I *can't* stay here! I'll not eat or drink—I'll find a way, some way, a short way. Oh, mamma! you'll be sorry, then.'

Again she began walking swiftly from room to room. Now up and down the floor of one; now to and fro across the floor of another, shifting her hands across her forehead with an uncertain movement.

' I *can't* be imprisoned here; I'm not a slave. Where is the nearest posting-house? I'll have my attorney; I'll have advice; I'll write to Mr. Coke; that can't be prevented; I'll leave this *now.*'

And she ran to the bedroom-door.

Mercy Creswell knew that it was secured, and running into her dressing-room, she adroitly bolted the door of communication between the two apartments.

Maud now found herself a prisoner in her room. She tried both doors with growing impetuosity, but they resisted her utmost efforts.

Her own maid had locked her in, by a trick, and she was securely imprisoned in her room. This outrage fired her so as, for the moment, to displace her panic.

' Open the door,' she cried, shaking the lock with all her fragile strength; ' Mercy Creswell, open the door,' she repeated again and again; and she heard the creak of the servant's shoe, faintly, as she stood holding her breath, close to the other side of the door.

' Open the door; how dare you treat me so? Am I to be insulted by my own servant? Let me out.'

Mercy heard her run to the window, and throw it up. More cadaverous than ever her face looked, as, in a momentary hesitation, she extended her dumpy fingers, that trembled visibly, to the bolt, but she changed her mind, and withdrawing her hand, ran instead to the brass handle that was fixed in the wall, pulled it, and a deep-toned bell sounded all down the gallery. She had remembered that the window, as it went up, drew with it a strong wire grating, which made it safe against all attempts to escape, or worse.

She stood in the gallery, and almost instantly two of those firmly knit, hardy women, whom we may call housemaids, emerged from a room at its further end, which was a sort of guard-room for the detachment in charge of that wing of the house, and up they came at a jog-trot; and almost at the same instant, for the alarm sounded also in the opposite direction, the iron door across the passage opened, and a keeper, a powerful man, in a barragan jacket, with a white scar across his brown forehead and nose, telling of old service, entered, clanging the door behind him.

'*Where* is the case?' he demanded.

'This here patient,' said Mercy, entering the dressing-room with her escort. 'She's bin a-going of it most wiolent, and threatens to hurt herself, and is took very nigh with a par-rokism.'

Beckoning them on, and waiting till they were ready to enter, she removed the bolt and unlocked the door, keeping herself in the rear.

'Who are you?' asked Maud, who was standing now in the middle of the room; 'I have been led to suppose this is my room. What do you all want here?'

'It was only, miss, because I was afraid you might be unwell, miss; and I could not undertake it without 'elp, Miss Maud, replied Mercy Creswell.

The man stepped in.

'By your leave, miss,' said he, looking with his shrewd quick glance at her hands, and then, with another, about the room; and then striding to the window, and shutting it down, he turned some little pins at the side, and said to Mercy:

'You should 'a fixed the window.'

'There's the grating though.'

'No matter,' he replied.

'What do you mean by shutting my window without my leave?' inquired Maud, with a fiery glance.

The man takes no notice of the question, but asks Mercy Creswell:

'Is there fire-irons, or anything hard and heavy, that way, here?'

'No, nothing,' answered she.

'But I ask you——' repeated Maud Vernon.

'I'll attend to you just now, miss,' said the man. 'Nor nothing sharp?' he said, as he continued his search.

'I'll mention your conduct. Who is in the house to whom I can make a complaint?' said the young lady, who was not accustomed to be treated so by servants.

She had directed her question to Mercy Creswell; but the man answered it, scarcely looking at her as he did so.

'To the doctor, please, miss, Doctor Antomarchi,' and he continued in the same even tone: 'You should not 'a left her alone; don't you know this 'ere number's entered questionable? Mr. Darkdale will put another with you if you want her. Look here.'

And he touched his thumb to his mouth, and turned over the leaves of a little book rapidly, and showed her something inscribed upon a page.

'Well, I *would* like another in *call*. She could sit in the next room, d'ye see; I'm not *fit* alone,' said Mercy Creswell, with nervous earnestness.

'I'll not remain here—I shan't stay—I'll go,' said Maud, going to the wardrobe and pulling the drawers open, and beginning to place her things upon the table close by.

'And ye shouldn't leave a thing like that here,' said the man, with a frown and a wag of his head, availing himself of Maud's having gone to a distant part of the room, and taking in his hand the silk cord of her dressing-gown, which lay on the back of a chair close by. 'You might 'a remembered Miss Bangles, it ain't so long ago. Put it out o' this, mind. Is there any bits of cord about ?'

'No, not one.'

'Tell some one to order me a chaise from the nearest place as soon as possible, and go and order it yourself,' said Maud to the man.

'Just now, miss, when we gets the doctor's orders.'

'Then I'll go on foot—I'll go this moment. Tell him I've left.'

The man looked at her with a sheepish smile, amused, and cleared his voice, and looked grave, not wishing that she should see any disposition to laugh.

'It won't do, miss; you can't go out without the doctor's order, and you must make your mind 'appy; for you can no more go out o' the door, without it was allowed, than you could walk through the wall. But it is easy to talk to the doctor, and tell him what ye wants; and if you persuades him, it will be all right, you know; and anyhow it can't do no one no harm.'

Maud walked about the room, agitated.

'Very good,' she said at last; 'tell him I should like to see him.'

CHAPTER LXXII.

DOCTOR AND PATIENT.

NEARLY ten minutes had passed, and Maud was sitting in her room, in profound gloom; torpid; without motion; with her eyes upon the floor.

Mercy Creswell, unable to divine what her thoughts might be, was only a few steps away, standing against the wall, with her arms folded across, and her eyes turned, with a nervous side-glance, without ever swerving, on the young lady.

In the room beyond that sat one of the athletic housemaids, who could have lifted Maud off her feet, and carried her about the house as easily as her hat and jacket.

At this, the sitting-room door, now came a knock.

Doctor Antomarchi was there; Maud was on her feet in a moment.

This doctor had the peculiar marble skin which is ascribed to the first Napoleon. Dark and colourless, his strongly pronounced under-jaw and thin lips, his delicate black eyebrows, and piercing, cold eyes, gave a character of severity and decision to his massive face, which inspired fear in all who were subjected to his authority.

Some little sensation of this kind modified Miss Vernon's agitated feelings, as he entered the room, and made his bow of ceremony, in obedience to her summons.

'Oh, Doctor Antomarchi!' she said, 'I will try to speak with moderation. I have been duped. I came here under the persuasion that I was on my way to Carsbrook, Lady Mardykes' house. I find that I have been wickedly deceived. I am a prisoner, and I can't escape. I don't know why I have been sent here. I am here, helpless, in the most awful place a mortal can be committed to—a madhouse. I have not a single friend or adviser to turn to, in this great danger. I am utterly alone. I have been brought up in a very lonely way, in the country, and I don't know very well what I ought to do in this dreadful case. May God help me!' Her lip trembled. 'You, sir, can have no wish to keep me here, if I am perfectly in my right mind; and, as God is my hope, I am not mad, nor ever was supposed to be! My good cousin,

Maximilla Medwyn, when I write to her, will come and tell you so. And you, I have heard, are learned, and clever, and can easily decide whether I tell you truth ; and if you find that I am what I describe, you can set me at liberty.'

'What you say is reasonable,' replies Antomarchi, not one muscle of whose stern face had shown a sign of life during Maud's appeal, and whose dark eye had shown neither light nor softening. 'Shall I say a word in private?' he added, glancing at the servant.

'Do—pray.'

He signed to Mercy Creswell to leave the room, which she did.

He then in a low tone, with an air of very marked deference, said :

'Your request is grounded on a supposition, which, if sustained by proof, would place you instantly at liberty. All you say is fair. As to the fact on which you rely, however, it is, I regret to say, more than disputed in the papers which have been placed before us; and while you remain here, which may be a very short time, I need scarcely say, you shall be treated with the greatest possible consideration, and everything done to make your sojourn as little disagreeable as possible. Would you object, Miss Vernon, to accompany me to the office downstairs. I wish very much, with your permission, to call your attention to a circumstance.'

The lady assented. Together they entered the gallery. Doctor Antomarchi took a key from his pocket, and opened the iron door which separated that portion of the long corridor, from which Miss Vernon's rooms opened, from the remainder of the gallery, passing westward.

In the wildest dream, no matter how fantastic the situation and strange the scenery, the dreamer follows the action of his vision with good faith, and the sense of incredulity slumbers. Here was a reality strangely horrible as any dream she had ever dreamed. She heard their tread on the boards, she felt the cold, smooth banister on which her hand rested, as they went down the private spiral stair, and yet, real as it was, it was an effort to believe it more than a vision.

Now she had arrived. The door was shut. When she had placed herself in one of the great chairs in the oval room, of which she and Doctor Antomarchi were the only tenants, he touched a bell, without speaking, and Mr. Darkdale entered.

Maud wondered what was intended. Antomarchi rose quickly, and two or three steps brought him to Darkdale's side. That slight dark man inclined his ear; and as Antomarchi concluded a few whispered sentences, he nodded, and immediately withdrew. Maud heard nothing of what passed.

The doctor returned, and sat down at the opposite side of the table.

'I think it desirable to impress upon you, Miss Vernon, two or three facts, which, while here, you will find it to your advantage to bear in mind.'

An intimidating change had come over Doctor Antomarchi's face, and he was speaking in stern, measured accents. His ceremonious manner was quite gone, and he was talking as a cold, insolent colonel might to a defaulting drummer-boy on the parade-ground.

'The inmates of that part of the house in which apartments are assigned to you, are generally quite competent to understand what I now say. It is my duty to treat you with what skill I possess; it is yours to submit; and submit you shall. I have heard of your language, of your violence, of your covert menace of forcing an escape, or committing self-destruction. Sufficient precautions are taken in this establishment to render that crime impracticable. There are people confined here whose desire to commit suicide amounts to a lust. They hope for nothing else, they dream of nothing else; they are persistent, they are crafty, and yet all their persistence, cunning, and wickedness are daily defeated with perfect ease and certainty. Violence here, leads necessarily to repression; contumacy, in the most trifling particulars, to increased restraint; and angry language, as tending in certain nervous states to produce corresponding action, necessarily to a treatment dispensed with before, that is intensely disagreeable. This, you understand, is not punishment; it is precaution, and a process, though painful, strictly of a sanatory kind. And now, you distinctly comprehend, that neither unmeasured language, nor violence of temper, nor threats of suicide, or of escape, ever fail to bring down on the patient who indulges in them consequences which are deplorable.'

All the time he thus spoke his eyes were fixed on those of the young lady, who felt the power of that indescribable coercion.

Under it thought grew vague, and the powers of will were lost.

'You will be so good, Miss Vernon, as to accompany me a little further,' said Antomarchi, his eye upon her, as he suddenly arose. The young lady, without answering, followed him.

Through a door at the side of this room, a short and narrow passage, tiled and lighted by a window over the door, conducted them to a small but lofty room, also tiled, the arrangements of which were singular.

It was lighted only from above, near the ceiling, by a long line of window scarcely a foot and a half in height. In the middle of the floor stood a small stout table, a little further stood a strong arm-chair, made of open bands of iron, muffled on the inside with india-rubber, the frame also being of iron. The entire chair was of open work. It was mounted on castors so enormous as almost to amount to wheels; and it was furnished with many straps and buckles. A Dutch clock ticked upon the wall.

In the corner of the room, beyond this, rose something that looked like a tall iron press, of some four feet square, which reached, or rather seemed to pass through, the ceiling. There was no other furniture in the room except two small shelves; and a piece of thick rug lay on the floor.

The portion of the room in which Maud stood was railed off from the rest. There was a bench there, on which he requested Miss Vernon to sit. He then left the room; and she heard the door locked behind her.

She was now perfectly alone in this oddly adjusted room. Could its mysterious and in some respects sinister furniture portend any coercion designed for *her?* This startling thought had just occurred to her, when another door in the room opened, and Doctor Antomarchi returned alone. The portion of the floor railed off was raised a little; and the rails rose therefore high from the tiling on which Doctor Antomarchi now stood.

Three or four steps across the narrow floor brought him to the railing, on which he placed his hand. His first sentence relieved her of this alarm.

'You are here, Miss Vernon, merely as a spectator, to witness, in part, the practice to which the refractory are subjected. There is nothing, in sultry weather like this, more refreshing than a shower-bath. You will see what it becomes when administered in a case of morbidly over-excited energies. In such a case it is vital to the patient, and to others, at whatever cost, to produce quiet and docility. The patient must, therefore, be overpowered, and the system must be brought down until decided prostration ensues. This is a powerful shower-bath. It is fed from an almost inexhaustible tank '—he went over to the tall iron structure in the corner, and opened its door—' and the fall is from a much greater height than one ever experiences in the ordinary bath. The patient upon whom you will see it exercised is a lady who has unhappily suffered, for an hour or upwards, under intense excitement, accompanied with perversity and violence. You shall see, in her case, how we reduce that unhappy state upon sanatory principles.'

Darkdale opened the room door and looked in.

'The patient is coming;' and he inquires, 'do you wish it now?'

'Yes,' says Antomarchi.

Maud heard a sound of feet on stairs descending, accompanied by a muffled gabbling and screaming, and the noise of furious hysterics.

CHAPTER LXXIII.

THE BATH.

SUDDENLY the door flies open. The sounds are close, are in the room, piercing, unnatural. The patient has an under-dress on, but a sheet envelops her, and muffles her cries. There are no less than four female attendants with her; three stalwart female nurses, housemaids, whatever their office, are round this sheeted figure. Two have their arms clasped firmly about her. Her arms are, evidently, secured, for her resistance is confined to writhing, jerking, dashing her head with violence, this way and that, and stamping on the floor, with loud shrieks, and incoherent ravings, menace, and supplication. The fourth attendant is, to Maud's surprise, Mercy Creswell.

'Your maid is to attend her,' said Antomarchi coolly. 'It will show you that she is a woman of nerve, and can do her duty.'

This impertinence did not fire Maud's pride, as an hour or two ago it would   A part of her nature had been reduced to a state of prostration.'

She was looking on with a painful curiosity. She had no idea, from the trifling programme she had heard, that feelings so strong as she soon experienced, were about to be excited.

'Come, bustle, girls : come, be lively,' said Mercy Creswell, who felt that she must do her devoir, under the severe eye of Doctor Antomarchi. 'Bring it up.'

She looked at the woman whose hands were disengaged, and pointed to the chair. This dumpy *femme de chambre* appeared suspiciously well up in the direction of this madhouse detachment.

The figure in the sheet, in the midst of her struggles and vociferations, was suddenly jerked back into the chair. The sheet, in Mercy Creswell's phrase, was 'whipped from over her head,' and in spite of her yells and wrestling, the straps were deftly brought into their places, and tightly buckled, so that she could now do no more than roll her head fiercely from side to side, and shriek her wild invectives.

Maud was shocked to recognise in this melancholy transformation the pseudo Duchess of Falconbury. Poor thing ! her grace was in a sorry plight, strapped down in the iron chair, and, spite of all her writhings and tuggings, unable to alter her position by a hair's-breadth, or even to jolt one leg of the heavy chair the smallest fraction of an inch off the ground.

She was talking at a screaming pitch, without a moment's rest. But not many moments were allowed her. The chair, with its burden, was rolled quickly into the bath, and the door shut. The shrilly uproar continued, but so muffled that Maud could now hear without effort, distinctly, all the doctor said.

'You have taken an ordinary shower-bath, I dare say, Miss Vernon, and found it quite long and heavy enough ? This, from its greater height, has a fall more than twice as heavy. Yours lasted only a fraction of a minute, this will descend, without interruption, for exactly thirty-five minutes. Yours, probably, contained between two and three stone weight of water ; this will discharge between eight and nine tons. You observe, then, that it is very different from anything you have experienced. Are you ready ?'

'Yes, sir,' answers Mercy Creswell, who looks a little pale. 'How long, please, sir ?'

'Thirty-five minutes,' said the doctor.

'But please, sir,' said Creswell, growing paler, ' that is five minutes longer than the longest.'

The doctor nodded.

'She never had it before, sir.'

'Better *once* effectually, than half-measures repeatedly,' remarked the doctor to Miss Vernon, with his watch in his hand. 'Take the winch,' he said to Mercy Creswell. 'When the minute-hand reaches half-past (keep your eye on the clock) you turn it on ; and when it reaches five minutes past, you turn it off. You are ready ? stay—wait—look to the minute-hand— now.'

As the doctor uttered the final direction, at the same instant Mercy Creswell turned the handle, and a rush commenced perceptibly louder and heavier than any heard in those toys of luxury, which don't deserve the name of shower-bath, in sight of these Titanic appliances.

For a time the fury of the patient seemed to increase. But it was not long. In Maud's ears, the monotonous down-pour grew louder and louder, as minute after minute passed. The yells became sobs, and the sobs subsided. And still the rush of water thundered on.

'Oh! my God! She's drowning !' cried Maud.

'You perceive,' said the doctor, ' when treatment of this kind becomes necessary, we don't flinch.'

'It is cruel; it is horrible; it is frightful cruelty !' cried Maud.

'Cruelty ! My dear Miss Vernon, have you no compassion for an honest keeper whom she would have killed, if she could ?' replied the doctor, on whose stern lips she sees, or fancies, something like a smile, a cruel pride that is vindictive.

'But her voice is gone ! For God's sake let her out,' pleads Maud.

'She has gone through twelve minutes,' said Antomarchi ; 'she has twenty-three still to go through. She will be taken out when the time is accomplished, not sooner.'

'She can't live through it,' Maud almost screamed. 'It is quite impossible. Mercy Creswell let her out. You are killing her ; I command you ; let her out. Must I stay here to see her *killed ?*'

Mercy Creswell makes no sign. She does not glance towards her mistress. She stares darkly straight before her, very pale, and looks in a sort of 'sulk.'

One of the younger women is crying, with her face toward the wall, and her apron to her eyes.

If one could get rid of the idea of extreme suffering, ay, and of danger, for it has turned out there *is* danger, this scene has its ludicrous side, and might be witnessed as merrily as, in old times, men stood by and laughed at the ducking of a witch.

The descent of the water thunders on like the roll of a hundred muffled drums; no sound of life, ever so suffering, ever so faint, ever so intermittent, is now heard from within.

Will that dragging minute-hand never make its appointed course and point to the second of her release?

At length the dreadful half-hour has passed; that seems like half a day; four minutes remain—the hand is measuring the last minute. Antomarchi's eye is on the second-hand of his watch—the last second is touched. 'Stop,' cries his loud voice, and the winch is turned.

The noise of the falling water has ceased. The door is open, the room is as still as the dead-house of an hospital. A great silence has come. In a whisper Mercy directs the women, who obey in silence.

The straps are unbuckled, and the 'patient' is lifted out, and laid on another chair in the midst of the room. She looks lifeless. Her long dark hair clings about her shoulders. Her arms hang helplessly, and the water streams over her—over her hair, over her closed eyes—in rivulets; over her pretty face, that looks in a sad sleep; over her lace and vanities; over her white slender hands, that hang by her sides, and over her rings, making little rills and pools along the tiles.

The imperturbable doctor, his watch in his hand, approaches and takes her wrist, and tries her pulse.

Mercy Creswell gently drew back her hair, and Antomarchi with a handkerchief dried her face.

The others drew a cord that opened the window, and admitted the fresh air.

After a time there was a little sob; and after an interval another, and then a great sigh, and then again another and another, long-drawn as that with which life departs.

There must be the agonies of drowning in all this; worse than common drowning, drowning by a slower suffocation, and with a consciousness horribly protracted.

And now there is the greater agony of recovery.

The doctor had returned to the side of the poor Duchess, who was now breathing, or rather sighing, heavily, and staring vaguely before her.

His fingers were again on her pulse.

'Give her the white mixture,' he said to Mercy Creswell, glancing at a phial which stands beside a cup on a table a little way off.

'Oh, sir, please, doctor, not this time, sir,' faltered Mercy Creswell. 'She ate no breakfast, I hear, sir, and she'll be very bad for hours after she takes the mixture.'

'Shake it first; pour it into the cup; and administer it to the patient. Do your duty, Creswell.'

She shook the bottle, poured its contents into the cup, and, with a frightened face, did as she was ordered.

This peculiar use of the shower-bath in the treatment of the insane is no fiction. The Commissioners in Lunacy preferred an indictment against the medical superintendent of an English asylum, for having, as they alleged, caused the death of a pauper patient, by subjecting him to a continuous shower-bath of *thirty* minutes' duration, and for having administered to him, soon after his removal from the bath, and whilst in a state of vital depression, a dose of white-coloured mixture, alleged to have contained two grains of tartar emetic.

The physician in this case resembled Antomarchi in no respect, except in being a man of attainments and experience. He was perfectly conscientious. The grand jury threw out the bill. A commission of medical men of eminence reinstated him in his office. But his theory was this, that in the awfully depressing malady of madness, if a patient is 'violent,' 'noisy,' 'excited,' and 'destructive,' 'quiet' and 'docility' are legitimately to be induced by 'overpowering' him, and 'prostrating the system,' by a continuous shower-bath of monstrous duration, followed up on his release from the bath by a nauseating emetic, still further to exhaust an already prostrate system. That practice is no longer countenanced by the faculty.

Antomarchi now said : 'The patient may go, Creswell ; you are to attend Miss Vernon as before. Miss Vernon, you can return to your rooms.'

He made her a bow, and in a moment more Maud and her *femme de chambre* had left the room.

'Miss Vernon, a spirited young lady,' mused Antomarchi. 'She has had her first lesson.'

CHAPTER LXXIV.

MISTRESS AND MAID.

IT is well when, even in after-life, we can see that our sufferings have made us better, and that God has purged the tree, and not cursed it.

This awful time in Maud's life will do a good work in her. Her character has suffered from the coldness of her mother, from occasional periods of parental caprice and coercion, and from long intervals of the indulgence of absolute neglect. God has found her a time and a place in which to think upon Him, and on herself. These awful days, if they lead her to see and to amend her faults, will not have passed in vain.

For four-and-twenty hours Maud never opened her lips to speak one word to Mercy Creswell. But the quarrel of the two sailors would not do here; and a little reflection tells Maud that Mercy Creswell, after all, has acted in this affair under orders, and in good faith, believing all representations made to her by so great and good a woman as Lady Vernon; and walking honestly in such light as she had. These silent relations would not be long endurable to Maud herself; and her anger against Mercy Creswell was not quite reasonable.

I do not wonder, therefore, that before the evening of the next day Maud was on speaking terms again with her maid. The situation was now distinctly before her mind; but hope, irrepressible, began to revive.

'Do you know, Mercy,' asked the young lady, after they had talked a little, and a short silence had intervened, during which she was in deep thought, 'upon what subject they say I am mad?'

'I don't know, indeed, miss; I don't know at all. Only Lady Vernon told me the doctors said so; and she had no doubt of it herself.' Mercy Creswell was speaking, now, without the preliminary hesitation which gave, while Maud was still in the dark as to the real relations in which they stood, an air of reserve and prevarication to all her answers. 'But, miss, it mayn't last no time. There was a lady sent away from here last week, quite right again, as had bin here only two months.'

'But is there nothing? Why were my scissors and pen-knives taken away? And the breakfast knives are silver, like dessert knives!'

'Oh, yes, miss! Yes, to be sure. It was said you threatened different times, to take away your life, miss. That was the reason.'

Another silence followed.

'Every girl, when she's vexed, wishes herself dead. But she does not mean it. I never did. I am foolish and violent sometimes; but I am not wicked. Mercy Creswell, do you care about me?'

'La! miss, I like ye well, miss, and always did.'

'Do people listen at the doors, here?' she said, lowering her voice.

'Not they, miss; they have no time—too busy—they don't care, not a jack-straw, what you're talking about, and if anything goes wrong there's the bell at hand. *That* will bring hands enough in no time.'

'For how long have you been here?' asked Maud.

'It will be five years next November, miss.'

'Then you can't be mistaken about anything here?' mused Maud. 'You must know all their rules. I wonder, Mercy, whether you care for me?'

'Yes, surely, miss,' she answered.

Maud was silent again, looking at Mercy thoughtfully.

'You were very young, Mercy, and I only a child, when we were together in Roydon nursery; but—I'm afraid—you have no affection for me?'

'Why will ye say that, Miss Maud; don't you know I always liked ye well? Affection! well, miss, I think 'twould be less than kind in me if I hadn't.'

Maud looked again thoughtfully at Mercy Creswell, and then on the ground, and then raising her eyes, she said:

'Do they often inflict that dreadful punishment that I witnessed yesterday?'

'The bath, ma'am? La! you wouldn't call that a punishment. There's nothing Doctor Antomarchi is more paticlar about than that—not one of us here dar' call it a punishment.'

'Well, half-drowning, or whole-drowning, as it may turn out, is that *often* inflicted in this place?'

'Well, Mr. Damian would not allow it, perhaps, twice in a year, when he's at home, and then only ten or twelve minutes, and no white mixture. But Doctor Antomarchi, he'd be harder on them—he's a man that won't stand no nonsense from *no* one.' Mercy nodded with a dark significance, as she said this. 'He won't spare neither high nor low. He may do as he pleases. La! no one ever minds what a patient says. The doctor has only to smile and shake his head, and whisper a word in the ear of father, or mother, or brother, or whoever comes to see that the patient is comfortable, and all his grumbling and complaints, they're just took for so much dreams, and nothings, and no one ever believed but the doctor.'

'It is very bad—it is horrible. I sometimes think, Mercy, that I will refuse to eat anything—that would soon force them to bring my friends about me, and once that were effected, I should inevitably get out.'

'Refuse your food, miss? La! bless you, child, why that dodge has been tried as often as I have fingers and toes,' exclaimed Mercy, with elegant disdain. 'They'd make ye as fat as a pig, in spite of all ye can do. They'd make ye take three quarts of strong soup a day, and two pints of good chocolate and cream, and porter, and jelly, and whatever would keep ye in high condition, and fatten ye quickest.'

'Do you mean they would torture me into compliance?' said Maud.

'Not I; I means no sich thing, miss; but I means this, for I 'ave seen it as often as I 'ave heard song or sermon; and there's three, no less, in the 'ouse, I do hear, at the present time, as gets their food that way, because they won't take it no other.'

'What way? Say how you mean?'

'By the stomach-pump. There was a patient in the dangerous part of the 'ouse, where Mrs. Fish is sent to now, as used to shut her teeth together, refusing nourishment, as fast as a padlock, and, my dear, twenty times I 'a seen it, three men at the hour for the meal, into her room, with the stomach-pump, and before you could count twelve, they would have her fast in a chair, her mouth as wide as a pitcher, and three half-pints of the strongest soup in her stomach, in spite of all she could say or do, in a twinkling; and when she saw, plainly, she was growing twice as fat as if she took her food like other people, she gave up the notion, and there was no more trouble with her. There's no good sulking here; they has ways and means for all; and no patient can do nothing against rule.'

There was another silence, and then Maud asked:

'Has Lady Mardykes sold her place? is this Carsbrook?'

'La! no, miss; this is Glarewoods, Mr. Damian's asylum. It

is like Carsbrook in a way, and it's not like it. They are both black-and-white houses. But Carsbrook is a beautiful house ; not so big as this great barracks ; but you never saw a prettier. There's nothing in this to look at, without they fits up two or three rooms, special, like these was done for you. It is a bare-looking place, and furnished very plain ; but Carsbrook is beautiful all through. It is too grand almost. You'd say 'tis a pity almost to walk on the carpets, or sit on the chairs.'

' But—but it describes exactly like this. The croquet-ground and everything.'

' Yes, it has a croquet-ground, with a hedge round it ; but it is shaped different ; round at the corners ; and it lies on t'other side of the house.'

' And the flower-garden round it,' says Maud, still a little bewildered.

' Ay, the flower-knots ; yes, they was laid out by the same man as settled them that's at Carsbrook. But as for all the rest, if you was to see the two places, you would not think there was two things about 'em alike ; no more there ain't.'

' Glarewoods—I think I have heard it mentioned—and Mr. Damian's name——'

' He's a hard man in some things, miss. But 'twould be well if all was like him,' she added, with a dark little nod.

She had already told Maud of his absence, and the uncertainty respecting the time of his return.

A time of great mental agony, however, measured by clock or calendar, is a time of great duration. The moment when her terrific discovery broke upon her, seemed now a long way off. The period of violent agitation was over, and a gloomy calculating listlessness had come instead. Almost without effort of her own, everything, in turn, that promised a chance of liberation, revolved in her mind, hovered there a little, and gave place to some new hope.

CHAPTER LXXV.

A DISAPPOINTMENT.

THERE was another silence now, and Maud got up and walked slowly about the room. At the piano, which she had not touched for two days, she lingered for a little, and now with one hand she softly struck a chord or two, as she went on thinking.

'I certainly saw Lady Mardykes here. There could be no deception, at least, about that. Does she know that I am here ?'

'No, miss; I'm sure she don't.'

'Why do you suppose that ?'

'Well, miss, ye won't say a word if I tells you—if you *do*, it might be the worse for me.'

'Certainly, not a word,' promised Maud, whose curiosity was excited.

'Well, miss, Doctor Antomarchi told me you wasn't to get into the croquet-ground, nor out of your own room, yesterday morning, till after Lady Mardykes was gone, and he told me the minute to keep ye to, and I did ; and something more ; after all, ye was as near meeting—La ! but ye was—as ever two was, in the gallery !'

'Perhaps she knew, but did not herself wish to see me ?' suggested Maud.

'No, not a bit; she's not that way ; no, she's very good-natured. She came all the way from Carsbrook the morning after you came, and yesterday, only to see about that poor young man, Mr. Vivian Mardykes, her husband's nephew. 'Twas him, on his way here, as overtook us near Torvey's Cross. 'Twas a very sad thing. He went mad after a fall from his horse out a-hunting ; and he was promised in marriage to a young lady near Oxford ; and Lady Mardykes took it to heart awful. He got well again, very near, for awhile, and he took bad after, and had to come back, as you saw. And to-day, they say, he's very bad—some inflammation that may kill him—and dear knows, 'twould be a mercy he was took.'

'Whose funeral was that I saw from my window the first night I slept here ?'

'That was Lord Corrington's second son ; I believe he drank, poor man ; he grew paralytic ; a deal on 'em goes off that way.'

'It was you,' said Maud suddenly, after another pause, ' who took away my penknives and scissors.'

' Well, it *was*, miss,' said Mercy, brazening it out with sullen resolution. ' I must do as I am ordered, and I *will*, and there's the whole story out.'

' How could you tell me all the untruths you did about that, and other things ?'

' La ! miss, if you was in my place, you'd do the same. We must humour patients, or we could not get on, no time.'

' Patients ! And you really think me mad ?'

' I'm not fit to judge, miss ; 'tis for wiser heads than me.'

A longer silence than before ensued ; Maud was thinking, as she leaned her head lightly on her hand.

It was a strange thought that even her companion had no faith in her sanity ; horrible that her own word went for nothing. How can she prove that she is *not* mad? Prove a negative ?

The excitement of terror rises in her brain, gush after gush.

The small vigilant eyes of Mercy Creswell watched her with a restless, sidelong scrutiny.

' Fetch me a glass of water,' said Maud, and sips some. ' Give me the eau-de-cologne,' she said, and bathes her temples and forehead.

For a good while there is silence, and Mercy Creswell stands, as before, eyeing her.

The young lady is better now.

Maud sighed and looked at her, and seemed on the point of saying something that lay near her heart, but changed her mind. ' Will Lady Mardykes be here again soon ?' she asked, instead.

' I told Mr. Darkdale to ask, on account of you, miss, for I did not want to get into trouble unawares ; and he told me she might not come for another month, or more, for the doctor promised to write to her, telling how Mr. Mardykes was getting along.'

Maud looked down again and sighed.

There was another silence.

Then she raised her eyes, and looked for a time earnestly at her humble companion ; and once more she asked her oft-repeated question :

' Mercy, do you really care about me ?'

' Why, miss, you knows I do. 'Twould be a queer thing if I didn't, sure. I always liked you, Miss Maud ; I always did, indeed.'

'If you care for me ever so little,' said Maud, suddenly standing before her, with her hand on her shoulder, and looking hard in her face, with eyes now cold and stern, with earnest horror, 'you will help me, Mercy, to escape from this place.'

'Escape, miss!' exclaimed Mercy, after she had gaped at her for some seconds in consternation. 'La, bless you, miss, all the wit in fifty heads would not manage that. They're wide awake, and lots of hands and eyes everywhere; and good locks, and safe windows, and high walls, and bell-wires in many a place, miss, ye would not suppose, that would ring, almost, if a fly walked over them. There's no chance of getting out that way; and anyhow, I could not have act or part in it, and I *won't*, Miss Maud; and you mustn't never talk that way in my hearing, miss, for I am bound to report it, and won't run no risks for nonsense. Ye must not be offended, miss, for I knows a sight better than you do, all about it.'

'If you won't aid me in that, at least you will manage to have a letter put in the post for me,' pleaded Maud. 'I must write to Mr. Coke, my attorney; and to my cousin, Miss Medwyn. I ask for nothing but inquiry. There can be no honest reason for refusing that.'

'I'm sorry, miss, to refuse you,' said the maid doggedly, 'but the rule is that all letters is subject to inspection—"subject to inspection" is the words in the order-book, and no letter from a patient to be conveyed to the post-office, "conveyed to the post-office," mind, "or by a messenger"—I'm telling ye the very words of the order—"except by the permission of the principal, or his rapperrasentative"—I'm telling you the very words, miss—"in the one case by the post-bag of the consulting-room," and he has the only key of it in the house, "and in the other by the messenger of the consulting-room for the day." Them's the identical words, I could say them in my sleep.'

'Then you won't run that risk for me?'

'I won't do that, miss; no, I won't.'

'Well, Mercy, you may, at least, do this,' Maud supplicated —'you may write yourself to my cousin, Miss Medwyn, and tell her I am here, and that I implore of her to come and see me without delay.'

'No, miss, I can't do that.'

'Not for me, in this extremity? It ain't much. Oh! think —think—take pity on me—you could not be so cruel.'

'I won't do it for no one, miss. You don't know this 'ouse, miss, like I does. It's no use a pressing of me. I *won't*, miss; and what's more, I couldn't, if I would. And don't say no more about it, or I must report it to the doctor.'

Mercy delivered this speech with a flushed face, and many a wag of her head, looking straight at the wall, and not at Maud.

'I'll tell you what, miss, if you be as you say,' resumed Mercy, after an interval, 'and has nothing to signify wrong with you—you'll not be long here. Only you must draw it mild — I mean, ye must 'ave patience, and do hevrything accordin' to the rules. Look at that poor foolish Mrs. Fish, jest puttin' herself in a tantarem with that creature Ap-Jenkins; it's jest like puttin' a light to one o' them fireworks; once they takes fire, away they goes, and none to hold them till they sees the fun out; and now she's out o' this side, beyond the cross-door, among the dangerous uns, and much stricter looked after; you'll not see her in the croquet-ground, very like, for a year to come again.'

Maud had made up her mind not to quarrel with Mercy, and here it required a little effort to avoid it.

It was dismaying to meet this frank rebuff, where she had begun to hope for sympathy and active aid. What sordid brutality it was !

But already Maud Vernon had grown more tolerant. In this strange seclusion, she had learned more of human nature, and had her sense of superiority more humbled, in two or three days, than in all her life before.

'Service is no inheritance, miss, as I've often heard say, and if *I* don't look to myself, who will? You know, miss, 'twould never do to get the sack from here, and not know where to turn to. But if ye'll jest have patience, and don't get into no rows, nor refuse your meals, nor your walking and dining, or whatever's ordered for you, nor never sulks noways, about nothing, you'll not be long till something turns up. Why should the doctor want to keep you here, miss, a day longer than is fit? There's never a room empty in this house; and one customer's money is as good as another's; so don't you think or imagine, if you're not a case for Glarewoods, you'll be here any time to speak of, and when you're on the convalescent list, you'll have more liberty, and ye'll be allowed to write to your friends. Only don't ye mar all by nonsense. If you're ever so well in your wits, you'll drive yourself out of them, so sure as ye take to moping, and sulking, and roaring, and raving. 'Tis best to be quiet, and orderly, and cheerful, and 'appy, and that's my advice to you, miss; be always pleasant and 'appy, while you stays at Glarewoods.'

CHAPTER LXXVI.

A FRIEND'S FACE, AND A MENACE.

IT was only about three days after this that Maud, having gone down for her accustomed walk in the croquet-ground, which she now took at a quick pace, with her veil closely drawn, so as to avoid the recognition of any of the unhappy people, whose society she now regarded with terror, had a rather agitating adventure.

On the ground floor the passages are a little complicated; and Maud, whose thoughts were, as often happened now, far away, missed the turn which would have led her direct to the terrace-door, and entered instead the passage that terminates in one of the doors of Doctor Antomarchi's room of audience.

The passage is pretty long, and the door into Antomarchi's room is at the further end of it.

That door was now open. Doctor Antomarchi was standing at the table speaking to a lady who had been listening in a chair at the opposite side, and was now rising, as it seemed, to take her leave. The figure and profile of that lady she distinctly saw, and, wild with excitement, she cried, 'Lady Mardykes!' and rushed toward the door.

What fatality seemed always to blast her hopes of liberation.

As she ran forward, she saw Lady Mardykes pass through a different door, which happened also to be open, in the evident belief that the voice proceeded from that direction; and at the same moment the picture was hidden. The pale face of Antomarchi appeared, and before she could reach it the door shut. Against its thick panelling she rushed; she beat it with her hands, she cried wildly again and again :

'It is I, Maud Vernon; hear me, take me, save me, Lady Mardykes, for God's sake don't go !'

It was vain; there was not a sound from within. They had

left the room; and Maud ran round the passage to reach the terrace-walk, determined, if they had gone that way, to overtake Lady Mardykes.

But the terrace-door, instead of standing open as usual at this time of day, had been shut, and without a key she could not open it; she screamed for help; she ran distractedly up and down the passage, and returned. She called down the long corridor toward the office of the register for help; she cried for Mr. Darkdale on the almost desperate chance that that grim minister might be moved to compassion in her extremity.

Her piercing appeals rang down the empty corridor, and produced no sign in return.

Half frantic, she ran round toward the great hall, and had it and the hall-door been unguarded, would have rushed from it in pursuit of her friend, and perhaps have even effected a momentary escape.

But that door was always safely kept. It was protected by a second door, which prevented access to the hall without the aid of the footman's key, who, of course, exercised due caution in using it.

An oval piece of plate-glass enables one to see the hall from inside that door, and availing herself of this, Maud saw through the barred window beside the hall-door Lady Mardykes get into her carriage, take her leave of Antomarchi, and drive rapidly away.

Beating her hands together, with a long cry of agony, Maud witnessed the disappearance of her friend, and then she turned, and with her hands over her eyes, cast herself down on the stairs, sobbing as if her heart would burst. She would have liked to die then and there. Why should she live on in that hideous captivity? No other chance would ever come; Mr. Vivian Mardykes was to be removed, that day, being quite disabled by severe bodily illness, to other quarters, and the occasional visits of Lady Mardykes to Glarewoods would totally cease.

The first paroxysm over, Maud hurried to her room, and without speaking to Mercy Creswell, threw herself on her bed, and wept with her face buried in the pillows.

In a little time, a knock came at the dressing-room door, and Mercy Creswell, perplexed and even a little dismayed by what she saw, went to answer it, and found Mr. Darkdale waiting in the gallery outside.

He there made her one of his brief, quiet communications, and departed.

Uncomfortably ruminating, Mercy Creswell returned, and sat down near the bed.

By this time Maud's tears had ceased to flow, and she was lying without motion. Mercy Creswell thought that she had fallen asleep. But it was not so; for hearing a faint sound, she half-opened her eyes, and saw Mercy Creswell making a sign to some one at the door.

Turning her eyes in the same direction, she saw two of the sturdy housemaids standing there.

On seeing her looking that way, probably at another sign from Mercy Creswell, they receded a step or two into the dressing-room.

In the apathy of her dejection, Maud did not care to ask why they were there. She turned again, and lay still; sobbing at intervals, although she was no longer weeping.

In a little while she heard a quick, but not a light step, with a creaking boot, cross the floor, and looking up she saw the dreaded face of Doctor Antomarchi, looking sternly down upon her.

'Your pulse, please,' he said, extending his hand.

She placed her wrist in his fingers, and in silence he made his trial of its throb. He then placed his fingers on her forehead for a moment.

'Does she complain of headache?'

'No, sir—do you, miss?' answered and inquired Mercy Creswell, in a breath.

'No,' said Maud faintly.

'No, sir, she don't.'

'Has she been talking violently?

'No, sir, not a word,' Mercy hastened to assure him; 'very quiet.'

He beckoned her to follow him to the next room, and there he said in tones which to her terror Maud distinctly heard:

'Report her demeanour and language to Darkdale, who will call at the door every half-hour, and at the end of two hours I shall let you know whether you are to prepare her for the oath.'

She heard Mercy ejaculate, in a horrified aside, 'Lord grant it mayn't!' and the energetic tread across the dressing-room,

and the door open and shut; and for the present Antomarchi
was gone.

Maud sat up trembling and weeping.

'Now, miss, do you only be quiet, and I think it won't come
to nothing,' urged Mercy, almost fiercely.

Maud continued to weep in silence.

After some time she got up, bathed her eyes and temples in
cold water, adjusted her dress, and sat down in the dressing-
room to await the result.

Did Antomarchi intend to inflict an atrocious revenge, and
did he interpose a two hours' suspense, only to enhance its
severity?

She would afford him no pretext or excuse. She sat still,
leaning on her hand, and spoke not a word.

At the end of two hours, Antomarchi appeared. He again
felt her pulse, put a question or two to Mercy Creswell, revolved the question in his mind for a minute or two, and then
announced his resolve.

'She can go on just as usual.'

'Thank God!' interpolated Mercy Creswell, in a fervent
whisper.

'You keep a strict watch upon her words and demeanour, as
before, and report to the man on duty when he passes. Mrs.
Macklin will send you one of the women on night-duty to
assist. These women remain with you for the present.'

With these words he left the room.

Well was it for Maud, I dare say, that Lady Mardykes was
to visit no more at Glarewoods. Had it not been so, Antomarchi might have thought a second, and still more impressive
'lesson' necessary, to prevent future attempts to force an interview with that lady.

Antomarchi's energetic soul was in his work. Mammon was
the god of his worship. He knew nothing of Macbeth's falter-
ings, for he divided his faith with no other divinity. The
world, the flesh, and the devil, he liked very well, as cognate,
but subordinate powers. But Mammon, the lord of all, the
foundation of his universe, the king of his paradise, he served
with an inflexible adoration.

He was seated, now, in his office, writing his daily despatch,
sometimes no more than a line, sometimes many sheets of paper,
to his principal, and, with special reservations and powers, his

partner, Mr. Damian, who was now making a quiet sojourn at Brighton.

Antomarchi commenced with a note of the expenditure of the establishment for the week just ended, and also of the sum lodged to its credit for the same time—a sum which might make many a poor man bitter, and many a rich one modest. Then came some details of his government; and then a word or two of particular patients.

'Miss Vernon of Roydon,' he said, 'has been, a second time, disposed to be violent. Her paroxysms have been, however, brief, and I think she will become, with judicious management, perfectly docile in a little time. In other respects her mental condition has, as yet, undergone no change.'

Then followed some sentences about other people; and then the doctor said:

'And now, dear Mr. Damian, may I beg to remind you how valuable you are to thousands, and how necessary a temporary quiet, a little further prolonged, is to your perfect restoration to health. I am doing my utmost; I delight in my work; if you have any confidence, therefore, in my zeal and capacity, do not scruple to prolong, as I entreat you will, your stay at Brighton, until you feel yourself a new man. If any case of difficulty should arise, rely on my instantly invoking your presence and direction. At present there is not one presenting a single anomalous feature, and the mechanism of the establishment works with the most perfect freedom and smoothness. If you were here just now you would find yourself, except for routine, without employment. We have had some fogs here, and knowing how that sort of atmosphere tells upon you, I determined to urge, as I now do, your giving the sea air a fair trial, and not leaving Brighton until its good work shall have been more than half done.'

That evening Mercy Creswell, entering the sitting-room where Maud was, made her short courtesy near the door, and with a mysterious air said:

'A message, please, miss, from Doctor Antomarchi.'

Darkdale entered the room with a very slight bow, and an eye that searched every corner in a moment. He said:

'I have been directed by Doctor Antomarchi to tell you, Miss. Vernon, that he considers such agitations as you threw yourself into this morning as in a high degree prejudicial to your health; that you must not seek interviews, while you remain at Glarewoods, with casual visitors to other patients; that another scene, such as that of yesterday, he must regard and treat as an outbreak of morbid contumacy'—here he paused while you might count ten—'indicating a condition which must be reduced by the usual sanatory process, and if necessary by others.'

He paused again for a like time.

Her old spirit for a moment flashed from Maud's eyes. She rose to her feet, flushed and trembling, on the point of uttering her wild defiance. But it was only a lighting up of a moment; and pretty Maud, covering her eyes with her hands, sat down and burst into tears.

Mr. Darkdale was not moved by such distresses. He was inured to the eloquence and pathos of the madhouse, and employed the interval, during which he thought her tears would prevent her hearing his message, in directing his shrewd glance upon everything in the room in turn.

There was, apparently, nothing to criticize, however, and when all was a little quieter, he continued in the same tone, as if there had been no interruption:

'He wishes you to understand that he will forward, through the post, any letters you may desire to write to your mother, Lady Vernon.'

'It's a mockery! it's a mockery! he knows it is. It is *she* who *keeps* me in this dreadful place. My God hear me! Will no one help me? Oh, sir—Mr. Darkdale, you are a man! Is this manly? You have children, perhaps, whom you love. If they should ever come, and they can't be more helpless, than I am, under the power of strangers, think how you would have them dealt with. All I ask for is light. Let some impartial people try whether I am mad or not. Let me have but a trial; no one loses liberty for ever, and the society of human creatures, and the sight of friends, and is buried in such a fearful place for life, without a fair inquiry. Sir, let me see my friends, and have a chance for my freedom, like any other prisoner.'

'I have no more power than you in the matter,' answered Darkdale dryly; 'anything you have to say on that subject you can mention to Doctor Antomarchi. I am in this house only like Creswell there, or, in a higher sense, yourself, Miss Vernon, to obey orders, or abide the consequences.'

Here there was a pause.

'Except to Lady Vernon, and transmitted by Doctor Antomarchi,' continued Mr. Darkdale, 'there must be *no* letters, he says peremptorily; and he must take measures upon **any** attempt to send, or even to write one. I have neither act nor part beyond that of simple messenger, you understand, in this.'

And so saying, with another slight bow, he left the room quickly.

CHAPTER LXXVII.

A NEW LEGEND OF THE ROSE AND THE KEY.

DAYS and nights came and passed in monotonous round. Sometimes arrived as unaccountably as a dream of heaven a half-hour of hope, almost of confidence; she knew not why; perhaps a happy spirit chanced to stand near. Sometimes came hours of the bleakest despair. Sometimes a frenzy of terror.

In external matters, one day was like another, except that on Sunday a pale little resident chaplain with a consumptive cough read the morning service and preached in the chapel.

Maud was free to attend or not as she pleased; and on Mercy Creswell's assurance that no troublesome ' patient ' was ever present, and that all was conducted as decorously as in the parish church, she went with a thick veil on, and heard our beautiful Liturgy; heard hymns sung by women's voices, sweet and melancholy, the voices of the forlorn, singing in their unconscious night and privation the praises of the Great Creator, who has promised, ' Behold I make all things new. Write, for these words are true and faithful. And there shall be no more death, neither sorrow, nor crying, neither shall there be any more pain : for the former things are passed away.'

And the pale little chaplain, with dark earnest eyes, and the slight peculiar cough, that denotes that the unseen messenger has been with him and told him lovingly that he must depart and be with the King in no long time, told them his message from the Book of Life; told them how short a time man has to live, and how full of misery he is; and spoke of that beautiful world, the light of which seemed already to shine from afar on his gentle face, and make its homely lines and its traces of grief beautiful.

She had never so listened to sermon before, and under her veil the tears are trickling fast.

It is alleged as a scientific fact, that a man may go into an oven, which I take to be something of the nature of a Turkish bath, and sit there with a raw mutton-pie suspended by a string in his hand, and come out, himself nothing worse, with the same mutton-pie perfectly well baked. We don't know what human nature can bear till it is submitted to experiment. As it grows late in life with us, we look back over the wide waste of years, and meditate on the things that have happened; through some of which we thought we could not have lived, and retained our reason, and yet here we sit, and in our right minds.

And so it is with Maud. Day after day she lives on, and wonders how she lives, how she has not lost her mind. Except when, now and then, as I have said, despair or terror seizes her, life moves on in a dream, stupid and awful, but still a dream.

Maud was permitted to live as much as she pleased to herself. She restricted herself to the society of her books, of her maid, and, when she could induce her to drink tea with her, of the old matron, whose simplicity and kindness pleased her.

One morning, taking her accustomed walk a little earlier than usual round the croquet-ground, she was astounded to see taking his leave of the philosopher Sidebotham, with whom he had been conversing, a face she knew. He was about the last person of her acquaintance she should have thought it likely to meet in that part of the world.

The figure was youthful and athletic, and the costume clerical. In fact, it was the curate of the vicar of Roydon, the Reverend Michael Doody, who stood before her, shaking, with his powerful leave-taking, the hand of the little discoverer of the perpetual motion, who swayed and skipped in that gigantic swing, and showed by a screw of mouth and brow, and a sudden ogle, the force of the Reverend Mr. Doody's gripe.

The good-natured curate, who had been away on a ten days' holiday, was here to make personal inspection of the great mechanist, at the request of a friend who took an interest in him.

He was now walking toward Miss Vernon on the side-walk that leads straight to the court-yard door, which he was approaching, with swinging strides, laughing to himself, as he looked down on the gravel-walk, and repeating the words 'perpetuum mobile,' in low tones, with an irrepressible chuckle.

Maud stood still; she felt on the very point of fainting. All depended on a word with him unobserved. If he were to escape her now, years might pass, and no such opportunity occur again. He was scarcely a hundred paces from her; for a moment all darkened, and she lost sight of him. When light returned, she saw him, at an interval of only 'twelve steps, approaching at the same pace, and still chuckling over his recent conversation.

She put back her veil, and before he could pass he heard a voice, nearly before him, earnestly repeat his name. He raised his eyes, checking his pace, and saw Miss Vernon, of Roydon. It was the face of a person who had suffered. She was pale, and looked at him earnestly, and even imploringly.

'Good—good heavens! Miss Vernon!' he said in a whisper, staring at her, himself suddenly pale, with a great frown.

'Will you give a message for me?'

'A hundred—send me where you like. Good God! Miss Vernon, I'm very sorry.'

'It is only this—they won't allow me to write, or to send a message to a friend, by my maid, and I ask you to do this—and you must not tell anyone here that you know me—I want only a chance. Do you know a place called War-hampton?'

'Lord Warhampton's place?'

'Yes,' she answered.

'I'll make it out—well?'

'You must see his son, Mr. Charles Marston, and tell him where you found me, and say I sent him this, and don't fail me in my trouble, and may God for ever bless you.'

And she placed in his hand a rose which she had plucked from the tree beside her, and at the same time passed on without turning her head again.

'Be the powers o' Moll Kelly!' exclaimed the curate, recurring, in deep amazement, to an ejaculation which he had not employed till now since his initiation into theology. 'The crayture! Bless us all! How close that was kept! Not one at Roydon, except her ladyship, has an idaya.'

He looked over his shoulder ruefully after the young lady, and saw her now in the distance.

'I'm not to tell them I know her. I'll not be looking that way after her.'

As he thus soliloquized he was folding the rose, which con-

stituted the principal ingredient in his message, carefully into a
letter, and placing it in his breast-pocket.

'Lady Vernon won't like it. But how can I help that? If
the poor young lady *is* mad, what harm can it do? And if she
bain't, it may do a deal of good. In that case, be gannies! I'll
have got into a pretty hot kittle o' fish. But what am I to do?
There is no refusing the crayture. I don't know where the
place is. But I'll go, if it's a hundred miles.'

So ruminated and resolved the curate, as, by favour of the
key of one of the keepers who constantly hover about the
croquet-ground, he passed out by the door that gives access to
the court, and got into his fly in front of the house, and drove
again to the railway-station, from whence he had come.

As Maud walked in a state of indescribable but controlled
agitation towards the lower walk that lies within the yew-hedge,
Antomarchi emerged from it. At sight of this man, whose eye
seemed everywhere, and to pierce all disguises, she felt as if she
would have sunk into the earth. She had drawn her veil
closely over her face; he might possibly fail to recognise her.
That, indeed, was not very likely. But he generally passed her
with a bow. And she hoped would do so now.

But he did not. He bowed and also stopped, and spoke to
her, fixing his eyes upon her.

Every vibration of that dreaded voice seemed to tremble at
her heart, and awake a separate terror.

'Have you seen,' he asked, with slow emphasis, 'an old friend
anywhere about here, Miss Vernon?'

Maud's veil covered her face so as to conceal the signs of her
alarm.

'Who is it—what old friend?' she asked.

He paused; perhaps there was something unconsciously careless in the tone of her inquiry, that quieted his uneasiness.

'I'm sure it is a mistake. They said the Duchess of Falconbury, as she calls herself, Mrs. Fish, had contrived to get in,'
and with another bow he went on.

He was nearly satisfied that Miss Vernon had not spoken to
the clerical visitor from Roydon, whose untoward arrival, together with her unusually early promenade in the croquet-
ground, might easily have resulted in such an occurrence.

Maud hurried back to the house.

Mercy Creswell remarked that she looked ill. No wonder.
Such a tumult in heart and brain. Oh! for a friend, however

humble, whom she dare trust ! With Mercy Creswell, in some sort a spy, she must be circumspect. She asked an indifferent question or two, and with a bursting heart, sat down, and played waltzes on the piano.

CHAPTER LXXVIII.

AT CARSBROOK.

I NEED not follow my rough but honest friend, the Reverend Michael Doody, all the way to stately Warhampton; nor thence, in pursuit of Charles Marston, to Lady Mardykes' house at Carsbrook.

It was not until the day after he left Glarewoods that his devious journey brought him to the door of the beautiful old mansion where that charming widow dispensed her hospitalities.

Ample time had passed for a careful consideration of the nature of his message, and of the best manner of communicating it.

In the library he saw the young gentleman alone, told his message, and delivered his significant token.

He had nothing, of his own knowledge, to add to the words of his message. He had been as much amazed to see her there, and almost as much horrified, as Marston was himself to hear the news.

He had seen her so short a time before she was immured in that place, that he could speak with confidence.

He was too much stunned, and too entirely engrossed by confused thought and horror, to thank the curate, as he afterwards remembered he ought to have done.

Mr. Doody declined to take luncheon. He must catch his train, or be a second day late, and get into a scrape with the vicar.

One stipulation the curate made.

'I know, of course, Mr. Marston, what I'm doing in bringing this message to you ; I suppose you are to do your endayvour to get Miss Vernon out of that house at Glarewoods; and, I suppose, that mayn't please Lady Vernon, and of course she could aisily put me out of where I am, and throw me a bit back in the world. So I hope you won't tell on me—that's all.

Don't tell any one living, when you're speakin' of this job, that Michael Doody *putt* his hand to it : or worse, *putt* his futt in it; don't so much as mintion my name.'

With this charge the curate would have departed ; but Charles Marston could not let him go so soon. He had to put him through I know not how many questionings. How Miss Vernon was looking ? How Miss Vernon was dressed ? Where Miss Vernon was walking when he saw her ? At last the honest curate could stand it no longer.

' Arra, bother ye, man ! Why, I told ye that six times over already. I haven't another minute ; good-bye to ye.'

And, exploding with laughter, he broke away, almost at a run, across the hall, nearly throwing the footman down the steps in his impetuosity, and, jumping into the fly, he bawled to the driver :

' Away wid ye, now, to the steetion.'

Charles Marston, who had followed him into the hall, thought him a little brutal, but very good-natured ; and perhaps he was right.

It had been an odd spectacle ; the florid curate, with his hat on, and a stick in his hands, running across the hall in peals of laughter, and Charles Marston, pale as death, and earnest as if his life hung on the event of the minute, pursuing him with a full-blown rose, by the stalk, in his fingers.

The curate was gone ; Charles Marston, with the precious rose still nodding in his hand, turned back, and stood thinking for awhile in the library, where this strange interview had just taken place.

He was horribly agitated. Here was the rose plucked by her own hand so lately. He pressed it to his lips. Sent to him, Charles Marston, with a message from her own lips. He laid it fondly to his heart.

Yes, here was the rose. But, alas for this pettifogging, crooked, vulgar generation ! where was the key ? His ancestor had but to lift his arm, take down his battle-axe, and ride out at the head of his men-at-arms and archers to the siege of the northern castle ; but here was no work for manhood or emotion. The lady must be rescued, alas ! by writs of *habeas corpus,* or commissioners ; and her best champion would be a competent attorney. Every man is a knight-errant in his love ; and like every other Quixote, intolerant of the mean and sober procedure of the well-regulated world. It was hard that this thing was feasible, if at all, without immense pummelling and slaughter, and that he could not even get badly wounded in the process.

He was glad that his sister, Lady Mardykes, was out taking a drive with some of her guests. It was clear that the more secret he could be the better. Lady Mardykes had received a note from Lady Vernon, on the day of Maud's expected arrival, saying that her daughter was not very well, that she required a little rest, and that with the advice of a physician, she would leave home for some weeks; perhaps a little longer, but that she hoped she would very soon be quite herself again.

A note to a similar effect had reached Maximilla Medwyn, but written it seemed, in greater depression, though, as respected Maud, with no despondency. Maximilla immediately wrote to offer her services as a companion to Maud; but Lady Vernon did not seem to want her; so she could not press it.

Miss Medwyn had left Carsbrook only a day or two before. Her absence was unfortunate. It involved loss of time; for she was the only person, being not only in emergency clear-headed and prompt, but acquainted with those 'friends of the family,' who might be usefully taken into council, and without whom he could scarcely hope a successful issue for his enterprise.

He leaves a little note for his sister, Lady Mardykes, accounting for his flight. A very dear friend of his is in trouble; he must go for a few days and try to be of use. But he won't let her off; she must receive him again when he returns.

Leaving this to account for himself, away he goes for Wybourne, to find Maximilla Medwyn at the Hermitage.

He does find her there that evening. She in turn is astounded and terrified. After the first eloquent half-hour, she begins to think more coolly.

'*Now* I understand, for the first time, a singular persecution to which Maud and I were exposed during our little tour in Wales. We were watched and followed everywhere by an ill-looking, canting man; his name was Lizard, and I saw him once shortly after at Roydon. I'm quite certain that man was instructed to follow us, and to collect information, and make notes of everything, we, that is to say, Maud, said or did which could be perverted into evidence of insanity. That is my conjecture and belief.'

So the old lady indignantly ran on:

'I can swear, and I fancy I have as good opportunities of judging as Mr. Lizard, that no person was ever of sounder or clearer intellect than Maud Vernon, and there never was anything the least eccentric, in either word or act, except what was natural to the high and wayward spirits of a girl emancipated for a brief holiday from the gloom and formality of a cold and joyless home. You and I are among the very last who saw her, before this amazing step was taken, and I think neither of us can have the slightest difficulty in pronouncing her as sane as ourselves. Mind,' she said a little later, 'I don't charge Barbara Vernon with acting, in this dreadful business, contrary to her belief. But she is the kind of person who believes whatever it pleases her passions should be true. She has a kind of conscience, and advises with it. But she bullies it into whatever shape she pleases. I never in my life met a person with the same power of self-delusion. There is no character more dangerous.'

At first Miss Medwyn recommended immediate recourse to Mr. Coke, the family attorney. On second thoughts, however, she took a different view. It was quite possible that Mr. Coke's mind was already charged with perverted evidence, and his adhesion secured for Lady Vernon's view of the question. Lady Vernon was artful and able in managing people; and her social influence was potent.

Ultimately, therefore, for a variety of reasons, she decided on old Richard Dawe as the safest person to consult and act with in this crisis. He was sagacious and taciturn. He knew Barbara Vernon thoroughly, and was not a bit afraid of her. He was attached to the family of Vernon; he was a man of inflexible probity, and where he took up a cause, he was a thorough friend and persevering.

It was a question, however, whether he would undertake the active direction of this. There were many things to make him hesitate.

Furnished with his address, and a letter from Maximilla Medwyn, Marston set out without losing a moment unnecessarily. And early next morning had an interview with Mr. Dawe.

You shall learn immediately with what results it was attended.

CHAPTER LXXIX.

AT ROYDON.

LADY VERNON was, as usual, busy in the library at Roydon, noting letters to be answered by her secretary, and answering others which she thought deserved the distinction of an autograph.

With a face marble-like and serene, she is promoting the conversion of the human race to Christianity. To make them all even as she is, is worth a great sacrifice. And, besides teaching them to walk in the light, and tend to heaven, she promotes, as we know, all sorts of benevolent designs, schools, mild reformatories, temperance associations, savings-banks on new and liberal principles, building societies for the poor, farms for their employment and sustentation, loan societies, convalescent hospitals, asylums for all sorts of deserving and suffering people.

If this pale, still lady, with the black hair and large grey eyes, had her way with the world, you would know it no longer. There would not be a sorrowful soul or a writhing body on earth. It would be a paradise; and heaven anticipated, one wide, universal heaven, musical with angelic joy and gratitude, would reign in every corner of the globe.

Ay, good reader, it would be all heaven; except that one small hell, very deep, very murky, in which motionless stands the white figure of her child.

In momentary reveries, as she pens her letter to the president of the Benevolent Society in Aid of Children, by death, or other causes, bereft of the tender care of parents, the eye of her spirit opens, and she sees, through the letter, beneath her feet, far below, in the nether earth, that pale hell, and raises her face momentarily, as if from the breath of a furnace.

She looks round on books and busts, and through the windows on the majestic trees, and is reassured by a sight of the material world about her.

'I have duties, some painful, but many happy,' she thought. 'I try to acquit myself of all.'

And when she looked on the long list of her charities and benefactions, and on the antique binding of the folio, containing no less than fifty-seven distinct addresses from as many admirable societies, each acknowledging with decorous panegyric her magnificent benefactions; addresses or resolutions proposed and seconded by bishops, eminent dissenters, and religious peers, amidst the unanimous applause of meaner Christians, could she feel otherwise than reassured ?

She could not say she was happy; some of her duties pained her; but she heaved over these latter a comfortable sigh, and her irrepressible self-esteem reasserted itself.

It was at this moment, just as she had resumed her writing, that her tall footman stood at the door, and informed her that Mr. Dawe and Mr. Marston had arrived in a chaise, and come in, and that they had asked particularly to see her.

'Did you say I was not very well ?'

'Yes, my lady.'

'I don't think those gentlemen can have understood—go and tell Mr. Dawe that I am not sufficiently well to see any one to-day.'

So said Lady Vernon, a little peremptorily, with her head high, and the footman backed from the door and vanished.

Lady Vernon sat, with a very still respiration, and her pen resting on her desk, without a stir, awaiting the issue of a diplomacy which she feared.

She could have had no difficulty if it had been any one else on earth. But with Mr. Dawe it was a different matter. His relations with her were very peculiar. His persistence was formidable. And she knew, if he thought himself right, he would, not very improbably, carry his point.

The hectic fires, those signals of danger, were already burning in each cheek, under her cold steady eyes.

'What detains him all this time ?' she asked, in her solitude, with an angry tap on her desk.

There is more suspense in this trifling situation than is pleasant. She is in the acutest irritation of impatience.

The footman returns, and finds her apparently busily writing.

'What is it ?' she asked, a little peevishly, glancing toward the door.

'Please, my lady, Mr. Dawe says that his business is particularly hurgent, and that you would be displeased, my lady, if he went away without hacquainting you with it.'

'Oh ! said Lady Vernon gently ; 'then you had better show him and the other gentleman, his friend, into the great drawing-room. And let some one tell Latimer that I want her, and tell Mr. Penrhyn that I should be obliged to him to come here for a few minutes.'

'Yes, my lady,' and again the footman disappeared.

The maid arrived before the secretary.

'Latimer, I may have to speak to Mr. Dawe about business; he's here now; and I don't feel strong, and I think the best thing I can take is a little sal-volatile, and do you just put some in water, the same quantity you did yesterday, and fetch it to me.'

'Yes, my lady—you're not looking very well—they should not come to trouble you about business now.'

'I think not, Latimer,' she answered. 'But it is old Mr. Dawe, and I suppose he fancies I should see him if I were dying; people are so selfish; but if I must I must, and at all events let me have my sal-volatile.'

'She's worriting herself over everything, and she looks as if she was a good half-ways into a fever this minute,' remarked Mrs. Latimer, straight and thin, in her black silk dress, as she hurried up the stairs to execute her message.

She had hardly gone when a knock came to the door.

'Come in.'

The secretary came in, with the peculiar drowsiness of air and face that tedious work, too long continued, bestows. He was not sorry of the little interruption, and an opportunity of lifting his head and shaking his ears, and although Jack was growing a dull boy, he smiled politely, and I think could have yawned at the same time.

'You wished to speak to me, Lady Vernon?'

'Yes. won't you sit down? I wanted to tell you that Mr. Dawe, with a friend, has called, and wants to talk with me about business; and I should be so glad to avoid it, if possible, I feel so poorly. So I'm going to ask you kindly to see him for me, and if it is anything that you can settle, I should be so much obliged if you would arrange it, as I really don't feel able to talk at any length to-day, and you could make him understand that.'

'Oh, certainly—of course he could not think—I have only to explain,' said the secretary, with polite peremptoriness.

'Thank you so very much,' she said, gladder of his confident prognostics than her pride would have confessed.

In came Latimer with the sal-volatile and water.

'Thanks,' said Lady Vernon. 'I'll take it now.'

And she drank it off.

'Well, my lady, I must tell you, you're not looking yourself; and don't you go and bother yourself about Mr. Dawe's business, my lady; it is a shame all the trouble they puts upon you.'

'I've sent Mr. Penrhyn to try whether he can't arrange it for me, and I'm in hopes he can. Thanks, that will do. Latimer; you can go.'

Mr. Penrhyn's return was delayed long enough to raise a strong hope in her mind that Mr. Dawe was, after all, avertable.

In a few minutes more the secretary returns.

'Well, what is it about?' asked Lady Vernon, affecting to raise her eyes from the letter she was *not* writing.

'Upon that point, Lady Vernon, I'm as much in the dark as when I left you——'

'Oh!'

'I pressed him all I could, but he insists he can open the matter only to you, Lady Vernon, and he seems a very obstinate old gentleman.'

The secretary, she fancied, was curious; but his eyes, as he related the result of his interview, were lowered steadily to the table.

'And I then asked him to write a note. I hope, Lady Vernon, I did as you would have wished?'

'Certainly,' said Lady Vernon. 'Thanks—and that is it?'

She extended her fingers to receive it.

It was a pencilled note, merely turned down at the corner. She did not open it.

'He is still in the drawing-room?'

'He and his friend?' acquiesced Mr. Penrhyn.

'Did he say it was anything of much importance?' she asked, looking wistfully at the note which she was, somehow, reluctant to open.

'No, not exactly; he said he must decline opening it—I think those were his words—except to you, Lady Vernon; and it required some little pressing to get him to write.'

'Yes—I dare say—and he indicated nothing more?' and she looked again wistfully at the note.

'Nothing. He is more of a listener than a talker. I don't think he uttered twenty words.'

'Yes, he *is* silent. Thanks, Mr. Penrhyn, I think you have done everything possible for me—thank you very much.'

'You don't wish me to return to him, Lady Vernon?'

'No, thanks, I'll look into this, and send him an answer just now. I shan't trouble you any more at present.'

So Mr. Penrhyn made his bow, and Lady Vernon was alone.

She knew perfectly what Mr. Dawe had come about. But her case was too strong. She defied him to pick a hole in her proofs. Was there not a responsibility and a duty?

She opened his note. It said:

'DEAR BARBARA,—

'I must see *you*. Your secretary will not do. What I have to say is too harrowing. You may anticipate.'

She read these words with a sudden chill and sickness; for the first time a maternal thrill, like a pain in an unknown nerve, stole through her. The words had touched a thought that had before been peremptorily 'laid.'

Has the miserable girl made away with herself?

She felt faint for a moment.

But the next words cleared his meaning up:

'I have preferred seeing you, and obtaining your prompt acquiescence, to taking a public step. If you deny me an interview, my next measure will be decisive. I shall not postpone action in this grave matter.

'Yours faithfully,

'RICHARD DAWE.'

She touches the bell.

'Show Mr. Dawe, but not the gentleman who came with him, into this room,' she said to her footman.

And now, leaning back a little, with her cold gaze fixed on the door, she awaits the conflict.

CHAPTER LXXX.

DEBATE.

THE servant announces ' Mr. Dawe.' And that swarthy little gentleman, with wooden features and black wig, walks in, and approaches. There is, as it were, a halo of darkness round him. His countenance shows no excitement; nothing but its customary solemn reserve.

The door closes.

Lady Vernon receives him standing, and does not sit again for some minutes. Mr. Dawe is thus kept standing; and thus the meeting acquires an odd air of formality. He steps up to her as if he had to announce nothing more important than a purchase of fifty pounds' worth of Three-per-Cent. Stock.

He extends his hand, as usual; but she does not take it this time.

This coldness, or severity, does not seem to disconcert Mr. Dawe in the slightest degree; in fact, he seems scarcely conscious of it.

' Your reluctance to see me assures me that you anticipate the subject on which I mean to speak,' he began.

' It might have assured you, if my words had not, that I was not well enough to see anyone. I can't be certain what subject you mean, but I am pretty sure it is nothing pleasant; you never trouble your head about anything pleasant.'

'That is rather true, Barbara,' he says, 'and this is *not* pleasant. Your daughter Maud has been placed in the madhouse at Glarewoods.'

' I have acted with too much reluctance; I have acted under strong pressure from my advisers; I have acted in obedience to urgent medical advice. She *is* an inmate of Glarewoods, under the care of that good and able man, against whom even you will hesitate to venture an ill word—Mr. Damian.'

' I know. But Mr. Damian is not there. He's at Brighton. Doctor Antomarchi, no worse and no better, I suppose, than an ordinary mad-doctor, received her, and has at present, and will have for some time to come, the sole control of that place. The fact has become known to your daughter's friends, who, believing her to be sane, wish to know why she is in a madhouse.'

' She is in a madhouse, I answer in the coarse terms you seem best to understand, because she is mad.'

'She's not mad, not a bid mad; not half so mad as you,' replied the little man sternly. 'The people who intimately associated with her immediately before her imprisonment in that place are convinced of her sanity, and prepared to depose to it.'

Lady Vernon's rising wrath subsided suddenly as these words opened a new vein of suspicion.

'Captain Vivian, you mean,' she said, growing deadly pale, with a smile of horrible scorn.

'No, I don't; I mean people who are more likely to be attended to,' he answered as sternly.

There was a silence. Lady Vernon looked down. She still thought that Captain Vivian was the mainspring of this untoward movement.

'You seem to think I am bound to give account to you of all I do,' she said, in sarcastic tones.

'You, Barbara, seem to think you are accountable to *no* one,' he retorted dryly.

'I am answerable to my God,' she replied, with flashing eyes. 'My stewardship is to Him, not to *you.* I'll give no account to you, further than to say, and *that* only to stop slander, that all responsibility is removed from me; that I have been directed by the advice of as able and conscientious men as are to be found in England; and that copies of the depositions, for I chose to reduce the evidence to that shape, are lodged with Mr. Damian.'

'May I see them?'

'He has got them, not I,' she said coldly.

Mr. Dawe grunted, after his fashion, and with brows more knit than usual looked down for a few seconds.

'You have the originals—you can let me see them?' he persisted.

'You have no more claim than any other person; perhaps less. I shan't show them to you without consideration; certainly not now, possibly never. Why, what motive,' she broke out fiercely, 'but the noblest, can a mother have in making so terrible a sacrifice of feeling?'

'*I*, and I *only*, know the existence of a motive,' said Mr. Dawe; 'and if Satan has put in your mind to do this——'

'Satan! How dare you talk of Satan to me, sir?' cried the lady in a choking voice, rising with a crimson flush, and stamping on the floor, with pride and hate in her face. 'Do you

know who I am ? Satan in *my* mind ! You wicked old man !
You *alone* know my secret. That's true. *Tell* it where you
will, and have done with these infamous threats. You may
wound, but you can't disgrace me. The world knows something
of me—the Christian world. I've done my duty in all things,
especially by my daughter ; and all the false tongues in England
shan't frighten me !'

'You ought to know me, Barbara, by this time. High
words, hard words, don't affect me, no more than flatteries do—
in at one ear and out at the other,' and he touched alternately
the sides of his black wig. 'Be reasonable. Your violence de-
prives you of the power of considering consequences. You *have*
a powerful motive, and motives, often unrecognised, control our
actions. I know what power the death of Maud unmarried
would give you by your father's will. I know what it would
enable you to do for Elwyn Howard—Captain Vivian, as we
style him—your son. I know the sad story of his birth, and of
your secret marriage, that turned out to be a nugatory one, with
that weak, strange man, Elwyn Howard, the vicar.'

'Stop, in God's name !—spare the dead. My noble Elwyn,
my pure, noble, heart-broken Elwyn—my first, and best, and
only beloved, in his grave !'

And she burst into shrill screaming sobs, and, wringing her
hands, walked to and fro in the room.

The little man in the black wig said nothing, but waved his
hand toward her again and again, as one beckons a child to be
quiet.

The paroxysm subsided, and she stood before him with stern
eyes.

'You come to me always like a messenger from the grave.
Have I ever seen you but for trouble ? Have you ever had
a pleasant or even a merciful word for me ? Have you ever
spared me one pang, or spared the dead or the living in your
mission of cruelty ?'

'If it be so, Barbara, the fault is yours, not mine. I believe
she is in her right mind ; and I have come to make you an
offer. Liberate her, and let her case be examined into here or
in London, with her own solicitor to watch her interests, and
such of her friends as she may choose to name to attend and
lend their aid. If you won't do this, I'll take a course you may
like less, for I'll not allow her to be immured there, without an
effort to set her free.'

'Then you propose to put me formally on my trial, in my own house, on a charge of having entered into a conspiracy to imprison my daughter in a madhouse?'

'You are a self-willed, impetuous woman, Barbara. You are intolerant of argument, and prefer error and illusion to truth when it stands in your way. Look into your heart. Is there nothing there to startle you? When you have done that, call up the past. Consider what happened. You would believe whatever favoured your wishes. You would listen to no warning. With headstrong infatuation you married Elwyn Howard without consent or knowledge of your parents. And have you ever known a quiet hour since? All are dead, but I, who knew your secret. Your father, your mother, your old nurse, and your husband; he made a cowardly and cruel use of it; but his cruelty does not justify yours, wreaked upon his and your child. No lesson instructs you. You are what you were— perverse, one-idead, headstrong. Where you have a sufficient motive, nothing will stop or turn you. You don't, perhaps, see the motives that rule you now. You dread, as well you may, the complication which your secret threatens. It would be a brief way of solving this horrible danger to hide Maud Vernon in Glarewoods for the rest of her days. Moreover, it would be a short way to a provision for the child you love, to consign the child you hate, to what must attend the incarceration of a spirited girl in such a place, an early death. You live in delusion, a serenity of egotism, from which the stroke of death alone will startle you too late. I will invoke in this case the intervention of the Chancellor, unless you consent to the proposition I have made you.'

With these words Mr. Dawe closed the longest speech he was ever known to deliver at a single spell; and in his face and voice there was something more threatening than either had ever evidenced before.

Whiter and whiter grew the handsome face of Lady Vernon as Mr. Dawe proceeded. She rose like an evoked spirit to his incantation, and stood with a countenance in which rage, and fear, and derision were blended with a force worthy of an evil spirit.

'I have listened to your hideous calumny till it is expended. Let it be your comfort that your last act has been in keeping with all your former malignant intercourse with me, and that you leave a broken-hearted woman with a curse and a falsehood, and a threat on your lips. It is our last meeting. I shall never hear your ill-omened voice again. I disdain your offers; I defy your threats.' She rang furiously at the bell. 'And I command you never more to enter this house, or to presume to claim acquaintance with me.'

She turned and walked away from him, into the room.

Hearing the door open, she turned again, and said to the footman, who had come in:

'This gentleman is going; show him to the hall-door.'

Dawe nodded sullenly at the door of the room, and said in his accustomed tones:

'I shall act strictly on what you have said to me: and as it can't be mended, I accept the terms you prescribe. Farewell, Barbara.'

The little figure in the black wig withdrew at his customary gait; his dark wooden face presenting its solemn furrows and accustomed carving, and his voice and his whole demeanour, dry and phlegmatic, as if nothing of interest had occurred.

Trembling, Lady Vernon sat down. There is always a 'devil's advocate' to pervert the motives and distort the conduct of the saints, and hers had just been with her. His insults still quivered in her nerves. Does not Satan plague scrupulous consciences with dubitations and upbraidings utterly fantastic? The 'still small voice' within her had been whispering vaguely the same thing that now she had heard croaked with coarse distinctness, by an external voice. It was this harmony and iteration that made that croaking voice eloquent, and when it ceased, left spotless Lady Vernon trembling.

CHAPTER LXXXI.

THE LIGHT APPROACHES.

In a situation in any degree resembling Maud's, a captivity in which all contact with the outer world, and all communication with friends, are effectually prevented, delays unexplained appears supernaturally long; time moves so slowly; the idea of neglect and oblivion is so often uppermost; and despair always so near.

One morning, some time after the scene at Roydon between Lady Vernon and Mr. Dawe, Mercy Creswell appeared before Maud with an unusually reserved countenance.

'You'll be wanting downstairs, miss, at twelve o'clock, in the doctor's office, to-day,' she said.

'And what is this for ?' asked Maud, startled.

'Well, miss, I do believe it is two gentlemen from the Lord High Chancellor as is come down to ask you some questions,' answered Mercy.

'Oh! oh! Really ?' faltered Maud, her heart beating fast with a secret prescience of a coming crisis. Her message had not been in vain, and here was the result of a powerful and friendly interposition.

'You need not be frightened, miss, they won't do you no harm. There was two came down here last year to see a very rich patient, and I dessay the Chancellor was making a nice thing of his money and estates, while he was locked up here; I should not wonder: anyhow, he would not let him out from here till he found he could not keep him shut up no longer. So before he took him out he sends his gentlemen down here, to make, as we thought, all the fuss they could about letting him away and home again to manage his own business, but home he went for all that. His name was Hempenfeldt, a tall thin man of fifty, with a hooked nose, and gold heyeglass, and used to wear a white hat and blue frock-coat, and buff waistcoat, and them varnish boots.'

Maud looked at her watch. It was past eleven.

'Did you ever see the Honourable Mr. Marston, Lady Mardykes' brother, miss ?' inquired Mercy, who had grown to be on easy terms with the young lady in her charge.

'Yes, I have. What about him ?' inquired Maud, as carelessly as if her heart had not fluttered up to her lips and dropped down dead again.

'Because I saw him, and a little black gentleman, just up to his elbow, talking to Doctor Antomarchi, and Miss Medwyn is in the waiting-room.'

Perhaps Mercy thought that these signs betokened the early liberation of Maud, and became more communicative as the likelihood of her again emerging into light, and becoming a personage in the living world, improved.

Maud knew now that battle was actually waged in her behalf, and that a few hours might see her free, and on her way to Wybourne with dear old Maximilla Medwyn.

But, oh! no; she would not allow herself to believe anything so incredible. It could not happen. To admit a hope so immense would be to insure a plunge into the deepest hell of disappointment. And yet that hope possessed her.

'Do you think Miss Medwyn will be allowed to see me?' asked Maud.

'I don't know, miss; they was jealous of you seeing any one; and I'm sure there's no good in *you* asking, whatever they may say when *she* does.'

Maud, being quite of the same opinion, made no move, well knowing that Maximilla would leave no stone unturned to obtain a few minutes' sight of her.

Mr. Darkdale arrived, with a knock at the sitting-room door. His business was to deliver a formal intimation from Doctor Antomarchi that Miss Vernon was to hold herself in readiness to come to his room at twelve o'clock, to answer some questions which two official persons would have to put to her, and to request that she would be good enough not to leave her rooms until his messenger should arrive to conduct her to his office.

In a state of suspense Maud awaited Antomarchi's summons in her sitting-room. Twelve o'clock came, and no summons yet. Ten minutes, twenty minutes, half an hour passed. The little timepiece in her room struck one.

Mr. Darkdale arrived a minute or two later. He looked stern and thoughtful. Mercy Creswell was summoned. She was to go alone with Mr. Darkdale. Miss Vernon was to be so good as to await her, or his, return where she was. These attendants would wait upon her in the meantime.

Two of the stalwart housemaids in the Glarewoods uniform entered quietly, and stood near the door.

Mercy Creswell looked a little disagreeably surprised at the occurrence; but she accompanied Mr. Darkdale in silence; and Maud remained in utter ignorance of all that was taking place downstairs, upon the issue of the ordeal that was to decide her fate.

In less than ten minutes Mercy Creswell returned, looking hot and agitated. The temporary attendants were withdrawn, and Maud, being alone with her maid, questioned her as to what was going on.

'I'm not to tell nothing about it, miss; them's my orders.'

'The inquiry is about me, ain't it? Surely you can tell me so much,' urged Maud.

'Well, yes, miss; it is about you, and not another thing will I say about it. Where's the use of me running that risk without no good to no one?'

Mercy was obstinate, and held to her resolution, spite of all Maud's importunities and promises of secrecy; and Maud in the burning fever of her suspense walked from room to room, and from window to window, unable to rest for a moment.

If she could only tell how it was going! By what right was she excluded from her own trial? How unfairly her case might be dealt with! And, oh! but to think of all that depends on the next hour.

In the waiting-room Mr. Marston and old Miss Medwyn had met Mr. Dawe, and were in high chat when Mr. Tintern was shown in. He had not perhaps expected to meet Miss Vernon's friends in such force. He knew only that he was to see Mr. Dawe there. He would have preferred not meeting Miss Medwyn. He smiled pensively, and shook hands and shrugged pathetically over the melancholy state of things which had called them there.

'And poor Lady Vernon, what a deplorable thing for her! Only think, a mother, you know, and all that kind of feeling; so awfully distressing! I know, for my part, I should rather lose a child by death outright, and be spared the anguish of such an affliction as this.'

He looked round upon them with a sad shake of the head, and a slow wave of his hand, which was intended generally to take in Miss Vernon, the lunatic asylum, its inmates and apparatus; and this pantomime terminated in a slight but expressive elevation of the eyes and hand, and another desolate shrug.

'Lady Vernon lives in hopes,' he continues, liking, I fancy,

to talk better than to be talked to, on this subject. 'She thinks
this will not be a very tedious—a—a—illness. All this is, of
course, quite dark at Roydon. No one there—I have not even
mentioned it to my wife—not a human being but I and Doctor
Malkin——'

'Ho! Doctor Malkin! Well, that does not surprise me,'
exclaimed Miss Medwyn, in an angry parenthesis.

'Not a living person but he and I, and Lady Vernon herself,
in all that part of the world, has the least idea there is anything
of the kind; and you know we may look to see her very soon,
I do hope, quite as we could wish.'

'Very soon, I should hope, Mr. Tintern; sooner even than
some of her friends expect,' says Maximilla, with a tart emphasis.
'She is under very special restraint here. They won't permit
me so much as to see her! What can be the reason of that?
I don't suppose I can hurt her; and as to my share of the
danger, I'm quite willing to risk that, ha, ha, ha!—poor little
Maud!' and with these words Maximilla Medwyn suddenly
burst into tears.

Mr. Tintern looked with much feeling at Mr. Dawe; but a
blacker shadow seemed to have gathered about that odd figure.

Mr. Marston, at the further end of the long room, was trying
to read some papers connected with the proceedings, but his eye
every moment wandered to the door through which he expected
the summons of a messenger from the commissioners.

Maximilla's tears disconcerted Mr. Tintern, who walked first
to the window, and then to Mr. Dawe, to whom, with another
shrug, he murmured:

'Most harrowing! No place for ladies, this!'

Mr. Dawe said 'H'm.'

Maximilla's sobs did not last long. A footman entered and
presented a little note to Mr. Dawe.

Mr. Dawe read it. The eyes of Mr. Marston and Miss
Medwyn are now directed on him very anxiously.

'It is all right,' said Mr. Dawe, in his dry tones.

'Thank God!' exclaimed Maximilla.

And Mr. Marston looked as if he would have said the same.

Mr. Tintern eyed them curiously. What was 'all right'?
He would have given something to know.

Mr. Dawe walked up to Maximilla briskly, and saying,
'Read that,' placed the note in her hands.

It said:

'DEAR MR. DAWE,

'I write a line, because I cannot leave the room where my papers are. I have very great pleasure in saying that Mr. Commissioner Steele and Mr. Commissioner Bunting make no objection, under the circumstances of this case, to your being present, although your request, coming from one who is not related to the family, is not usual; and the only condition imposed is, that you make no public use of what you are permitted to witness; and they reserve, of course, the right of dispensing with your presence at any time. I write this with pleasure, as I look upon your presence as a protection to myself.

'Yours truly,
'MICHAEL ANTOMARCHI,

'P.S.—You are at liberty to accompany Mr. Tintern when the commissioners send for him.'

This summons was not long in coming.

Mr. Tintern looked with an air of studied curiosity and polite surprise at Mr. Dawe as that gentleman accompanied him.

Mr. Dawe did not care. Those looks did not overpower him.

CHAPTER LXXXII.

BEFORE THE COMMISSIONERS.

THEY found the commissioners, with Doctor Antomarchi, in the oval room, to which the servant conducted them.

Mr. Commissioner Steele is a tall, gentlemanlike-looking man, with a dark face, closely shaved, black curly hair, a little streaked with white, growing close over his broad but not high forehead. He looks at them with eyes nearly shut, and a little frown, after the manner of near-sighted people, and he is twirling, round his finger, an eye-glass. He rises, and receives these gentlemen with a short bow; so does Mr. Commissioner Bunting, a short and fat gentleman of sixty, who represents medical science on this commission, being, in fact, an apothecary. He follows Mr. Steele in this, and stands in awe of him, as being a great gentleman, with influential friends; and he seldom

ventures an opinion, and then only in a whisper in his ear.
Mr. Steele looks to Doctor Antomarchi to explain Messrs.
Tintern and Dawe. The doctor, who has seen them before,
does so.

'Oh! Mr. Dawe? The gentleman who wishes to be present
on behalf of Miss Vernon?' asked the commissioner.

'Yes,' said Antomarchi.

'Have you considered, Doctor Antomarchi,' hesitated Mr.
Tintern, ' whether Lady Vernon would quite wish that arrangement? The young lady's mother,' he explains to the commissioners, ' she is naturally extremely anxious that as little as
possible of this very painful case should become generally
known; she wished it, in fact, as private as possible.'

'Yes; but in this case it is not a simple relation of mother
and child,' said Mr. Steele fluently, while arranging his papers.
'The young lady has quite different interests, and on a very
great scale; and it is only reasonable that some one, in whom
her relations have confidence, should be permitted, in her interest, to hear what passes. Mr. Tintern, you are a magistrate?'

'Yes, sir.'

'The depositions in this matter were made before you?'

'They were, sir.'

'We don't usually come at our facts in that way; but it can
do no harm looking into them. You have brought with you
the original depositions?'

'Yes, sir.'

'Be so kind as to hand them to me. Thanks; Mr. Dawe,
while I read these, you can read the attested copies which Doctor
Antomarchi will be so good as to give you.'

Doctor Antomarchi placed the papers before Mr. Dawe, who
received them with one of his stiff bows, and read them with
characteristic care.

'Lady Vernon is not here?' asked Mr. Commissioner Steele.

'No,' answered Antomarchi.

'Nor that man, Elihu Lizard?'

'He is not here.'

'These affidavits are very strong. Lady Vernon deposes that
her daughter, the subject of this inquiry, has for some years
exhibited a growing eccentricity and violence, which have caused
her extreme anxiety; that latterly these peculiarities had, in her
opinion, become distinctly morbid, and that on a certain evening,

the date of which she states, Miss Vernon intimated an intention of putting an end to her own life. That this had been preceded by two distinct occurrences of a similar kind, within little more than a year antecedent to the final threat of this sort at Roydon Hall.'

The commissioner paused and looked at Mr. Dawe.

'Doctor Malkin, the family physician, states that the young lady is of a highly nervous temperament, with strange ideas, such as are popularly termed flighty, that she is hysterical and impetuous, and without sufficient self-control to counteract the obvious tendencies of such a mental and nervous condition. That with this knowledge of predisposing causes at work, he cannot refer the facts set out in Lady Vernon's and Elihu Lizard's depositions to any cause other than insanity too inconsiderably developed to be safely committed to any but the constant supervision and treatment of an able physician, residing under the same roof, and experienced in the treatment of insanity. He says he cannot undertake the responsibility of advising Lady Vernon to keep the young lady at home, an experiment which has often been attended, he remarks, especially when suicidal tendencies have existed, with fatal consequences. That is very strong, you observe,' he said, throwing his head back, and glancing at Mr. Dawe.

Mr. Dawe grunted.

'You think that very strong ?' said the commissioner.

'No,' said Mr. Dawe, 'I don't mind Lady Vernon; and the Roydon doctor is in her pocket. He thinks what *she* thinks, and *she* thinks whatever she likes.'

Mr. Commissioner Steele popped his glass in his eye and stared at this outspoken little man, as he might at a curious specimen in a managerie ; and then he resumed.

'Well, here's Elihu Lizard,' said the commissioner, who had opened another paper ; 'I think *here*, perhaps, it will be as well to ask Miss Medwyn to be good enough to come in ; she may, possibly, have something to explain.'

Mr. Steele leaned back in his chair, and Doctor Antomarchi again touched the bell, and the servant in a minute more announced Miss Medwyn.

The commissioner rose and made his bow. So did Mr. Bunting as before. Miss Medwyn glanced shrewdly at Mr. Steele and his brother commissioner, to ascertain what manner of men the judges might be.

' I'll tell you what Elihu Lizard states, if you please, Miss Medwyn, and you can make any remarks that strike you,' says Mr. Steele.

' So I shall,' said Miss Medwyn.

' He swears he followed Miss Vernon from place to place.'

' Who sent him?' asked Miss Medwyn.

' I know no more than the affidavit states; Mr. Dawe has the copy. The witness found that she acted with very marked eccentricity during a tour she made with her cousin, that was you, Miss Medwyn ; she concealed her name, and passed herself off as a Miss Maud Guendoline ; she represented herself as being, and the deponent seems to think, for the time, actually believed the statement, obliged to make her livelihood by selling her water colour sketches ; she told people that she was miserably poor, and, in social position, extremely humble ; and Elihu Lizard believes that, at the time, she seriously thought that all these statements were true.'

' She thought no such thing,' said Miss Medwyn. ' It was all done in the spirit of frolic ; just what any young creature a little wayward, and quite wild with spirits, as she was, in the enjoyment of a little holiday, might do ; and no one ever dreamt of supposing her mad.'

' Did she tell you, Miss Medwyn, during your excursion, at any time, that she did not believe these representations herself?'

' No, certainly, it was quite unnecessary ; she knew that such an idea had never entered my mind.'

' You have a strong opinion, then, in favour of Miss Vernon's sanity?'

' It is not an opinion, I am quite certain of it.'

' But suppose it were proved to you that she has, at three distinct times, threatened her own life while at Roydon ; and that once, since she came here, she has not only threatened, but attempted it ; would not that modify your opinion as to the expediency of removing, at once, all restraint and superintendence in her case?'

' It's quite untrue. I have no other answer. It is utterly false.'

' I only say, as a supposition, *suppose* it were proved——'

' It would not make the least difference ; I could not believe it,' she answered peremptorily ; ' I never shall.'

The commissioner smiled and shook his head.

Mr. Bunting smiled and shook his head.

'There is another odd circumstance deposed to here,' he resumes ; ' at a ball at a place called Wy—Wymering, I think it is ; where she went with—with *you*, Miss Medwyn, to join the party of a Mrs. Tintern——'

'My wife,' interposed Mr. Tintern softly. ' She was not able to go ; but *I* went with them, and it was *her* party all the same.'

' Oh ! I see, thanks ; where Miss Vernon went to join Mrs. Tintern's party,' continued the commissioner, ' she insisted on visiting the gallery of the town-hall, before the company had assembled, and once, in an unreal character, she presented herself as your servant, the deposition says.'

' That was precisely in the same spirit ; a mere whim ; she had been looking forward, for a long time, to the ball, and was in such spirits, poor little thing !'

Miss Medwyn was as near as possible crying again, and had to pull up suddenly.

The commissioner offered no criticism on Miss Medwyn's explanation. And after a little silence, for he saw she was agitated, he asked :

' Perhaps you would like to look over Lady Vernon's statement ? There is no objection.'

Miss Medwyn thanked him, and took the paper, which she read over, her face frowning a little, pale and scornful as she did so.

When she had conned it over, and returned the paper, he asked :

' Have you anything, Miss Medwyn, by way of explanation, or generally, to state which you think might throw light on this inquiry ?'

Miss Medwyn had a great deal to say, and said it, more than once, with great volubility, and in high scorn of all opposition. When her harangue was over, the commissioner thanked her very much, and rose, with a bow or two, and Doctor Antomarchi politely conducted her again to the waiting-room, where Mr. Marston received her with intense anxiety.

Mr. Dawe had, on hearing his narrative, peremptorily forbidden his appearance as a witness, and blew up Maximilla roundly, in his proper laconics, for having permitted all that masquerading, which now furnished the chief material of the case.

Maximilla answered that she *could* not have prevented it ; and that if that had never happened, still a case would not have been wanting, because it was plain, from different things in Barbara's statement, that she had employed people to watch Maud wherever she went.

As Mr. Marston and Maximilla Medwyn were now conversing, Mr. Dawe, whose chief object was to note carefully in his memory the facts on which the theory of Maud's insanity was based, with a view to action of a different kind, should this measure fail, had the pleasure of listening to Mercy Creswell's description of what she had termed Maud's 'parrokism.'

Then came an account of her attempt to get into the hall in pursuit of Lady Mardykes ; her throwing herself on the stairs, and what was called her violence, and ultimate reduction to submission under moral influences. Then Dr. Antomarchi made his statement, stronger, abler, more learned than the opinion of Doctor Malkin, and in conclusion he said :

'This is a case, I admit, of which I should be happy to be relieved. It is a case round which family feuds and jealousies gather and prepare for battle. We have never been in litigation here ; and although I cannot conscientiously recommend Lady Vernon to take the young lady home, I should be very much obliged if she would remove her to some other house.'

CHAPTER LXXXIII.

MAUD IS SUMMONED.

'I SHOULD like now,' said the commissioner, 'to see the young lady herself ; and after that, Doctor Antomarchi, if you please, we could have a few words with you. Mr. Dawe, are you acquainted with Miss Vernon ?'

Mr. Dawe assented.

'What do you say, Doctor Antomarchi, to Mr. Dawe remaining, while Miss Vernon answers a few questions ?'

'I should be most happy if I were not certain that in her present state a meeting of the kind would be, as respects the progress of her recovery, almost the worst thing that could happen to Miss Vernon. I speak with the responsibility of her medical adviser; and I must request Mr. Dawe to withdraw, unless you, sir, should direct otherwise.'

'Then, Mr. Dawe, I must ask you to retire,' says the commissioner, making him a little bow.

Mr. Dawe rose, and returned it with a nod ; the servant conducted him to the waiting-room ; and Doctor Antomarchi turned the key in the door through which he had retreated.

Dr. Antomarchi and Mr. Commissioner Steele had a little bit of earnest conversation. The long period of Miss Vernon's suspense at length expired.

Never did imprisoned lady in the Reign of Terror hear herself summoned to the presence of the tremendous Fouquier Tinville with a colder pang of horror than unnerved Maud Vernon, as the tap at her door intimated that the time had come, and her presence was required by the commissioners.

'Are there many people in the room ?' Maud asked, rising quickly, very pale, and feeling a little dizzy.

'Only the doctor, please, miss.'

The young lady followed the servant ; Mercy Creswell stumping after, with a supernaturally solemn countenance.

Maud did not know how she reached the office door. At sight of that well-known barrier, its well-varnished panels and oak veining, her heart bounded as if it would suffocate her.

'Wait a moment,' she whispered to the man who was about opening the door to announce her. 'Not yet ; just a moment.'

She must not seem flurried. All for her depended on her perfect self-possession in presence of this stranger, who held the key of her prison.

She signed to the man, who opened the door, and she heard her name announced.

Now she is in the room. She sees Antomarchi rise and make her a very grave and ceremonious bow. She turns from that smooth bust that frightens her, to the principal commissioner, who had also risen, and makes her a less elaborate bow. Dark, intelligent, energetic, narrow, utterly unsympathetic, in the face of her judge. Instinctively she is dismayed by it.

She sits down, hardly knowing what she does, in a chair opposite the commissioners. Mr. Steele asks her some questions, the purport of which she does not distinctly catch. She sees nothing but that cold, shrewd, self-complacent face, which dismays her.

The stern ringing voice of Antomarchi repeats the question,

and she turns. He is looking at her. She finds herself under the spell of those baleful eyes.

'Mr. Commissioner Steele asked you whether you are aware that you are sworn to have on three distinct occasions, at Roydon, threatened to take away your life?'

'I was not aware, that is, I don't know, what is said against me,' she says with an effort, and a little confusedly.

'May I ask her a few questions?' inquires Antomarchi.

'Do, pray,' acquiesces the commissioner.

He bowed to Mr. Steele, and then said:

'Be so good as to look a little this way.' She had averted her eyes. 'I want to be assured that you hear me.'

She submitted, and he proceeded.

'You are frank, Miss Vernon, and would not mislead this inquiry. Did you not intend to commit suicide at Roydon?'

Miss Vernon faltered; she tried instinctively to raise her hand to her eyes, but she did not raise it higher than her throat, where she felt a great ball rising.

'I'm sorry to press you, but we must accept your silence as an admission,' said the cold bass of Antomarchi. 'Is it not true,' he persisted sternly, with his powerful and practised eye upon her, 'that you intended suicide three distinct times, when at Roydon?'

'I—I can't,' faltered Maud.

'I know you can't,' he repeated, 'and you could not *there*, I believe.'

'I could not there—I believe—if—if—What am I saying? Oh, God! *what* am I saying?'

'Never regret speaking candidly to friends ; Mr. Commissioner Steele, of whom you seem so much in awe, can have no object in this inquiry, but what tends to your good. Now, as to what occurred *here*—upstairs — when you told Mercy Creswell you would make away with yourself, and she locked you into your room in consequence, and you then threw up the window. Come, be frank, Miss Vernon, did you not do so with the intention of taking away your life, by throwing yourself from it? You confessed it.'

She could see nothing but the direful eyes that paralyzed her.

'Did I—did I confess it? I confessed——' she murmured, with white lips.

'You did—that's right—it is hardly necessary to do so again, but if you can deny it, or explain it, you are at liberty to do so.'

Mr. Steele was, while this was passing, with a very faint smile, not ill-natured, but which seemed to say, 'Ay, ay, just as I thought,' glancing at his notes, and marking the papers before him with his pen, and saw nothing of the fatuized look that had stolen over Maud's face ; and if he had, would have attributed it to her imputed mental condition.

Mr. Bunting had an immense opinion of this house, and never dreamed of doubting an opinion of Antomarchi's.

'You *can't* explain or deny it—I am to infer *that*,' persisted Antomarchi ; 'you *can't.*'

'I can't—can I ?—I can't—oh ! what is it ?—I feel so strangely.' She shook her ears as if a fly was humming at them, and lifted her pretty fingers towards her temple vaguely.

'You say you can't, and that is quite enough—I expected no less from your candour ; and as you say you feel a little oddly, it will perhaps be better that you should return to your room, if Mr. Commissioner has no objection?'

'Certainly not,' acquiesced the official, who, with half-closed eyes, is now eyeing Miss Vernon curiously.

'You may go, Miss Vernon ; see Miss Vernon to her room,' said Antomarchi to the servant. 'Instantly, please ; she is agitated.'

Maud was standing now, and looked a little about her, bewildered, as if newly awakened from sleep.

'Oh ! what is it? What have I said? Let me remember——'

'Never regret having spoken truth, Miss Vernon,' said Antomarchi ; 'you must go,' he said sternly to her, and added quickly in a whisper to Mr. Steele, 'If she stays we shall have a scene.'

The commissioner, who had no fancy for anything of the kind, rose at the same moment and made a hasty bow.

Mr. Bunting rose abruptly, also, inclined his bald head toward Maud, and buried his double chin in his chest.

'Oh, sir ; no, don't send me back ; have mercy on me. It is false,' she screamed. 'If I said anything against myself I retract it all. You are here to try me ; God sees us ; oh, my last hope !'

This last cry was heard in the passage, as the door shut ;

and the commissioners and Doctor Antomarchi were left *tête-à-tête.*

The doctor smiled and shrugged.

Retract, retract; they all retract after an admission. People who don't know something of them, as you and I do, and Mr. Bunting, of course, have no notion how much cunning belongs to that state, and how little scruple. You see the excitement she has gone away in, and simply from having seen you and me! What would it be if she were to see an intimate friend? How could we separate tnem? And yet, I venture to say, Miss Medwyn thinks it a hardship she has not had an interview with the young lady—I should not wonder if the patient became violent; I rather expect to be sent for.'

This, and a good deal more, said Doctor Antomarchi; and, after some conversation, invited the commissioners to luncheon, which those semi-judicial functionaries agreed to partake of; and over it Mr. Commissioner Steele relaxed, and conversed about fifty things, very pleasantly, and laughed over the agreeable doctor's amusing stories. While upstairs, Maud Vernon, on her knees, with her face buried in the coverlet, writhed and sobbed wildly in the solitude of an immeasurable despair.

CHAPTER LXXXIV.

DOCTOR DAMIAN.

MR. TINTERN had more than was pleasant to think of, as he glided homeward upon the rails. His matrimonial plans for his daughter had found in that young lady a very supplicatory but stubborn resistance. He could divine no reason for it; and he took to sulking and bullying by turns. It was very desirable to establish his daughter just now, and to secure the particular son-in-law who sought the young lady's hand, because he was very wealthy, and, in consequence of peculiar circumstances, in a position to make certain difficulties of a very pressing nature easy to him. He had 'gone into a mine,' which was insolvent; and he had made the directors an offer, by way of compromise, which would save him; and his intended son-in-law was one of these directors. There was another trouble, a foolish bank speculation, in which he had also a potent influence, and might modify the urgency and rapidity of coming calls, of which Mr. Tintern, as well he might, stood much in fear.

Mr. Tintern, therefore, in his homeward drive, had ample matter for agreeable reflection. For Mr. Tintern, however, there was a little surprise in store. On his arrival at the Grange, he asked for Miss Ethel. There was an inexplicable cloud over the household. The servants were solemn and laconic. No one knew, distinctly, where she was; and all were agreed in referring him to Mrs. Tintern, who was not very well, and in her room.

Up the stairs, with very uncomfortable qualms and vague misgivings, he ran; and, in the darkened room of his wife, learned that Ethel had eloped!

All was mystery. Mrs. Tintern had not a great deal of energy or judgment in an emergency. She had sent a carriage express to the town of Roydon to bring the Reverend Mr. Foljambe, the vicar, and Mr. Puntles, the antiquary, to advise her in her perplexity. The assistance of these admirably selected counsellors did not result in very much; except, indeed, that the occurrence became speedily well-known throughout the whole town of Roydon.

A sage servant, on a steady horse, was sent off, at a jog-trot, to the nearest railway station to make inquiry, and returned some hours later a little tipsy, and in other respects as wise as he set out.

The only clue to the mysterious disappearance of the young lady was that a carriage had been seen for some time on the narrow road in the rear of the Grange, where the wooded ground affords the closest cover for an unobserved approach. The same carriage had been seen, or one very like it, in the village of Crowpton, near which five roads meet; and here, in bewilderment, the pursuit was, after a time, abandoned.

When Mr. Tintern arrived, nearly five hours had passed since Miss Tintern's flight. That did not deter him, however; he started without delay, and did not return until late next day, to find that Mrs. Tintern had received a short and rather distracted letter from her daughter, who was, in fact, married to Captain Vivian. For many hours after his arrival, under this great blow to all his plans of extrication, Mr. Tintern quite forgot Roydon Hall and its concerns.

Lady Vernon was, however, far too important an influence in

the general scheme of his speculations to be long out of his thoughts. Lady Vernon, therefore, had a note from him, a part of which she did not very well understand, not at all in Mr. Tintern's usual natty style.

It said that not knowing whether Lady Vernon was well enough to see him, he had been compelled, without even taking off his hat at the Grange, to run on upon business of the very most momentous kind. He had been in attendance at Glarewoods, and he and Antomarchi were both of opinion that the commissioners took precisely the same view of the case in which so many concur, who are profoundly and painfully interested in the case of Miss Vernon. 'Captain Vivian, whom, owing to special circumstances with which I shall acquaint you, I cannot, for a moment, dismiss from my thoughts, has behaved like a villain. It pains me to apply that term to any person who was ever honoured by your notice or consideration.'

At that moment, not a living creature, except Mr. and Mrs. Tintern, and the absconding lover, was aware that Captain Vivian had any but the slightest acquaintance with Miss Ethel Tintern, or dreamed of connecting her disappearance with him.

Lady Vernon, who was always perfectly up in the Roydon news, without making the least apparent effort to learn it, had heard of Ethel's flight, without knowing whether quite to believe it or not, or, in any case, caring about it. Mr. Tintern's words respecting Captain Vivian—Elwyn, as she called him—she, with a morbid terror, referred to the suspicion that was nearest her own heart. Fate seemed driving her into a corner. Must she avow the grand folly and humiliation of her life? Must that proud, conspicuous woman stand in the gaze of the world in that abject penance?

In the meantime Mr. Marston, furnished with a report of what had taken place before the commissioners, noted down from the careful narrative of Mr. Dawe, ran up to London that night to talk the matter over with an able Chancery Q.C., who always lingered late in town, and who was leader in all the Warhampton business. This gentleman knew Mr. Steele officially, and could estimate the view he was likely to take.

'Damian's establishment and Damian's opinion stand very high in our court,' he said. 'Antomarchi has only appeared once or twice, second fiddle, you know; Damian's thinking the statement sufficient will go a great way; and the evidence is so strong and clear——'

'So plausible and audacious,' said Marston.

'That I am quite satisfied,' continued the barrister, 'there is not a chance of succeeding by a commission *de lunatico*. I don't think by *habeas corpus*, at common law, with such evidence, you would have the smallest chance, either. You must lie by for a time, and if it be as her friends think, the medical people there will find it out, and all ultimately be as you would wish. But I should not advise public proceedings. They would fail; and the young lady occupying so conspicuous a position, the affair would become the talk of all England. It is better to wait.'

A gloomy and distracted letter Marston wrote to Maximilla Medwyn; and one as gloomy, but more reserved, to Mr. Dawe.

What was he now to do? Inaction in such a state of things was simply intolerable!

A few hours later saw him at Brighton, on the door-steps of the house in which Mr. Damian for the time resided; it was night, and the moon shining, and a thin chill mist made sea, and shipping, and houses vague.

'Can I see Doctor Damian?' he asked of the servant who opened the door.

'If you please to wait a moment, sir, I'll inquire; who shall I say?'

'He does not know me, and my name will hardly help him; give him this card, however, and say that I call upon urgent business connected with Glarewoods. I'll wait here till you come down.'

He stood on the steps, looking toward the sea, wondering whether Mr. Damian would see him, and without any distinct plan as to how to order and arrange what he had to say.

The servant returned; Doctor Damian would see him.

He followed to the drawing-room, in which were an unusual number of candles burning, and for the first time saw Doctor Damian, of whom he had heard a great deal in the course of his life.

Standing at some distance was a tall, lean man, broad-shouldered, erect, with hair white as snow, a broad square forehead, and a resolute face.

He had heard that this man was benevolent and pious. He saw nothing in his face but cold command and rigour.

He placed a chair for Mr. Marston, with a slight bow, and asked him, by name, to sit down.

'You are a son of Lord Warhampton, I conjecture from the

address upon your card?' said the old man, in a voice still clear, and, like his aspect, somewhat stern.

Mr. Marston assented, and the doctor, taking a chair, asked him to state the object of his visit.

Doctor Damian listened to the young man's fluent and sometimes vehement address with a countenance unmoved and impenetrable.

'We have never had at Glarewoods a single case of fraudulently imputed insanity,' he said with cold decision. 'The statement on which Miss Vernon was admitted, and furnished in the unusual form of attested copies of affidavits, was conclusive upon that point; I assume them to be true; you mention the inquiry just held at Glarewoods, on the motion of friends and relations, under the eighth and ninth Victoria, chapter 100. I have heard from Antomarchi on the subject. Have you about you the report you said you had of what occurred there, and if so, can you permit me to read it?'

Mr. Marston placed the paper in his hands. He glanced through it. Mr. Marston could not help admiring the large, cold grey eyes with which the old man read it. To judge by his countenance it had not made the slightest impression upon him.

'When shall we have the commissioners' decision?' he asked.

'In a day or two, I believe,' he said.

'And what particular request, Mr. Marston, do you urge upon me?' he inquired.

'I want you, with the immense powers you possess in this matter, to recognise the awful obligation so obviously imposed on your conscience, and to take the task of inquiry into your own hands.'

The old man smiled coldly.

'You are frank, Mr. Marston. You may fail to persuade, but you don't mince the matter.'

'I hope, Doctor Damian, I have not spoken too strongly; I would not offend you for any consideration.'

'I am never offended, sir, by bluntness. Will you take some tea, sir, or a glass of sherry; or will you allow me to order some supper? it is later than I thought.'

All these hospitable offers were declined with thanks.

'I don't say I'm not obliged to you, Mr. Marston, for this call; but you must remember that I speak with a knowledge of Doctor Antomarchi's great ability, and of the statement on which the patient was received at Glarewoods. I quite accept the responsibility that rests upon me; but, from a rather long experience, I can assure you that relations are often very much at issue upon the question of a patient's insanity, when a medical man can entertain no doubt either of its existence or of its very advanced development. I shall bear your request in mind. That is the utmost I shall say. But I counsel you not to be sanguine. I don't share your hopes.'

'But, Mr. Damian, you will not let the matter rest?'

'I shall make the inquiries necessary to satisfy the friends and relations whom you represent, sir; I shall say no more on the subject.'

There was something harsh in the tones in which this was spoken that warned Charles Marston that he might possibly do wisely to forbear any further pressure. The old gentleman was accustomed to command, and his air and looks were peremptory.

'Not much sympathy there,' thought Charles Marston, as, with a heavy heart, he descended the steps and walked back toward the London railway.

CHAPTER LXXXV.

THREE DOCTORS.

A LETTER reached Mr. Dawe two days later, from his solicitor, stating that the commissioners had pronounced strongly against removing Miss Vernon from the restraints of her present position.

This letter made its dismal tour of the three principal promoters of the inquiry; from Mr. Dawe to Miss Medwyn it flew, and from Miss Medwyn to Mr. Marston.

Charles Marston, on receipt of it, took wing instantly for the Hermitage, in the vague pursuit of sympathy, and longing for some one to talk to.

There are situations and states of mind in which it is quite impossible to remain stationary; a universal irritation of the nervous system, which can only be subdued by overpowering bodily fatigue, and in which sanatory nature instinctively impels to change and exertion.

Things were looking very black. He was not aware, until

the adverse result was actually made known, how much hope he had secretly cherished.

Whirling up the embowered avenue of the quiet Hermitage, with four reeking horses, at a canter—he would have had six if they would have brought him there five minutes sooner— Charles Marston reached the steps of the old-fashioned house ; and running up them, he thundered and rang at the hall-door as impetuously as if his best-beloved lay within, in the agonies of death, and he had arrived with a specific in his hand.

On learning that Miss Medwyn was in the drawing-room, without waiting to be announced, he hurried to the room, and found her with Mr. Dawe, who had arrived only ten minutes before.

Mr. Dawe had other things beside this to trouble him. A letter had reached him from Captain Vivian, in whom, by a kind of adoption, he took a very near interest, relating what had occurred. Mr. Dawe was angry. He had been tricked in return for years of kindness.

Why should he be surprised or wroth ? If it were not that every child of earth must learn wisdom for himself in the school of pain and labour, and if experience were orally communicable, as old people are prone to fancy, and if youth were less conceited and selfish, comparatively few foolish things would be done, and this life would lose, in a large measure, its efficacy as a place of discipline.

Thus, in the rough, the coarse old comedy is true ; a great gulf separates age and youth. The youngsters will, to the end of time, prefer new lamps to old : they will trust their own senses, not yours. Buzz in the ears of your brood that flame burns and cobwebs catch. Their senses tell them that candle-light and warmth are pleasant, and liberty to fly high or low as one pleases ; and, therefore, your love may as well be silent on those subjects. Otherwise you become, in their eyes, but a venerable muff and a bore. Nature has ordained that their nerves shall quiver, as yours have done, and their hearts thump with fear ; and when their turn comes they will scorch their wings, as you have, and make acquaintance with the spider.

Mr. Dawe is going on with this particular news, for reasons which he well knows, to Lady Vernon. She may or may not see him, as she thinks fit ; but she ought to hear it as soon as he ; and he is not deterred by her fierce language of a few weeks ago.

'I must see Lady Vernon first, upon quite another matter,' said Mr. Dawe, therefore, mysteriously. 'But I will meet you, Mr. Marston, in town, at my attorney's, this day week. I have put my hand to the plough, and will not look back.'

'Could you not name an earlier day?' urged Mr. Marston.

'This day week, if you please,' said Mr. Dawe.

'And where will a letter find you in the meantime?' asked active Miss Medwyn, who rather likes writing notes.

'I shall sleep, to-morrow night, at the Vernon Arms; and I may not leave Roydon till evening. I have business in the neighbourhood.'

And so Mr. Dawe took his leave.

A week's wait, to a man upon the rack, is a good deal. It was quite impossible that Charles Marston should be quiet all that time.

Maximilla liked his impatience, and sympathized with all his unreasonableness.

'Quite accidentally,' she said, 'I heard such a character of Doctor Antomarchi, from our rector, here; he had a cousin who was confined at Glarewoods, and discharged about a year ago; and he says that Doctor Antomarchi is quite a charming person, and the kindest man you can imagine; and he thought Mr. Damian, on the contrary, a severe man, with hardly a human sympathy, although his establishment is conducted on very genial and indulgent principles. His view of Mr. Damian corresponds very much with your impression, on seeing him at Brighton. He thought him conscientious, but cold and stern. Now, I have taken a whim into my head; I don't know why, but I do fancy if we went to Glarewoods and saw Doctor Antomarchi, to-day, some good might come of it. I think he would allow me to see Maud, and I have been two or three times on the point of ordering the carriage, and setting out for the railway.'

Full of this whimsical presentiment I shall leave her, still in conference with Charles Marston, who is only too well pleased to find the active old lady almost as restless as himself.

Night descended on Glarewoods, and all the country round. Moonlight falls on lofty masses of foliage, and dark yew hedges, on high, carved chimneys, steep roofs, and black oak cage-work, with white plaster between. From long rows of windows overlooking the croquet-ground peeps the peculiar soft light emitted through the dull globes fixed in the ceilings of the patients' rooms. This was not one of the festive nights at Glarewoods, and neither ball nor concert stirred the strange gaiety of the colony that dwells there.

The great house, with its sylvan surroundings, looks all serenity and happiness; more like fair Belmont, as Lorenzo and Jessica beheld it in the moonlight, than a madhouse.

A visitor is closeted with Antomarchi. It is Doctor Malkin, who has come from Roydon, to talk and hear, on Lady Vernon's behalf, all that it may at this moment concern her to communicate or to learn.

They have had their conference, and have dined together. They are sitting now at an open window, looking out on the moon-lighted croquet-ground. A small round table, with decanters and glasses on it, stands close by; they are sipping their claret, with their eyes turned toward the drooping flowers and dewy foliage, while they talk for a minute longer about Miss Vernon.

Candles are burning at the further end of the room. They prefer the open window and the moon.

'You and Miss Medwyn are at issue respecting the young lady's state of mind,' said Antomarchi.

'I am a very secondary opinion on the question,' answered Malkin, peering into the claret in his glass; 'you may observe that I contribute, myself, next to nothing to the proof, and rest my opinion entirely upon the assumption that the evidence on which I found it is strictly true; and I have been looking the subject up, and I'm not afraid to maintain that opinion anywhere.'

'Nor am I; nor is Damian,' said Antomarchi. 'She is violent; she was troublesome this morning. To-morrow, at twelve, I have arranged to give that young lady a lesson that will a good deal tame her.'

'It is a very sad case,' murmured Doctor Malkin, still looking down with a gloomy shake of his head.

'Very,' echoed Antomarchi abstractedly.

And there followed a silence, during which Darkdale enters the room.

'Miss Medwyn, the old lady who was here before the commissioners,' Mr. Darkdale said softly, leaning over his shoulder, 'is in the waiting-room, with a friend, and hopes that you will see her, and desires me to say, that she is most anxious to visit Miss Vernon, for ever so short a time, in her room.'

'Tell her I regret I can't possibly permit an interview with Miss Vernon ; but that I shall be very happy, in a few minutes, to see Miss Medwyn in the waiting-room.'

'I remember you, Antomarchi, in Paris,' said Doctor Malkin, as soon as Darkdale was gone. 'You and I have played billiards there, and could hardly afford our demi-tasse of coffee after. I little fancied I should see you what you are. I wish you would tell me your secret ; what god do you worship ? Æsculapius, Fortune, Satan ? Do give a poor devil a wrinkle.'

'Fill your glass ; take comfort ; I'm not quite so prosperous as you fancy. I have burnt my fingers a little in that cursed thing that old Tintern went into ; but, as you say, I am making way, notwithstanding.'

'Making way ? Why, my dear fellow, you know all this must belong to you, it *must*, and managed as you would do it, it is the revenue of a principality. When does old Damian return ?'

'In a month, perhaps ; perhaps in six ; perhaps *never*,' says Antomarchi, who is in a state of luxurious good-humour. 'It is high time he should take a little rest ; it is only fair. He can't be many months at this side of seventy, and he may sing *Non sum qualis eram.*'

'I am not what I used to was,' translated Doctor Malkin facetiously.

'He does not like work as he used,' continued Antomarchi, 'and he has confidence in me ; and he feels he need not fatigue himself as he used ; he may take his ease, and yet all go well.'

'All go *better*,' said Malkin.

'I did not say *that ;* but it is not a great way from the truth. He is sometimes a little bit in one's way ; but his name in the concern is valuable, and he is a good man ; and always, at least, *means* well.'

'He'll make over the whole concern to you before a year, on an annuity, and he won't live three years after ; and then you are monarch of all you survey ! You'll be wanting a sharp fellow to play second fiddle, eh ? And if you think *I* would answer, it is the kind of thing I should like.'

'First make me "monarch of all I survey." It would be idle choosing my man Friday till I get upon my island.'

A slight noise at the other end of the room attracted the eyes of both. They saw a tall, broad-shouldered man in a short black cloak, with a resolute face, and hair white as snow, standing near the door, hat in hand, as if off a journey.

With an odd sensation, for he did not know at what moment he had entered, Doctor Malkin, sitting in the moonlight with his claret glass in his fingers, recognised Mr. Damian, exhibited, like a figure of Schalkin's, partly in deep shadow, and partly in the oblique candle-light.

CHAPTER LXXXVI.

LIGHT.

'How d'ye do, Doctor Malkin?' said Mr. Damian, with a short nod. 'I called at Roydon Hall to-day, only an hour after you had left it. How d'ye do, Antomarchi?' Antomarchi had walked up to him, and extended his hand, which Damian took, and shook civilly, but with no great fervour. 'I have come here to-day,' he continued, 'about Miss Vernon's case; I'm not quite satisfied about it. I ought to have stayed perhaps to see her. We could then have consulted. But it seemed on the statement a very clear case. Had I known that her family were divided on the point, I should have thought twice.'

'I can't say *that*,' said Antomarchi promptly. 'There is no division of the family, sir; but one dissentient, an old lady, Miss Medwyn, who said her say here, and nothing in it. Mr. Dawe is no relation, Mr. Marston is none; although,' he sneered, 'I'm told he has no objection to become one.'

'I had a letter from Mr. Dawe this morning,' said Damian.

'He's a very strong partisan,' observed Antomarchi, with a faint smile.

'Yes,' acquiesced Damian, and turned to Malkin.

'You recollect, sir, the substance of your statement?' said Damian. 'May I put two or three questions to you upon it?'

Damian sat down, and he and Malkin had a short talk; and Damian thanked him in a gentle abstraction, like a man who is meditating on the materials of an hypothesis.

A few minutes later, Doctor Malkin had taken his leave, and was on his way to the railway. He did not care to get deeper than was necessary into this business.

Damian was still sitting in his cloak, his white head leaning on his hand, thinking.

On a sudden looking up, he said gently :

' We may as well see the young lady now.'

' Don't you think, sir, it may be a little late ?' suggested Antomarchi.

Damian looked at his watch.

' I think not; only a quarter past eight,' said he. ' Let the young lady decide. I shall send the message, *so.* We can see her in the office.'

Thither they went.

' I am very glad on my own acccount you have come, sir. I was glad to have even Mr. Dawe, the other day ; when a question *is* raised, it is not pleasant to be quite alone.'

' I'm sure of it,' said Damian.

He touched the office-bell, and told the servant to send Mr. Darkdale to him.

He charged that officer with his message to Miss Vernon ; and when he had gone, he sent for the ' register' and the ' ledger' of the establishment ; and those ponderous folios were brought in and laid upon the table.

' You will see in the ledger a reference to a letter of Lady Vernon's, it is intended only for *your* eye and mine,' said Antomarchi, a little grimly, his head higher than usual.

' In the *ledger ?* You mean the register, I suppose ?' said Damian.

' No—the ledger,' said Antomarchi coolly.

' Then it refers to *terms,*' said Damian.

' Certainly ; this is it.'

He had taken from the office-desk a letter, which looked more like a law paper, folded attorney fashion, and he placed it on the ledger which was before Damian.

At this moment the door opened, and Miss Vernon, followed by Mercy Creswell, came in.

The young lady was looking pale and ill.

Damian stood up, and received her with a bow, courteously, and, taking her by the hand, he led her to a chair.

' Don't be frightened, Miss Vernon,' he said. ' I merely want to talk a little with you, and to ask you how you are ; and I assure you there is nothing to make you the least uncomfortable in anything that has passed between Doctor Antomarchi and me. Therefore, you must not be nervous ; and if you would prefer to-morrow, or any other time, we can put off our little conversation, and there is nothing critical in it, we can repeat it as often as you please; so that should you feel nervous or put out at one time, you will not be so at another; and I make every allowance for a little flurry and embarrassment.'

'I should much rather you ask me any question you please, *now;* but not here.'

'And why not here?' he asked, with a smile.

'I can't answer collectedly while Doctor Antomarchi fixes his eyes on me; I am nervous while I am in the same room.'

Antomarchi smiled oddly and shrugged, looking at Damian.

'Perhaps, Antomarchi, you would kindly leave us for a little——'

'*Certainly*,' he exclaims with sudden alacrity, and another little shrug; and so he leaves the room.

Then Damian, not looking at her otherwise than a well-bred old gentleman might, began to tell her of his journey, and fifty other things, and so drew her into talk, and now and then, adroitly, he insinuated a question; and after fifteen minutes or so, at the end of their interview, he said:

'You would be glad to hear I have no objection to your seeing Miss Medwyn, or any other friend who calls; you may write to any one you please, and your letters shall reach you without being opened; and your stay here will be a short one.'

Old Mr. Damian, wrinkled, haggard, white-haired, as he spoke these words, looked, she thought, like an angel of light. She could have fallen on her knees, and kissed his feet.

He talked a little more, encouragingly and kindly. Maud could say nothing; she was crying vehemently.

By his direction Mercy Creswell returned; and to her he put many questions; all which she answered with the directness of fear. So she, in turn, was dismissed.

A few minutes more and he was sitting there alone, leaning on his hand, which shaded his eyes, in deep thought. He touched the bell, and sent for Antomarchi.

'Where is the letter you spoke of? Oh, *here*,' said Damian.

He put on his glasses, and untied the red tape, and opened the paper.

'This is an agreement,' he observed.

As he read on, he drew back his head a little from it, as if he had seen a centipede or a wasp on the page. He knit his brows and held it closer to the candle, and his countenance darkened as he read on; and when he had come to the end, with the same severe aspect, he read it over again more rapidly, and threw it down on the table. Then he looked to the index of the huge ledger, and opened at the 'folio' indicated as that containing the account of Lady Vernon of Roydon, for her daughter, Miss Maud Guendoline Vernon, for residence, expenses, advice, etc., etc. [See letter, August the 19th, 1862.] He let the ledger shut with a heavy slap, and took a turn or two in silence up and down the room.

Damian stopped at the other side of the table, looking stern and pale, and said :

'The evidence in Miss Vernon's case looks very well on paper. But it won't stand the test. I saw Lady Vernon to-day. I sifted hers. She could not evade my questions. Those threats of suicide melt into mere follies of temper. I have examined Creswell respecting the alleged threat and attempt *here. That* was temper also. The girl had no more real idea of killing herself than Creswell had. If I had not believed her mother's testimony on the point of suicide, I should have insisted on evidence of more developed symptoms than are set out in the statement. You observe there is no pretence of any delusion !'

Antomarchi assented and said :

'But that is not necessary to constitute insanity.'

'No, quite right,' said Damian. 'We need not to be told, at this time of day, that delusion is not necessary to constitute insanity. We have had here,' he pondered, 'too many cases of melancholia, of mania in its slighter degrees, and of suicidal mania fully developed, to require the presence of delusion as a test. But there is no impulse to suicide here. The evidence of Elihu Lizard without this is not enough. It is explained away by the statement, very clear and sensible, of Miss Medwyn, which reached me last night in a letter from Mr. Dawe, and I am informed that Elihu Lizard is in custody, the judge before whom he appeared in a will case having directed a prosecution for perjury against him.'

'Really? Why, he was a shining light in the religious firmament,' observed Antomarchi, with an effort, and a grim smile.

'Lastly, I have had a long conversation with the young lady. It has satisfied me. She shall leave us forthwith.'

Antomarchi smiled, but his face darkened.

'I am very glad, sir, you take so decided a view. I told the commissioner, Mr. Steele, and all Miss Vernon's friends, that I should be for my part only too glad to be relieved of the responsibility. It is an ugly case.'

'It was *not* an ugly case,' said old Damian, sternly, 'until that letter was written and received. Has it been acted upon?'

'Of course; there has been the outfit, and the furniture, and decoration.'

'How much money has been paid?'

'Two thousand five hundred pounds.'

'And all the plate, china, furniture, and so forth belong to this establishment, and five thousand a-year for the maintenance of one girl!'

'With servants and carriage for her exclusive use,' said Antomarchi.

'All which would not have cost us seven hundred a year,' added Damian. 'I wish I had known of the existence of that letter to-day,' and Damian struck the knuckles of his open hand upon it sharply; 'and I should have held different language to my Lady Vernon.'

Damian turned and resumed his impatient walk up and down the room.

'If I had thought it the least excessive, I should have been the last man to agree to it, as little likely, I hope, as you, sir,' said Antomarchi sternly.

'It can't bear the light,' said Damian. 'It is a very black case.'

'You'll please not to apply such terms to anything *I* have sanctioned,' said Antomarchi. 'I suppose we are to do something more than simply pay expenses here? I rather think we have a right to profits; and considering all our labour and responsibilities, *large* profits too. I might have hid that letter from you, if I had been what you, I think, dare not insinuate.'

He might have added that he had seriously thought of doing so, but rejected it as too hazardous a game.

'I have passed through life with honour,' continued Damian. 'To think that my house and name should be abused to such a purpose!'

Antomarchi's pale face glared angrily after the old man as he walked toward the upper end of the room.

'It *is* the right course,' mused Damian gloomily to himself. 'I have been long enough here. I think I shall relinquish it.'

Antomarchi heard these words with a presentiment that the retirement which he had long looked forward to was imminent.

After an interval, Damian arrested his walk suddenly, opposite to Antomarchi, and looking him sternly in the face, he said :

'I shall break up this establishment.'

'Break it up ?' There was a long pause here. 'Transfer it, I fancy you mean,' remarked Antomarchi.

'Transfer it ; to whom ?' said Damian.

'To me, of course,' answered Antomarchi insolently.

'Certainly not,' answered the old man ; 'we part, you and I, forthwith.'

'You'll think twice before you try that,' said Antomarchi, his black beard and brows looking blacker as his face whitened and his eyes gleamed.

'*More* than twice. I can take no step till to-morrow ; but *then* I'll do it.'

'See, old man,' said Antomarchi, with a voice of constrained fury, so intense that he might have been on the point of striking him ; 'I have given many of the best years of my life to maintaining your enormous revenues, and, by my priceless exertions, supporting your undeserved reputation. I have no notion of being *sold* by you. I'm a partner, and if you presume intentionally to hurt the business of this concern, to the value of a guinea, I'll make you repent it.'

'My powers, under our deed, are clear ; I mean to act upon them,' said Damian, with cold decision.

'You mean to say that letter is a covenant to *bribe* us ; that I have sold myself to a *conspiracy*, of which Lady Vernon is the mainspring, and her daughter the victim, and that your superior conscience and delicacy interpose to save her ? I'll compel you to define,' thundered Antomarchi.

Damian made him no answer.

'You have lost your head, sir, and as your partner, I shall look after my property, and see that you are restrained from inflicting the injury you meditate. I have more lines of attack than you are, perhaps, prepared for.' Antomarchi smiled with a baleful eye on the resolute old man as he said this. 'You have taken the letter,' he added, 'you will be good enough to replace it in the office-desk.'

'One moment,' said Damian, who had been writing a few

lines on two sheets of note-paper, and now rose and touched the bell. He desired the servant to send Mr. Darkdale, who forthwith was there.

'Take this copy, Mr. Darkdale, and compare, as I read the original aloud. Doctor Antomarchi, this is addressed to you.'

And he read aloud a formal notice of the dissolution of partnership, which he then handed to Antomarchi.

'And take notice, Mr. Darkdale,' said Antomarchi, 'original and copy are no better than waste paper.'

'To-night, or to-morrow, which you please, you shall have a cheque for the liquidated sum, to which, on retirement, you are entitled by the deed,' said old Damian, as he withdrew, with the grim formality of a bow.

Antomarchi laughed with stentorian scorn. He was not a devil to be easily cast out. His cool and vigorous head was machinating mischief.

In the meantime, having learned that Miss Medwyn was in the waiting-room, Damian proceeded thither, and having heard her request, instantly granted it, shook Mr. Marston by the hand, and added :

'I have now considered Miss Vernon's case, and I am clear that she is and always has been of perfectly sound mind.'

After immense jubilation, and a tempest of tears from Miss Medwyn, came the happy thought.

'And she may leave this, with me, to-night ?'

'I see no objection ; but you must give me a letter to say that you receive her only till her proper guardians shall have made their wishes known.'

CHAPTER LXXXVII.

THE ANTE-CHAMBER.

I NEED not trouble you with details. That night Maud Vernon was free, and slept under the roof of the pleasant Hermitage.

Charles Marston passed the night at the Star and Garter, at Wybourne, whence he popped in upon the party at breakfast.

Never was so happy a breakfast ; never was known, before or since, so delightful a ramble as followed, among the self-same grassy slopes and lordly trees, near the ivy-bound walls and arches of the ruined manor-house at Wybourne, among which Charles Marston had on a tumultuously happy afternoon, in the early summer, avowed his love for the beautiful stranger, who was then a mystery.

Let us leave them to their happy recollections and foolish talk, and follow a less romantic rambler to his destination.

Mr. Dawe had driven through the town of Roydon the day before. His carriage pulled up at the door of Doctor Malkin. But the physician was making a visit to Lady Vernon, preliminary to his departure for Glarewoods.

Old Mrs. Foljambe, very hot, in a fusty suit of black, for she has just lost a grand-nephew, passing on the dusty road dolorously in the sun, recognises Mr. Dawe, and stops and gives him her fingers, which she leaves in his hand, so that without a very marked rudeness he can't dispose of them, and regain his liberty, while she recounts the vicissitudes of the young man's protracted illness and traits, also of his nurse's, Mrs. Marjoram's, devotion ; and she strongly recommends her to the benevolent protection of Mr. Dawe ; and then she says that Lady Vernon is ill, she understands ; she met Doctor Malkin only an hour ago, 'and he said she can't see visitors, although he was good enough to add that a visit from me would cheer her ; but she is not equal to it.'

'She's ill, eh ?' said Mr. Dawe, changing his plans, and thinking of taking Mr. Tintern first.

'Yes, she's ill,' answered the lady. And hereupon Mrs. Foljambe fell into a melancholy reverie or vacancy, looking at the wheel-tracks on the road, and Mr. Dawe was stealing his hand away, but the slight movement recalled her. I think she had forgot in the meantime what they were talking upon, for she looked about a little dazed, and she said gently, 'That is the house, with the tree near it, you see,' and she nodded toward a particular house, and then her lack-lustre eyes lighted mournfully on Mr. Dawe, who with laudable presence of mind plucked his hand away to point towards the house she had indicated.

'Is that it ?' he asks.

'Yes, they lived there, Anne Pluggs and Julia Pluggs, most respectable poor women ; there were two. They had been in situations as cooks, and Mr. Foljambe thought them most deserving women, and so did I; and about sixteen years ago they gave up the house and went to Coventry.'

'Yes, you told me that,' interrupted Mr. Dawe, who knew the story, 'and they set up a pastrycook's shop, I know, and—good-bye, ma'am—they are doing very well. Pray present my best respects to the vicar.'

Mr. Dawe, full of his coming interview with Mr. Tintern, got into his vehicle without trusting his hand again on Mrs. Foljambe's and ordered the man to drive to the Grange; and Mrs. Foljambe laid her hand, in a shabby black glove, on the window, and said, with a sigh:

'And they sent us a present of mince-pies last Christmas. Wasn't it thoughtful?'

'Very,' said Mr. Dawe sternly, and made a bow, and the horses got into motion, and Mrs. Foljambe was left musing.

Mr. Dawe, in due time, reached the Grange, but his talk with Mr. Tintern was not satisfactory.

He had some difficulty in finding him. He was taking a furious walk in his wide plantations, switching the heads off nettles, kicking the withered cones of the pines when they came in his way, and jabbering fiercely to himself. He found him, at last, in the depths of his solitudes of pine and larch.

Mr. Tintern knew nothing about the 'young people,' and desired to know nothing. He hoped to God he might never see his daughter's face again. He hoped they might come to the workhouse, and he had many other pleasant things to say in the same vein.

Mr. Dawe talked as if he took an interest in the young man, and confessed that he intended doing something handsome for him, if Mr. Tintern would contribute in a fair proportion; and now came Mr. Tintern's bleak and furious confession of ruin, as he stood white under the black shadow of his pine-trees, shaking his walking-cane in his clenched fist in the face of an imaginary persecutor, and making the brown colonnades of his sober trees ring with threats, and boasts, and blasphemies; and then the thin old coxcomb, overcome by self-commiseration, on a sudden broke down, and began to cry hysterically.

'I say it's awful; you ought to consider; it was you who brought that d—d fellow down here; and he has been more than half the ruin of me; and now that the thing is past cure, I think you are bound to use your influence with Lady Vernon to exercise her power of appointment under the will in my favour.

It would enable me to do what you wish—for I could raise money on it, and she might as well do that, as give it to strangers, or let it go to charitable institutions, that no one cares a curse about. I wish you would—won't you? *Do*, like a good fellow; *promise* me; and, upon my soul, if I get it, I'll make whatever settlements you ask me, in reason. You may believe me; by Heaven I will!'

Perhaps Mr. Dawe was thinking in the same direction, for he grunted rather in the tone of assent. And having heard enough of the sort of declamation in which Mr. Tintern shone just then, and observing that the sun was near the horizon, he took his leave, simply promising, in perfect good faith, to see what could be done, and so made his escape; the conversation had never once touched upon the situation of Miss Vernon. Mr. Tintern's egotism was absorbed, for the present, by his last and greatest misfortune.

It was too late, by the time Mr. Dawe reached the town of Roydon, to think of going up to the Hall, to try whether Lady Vernon would see him. He therefore put up for the night at the Vernon Arms, and next day walked up to Roydon Hall.

On the avenue he was met and passed by no less than two carriages. These visitors had been merely leaving cards, and inquiring how Lady Vernon was. A rumour had got abroad that she was ailing, and the county, we know, could not spare her.

Mr. Dawe, with his usual forecast, had come provided with a note, at which, he thought, her doors would most likely open to him.

In the meantime he stood upon the steps, looking down the avenue, between the double files of lordly trees, whose foliage was already thinned and yellowed in the suns and winds of autumn.

That queer little black-wigged man had, perhaps, his feeling of the picturesque, as handsomer people have. He had paid more than you would have thought for the exquisite little landscapes that hung upon his walls at East Mauling. I should not wonder if he had his secret poetry, and deeper still, his secret and early romance. It is hard to say what may be in a man so reserved as he, and so sensitive, that he takes vows of silence, and wears the habit of a cynic.

The footman now comes to say that Lady Vernon will see him; and he follows, not to his left, as he enters, where, at the front of the house, lie the long suite of drawing-rooms, but to the right, beyond the shield-room, where, at the rear, a different suite of rooms is placed.

Into one of these he is shown ; a square room with a single window, through which you see the funereal yew worked into cloistered walls and arches, and a sombre tree standing near, which keeps the room in perpetual shadow. The heavy curtains hide part of the window, and increase the gloom. Some bygone Vernon seems to have got up this apartment under a caprice of melancholy.

There are three pictures, with something *funeste* in each. The first represents a frowning forest glade, that looks as if sun had never shown there, nor bird sung in its leaves ; such a forest as Dante may have seen ; with a black marble tomb with sombre underwood, and weeds drooping over it, near the front, and a solitary figure like a shadow looking back upon it, over his shoulder, and gliding away among the obscure trees into the deeper darkness. Opposite the window is a fine picture of Cleopatra fainting, with the asp to her bosom. And at the right, scarcely a foot between the floor and the lower end of the frame, hangs a large repulsive painting of the death of Sapphira. It is powerful, but odious. She lies distorted on the oak flooring, a strip of tapestry, with Dutch anachronism, torn in her convulsive fall from the wall in her dead hand, her jaw fallen, her eyes nothing but white; almost the only light in the picture is that one beam which strikes on the bald head of Peter, who looks ferocious as a brigand. The 'young men,' who are stooping to carry her out smile like ghouls, in cynical sympathy with the dealer of death ; and behind, row after row, till they disappear in the deepening shadow, the spectators, like ghosts awaiting judgment, stand with dim long faces, white and horror-stricken.

He has time enough to examine these saturnine old pictures, and has more than once peeped at his watch.

At length the thin figure of Latimer, in her accustomed black silk, appears in the doorway close beside the evil-minded 'young men,' and the corpse in the shadow ; and she looks like a lean matron introduced to show them the way to the dead-house.

'Please, Mr. Dawe, sir, her ladyship has a bad headache ; nothing more, she desires me to say ; but she is not equal to much exertion, and if you would please to excuse her dressing-gown and slippers, and to make any business you may have as short as you can, she would feel it a kindness.'

'Certainly, not five minutes if I can help it,' said he.

'This way please, sir.'

And she led the way into a darksome, but long and stately room.

The shutters of the window next the door are partly open, but the blind down. Those of the remaining two are closed, and the curtains also. The whole room therefore is lighted by less than half a window; and so imperfectly at the upper end, that on first coming in you could not discern objects there.

CHAPTER LXXXVIII.

LADY VERNON LEAVES ROYDON.

'THIS is Mr. Dawe, please, my lady,' says Latimer, and withdrew softly.

'How do you do, Mr. Dawe?' says the well-known sweet voice from the darkened part of the room; 'I'm suffering from headache; but take a chair, where there is a little light, and I'll come as near as I can bear.'

He saw a white figure moving slowly towards him; and soon it emerged in the twilight; and Lady Vernon appeared. She had a loose grey dress on, of a very thick soft silk. She pointed to a chair more in the light, which accordingly Dawe took; she herself sat down, and appeared a little out of breath.

He was shocked at the change he observed. She had grown thin, and it seemed to him stooped, and was deadly pale, except for a hectic spot in each cheek, which used to come only with agitation. Her eyes looked larger and fiercer, but had the glassy look that strangely suited her peaked features.

She looked sinister as the woman of Endor. He thought the hand of death was on her.

He relented, though his brown corded face and prominent eyes showed no sign, and he said:

'You look ill, Barbara; you must be ill. Who is attending you?'

'No one; I prescribe for myself; it is not anything serious; and I know what suits me.'

'You ought to have the best advice from town,' he persisted. 'And, and, Barbara, I have known you in your cradle; I have had you on my knee; you'll shake hands with me.'

He had approached, with his brown hand extended.

'Another time; not to-day,' she said coldly; 'pray take my own account of it; I am *not* seriously ill; and be kind enough not to tell my friends that I am dying; I'm bored to death by calls and notes; I shall be quite well in a week. What about Elwyn? *Do* say at once; I implore of you, come to the point.'

'I find that Elwyn Howard, or Vivian, your son, is the person who has married Miss Ethel Tintern.'

'I knew it, I guessed it,' she said, after a pause. 'There is always a shock when surmises turn out true; but I was sure it was so. I am glad and grieved—I hate the Tinterns.'

'I had a letter this morning from Miss Medwyn,' says Mr. Dawe. 'She says that Damian pronounces Maud perfectly well, and has sent her away in Maximilla's care from Glarewoods.'

'Mr. Damian is doting; but that doesn't excuse his writing libels,' said Lady Vernon, flushing all over a bright scarlet, and then growing deadly pale. 'I had a letter of insinuation and insult from him this morning, which he shall rue. I'm glad Maud is set at liberty without my sanction; let her kill me, or kill herself; what does it matter, compared with the tragedy she threatened, and which is now impossible?'

Mr. Dawe nodded, and in a few moments said:

'I have seen Mr. Tintern.'

'The wretch!' whispered she, looking down steadfastly on the floor; you might have fancied a Canidia looking down on the blood of her enemy. 'He was the contriver of all that misery. He thought that you would provide for the young man. He is utterly false.'

'I believe he had quite other intentions for the young lady,' said Dawe.

'*Don't* believe it; what better could a country squire do for his daughter? Mr. Tintern never goes straight to anything. You never discover what he intends, except by his bad acting. And to think of their having caught my beautiful boy in their toils! When he came here ill, he looked so like my own noble Elwyn, the sight of him almost broke my heart. You must bring him to see me; I have made up my mind to tell him everything. He shall know his father, and his poor, broken-hearted mother.'

'Well, Barbara, I fear you are exerting yourself too much One thing I mention for your consideration. Use your power of appointment under the will in favour of Tintern, and you can dictate his settlements for your son, and thus provide for him handsomely.'

'It is too late. I executed a deed which excludes him irrevocably ; and it is in Mr. Coke's custody.'

There was a silence here of some seconds.

'You might have consulted me, or some one, with more caution than yourself, Barbara, before taking such a step,' said Dawe, at length.

'It *is* taken, and no power on earth can recall it,' she said coldly.

'It is a pity,' said Dawe. After a short silence, 'I am told there is not a nicer girl in England than Ethel Tintern.'

'I hope she mayn't live long,' said Lady Vernon, in her cold tones. ' "Vengeance is mine ; I will repay, saith the Lord." Let His justice be done, and my poor Elwyn released from the wicked conspirator who deceived him. Ill as I am,' she continued, after a pause ; 'I have written to Mr. Coke to come down to consult upon the letter of that slanderous old man, Mr. Damian ; I have walked with God all my days, why will He not spare me one drop in this dreadful cup ? I have lived a life of virtue. I have done my duty. I have nothing to retract ; nothing to repent of. I will see Maud's face no more. She has never been a child to me. She has been the source of half my misery. Another parent would leave her with a curse. I turn from her in silence. Good people understand and honour me. The wicked I trample under my feet. "These speak evil of those things which they know not." ' She made her quotation with a low utterance, and with a slow and bitter emphasis. She was talking, as it were, to herself. ' "Woe unto them, for they have gone in the way of Cain, and perished in the gainsaying of Core. These are spots in your feasts of charity. Trees whose fruit withereth, without fruit, twice dead, plucked up by the roots ; wandering stars, to whom is reserved the blackness of darkness—for ever." '

She turned as she said this, and Mr. Dawe thought she was weeping, for he observed one or two little sobs.

Latimer, a minute after, in the adjoining room, heard a hoarse voice calling her in strange, loud accents. At sound of this discordant summons, through Latimer's brain, with a sure omen, flashed a dreadful suspicion.

Now she is in the room, she does not know how, stooping over the chair, calling distractedly, ' My lady ! my lady !' in an ear that will never hear sound again. She is holding her up in the chair, but the head sinks and rolls, this way or that, as its weight inclines. ' 'Tis a faint ! 'tis a faint ! my God ! 'Tis only a faint !' Latimer cries wildly in her terror.

Mr. Dawe has thrown open the shutter, the window itself ; and the fitful autumn air eddies in, and the elegant little lace coiffure and its long, dark, grey-and-blue silk ribbons flutter about the dead face and open mouth. Mr. Dawe has sprinkled water on her face—dashed water. It streams over it as it would over a marble bust.

Latimer despairs ; she cries out the awful name of the Creator. ' What is it, what is it? Is she gone? Oh ! she's gone, she *is* gone ! she's *gone !*'

Mr. Dawe at the door is calling for help, and soon many feet and voices are in the room. Strange liberties are taken with awful Lady Vernon's sanctuary. The shutters thrown open, the curtains dragged back, furniture wheeled out of the way, huddled together. ' My lady's ' Bible lies flat on its face on the floor with its covers open, beside a gilt candlestick and broken candle ; broken, too, lies the pretty malachite paper-cutter which dead and buried Vicar Howard owned long since, which he had given her three-and-twenty years ago, and which ever since his death has always been beside her. On the carpet are strewn letters and two or three books, and the gold mounted ink-bottle lies on its side on the rich table-cover, as it were in a swoon, and bleeding ink profusely, quite neglected.

The great and faultless Lady Vernon is by this time cooling and stiffening rapidly, on the sofa, a shawl over her feet, her head propped with the pillow, and something under her chin to close her mouth. There are no disclosures of 'making up.' The tints on her cheeks fade naturally into the proper hue of death ; and her fine teeth were all her own. Her large grey eyes are now, one at least, quite shut ; there is a little glitter perceptible under the lashes of the other. This solitary lady, with one great and untold affection among the living, one passionate affection among the dead, is more alone than ever now. Her pride, her passion, her strong affections, her wickedness, the whole story of her life, signed, sealed, and delivered, and passed out of her keeping now.

A servant is galloping by this time half-way to Shillingsworth to bring the doctor, the Roydon doctor not yet having returned, and Mr. Dawe wishing some skilled inspection in the case of so great a lady.

All goes on as usual. The little town recovers from its momentary stupor. The scepticism of startled people subsides, and the great conviction is established. Lady Vernon of Roydon is dead.

Mr. Dawe remains at the Vernon Arms ; Mr. Coke arrives, letters are flying in all directions. Lady Vernon's will has never been executed. She had not been able quite to make up her mind upon some points, and had no idea that her hour was so near.

The letters that radiate from the Hall to many scores of other homes, chiefly of the great, announce that the physicians agree in referring the sad event to heart-complaint, developed with unusual rapidity.

CONCLUSION.

THE remainder of my story pretty nearly tells itself.

In Lady Vernon's secret marriage with the vicar, Elwyn Howard, there was no taint of guilt. There was extreme rashness. Each honestly believed that the artful person whom he had married in his romantic nonage, and lived with little more than a week, had been dead for years. Her own family had not only published her death, but sworn to the fact, and actually administered some trifling property of hers. It was not until after his marriage, not his seeking, but urged upon him by the wayward and impassioned girl, that the dreadful uncertainty of the situation was for the first time suspected. The story is curious, but true. The spoiled girl had revealed her marriage to no one. It was not until circumstances compelled her to choose between confidence or exposure, that she disclosed her situation. Mr. Dawe was the sole confidant of her parents in this dark emergency in family history. By his advice the young lady and her father set out as if for a short tour on the Continent. The journey diverged and really ended in a sequestered place near a little Welsh village. Here the child of this ill-fated and invalid marriage was born. Mr. Dawe undertook to direct every particular respecting its early care, its subsequent education, and final position in life.

They were to leave in a day or two, and to return home, in a little time, by a very wide circuit, having taken every precaution necessary for a complete mystification of the good gossips of Roydon, when who should light upon them, traversing a path through the very grounds of the house they inhabited, but about the most unlikely man in the world to be found in that seques-tered corner, Sir Amyrald Vernon, the young lady's rejected suitor. He saw signs of alarm and agitation in both, on recog-nising him, by no means to be accounted for by an accidental meeting with a rejected lover.

They departed; but he remained, and without disclosing their real names, he made himself master of their secret. He tracked Mr. Dawe, and insisted that he should be taken into confidence, and took such a tone, that with the advice of the young lady's father, Mr. Dawe told him the facts of the case, which, painful as they were, yet supplied an answer to suspicions of a more degrading kind.

It was the possession of this secret that enabled him, after the death of the vicar, to bend that proud young lady to his will.

I now turn to Charles Marston and Maud Vernon, who, in due time, there being no longer any let or hindrance, were united. At present they live very much abroad; and when in England they do not stay at Roydon, which the young lady associates with many painful recollections, but at their beautiful house of Darrel Abbey.

Doctor Malkin was one of those persons whom Lady Vernon's death disappointed. He wishes very much he had been a little less active in managing that Glarewood's affair. But who could have supposed that Lady Vernon would have died before the appointments she intended for him were filled up? He has no liking for the young lady. But for reasons of his own he never hints at that secret, and the good people of Roydon had been led to believe that she was, during her absence, making a little tour for her health.

Antomarchi, finding old Damian resolute against committing to him, after the disclosures of which he took so strong a view, a trust so awful as the autocracy of such an empire as Glare-woods, took steps in the Court of Chancery to restrain Mr. Damian from breaking up that establishment, and selling the house and grounds.

This attempt recoiled upon himself. The court read him an astounding lecture on the facts. The press took it up; and that able adventurer found that England was no longer a field for his talents.

I have heard various accounts of the after career of that brilliant rogue, some of which represent him in sore straits; others, following dark and downward paths, picking gold and silver, 'on Jews' ground,' but in danger, all the while, of breaking his neck, and quite lost sight of by the decent upper world.

Mr. Tintern is not quite ruined after all, but he has had to sell nearly all his estates, except the Grange, and a rental of about seven hundred a year. He lives in France, and refuses to see Ethel; and I heard this morning from old Puntles, whom I happened to meet, that he has just had a slight paralytic attack. His temper continues precisely in the state in which his misfortunes left it.

The Reverend Michael Doody has been presented to one of the comfortable livings in the gift of the Roydon Vernons. He is a good deal sobered, and has lost something of his wild spirits and eccentricities. But his energy and good-nature are unabated. It is said that he has cast eyes of affection on a niece of Mr. Puntles. But of this I have heard only as rumour, and must, therefore, speak with reserve.

Vivian and Ethel are as happy as any two people, except perhaps Charles Marston, now Lord Warhampton, and his affectionate and beautiful young wife, can be. Charles and Maud have, indeed, little on earth to desire, for an heir is born to the title of Warhampton, and that heir is not without merry little companions in the nursery. Maximilla almost lives with her old friend Maud, and over the gateway of Warhampton stands, in well-chiselled relief, the time-honoured device of

THE ROSE AND THE KEY.

THE END.

A CATALOGUE OF
SELECTED DOVER BOOKS
IN ALL FIELDS OF INTEREST

A CATALOGUE OF SELECTED DOVER
BOOKS IN ALL FIELDS OF INTEREST

RACKHAM'S COLOR ILLUSTRATIONS FOR WAGNER'S RING. Rackham's finest mature work—all 64 full-color watercolors in a faithful and lush interpretation of the *Ring.* Full-sized plates on coated stock of the paintings used by opera companies for authentic staging of Wagner. Captions aid in following complete Ring cycle. Introduction. 64 illustrations plus vignettes. 72pp. 8⅝ x 11¼.   23779-6 Pa. $6.00

CONTEMPORARY POLISH POSTERS IN FULL COLOR, edited by Joseph Czestochowski. 46 full-color examples of brilliant school of Polish graphic design, selected from world's first museum (near Warsaw) dedicated to poster art. Posters on circuses, films, plays, concerts all show cosmopolitan influences, free imagination. Introduction. 48pp. 9⅜ x 12¼.
23780-X Pa. $6.00

GRAPHIC WORKS OF EDVARD MUNCH, Edvard Munch. 90 haunting, evocative prints by first major Expressionist artist and one of the greatest graphic artists of his time: *The Scream, Anxiety, Death Chamber, The Kiss, Madonna,* etc. Introduction by Alfred Werner. 90pp. 9 x 12.
23765-6 Pa. $5.00

THE GOLDEN AGE OF THE POSTER, Hayward and Blanche Cirker. 70 extraordinary posters in full colors, from Maitres de l'Affiche, Mucha, Lautrec, Bradley, Cheret, Beardsley, many others. Total of 78pp. 9⅜ x 12¼.   22753-7 Pa. $5.95

THE NOTEBOOKS OF LEONARDO DA VINCI, edited by J. P. Richter. Extracts from manuscripts reveal great genius; on painting, sculpture, anatomy, sciences, geography, etc. Both Italian and English. 186 ms. pages reproduced, plus 500 additional drawings, including studies for *Last Supper,* Sforza monument, etc. 860pp. 7⅞ x 10¾. (Available in U.S. only)
22572-0, 22573-9 Pa., Two-vol. set $15.90

THE CODEX NUTTALL, as first edited by Zelia Nuttall. Only inexpensive edition, in full color, of a pre-Columbian Mexican (Mixtec) book. 88 color plates show kings, gods, heroes, temples, sacrifices. New explanatory, historical introduction by Arthur G. Miller. 96pp. 11⅜ x 8½. (Available in U.S. only)   23168-2 Pa. $7.95

UNE SEMAINE DE BONTÉ, A SURREALISTIC NOVEL IN COLLAGE, Max Ernst. Masterpiece created out of 19th-century periodical illustrations, explores worlds of terror and surprise. Some consider this Ernst's greatest work. 208pp. 8⅛ x 11.   23252-2 Pa. $6.00

DRAWINGS OF WILLIAM BLAKE, William Blake. 92 plates from Book of Job, *Divine Comedy, Paradise Lost*, visionary heads, mythological figures, Laocoon, etc. Selection, introduction, commentary by Sir Geoffrey Keynes. 178pp. 8⅛ x 11. 22303-5 Pa. $4.00

ENGRAVINGS OF HOGARTH, William Hogarth. 101 of Hogarth's greatest works: *Rake's Progress, Harlot's Progress, Illustrations for Hudibras, Before and After, Beer Street and Gin Lane*, many more. Full commentary. 256pp. 11 x 13¾. 22479-1 Pa. $12.95

DAUMIER: 120 GREAT LITHOGRAPHS, Honore Daumier. Wide-ranging collection of lithographs by the greatest caricaturist of the 19th century. Concentrates on eternally popular series on lawyers, on married life, on liberated women, etc. Selection, introduction, and notes on plates by Charles F. Ramus. Total of 158pp. 9⅜ x 12¼. 23512-2 Pa. $6.00

DRAWINGS OF MUCHA, Alphonse Maria Mucha. Work reveals drafts-man of highest caliber: studies for famous posters and paintings, render-ings for book illustrations and ads, etc. 70 works, 9 in color; including 6 items not drawings. Introduction. List of illustrations. 72pp. 9⅜ x 12¼. (Available in U.S. only) 23672-2 Pa. $4.00

GIOVANNI BATTISTA PIRANESI: DRAWINGS IN THE PIERPONT MORGAN LIBRARY, Giovanni Battista Piranesi. For first time ever all of Morgan Library's collection, world's largest. 167 illustrations of rare Piranesi drawings—archeological, architectural, decorative and visionary. Essay, detailed list of drawings, chronology, captions. Edited by Felice Stampfle. 144pp. 9⅜ x 12¼. 23714-1 Pa. $7.50

NEW YORK ETCHINGS (1905-1949), John Sloan. All of important American artist's N.Y. life etchings. 67 works include some of his best art; also lively historical record—Greenwich Village, tenement scenes. Edited by Sloan's widow. Introduction and captions. 79pp. 8⅜ x 11¼. 23651-X Pa. $4.00

CHINESE PAINTING AND CALLIGRAPHY: A PICTORIAL SURVEY, Wan-go Weng. 69 fine examples from John M. Crawford's matchless private collection: landscapes, birds, flowers, human figures, etc., plus calligraphy. Every basic form included: hanging scrolls, handscrolls, album leaves, fans, etc. 109 illustrations. Introduction. Captions. 192pp. 8⅞ x 11¾. 23707-9 Pa. $7.95

DRAWINGS OF REMBRANDT, edited by Seymour Slive. Updated Lipp-mann, Hofstede de Groot edition, with definitive scholarly apparatus. All portraits, biblical sketches, landscapes, nudes, Oriental figures, classical studies, together with selection of work by followers. 550 illustrations. Total of 630pp. 9⅛ x 12¼. 21485-0, 21486-9 Pa., Two-vol. set $15.00

THE DISASTERS OF WAR, Francisco Goya. 83 etchings record horrors of Napoleonic wars in Spain and war in general. Reprint of 1st edition, plus 3 additional plates. Introduction by Philip Hofer. 97pp. 9⅜ x 8¼. 21872-4 Pa. $4.00

THE EARLY WORK OF AUBREY BEARDSLEY, Aubrey Beardsley. 157 plates, 2 in color: *Manon Lescaut, Madame Bovary, Morte Darthur, Salome,* other. Introduction by H. Marillier. 182pp. 8⅛ x 11. 21816-3 Pa. $4.50

THE LATER WORK OF AUBREY BEARDSLEY, Aubrey Beardsley. Exotic masterpieces of full maturity: *Venus and Tannhauser, Lysistrata, Rape of the Lock, Volpone,* Savoy material, etc. 174 plates, 2 in color. 186pp. 8⅛ x 11. 21817-1 Pa. $5.95

THOMAS NAST'S CHRISTMAS DRAWINGS, Thomas Nast. Almost all Christmas drawings by creator of image of Santa Claus as we know it, and one of America's foremost illustrators and political cartoonists. 66 illustrations. 3 illustrations in color on covers. 96pp. 8⅜ x 11¼. 23660-9 Pa. $3.50

THE DORÉ ILLUSTRATIONS FOR DANTE'S DIVINE COMEDY, Gustave Doré. All 135 plates from Inferno, Purgatory, Paradise; fantastic tortures, infernal landscapes, celestial wonders. Each plate with appropriate (translated) verses. 141pp. 9 x 12. 23231-X Pa. $4.50

DORÉ'S ILLUSTRATIONS FOR RABELAIS, Gustave Doré. 252 striking illustrations of *Gargantua and Pantagruel* books by foremost 19th-century illustrator. Including 60 plates, 192 delightful smaller illustrations. 153pp. 9 x 12. 23656-0 Pa. $5.00

LONDON: A PILGRIMAGE, Gustave Doré, Blanchard Jerrold. Squalor, riches, misery, beauty of mid-Victorian metropolis; 55 wonderful plates, 125 other illustrations, full social, cultural text by Jerrold. 191pp. of text. 9⅜ x 12¼. 22306-X Pa. $7.00

THE RIME OF THE ANCIENT MARINER, Gustave Doré, S. T. Coleridge. Dore's finest work, 34 plates capture moods, subtleties of poem. Full text. Introduction by Millicent Rose. 77pp. 9¼ x 12. 22305-1 Pa. $3.50

THE DORE BIBLE ILLUSTRATIONS, Gustave Doré. All wonderful, detailed plates: Adam and Eve, Flood, Babylon, Life of Jesus, etc. Brief King James text with each plate. Introduction by Millicent Rose. 241 plates. 241pp. 9 x 12. 23004-X Pa. $6.00

THE COMPLETE ENGRAVINGS, ETCHINGS AND DRYPOINTS OF ALBRECHT DURER. "Knight, Death and Devil"; "Melencolia," and more—all Dürer's known works in all three media, including 6 works formerly attributed to him. 120 plates. 235pp. 8⅜ x 11¼. 22851-7 Pa. $6.50

MECHANICK EXERCISES ON THE WHOLE ART OF PRINTING, Joseph Moxon. First complete book (1683-4) ever written about typography, a compendium of everything known about printing at the latter part of 17th century. Reprint of 2nd (1962) Oxford Univ. Press edition. 74 illustrations. Total of 550pp. 6⅛ x 9¼. 23617-X Pa. $7.95

THE COMPLETE WOODCUTS OF ALBRECHT DURER, edited by Dr. W. Kurth. 346 in all: "Old Testament," "St. Jerome," "Passion," "Life of Virgin," Apocalypse," many others. Introduction by Campbell Dodgson. 285pp. 8½ x 12¼.   21097-9 Pa. $7.50

DRAWINGS OF ALBRECHT DURER, edited by Heinrich Wolfflin. 81 plates show development from youth to full style. Many favorites; many new. Introduction by Alfred Werner. 96pp. 8⅛ x 11. 22352-3 Pa. $5.00

THE HUMAN FIGURE, Albrecht Dürer. Experiments in various techniques—stereometric, progressive proportional, and others. Also life studies that rank among finest ever done. Complete reprinting of *Dresden Sketchbook*. 170 plates. 355pp. 8⅜ x 11¼.   21042-1 Pa. $7.95

OF THE JUST SHAPING OF LETTERS, Albrecht Dürer. Renaissance artist explains design of Roman majuscules by geometry, also Gothic lower and capitals. Grolier Club edition. 43pp. 7⅞ x 10¾   21306-4 Pa. $3.00

TEN BOOKS ON ARCHITECTURE, Vitruvius. The most important book ever written on architecture. Early Roman aesthetics, technology, classical orders, site selection, all other aspects. Stands behind everything since. Morgan translation. 331pp. 5⅜ x 8½.   20645-9 Pa. $4.50

THE FOUR BOOKS OF ARCHITECTURE, Andrea Palladio. 16th-century classic responsible for Palladian movement and style. Covers classical architectural remains, Renaissance revivals, classical orders, etc. 1738 Ware English edition. Introduction by A. Placzek. 216 plates. 110pp. of text. 9½ x 12¾.   21308-0 Pa. $10.00

HORIZONS, Norman Bel Geddes. Great industrialist stage designer, "father of streamlining," on application of aesthetics to transportation, amusement, architecture, etc. 1932 prophetic account; function, theory, specific projects. 222 illustrations. 312pp. 7⅞ x 10¾.   23514-9 Pa. $6.95

FRANK LLOYD WRIGHT'S FALLINGWATER, Donald Hoffmann. Full, illustrated story of conception and building of Wright's masterwork at Bear Run, Pa. 100 photographs of site, construction, and details of completed structure. 112pp. 9¼ x 10.   23671-4 Pa. $5.50

THE ELEMENTS OF DRAWING, John Ruskin. Timeless classic by great Vitorian; starts with basic ideas, works through more difficult. Many practical exercises. 48 illustrations. Introduction by Lawrence Campbell. 228pp. 5⅜ x 8½.   22730-8 Pa. $3.75

GIST OF ART, John Sloan. Greatest modern American teacher, Art Students League, offers innumerable hints, instructions, guided comments to help you in painting. Not a formal course. 46 illustrations. Introduction by Helen Sloan. 200pp. 5⅜ x 8½.   23435-5 Pa. $4.00

THE ANATOMY OF THE HORSE, George Stubbs. Often considered the great masterpiece of animal anatomy. Full reproduction of 1766 edition, plus prospectus; original text and modernized text. 36 plates. Introduction by Eleanor Garvey. 121pp. 11 x 14¾.   23402-9 Pa. $6.00

BRIDGMAN'S LIFE DRAWING, George B. Bridgman. More than 500 illustrative drawings and text teach you to abstract the body into its major masses, use light and shade, proportion; as well as specific areas of anatomy, of which Bridgman is master. 192pp. 6½ x 9¼. (Available in U.S. only)
23402-9 Pa. $3.50

ART NOUVEAU DESIGNS IN COLOR, Alphonse Mucha, Maurice Verneuil, Georges Auriol. Full-color reproduction of *Combinaisons ornementales* (c. 1900) by Art Nouveau masters. Floral, animal, geometric, interlacings, swashes—borders, frames, spots—all incredibly beautiful. 60 plates, hundreds of designs. 9⅜ x 8-1/16.   22885-1 Pa. $4.00

FULL-COLOR FLORAL DESIGNS IN THE ART NOUVEAU STYLE, E. A. Seguy. 166 motifs, on 40 plates, from *Les fleurs et leurs applications decoratives* (1902): borders, circular designs, repeats, allovers, "spots." All in authentic Art Nouveau colors. 48pp. 9⅜ x 12¼.
23439-8 Pa. $5.00

A DIDEROT PICTORIAL ENCYCLOPEDIA OF TRADES AND IN-DUSTRY, edited by Charles C. Gillispie. 485 most interesting plates from the great French Encyclopedia of the 18th century show hundreds of working figures, artifacts, process, land and cityscapes; glassmaking, paper-making, metal extraction, construction, weaving, making furniture, clothing, wigs, dozens of other activities. Plates fully explained. 920pp. 9 x 12.
22284-5, 22285-3 Clothbd., Two-vol. set $40.00

HANDBOOK OF EARLY ADVERTISING ART, Clarence P. Hornung. Largest collection of copyright-free early and antique advertising art ever compiled. Over 6,000 illustrations, from Franklin's time to the 1890's for special effects, novelty. Valuable source, almost inexhaustible.
Pictorial Volume. Agriculture, the zodiac, animals, autos, birds, Christmas, fire engines, flowers, trees, musical instruments, ships, games and sports, much more. Arranged by subject matter and use. 237 plates. 288pp. 9 x 12.
20122-8 Clothbd. $14.50

Typographical Volume. Roman and Gothic faces ranging from 10 point to 300 point, "Barnum," German and Old English faces, script, logotypes, scrolls and flourishes, 1115 ornamental initials, 67 complete alphabets, more. 310 plates. 320pp. 9 x 12.   20123-6 Clothbd. $15.00

CALLIGRAPHY (CALLIGRAPHIA LATINA), J. G. Schwandner. High point of 18th-century ornamental calligraphy. Very ornate initials, scrolls, borders, cherubs, birds, lettered examples. 172pp. 9 x 13.
20475-8 Pa. $7.00

ART FORMS IN NATURE, Ernst Haeckel. Multitude of strangely beautiful natural forms: Radiolaria, Foraminifera, jellyfishes, fungi, turtles, bats, etc. All 100 plates of the 19th-century evolutionist's *Kunstformen der Natur* (1904). 100pp. 9⅜ x 12¼.   22987-4 Pa. $5.00

CHILDREN: A PICTORIAL ARCHIVE FROM NINETEENTH-CENTURY SOURCES, edited by Carol Belanger Grafton. 242 rare, copyright-free wood engravings for artists and designers. Widest such selection available. All illustrations in line. 119pp. 8⅜ x 11¼.
23694-3 Pa. $4.00

WOMEN: A PICTORIAL ARCHIVE FROM NINETEENTH-CENTURY SOURCES, edited by Jim Harter. 391 copyright-free wood engravings for artists and designers selected from rare periodicals. Most extensive such collection available. All illustrations in line. 128pp. 9 x 12.
23703-6 Pa. $4.50

ARABIC ART IN COLOR, Prisse d'Avennes. From the greatest ornamentalists of all time—50 plates in color, rarely seen outside the Near East, rich in suggestion and stimulus. Includes 4 plates on covers. 46pp. 9⅜ x 12¼.   23658-7 Pa. $6.00

AUTHENTIC ALGERIAN CARPET DESIGNS AND MOTIFS, edited by June Beveridge. Algerian carpets are world famous. Dozens of geometrical motifs are charted on grids, color-coded, for weavers, needleworkers, craftsmen, designers. 53 illustrations plus 4 in color. 48pp. 8¼ x 11. (Available in U.S. only)   23650-1 Pa. $1.75

DICTIONARY OF AMERICAN PORTRAITS, edited by Hayward and Blanche Cirker. 4000 important Americans, earliest times to 1905, mostly in clear line. Politicians, writers, soldiers, scientists, inventors, industrialists, Indians, Blacks, women, outlaws, etc. Identificatory information. 756pp. 9¼ x 12¾.   21823-6 Clothbd. $40.00

HOW THE OTHER HALF LIVES, Jacob A. Riis. Journalistic record of filth, degradation, upward drive in New York immigrant slums, shops, around 1900. New edition includes 100 original Riis photos, monuments of early photography. 233pp. 10 x 7⅞.   22012-5 Pa. $7.00

NEW YORK IN THE THIRTIES, Berenice Abbott. Noted photographer's fascinating study of city shows new buildings that have become famous and old sights that have disappeared forever. Insightful commentary. 97 photographs. 97pp. 11⅜ x 10.   22967-X Pa. $5.00

MEN AT WORK, Lewis W. Hine. Famous photographic studies of construction workers, railroad men, factory workers and coal miners. New supplement of 18 photos on Empire State building construction. New introduction by Jonathan L. Doherty. Total of 69 photos. 63pp. 8 x 10¾.
23475-4 Pa. $3.00

THE DEPRESSION YEARS AS PHOTOGRAPHED BY ARTHUR ROTH-STEIN, Arthur Rothstein. First collection devoted entirely to the work of outstanding 1930s photographer: famous dust storm photo, ragged children, unemployed, etc. 120 photographs. Captions. 119pp. 9¼ x 10¾.
23590-4 Pa. $5.00

CAMERA WORK: A PICTORIAL GUIDE, Alfred Stieglitz. All 559 illustrations and plates from the most important periodical in the history of art photography, Camera Work (1903-17). Presented four to a page, reduced in size but still clear, in strict chronological order, with complete captions. Three indexes. Glossary. Bibliography. 176pp. 8⅜ x 11¼.
23591-2 Pa. $6.95

ALVIN LANGDON COBURN, PHOTOGRAPHER, Alvin L. Coburn. Revealing autobiography by one of greatest photographers of 20th century gives insider's version of Photo-Secession, plus comments on his own work. 77 photographs by Coburn. Edited by Helmut and Alison Gernsheim. 160pp. 8⅛ x 11.
23685-4 Pa. $6.00

NEW YORK IN THE FORTIES, Andreas Feininger. 162 brilliant photographs by the well-known photographer, formerly with Life magazine, show commuters, shoppers, Times Square at night, Harlem nightclub, Lower East Side, etc. Introduction and full captions by John von Hartz. 181pp. 9¼ x 10¾.
23585-8 Pa. $6.95

GREAT NEWS PHOTOS AND THE STORIES BEHIND THEM, John Faber. Dramatic volume of 140 great news photos, 1855 through 1976, and revealing stories behind them, with both historical and technical information. Hindenburg disaster, shooting of Oswald, nomination of Jimmy Carter, etc. 160pp. 8¼ x 11.
23667-6 Pa. $5.00

THE ART OF THE CINEMATOGRAPHER, Leonard Maltin. Survey of American cinematography history and anecdotal interviews with 5 masters—Arthur Miller, Hal Mohr, Hal Rosson, Lucien Ballard, and Conrad Hall. Very large selection of behind-the-scenes production photos. 105 photographs. Filmographies. Index. Originally Behind the Camera. 144pp. 8¼ x 11.
23686-2 Pa. $5.00

DESIGNS FOR THE THREE-CORNERED HAT (LE TRICORNE), Pablo Picasso. 32 fabulously rare drawings—including 31 color illustrations of costumes and accessories—for 1919 production of famous ballet. Edited by Parmenia Migel, who has written new introduction. 48pp. 9⅜ x 12¼. (Available in U.S. only)
23709-5 Pa. $5.00

NOTES OF A FILM DIRECTOR, Sergei Eisenstein. Greatest Russian filmmaker explains montage, making of Alexander Nevsky, aesthetics; comments on self, associates, great rivals (Chaplin), similar material. 78 illustrations. 240pp. 5⅜ x 8½.
22392-2 Pa. $4.50

HOLLYWOOD GLAMOUR PORTRAITS, edited by John Kobal. 145 photos capture the stars from 1926-49, the high point in portrait photography. Gable, Harlow, Bogart, Bacall, Hedy Lamarr, Marlene Dietrich, Robert Montgomery, Marlon Brando, Veronica Lake; 94 stars in all. Full background on photographers, technical aspects, much more. Total of 160pp. 8⅜ x 11¼. 23352-9 Pa. $6.00

THE NEW YORK STAGE: FAMOUS PRODUCTIONS IN PHOTO-GRAPHS, edited by Stanley Appelbaum. 148 photographs from Museum of City of New York show 142 plays, 1883-1939. *Peter Pan, The Front Page, Dead End, Our Town,* O'Neill, hundreds of actors and actresses, etc. Full indexes. 154pp. 9½ x 10. 23241-7 Pa. $6.00

DIALOGUES CONCERNING TWO NEW SCIENCES, Galileo Galilei. Encompassing 30 years of experiment and thought, these dialogues deal with geometric demonstrations of fracture of solid bodies, cohesion, leverage, speed of light and sound, pendulums, falling bodies, accelerated motion, etc. 300pp. 5⅜ x 8½. 60099-8 Pa. $4.00

THE GREAT OPERA STARS IN HISTORIC PHOTOGRAPHS, edited by James Camner. 343 portraits from the 1850s to the 1940s: Tamburini, Mario, Caliapin, Jeritza, Melchior, Melba, Patti, Pinza, Schipa, Caruso, Farrar, Steber, Gobbi, and many more—270 performers in all. Index. 199pp. 8⅜ x 11¼. 23575-0 Pa. $7.50

J. S. BACH, Albert Schweitzer. Great full-length study of Bach, life, background to music, music, by foremost modern scholar. Ernest Newman translation. 650 musical examples. Total of 928pp. 5⅜ x 8½. (Available in U.S. only) 21631-4, 21632-2 Pa., Two-vol. set $11.00

COMPLETE PIANO SONATAS, Ludwig van Beethoven. All sonatas in the fine Schenker edition, with fingering, analytical material. One of best modern editions. Total of 615pp. 9 x 12. (Available in U.S. only) 23134-8, 23135-6 Pa., Two-vol. set $15.50

KEYBOARD MUSIC, J. S. Bach. Bach-Gesellschaft edition. For harpsichord, piano, other keyboard instruments. English Suites, French Suites, Six Partitas, Goldberg Variations, Two-Part Inventions, Three-Part Sinfonias. 312pp. 8⅛ x 11. (Available in U.S. only) 22360-4 Pa. $6.95

FOUR SYMPHONIES IN FULL SCORE, Franz Schubert. Schubert's four most popular symphonies: No. 4 in C Minor ("Tragic"); No. 5 in B-flat Major; No. 8 in B Minor ("Unfinished"); No. 9 in C Major ("Great"). Breitkopf & Hartel edition. Study score. 261pp. 9⅜ x 12¼. 23681-1 Pa. $6.50

THE AUTHENTIC GILBERT & SULLIVAN SONGBOOK, W. S. Gilbert, A. S. Sullivan. Largest selection available; 92 songs, uncut, original keys, in piano rendering approved by Sullivan. Favorites and lesser-known fine numbers. Edited with plot synopses by James Spero. 3 illustrations. 399pp. 9 x 12. 23482-7 Pa. $9.95

PRINCIPLES OF ORCHESTRATION, Nikolay Rimsky-Korsakov. Great classical orchestrator provides fundamentals of tonal resonance, progression of parts, voice and orchestra, tutti effects, much else in major document. 330pp. of musical excerpts. 489pp. 6½ x 9¼. 21266-1 Pa. $7.50

TRISTAN UND ISOLDE, Richard Wagner. Full orchestral score with complete instrumentation. Do not confuse with piano reduction. Commentary by Felix Mottl, great Wagnerian conductor and scholar. Study score. 655pp. 8⅛ x 11. 22915-7 Pa. $13.95

REQUIEM IN FULL SCORE, Giuseppe Verdi. Immensely popular with choral groups and music lovers. Republication of edition published by C. F. Peters, Leipzig, n. d. German frontmaker in English translation. Glossary. Text in Latin. Study score. 204pp. 9⅜ x 12¼.
23682-X Pa. $6.00

COMPLETE CHAMBER MUSIC FOR STRINGS, Felix Mendelssohn. All of Mendelssohn's chamber music: Octet, 2 Quintets, 6 Quartets, and Four Pieces for String Quartet. (Nothing with piano is included). Complete works edition (1874-7). Study score. 283 pp. 9⅜ x 12¼.
23679-X Pa. $7.50

POPULAR SONGS OF NINETEENTH-CENTURY AMERICA, edited by Richard Jackson. 64 most important songs: "Old Oaken Bucket," "Arkansas Traveler," "Yellow Rose of Texas," etc. Authentic original sheet music, full introduction and commentaries. 290pp. 9 x 12. 23270-0 Pa. $7.95

COLLECTED PIANO WORKS, Scott Joplin. Edited by Vera Brodsky Lawrence. Practically all of Joplin's piano works—rags, two-steps, marches, waltzes, etc., 51 works in all. Extensive introduction by Rudi Blesh. Total of 345pp. 9 x 12. 23106-2 Pa. $14.95

BASIC PRINCIPLES OF CLASSICAL BALLET, Agrippina Vaganova. Great Russian theoretician, teacher explains methods for teaching classical ballet; incorporates best from French, Italian, Russian schools. 118 illustrations. 175pp. 5⅜ x 8½. 22036-2 Pa. $2.50

CHINESE CHARACTERS, L. Wieger. Rich analysis of 2300 characters according to traditional systems into primitives. Historical-semantic analysis to phonetics (Classical Mandarin) and radicals. 820pp. 6⅛ x 9¼.
21321-8 Pa. $10.00

EGYPTIAN LANGUAGE: EASY LESSONS IN EGYPTIAN HIERO-GLYPHICS, E. A. Wallis Budge. Foremost Egyptologist offers Egyptian grammar, explanation of hieroglyphics, many reading texts, dictionary of symbols. 246pp. 5 x 7½. (Available in U.S. only)
21394-3 Clothbd. $7.50

AN ETYMOLOGICAL DICTIONARY OF MODERN ENGLISH, Ernest Weekley. Richest, fullest work, by foremost British lexicographer. Detailed word histories. Inexhaustible. Do not confuse this with *Concise Etymological Dictionary,* which is abridged. Total of 856pp. 6½ x 9¼.
21873-2, 21874-0 Pa., Two-vol. set $12.00

A MAYA GRAMMAR, Alfred M. Tozzer. Practical, useful English-language grammar by the Harvard anthropologist who was one of the three greatest American scholars in the area of Maya culture. Phonetics, grammatical processes, syntax, more. 301pp. 5⅜ x 8½.   23465-7 Pa. $4.00

THE JOURNAL OF HENRY D. THOREAU, edited by Bradford Torrey, F. H. Allen. Complete reprinting of 14 volumes, 1837-61, over two million words; the sourcebooks for *Walden*, etc. Definitive. All original sketches, plus 75 photographs. Introduction by Walter Harding. Total of 1804pp. 8½ x 12¼.   20312-3, 20313-1 Clothbd., Two-vol. set $70.00

CLASSIC GHOST STORIES, Charles Dickens and others. 18 wonderful stories you've wanted to reread: "The Monkey's Paw," "The House and the Brain," "The Upper Berth," "The Signalman," "Dracula's Guest," "The Tapestried Chamber," etc. Dickens, Scott, Mary Shelley, Stoker, etc. 330pp. 5⅜ x 8½.   20735-8 Pa. $4.50

SEVEN SCIENCE FICTION NOVELS, H. G. Wells. Full novels. *First Men in the Moon, Island of Dr. Moreau, War of the Worlds, Food of the Gods, Invisible Man, Time Machine, In the Days of the Comet.* A basic science-fiction library. 1015pp. 5⅜ x 8½. (Available in U.S. only)
20264-X Clothbd. $8.95

ARMADALE, Wilkie Collins. Third great mystery novel by the author of *The Woman in White* and *The Moonstone.* Ingeniously plotted narrative shows an exceptional command of character, incident and mood. Original magazine version with 40 illustrations. 597pp. 5⅜ x 8½.
23429-0 Pa. $6.00

MASTERS OF MYSTERY, H. Douglas Thomson. The first book in English (1931) devoted to history and aesthetics of detective story. Poe, Doyle, LeFanu, Dickens, many others, up to 1930. New introduction and notes by E. F. Bleiler. 288pp. 5⅜ x 8½. (Available in U.S. only)
23606-4 Pa. $4.00

FLATLAND, E. A. Abbott. Science-fiction classic explores life of 2-D being in 3-D world. Read also as introduction to thought about hyperspace. Introduction by Banesh Hoffmann. 16 illustrations. 103pp. 5⅜ x 8½.
20001-9 Pa. $2.00

THREE SUPERNATURAL NOVELS OF THE VICTORIAN PERIOD, edited, with an introduction, by E. F. Bleiler. Reprinted complete and unabridged, three great classics of the supernatural: *The Haunted Hotel* by Wilkie Collins, *The Haunted House at Latchford* by Mrs. J. H. Riddell, and *The Lost Stradivarius* by J. Meade Falkner. 325pp. 5⅜ x 8½.
22571-2 Pa. $4.00

AYESHA: THE RETURN OF "SHE," H. Rider Haggard. Virtuoso sequel featuring the great mythic creation, Ayesha, in an adventure that is fully as good as the first book, *She.* Original magazine version, with 47 original illustrations by Maurice Greiffenhagen. 189pp. 6½ x 9¼.
23649-8 Pa. $3.50

UNCLE SILAS, J. Sheridan LeFanu. Victorian Gothic mystery novel, considered by many best of period, even better than Collins or Dickens. Wonderful psychological terror. Introduction by Frederick Shroyer. 436pp. 5⅜ x 8½.   21715-9 Pa. $6.00

JURGEN, James Branch Cabell. The great erotic fantasy of the 1920's that delighted thousands, shocked thousands more. Full final text, Lane edition with 13 plates by Frank Pape. 346pp. 5⅜ x 8½.
23507-6 Pa. $4.50

THE CLAVERINGS, Anthony Trollope. Major novel, chronicling aspects of British Victorian society, personalities. Reprint of Cornhill serialization, 16 plates by M. Edwards; first reprint of full text. Introduction by Norman Donaldson. 412pp. 5⅜ x 8½.   23464-9 Pa. $5.00

KEPT IN THE DARK, Anthony Trollope. Unusual short novel about Victorian morality and abnormal psychology by the great English author. Probably the first American publication. Frontispiece by Sir John Millais. 92pp. 6½ x 9¼.   23609-9 Pa. $2.50

RALPH THE HEIR, Anthony Trollope. Forgotten tale of illegitimacy, inheritance. Master novel of Trollope's later years. Victorian country estates, clubs, Parliament, fox hunting, world of fully realized characters. Reprint of 1871 edition. 12 illustrations by F. A. Faser. 434pp. of text. 5⅜ x 8½.   23642-0 Pa. $5.00

YEKL and THE IMPORTED BRIDEGROOM AND OTHER STORIES OF THE NEW YORK GHETTO, Abraham Cahan. Film *Hester Street* based on *Yekl* (1896). Novel, other stories among first about Jewish immigrants of N.Y.'s East Side. Highly praised by W. D. Howells—Cahan "a new star of realism." New introduction by Bernard G. Richards. 240pp. 5⅜ x 8½.   22427-9 Pa. $3.50

THE HIGH PLACE, James Branch Cabell. Great fantasy writer's enchanting comedy of disenchantment set in 18th-century France. Considered by some critics to be even better than his famous *Jurgen*. 10 illustrations and numerous vignettes by noted fantasy artist Frank C. Pape. 320pp. 5⅜ x 8½.   23670-6 Pa. $4.00

ALICE'S ADVENTURES UNDER GROUND, Lewis Carroll. Facsimile of ms. Carroll gave Alice Liddell in 1864. Different in many ways from final Alice. Handlettered, illustrated by Carroll. Introduction by Martin Gardner. 128pp. 5⅜ x 8½.   21482-6 Pa. $2.50

FAVORITE ANDREW LANG FAIRY TALE BOOKS IN MANY COLORS, Andrew Lang. The four Lang favorites in a boxed set—the complete *Red, Green, Yellow* and *Blue* Fairy Books. 164 stories; 439 illustrations by Lancelot Speed, Henry Ford and G. P. Jacomb Hood. Total of about 1500pp. 5⅜ x 8½.   23407-X Boxed set, Pa. $15.95

HOUSEHOLD STORIES BY THE BROTHERS GRIMM. All the great Grimm stories: "Rumpelstiltskin," "Snow White," "Hansel and Gretel," etc., with 114 illustrations by Walter Crane. 269pp. 5⅜ x 8½.
21080-4 Pa. $3.50

SLEEPING BEAUTY, illustrated by Arthur Rackham. Perhaps the fullest, most delightful version ever, told by C. S. Evans. Rackham's best work. 49 illustrations. 110pp. 7⅞ x 10¾. 22756-1 Pa. $2.50

AMERICAN FAIRY TALES, L. Frank Baum. Young cowboy lassoes Father Time; dummy in Mr. Floman's department store window comes to life; and 10 other fairy tales. 41 illustrations by N. P. Hall, Harry Kennedy, Ike Morgan, and Ralph Gardner. 209pp. 5⅜ x 8½. 23643-9 Pa. $3.00

THE WONDERFUL WIZARD OF OZ, L. Frank Baum. Facsimile in full color of America's finest children's classic. Introduction by Martin Gardner. 143 illustrations by W. W. Denslow. 267pp. 5⅜ x 8½.
20691-2 Pa. $3.50

THE TALE OF PETER RABBIT, Beatrix Potter. The inimitable Peter's terrifying adventure in Mr. McGregor's garden, with all 27 wonderful, full-color Potter illustrations. 55pp. 4¼ x 5½. (Available in U.S. only)
22827-4 Pa. $1.25

THE STORY OF KING ARTHUR AND HIS KNIGHTS, Howard Pyle. Finest children's version of life of King Arthur. 48 illustrations by Pyle. 131pp. 6⅛ x 9¼. 21445-1 Pa. $4.95

CARUSO'S CARICATURES, Enrico Caruso. Great tenor's remarkable caricatures of self, fellow musicians, composers, others. Toscanini, Puccini, Farrar, etc. Impish, cutting, insightful. 473 illustrations. Preface by M. Sisca. 217pp. 8⅜ x 11¼. 23528-9 Pa. $6.95

PERSONAL NARRATIVE OF A PILGRIMAGE TO ALMADINAH AND MECCAH, Richard Burton. Great travel classic by remarkably colorful personality. Burton, disguised as a Moroccan, visited sacred shrines of Islam, narrowly escaping death. Wonderful observations of Islamic life, customs, personalities. 47 illustrations. Total of 959pp. 5⅜ x 8½.
21217-3, 21218-1 Pa., Two-vol. set $12.00

INCIDENTS OF TRAVEL IN YUCATAN, John L. Stephens. Classic (1843) exploration of jungles of Yucatan, looking for evidences of Maya civilization. Travel adventures, Mexican and Indian culture, etc. Total of 669pp. 5⅜ x 8½. 20926-1, 20927-X Pa., Two-vol. set $7.90

AMERICAN LITERARY AUTOGRAPHS FROM WASHINGTON IRVING TO HENRY JAMES, Herbert Cahoon, et al. Letters, poems, manuscripts of Hawthorne, Thoreau, Twain, Alcott, Whitman, 67 other prominent American authors. Reproductions, full transcripts and commentary. Plus checklist of all American Literary Autographs in The Pierpont Morgan Library. Printed on exceptionally high-quality paper. 136 illustrations. 212pp. 9⅛ x 12¼. 23548-3 Pa. $12.50

AN AUTOBIOGRAPHY, Margaret Sanger. Exciting personal account of hard-fought battle for woman's right to birth control, against prejudice, church, law. Foremost feminist document. 504pp. 5⅜ x 8½.
20470-7 Pa. $5.50

MY BONDAGE AND MY FREEDOM, Frederick Douglass. Born as a slave, Douglass became outspoken force in antislavery movement. The best of Douglass's autobiographies. Graphic description of slave life. Introduction by P. Foner. 464pp. 5⅜ x 8½. 22457-0 Pa. $5.50

LIVING MY LIFE, Emma Goldman. Candid, no holds barred account by foremost American anarchist: her own life, anarchist movement, famous contemporaries, ideas and their impact. Struggles and confrontations in America, plus deportation to U.S.S.R. Shocking inside account of persecution of anarchists under Lenin. 13 plates. Total of 944pp. 5⅜ x 8½.
22543-7, 22544-5 Pa., Two-vol. set $12.00

LETTERS AND NOTES ON THE MANNERS, CUSTOMS AND CONDITIONS OF THE NORTH AMERICAN INDIANS, George Catlin. Classic account of life among Plains Indians: ceremonies, hunt, warfare, etc. Dover edition reproduces for first time all original paintings. 312 plates. 572pp. of text. 6⅛ x 9¼. 22118-0, 22119-9 Pa.. Two-vol. set $12.00

THE MAYA AND THEIR NEIGHBORS, edited by Clarence L. Hay, others. Synoptic view of Maya civilization in broadest sense, together with Northern, Southern neighbors. Integrates much background, valuable detail not elsewhere. Prepared by greatest scholars: Kroeber, Morley, Thompson, Spinden, Vaillant, many others. Sometimes called Tozzer Memorial Volume. 60 illustrations, linguistic map. 634pp. 5⅜ x 8½.
23510-6 Pa. $10.00

HANDBOOK OF THE INDIANS OF CALIFORNIA, A. L. Kroeber. Foremost American anthropologist offers complete ethnographic study of each group. Monumental classic. 459 illustrations, maps. 995pp. 5⅜ x 8½.
23368-5 Pa. $13.00

SHAKTI AND SHAKTA, Arthur Avalon. First book to give clear, cohesive analysis of Shakta doctrine, Shakta ritual and Kundalini Shakti (yoga). Important work by one of world's foremost students of Shaktic and Tantric thought. 732pp. 5⅜ x 8½. (Available in U.S. only)
23645-5 Pa. $7.95

AN INTRODUCTION TO THE STUDY OF THE MAYA HIEROGLYPHS, Syvanus Griswold Morley. Classic study by one of the truly great figures in hieroglyph research. Still the best introduction for the student for reading Maya hieroglyphs. New introduction by J. Eric S. Thompson. 117 illustrations. 284pp. 5⅜ x 8½. 23108-9 Pa. $4.00

A STUDY OF MAYA ART, Herbert J. Spinden. Landmark classic interprets Maya symbolism, estimates styles, covers ceramics, architecture, murals, stone carvings as artforms. Still a basic book in area. New introduction by J. Eric Thompson. Over 750 illustrations. 341pp. 8⅜ x 11¼.
21235-1 Pa. $6.95

GEOMETRY, RELATIVITY AND THE FOURTH DIMENSION, Rudolf Rucker. Exposition of fourth dimension, means of visualization, concepts of relativity as Flatland characters continue adventures. Popular, easily followed yet accurate, profound. 141 illustrations. 133pp. 5⅜ x 8½.
23400-2 Pa. $2.75

THE ORIGIN OF LIFE, A. I. Oparin. Modern classic in biochemistry, the first rigorous examination of possible evolution of life from nitrocarbon compounds. Non-technical, easily followed. Total of 295pp. 5⅜ x 8½.
60213-3 Pa. $4.00

PLANETS, STARS AND GALAXIES, A. E. Fanning. Comprehensive introductory survey: the sun, solar system, stars, galaxies, universe, cosmology; quasars, radio stars, etc. 24pp. of photographs. 189pp. 5⅜ x 8½. (Available in U.S. only)
21680-2 Pa. $3.75

THE THIRTEEN BOOKS OF EUCLID'S ELEMENTS, translated with introduction and commentary by Sir Thomas L. Heath. Definitive edition. Textual and linguistic notes, mathematical analysis, 2500 years of critical commentary. Do not confuse with abridged school editions. Total of 1414pp. 5⅜ x 8½.
60088-2, 60089-0, 60090-4 Pa., Three-vol. set $18.50

Prices subject to change without notice.

Available at your book dealer or write for free catalogue to Dept. GI, Dover Publications, Inc., 180 Varick St., N.Y., N.Y. 10014. Dover publishes more than 175 books each year on science, elementary and advanced mathematics, biology, music, art, literary history, social sciences and other areas.